Beethoven, Then and Now

Beethoven, Then and Now

Fred Gaertner

Cover Illustrations By: Earlene Gayle Escalona.

Library of Congress Control Number:		2014915814
ISBN:	Hardcover	978-1-4990-6819-1
	Softcover	978-1-4990-6818-4
	eBook	978-1-4990-6820-7

Part 1 is autobiographical with historical characters and events.

Part 2 is fictional and the names of characters, places and incidents are the products of the author's imagination.

This book was printed in the United States of America.

Rev. date: 11/05/2014

To order additional copies of this book, contact:
Xlibris
1-888-795-4274
www.Xlibris.com
Orders@Xlibris.com
549287

To those

individuals who are uncertain as to

whether life continues after death.

May this story reassure them that

their present life proceeds

meaningfully throughout eternity.

Best wishes
from the author,
Fred Gaertner

Part I

BEETHOVEN THEN (1770–1827)

The Final Earthly Years

Total of *16 Earthly lives*, culminating in *Beethoven's 57 years on Earth*:

Years for each life:
63
74
55 w
72
60
53
87 w
61
59 w
66
72
18 w
69
60 w
65

934*

5 lives as *women*: 279 years
10 lives as *men*: *655* years
Total years prior to Beethoven: 934 years*
Beethoven's span 1770–1827: *57 years*
Total First-Order time: 991 years

Chapter 1

Part 1 of my narrative flows from the stream of total recall, and is not the feeble attempt of an aged mariner to plot the misty origin of his life's voyage. Beethoven's first day on Earth comes as vividly to mind as does my last hour of consciousness in Vienna.

Attraction toward music was natural, for I was planted in a musical garden. Grandfather and Father were both court musicians, and the Bonn of my youth did little to discourage a musical career.

Grandfather came to Bonn at the invitation of Elector Clemens August, by whose official decree he became a court musician in 1733. This same year he married Maria Josepha Poll, a girl of nineteen, two years his junior. Their first children died in infancy. In 1740 came Johann, my father, the only child to survive. I never knew Grandmother, though Father would speak of her occasionally, blaming her addiction to alcohol on the loss of her children and on her husband's preoccupation with music, court life, and matters outside their home.

Grandfather's musical abilities flourished, and in 1761, he became "Herr Kapellmeister." His main talent was his voice, though he was also proficient in piano and violin. He personally supervised the training of my father and prepared him for service in the court chapel as a boy soprano. Father remained a court musician and developed sufficiently as a singer and violinist to be granted a salary in 1764. Private teaching augmented his flimsy hundred thalers per year, until the resulting financial prowess encouraged him to propose marriage to my mother in 1767. She was Maria Magdalena Kewerich, twenty-year-old daughter of the head cook at the Ehrenbreitstein castle and widow of Johann Laym, whom she had married in 1763. My parents' first child was Ludwig Maria, who lived less than a week of April 1769. I arrived twenty months later and, according to custom, inherited my little brother's name.

Since I am to relate only those incidents from Beethoven's Earthly life that have directly influenced later years, there is little to mention about my first few months—little, except perhaps a word of warning to parents, grandparents, and babysitters who aren't too careful about their verbal assaults upon tiny infants. It's true, such babies do not understand your words, nor will they remember them during their Earthly pilgrimages. With complete indifference, they respond to a heartless insult with smiles, unintelligible cooings, even slobbered kisses. But what about the subsequent miracle of total recall? Since March 26, 1827, I have been intimately conscious of my *total* of sixteen Earthly incarnations, including that *final* one as "Beethoven." In the fifty-seventh day of that span, I was awakened by Grandfather's huge forefinger tucked under my chin. My eyes adjusted as his boundless countenance moved closer and closer. At last, in resonantly muted baritone, came the fatal words:

BG. God in heaven, what an ugly bastard!

Since Grandfather died one week after my third birthday, it was not possible for me to remember much about him during my Earthly years. Although I held him in great esteem, such worshipful feelings were not based upon personal recollections. I took pride in Grandfather because his career seemed to succeed at each point where my father's failed. Grandfather became chapelmaster; Father did not. Grandfather's salary approximated a living wage; Father's did not. Grandfather was a connoisseur and merchant of wine; Father became its obedient servant. Grandfather was endowed with a healthy measure of pride and self-confidence. He seized upon his musical abilities and through their development won at least the admiration and respect of his fellows. Father was an impotent dreamer. From his bottle, he would pour pure pessimism to inspire long periods of helpless inactivity.

Fifteen months later, it was this same loving Grandfather who held me on his knee at the piano. He struck a chord, the first musical sound to reach my ears. A look of disappointment shaded his face as my attention concentrated upon his nose. He countered with a second triad. A third . . . crescendo! A fourth . . . to no avail! My glance remained upward, toward the moistness that twinkled in his eyes. Then from my elbow down, my right arm disappeared into his huge hand, and we played my first scale. Grandfather sang along with our instrumental accompaniment:

BG. C-D-E-F-G-A-B-C . . .

Three years later, I would have realized that there was a relation between his lyrics and the ivory-edged "workbench" at which we sat.

Shortly after Grandfather's death, Father petitioned the Electoral Grace for an increase in his allowance. He contended that his salary was not sufficient to provide for his own family and at the same time meet the expenses of cloistering his hopelessly alcoholic mother. Father "tactfully" hinted that he was fully capable of assuming Grandfather's position and that his increase in pay would be simply a matter of reallocating a portion of the allowance vacated by the former chapelmaster. Father was optimistic regarding the outcome of his petition, so much so that our family moved from the humble place of my birth into a much better dwelling in the Dreieckplatz. While living here, another son was born in April 1774, his name Casper Anton Carl.

Life in the Dreieckplatz was pleasant and musical. We had inherited Grandfather's piano, violin, music books and tasteful furnishings. It was here that my "formal" training began as Father taught me the rudiments of piano and violin. He seemed quite impressed by my musical memory and attempted to develop it by playing a little game. I would stand across the room with my back to the piano. Father would play a melody two or three times, depending on its length. I would then jump to my position on a little footstool in front of the clavier and attempt to reproduce his tune. Even this harmless game made some interesting disclosures about my native ability. I did *not* have absolute pitch; usually the first tone of the theme had to be spelled out. I did have a good sense of relative pitch; once on the right track, I rarely lost a melody. Soon the "game" gave way to a serious program of ear training. Father would play two, three, sometimes four tunes at once, and I was expected to play back any one of them. Two years later, when my piano technique caught up with my ears, it was easy for me to reproduce entire pieces (of modest length) simply by hearing them played once or twice and being told the proper key.

At long last my father's courageous optimism was met head-on by the storm of reality, a tempest from which he never fully recovered. His petition was not granted. His hopes and dreams of greater responsibility and higher pay did not materialize. It's difficult to believe that a single disappointment in a father's plans could directly influence the life of his son, permanently. But such has been the case. I often wonder what would have happened to me if Father had received the promotion he sought. No doubt our family would have settled back in quiet comfort and I would have continued to be the little boy who played musical games at home and at court. But there was no calm resolution of Father's problem. His personal plans remained frustrated to the end of his present days, and such intolerable frustration defined the image I was to occupy in his mind. This image developed swiftly—almost overnight. Rather than see himself as the chapelmaster's son who could never become chapelmaster, he preferred the role of father to a little musician who, with "proper paternal guidance," could be made to outperform Mozart. And once he viewed himself as "father of a Mozart," the vision became fixed and immovable.

While still living in the Dreieckplatz, I noticed that the strictness of Father's tutelage was increasing. My violin lessons, and especially my piano lessons, seemed endless to a boy of five; neither had the slightest resemblance to a game. In one mighty grasp, my teacher had squeezed all the fun out of music.

Early in 1776, Father had a clear vision of the permanent impairment of our family finances. Consequently, we moved from the Dreieckplatz to the Fischer house in the Rheingasse, a much cheaper place down by the river and the same spot formerly occupied by Grandfather. Following this move, my daily life became a rigid schedule with music as the chief attraction. In addition to lessons and ear training, something new was added—hours and hours of practice! When I grew tired of the drudgery and complained to Father about it, his stock reply was something like:

BF. Good little boys do what they are told! When you are older, you will be glad that you learned how to work.

Father's inflexible severity would often send me running and weeping to my mother's knee. I would bury my head in her lap and absorb every word of comfort that fell from her lips. Even as our tears mingled, she would never side with me against my father's demands. She felt that his requirements were just, and yet in some beautiful way, she sensed my urgent need for sympathy and understanding.

As the sixth year rolled by, my questions became more insistent:

B. Why, Mother? Why must I spend so much time at the clavier? Why is Father so determined? Why do other boys my age seem to come and go as they please?

In response to these questions, Mother mentioned for the first time the name of Mozart.

BM. In the city of Salzburg, there is a great musician whose name is Mozart. In all the world there is no greater pianist. As a composer, he holds the same high rank. Your father believes that Mozart's musical ascent was due partly to his inborn genius, but mainly to his ability for demonstrating remarkable musicianship at a very early age! Father senses that you too show promise as a pianist, and that if you work hard and can make your debut while still a boy, you will come to enjoy the honor and good fortune that are now Mozart's.

And thus, quite innocently, was planted the seed of my personality, the root of my character, the force that patterned Beethoven's life on Earth. I was not an ordinary boy; I was a young Mozart patiently waiting and working for his birthright to fame, fortune, and world renown. Mother's explanation of Father's demands was good in that I was now able to accept my daily schedule with greater confidence and fewer questions. However, such reasoning led me to a profound hero worship of Wolfgang Amadeus Mozart! Not that it's bad for a boy to have a hero, but the more I learned about my prototype, the greater opinion I came to have of myself. Thus, indirectly, I built up such dreams of fame, success, power and glory, that the world of reality never proved large enough to contain them!

Chapter 2

On the first of October 1776, another brother was born—Nicholas Johann. Little effect the blessed event had upon my routine! I continued to practice the clavier ten hours a day until the spring of '77, when I was enrolled in the Tirocinium, a Latin school whose curriculum was designed to prepare students for the gymnasium. Besides elementary studies, my main subject was Latin. Arithmetic was considered of such slight importance that I was taught addition, but never the intricacies of multiplication.

My days in the Tirocinium lasted only until 1781, at which time all other studies were abandoned for music. These days in school were not happy ones. Perhaps they would have been, if my practicing schedule had been suitably modified. But how could this be? Interrupt the career of a Mozart? Of course not! I was expected to attend school daily and to devote all free time to an undiminished load of musical responsibilities.

Father's determination rewarded me with such proficiency upon the clavier that by the spring of '78, he was ready to present his "gift" to the musical world. I played in three concerts: two at court and one in the Sternengasse concert room. Father understated my age, advertising me as his "little son of six years." In spite of this two-year deception, my offerings of rococo trios and concertos were received with little more than "polite" applause. There were head pats for me and handshakes for Father, but no improvement in our financial position. Nor did the heavens emit the slightest ray of soft gentle light to come down and settle about my head and shoulders. I remained a tiny musician who had practiced the piano, who had played in public, and who was destined to return immediately to his practice.

During the winter that preceded this uneventful debut, I began to balk under the combined weight of schoolwork and piano practice. Was there not some way I could restore the spirit of play to my boyhood? How could I escape the arid wasteland of my traditional repertoire? Father was beyond musical games; it was now up to me. I began to experiment with the gentle art of improvisation. What fun! The simple tunes that hummed themselves in my head could now be shared with others. Did Father appreciate them? I'll say he did! He threatened me with ear boxing and confinement in the cellar if I didn't "play according to the notes!"

But my concert in the Sternengasse modified his attitude toward musical daydreaming. No longer was improvising a mortal sin and total waste of time, but perhaps a necessary prerequisite to original composition. And Father assured me that my debut of March 26 would have been as successful as Mozart's—if only there had been some compositions of my own to perform.

Since Father knew little of composition, he set out to find me a teacher. His first choice was Gilles van den Eeden, the old court organist who had been in the electoral service for fifty years and had been a good friend of Grandfather. These lessons began in June '78. Although Van Den Eeden promised to teach me thorough bass, his instruction was chiefly in piano playing and organ. He told Father that he was preparing me to be his successor as court organist. Since Father was mainly interested in some original compositions to go with my next recital, these lessons were terminated the following October. Paternal supervision resumed as before—no lessons in composition!

Several biographers have preserved a rumor that my mother never smiled. One naturally suspects never to be an absurd exaggeration. However, the belief is absolutely correct when related to her days on Earth that followed February 1779. On the twenty-third of this month, she gave birth to her first daughter, Anna Maria Franciska; in less than five days, the little girl was dead. Of the entire chain of sorrows shouldering my dear mother, this cruel link went the farthest to convince her that married life was nothing but a veil of tears. All subsequent attempts on my part to penetrate her cheer-defeating gloom ended in more tears—never a smile!

My next teacher was the talented comedian, Tobias Friedrich Pfeiffer, who came to Bonn as a member of the Grossmann Theatrical Company in the summer of '79 and found lodgings in our home. Like Van Den Eeden, Pfeiffer taught piano—very little composition. But he had a profound love for the art of music and a sincere appreciation for composers. His interesting and humorous stories about creative musicians kindled my imagination. For the first time, I came to see something in a musical career besides endless hours of drearisome practice. In the years that followed, I had more knowledgeable instructors than Pfeiffer, but none could equal his ability in teaching the beautiful, simple, mystical love that exists between a musician and his art.

It was during the Pfeiffer days that Father began to drink excessively. Perhaps the increase in his libation was brought about by the disappointment of my debut, or by the unfriendly realities of his own professional life, or by his "failing" eyesight—a peculiar condition in which his vision constantly improved its focus on the world's ugliness and injustice, but became progressively blind to its countless images of hope and beauty. At any rate, Father approached the bottle with a determination and gusto that would have made his mother proud.

Prior to Father's intemperance, his drab severity was punctuated by welcome reliefs: a pun, a joke, a laugh, some horseplay. But these bright and cherished high spots were swiftly washed away by the wave of wine that crested over his life. What remained was dark, cold, sad, unreal, unloving. Could such a distorted residue respond to the open arms of a child? No! But Mother was there, ready and waiting. Had she not been, I doubt if my emotions could have survived their first decade. I loved Mother; I respected Father. My respect for him sprang from a sense of duty, not from love. Such regimented devotion to Father was always accompanied by companion feelings that ranged from fear to hatred. How could I love a father who heaped mountains of inexcusable suffering upon my poor mother? How could I love a father who carefully groomed me as a Mozart while preparing himself for the role of superb teacher, proud parent, concert manager, and custodian of all funds? How could I love a father who subjected me to the cruel lessons of the Pfeiffer period? Several times each week, Father would come stomping into my midnight dreams with the bark of a dog and the breath of a bottle. He'd grab me from my bed and drag me to the clavier. There, he and Pfeiffer would keep me busy until five or six in the morning. Then followed several hours of what seemed more like recovery than sleep, after which I was awakened and sent to school. Is it any wonder that I sat in class absolutely dazed? What Krengel called my "stubborn resistance to learn" and my "contented stupor" were not due to obstinacy. I was simply reacting to the severe piano lesson that had been pounded into me the night before.

Try as Father did, he was unable to find me an instructor in composition. His plans for my Mozartian debut were pushed farther into the future, but not abandoned. He permitted a temporary compromise. If I were not to become a royal prodigy, then perhaps at least I could inherit Van Den Eeden's post as court organist. Even an organist's wages were better than none at all. Father hesitated to send me back to the ancient Van Den Eeden; instead we visited the Franciscan Cloister in Bonn, hoping to obtain some sort of instruction in organ. Father found just the man he was looking for in Friar Willibald Koch. I became Koch's pupil in the Fall of '79 and, thanks to my piano technique, made sufficient progress to be named his assistant the following Christmas. In this capacity, I was subsequently introduced to the nearby Cloister of Minorites, who offered me the post of regular organist for their six o'clock morning mass. My pay was the usual zero thalers, but I was happy to take the job since the Minorite instrument was far superior to that of the Franciscans.

Three months later, on a beautiful spring morning in 1780, I was bouncing my way to school. I was able to "bounce" because there had been no piano lesson the night before. As I passed by the Zehrgarten, I bumped squarely into Friar Koch:

K. Ludwig, you must come with me. I have a great surprise for you!

I tried to study the expression in his face, but the early May sun blinded my efforts into a helpless squint.

B. You mean . . . ?
K. Yes! Skip school today. This is far more important!
B. But my father?

Koch anticipated my doubts.

K. Your father will understand. And so will Herr Krengel.

I needed no further encouragement. In spite of my "springy" readiness for a day in class, I would much prefer spending a morning with dear Koch. To my astonishment, we did not join the Franciscans, but found our way to a quiet spot near the Minorite organ.

B. What's the surprise, Friar Koch?
K. In a few moments, Ludwig, through that door will enter Bonn's newest and greatest musician! For several months he has wanted to try this organ. He comes this morning and you must hear him!
B. Why?
K. Because I have no doubt that he will soon become your master!

We waited about five minutes, and there entered a small stooped man with a burning brightness in his eyes. He passed by us as though we weren't there. I noticed a spring in his step, just like the one I was feeling myself.

The next forty-five minutes were filled—running over—with the greatest inspiration I had yet heard. He played as ten men. The colors of the rainbow sang in my ears. The "god of harmony" spoke to me for the first time. How could the organ that I had played for three months suddenly sound so different? I wanted to laugh, to cry, to run, to sit immovable. My spine vibrated like a sixteen-foot diapason. I could no longer cope with the mixture of my emotions. When I cried audibly, Friar Koch took me by the hand and led me into the garden.

K. Why are you crying, Ludwig?
B. Because . . . because it's too beautiful!
K. Wouldn't you like to meet such a fine Maestro?

I responded with a silent downward glance, which Koch correctly interpreted.

K. Very well, Ludwig. You will meet him later. Your father will see to that.

As we walked from the chapel, the entire edifice vibrated with beautiful music—a transfigured structure, touched by the hand of J. S. Bach. When I was again able to speak, I turned to Friar Koch.

B. Who was that man?
K. His name is Christian Gottlob Neefe!

Chapter 3

Koch's words were prophetic; in September 1780, I became a student of Neefe. Although Father still talked and dreamed of a Mozartian debut with compositions of my own, he gave Neefe specific instructions that I was to be trained exclusively in organ. How convenient! I would succeed Van Den Eeden as court organist and evolve into a much-needed income-producing member of our little family. I was proud to study organ with Neefe. How different he was from my other teachers. Instead of telling me how to play a passage, he would show me how. Instead of words, music, played with a fearsome organ technique that I was never able to equal.

On February 15, 1781, Neefe was officially appointed court organist in the elector's service. This unhoped-for replacement of Van Den Eeden dashed our careful plans to the ground. The financial loss was especially hard-felt since a new little brother, August Franz Georg, had arrived one month before. Naturally, there came drinks for Father and tears for Mother. A short-lived sequence since Neefe paid a redeeming visit to our home on the twentieth. Sensing my parents' disappointment, he described the ever-increasing weight of his musical responsibilities, his potential need for an assistant, and his willingness to train me for the job. Father was totally appeased when Neefe explained how my services would be accepted as full payment for his tutoring and that the post would eventually carry a salary. He also agreed to include some lessons in composition, and back into the works went Father's plan for Mozart II!

Regardless of how fully absorbed I had become in musical training during the first decade of my life, I still managed to find a little time for games, hikes, and daydreaming. Under the new arrangement with Herr Neefe, all except music was vanquished from my remaining days in Bonn. Even my career at the Tirocinium quickly withered and died. How did Neefe inspire such unreserved devotion to duty? Not by threats, browbeating, or fits of temper. He simply set a good example himself, being literally wedded to music and the arts. He had a fine talent and was driven from one day's achievement to the next by an unlimited aspiration. What a contrast to Pfeiffer and my father. They talked constantly of great achievements, but attempted nothing themselves. Neefe taught the joy of total sacrifice to the Divine Art—he taught it by the way he lived his own life. Each day seemed for him a new adventure; each new project, a creative challenge. Oh, to live my life on such a plane! I wondered if Mozart himself could have been as great an inspiration as my man, Neefe. I was determined to accept each responsibility he placed upon my shoulders—to accept it and come back for more.

My instruction in piano was centered about Bach's *Well-Tempered Clavichord.* There were sonatas, rondos, and a concerto, but for the *most* part, preludes and fugues by Bach. Father's patient training of my musical memory was here put to use, and within a year, I could play much of the *Clavichord* by heart. My "lifelong" preference for instrumental forms sprang chiefly from this early acquaintance with Bach's great work.

Neefe's course in composition was likewise Bachian, being founded upon the theoretical studies of Carl Philipp Emanuel Bach. Again, how different from my studies with Pfeiffer. Only now did I come to realize the importance of form, structure, and continuity. My biggest adjustment was to a new type of criticism. Pfeiffer was always complimentary and encouraging; Neefe was merciless and cruel, but honest!

Toward the end of June 1782, Neefe journeyed to Münster with the Grossmann Theatrical Company. During his absence, I substituted as court organist and absolutely thrived on the added responsibilities. But I had yet to earn my first florin. I had yet to be of any help to my struggling parents in their brutal fight for economic survival.

For Neefe's return, I planned a little surprise; finishing touches were added to a set of nine pianoforte variations on a march by

Dressler. Instead of me surprising my teacher, *I* was the one to be surprised. He read through the entire score, thoughtfully stroking his chin. Of course, there was no praise, but neither was there the usual tirade of "constructive" criticism. He made a few suggestions as to voice leadings, then laid the opus on his desk. We concentrated on a Bach fugue, and I soon forgot about my "masterpiece." The last repercussion of my boomerang-like surprise occurred nearly a year later. Out of the clear blue, Neefe placed in my hands an engraved copy of the little variations. Imagine my pride, the first work of Ludwig van Beethoven—in print! Surely I was now but a single step behind Wolfgang Amadeus Mozart!

After Neefe's return, my duties as assistant were light. I had time for theory and composition and began to think in terms of more elaborate variations, some chamber music, perhaps even a piano concerto of my own. How close to Father's dream!

The relative leisure of this period engendered my first clear consciousness of the social order. On one hand, I saw the wealth and glitter of the Court of Cologne; on the other, I saw the poverty and suffering of my parental home. Enrollment in either class was simply an accident of birth. Because of my birth, I was excluded from the nobility; my only approach to them was as a servant. Because of my birth, I was shackled to a poverty that seemed impossible to rise above. I rejected membership in either class. There must be some middle ground. There must exist a nobility to which I could aspire, a true nobility that is earned, not inherited!

My suspicions of a sacred in-between plateau were confirmed by a young friend who came my way in the fall of '82, his name Franz Gerhard Wegeler. I was immediately attracted to this lad of seventeen. Not only was he interested in music and science, but (through birth) shared with me a common poverty. He was determined to rise above his lowly state—to reach the lasting nobility of intellectual achievement. What more perfect encouragement could there be for my own resolution? I had found a true brother-in-arms!

In the spring of 1783, Electoral Chapelmaster Lucchesi was granted a leave of absence. For the balance of the theatrical season, poor Neefe was in charge of all church music and court music. Needless to say, he called upon me for increased assistance. Before I realized what happened, I was seated in the theater orchestra conducting rehearsals from the pianoforte. Is it any wonder that I developed sight-reading capabilities? I had to guide entire performances by playing from the score. It was here that I first made practical use of my training—an opportunity to savor the possibilities of applied music. By June '83, I had been exposed to a considerable cross section of the light and superficial music of Bonn's stage. Its contrast to my studies in Bach, Handel, and Mozart established for me a permanent sense of values. From this experience grew my "lifelong" abhorrence of cheap music—music of the hour. I thanked sweet fate that Mozart was still my goal and Neefe was still my teacher.

In spite of what some artists and sculptors pretend to see, I was not handsome. I had a very dark complexion that encouraged unflattering nicknames. My chest was well developed for a thirteen-year-old. My arms were strong, could easily lift my weight. But my legs were short and kept me well below average height. They grew round as a linden tree, but unfortunately not as tall. A siege of smallpox two years earlier sprinkled my face with unsightly "craters of the moon." To top off this lack of beauty came a growth of hair, which in five years transformed me into the typical "hairy ape." I had more hair on my shoulders and hands than many a poor Earthling could boast on his scalp. And yet in spite of this ominous inventory of physical hindrances, I knew that deep within dwelt the desire and ability for intellectual achievement. Hopefully, the light of my efforts would someday shine from my eyes and lead me into the arms of a beautiful girl!

The end of the 1782–83 season brought welcome leisure to unleash a new inspiration for study and composition. I do believe that I could have achieved Father's dream this summer had it not been for the sadness and gloom that surrounded me at home. In the middle of August, my youngest brother died, and conditions became absolutely paralytic.

For the coming season (1783–84), Max Friedrich assumed financial responsibilities of the theater. Consequently, Director Mme Grossmann went all-out to please the elector's dramatic tastes, which were decidedly operatic. This provided Neefe with an even busier season than before. He had daily rehearsals of opera and was still substituting for Chapelmaster Lucchesi. My duties became correspondingly heavier, so much so that Father encouraged me to petition for an appointment as assistant court organist. Until I received such official status, there would be no hope for compensation. On the last day of February 1784, my petition was granted, thanks no doubt to the kind interventions of Neefe and Salm-Reifferscheid. I was now a regular member of the court chapel, but still without pay! The question of my salary had not been decided when, on April 15,

Elector Max Friedrich died. His death brought abrupt changes in Bonn's music circles. The theatrical company was dismissed with a month's pay. Lucchesi returned as chapelmaster. Neefe was reduced to the position of organist/teacher. And I became, once again, a full-time student, but a student who had had a taste of professional musicianship.0 I had glimpsed my future. And I was now listed in the official register as assistant court organist, even though Neefe had no need for an assistant.

Had Max Friedrich continued to live, Lucchesi would not have hurried home in fear of his job, Neefe would have remained overloaded, and I would have continued as cembalist in the theater orchestra. Perhaps I would have blossomed into an operatic composer. However, under the new scheme of things, I resumed the serious study of piano and composition, fragments of the E-flat Piano Concerto took shape, and the Mozartian goal loomed once more into imminence. Apparently Father had gotten to Neefe; for now, even my teacher thought of me as an aspiring Mozart. He encouraged me to be as much like my prototype as possible. His main reason appeared to be the profoundly worshipful feelings held for Mozart by the new elector, Max Franz. The closer I approached Mozart, the greater would be my promotional opportunities at court. At any rate, starting with July, I was under an annual salary of one hundred thalers—just half the amount my father received after twenty-eight years of service! All I did for my pay was share the chapel organ with Neefe. Thus began a sequence of three years in which most of my time was spent composing, practicing and studying.

Chapter 4

In addition to the musical developments of this period, there were important social contacts—friendships made that lasted across the decades until the closing scenes in Vienna. First came Franz Ries, leader of the court orchestra and a good friend of Father's. He condescended to give me violin lessons, and how he managed to put up with my scrapings and scratchings, I'll never know. But at the close of the three-year period of which I now speak, it is this loving Ries who helps our family through its greatest financial crisis and proves himself to be far more than a mere teacher of violin.

By the end of 1784, I had gotten to know most of Ries's students; and three of them became my own first piano pupils, providing a welcome supplement to the annual one hundred thalers. It was a long time between quarterly payments!

Among my fellow violin students was a young chap of ten named Stephan von Breuning. I hadn't seriously considered him as a pupil until Wegeler struck up an acquaintance with the boy, getting to know not only Stephan but also the rest of his family, which was of highest social rank. He described a wonderful mother whose husband had died in the palace fire of '77. Besides Stephan, there were three other children: Christoph, who was thirteen; Eleonore, twelve; and a younger brother, Lenz, who was seven. Wegeler assured me that as "assistant court organist to the elector of Cologne," I would be welcomed into their family circle and gain four new students of piano.

On February 9, 1785, accompanied by Wegeler, I took the fatal step and there opened for me a view of family relations that to date had existed only in my dreams. Here in the Münsterplatz were people who occupied the precise social plateau to which I aspired. They had comfortable wealth and yet none of the aloof snobbishness of court nobility. My welcome as Wegeler's friend was warm and sincere. It would have been the same were I a prince, a priest, a king, or a pauper. At first, my dark complexion, short stature, and square-edged manners seemed to amuse the children. They kept their distance. But soon our conversation turned to music and led me to the piano and a half hour's improvisation. My playing, not my words, won me the full acceptance of the family; and I was engaged as a teacher for Eleonore and Lenz.

With three hundred thalers per year, three measures of grain, and income from fourteen private students, Father concluded that our family was far too wealthy to continue living in the Rheingasse. On the first of May, we moved to No. 462 Wenzelgasse, a more cheerful home near the Minorite Church. This continued to be our family dwelling place for the remaining years in Bonn.

One year later, almost to the day, Mother gave birth to her last child, Maria Margaretha Josepha. I hoped my darling new sister would compensate Mom for the loss of little Anna Maria. But not even a baby girl angel could penetrate the dark clouds of Mother's pessimism. Pitiable sadness had become her permanent way of life.

The next year had much in common with its two predecessors. A small proportion of it was spent as organist and piano teacher. For the most, I continued to be cast in the role of student—a student of piano, violin, theory and composition. Neefe continued as he had begun, every inch a taskmaster. The first noticeable change in routine was due to father. With the arrival of 1787, he realized that I had turned sixteen (which meant fourteen, according to his calendar) and would soon be too old for the scant clothing of a child prodigy. It was now or never! But how could he present me to the world? Another local debut? No! Although my technique for playing and improvising had improved and the E-flat Concerto was approaching its final form, there were still no creative masterpieces in my name. I had failed to grow like a Mozart. What could be done?

Father and Neefe had many talks about my next step and always came to the same conclusion. I must journey to Vienna and become a student of Mozart. What better way to descend from a Master than as his pupil? Some plan! Its mere contemplation brought me weak knees, a fluttery stomach and dangerously loose bowels. Though my first intestinal disorders occurred at this time, I refuse to blame the next forty years of diarrheic disturbances entirely on the might of Herr Mozart's musical personality. However, if the great Maestro could thus affect me from faraway Vienna, I wondered what would be the result of meeting him face-to-face!

Back in 1787, a journey from Bonn to Vienna was no easy undertaking, especially for a member of a family in our financial condition. I had saved my entire first-quarter salary and, in reply to a petition for leave of absence, had received the second-quarter payment in advance. Father and I scraped together fifteen florins from our private teaching, and good old Neefe managed a gold ducat for my going-away present.

The journey was made in a public post coach, which square-wheeled its way along the Rhine as far as Ehrenbreitstein, then through Frankfurt, Nuremberg and Linz to Vienna. As I jolted along, my hopes hit an indeterminate sequence of highs and lows. I tried to imagine what it would be like to finally behold the man whose example had become my justification for existence. Would he embrace my talent with words of praise and encouragement? Would he take me under the wing of his personal guidance? Or would he tower above me as a mighty Thor, casting perfected thunderbolts on the naked strivings of a poor boy from Bonn? Would I return victoriously to my mother's arms? Or would her terrible cough continue to worsen (as it had since Maria's birth) and call her from me before I had a chance to offer anything but dreams and promises? Not even the sunny confidence of Father Rhine could interrupt this alternating current of my thoughts.

The seventeenth of April welcomed me to Vienna, and I spent the entire day trying to squeeze suitable lodging into the restricted dimensions of my budget. Not until the following Sunday morning did I first go Mozart hunting; this seemed to me the best time in the week for a busy Master. Under my arm, I proudly carried the *E-flat Concerto*, three *Bagatelles* and Neefe's engraving of my baby variations. My memory was stuffed to the fingertips with Bach fugues and two sets of teenage Beethoven variations, still in a semi-improvisatory state. As I crossed into the Schulerstrasse, the sound of beautiful quartet music convinced me that "1846" was the correct address. I climbed the dark flights of stone steps that led to Mozart's rooms and stood before the one remaining door that separated me from the living inspiration of my entire youth. My first inclination was to run, the next was to proudly announce my arrival with a bold fortissimo knock; but then, how could I interrupt such inspired goings-on, perfect music which I later came to know and love as the Master's "*Hunting Quartet*?" For a while, I stood in an opposite doorway, soaking up the tones. Suddenly, the very walls of the deep stairwell seemed to develop huge unfriendly eyes that stared me into self-consciousness. I descended to the street and walked toward St. Stephen's Church, planning to reappear after the quartet. My return was not greeted by encouraging silence, but by pianoforte accompaniment to a soprano voice of operatic stature. Then came clapping, laughing and dancing to a minuet. This was not a home. It was a music center! I would return the next day.

Monday's knock was answered by a slight but splendid man. He dazzled like a king in a bright red dress coat, which had jewels for buttons. His point lace ruffles and silver buckles made me think that I had inadvertently aroused His Imperial Majesty. All that was missing was the powdered wig; instead there was a mound of natural blond hair that was drawn straight back into a stringy tail held neatly in place by a tight black ribbon. I managed to pry a question from the dryness in my throat.

B. Herr Mozart?
M. Yes, indeed. And what young devil have we here?
B. Not a devil, Sir! I am Beethoven. I have come from Bonn to see you.
M. Oh yes! Just last week I received a post from your elector. He introduced you and included some fine commendations from Herr Neefe and my friend Waldstein. Come in! I must hear you.

We entered a large room that seemed small because of its crowded contents. Stuffed into the corners were a piano, a full quartet of strings, some woodwinds, two writing desks (one so tall that you would have to stand in front of it to employ its use), two sofas, three chairs, a billiard table, and a miniature stage. Unbelievably, the center of the room was an open space. This explained where the quartet playing and dancing of the preceding day had taken place. Mozart offered me a chair and explained that he had guests in an adjoining room and would return as soon as he had excused himself. His polished manners, his graceful walk, his entire physical body possessed a rhythm and charm that made me feel clumsy and awkward. I was surprised at his smallness. Not the giant I had feared—just a thin little man with a very large nose. He returned, offered me the piano, and pulled up a chair for himself.

M. What have you brought *with* you?
B. Bach fugues . . . two sets of variations which Herr Neefe—
M. *What*?! (*He interrupted before I could mention my concerto.*) You come to me without any *Mozart*? You *are* a scamp!

He jumped to his writing table, fidgeted through a topsy-turvy stack of manuscripts, then handed me a bulky score. Its cover sheet contained the words: "*Concerto in C,* Written to Please Herr Mozart by Wolfgang Amade' Mozart." While I pondered over this strange title, he opened the score and thumped a nervous finger at the piano part.

M. Here . . . try *this*!

I had never seen such perfect manuscript—a pleasure to read at sight. No challenge at all, compared to my mortal struggles at Grossmann's. At first I was kept busy trying to apply all of Neefe's pedantries to the music before me. But in the slow section, I could turn several times and observe Mozart. The nervous rhythms of his hands and feet were quieted by a deep abstraction that had come upon him. His bony chin rested in the chubby fingers of his right hand while the pupils of his eyes moved upward and disappeared beneath half-closed lids. Whatever he was contemplating was deep, and sad and mystical. I could see it was not my playing that held his attention. This bothered me. My sole purpose was to make a favorable first impression. As gracefully as possible, I terminated my Mozart reading and asked the Maestro for a theme upon which I could improvise. A pink concentration replaced the white abstraction in his face; I knew he was composing! In less than a minute, he stood beside me at the piano and played the newborn text. It contained an interesting melody, a pregnant rhythm and a trick. The trick was a subtly hidden countertheme that wove its way between the alto and tenor parts. I knew he thought I would never discover it, but thanks to Father's hearing game, it sang to me clearly and enticingly with handfuls of tempting possibilities. Now *I* became the one who was fully abstracted; the music at hand crowded all else from my mind. There was no room for doubt or fear. No thoughts of time or place, of an anxious father, of a sickly mother, or of the great Maestro who listened nearby. Only the music remained, and it poured from my fingers with a determined variety of patterns.

I was brought back to consciousness by two hands placed on my shoulders—hands of the greatest musician in the world. I looked up into Mozart's face, and had he not spoken a single word, the approval in his eyes would have sufficed. But he turned to the doorway that was now filled with staring guests.

M. Watch this young chap. He'll make a noise in the world. And we'll *all* sit up and listen!

(*His quiet smile beamed down at me.*) And now, young man, I must return to my company. Stanzi will be away this Friday. If you come in the afternoon, I should like to discuss what you've done and your future plans. I might even challenge your respect for billiards.

I had descended a dozen steps when he called me back to hand me some staff paper.

M. Here, take *this*. I'm anxious to see how much of your improvisation can find its way to paper.

I bounded into the Schulerstrasse. The happiest boy in Vienna wanted to sing, to dance, to clap his heels in the air, to hug the first stranger who came along and shout in his ear,

B. I am Beethoven, pupil of Mozart!

After the novelty of my new title had had its effect, I found myself sitting quietly in my little room, staring at empty music paper. How much I had grown to depend upon a keyboard! I scratched down the Master's theme, but could not go on without a piano. For two days I tried to recall the inspiration that had flashed through my mind at Mozart's; pitiable fragments were all that returned. And yet Friday was approaching, and I had to have something to take with me. I decided to forget my cursed improvisation and spend the remaining time in writing a set of variations on Mozart's theme. When Friday afternoon called time on my frantic efforts, I realized that I could have used another week to patch up deficiencies. But such is life! When hoping for time to pass, it caterpillars along like a sleepy cecropia, but try to hold it back an hour, it flexes new-sprouted moth wings and flies away. I arrived at No. 1846 with great misgivings.

This time, Herr Mozart was not dressed for a party, but relaxed in the loose-fitting comfort of what must have been an old and favorite dressing gown. His eyes spotted my score.

M. Ah, you brought me your improvisation.
B. No, Herr Mozart.
M. Something else then. Good! Let me see it.
B. I am ashamed of it.
M. A composer ashamed of his own score? You are a knave, but an honest one. Very well. If it is a bad score, it must be punished, and the only way to punish a bad score is to ignore it. Sit down, I have a surprise for you.

He seated himself at the piano, and his playing of the next thirty-five minutes shook my self-confidence until it blushed at the very thought of a musical career. How humiliating! For nearly a week, I had tried without any success to recall Monday's improvisation. And here was Mozart, with the technique of liquid sunshine and the sensitivity of moonlight, recreating the entire piece exactly as I had dreamed it five days earlier. Was there any hope for me at all?

When he finished playing, he took down a friendly bottle of Rüdesheimer wine and poured us each a glass. Looking me straight in the eyes, he winked.

M. Let's talk now and save the billiards for another time. (*He pulled his chair closer and continued.*) I'm glad you've come to Vienna. This is the best place in the world for young musicians. Paris sings of her revolution; London holds out her enticing gold. But Vienna offers you her love—the love of a beautiful woman. She is not always expedient and proper, but always a woman, always beautiful. Breaking away from Bonn won't be easy. Your parents will plead for your return, you'll be homesick. When you least expect it, Max Franz will cut off your salary, and you'll wonder where on earth the next florin is coming from. But courage! Remember that poor Mozart suffered identical pangs when he left Salzburg and came here to woo the lovely lady. To this day, my beloved emperor has never offered me the dignity of a court position. He respects me as a pianist, but thinks my compositions are "too modern" to be taken seriously. He stands in his imperial box and shouts "Bravo, Mozart!" at the conclusion of my *Figaro*, but offers me no appointment. His musical court is ruled by a clique of bloodthirsty Italians who think nothing of cutting out my heart to get at my reputation. They convince Joseph that *Figaro* is a novelty and should be quickly shelved in favor of more "proper" operas by Martini, Righini, and Salieri. I had to journey clear to Prague to find a suitable home for my dear *Figaro*.

B. How can you love such a lady? (*I interrupted.*) She slaps your face!

M. Ah, but she's beautiful! She offers you pride and a feeling of independence and social status. Within her loving arms are to be found the best musicians in Europe. Haydn comes to play quartets with me in this very room. She's happy to share with you the finest musical instruments, the best orchestras, perfect theater, the promise of a national opera born and bred on German soil. She embraces the best-educated musical public in the world and sends to your door a host of wealthy patrons who are eager to sponsor private concerts and to pay for lessons. Now can you love her a little?

I managed a weak affirmative, and then Mozart asked for a more detailed description of my musical background than was provided in the letters of introduction. I dwelt long and lovingly on Grandfather's career, but carefully understated the frustrated efforts of Father and the poverty-ridden conditions of our home life. The Maestro was pleased to hear of Neefe's strong pedagogical preference for Bach, but seemed most interested in my applied musical experiences at Grossmann's. He then pressed me for a precise statement of my musical goals, and it was impossible to behold the pale penetration of childlike kindness in his face without being perfectly honest.

B. It is my dream, Herr Mozart, to become as great a musician as yourself. And it is my parents' dream that my career may begin as yours began.

M. (*From the Maestro, with penetrating eyes.*) For *monetary* reasons?

B. Not entirely . . . one *must* make a strong beginning.

Mozart filled our glasses from the halfway mark.

M. Good! I hope your career will never become enslaved to a bag of ducats. Of course, a musician must be paid for his work, but he daren't confuse compensation with inspiration. I must admit . . .

financially, my own career has been a disappointment. Stanzi and I never seem to have enough money for the simple pleasures we enjoy. But there is still hope; after all, Gluck is an old man. Perhaps I shall receive his appointment, and think how happy we could be on such a fine salary. But an artist should not be concerned with finances. After all, things will be *some* way. If I must give music lessons to survive, so be it! If I'm to enjoy a beautiful home and garden, good. If not, well . . . the career of a musician has its own rewards. Now let's talk about your future. You come to Vienna to study with Mozart. Very well, I accept you as a student. I accept you as you are, not as you and your parents dream yourself to be. I cannot make a child prodigy out of you because you are not a child prodigy. I cannot make you a precocious young soloist because you are not a precocious young soloist. Next week, when my little Hans Hummel returns, you must hear *him* play. He is only eleven, and yet his delicate and sensitive piano makes yours sound like all fists and thumbs!

Temper boiled its way from my soul to the tip of my nose. If I had remained silent, the thumping in my ears and the pounding of my heart would have spoken for me. Putting down the wine, I stood by my chair, practically at attention.

B. Herr Mozart! I come to you for help and encouragement. At the thought of being your pupil, I am as proud as any mortal has ever been. But you take everything from me. You must understand how I feel. I can put up with almost anything except insurmountable competition. When Herr Neefe displays his masterful organ technique, I can feel my career running to an opposite path. And now, you outshine me in *every* respect. I can't recall my own improvisation, you play it back note for note. Your piano technique is greater than mine. A little boy's technique is greater than mine. Your gift as a composer—

M. Is greater than yours. So what? Does this mean that you have no right to a musical career? Sit down, boy. Your sensitivity is showing, and I'm proud of you.

We traded chairs, and Mozart continued.

M. I pass judgment on you as your teacher, and I reserve the right to be perfectly frank with my students. If you can't stand my sharp tongue, you won't survive as my pupil.

B. It's not your tongue I fear, Herr Mozart. It's your talent. You are heavens above me!

M. Must you be above everyone else to feel comfortable?

B To me, a career is like a competitive race. If I cannot carry the torch a few steps farther than my contemporaries, what purpose do I serve?

M Very well, Ludwig. Run your race! Carry your torch! But must you lead all contestants from the start? I dangle little Hummel before your ears to discourage your dreams of prodigy, not to demoralize your musical ambitions. What counts in a man is his achievement, not his native endowment. My talent is enormous, but without strenuous application, I would achieve little. Perhaps your talents are less than Hummel's and mine, but through work, self-discipline, and sacrifice, your final achievement could well leave us both behind! Concentrate on the race, and don't worry so much about who's winning. Let me see that bad little score you brought.

Mozart nervously bit his lips and made sour grimaces as he read through the pages.

M. This is very poor. You would never become my student on the basis of such a piece. But how frail it is compared to the personality of your improvisation. As soon as that bold and independent spirit of yours reaches paper, Beethoven the composer will emerge. I want you to write me a minuet, a fugue, and a rondo. And mind you, they must sound like the Beethoven I respect—not like exercises in thoroughbass.

B. How about Beethoven, the pianist?

M. Don't worry about him! With a little patience, we'll polish off his rough edges and he'll do all right as a young man—not as a boy wonder.

B. When should I return?

M. Hmm . . . this is a very bad time for me. I'm up to my neck in a new opera, and my dear father's health is precarious. Suppose we don't make a definite appointment. Stick with your assignment until the pieces represent your best work . . . until they sound like last Monday. Then come back and we'll set up a definite schedule.

Walking from the Schulerstrasse, I felt as though I had left my own weight in golden dreams standing on Mozart's doorstep. I hurried back to my little room near the Hofburg and settled down to a week's work that took thirty-seven days for completion. Only three pieces, but I was determined to achieve perfection!

First, a minuet. I decided to write a half dozen and then select the best one for Mozart. The writing was easy enough, but when the time came to choose my favorite, I could find none. All six were average compositions—products of a schoolboy. None contained the slightest bolt of improvisatory splendor.

Forget the minuet! I turned to the problem of writing a good fugue. Three attempts led to the careful application of Neefe's rules, but not to inspired music. A sickening fear came upon me—imagine returning to Mozart with three poor pieces as bad as the first one I had shown him! There was a difference. This time I was not fighting a Friday afternoon deadline but could take as much time as was needed to do my best work. An evolutionary approach suddenly tempted me into following its path and seemed more promising than rules. I turned to the *Well-Tempered Clavichord* and copied out *five* of the twenty-one Bach fugues I had memorized—quite a feat for me, without a piano! Next came five days of painstaking analysis, limiting myself to one day per fugue. Each subject and countersubject, each augmentation and diminution, each selection of intervals, each rhythmic and sequential pattern was carefully scrutinized. I began to see the difference between a fugue and great music written in the *form* of a fugue. Father Bach was more than the following of rules. His music was his personality—a pillar of strength, honesty, devotion, sincerity, beauty. And most important, he spoke in a polyphonic language that was neither assumed nor affected, but absolutely natural to him in every way. My problem was to discover how he was able to breathe his spirit into a skeleton of inanimate rules and transform it into the immortality of living music—music that portrayed his very being! From this I hoped to learn how to stamp Beethovenian scores with Beethoven's personality. Only then would my written pieces take on the improvisatory flair appreciated by Mozart.

After my studies in Bach, I wrote four fugues. Each displayed more "living" music than those that sprang from Neefe's teaching, but none contained the uniqueness of inspiration so easy to capture in extemporaneous playing. Composing another fugue wasn't the answer. I chose the best of the four and attacked it with a week's barrage of editing and rewriting in the form of insertions, alterations, contractions, deletions, substitutions, expansions. The cold austerity of a "correct" fugue finally gave way to the blood and suffering of patient revision. Though cast in the framework of Bach, many of its sections now contained the spontaneity of improvisation. Here and there were snatches of newness that were the first appearance of my own personality on paper. I was proud of this work, even though its birth cost me ten days of suffering and anxiety. If this were the price I must pay to get real Beethoven into writing, so be it!

I chose one of my six "average" minuets and exposed it to the same write, rewrite, and rewrite-the-rewrite technique. In two days, the much worked-over little dance was worthy to stand beside my fugue, and there remained only the problem of a rondo. Instead of composing an entire piece and then subjecting it to revision, I decided to do my rewriting as I went along. The initial sketches were carefully reshaped until they pleased me, then the rest of the composition progressed quickly and agreeably. The end of the rondo was the end of my assignment, and I was ready for Mozart!

When I returned to the Schulerstrasse, my teacher's apartment was quiet and empty. He had moved away. Following neighbors' directions, I journeyed out to the Landstrasse where I found Herr Mozart sitting in the delightful garden of a tiny cottage. With him was a "youngish" woman whom I assumed to be Frau Mozart. Their backs were toward the gate, and they did not hear me enter. For several minutes, I stood beneath the beautiful rose arbor and stared upward through young leaves at a sky of spotless blue. Dozens of pink buds danced and sang to the world that the first week of June had arrived. I hoped that the Mozarts would notice me, but neither turned my way. Our initial meeting crossed my mind, and I whistled the tune that the Maestro had given me to improvise upon. Before turning around, he had already joined me in whistling the countertheme. When our eyes met, the duet ended and he greeted me:

M. Good morning, young Beethoven, it's nice to see you again. Come into our little paradise.

I hope my expression did not betray my surprise, but I was shocked to see the change that had taken place in Mozart. His dear face was all nose and eyes, and he was even whiter and thinner than he was when I had last seen him. Before he mentioned it, I knew that his father had either died or was much worse.

M. You must meet my strict but inspiring hausfrau. Stanzi, this is Beethoven, my newest pupil—a true diamond in the rough.

I bowed and kissed her extended hand. She combined the charm and poise of a Madame von Breuning with a childlike ease of manner that I had never observed in a full-grown woman. With delightful composure, she kissed her husband on the forehead, tweaked his nose, and turned again toward me.

S. Young man, into your hands I commend my dear Mozart. See what you can do with him. He sits brooding and philosophizing over the death of his father. Neither Don Giovanni nor I can entice him away from his profound and melancholic thoughts. I keep telling him that he will never be happy again until he returns to his music.

She curtseyed to me like a dainty little girl.

S. I leave you now, please talk shop. See if you can inspire the Muse in him once more!

Mozart eyed her worshipfully as she "daintied" her way from the garden into the house.

M. Dear Constanze! She really understands me better than you would suppose. She knows that it is not my nature to be morose or sad. I am my best at happy parties among chattering friends and sparkling punch bowls. I much prefer a stein of pilsner to the bread and water of contemplation. She knows that I'm the life of any party and would not have me otherwise. . . . Ah, but the death of my dear father is another matter. He was not only a loving parent, but the discoverer of my talents too, the well-taught teacher of my early days, the careful guide of my first ambitions, the constant inspiration of my prodigy career. Am I now to go on pushing my little pen as though nothing has happened?

B. I think I understand how you feel, Herr Mozart.

M. How can you?

B. Last month I received two letters from home. Each spoke of the worsening condition of my dear mother, and we now know that she is not strong enough to win her battle against consumption.

M. I'm sorry to hear this. I can tell that you are close to your mother and that you will miss her. You will feel deprived and resentful at her being taken from you. But perhaps your attitude toward death will change as you grow older. Mine has!

B. Death is the cruel surrender to fate that each of us must eventually make.

M. Death is our reward for having lived. It is the goal of our life, a good and true friend of mankind.

B. It is the merciless end of our dreams and hopes—a foul injustice rearing its ugly head amidst the otherwise beautiful scheme of creation.

M. Dear Beethoven, five years ago I would have agreed with you perfectly. But not now! I can no longer view death as a cruel monster patiently waiting to deprive us of all joy and beauty. I see her not as the end of things, but as an open door to a new beginning.

B. New beginning! How can you find a new beginning in an open grave?

M. I can't point it out to you, but I know it's there! For several days, I've been rebuilding my life in the inspiring assurance that my father is now safe and free from pain and suffering. As Stanzi has observed, such reconstruction takes time. Soon the picture will be complete. I shall return to my work, and return with enough inspiration for the rest of my days. A few weeks on my new opera, then I'll be ready even for the pangs of pedagogy. Could you return about the first of next month? Things will surely be back to normal, and we'll fit you into my schedule.

B. Do you not have time to review my assignment?

M. Certainly! Let's see what you have.

I handed Mozart the three pieces—minuet on top, rondo in the middle, and the dessert last. As I expected, he opened the scores in his lap and read them through on the spot. Any old day, *this* musician needed a piano to hear music. His concentration brought a radiant glow into his face. Eagerly, I watched for the first nod of acceptance . . . for just a tiny wink of approval. I felt my hands grow cold and my toes curl with anxiety. If only he would say something!

He seemed to hear with his whole body. His head, eyebrows, lips, hands, and feet were all in motion. At last! Thanks to a tricky little contrapuntal rhythm in the third section of the fugue, the heart-stopping silence was shattered by words from heaven:

M. This is fine, Ludwig . . . very fine!

Think of it! The king of music had looked into my score and found something that pleased him. Six little words of encouragement, but how valued they were! I could now accomplish all things. Never again would I doubt the authenticity of my mission. The joy of this moment assured me that my parents had been correct and realistic in their dreams for my future. My career was launched; I would now never turn back—no matter *what* the odds!

When Mozart finished "hearing" the fugue, he looked up with a twinkle in his eye.

M. You've done a fine job with your assignment, young man. In my long career, I've heard many brilliant masters of extempore playing. Usually when these musicians attempt to write down their pianistic rhapsodizings, only sad sequences of trite clichés come to paper. This has not been the case with you. Somehow you've managed to catch the fire and spark of your improvisations. Tell me the story behind your success.

My rewritings for the fugue and minuet were destroyed, but fortunately, I had intact the entire set of work papers for the rondo. I handed these to Mozart; he studied them carefully.

M. This is amazing, Ludwig. You begin with naively crude ideas and then evolve genuine originality out of nothingness! I would never have believed that such natural spontaneity could result from such painstaking revision. In my own case, the entire act of composition takes place within my mind. The original ideas, the rough boundaries, the first statements, the modest revisions . . . the finished piece. All the work is done before I take pen in hand. In your case, the very act of composition awaits your determined revisions. So . . . this is not a matter of right-or-wrong technique, but simply an example of individual differences. I'm not the first to predict great things for your future, nor will I be the last. But just let me say this. You are young and determined. You've found a method of composition that really works. Your pianistic skill is above average. If you roll up your sleeves and keep working, there is no limit to the success you will achieve for our art and for our Fatherland. I'm sorry to delay our first lessons together, but I know you understand my situation. I wish you'd spend the next several weeks working out some preliminary sketches for a piano concerto. We'll complete it during the summer and polish up your piano technique. If all goes well, this coming season should witness your debut as pianist and composer. Vienna will give you her official welcome, and I know you'll consider making her your permanent home . . . or at least the center of your musical activities. Leave your assignment with me. When you return, I'll show you how I would have handled a few spots here and there. I do this not to teach you to write like Mozart, but to put you on the defensive. From our discussions (and arguments) you'll learn why you do what you do, and whether or not you wish to modify your technique.

We shook hands and walked toward the little opening in the hedge, Mozart's arm about my shoulder. As we parted, came his final words:

M. Take care, work hard, and *do* receive good news about your mother!

That afternoon, I was suddenly struck by the full realization of how successful my trip to Vienna had been. I came, hoping at best for Mozart's appraisal of my work, a few lessons, and perhaps an entree into the music circles of Vienna. Instead, I was accepted as a regular student of Mozart. The great Maestro was already planning my Vienna debut. He promised me a list of eager and well-paying piano students. His opinion of my progress was honest, sincere—encouraging. And I could afford to be extremely optimistic about my latest assignment: sketches for a piano concerto! On July first, instead of returning to the Maestro with sketches, I hoped to surprise him with a complete composition. All I had to do was pass my *E-flat Concerto* through the same careful revisions that had transformed my fugue and minuet into acceptable music and hope for the best. Wonderful prospects, but what sad reverses lay ahead!

During the second and third weeks of June, I received three letters from home, each more ominous than its predecessor. The last, posted June 15, insisted that if I did not leave for Bonn at once, I would never again see my mother alive. Think of it. Here in Vienna, the door to my career opened wide and invitingly. At the same time, in Bonn, the door to the one whom I most loved was closing forever. I had no alternative but to fly to her arms and offer whatever comfort she could find in my heart. Small payment for a dear mother whose sole ambition was to love her family and to sacrifice her life for it. Fate was kind to me in one respect. He gave me no hint as to the long and wearisome path that would lead me back to Vienna. Nor did he tell me that my return, five years later, would find an entirely different city. Still happy and gay on the surface, still opening friendly doors to visiting musicians, but a city whose true musical spirit had become as cold and inaccessible as the unmarked grave of Wolfgang Amadeus Mozart!

Chapter 5

While in Vienna, I wrote nothing to Bonn concerning my conversations with Mozart. I wanted to be sure of their outcome; then I would surprise our entire family. When I arrived home, Father had heard nothing of Mozart's encouragement, nor of his plans for my debut. And yet his first words to me did not concern my career:

BF. Ludwig, you must run to your mother. She lives just for your return.
B. Is there no hope?
BF. Only the hope that she will not linger on in her pain and suffering.

I was shocked by the cruel heartlessness that could wish my mother dead, but shock melted into sympathetic agreement the instant I stood by her bed. How little remained of her former self. The pitiable frame she occupied was more dead than alive, and the gray pallor of death had practically erased her loving features. I held her hands in mine; I gently stroked her moistureless brow. For long minutes she slept while I patiently awaited the opening of her eyes. Only in them could I hope to find once more the heart-warming approval of a mother's smile.

At last she awakened and looked up into my face. No smile in those poor eyes—just the glassy stare of physical suffering! Using all her strength, she raised her hand to feebly outline my forehead, cheek and chin. This convinced her that it was I who knelt by her bed. (Think of it! Two years earlier, Mother could lift me off my feet into her arms. Now she could scarcely raise her own hand!) Her lips trembled.

BM. Ludwig! . . . Dear Ludwig! . . . You've come home to me! (*Tears ran down her cheeks.*) What . . . what will happen to you now . . . now that I am gone?

B. Dear soul . . . you are not gone! You've been ill, that's all. In a few weeks you'll be strong again. You'll be up and around the house. In September, I'll take you with me to Vienna, where you'll meet Herr Mozart. He has accepted me as his student and predicts great things for this Fall. He even talks of my debut. Just try to tell me that our dream is not coming true.

I paused for her reply—there was none. Her heavy eyelids had closed again; she was asleep. With my lips and my tears, I kissed her withered hands, knowing that for only a short time would they escape the cold stillness of death. She had spoken the truth. She *was* gone. What would happen to us now? I could scream out the hallowed name of "Mother" from one nation to the next, and nowhere on Earth was there a single voice to answer my cry. How could Mozart call such cruel separation the "true friend of mankind"?

Mother lingered on through five more weeks of coughing, gagging, gasping, suffering—utter exhaustion. She never gained enough strength to be receptive to my good news from Vienna. She died on July 17, totally unconcerned that her son had become a pupil of the greatest musician on Earth!

For the next five years, I remained in Bonn and waged my first battles against the swiftly developing specter of a cruel fate that was "out to get me." His initial blows were the death of my mother and my separation from Mozart. These were the worst. But they were followed immediately by an uninterrupted sequence of nagging frustrations, calculated to add insult to my injuries. First came poverty, financial embarrassment of the direst sort. We had always been poor, but never to the extent of actual fear for the survival of our family. Completing my journey from Vienna, I had to borrow money from the Schadens in Augsburg. I arrived home in debt, without a penny, having spent six months' pay and all my earnings from teaching. My third-quarter salary was not due until August, and Father's petition for an advance had been ignored. What could we do? At this time I didn't know the Breuning family well enough to ask them for help; besides, they were away for the summer. Father had sold most of his personal effects and was now auctioning off Grandfather's modest treasures and even my dead mother's clothing. What a disgrace!

Concurrent with this outburst of rank poverty came the first real impairment of my health. I suffered a serious spell of asthma that lasted through the summer. Because of our vivid experience with Mother, my imagination quickly transformed this asthmatic condition into the advanced stages of consumption.To me, my cough sounded as final and fatal as Mother's. The belief that my illness was mortal engendered feelings of deep depression and hopeless melancholy. Four months later, the same gamut of despair was rerun upon the death of my little sister on November 25, 1787.

Father never recovered from the loss of his wife and daughter. He gave up all hope for our future and proceeded to drink his way through 1788 and 1789. Since I had promised my dying mother that I would protect our little family from his incurable weakness, I petitioned the elector for the chance to assume full responsibility for our financial affairs. I sought to have Father's salary paid to me so that I could protect it from alcoholic conversion. On November 20, 1789, came the decree. What a disappointment! Only half of his salary was transferred to me, his services at court were terminated, and he was threatened with banishment from Bonn if he didn't mend his ways. The stupid document asked the impossible. It took away his job, provided him with drinking money, and insisted that he give up drinking. This was no victory for me. After all, he was still my father; I had the need and the right to feel proud of him. And yet there he was, reduced to less than a man: no profession, no pride, no self-confidence, no hope. Just a broken-down drinking machine with sufficient funds to keep on "running!"

No doubt about it, these final years in Bonn contained a downward current that swept me toward the brink of suicide. Such release would have been too tempting to resist had there not been a countercurrent, a warm stream of slowly rising optimism that finally crested at such heights as to enable me once again to turn my steps toward Vienna. My self-confidence gradually metamorphosed into manly proportions. By 1792, I could stare fate straight in the eye and accept, without reservation, whatever he had to offer.

The first rung of this upward climb is attributable to Franz Ries. He visited us on the day of Mother's death, offering his sympathy and financial aid. Thanks to him, we were able to provide a decent burial for Mother and, four months later, the same for little Margareth. Ries helped us with food, clothing, and rent. He employed a housekeeper for our part-time use, enabling Father, Carl, Johann, and me to remain together in the Wenzelgasse. From Ries, I learned how a true friend should act and the inestimable value of having true friends. During the final five years in Bonn, my circle of loved ones widened and deepened. It came to include those Earthlings who remained closest and dearest to my heart. At the top of the list were Wegeler, the von Breunings, and Waldstein.

Wegeler was exceptionally helpful to me from the time of Mother's death until his departure for Vienna in September 1787. Together we would take extended walks through the palace gardens and along the Rhine. His continued reassurances gradually had their effect. I came to visualize my departed mother in the unfading colors of true optimism. Indeed, my living picture of her was probably much like that which Mozart was reconstructing of his father. Thanks to Wegeler, I was able to survive the loss of this dear soul who gave me life and carefully nurtured it through early storms. The good doctor further convinced me that my "fatal consumption" was nothing more than a psychosomatic inflection of a stubborn asthmatic condition, a distortion inspired by the painful image of Mother's suffering. I must interrupt myself to confess that Wegeler did not use the word *psychosomatic*. It had not yet been invented. At any rate, I came to see my illness as 90 percent imagined and 10 percent real. This favorable ratio quickly reduced it to my own size. I fought back and won. My high opinion of Wegeler never diminished. He was not like ordinary doctors, helpless without their little bottles of medicine. He was a natural-born physician who could relieve much suffering by his words alone!

My biographers have made quite an issue of the wonderful "second home" I found with the Breunings in the Münsterplatz. They are absolutely correct, but I should like to clear up a point. My "second home" did not materialize until after Mother's death. Prior to the Fall of '87, I had become a regular visitor, but only as a piano teacher for Eleonore and Lenz. Now things changed. Madame von Breuning sensed the profoundness of my sad loss. Through her, the very personality of their home opened its arms and reached out to embrace me. I spent more days in their midst than in the gray gloom of Father's shadow. I don't wish to imply that I willingly turned my back on my own family in their hour of need. Far from it! I constantly had them in mind. But if I were ever to be of financial help to them, I had to keep alive the hopes and dreams of my early youth—keep them alive until they could be fulfilled. And certainly our deathly little apartment in the Wenzelgasse was not the place for nurturing artistic ambitions. The Breuning home was! There I now freely moved about as one of the family. They all respected my musical abilities, but soon discovered how woefully neglected my training had been in every other aspect of culture and education. Without embarrassment, I was led to the enjoyment of art, poetry, and literature. Emphasis was upon the classics—especially Homer, Plutarch, and Plato; occasionally, some "moderns" crept in: Klopstock, Schiller, Goethe. I could feel myself growing. Even my poor French was brought under the polishing cloth, and the able guidance of Canon Lorenz von Breuning would often turn our fireside discussions to philosophy and religion.

Each summer the family would spend six weeks visiting Uncle Philipp von Breuning at Kerpen. On three such occasions, I was invited along for a two weeks' vacation in the country. During these reviving excursions, I learned perhaps the most important lesson of my youth. I discovered that for me, the direct revelations of God were to be found in nature—not in the clamor and hurry of city streets, nor in the musty chancel of a cathedral, but in the song of birds, the quiet green of growing things, the unchanging confidence of rocks and stones, the effervescent choir of a mountain brook, the eternal sound of wind and thunder. My lesson was well learned. For my remaining years of *this* incarnation, each summer was another invitation to come to the country.

In the spring of '88, on the Münsterplatz, I first met Count Ferdinand von Waldstein. The Breunings had talked me into an improvising séance. At its conclusion, I turned to acknowledge my applause. There stood the family and a handsome young stranger, who was not present at the beginning of my performance. He was clothed impeccably in the Austrian tradition and wore a beautiful red jacket, reminding me of Mozart's. He stepped forward, and Madame von Breuning introduced us. Said Waldstein,

W. You must forgive our devious plot for smuggling me into your audience, but Madam thought perhaps you would be reluctant to improvise before a total stranger.

B. I am indebted to you for your applause.

W. Not in the least. Handclapping is no payment for such a performance. But you *are* indebted to me!

B. So?

W. For a letter. A letter that I wrote on your behalf to my dear friend, Mozart.

B. Now I remember! I do remember hearing your name. Mozart spoke of a glowing recommendation he had received from his friend, Waldstein. . . . But how could you recommend someone you had not heard?

W. I did so on the strength of Herr Neefe's authentication. Such an organist's word is good enough for me! You see, two years ago I was planning to begin my novitiate in the Teutonic Order at Ellingen. Since your elector is Grand Master of this order, I knew that I must eventually move to Bonn. Last Spring I came for a short "tour of inspection," and, being a pianist of sorts, immediately sought acquaintances among your musicians. Neefe was the first, and he told me of his plan to send you to Mozart. I must admit that ever since I wrote my letter, I've been anxious to hear you. I feared that perhaps my words were a bit too flattering; now I see them as a gross understatement!

B. I am indebted to you. Meeting Mozart has been the high point of my life! How shall I *ever* repay you?

W. Just let me go on listening to your playing, that's how!

While Waldstein's influence caused the first explosion of erotic feelings in my life, sex did not find physical expression during my stay in Bonn. Father's warnings were too dark, Madame von Breuning's example was too bright, my career was too demanding, our finances were impossible. Had it not been for these restraining influences, my departure from home in 1792 would have been witnessed by four wives and at least that many offspring!

During our last years together, Father made no conscious effort to dampen my enthusiasm for a musical career, nor was he able to offer any encouragement. He simply continued to exist, a shadow of his former self, a poor man without any purpose in living. Brother Carl followed in the family tradition and was being trained as a court musician. Brother Johann decided that three musicians in our family were three too many. He would become a pharmacist and was accordingly apprenticed to Hittorf, the court apothecary.

My musical development from 1788 to 1792 was largely a matter of my *own decision*. Father was no longer at the helm, though Neefe still exerted his Bachian influence as teacher and adviser. At court, I continued to be assistant organist and performer of clavier concertos. Also I was placed as violist in both court orchestras. This "on-the-spot" orchestral experience led ultimately to my career as a symphonist. Many of the pieces that appeared in Vienna during and after my studies with Haydn, Albrechtsberger, and Salieri were actually products of my last years at home. They were sketched and composed in Bonn, polished and revised in Vienna.

Regardless of what my efforts and determination succeeded or failed to accomplish, my dream remained the same. Someday I would return to Vienna and Mozart. Alas. Sad news from Austria. Mozart was dead! Now what could I plan for future goals? Vienna would never be the same; it had lost its chief claim to greatness. With tearful pessimism, I ran to Waldstein and dumped my latest problem squarely in his lap.

B. What am I to do now? The light of music has gone out! The door to my career is slammed shut—forever! Vienna can offer me no hope at all!
W. On the contrary, it is now more important than ever that you go there.
B. Why?
W. Austrians are now lost without a great musician to worship.
B. What can *I* do?
W. Go to Vienna. Replace Mozart in their hearts by acting like a Beethoven!
B. You make it sound so easy.
W. For you it will be easy. Just do it!

The decision was final; I would go to Vienna. To the Austrian capital, I proudly carried a delightful autograph album that was presented to me on the first of November 1792 during a farewell party in the Münsterplatz. I treasured each precious inscription, but my favorite has remained the one that proclaimed the greatest faith in my future.

> Dear Beethoven, you are now going to Vienna in fulfillment of the wish so long awaited. Mozart's genius weeps and grieves over his death. It sought refuge in Haydn, but finds no permanent place there. It now seeks refuge in another. With the help of diligent labor, you will surely receive the spirit of Mozart from the hands of Haydn.
>
> Your true friend,
> Waldstein

Chapter 6

Brother Johann was able to borrow his employer's handcart. In this rickety conveyance, I wheeled my Earthly possessions to the local post house, where they were strapped on top of the heavy mail coach in which my journey would begin early next morning. These dubious treasures consisted of three large cases of music and one bulky box of old clothes. Into the latter were squeezed Grandfather's silver saltcellar and an old quilt belonging to Mother.

Knowing that there was little chance of my family rising at 5:00 AM to see me off, I returned home from the Breunings' party in time for our farewells to be spoken the night before. We had an early supper—our last meal together in the Wenzelgasse. After dinner, Father opened his sole surviving bottle of Grandfather's Mosel and toasted my journey. I then shook my brothers' hands and brightened their faces with a promise to send them money from Vienna. Carl left with his violin, and Johann went to look after his cart. Instead of sitting there staring at each other, Father proposed a farewell walk.

We rambled past the Minorite Church, and I was reminded of my first visit there with Friar Koch. Since Father was directing our promenade, I had a pretty good idea where it would lead us. Sure enough. Down to the old Fischer house in the Rheingasse. There was the fence where I once practiced archery with my boyhood comrades. There was the sandy spot where I played marbles. There was the old roost from which I stole Frau Fischer's hen. And there was Mother's little garden neatly composted for the coming winter. How sad to return, how sad to leave. There was the little door from which Father's huge voice would bark at me and call me from my games. He was such a giant then. Now he seems so small. His powerful walk was suddenly the unsteady stumble of a little old man. With each step, I heard him scraping at my side. The quiver in his voice seemed actually to fear the cold stillness of a new November night. We passed by a silhouette of painted roofs. A quaint tower bell chanted the hour, and we could barely make out the gray masses of old houses sloping their way toward the river. At a turn in the road, we came upon the single lamp that clearly lighted the sign of the Red Ox. Father quickened his step and grated his coarse old hands in an attempt to warm them. I knew just what he was going to suggest.

BF. Ludwig, do you know something? You know what's the best thing in all the world for a cold night like this?
B. Yes, Father—a liter of punch served piping hot at the Red Ox.
BF. He reads my mind! How did you know? Here we are. Let's go in.
B. (*I grabbed his cold hand and pressed a florin into its palm.*) You go in, Father. I think I'll walk on a bit.

We embraced in a long-overdue *bear hug*, and I promised him good news from Vienna. Father entered the café; I walked toward the river.

It was a clear night, remarkably clear for this time of year. I had expected the usual milky mist through which the murmuring Rhine could be heard, but not seen. Instead, there was a pale moonlight dancing over crusted fields. The glimmering face of the old river was filled with stars. How eternal he was! With his unchanging song, he had welcomed Grandfather to this very spot. He now sings over my mother's grave, watches over Father, and sends me to a far city. Always the same, I shall never forget him! The path was deserted as I stumbled over its pebbles. I sat on the frosted slope for a final picture of my life's companion. There on his opposite bank were the tall dark trees, shivering their bare branches in the cold. The freezing wind reddened my cheeks, made my face tingle, and brought an ominous reply from nearby alders. I stared long and lovingly at his coveted Siebengebirge, those dear peaks that forever sheltered the dreams of my youth. It was now time to leave. What a strange way to have spent my last evening in Bonn. Wouldn't things have been better in the Münsterplatz? Or in the Zehrgarten? No. I have never regretted how

I spent these last hours at home. They were wisely used. I had said good-bye to Father Beethoven, I had said good-bye to Father Rhine, and I never saw either of them again!

My post chaise left Bonn before daybreak on the morning of the second of November. The first twenty-six hours, from Bonn to Frankfurt, were the most enjoyable. I was least tired, and the large gray Wagen was heavy and well hung. The horses were fast and spirited; Gruig, the postillion, changed them often enough to keep them that way. Thanks to his excellent driving, we smashed right through the Hessian army, going like the devil. For his skill and bravery, we tipped him an entire thaler. Also during this first day, I made the acquaintance of a strange little man with whom I shared expenses. He was Vincenz Blumberg, a violin maker on his way to Königstein. What an absolute picture of meekness and mildness! His long thin face looked like it was squeezed from a tube and was made even longer and thinner by the quaint little Santa Claus cap that he wore. For five hours, he sat carefully nursing a hatbox on his knee. When we stopped for our second change of horses, he jumped from the cab and quickly returned with two large steins of dark well-crested beer. He opened his carefully protected package. It contained exactly what my nose had suspected: fresh round loaves of rye and thick juicy slices of rose-pink ham. What an appetite! What a meal! I ate half the contents of Blumberg's lunch box, and he still offered me more. Our only arguments concerned the coach windows; I wanted them open, he wanted them closed. Each time I lowered my window, he'd forget his meek little image and pull his cap so far down over his ears that I thought the point of his head would break through the tassel. Then he'd shout like a lion,

VB. Damn it! Close the window! That draft's enough to catch us both our death!

At Frankfurt, I said good-bye to my "friend" and changed coaches for Vienna. The second vehicle looked just like the first, but to my sorrow, there were sad differences. It was shorter and "bouncier," hadn't the trace of a spring! The stern Viennese coachman rarely changed horses, and consequently we seldom did better than a "slow walk." What a trip! Neither window would open, and I was obliged to spend five impossible days in a smelly, lurching "hen coop."

On November 8, 1792, I arrived in Vienna and found suitable board and lodging at the home of a printer, Anton Strauss. His dwelling was at 45 Alsergasse in the suburb of Alser. My journey had made serious inroads upon the 25 ducats; but there still remained enough money for food, rent, new clothing, a writing desk, and a down payment on a fine old piano that I located in the Graben. Since the heavy grand couldn't be moved into my attic room, I moved to the ground floor with no increase in rent. Strauss assured me that he'd rather lose a few florins' house rent than pay for a new ceiling.

Waldstein's words of encouragement still echoed brightly. I hoped for imminent recognition and financial success in Vienna. After all, was I not court organist and pianist to the new emperor's uncle? Had I not already been heard and appreciated by those of the Austrian nobility who had visited Bonn? Was I not soon to become a pupil of Haydn, the most respected musician in the capital? Were my pockets not bulging with letters of introduction from Count Waldstein? Letters that should open doors into the highest circles of Viennese society, excepting the Imperial House itself. Outwardly, I became an absurd coating of naive optimism; but within, there still remained the bitter twangs of doubt. Was I really Mozart II, or a monstrously proportioned ambition structured on shifting sands? Within a year, I should have my answer.

It was no accident that I sought living quarters in the Alservorstadt. At the upper part of this street was the palace of Prince Karl Lichnowsky, the first nobleman on Waldstein's list of hopeful contacts. One week after my arrival, having "polished up" my wardrobe, I knocked on Lichnowsky's huge courtyard gate. It looked more like the entrance to heaven than the doorway to a mere town palace. I was disappointed. My knock was not answered by St. Peter, but by a snobbish lackey dressed in the family livery.

L. Yes?
B. I am Beethoven. I've come to see Prince Lichnowsky.
L. So?

I could have stuck my foot up his ——.

B Suppose you give him this *reference*. It's from *Count Ferdinand von Waldstein.*
L. As you wish.

He jerked his mittened hand through the gate, grabbed my letter, and disappeared with it through the baroque facade of the white stone palace. For fifteen impatient minutes, I waited and studied the enclosed courtyard. The opposite boundary was an ornate garden wall. Into its arches were recessed two inactive fountains and a dozen life-size statues ranging from saints to fallen women. In all their nudity, they pretended to ignore the weather, but the stone-cold color of their smiling faces gave them away. The sky turned from gray to black and decided to present us with winter's first snow. The lacy flakes came dancing down, playfully nudging one another for a choice spot on the tip of my nose.

At last the flunkey returned with another servant at his heels. The second looked at the first and then at me: "Is this the man?"

"Yes," replied the first as he rattled open the gate. I stepped in, and for long careful seconds, the newcomer brought me under his myopic stare. He suggested that I follow him into the palace.

In the anteroom, I parted with my new apple-green hat and greatcoat. We then entered an enormous high-ceilinged corridor whose damp marble walls were hung with ornate mirrors and damask tapestries. We ascended a polished marble staircase of unbelievable grandeur. Then came a long slippery corridor whose blasts of frigid air threatened the dim yellow flames of my guide's candlestick. Suddenly we entered a magnificent drawing room, decorated in the most lavish detail. Its cool white woodwork contrasted beautifully with heavy gilt ornamentation. On the walls were kingly portraits, huge mirrors, and brocades of delicate blue. Hundreds of wax candles burned in crystal sconces and chandeliers. Their cheerful light defied the winter sky whose dirty face peered through the double casement windows. Quiet, fuzzy carpets supported countless pieces of priceless French furniture. A tempting gilt table was overloaded with fruit and sweets. Instead of a fireplace, there was built into the wall a towering stove of white and gold porcelain. In front of this palatial hearth stood the prince I had come to see.

Lichnowsky was tall, thin and slightly round shouldered. His artistic face was clean shaven, like a priest. He had black Spanish eyes with enormous pupils, a shock of unruly dark hair slightly receding at the temples, and heavy eyebrows that he labored into a questioning arch. What a fantastically shaped nose: thin and straight as it grew between his eyes, big and bulbous as it moved down and out. This fleshy appendage would wrinkle up and move as he formed his words. Above a strong and manly chin, his prominent lips rested naturally in a faint but constant smile. He wore a gray fur-collared coat that beautifully framed his immaculate neckpiece and a solitary gold medallion. He walked toward me, extending his hand.

L. Herr Beethoven, I'm Prince Lichnowsky, and I welcome you to Vienna.

We shook hands and seated ourselves on a comfortable divan. The prince turned his head and mumbled a few words to my near-sighted escort, who then bowed and left the room. Our eyes met again and Lichnowsky continued.

L. Waldstein tells me that you were accepted as a pupil of Mozart. What a pity that he's now dead. Our city will never be the same! You know, we Lichnowskys were great sponsors of the little Maestro, and we now feel that we've lost one of our family. He played often in this room (*he nodded toward a gaudily ornamented clavier*) at that *very* keyboard!

Suddenly, we were surrounded by a semicircle of indistinguishable lackeys. One provided napkins for our knees. Another brought gilded cups and saucers. Another held a silver pot of steaming coffee. A fourth brought sugar. A fifth, cream. Still another extended a tempting tray of mouth-watering kuchen. Even old "myopia" had returned to supervise the regiment.

The delicious strong coffee soon made me forget that I had waited fifteen minutes in the snow. Lichnowsky asked me about my visits to Mozart. I related these in considerable detail, and he seemed to enjoy my stories more than his kuchen. Since I was doing most of the talking, the prince finished his refreshment while I was still reaching for more. He used the ensuing minutes to light an appetizing pipe of good-smelling tobacco.

As soon as I had inhaled the last crumb on my plate, Lichnowsky smiled and winked at me through puffs of smoke.

L. Let's hear you play something.
B. Anything special?
L. I'd love to hear some Mozart.
B. Except for parts of the D Minor Concerto, I haven't memorized any of his pieces. Play me a few of your favorite Mozart themes.

The prince stood at his kingly clavier and played two themes from Figaro and two from Don Giovanni. On these, I improvised for nearly an hour. When I finished, the prince jumped from his armchair and clasped my hands. He made no effort to conceal the tears in his eyes.

L. Wonderful! Wonderful! Mozart has come back to us. Except at his hands, I've never heard such improvisation. Just wait 'til the countess and the princess hear you. They'll put a crown on your head.

Lichnowsky invited me to return on Friday morning for a musical treat. I did, and it was! Two quartets by Mozart and one by Förster were performed by an amazing adolescent ensemble. The ages of these youngsters ranged from fourteen to seventeen, and I was proud to make their acquaintance. They included Ignaz Schuppanzigh, first violin; Louis Sina, second violin; Franz Weiss, viola; and Nicholas Kraft, cello.

I was invited back the following Friday and requested to perform after the regular string concert. I played some Bach *Clavichord* and then asked Schuppanzigh to make up a tune on his fiddle. Using this spontaneous but tiny tidbit, I improvised at the piano for half an hour. My acceptance was not unlike that at the Breunings'. There were handclapping, backslapping, handshaking, even tears and absolute drooling from an eccentric, grandmotherly soul who turned out to be Lichnowsky's mother-in-law, the Countess Wilhelmine Thun. She had been an admirer and patroness of Mozart, and I had no doubt that she was about to transfer a year's pent-up affection for the deceased Maestro to her latest "discovery." This was very gratifying. In the heart of at least one Viennese, I could become a substitute for Mozart!

The Lichnowskys took such an immediate and personal interest in my career that I was invited to move into their palace. Then they seemed shocked at my behavior, simply because I treated them as though I were every bit their equal. The prince took me aside for a little "talking-down."

L. See here, Ludwig, you don't behave like a musician!
B. And how is that?
L. Like a young Mozart, or a young Haydn.
B You mean like a servant?
L. No, not a servant. What I'm trying to say . . . well . . . you've been in our home only two weeks. Yet you move about with all the

pride and conceit of a spoiled son or grandson. You seem to take us for granted, as though you knew all along that you would come here to live. Perhaps--

B. Prince Lichnowsky, are you asking me to leave?

L. Heavens no! This is farthest from my wish. The princess, the countess, and I find great delight in having you here. We just don't understand your reactions to us. Is there perhaps some basis for resentment?

B. I am reacting to you as I've been taught to react.

L. By whom?

B. By my dearest friends on Earth—the Breunings and Waldstein.

L. And what did they teach you?

B. They taught me to respect my fellowmen for what they really are, not for their possessions or inherited wealth. They taught me that true nobility is a quality of heart and mind, not some worthless chattel to be transferred by deed or title.

L. Then there's nothing personal?

B. Of course not. I am fond of all three of you and proud to live within your gates. I feel that your beautiful home is the open door to my career.

Lichnowsky smiled, cleared his throat, put one hand in mine, and the other on my shoulder.

L. Then think no more of it. We'll understand you now.

B. Good! After all, can I help not being born a prince?

L. I'm not so sure you weren't, my boy. I'm not so sure you weren't!

For me, the Lichnowsky palace was Vienna, and I was now on the inside of the gate looking out. This observation became the theme of an optimistic letter that I intended to send out as a Christmas greeting. Before I could post my glad tidings, I received a letter from Bonn that choked the breath out of my Christmas spirit. Father had died suddenly on December 18, 1792. I was numbed by this news, didn't want to see anyone or speak to anyone. I walked aimlessly through the streets of Vienna: the Hof, the Kohlmarkt, the Graben, the Stock-im-Eisen Platz, the Hoher Markt. I climbed gray steps. I knocked at a door. There were tears in my eyes. The door opened, and I was snapped to consciousness by the rasping voice of a skeletal man.

Oc. Yes? What do you want?

Suddenly, I realized that my thoughts had turned to Mozart at the hour of his father's death. I had remembered his encouraging words. Unconsciously, my walk had returned me to the Schulerstrasse, where I had knocked on this very door which five years earlier had opened on the Maestro. The occupant's impatience continued.

Oc. What are you doing here? Whom do you seek?
B. Never mind. The man I seek is not here.

He slammed the door, but not in time to prevent my hearing his final words:

Oc. I have no time for a madman!

A madman. Think of it; my stay in Vienna had scarcely exceeded a month, and I had been called a "madman." Before my Earthly days had run their course, there were to be others of like opinion.

In December 27, the Lichnowskys took me to a concert at the palace of Prince Lobkowitz. To my delight, Mozart's *Concerto in D Minor* was performed by Franz Joseph Haydn. At its conclusion, I was brought before the prince and the Maestro. I couldn't get over how much Lobkowitz resembled my father. He had the rough red complexion and the coarse features of a peasant. His forehead, his eyes, his nostrils, his chin, his cheeks—his entire face was round and manly proportioned. His thick unruly hair reminded me of my own. But aside from the Rhenish features, everything else about this man was strictly a prince. In manners, dress and polish, he was another Lichnowsky, differing from him mainly in his gay disposition and humanizing simplicity. At the slightest inducement, he would laugh like a horse and shake convulsively from stem to stern. Lobkowitz believed every word Lichnowsky told him about my improvisatory skill and invited me to perform in his palace. Haydn seemed surprised by my sudden reappearance, but was pleased when I complimented him on the sensitivity of his performance. He offered to begin my lessons the first of the year.

In January 3, I showed up at Haydn's apartment in the Hamberger house. "Papa" decided to instruct me in two subjects at once: counterpoint and theory of harmony. For the first three months of '93, all went well. I had two lessons a week and found Haydn's instruction thorough and conscientious. Much of the material had been adequately covered by Neefe, but no matter. I would toe the line and not complain. I would play the role of "model student"—student of the greatest living musician in Europe!

My determination "paid off." By the end of March, I found myself with eight piano pupils and a record of eleven private performances at the palaces of Lichnowsky and Lobkowitz. What magic worked these miracles? The name of the venerable "Papa." I was not just a young pianist from the Rhine. I was Beethoven, pupil of Haydn!

Thanks to recitals, piano pupils and the Lichnowskys, my finances began to improve. Not to the extent that I could be of any immediate help to my brothers, but I hoped eventually to establish them both in Vienna. Franz Ries signed for my first-quarter salary and forwarded me the sum, a disappointing twenty-five thalers. Did this mean that Max Franz had terminated the contract which was in effect while Father lived? I wrote the elector at Münster, begging him to continue paying me a portion of Father's salary so that I might feed, clothe and educate my two younger brothers. My request was approved. In June, I received an additional twenty-five thalers for the first quarter and fifty for the second. This quarterly payment was repeated three times, and that was it! No doubt the elector meant well. But the sea of troubles that rushed upon him from the West swept away our little agreement. I never received another penny from Bonn!

By April, I noticed a decline in the quality of Haydn's teaching. He began planning for a second trip to London, and immediately his own career loomed into such prominence that he gave little thought to our lessons. His teaching became more philosophical than musical. He would talk in vague abstractions about form, style and emotionalism in music. Recalling our conversations, I now realize that the apologies of "Papa" for the gay spirit of his church music amounted to a prophetic anticipation of the yet-unborn romantic movement in our art. Each successive tuition devoted less time to discussing and correcting exercises. Entire lessons sped by, and I would remain on the same assignment!

As anxious as I was to write music of my own, I felt that I must first undergo a thorough training. I had to discover whether books of rules had anything of real value to teach me. And here I was with the greatest living composer, and he was unable to stick to the business at hand. Perhaps this observation was characteristic; the greater the composer, the less respect for rules. An interesting theory, but I had to find out for myself.

I soon grew dissatisfied with Haydn; he had promised to teach me the theory of composition and was not doing so. My incensed feelings tempted me to tell him off in no uncertain terms, but fortunately, a better judgment discouraged the outburst. Was he not largely responsible for my acceptance to date in the musical capital? Would his magic name not open yet other doors? I gnashed my teeth, bit my lips and continued to show up twice a week for studies in the *philosophy* of music.

Frequently my lessons would evolve into long walks on the Wasserkunstbastei with Haydn. I would usually treat him to some nonalcoholic brew: coffee or chocolate. Over this cup, he would continue to philosophize:

H. So you're going to stay in Vienna?
B. Yes, Maestro. To me, it is the musical capital of the world!
H. There are other musical capitals.
B. Not according to Mozart.
H. Mozart was thinking in terms of instrumental music. In this respect, Vienna has no rival. But you'd better not try to interest her in Beethoven opera or Beethoven church music.
B. Why?
H. Her taste for opera is strictly Italian, and she has no taste for church music.
B. I think I can do as well as Salieri.
H. I don't know. Mozart tried, and he came in second to the imperial chapelmaster. If you're that much interested in vocal music, you'd better concentrate on oratorios and come with me to London.
B. My contacts here with the nobility are so promising.
H. Maybe so. But you'd better specialize in instrumental forms. Nowhere on Earth is there such cultivated taste or insatiable demand for new symphonies and chamber pieces. You'll probably find a ready market for new scores, even while your name is comparatively unknown.
B. What more could I ask?
H. Well, take the matter of public performances. In London there's a regular musical public which attends from twenty to thirty concerts each season. As a young pianist, how does that sound to you?
B Are there no public concerts in Vienna?
H Only those established by Salieri and Gassmann: two at Christmas and two at Easter. Why not come with me to London?
B. First I'd like to do a little growing right here in my own garden.

By the end of the 1792–93 season of "private" concerts in Vienna, I felt that my career as a virtuoso had been successfully launched. Rumors of my pianistic prowess radiated from the palaces of Lichnowsky and Lobkowitz. I found the doors of other Viennese salons opening to the elaborate boasts of my sponsoring princes.

As my first year in Vienna came to an end, I felt pretty well adjusted to life in the big city. Through 1794, I continued to write pianoforte variations. This was the form best reflecting the virtuoso style of my improvisations. I also spent considerable time working on three piano sonatas, a piano concerto, and three pianoforte trios. Although these works were begun in Bonn, they were still far below the state of perfection to which I hoped to bring them. This called into practice my Mozart-inspired technique of making revisions, revisions, and more revisions!

Before Haydn left for London, he made arrangements for me to continue my studies under the stern old academician, Johann Georg Albrechtsberger. Starting in February, I had three lessons a week from this master-teacher. My course of study included five species of strict counterpoint; two-, three-, and four-part fugue; double counterpoint and fugue; triple counterpoint and fugue; canonic imitation; and tons of contrapuntal exercises in free-voice settings. Albrechtsberger was impossible to know socially (just the opposite of Haydn and Schenk). He was a tall, cold, clever, correct, and disagreeable man. If ever a teacher possessed a pair of icy and brutally staring eyes, it was this man! He had a contemptuous way of biting off his words and spitting them at you. Even an ordinary "Good morning!" sounded like the insulting basis for an argument! I was his pupil and nothing more. In fact, he was so aloof that if I had studied with him for thirty years, I would have known him no better than I did after the first week of lessons. What kept me going to him? His uncanny tutorial ability. As a master of theoretical studies, he was second to none. He could take a book of dry rules and invest it with unbelievable interest, charm and immediacy! Although he seemed to hear with his eyes instead of his ears, his vigorous teaching and boundless knowledge of counterpoint kindled my deep interest in the subject. Today, beyond the grave, it still burns brightly. Albrechtsberger thought little of my original compositions, and I cared even less for his criticisms of them. I learned early to pay no attention to the opinions of theoretical musicians. There is no poorer judge of an original composition than a teacher of composition!

If I discounted Albrechtsberger as a critic, I worshiped him as a theoretician. Compared to his musical acumen, even Neefe and Schenk paled into inadequacy. Since my newest mentor provided all that I hoped for in a teacher of composition, it was no longer necessary to continue lessons with Schenk. But how could I gracefully depart from such a fine man who had offered me his tuition free of charge? I decided to wait for some acceptable excuse.

In January of '94, Haydn had introduced me to Prince Nicholas Esterhazy. Nicholas was the grandson of the prince in whose service Haydn had spent thirty years at Esterhaz. When the elder Nicholas died in 1790, his son, Prince Paul Anton Esterhazy, dismissed most of the musicians from the estate, including Haydn. This was fortunate for "Papa," for he was provided with the annuity that enabled him to make his rewarding trips to London. Paul died in January 1794 and was succeeded by his son, Prince Nicholas. This young man of thirty inherited his grandfather's love for music and promptly reengaged an orchestra at Esterhaz. In later years, he became a zealous promoter of church music, and the best composers of Vienna were commissioned to write masses for his chapel. In May 15, I received an invitation from Prince Nicholas to spend June and July with him at Eisenstadt. Just what I was waiting for! A chance to leave Vienna for a couple of months and, upon returning, to resume my lessons with Albrechtsberger, but not those with Schenk.

The end of 1794 brought some happy reunions. In October came Wegeler to begin a two-year study of medicine. He was astonished by the many comfortable luxuries that surrounded me at Lichnowsky's. With the stern look of a pedant, he shook his finger and criticized my stay in the capital as having transformed a shy little boy into a conceited monster! I tweaked his nose and replied, "My good Wegeler, if you must criticize me, you should first learn to distinguish between conceit and self-confidence!"

October also brought Lenz von Breuning to Vienna. He studied medicine from 1794 to 1797, during which time he once again became my piano pupil.

Brother Carl joined me in time for the two of us to celebrate Christmas together. In January of '95, I procured him an appointment as violinist and teacher. The position offered such slight remuneration that it was necessary for him to supplement his income by a heavy schedule of private teaching. My growing reputation assisted Carl in obtaining new pupils, but even so, he remained a poor example of economic maturation. Often I would throw handfuls of florins in his direction. No doubt such fraternal dependence hurt Carl's pride, for he later entered the civil service as "Kassa-Officier" and, by working hard at both jobs, was able to hack his way to financial stability.

Before Haydn's second tour, he introduced me to Royal Imperial Chapelmaster Salieri, who offered gratuitous instruction to capable musicians of small means. Haydn strongly recommended that I become Salieri's pupil. If my ambitions were to give public concerts and to compose operas, the chapelmaster would be a good man to know. He was in charge of the Burgtheater concerts and was the greatest living operatic composer. My subsequent and spasmodic "visits" with Salieri never became regular enough to be called "lessons"; however, they pretty well managed to exhaust such topics as song composition and the setting of Italian operas.

Thanks to Salieri, I was invited to perform in the annual Tonkünstlergesellschaft concerts given in the Burgtheater on the last three days of March 1795. These were my first public appearances as pianist and composer. One would naturally expect such a dramatic step upward to present a profound and difficult emotional adjustment. Actually, it did not. I had appeared in so many private salons, had developed such a firm self-confidence, and had so completely mastered the art of concentrating on the music at hand that these concerts were just another event in my professional career. To be sure, I was not unimpressed by the staggering beauty of the R. I. Court Theater. Never had I performed in such an immense hall with its crown-crested royal box, its cherubim-laden stalls, its frosty white balconies, its wall-length mirrors, its satiny parquet, and oh yes, its tide of hat-waving, flower-throwing humanity—those dear Viennese who were soon to become my respectful public. On the twenty-ninth, I played the world premiere of my *Piano Concerto in B-flat.* On the thirtieth, I improvised at the pianoforte. On the thirty-first, I performed the Mozart *Concerto in D Minor* in a concert of Mozart's music arranged by his widow. Prior to these concerts, I had not been able to share Mozart's vision of Vienna as a "beautiful woman." But now I saw her clearly! She clapped. She stood. She extended her arms. She embraced me. I fell in love with her. Within the short span of three days, I had become a first citizen of the music capital of the world!

With such applause ringing in my ears, with such spontaneous public acceptance of the *B-flat Concerto,* there seemed little need for further personal instruction. On April 15, I terminated my studies with Albrechtsberger. Under his careful systematization, I had been exposed to the rules of my craft. I knew them well. And if I now chose to lay many of them aside, it would not be out of ignorance, but because my ears told me to do so. I still owe a debt of gratitude to Neefe, Schenk and Albrechtsberger—men who really knew the theory of composition and cared enough to direct and systematize my studies. But most of all, I owe my Earthly success to that composer-predecessor, Wolfgang Amadeus Mozart. I evolved from him as directly as a son from his father. I approached each new form with a score by Mozart in one hand and a pen in the other. Without his works as models, I would have lacked the courage to be myself! My subsequent discussions with Förster about string quartet technique were likewise more conversational than tutorial. I learned much from him, but not in the academic garb of a student. My formal training as a composer came to an end when I said good-bye to Johann Georg Albrechtsberger.

By the middle of May 1795, I felt that my trios had been sufficiently revised, adequately performed, and were now enough in demand to warrant their publication as Opus 1. Through van Swieten, I had gotten to know Artaria, the publisher, who threatened to print these works if I could produce a promising list of subscribers. On May 16, the trios were advertised in the Wiener Zeitung. Within four days, 123 persons subscribed for 241 copies. Needless to say, a contract with Artaria & Company was signed in May 19.

Having attained "preeminent" success as pianist and composer, I decided to marry and settle down. The object of my newest matrimonial maneuverings was Magdalene Willmann, a casual acquaintance from the Bonn days. She was a beautiful and talented musician who was now engaged in Vienna to sing German and Italian opera at the court theater. I had great visions of our professional endeavors becoming instantly and dramatically entwined. Magdalene had no such visions; she snubbed my written proposal and rushed on with her own career as completely independent of me and mine as though I had never made known my amorous intentions. I shed a tear, burst out laughing, and went back to revising sonatas and the *B-flat Concerto*.

My work on the first three piano sonatas was completed in time for Haydn's return from London. I played their première performance at Lichnowsky's in the presence of "Mr. Joseph Haydn, Docteur en Musique," to whom they were dedicated. Because of the enthusiasm of "Papa," the sonatas were accepted for publication as Opus 2.

Three unrelated events brought 1795 to a close. Brother Johann arrived in Vienna, where for the next ten years he pursued his career as apothecary. (His traveling companions were Stephan and Christoph von Breuning who had come to visit their younger brother.) To obtain complete freedom in my dressing and eating habits, I moved from Lichnowsky's palace to the Ogilvy house in the Kreuzgasse. (I had decided that I was not a prince and had no business living like one. When the spirit moved me to compose, I had more important things to think about than whether or not I was properly dressed and shaved in time for the next meal.) My fourth "public" appearance took place in the tiny Redoutensaal on December 18. Haydn and I participated. He conducted his newest London Symphonies, and I gave a second performance of my *B-flat Concerto.*

Chapter 7

So far as my career is concerned, the years 1796 and 1797 were a period of quiet growth and stabilization. New compositions were added to my list. New pupils arrived. My first concert tours were launched. Finances continued to improve. New friends joined the circle. Some old friends were bidden farewell. Now the details.

The year 1796 began with a professional visit to Prague. Lichnowsky was both inspiration and companion for the trip. He described Prague as a friendly town that made up for its lack of royal or imperial court by having an inordinate number of private salons, concert rooms whose doors should swing wide in welcome to a visiting virtuoso, especially during the gala Christmas holidays. Lichnowsky promised me a reception comparable to Mozart's seven years before. Although the prince was letting his optimism run wild, my first tour did turn out to be a warm and encouraging success. I gave seven private concerts in six days, returning to Vienna as a conquering pianist with a fat round purse and a like-proportioned ego.

Such a triumph naturally led to immediate plans for a second tour. Lichnowsky was returning to Prague on the fifteenth of February, and I would go with him.

During the five weeks between these trips, I made the acquaintance of Freiherr Nikolaus Zmeskall von Domanovecz. "Count Z.," as I usually called him, was a Bohemian nobleman from the Royal Hungarian Court Chancellery. He was an expert cellist and a permanent fixture at Lichnowsky's musical parties. Although ten years my senior, Zmeskall turned out to be among the best and longest-lasting of my Viennese friends. He had none of the cringing servitude or excessive humility that began to characterize my growing flock of admirers. He respected my talent and my ambition, but thought of me as just another man and fellow artist—not some cool, distant object of idolatry. He stood up boldly to my quips and "quiddities," usually coming back with some beauties of his own. One time I addressed him as "Baron Muckcartdriver." His reply: "Yes, 'God,' what do you want?"

Zmeskall encouraged me to extend my second tour farther north, especially to Berlin. He pictured musical opportunities at the court of King Frederick William II in such glowing colors that I felt strongly inclined to go there. In the event these plans did materialize, I thought it advisable to have some new compositions to take with me. Accordingly, I completed the preliminary sketches of two sonatas for piano and cello.

In February 15, I returned to Prague with Lichnowsky. He remained only a week; however, I stayed on until April 20, giving private concerts and completing the cello sonatas that were to become Opus 5. I then toured through Dresden and Leipzig on my way to Berlin, arriving there in May 11. My reception at the Prussian Court was so rewarding that I lingered on until the end of the 1795–96 concert season. During this visit, I performed five times at court and gave an equal number of private concerts, besides two improvisatory sessions at the Singakademie. Three of my court appearances were before Frederick William himself, who graciously accepted the dedication of Opus 5. I gave these sonatas their world premiere with the help of Jean Pierre Duport, first violoncellist of the king. In return, I was offered the position of Royal Master of Chamber Music, a permanent post left vacant by the dismissal of Johann Friedrich Reichardt for his revolutionary political views. I humbly declined the king's offer because I still felt that Vienna and my career were somehow inextricably entwined.

At the height of my Berlin concerts, I met two great pianists. The first was Friedrich Heinrich Himmel. Though only five years older than myself, he held the position of royal pianist and composer. The second was Prince Louis Ferdinand, nephew of the king and two years my junior. Prince Louis was the greater of the two, a first-rate pianist in the Mozart tradition. Himmel was finished, polished, pleasing, and elegant, but lacked those certain unnamed traits that distinguish a true virtuoso from a mere supertechnician.

At my final concert, Frederick William presented me with a going-away present fit for an ambassador: a solid gold snuffbox filled with Louis d'ors. Arriving home with such a gift under my arm, is it any wonder that I went straight to my dear damnably devoted "Baron Muckcartdriver"? I knew that the good "Count Z." would lose no time in cutting me down to my proper size!

By now, Wegeler had left Vienna and my only remaining friends from Bonn were Stephan and Lenz von Breuning. In September of '96, Stephan also left the capital. He went to Mergentheim for his appointment in the Teutonic Order. A month later, my supply of Bonnians was happily replenished when Andreas and Bernhard Romberg came to Vienna from Italy. They were indirectly forced homeward by the rapid progress of the French army. These two cousins stayed on until the following February, during which time we had lots of fun discussing the old days in Bonn and trying over my newest chamber music.

The 1796–'97 season was a busy one. Although I now lived in the Ogilvy house, I still circulated freely among the Lichnowskys, maintaining a heavy teaching assignment and an even heavier schedule of private concerts involving another professional tour, this time to Pressburg and Budapest. New chamber pieces were completed so that my list now included a string trio, a string quintet, a sonata for four hands, the fourth piano sonata, a serenade for strings, and a quintet for piano and wind instruments. With the exception of the last-mentioned quintet, these works were all published during 1797. They bore the respective opus numbers: 3, 4, 6, 7 and 8. Artaria also published my first really popular work—a two-year-old song called "Adelaide," based upon the exquisite poem by Friedrich von Matthisson. Thus as teacher, pianist and composer, I continued to enjoy an encouraging upward swing in my finances.

In the fall of 1797, I said good-bye to my one remaining personal contact with the earlier days. Dear Lenz von Breuning had completed his studies and was returning to Bonn. Little did I think that I would never again cast Earthly eyes upon him. The following April, I received news of his death. Why? Why should such a fine young man be ruthlessly snatched from us at the very outset of his career? How could a loving God permit such cruel fate to strike at the Breunings? I found no answers to my questions. If only I had known then what I know now, the dark resentment that came to fill my heart would have been replaced by the light of hope and the patience of true understanding.

Chapter 8

The next convenient segment of my Earthly days is the five-year sequence from 1798 through 1802, which brings us to the conclusion of what biographers call the "first period" of my creative life.

On February 5, 1798, the new French ambassador arrived in Vienna. He was General Jean Baptiste Bernadotte. As I mentioned earlier, my political philosophy at this time was confused and uncertain. I respected the Viennese nobility for the encouragement and financial aid they bestowed upon my career. I also admired the spirit of the French Revolution with its promises of freedom, equality and opportunity for all men of Europe. Bonaparte the consul was my ideal hero, a giant who could bring order and sanity to the confusion and revolt that were France. Now came Bonaparte's representative to our capital. I could hardly wait to meet him and jumped at the opportunity to appear in his salon. The first concert was devoted to my trios, Opus 1. At a second concert, three days later, I soloed a prefinal version of my newest sonatas—those which were soon to become Opus 10. Bernadotte invited me to remain after the concert. In spite of his bad German and my bad French, we were able to communicate our way to a genuine friendship. He introduced me to many of the artists and intellectuals in his train, including the great violinist, Rudolph Kreutzer. All these men had been converted to the new ideology and were eager to proselytize for it.

One evening early in March, I was improvising for Bernadotte. Feeling especially heroic, I bore down on an extensive passage of pure emotionalism. At the peak of its ravings, the general stood behind me, tilted my hat down over my eyes until it fell to the keyboard, slapped me on the shoulders, and burst out laughing.

Otte. You are the one to do it!
B. The devil take you, Frenchman! What's the matter with you?
Otte. We had to come to Vienna to find you, but you're the man to do it!
B. Do what?
Otte. You are the one composer fit to commemorate the greatest hero of our age!
B. Bonaparte?
Otte. Bonaparte! In your playing just now, I heard the very spirit of our revolution. If you were to write a grand symphony in such a style, it would symbolize everything we stand for! Paris would accept you as her own, Napoleon would embrace you, your place in history would be secure!

The idea of a Bonaparte symphony resolved itself six years later with the completion and premier of *Synfonia Eroica,* Opus 55.

Since my arrival at Lichnowsky's, I had observed a constant improvement in the Schuppanzigh Quartet. By 1800 standards, these young men were fast becoming a group of real professionals. Their inspiring growth led me to consider writing my own first quartets. And thanks to my former teachers, I approached the task with a fearsome humility, hopefully climbing my way to self-confidence by reading the quartets of Haydn, Mozart and Förster. This was not enough. I needed some firsthand experience in quartet playing, a chance to pick up the bow. I tried dubbing in for Weiss or Sina, but the results were always the same: rounds of laughter, or else my suffering companions would run from the room, screaming for mercy. How could this be? How could an aspiring orchestral composer bring nothing but disruption to a well-organized quartet? I had no choice but to submit to a teacher of violin. Haydn had told me to look up Wenzel Krumpholz if I ever needed help in this direction. Exactly what I did. I found Krumpholz to be less a virtuoso than Kreutzer; however, his technique was what I like to call "comfortable"—a beautiful singing tone that never got in the way of his music. Krumpholz succeeded in grinding down the roughest and most objectionable spots in my violin playing, at least to the extent that I could now occasionally participate with Schuppanzigh. Without this experience, I would have met insurmountable difficulties in composing the quartets, Opus 18. Krumpholz turned out to be another idolater, tempting me to toss him aside as one more fool, too weak for friendship. However, behind his worshipful glances, I soon discovered a profound musical intellect, not in the Albrechtsbergerian sense, but in the realm of applied music. He had a flair for constructive criticism; and in discussing new compositions, I always found his opinions honest, intelligent and free from flattery. Our friendship was secure.

My next public appearance was in April '98, when Salieri reengaged me for the spring "Widows and Orphans Concerts." Haydn conducted his Seven Last Words, and I performed my *Piano Quintet, Opus 16.*

In April 5, I first heard Vienna's newest "fast gun." He was Joseph Wölffl from Salzburg. As is the case with every old well-established "fast gun," I eventually had to meet my match. A single concert at Lichnowsky's convinced me that he had arrived—the first serious threat to my career. Wölffl was two years younger than myself and had been a pupil of Mozart's father. He had served Count Oginsky in Warsaw, where he achieved a fine success as pianist, composer and teacher. His very physical attributes favored the career of piano virtuoso. Each arm appeared as a gigantic hand from the elbow down. He had powerful shoulders and knew how to use them. As he hovered over the keyboard, conquering impossible passages with childlike ease, there was no doubt that his extraordinary technique was in complete command. His only thoughts were toward correct interpretation.

My initial reaction to Wölffl (besides an attack of diarrhea) was a kind of "I'll-beat-you-ishness," which sprang from the very core of my life's plan. Was I now to permit an outsider to stand between me and the throne of Mozart? Never! I had to remain Vienna's "number one" pianist; I would meet Wölffl head-on, even if it meant my defeat.

In preparation for the inevitable dual, I spent six weeks greatly perfecting my piano playing. As of June first, my technique reached its highest state of development, a degree of proficiency that I would not again enjoy until after my death.

In the summer of '98, I played against Wölffl not once, but a dozen times. Our duals took place in Baron Raymond von Wetzlar's beautiful villa on the Grünberg. We would seat ourselves at separate pianos, performing alternately. Wölffl would win each round of playing from the printed page; I was correspondingly victorious when our task was to improvise. Thus, neither of us won a complete victory over the other. Each respected the other's strength and weakness. We became and remained good friends.

Because of my aroused interest in string quartets, I was anxious to get to know firsthand as many good fiddlers as possible. One such crossed my path on the evening of May 8 at the Lobkowitz palace. He was playing first violin in a set of Mozart quartets, which I found especially soothing to my nerves during those days of intensive piano practice. I went up and stood beside him so that I could better study his technique. This made him nervous, but he seemed to appreciate my turning pages for him. I was truly impressed by his sensitivity, which sounded like the makings of another Krumpholz. His eyes twinkled, a pleasant reminder of my first meeting with Waldstein. Since I had to leave before the concert was over, I asked Lobkowitz to invite the young man to visit me the following evening in the Ogilvy house. This the young man did, and he brought his fiddle with him. He turned out to be Karl Friedrich Amenda, a theology student from the University of Jena. Although he looked considerably younger than myself, he was just my age. He had completed a three-year course in music, had gone on tour, and was now hoping to establish himself in Vienna. We played together my sonatas in D and A, after which I decided to demonstrate my newly acquired "mastery" of his instrument. At first he listened politely. Then he caught the glimmer in my eye.

A. Have mercy . . . quit! I haven't heard such scrapings since my earliest student days.
B. So? A violinist, and you don't appreciate great violin playing?
A. That's just it! I do appreciate gr—
B. Then why do you interrupt me?

There was a moment of awful silence, during which my assumed look of sternness convinced poor Amenda that I was serious. I stared him down mercilessly, until the boyish innocence of his expression melted my face into an unconcealable grin. I poked him with the neck of his instrument, and the two of us burst into a marathon of laughter. Then we went for a walk, the first of many. In fact, we went walking together so often that by the spring of '99, if I ventured into the Graben alone, people would stop me and ask, "Where is the other one?"

What attracted me to Amenda? It was not just his good violin playing and his critical appreciation of my work. It was the amiability and true nobility of his character. The better I got to know KF, the more I liked him. By the end of '98, he occupied a choice spot in my little circle of dearest friends. Then came the death of his brother and resulting family responsibilities that called him home to Courland in the fall of '99. Though we corresponded by mail, the two of us never again went walking on Earth. I have no doubt that if Amenda had remained in Vienna, we would have continued to be as close as brothers. Not even the imminent development of my staggering crop of eccentricities could have driven such an understanding friend from my side.

The climax of the 1798–99 season was another concert tour of Prague. There I spent the last two weeks of October giving six concerts in private salons and two public concerts in the Konviktssaal. At the first public concert, I performed, among other things, the world premier of my *C Major Concerto.* At the second concert, I played a final revision of the *B-flat Concerto,* which was completed just in time for the rehearsal.

By the end of 1799, my expanded circle of friends included three additional virtuosi. First came Domenico Dragonetti, the greatest contrabassist known to history. (Had it been his purpose to find some serious competition, he would have had to wait a hundred years for the arrival of Serge Koussevitzky.) On his way to London, he stopped off in Vienna for the second and third weeks of April. Amenda assured me that our great visitor could actually perform cello passages on his huge instrument. This I couldn't believe. I invited Dragonetti to visit me in the Kreuzgasse and make good his boast. He did. He came, and we played together my "Cello" *Sonata in G Minor.* I was absolutely overcome with emotion, couldn't take my eyes off the man! He performed miracles that I knew were impossible for his instrument. In thirty minutes, I found out more about basses than I had learned in thirty years of study and observation. Without Dragonetti's astounding technical demonstration, I would not have had the courage (six years later) to pen a certain Scherzo for a certain Fifth Symphony!

The second virtuoso was Johann Nepomuk Hummel, the little boy whom Mozart had dangled before the jealous eyes of my earliest ambitions. He was a big boy now. He had returned to Vienna in 1795, concluding a six-year concert tour with his father, to become a piano student of Albrechtsberger and Salieri. After four years of study and private concerts, the time had arrived for his public debut. The entire affair was under the direction of Ignaz Schuppanzigh and was to occur on April 28 in the Augartensaal. "Milord Falstaff" insisted that I attend and introduced me to young Hummel after his concert. I did not appreciate Hummel's original compositions. They sounded like watered-down and warmed-over Haydn. I did admire his playing, a carbon copy of Mozart. His technique was light, clear, brilliant, perfect!

The third of the trilogy was also a pianist, John Baptist Cramer. In September 5, I received a note from Haydn proclaiming that the greatest pianist in the world had arrived from London and was planning to spend the winter in our city. I had often heard "Papa" speak of Clementi's great pupil and was anxious to hear him. We met at Lichnowsky's on October 3. Cramer tactfully maintained that he was not on a concert tour but was merely visiting the continent to observe great pianists. With this buildup, he asked me to play something. I went to the piano and from eleven sheets of hen-scratched Beethovenian hieroglyphics gave the premiere performance of my newest sonata, a neatly structured device which in two months would be sent into the world as *Sonate Pathétique*, Opus 13. Between its second and third movements, Cramer burst into applause—wouldn't let me go on until I had repeated the *Adagio cantabile.* At the end of the Rondo he stood, shook my hand, and showered me with compliments.

C. I now have a new favorite sonata. It's unlike anything I've ever heard, an absolutely *new* voice in piano music! You must send me a copy as soon as it's printed. I'll have everybody in London playing it!

Lichnowsky interrupted the eulogy.

L. Now Sir, let us hear *you* perform.
C. What would you like me to play?

The prince handed Cramer a copy of Eder's engraving of my Opus 10.

L. Try one of these.
C. Ah, good! More sonatas by Beethoven. Let me look them over.

He went to a far corner of the room, sat facing the wall and studied the scores in minute detail. . . . At last he seated himself at the piano, returning Lichnowsky's music.

C. Here. I think I can manage without *these.*

Cramer began a *masterful* interpretation of my *Sonata No. 5 in C Minor.* Although he had never seen the score before, in less than half an hour, he had read it through and was now performing it from memory. Within a few minutes, I found myself in perfect agreement with Haydn. Cramer *was* the king of pianists. He combined the very best qualities of Wölffl and Hummel into a single all-embracing technique. If my ascension to Mozart's throne required me to outperform Cramer, I knew then and there, I would have to settle for a lesser goal.

I began the new century by moving into new quarters: No. 241 in the Tiefen Graben. The big event of 1800 was the first public concert given in Vienna for my own benefit! I spent three months preparing for it. The concert was given on Wednesday, April 2, in the Royal Imperial Court Theater beside the Burg. Its duration was Gargantuan, beginning at 6:30 PM and lasting until midnight. The list included a Mozart symphony, an aria and duet from Haydn's *Creation,* and my own infernal *Septet, Opus 20.* As if these weren't enough, I "rounded out" the evening by performing the Viennese premiere of my *C Major Concerto,* by improvising for an hour, and by conducting the world premiere of *Symphony No. 1.*

How was the concert received? Musically and financially it was a great success. Prior to 1800, few public statements were made regarding my works. Those that I found were negative and demoralizing. I was an "upstart," a seeker of "novelty at any price," an "impossible noisemaker," a "corrupter of musical morals." I concluded that my compositions would never be appreciated during my lifetime. To hell with these "Leipzig oxen!" I would read their drivel, but continue to write exactly as I pleased!

Then came a miracle. In the February issue of the *Allgemeine Musikalische Zeitung,* my *Sonate Pathétique* received a favorable criticism. I thought they'd made a mistake, couldn't believe my eyes! But no, this was the beginning of a new trend. Their reviews continued to improve until by 1810, I could open their paper almost any month in the year and read what a "smart boy" I was. The April second concert was at least "acceptable in their sight." They admired the first two movements of the concerto, they praised the septet, they liked the novelty and wealth of ideas in the symphony, but thought that my "overuse" of woodwinds made the orchestra sound too much like a military band!

On April 18, I was invited to play in a concert given by Johann Stich, the Bohemian horn player. As in the case with Dragonetti, I was eager to meet the famous "Punto." Great orchestral virtuosi such as these could teach me more about their instruments in a few hours than I could learn from years of study and conducting. I promised Punto a new horn sonata for our concert. It was "new," all right! So newly born that my part had to be played from a few illegible scratches. In spite of all this "rush-rush," the sonata received enthusiastic applause and was immediately repeated!

In the summer of 1800, there began a ritual which I observed almost uninterruptedly until the year of my death. At the end of each musical season, I would follow the example of my aristocratic brethren and exchange the work-stopping heat of summertime Vienna for the cool comfort of surrounding countryside. I did this not just for a vacation or to indulge my "Bonn-Breuning-inspired" passion for walking in the woods. I wanted to escape from the interruptions and sociabilities of a musical career, to plunk down in the midst of some uneventful landscape and concentrate entirely upon composition.

In July 10, I took up quarters in Unter-Döbling, an hour's walk from town. Following the "advent" of J. B. Cramer, I no longer aspired to become No. 1 piano player. However, I still hoped to tour the world as a pianist and composer. For such a trip, I needed a new concerto—something entirely different, absolutely unique! Consequently, my first "stay in the country" was devoted mainly to piano practice and to the composition of *Concerto No. 3 in C Minor.* By Fall, the piece was ready for final revision and a trip to my copyist. It was not my plan to release this work for publication. I would raise it as my own "child" and use it for touring. Although my dreams of worldwide concerts did not materialize, I kept this concerto "at home" until 1804 when it finally became Opus 37.

In late September, I returned to the Tiefen Graben to say "hello" to a new friend and "good-bye" to an old one. Krumpholz introduced me to twenty-year-old Johann Doležalek, who arrived from Bohemia to become a pupil of Albrechtsberger. The young pianist and cellist stayed on for fifty years as one of the best teachers in the capital. Of all the inhabitants of Lichnowsky's realm, Franz Anton Hoffmeister was among the first that I had gotten to know.

He became deeply interested in my career, no doubt because of his own similar experience as a young Viennese student. Although at that time a popular and prolific composer, he liked nothing better than to hobnob with the newest generation of composer hopefuls. I now shook his hand and sent him off to Leipzig, where he founded the publishing firm of Hoffmeister & Kühnel. Within six weeks, he was writing me for manuscripts. His house remained faithful through all the storms of my "marketing" career and never lost interest in new Beethoven compositions.

The year 1801 was a slim year for concertizing. There were the usual private performances, but I played only once in public. The latter event took place on January 30, in the Redoutensaal of the imperial palace. Haydn directed the orchestra; Madame Frank, Madame Galvani (that girl who wouldn't marry me), and Herr Simoni sang; Punto and I were the instrumental soloists. To hear Madame Frank tell it, you'd think the entire concert was for her benefit. Actually it was not. It was the last of a series of public concerts given to raise funds for the poor wounded soldiers who were now stuffing the hospitals of Vienna. Their conditions had become atrocious ever since the disastrous battle of Hohenlinden on December 3, 1800!

This year, I did not plan another public concert for my own benefit. There were two reasons. First, I had argued with the Burgtheater orchestra. I thought their responsiveness of the preceding second of April was an abomination; they thought the same of my conducting. The net result of our mutual intolerance was that I was not to be invited back again. (Perhaps I would have tried the new Theater-an-der-Wien had it not been still under construction.) The second reason, I was commissioned to compose ballet music for the court stage. My immodest little *Septet, Opus 20* was to be thanked for this important assignment. In one year, it had become obscenely popular and carried into every music room its dedication to Empress Maria Theresia. Out of gratitude, the royal family had appointed me to collaborate with Salvatore Vigano in producing *The Men of Prometheus.* Our collaboration ended on March twenty-eighth when *Prometheus* was given its first performance in honor of the prima ballerina, Fräulein Cassentini. The work was staged twenty-nine times in two years and proved happily remunerative both to Vigano and myself!

At the turn of the century, short sacred cantatas had entered a period of great popularity in Vienna. Everybody was writing them, including Haydn and Salieri. Why not Beethoven? I decided to compose one for my next concert and began by cribbing together some words. Help was soon needed in this phase of the operation, and thanks to *Prometheus*, Franz Xaver Huber stood ready and willing. The result of our collaboration was a satisfactory text, *The Mount of Olives*, which went with me into the country as my "project for the summer." This year I chose the cool purple shades of the Schönbrunner Hofgarten at Hetzendorf. In the thicket of this delightful forest I discovered a remarkable oak. Twenty inches above the ground it branched out into two separate trees. This convenient "doubling" provided an inviting chair, or should I say throne? A throne upon which the "Great Mogul" seated himself and wrote the entire score of his newest oratorio.

In the fall of 1801, I returned to the Wasserkunstbastei and to the two important pupils of my Earthly pilgrimage. Franz Ries had written me that his son, Ferdinand, was "ready for launching." Since I could never forget the father's kindness to our family, I aided young Ries in every way possible. As soon as he arrived in Vienna, I helped him with his finances and took him under my tuition as the first nonpaying male piano student. He wanted me to instruct him in composition; but I refused, having neither the ability nor the patience to teach counterpoint. As a pianist, however, Ries made great progress. I was proud of him and, within six weeks, predicted that he would be the first pupil of Beethoven to perform in public!

My other new student was Carl Czerny. We were introduced by Krumpholz, who had gotten to know the family and greatly admired young Carl. Like Ries, Czerny was taught gratis, and soon he too was doing battle under the "pupil of Beethoven" banner. I could never choose a favorite between these young men. In matters of technique and interpretation, each tied the other for first place. As every serious pianist discovers, Czerny is the author of finger exercises—mountains of finger exercises! I wish to clear my name from any involvement in the conception of these torturous devices. With me, Carl studied piano, not composition! If you can't love Czerny for his etudes, you must at least respect him as a piano teacher. A teacher who would soon nurture the greatest pianist ever to walk the face of Earth, Franz Liszt!

The year 1802 brought serious thoughts of another public performance by and for Beethoven. The new concerto and cantata could easily be readied in time for the concert. However, the same stumbling block of the preceding year defeated my plan; I could not obtain use of the hall! Baron Von Braun, director of the theater, assured me that important events filled every available spot in the calendar. He said that I should have informed him of my plans early in September—important events! A bunch of mediocre show-offs whose collective talents were those of a spoiled child!

Very well! If my desire to perform was frustrated, I'd simply work twice as hard on an alternate goal. I went "all out" for composing! Final revisions were made in the concerto and oratorio to make sure they'd be ready for the next concert season. I worked twelve hours a day on three new violin sonatas and a sequence of piano pieces that included two sonatas, two sets of variations on original themes, and seven bagatelles.

This increased production resulted in such a storm of petty mechanical and financial details that I soon felt the need for a business manager. Who could fill the job? He had to have a mind for business, had to be musically trained, had to be someone I could trust. After a little cogitation, Brother Carl was summoned to the Hamberger house. He had ample leisure, experience in public office, and a good musical background.

Carl proved ideal for the job. We had our little arguments over which publisher should receive what composition, but these spats were short-lived. After all, we were brothers! Carl kept accounts with eight publishers. He directed the copyists. He examined proof sheets, supervising their correction and revision. He wrote business letters, checked on my annuity income, expedited commissions, and arranged appointments. What was the good of all this? Well, the "Great Mogul" was freed from countless vexing distractions. He could be off on his own, pounding over the hills, chasing musical rainbows. And (miracle of it all) every once in a while, he'd catch one!

Specializing in composition brought me to my *Second Symphony* in time for the summer of 1802. I moved to rooms in a large peasant house at Heiligenstadt. This ideal resort offered fresh air, sunshine and bathing. A few minutes' walk (in the opposite direction from Vienna) opened my eyes on a scene of piercing beauty and seclusion; a solitary valley of half-wild woods, open fields and gurgling brooks; a hallowed spot that inspired *Symphony No. 2* and called me back six years later to do the same for the *Pastoral Symphony*.

Returning to Vienna, I moved into the "Red House" on the St. Petersplatz. Such maneuvering placed me in the same building with Emanuel Aloys Förster. Next to Albrechtsberger, I regarded Förster as the best counterpoint teacher in Vienna and absolutely the greatest authority on string quartet composition. Although Schuppanzigh's strivings for perfection and Lichnowsky's background of Italian strings were strong inducements for me to write my own quartets, it was Förster who provided me with the necessary technical skill. I learned from him not as a formal student, but simply by attending his "quartet meetings" and listening to the great Master theorize.

Even so, after struggling through Opus 18, I still felt that I had much to learn. My best move was to the "Red House," where I would be exposed to the bells of St. Peter's, to the bells of St. Stephen's, and to the continuing lectures of a great theoretician. Förster never charged for his services. Consequently, he thought nothing of sending me his little son for free piano lessons. I had been spoiled by the serious adulthood of Czerny and Ries, thought I'd never adjust to a six-year-old. Because of the child's age, his father preferred five short lessons a week to one or two long ones. Each morning at daybreak, the little boy would tiptoe down three flights of stairs and tap for his lesson. I tried to be patient, but usually found myself belching tyrannical threats exactly like those vomited at me by Father and Pfeiffer twenty-six years earlier in the Rheingasse. One morning, I became so vexed by the disobedience of his little fingers that I "spanked" them with a cast-iron knitting needle. He jumped off the bench and ran from my room, screaming that he'd never come back! He never did. Not until the next morning.

As I mentioned earlier, 1802 brings us to the end of my "first period" compositions, a series that begins with pure Rococo sounds and ends with some carefully disciplined Romantic colors. Surprisingly, even this modest transition was enough to lose many of my "older" audience. They were looking for "pure Mozart" or "pure Haydn" and couldn't find either in my newest works. I was compensated for their loss by gaining "young" admirers, my first favorable reviews in the *Allgemeine Musikalische Zeitung*, and an unbelievable increase in the marketability of my music. I could have sold everything I composed ten times over! My publishers no longer bargained with me. I asked a good price, and they paid it.

Viewed from the other side of the grave, it's interesting to see how most of my original opinions of these works have changed. Today I'm no longer placed defensively on their behalf. I can freely admit that taken as a group, the first thirty opuses are a rather sorry lot! They were my "growing-up" exercises, but without them, I could never have reached the better things that followed. The Quartets, Opus 18 were an absolute prerequisite to the ultimate *C-sharp Minor*. Symphonies 1 and 2 enabled me to stretch a canvas big enough for the *Eroica*. Three careful attempts of the period taught me what a piano concerto should be. *Prometheus* and the *Mount of Olives* pointed their anemic fingers toward the stage. And two sets of piano variations finally pushed open the door to my "second period."

From the first thirty-two years, there are only a few compositions that I presently esteem to be more than "growing-up" music. They are three piano sonatas: the *Pathétique*, the *A-flat*, and the *Moonlight*. *Sonate Pathétique* burst into my consciousness from relatively simple preliminary sketches. In spite of the interest created by its spanking-new *cyclical structure*, I had to wait several years to fully appreciate the resulting music. My attitude toward the opus gradually improved, probably because of favorable comments from Cramer, Amenda, Krumpholz, Reicha, Wölffl, Hummel, Ries and Czerny. While on Earth, I never became fully reconciled to the *A-flat Sonata*. Its *Marcia funebre* was good enough, but the opening variations sounded too "folkish," the rondo followed too much the path of J. B. Cramer, and the separate movements didn't seem to "belong." Today, the story is different. When I play the *A-flat*, I don't go looking for unity and coherence. I enjoy it as a suite, a loose-knit collection of little old pieces that are obvious, folkish, unsophisticated and honest. The *Moonlight Sonata* arrived as a welcome addition to my list. I was proud of it, especially the last movement.

Then something unexpected happened. Its opening *Adagio sostenuto* suddenly exceeded all the bounds of respectable popularity. Everywhere I went it was "the *Fantasia in C-sharp Minor*, the *Fantasia in C-sharp Minor*, the *Fantasia in C-sharp Minor*!" Hell! You'd think I'd never written anything of value except the first movement of this sonata! And for the life of me, I couldn't understand its claim to fame. It was nothing but a "tum-ta-tum" rhythm, woven through a sequence of mushy chords that emoted along for five minutes above a well-behaved bass line! Yet on and on came the requests, down and down came the tears. Disgusting! The more my public clamored for this *Fantasia* the less I thought of the work. In fact, my dislike for its first movement eventually spread to the entire sonata, and I went to my grave thoroughly detesting the one and only Beethoven piano piece that was able to gain the admitted acceptance of Frédéric Chopin!

Today I no longer despise the *Moonlight* for her world renown, but see her as a beautiful daughter who has gone out and "made good." If she throws many of my other children into the shade of unpopularity, I don't worry. These bashful and less talented offspring receive exactly what they deserve!

Chapter 9

No doubt I've given the impression that the five years from 1798 through 1802 were an unadulterated blend of new friends, new apartments, new compositions, and new concerts. Actually they were more. They were responsible for the emergence of my first fully articulate personal philosophy—a power morality strong enough to cope with the hatred of jealous musicians, the disappointments of unrequited love, and a frightening specter of the permanent degeneration of my physical health.

This first Beethovenian philosophy didn't spring up overnight, but required a full decade of Viennese life to bring it into being—five years of growth and acceptance to nurture its prenativity, then five years of musical victories to confirm its birth. I didn't actually choose the philosophy of power as my own. It wasn't a matter of waking up one morning, deciding to be a superman, putting my hand into the hand of Friedrich Wilhelm Nietzsche, and walking boldly into the pages of history to kick fate in the pants every time he bent over. Instead, I simply grew into this philosophy and found each step of the way as natural as breathing. When the harshness of childhood first forced me to my knees under the weight of Father's lessons, I needed strength to go on. I looked deeply into the little boy that I was and found there the strength for another piano lesson. Thus encouraged, I continued to look within myself for the power to meet life's challenges. And for twenty-five years, until the summer of 1802,

I was not disappointed. Is it any wonder that I soon became the proud and kingly feathered peacock so easily recognized by Haydn and Breuning as the "Great Mogul"?

By my own strength, I survived Father's lessons and assumed the duties of Neefe. By my own strength, I knocked at Mozart's door and didn't run away when he opened it. By my own strength, I returned to Bonn and suffered the death of my angel mother. By my own strength, I continued to grow and didn't faint at the first clear visions of future goals. By my own strength, I played my way into the highest ranks of Viennese society and made no concessions for birth or class. By my own strength, I denied myself nothing, cheerfully made enemies among my rivals, earned and spent money freely, took no pains to humor my patrons or publishers, fully exploited my talents for personal glory. By my own strength, I ascended the throne of Mozart and enjoyed sitting there!

What did the world look like through the eyes of such a "strong" man? It was a small place, crowded with emptiness. I was looking for men with a passion for heroic achievement—men who were willing to sacrifice their lives for a noble cause, men who believed in themselves even though they were not yet known to universal fame. What did I find? A bunch of mosquitoes! Cowards who came in and went out with the tide. Weaklings who borrowed even their thoughts and emotions from other men. How could I find a place in my heart for such creatures? It was not long before the "Great Mogul" developed a profound contempt for the bulk of his fellowmen and began fighting them with a barrage of bad puns, provincial manners, horseplay, and "hearty free words" of about four letters. (At this time, my contempt had not yet reached the furniture-throwing stage.)

I was also looking for a way to consciously relate my life to God. What did I find? When I turned to the church of my youth, I found a Procrustean religious system whose ecclesiastical dogmas could never be reconciled to the new "republican" views that swept through my life. When I turned to nature, the results were quite the opposite. It was easy to find God under a starry sky or in the rainy splash of a new green countryside. And what a God he was! Small enough to notice me, human enough to smile, big enough to believe in man's humanity, kind enough to offer me my talent and his encouragement, yet boundless enough never to be squeezed into a robe and beard, nor placed on a showy pedestal, nor assigned the thankless task of distinguishing good men from bad men!

Naturally, the eyes of such a "powerful" man were not blind to feminine beauty. They had proven themselves otherwise in earlier days when, to no avail, they coaxed me to participate in the appetizing sex orgies of Grossmann's troupe. And now here I was in Vienna, far from the inhibitions of home. Gone were the restraining influences of Bonn. The class 1–class 2 distinctions of Father's warnings suddenly appeared as a youthful disillusionment. I began to look at a woman through Waldsteinian eyes, seeing her as just another material object reflecting the glitter, the superficiality, and the licentiousness of Viennese society. She was a burning symbol of the very world I had come to conquer. Her tempting lips smiled a sensuous smugness. She knew full well that my victory would never be complete without including her. What was my plan of "attack"? I had neither the body of Adonis nor the speech of Cyrano de Bergerac, but I had the music of Beethoven. If my improvisations could win the acceptance of princes, then why not the love of this woman? I would extemporize my way into her affection, into her parlor, into her bed. This is exactly what I did. The little tour de force was accomplished twelve times during my first three years in Vienna. My conquests included one delectable farm girl, seven eager piano students, and four willing ladies in "waiting." Then the enjoyable routine came to an abrupt halt, never to be repeated. As of November 1795, I had had my last cohabitation with a woman of Earth. My Casanova career had ended, not because of some inexplicable pride in having achieved a "round dozen," but because of the shocking arrival of a greenish-red chancre which all but duplicated one of the pictures in Father's antisex campaign. The belief that I had contracted a venereal disease convinced me of Father's wisdom. For the rest of my Earthly days, I looked at womankind through his eyes and had a genuine hatred for any girl whom I suspected of unchasteness or excessive sensuality. My own experience had convinced me that sexual gratification without the union of souls was a bestial thing. After a moment of pleasure, there remained no trace of a noble sentiment. Only remorse and penitence.

I was determined to protect my brothers from a fate such as mine. Several weeks before they came to Vienna, I wrote each a letter warning them to "beware the whole tribe of evil women!"

This newest addition to my roster of physical woes sent me on a "lifelong" quest for the ideal medical man. I changed physicians and surgeons almost as often as I changed living quarters. Several of my less sensitive biographers (whom I've had harpooned in northern waters) have dismissed this chain of events as prima facie evidence of old Beethoven's hypochondriacal tendencies. So I was a hypochondriac, was I? I'd like to shoulder any one of these eminent "snoopers" with my particular combination of smallpox, typhus, bad ears, sore eyes, rheumatism, syphilis, asthma, gout, colic, jaundice, and chronic diarrhea. Then we'd sit back, serenely fold our hands, and wait. If the beneficiary of my choice legacy went on living at all, I'm sure he'd spend at least some of his time thinking and complaining about his wretched physical condition. And in all fairness, I don't believe we would criticize him for his "self-pitying fancies of ill health"!

Of all my physical maladies, deafness caused the most suffering. How could it have been otherwise for a musician? Most doctors considered my ear trouble to be a tertiary symptom of syphilis; several treated it as the aftermath of typhus or as a companion ailment to my intestinal disorders. Regardless of who was right and who was wrong, the hideous affliction showed up in the summer of '98 and plagued me for my remaining days in an Earthly body. Its first symptoms did not appear amid melodramatic surroundings. I was neither dueling with Wölffl, nor arguing with the Burgtheater Orchestra, nor playing the *Moonlight Sonata* for my "immortal beloved." I had simply been for a long walk with *Amenda*, and our tempo had been Allegro con fuoco. Returning to the Kreuzgasse and finding myself in a heavy sweat, I opened the windows, stripped to the waist, poured a pitcher of cool water over my head, and fell across my bed, exhausted. In thirty minutes, I was awakened by a noisy thunderstorm that had brought cool breezes into the room, blowing across my chest. I had slept open-mouthed and now felt as though there was a bone caught in my throat. After repeated hawking, I successfully dislodged the obstruction and spat it through an open window. The aftermath of such heroic achievement was a ringing in my left ear. This responded favorably to the twistings and turnings of my little finger.

Next evening at supper, the ringing returned and did not respond to my treatment. It bothered me until bedtime and was still there the next morning. Thus it went for the rest of 1798—always in the left ear, a combination of ringing, whistling, and buzzing. This would last from two to forty-eight hours, then disappear for several days or several weeks. By February '99, the condition was much the same, except that it now occurred in both ears. During these ringing spells, my hearing was naturally impeded; at other times I could hear as well as ever. The year 1801 brought the really frightening development! Starting from April tenth, each siege of ringing was followed by two to ten hours of practically total deafness, during which time I could hear only the very lowest tones of singers and instruments. If I stood at some distance, I heard nothing at all. The fear of permanent deafness was enough to send me looking for a good surgeon. I went to Dr. Vering on June first and remained under his care for seven months. He did everything but operate, prescribing pills for my belly, painful vesicatories for both arms, and a kind of tea for my ears. The sounding in my head became less, but my hearing did not improve. Both duration and frequency of the deaf spells increased. Even so, as late as 1819, there were still some good days when I heard speech and music with almost normal clarity. However, from 1820 until my death, I was for all practical purposes totally deaf! Once in a long while I heard a few very low sounds and, when composing, managed to hear tones by placing one end of a wooden rod in the piano sound box and the other between my teeth.

If the supposed contraction of syphilis ended my quest for promiscuous love, it had the opposite effect upon my desire for a worthy "class 1" woman. Since Vering and, later, Schmidt both agreed that my disease had passed beyond its contagious and transmissive stage, I began once again to long for the joys of matrimony. In my mind, there arose a carefully studied picture of this "girl of my dreams." She had the face of impish loveliness, the charm and beauty of a Diana, the sacrificial love of my mother, the culture and refinement of Madame von Breuning. Some girl! No wonder I spent ten years searching and never found her.

Not a few musical historians have tried to discover the identity of Beethoven's "immortal beloved," the girl idolized in a certain love letter that showed up in the Schwarzpanierhaus after my death. They assume that this "immortal beloved" was the one and only girl ever to occupy the "place of places" in my heart. They are wrong! Of course, she dwelt there, but only while I thought we were madly in love. When I learned otherwise, she promptly relinquished the spot to my next lover. It would be more correct to proclaim the true "immortal beloved" as a beautiful creature of my imagination, ein schönes Stück, whom I dearly sought to know, to love, to marry. For ten years, I searched among the women of Earth. Half a dozen times I thought for sure I had found her, but without exception, after a few months of blissful hope, each dainty sculpture showed her tiny feet of clay and dissolved into fragments. By 1812, I had become too much the eccentric musician, too much the "set in his ways" bachelor, too much the "Great Mogul" to have any further hopes for marriage.

How could I expect any girl to live with my erratic temperament, my frequent bursts of rage, my total inability to cope with regularity or restraint? Conditions being what they were, I embraced the Divine Muse as my "immortal beloved" and found her to be the best choice after all. Surely no other girl could have made a place in her heart for the likes of me.

Countess Giulietta Guicciardi was the first to become involved in this final sequence of Beethoven's Earthly love affairs. We met at the Brunsvik's in October 1801; she was sixteen, and I was twice her age. It didn't take me long to notice her charm and vivacity. She had a pretty, dollish face that was accented by huge velvety soft black eyes. Her powdered forehead was temptingly banged in curls of rebellious gypsy hair. She smiled not alone with her rosebud lips, but with her entire face. Although her pose was that of a little girl, she was a goddess of coquetry. By using her inexhaustible array of girlish vanities, she could say, "Come here, Darling" in a thousand different ways without speaking a word. Besides her physical attractiveness, she had unusual pianistic abilities. Within a month, I knew that we were really in love; not the old story of just another musical maiden dazzled by the glitter of my reputation. She admired my playing, my compositions, my improvisations; but more important, this girl was in love with me!

On January twelfth, after a party at Brunsvik's, I offered her my hand. She accepted. There remained only the matter of her parents. Her mother consented to our marriage, but not her father. He had three objections. First, I had no permanent appointment. Second, he felt that I was too temperamental and misanthropical to make a good husband and father. Third, I had neither title nor wealth, and since the Guicciardis were not affluent, he considered it doubly necessary for Giulietta to marry a man of means. The thought of elopement crossed my mind, but I sensed that Giulietta was not a girl to disobey her father. I would wait for her decision. It came on the evening of January twenty-fifth. I answered my door and was delightfully surprised to find Giulietta. We embraced. She explained that her father had brought her to tell me something of great importance and that she couldn't stay long because he was waiting for her in their carriage. I knew what was coming. Her tearful adieu was exactly as Hollywood might have imagined it. She complained of not having words to express what was in her heart. She asked me to play something—hardly the mood for a minuet! I played the *Funeral March* from my *A-flat Sonata.* As she stood behind me, a few sobs were all that came from Giulietta. She begged me to go on, and I switched to the first movement of the *Moonlight Sonata.* This did the trick. Its somber spell opened her heart to the final words of our love:

G. Dear Louis . . . I don't want you to think of me as a little girl who must always obey her father. I love him, but it is not Papá who comes between us. He worries about your lack of position; I see you as Mozart's successor. He complains about how wretched our finances would be; I have no fear of poverty. He says that you're a revolutionist, filled with anger and hatred; I hear more honest passion, more freely given love in the beautiful piece you now perform than I could hope to find among all the petty and hypocritical deeds committed in the name of human kindness by a whole generation of lesser men. It is not my father, but another woman who drives us apart. Her name is "music," and I know that she will always claim first place in your heart. I wouldn't mind a little competition from an ordinary girl, but not from a goddess. Perhaps you would condescend to love me for a while, but soon enough you'd recognize me as the creature who stood between you and your goddess. What an unloving spot for me to occupy! No, Louis, it is best for both of us that we say adieu. Good-bye, love. God bless you!

I played to the end of the *Adagio sostenuto* and didn't bother turning around. She was gone.

I would never have permitted Giulietta to simply turn and walk out of my life had it not been for the prospects of total deafness that crashed down upon me at this time. Could I honestly implore her to stay, when I hadn't the courage to share with her the horror of my abominable secret? I hadn't told anyone except Amenda, Wegeler, and my physicians. How could I? How could I stand on the roof of the Hamberger house and shout to all Vienna, "I am the Beethoven who has outextemporized the pianists of Europe! I am the Beethoven who has come from Bonn to recompense you for the loss of Mozart! And incidentally, I am the Beethoven who will soon be totally deaf!"

This didn't make sense. It seemed to me that an admission of deafness would stamp me a charlatan and shake the very foundations of my career.

By 1802, there was no longer any doubt that my ear trouble had become a chronic condition. Nor was there any assurance that my deaf spells would continue to be alleviated by periods of almost normal hearing. I feared the worst—total deafness! If Giulietta's father sensed that I was unqualified for matrimony, it's too bad that he couldn't have known the reason behind it all. I cursed God to his face, not because I felt that my affliction was the punishment of a bad little boy, but because it seemed as though he had abandoned me to the most cruel and casual whim of fate. Why should I suffer the senseless torments of deafness? Taste, sight, the loss of a limb, I could accept this. But why my hearing? No man of Earth depended more upon his ears than I!

Being vexed by the lack of improvement in my condition, I decided to change physicians. Eight days before Giulietta's farewell, I became a patient of Dr. Johann Schmidt. It was this doctor who later advised me to spend the summer of 1802 at Heiligenstadt. He knew that such quiet countryside would spare my hearing as much as possible and that this quaint village was in easy reach of his care. From May through the middle of September, things went reasonably well. I stopped worrying about my physical ailments and completed a new symphony.

Then came the morning of September twelfth, which brought Ferdinand Ries for a piano lesson. Since I was in the midst of my first crippling deaf spell of the summer, I suggested a walk instead. Ries seemed agreeable. We directed our steps away from the spires and gables of the imperial city and walked toward the western horizon with its thick black forests, tempting vineyards, and brightly painted hunting lodges. After we had rambled about an hour, Ries stopped in his tracks and turned toward me. I could see that he was speaking, but heard only a few mumbled syllables. Trying to disguise my weak hearing, I feigned absentmindedness.

B. What was that, Ries? What did you say?

He looked directly into my face and repeated himself. I cupped my ears and watched his lips, but still made nothing of what he said.

B. I'm sorry, boy. You'll have to speak louder. I've got a kind of "ringing" in my head this morning.

This time, Ries shouted. And through my stopped-up ears came the faint dim echo of his fatal words.

R. The piping. Don't you hear it, Master? There must be a herdboy in the valley. He plays his flute!

We continued to exchange stares, and I knew that my fate was no longer a secret from Ries.

B. I hear no flute. Try to understand me, Ries. I'm now sailing through dangerous waters and must be alone. Don't come to me again until I send for you.

I turned from my pupil and walked toward Heiligenstadt, not without observing a moisture in his eyes that I had never seen there before. On my way back, it was as though the full impact of total deafness struck me for the first time. I could feel the clumping vibrations of my footsteps, but I heard nothing! I could see the silver fluttering of leaves, but couldn't hear the wind that set them dancing. I could see the freedom of frolicking birds, the playful dancing of an early autumn brook, but I heard neither of their songs.

This deaf spell turned out to be the longest I had yet experienced. It lasted from September tenth until the twenty-eighth. Then came three days of very weak hearing capabilities, which were followed by the usual sequence—a storm of ringing and buzzing that scraped and screamed from October second until my return to Vienna. During this isolated month of self-imprisonment, my philosophical views underwent a major change. The morality of power of the "Great Mogul" was brought trembling to its knees. I had come face-to-face with an evil demon whom no amount of personal strength or self-will could master. And worst of all, he now demanded the full recognition of his powerful grasp upon my life. If I could not conceal his presence from a devoted student like Ries, think how much less I could hide him from my jealous and hateful rivals. They would now clap their hands together and cry for my blood:

"He conducts our orchestras and can't hear their performances. He composes music and can't hear what he writes. He plays the clavier and can't hear his own false tones. He pretends to be a Mozart. Mozart had the greatest ears in the world, and this man has none at all!"

After three weeks of lonely walking, thinking, meditating, and brooding, I concluded that all my ambitious dreams were hopeless. Deafness had robbed me of everything. It put an end to my plans for an extensive tour with the *C Minor Concerto.* It made successful conducting impossible. If I could neither play nor conduct, where was the incentive to compose? Deafness placed financial security and marital happiness well beyond my reach. It separated me from all the joyous recreations of human society. It cut off my talent and creative visions from what could have been their most beautiful years of development. It proved my power morality to be a failure, my self-confidence, a disillusionment. By my own strength, I could do exactly nothing at all! I surrendered myself to this devil. If he was out to crush my spirit, he had succeeded. There remained nothing but an irresistible urge to abandon the struggle, to put an end to my miserable life!

This I would surely have done had it not been for a startling discovery. Upon giving up everything that I possessed—my Mozartian throne, my friends and pupils, my beloved art—I found that something still remained. Deep within, as though planted at birth by some mysterious hand, was an indestructible energy, a creative power demanding that my life be lived to its bitter conclusion. If death should come before I had the opportunity to unfold all my artistic capabilities, I would be content facing him with courage and with gratitude for liberating me from a state of perpetual suffering. But one thing was certain. Death would not come by my own hand!

Having resolved to go on living, I stooped over, picked up the fragments, and spent the first ten days of October piecing together what was left of the "Great Mogul." What did he look like now? He was a king with a new philosophy. No longer did he aspire to be Vienna's strong man, whose sheer physical defiance was the absolute master of his destiny. Instead he would pay the higher price of true heroism. And this was no condescension, for he realized that a hero was a strong man who had even the strength to suffer! He would return to Vienna and embrace the duties and obligations of his profession. He would no longer keep the secret of his deafness. He would earnestly try to stop brooding over his poor health. If the suffering became too great, he'd try to laugh until he could find something to laugh about. (After all, his rough old Rhenish wit had seen him through many an earlier storm.) He would not give up his hopes for marital bliss; perhaps some girl could find happiness in sharing him with his "goddess." He would continue to play and conduct until he was certain that deafness had made each of these treasured occupations absolutely impossible. He would devote most of his efforts to composition—composing for the sake of the music and not to display his orchestral or pianistic virtuosity. Thanks to the childhood training of his ears, no amount of deafness could now prevent his "mind's ear" from hearing what he committed to paper. To compensate for the limitations imposed upon his conducting and playing, he decided to go "all out" for another new symphony—this to be the greatest of his career. *Symphony 3* would be a complete break with the past, so extended in structure and so broad in scope that it would embrace the entire spirit of the French Revolution. It would satisfy Bernadotte's request and proclaim the Jacobinic message in a language that could be heard and understood by all men. The "Great Mogul" would model this garment on his own back and then carefully watch as Napoleon Bonaparte tried it on for size!

Chapter 10

The beginning of the 1802–03 season found me with enough new material to promote another public concert for my own benefit. But this wasn't an easy matter to arrange. Public concerts in Vienna were still few and far between. There were Salieri's annual Tonkünstlergesellschaft concerts given at Christmas and Easter in the Royal Imperial Court Theater, there were Schuppanzigh's series of summer concerts given Thursdays in the Augarten, and that was it! The only other possibility would be to obtain use of the brand-new Theater-an-der-Wien. But how could I ever manage this?

The new Wiener Theater was under the direction of Emanuel Schikaneder who engaged Henneberg and Seyfried as conductors. For years, this company had been in lively competition with the court theaters, and now because of the opening of Schikaneder's new building, this rivalry became even keener. The court theaters were owned and managed by the court banker, Baron Von Braun, who employed Liechtenstein and Weigl as conductors. Each manager tried to outdo the other. Each sought some new attraction that would catch and hold the biggest share of the music public for his particular theater. For three years they searched in vain. The smooth tried-and-proven styles of Salieri, Seyfried, Henneberg, and Weigl had been worn thin by constant use. Their new works would bring capacity crowds for a few days, and then attendance would quickly fall below the level of profitable production. If either theater were to survive, a new breed of operatic composer had to be found.

Such a new spirit was discovered in the person of Luigi Cherubini, Parisian composer and teacher. In 1802, his operas burst upon us like a bombshell, their originality finding immediate acceptance among the Viennese. His first import was an opera called *Lodoiska,* produced by Schikaneder on March 23. Its success was record-breaking. In the true spirit of "competitive enterprise," Von Braun lost no time in securing a Cherubini score for his theater. Schikaneder was not to be outfoxed. He applied to Cherubini for another score. The net result of all this careful throat-cutting was that *Die Tage der Gefahr* opened at both theaters on practically the same day in the middle of August. But even such dual presentation had no ill effect upon the financial success and instant popularity of this new opera. Cherubini's theatrical works continued to appear in Vienna through the rest of the year. *Medea* was produced in November, and *Der Bernardsberg* in December. I heard all these scores and delighted in their crisp newness and their ability to please the public. By 1803, I ranked Cherubini second only to Mozart as an operatic composer!

I was still lusting after the new theater building, wondering how I could negotiate a Beethoven concert, when Von Braun solved my problem for me. He journeyed to Paris and signed Cherubini to compose operas for his stage alone. Poor Schikaneder had to do something to even his score with the baron. In January 1803, he turned to Abbé Georg Joseph Vogler and to me, contracting the two of us to write operas exclusively for his stage. The terms of our agreements were perfect. We were to receive 10 percent of the receipts from the first ten performances, free lodgings in the theater building, and, what most appealed to me, the use of his stage for an occasional public concert! Since my success as an instrumental composer was fast approaching that of Mozart and Haydn, I believed that I could eventually outwrite "Monsieur" Cherubini in the field of opera. And how rewarding it would be to "cash in" on my share of his lucrative theatrical audiences!

On March 1, 1803, Brother Carl and I moved into No. 26 Theater Building An-der-Wien. Because we still worked together in many ways, it seemed silly for the two of us to go on living in separate apartments. Carl was now in complete charge of my business correspondence; he supervised my two part-time copyists and helped with much of the proofreading and arranging. He also advised me in financial matters.

Two days later, Schikaneder informed me that I would have the use of his stage on April fifth. My dreams for another Beethoven concert became a definite reality! All thoughts of beginning an opera were put aside until after this important public appearance. I spent the entire month of March reconstructing my sadly eroded piano technique and working on *Sinfonia Bonaparte*, which by now had far exceeded the structural boundaries imposed upon either of its two predecessors. My "touch and go" hearing continued as usual with its alternating "good spells" and "bad spells." I couldn't help wondering and worrying about how it would behave itself on the day of the concert.

On April fourth at 5:00 AM, the door opened and in came Ries. I had asked him to show up early because I knew there would be a lot of last-minute rushing. He helped me complete the trombones; and then while I was washing, shaving, and dressing, we talked about the day's prospects.

R. How is your hearing, Maestro?

B. Not bad, Ries. It's been normal for almost two weeks. Surely it will hold out for another day!

R. How's the new concerto? I'm so anxious to hear it.

B. You'll do more than hear it! I want you to make your debut with this piece. I'll arrange with Schuppanzigh for you to perform it in the Augarten. You'll be my first pupil to play in his own public concert. This will make me very proud of you.

R. Then by all means let me hear it. If this concerto is to become my specialty, I have the right to a private performance! How could I better learn its correct interpretation than from the composer's own hands?

B. Not from mine, Ries. I'm afraid my days of teaching by example have run their course. Between deaf spells and an unprecedented devotion to *Sinfonia Bonaparte,* I find that my poor old technique has lost much of the careful discipline pounded into it by my father. I can still "hear" a correct performance, but unfortunately, my fingers won't behave according to my ears.

R. You're being too self-critical, Master. If you never practiced another hour, you'd still be the best pianist in all Vienna!

B. It's kind of you to say this, Ries. I appreciate your encouragement.

R. I'm not flattering you. I mean what I say. Your playing has transcended the petty cares of technique. While most of us are completely occupied with the mechanics of translating notes into tones, you concern yourself with more important matters. When a composition falls beneath your hands, its very soul is made to shine! Why should you worry about a handful of bastard critics who entirely miss the glory of your interpretations for the sake of a few wrong notes and faulty leaps? Away with these wretches! If such men were transported to Michelangelo's Chapel, they could do nothing better than glance upward, scratch their heads, and complain about the cracks in the ceiling!

B. Dear Ries . . . you make me feel like a king.

R. Then my words are not entirely inadequate

B. Very well. I'll play the concerto for you. Perhaps another trip through will help today's rehearsal.

R. May I follow you in the score?

B. I have no score. The original manuscript is at the Bureau d'Arts et d' Industrie, and Seyfried has the orchestral parts. These sketches are all I have.

I handed my abbreviated notations to Ries; he fumbled through them nervously.

R. You mean to say you're going to play and conduct from this? Why, it's nothing but a dozen pages of scribbling!

B. On the contrary. It shows all entries of the solo part and traces the main themes. Suppose you turn pages for me.

R. You're joking. No one could know when to turn these pages!

B. When I nod, you turn. It's as simple as that.

I played through the solo and orchestral passages of the opening *Allegro*, humming the accompaniment as I went along. Since I hadn't time to write a cadenza, I substituted a ten-minute improvisation (on themes from this movement), which led smoothly into cadential patterns of arpeggios, octaves and scales. Before beginning the *Largo*, I turned to Ries.

B. Now tell me what you think. I want your honest opinion.

R. So far, it's the finest concerto I have ever heard. Its melodies are beautiful and sensitive. You've given the pianist important things to say—not just busy work.

B. And my playing?

R. You're not quite the technician you were two years ago. But even so, your interpretive powers are more than adequate.
B. Good! This is what I wanted to hear. Now comes the *Largo.*

Before I could complete the opening solo passage, Brother Carl entered and interrupted.

Ca. You two had better stop for breakfast. Seyfried comes in half an hour!

As it happened, Ignaz Ritter von Seyfried arrived twenty minutes early and joined the three of us for a modest pre-rehearsal breakfast consisting of twelve servings of bread soup, two bottles of Sankt Georger, and twenty-seven large eggs. As we consumed this dainty repast, our conversation turned from wines to apartments to housekeepers to girls to finances to politics to Napoléon. From Napoléon, it was a natural transition to current goings-on with *Symphony 3* and plans for the day's concert.

Seyfried had spent the preceding week rehearsing small groups of players and singers. He was very pleased with their progress, considering the limited experience many of these musicians had had in ensemble playing. He was optimistic about the final rehearsal, but advised me to go out of my way to be patient, encouraging, tactful, and understanding. Quite an order for a big old "Mogul" who had always been more interested in the quality of a performance than in the psychological well-being of his musicians. Seyfried and I argued at some length over what should and shouldn't be included in the program. I favored a longer list on the theory that people would appreciate more music for their money. Seyfried believed that fewer pieces would enhance the overall performance. Our final agreement was a compromise. The concert was to begin at six o'clock with *Symphony 1* and *Concerto 3.* After a twenty-minute intermission, Seyfried would conduct *Symphony 2,* to be followed by my improvising at the pianoforte until 9:00 PM on themes from *Prometheus. Mount of Olives* would then conclude the program. I was to play and conduct *Concerto 3*; Seyfried would direct all the other numbers.

The four of us arrived downstairs at 8:00 AM, where we found Prince Lichnowsky wringing his hands in anticipation of the first and only general rehearsal. No doubt about it, he had put the fear of God into the orchestra. They were all tuned up and ready to go.

Seyfried began with *Symphony 1* and *2*; I was very pleased with his results. At 9:30 AM, I seated myself at the clavier to begin rehearsing the concerto. I beckoned my pupil.

B. *Ries*! Come and turn pages.

Seyfried jumped in front of him.

Se. That won't be necessary. I can manage perfectly well.

I looked at Ries, Ries looked at me. Our exchange of glances confirmed mutual belief that Seyfried needed a lesson in humility. We knew exactly what was going to happen to him, and it did! As we began playing, he casually "eyed" my abbreviated manuscript, pretending not to be frightened by it. But soon he was openly staring at its impenetrable maze. Huge beads of sweat appeared from beneath careful locks and zigzagged their way down his corrugated brow. Poor Seyfried! I knew he was hopelessly lost. He no longer watched the score, but intensely studied my face for some friendly little clue as to when he should turn the page. I gave him none and thoroughly enjoyed his suffering. When he had missed his cue, I stopped playing and so did the orchestra. All eyes turned to me and then to my embarrassed assistant.

B. What are you waiting for, my personal invitation to turn the page?
Se. I couldn't find where you were.
B. What am I to think of a conductor who can't even follow a score?
Se. A score, yes! But not such impossible scribbling!
B. Perhaps now you will permit me the services of my pupil?
Se. By all means! Only your own pupil could read that score!
B. Ries! Come and turn pages.

Aided by my carefully concealed winks and nods, Ries performed his office well to Seyfried's utter astonishment. Our rehearsal of the concerto was a fine success, playing each movement twice.

At 5:00 PM, Prince Lichnowsky invited Breuning, Seyfried, Ries, Carl, and me to join him at the Swan for a preconcert supper. More Tokayer was served, and by the time our meal ended, I was in the best of spirits. Seyfried and I sat next to each other, and after an initial "cold spell," the two of us finally fell into conversation:

Se. Herr Beethoven, I sense the return of your optimism.
B. I'm always optimistic about the premieres of my newest works. If they please me, I know they will please others. I have great hopes for this evening, why do you think I raised the prices of seats? But, Seyfried, you should embrace my newest—*Sinfonia Bonaparte*.Wait 'til you hear it. It's entirely different from anything I've ever done. It frightens me.
Se. Oh, it can't sound that bad.
B. That's not what I mean. I begin with a few simple borrowings from *Prometheus* . . . some heroic themes to portray the victory of man's revolutionary spirit. And from these, there grows a work of such scope and import that I fear I shall never again be able to do its equal.
Se. Well, at least you should be glad that you are the one who sets the standard. What if *Sinfonia Bonaparte* were being written by some Frenchman, or some Englishman?
B. A good point, Seyfried.
Se. When will it be finished?
B. This summer. If it takes ten movements, I'm determined to finish the work this summer. By the way, are you turning pages for me this evening?
Se. No Sir! One humiliation is enough. If Ries is such a good score reader, let him do the job.
B. It would look much better if I were assisted by the conductor.
Se. No! I refuse.
B. Dear Seyfried, it was all a joke, a little conspiracy to take down our "tyrannical" leader.
Se. You mean . . .?
B. Yes! Ries would never have known when to turn a page except for a blink from old Beethoven.

We laughed heartily, and Seyfried agreed to assist me in the concerto.

The concert began on the stroke of six o'clock and lasted until eleven-ten. Some program! Thanks to a fully packed house, I netted 1,800 florins. The instrumental pieces were well-received, but the oratorio was considered a novelty and found only modest acceptance.

I spent the summer of 1803 among the beautiful vineyards of Oberdöbling—a half hour's walk up the mountain from Heiligenstadt. Here I completed the sketches for my best symphony, though there was still much to be done on its full score when I returned to Vienna, September fifth. Since I was under contract to write an opera, I also spent many summer hours looking for a suitable libretto. *Romeo and Juliet, Macbeth, Faust, Alfred the Great, Bacchus, Julius Caesar—all* these were carefully considered and then rejected. By August, my choice had narrowed to *Alexander the Great,* a text by Schikaneder, or *Leonore,* an original French text by Bouilly, which had been done into German by Sonnleithner and called *Fidelio.* I did a little sketching on each of these librettos and then put both aside in favor of *Symphony 3.* At this point in my career, desire for *Bonaparte*'s completion loomed above all else. I would finish the symphony and then go to work on *Alexander,* or *Leonore,* or perhaps on some text of my own.

Four days after my return to the theater building, I was busily orchestrating *Bonaparte* when Breuning entered with a stranger.

Br. Ludwig, I'd like you to meet a young friend of mine who hails from Ehrenbreitstein: Willibrord Joseph Mähler.

B. Welcome to any friend of Breuning's. You'll have to excuse the wild disorder of my apartment. I've been away all summer . . . you know how it is.

Breuning interrupted.

Br. Don't apologize, Ludwig. I've already warned Mähler about what a helpless bachelor you are.

B. That's not true, Breuning. The old place is often eruptive, but not this bad. Carl returns on the fifteenth, and he helps me with such things. Are you a musician, Mähler?

Mä. In a modest sense, yes. I write songs and piano pieces. I write poetry, I sing, I paint. I'm a dilettante of all the arts, but unfortunately, a master of none!

B. Mähler, I advise you to specialize. Pick out a favorite and concentrate on it. Any art form is like a beautiful woman. If you would win her love, you must devote yourself to her and to her alone. At a very early age, I was forced to specialize in music. There have been times when I cursed the narrowness of my training and the limited perspective of my outlook. But now, when I reflect upon a tortuous ascent of over thirty years, there is nothing I would exchange for my talent. Nowhere do I find greater happiness than in the practice and display of my art.

The more I suffer and sacrifice for her, the greater pleasure she brings me. Specialize, Mähler. There's no finer reward in life.

Mä. This is easy for you to say, Maestro, because your talent in music is so great.

B. The very words I spoke to Mozart when I first met him. And do you know what he said? He said that it's not a man's original endowment that counts, but rather his love for his craft and his willingness to sacrifice for it. These ultimately determine an artist's creative stature. I fully agree with Herr Mozart on this matter.

Breuning interrupted with a change in topic.

Br. How are the ears behaving these days?

B. Pretty well, Stephan. I had several bad spells this summer, one lasting for more than two weeks. But each period of deafness is followed by a return to normal hearing. And the dependability of this sequence has subdued much of the initial horror of my malady. When a deaf spell comes, I go on about my business—no longer paralyzed by the fear of never hearing again.

Br. Have you finished your opera?

B. No. I'm still looking for a good libretto. I must find something that pleases me, for the inspiration of an entire opera follows directly from its text. Right now, *Symphony 3* commands my full attention.

Br. Is this the one on Bonaparte?

B. Yes. It all began when General Bernadotte suggested that I was the one who should commemorate their leader in music. I approach the task with great purpose because of my high regard for Bonaparte.

Br. Ludwig! How can you admire a man who invades our Fatherland?

B. Napoleon is an invasion of liberation, not the yoke of bondage. He offers us freedom from the inequalities under which we live, from the injustices poured upon us by bastard kings, ruling through the "grace of God." Napoleon is like the greatest of Roman consuls. If he has his way, Europe will become a federation of free republics. No man will be exploited by other men, and each of us will share in the honor and dignity of being human. We shall never again be ravaged by war, for when every man is assured his honor and freedom, who will there be to fight a war?

Br. Napoleon undermines the very nobility who sponsor your music.

B. I'm naive enough to believe that my art would flourish in a republic as well as in a monarchy.

Br. I suppose you're right, Ludwig. There is much to be said for the French Revolution. It is directly responsible for most of the reforms which now come to us from our "benevolent" rulers. But reforms should come from above, not from the revolutionary masses. Like many Germans, I'm a strong supporter of the French cause, so long as it remains on French soil. They have no right to impose their system upon us.

B. But Breuning, your viewpoint is too restricted. How can we ever achieve a "world republic" unless the French are bold enough to export their revolution?

Br. Who wants a "world republic"?

B. I do! I'm damn tired of being a little German surrounded by little Frenchmen and little Italians. I want to be a "world citizen," living under a constitution big enough to embrace all humanity!

Br. Ridiculous!

B. Not at all. And in this republic there'd be one great "Bureau of Art" to which I would send my compositions and thence receive whatever money I needed. No longer would old Beethoven have to hawk his wares like some overzealous potato peddler.

Br. You're being idealistic, Ludwig. Wait and see. When the French set foot in Vienna, you'll be out there fighting them with the rest of us!

B. I don't think so. I can't see myself taking up the sword for this kind of battle; not for some king or pope or prince. But the world of art, the intellectual kingdom, this is a different matter. If liberty and progress are challenged here, then let me be the first to offer my life in their defense. Mähler, whose side are you on?

Mä. I'm afraid I agree with von Breuning. France has much to offer the rest of the world. But it should come to us naturally from their example—not be forced upon us by a tyrannical militarist!

B. Bah! You're both too conservative.

Mähler turned toward Breuning.

Mä. I wonder if Herr Beethoven would play something for us? He has composed my favorite piano sonatas. (*As Mähler continued, his eyes met mine.*) And how I would enjoy hearing him play one of them.

B. I think I'll try my new symphony on you two. But how about lunch, have you eaten?

Br. Be our guest.

B. Thanks, Stephan. But since Carl has been away, I've gotten into the habit of working straight through. Let's compromise. I'll give you a little cheese and wine. Then I want your opinion of *Sinfonia Bonaparte.*

While we ate and drank, I questioned Mähler about his days in my boyhood town. He had no recollections of Mother's family, but I enjoyed his colorful remembrances of Father Rhine. Our conversation soon turned to Beethoven's career, and I had to admit that my fine circle of aristocratic friends was largely responsible for the phenomenal growth of my reputation. It was this admiring band of royal followers who linked my name with Haydn and Mozart.

After our baby bacchanal, I played the last movement of *Symphony 3* and then improvised on its themes for a full hour. When I finished, Breuning and Mähler clapped and shouted their approval. I promptly sent them away, returned to my orchestration, and worked for eight hours without interruption. Such a prolific response as this was characteristic of my remaining years on Earth. Without exception, I continued to find my greatest inspiration for hard work in the sincere plaudits of friends!

Chapter 11

My tutorial association with Archduke Rudolph Johann Joseph Rainer began early in 1804. If I grew to regard aristocratic sponsors as mere "strings upon which I played," then certainly this pianistic archduke of fifteen years was the highest positioned and most influential "string" ever to come my way. I was now young Rudolph's personal choice for a music teacher. In one year of piano lessons, he was able to develop interpretative powers comparable to those of Ries. Rudolph became a powerful friend and my most generous patron. His interest in my career proved more rewarding than even the combined efforts of Lichnowsky and Lobkowitz.

In spite of von Braun's generosity (permitting Carl and me to stay on, rent-free), I soon became dissatisfied with the theater building as a place of residence—too much hubbub to get any work done. When I asked Breuning for his advice, he recommended the "Rothes Haus," a wonderful building into which he had just moved. Carl and I took an apartment there on March first, and it turned out to be a fine place to live and work. We also kept our theater residence, which served as a combination piano studio, office, choir room, dining hall, and editorial factory.

After a month of this arrangement, Carl decided that the Rothes Haus was too far from his office. He moved to a more convenient location on the Hohen Markt, but still spent much time with me at our "business quarters" in the theater building. Not far from the

Rothes Haus was an enormous structure called the House of the Black Spaniard. Hard to believe, but in twenty-three short years in a modest apartment of that very Schwarzspanierhaus I would close my eyes for the last time on Earth!

In the theater building on the afternoon of May 23, 1804, Lichnowsky and I were discussing plans for the first rehearsal of *Sinfonia Bonaparte.* He thought that my dedication to Bonaparte would be considered an open defiance of our emperor. He advised me to change the title page, and we were arguing over the matter when Ries entered. The young man had run himself out of breath and stood panting in the doorway. I couldn't resist quoting Macbeth.

B. Get thee hence, thou pale-faced loon!
R. Master! Have you heard?
B. That the woods began to move?
R. That Napoleon is now emperor of France!

I grabbed Ries by his right arm.

B. You jest! You must be joking!
R. No, Master. Everyone in the Graben is shouting about it. I even stopped by the Swan to make sure. The first consul is now emperor of France! He was crowned on the eighteenth . . . five days ago.
B. I'll be damned!

Lichnowsky mumbled something, but his words were no match for my loud profanity. I looked for something to break . . . to kill . . . to destroy! The careful copy of *Bonaparte* caught my eye. I ripped off its title page, tore it into shreds, and deposited these in an unemptied chamber pot.

B. This for the emperor of France! Never again will I put my faith in another man! As sure as I do, he turns out to be nothing but an ordinary mortal. He'll not have *my* composition! *Sinfonia Bonaparte* was inspired by a great man. One who heard the cry of his own generation and was not afraid to answer it. A man who tamed the revolution and offered us the hope of a republican millennium with liberty, equality, and fraternity FOR ALL! And what happens to this "hero of our age"? A single draught from the cup of absolute power, and he becomes an ordinary mortal who will trample the rights of others for the sake of his own ambition! He will exalt himself and become a tyrant! I can't believe that Frenchmen will tolerate another king. If they do, then the hope of Europe is lost! Thank God for the steamship; if need be, I shall sail to America and find me a republic.

Ries tries to be humorous.

R. I can imagine how the American Indian will appreciate your music.

B. So be it! I'd rather play for savages than live out my days under the heel of some self-appointed king!

Lichnowsky recovers from his silence.

L. Then Bonaparte . . . he's no longer honored by your symphony?

B. Not in name, but in spirit. I shall call my new work *Synfonia Eroica*, to commemorate the passing of a great hero!

Since Lobkowitz, in a sense, commissioned the *Eroica*, its initial rehearsal took place in his palace on the afternoon of May twenty-fifth. What a difference I found between the cold austerity of imagined sounds, and the warm vibrations of actual timbres! My favorable impressions were so pronounced that for twenty years I held the *Eroica* to be my masterpiece—the perfect symphony. What do I think of it today? Well, after two hundred years, I've "written off" the two final movements. But the balance of this work is a different matter. Today I am as proud of the opening *Allegro con brio* as I was the day it was finished. If I were to revise this movement, I wouldn't change a single note of its development, its recap, or its coda. They are perfect. The same goes for the *Marcia funebre.* No amount of rewriting could improve its stature; it says exactly what it was meant to say. Its high point is, of course, the *Minore,* with a dazzling triple fugue. In two hundred years, I have yet to exceed the fresh and luminous import of these terrifying measures. They were inspired by Bach and could have been written by him.

Of all my Earthly creations, there are scarcely two dozen pieces that I would rank with the opening movements of this symphony. Such music is great music, and the author knows this at the hour of its completion. He doesn't need to wait for the gushing approval of friends, for favorable reviews, or for the plaudits of a confirming audience. Such music "sings" from the written page, embracing its creator's dearest wish—the hope that he had had something worthwhile to say and the ability to say it. The first public hearing of the *Eroica* occurred one year later in the Wiener Theater.

During my stay in Baden, Ries commuted regularly for his lessons. The time was swiftly approaching when "Beethoven's pupil" would make his public debut. As promised, I had arranged with Schuppanzigh for Ries to perform my *C Minor Concerto* in one of the regular Augarten Thursday concerts.

Johann managed to rent summer lodgings for me at Döbling. I moved there in August and stayed for three months. Instead of being surrounded by people, my companions were the sky, fields, rocks, trees and vineyards. Not even deaf spells could make me suspicious of friends such as these. Wishing to recover from my siege with *Symphony 3*, I spent this entire summer on piano sonatas: the *Waldstein*, the *F Major*, and the *Appassionata*.

Early in October, I asked Ries to begin looking for a suitable apartment in the city, something as close as possible to Lichnowsky's. I also planned to continue using my free office-studio at the Wiener Theater. Ries found me an ideal spot on the Mölkerbastei, a fourth-floor suite in the tall many-chimneyed structure known as the Pasqualati House. I moved in on October 31 and was surprised to discover how much an old spiral staircase reminded me of the stone steps leading to Mozart's apartment. Upon reaching my "eagle's nest," I found bright cheery rooms, lots of sunlight, fresh breezes, and a dazzling view of the Wienerwald. Through Baron Pasqualati, it was possible to engage a servant for a very modest price. The lad's chief responsibility would be to "stand guard" before my sanctum sanctorum and admit no strangers. All uninvited guests were to be referred to my "visiting hours" in the theater building. Only through such antisocial tactics could I hope for a productive season of creative seclusion.

As if all this weren't enough, the Pasqualatis turned out to be great music lovers. They developed a passion for my compositions and took a genuine personal interest in my career. Nevertheless, in spite of ideal conditions, I had become too much the perennial mover to settle down here once and for all. Periodically I was to depart from the baron's and then return like some migrating bird. The old boy seemed to understand my nomadic tendencies better than I did myself. Each time I'd move away, he'd shake my hand and offer a consoling reassurance: "Never mind! We know you'll come back.

And when you do, your apartment will be here waiting for you. We couldn't think of renting it to anyone but Beethoven!"

November 5 was a cold gray day. As usual, I spent the afternoon walking the streets with my little sketchbook in hand. Only when stomping through the out-of-doors would my best thoughts come to me. I'd hum them over in my mind until I was reasonably sure, then I'd stop in my tracks and pencil them into my notebook. Since I had never learned to write with bemittened hands, this operation could be quite painful in cold weather. I would have much preferred Heiligenstadt with its inspiring summertime views of the blue Danube and the purple Carpathians. But during winter months, the best I could hope for were the blackish bare streets and parks of Vienna.

By evening, the cold weather and I had worked up an enormous appetite, and I decided to treat myself to a fine fish dinner. Since oysters at the Swan were getting too stale even for me, I tried the White Ox where Krumpholz guaranteed that the city's best Newfoundland white salt cod was served. The main dining room was large and cheerful. Although it was nearly filled to capacity, there wasn't a soul whom I recognized. Spotting a cozy table by the fireplace, I went over and wearily fell into one of its two chairs. A golden goose turned slowly on a spit, filling the entire room with the salivating "come and eat me" smell of its crisping flesh. But no matter—by now I had become so fond of seafood that not even a smelly "Mother Goose" could alter my fishy intent. I ordered a double serving of cod, which was, of course, prefixed by a gluttonous assortment of appetizers: bread soup, olives, anchovies, and champagne. As I stared through clouds of rich tobacco smoke, I noticed a life-size portrait, oak framed on the opposite wall. Before I could study the picture more closely, I was pleasantly shocked by the sudden appearance of Stephan von Breuning. He had just arrived and had chosen a small table beneath the colorful painting. Though dying to go over and shake hands with him, I jerked my head in the opposite direction and bent closer than ever to my bowl of soup. I could no more have gone to Breuning than I could have wished away my bad hearing. Our friendship had ruptured, and my stubborn pride absolutely prohibited me from taking an initial step toward reconciliation. I had made up my mind to finish eating, to rise, and unconcernedly walk away. But thank God, before I could act out such a deceitful plan, my lentil slurping was interrupted by the weight of a hand on my left shoulder. I looked up.

B. von Breuning! You old devil!

Br. If you won't answer my letters, perhaps you'll at least share a bottle of Melniker with me.
B. Any time, Stephan. Pull up a chair.
Br. I suppose you're still angry with me . . . and what a stupid thing for us to argue about! I should never have lost my temper!
B. No, Stephan, I'm the old bear! The fault is mine. Forgive me if I have pained you, and believe me, I've suffered nonetheless myself. The thought that I would never again see you has made me realize how dear to my heart you are and always will be.
Br. Our dispute is forgotten?
B. Of course! How could I remember your loving mother and have it otherwise?
Br. You really liked my mother, didn't you?
B. Now there's an understatement! Mozart, your mother, and mine—these are the treasures of my life. They are my inspiration for each new work . . . for each step forward!

We wined and dined for nearly two hours, then strolled from the White Ox, once again the best of friends. I felt twice as tall and ten times happier than when I had embarked upon what was to have been just another meal.

During the next few years, Breuning and I were frequent companions. Though I never again moved into his apartment, I would often go there for meals. Such visits to the Rothes Haus were especially convenient when my busy schedule kept me long hours at the theater building.

On December 27, Baron von Braun reinstated my commission to write an opera for his theater. I got out my preliminary sketches for both *Alexander the Great* and *Leonore*. After three days' careful studying, burrowing, and calculating, a final decision was made in favor of *Leonore*; this in spite of the fact that its author was no longer director of the Wiener Theater. A good "businessman" would say that I had chosen inexpediently, that I had given Director Schikaneder a slap in his thick face. I couldn't help it! Of the two texts, only *Leonore* succeeded in deeply touching my emotions. And from earlier days as cembalist, I had learned to beware the operatic composer who had not been genuinely moved by his chosen libretto.

The arrival of 1805 was celebrated by launching six months' hard work on *Leonore*. With the exception of 1793, no year brought higher hopes or greater expectations. I believed that I had chosen an ideal story—that through it, the power of the *Eroica* could be brought to the operatic stage. I believed that my *Leonore*'s novelty would be an easy match for the best works of Luigi Cherubini, and through this competition, I should win my share of his fame and fortune. To these rewards would be added the crowning gift of all—a sweet, smiling "hausfrau." Why not? I was still young enough to marry—a mere "boy" of thirty-four!

Chapter 12

The first five months of 1805 were a period of creative fertility. They witnessed final shaping of the *Appassionata,* as well as the complete sketching of *Leonore.* The *Fourth Piano Concerto* was begun, and sketches were continued for two movements of the *C Minor Symphony.* The only professional interruption in this productive flood tide occurred on Sunday evening April 7, when I conducted the first public performance of *Symphony 3* in Director Clementi's concert at the Theater-an-der-Wien. The *Eroica* came late in the program, which probably explains why it seemed unduly long to most Viennese concert goers. Halfway through the *Marcia funebre* the mouth belonging to one pair of tired ears cried out from the gallery: "I'll give another kreutzer if the damn thing will only stop!"

When the "thing" finally did stop, the applause was so meager that I walked from the stage without acknowledging it. This didn't bother me in the least since I had already formed my exalted opinion of Opus 55, and no amount of unfavorable criticism could induce me to change it in any way!

In June 15, I said good-bye to Baron Pasqualati with the understanding that I would return to his house in the Fall. Once again, I chose Hetzendorf for a summer retreat, where I spent an entire first week renewing acquaintances with the many pastoral delights of Schönbrunn Garden. Then came the time for good hard work. I "opened an office" under the same crotched oak where four years earlier I had finished the *Mount of Olives*. Perched beneath this grand old "philosopher," I transformed sketches for *Leonore* into a finished opera. Quite an accomplishment for eleven weeks! There were several factors contributing to this productive outburst: the joy of arriving in the countryside, my sporting ambition to rival Cherubini in his own field, and my temporary freedom from the routine interruptions of a musical career. At dear green Hetzendorf, there were no concerts to prepare for, no contracts to wrangle over, no brothers to argue with, no fancy pupils' fussy schedules to interrupt my work. Not even Ries came for lessons; I had wrapped him up in my best recommendations and sent him off to Silesia for the summer. There he would gain invaluable performing experience as Lichnowsky's chief pianist.

My return to Vienna was accompanied by the finished score of my opera and by complete preliminary sketches for the *G Major Piano Concerto.* Though I had great hopes for *Leonore,* I was too inexperienced as an operatic composer to form any definite preperformance opinion of the work. *Concerto No. 4* was a different story; I considered it the answer to a twenty-year quest. Counting early unpublished efforts, the *G Major* was my seventh attempt to write a good piece in this idiom. Since my first teenage performances with the Cologne Orchestra, I had felt that a true concerto should rise above the limitations of a virtuosic piano piece set against the stupid murmurings of an inferior orchestral accompaniment. The piano part should be concerned with more important things than "showing off"; the orchestra should have more to do than "fill in." Each should make important contributions to the overall structure. Each should complement the other. But it's one thing to philosophize about what a good concerto should be and quite something else to compose one. Nevertheless, in the summer of 1805, I achieved my ideal. To be sure, these latest sketches lacked the psychic powers of *Symphony 3,* but they did strike a good balance between musical values and technical display. *Concerto No. 4* was my new standard. If I wrote another, it would have to be at least as good as this one and say at least as much—or else not live to see the press.

The morning of September 13 began, as most mornings did, with another superhuman but unsuccessful attempt to obtain a reputably close shave. Always the greatest difficulty was in trying to fit the width of my face between cracks in my mirror. I was using a cracked glass because there wasn't a whole mirror in the entire apartment—each had been ruined by repeated crashes to the floor when I had tried to nail it to the wall near the window. There seemed to be nothing that made me feel quite so clumsy as an article made of glass. I was actually uncomfortable until I had tripped over it, fallen over it, or in some way mashed it to pieces. At any rate, I had lathered my face from eyes to Adam's apple and was squinting grimaces into a cross-grained mirror, when Ries entered the apartment. We met in a grisly hug during which, completely forgetting the condition of my face, I transferred most of the lather from my left cheek to his. Did we laugh!

R. Really, Master, that's quite a soapy welcome!

B. When a young scamp stays away twelve weeks at a time, he needs a good "lathering." Eh, Ries?

R. If you say so, I'm sure I do. How was your summer?

B. Very fine! I completed both the opera and the concerto. They are more like the *Eroica* than earlier pieces, and I doubt if either will add much to my popularity. Oh well, I'd rather forge onward and upward, continuing to fight rather than meekly basking in the glory of early symphonies and a septet. If it takes my public ten years to follow, I can wait.

R. I don't think I'd worry about popularity. The young people are on your side. They are eager to hear your symphonies and to play your sonatas. They mention your name in the same breath in which they speak of Haydn and Mozart.

B. This may be true. But their enthusiasm is for my earlier works, not for the *Eroica* and what follows.

R. Then why don't you continue writing traditional music? Keep up your reputation; you'll remain popular and financially secure. You'll still have time for an occasional exploratory masterpiece.

B. Is my favorite pupil asking me to write potboilers?

R. Why not? Mozart did!

B. If he did, it was for the sake of his starving family. No, Ries. I'll not write "down" to the common herd; I'll not prostitute my art! I see music as a beautiful young girl, her safety and well-being entrusted to me by Mozart himself. Like most Europeans, this girl seeks freedom from the bonds of her past. It is my duty to help her in every way that I can.

R. What an idealist! How about Beethoven? How about *your* bondage, *your* freedom, *your* career?

B. Ries! You know me better than this. I'll always be a self-centered little boy who thrives on fat commissions and loud applause. If I'm long deprived of either of these precious rewards, I'll be writing the noisiest pots that ever boiled! But let me tell you this. As soon as my public is reestablished, as soon as they bring me the ducats I need, I'll immediately return to that which is noble, high and best. I'll not be satisfied until I've carried my dear sweet girl to safer ground than that on which she now stands.

R. I hope I *live* to play the new concerto.

B. What do you mean?

R. I'm about to be drafted into Bonaparte's army.

B. Don't be ridiculous!

R. It's true! I'm of age and a citizen of Bonn, which is now under French rule. This makes me eligible for conscription.

B. I'd tear up the damned notice and throw it in Napoleon's face!

R Then my poor family would be ruined; they'd be at his mercy.

Ries was drafted a month later. He left for Bonn in October 14, and I was greatly sorrowed by the departure of this young musician. He was my dear friend and best pupil, constantly encouraging me in every new work.

An ugly event of the preceding month made our farewell especially poignant. In September 15, I attended a morning concert in the Augarten with Ries, Lichnowsky, Schikaneder, and von Braun. After the musicale, we had breakfast together, and I couldn't resist extolling the virtuous *Leonore*. Apparently my enthusiasm was too much; nothing would appease my friends but a drive to the Pasqualati House for a private preconcert performance. I was anxious to get their opinion, and we had climbed clear to the fourth-floor apartment before I remembered a certain vow.

B. Ries must go away!

Lichnowsky tried to be diplomatic.

L. Don't tell me you two haven't "kissed and made up"!

B. We've made up, but there'll be no more treachery between us. Ries knows that I'll not play for him again.

L. Be reasonable, Ludwig. There's no treachery here—just love and admiration for your music. If anyone should be told to leave, it is I. I'm the one who practiced the little piece behind your back . . . not Ries!

B. If you wish me to play the new opera—

Before I could restate my unconditional demand, Ries broke his tearful stare, turned on his heels, and left the room. He had no sooner gone than the remaining visitors formed themselves into a jury of my peers. They judged my dealings with Ries as unfair, irrational, illogical, exaggerated, unjust. I'm sure they would have gone on indefinitely, but I didn't stay to listen. I thanked them for their deep concern in a matter that was none of their business, then stormed out of my apartment. As I descended the stairs, I could still hear them chattering like three disjointed bassoons—Allegro con fuoco e molto staccato!

No doubt the Napoleonic scourge would have swept across Vienna in the Fall of 1805 regardless of the life and plans of Ludwig van Beethoven. Nevertheless, it seemed to my self-centered little soul that the entire bloody business had but one specific purpose in mind. Bonaparte and his armies had come from Paris to Vienna for no other reason than to ruin the première of my *Leonore.* Gone were the delightful audiences who would have met me at least halfway in bridging the gap between Mozart and Beethoven. In their place came a houseful of Frenchmen who were expecting something bright and fluffy a la Cherubini. *Fidelio* was just the opposite—grim, philosophical, and in a foreign tongue. Is it any wonder that the *Fidelio* production folded in November 22 after only three performances? Stage manager George Friedrich Treitschke offered his encouragement.

T. Never mind, Ludwig. Your opera has suffered a retreat, not a defeat. She will live to fight another day. Remember, it took the entire French army to bring her to her knees. With your patience, *Fidelio* should be able to regroup, consolidate, and prepare her counteroffensive. She will eventually sing her way into the hearts of men.

As things turned out, Breuning and I were the ones to make the real revisions in *Fidelio.* By the following Spring, we had trimmed it to an opera of two acts. But only one of three condemned pieces was actually omitted—*Vive le Grand Mogul!*

Chapter 13

Breuning's condensation of *Fidelio*'s script was completed on February 18, 1806, and I began adjusting the music accordingly. Instead of merely rewriting a difficult woodwind section of the original overture, I decided to compose a brand-new piece. The result, now called *Leonore No. 3*, was a vastly extended structure whose dramatic proportions, I hoped, would raise the artistic stature of the entire score. By the first of March, with the revision of *Fidelio* far from completed, Baron von Braun grew impatient.

V. Br. Herr Beethoven, I have set aside the best night of the season for the presentation of your revised opera. Saturday, March twenty-ninth should draw a fine house because it is our last performance before Holy Week. If your score is not ready by this date, it will not be given at all.

The good baron's threat provided all the impetus I needed. It inspired a brilliant flow not only from my pen but from my bowels too. Such dual "efficiency," born of *Fidelio*'s first revision, became and remained a characteristic of my Earthly creative efforts. Every time that I was commissioned to complete a work by a specific date, my endeavors were thwarted by crippling attacks of diarrhea! I complained so vehemently to poor Zmeskall that he suggested shortening the legs of my writing desk. This, he assured me, would enable Beethoven to continue composing while comfortably seated on his chamber pot. Some throne for the "Great Mogul"!

The completed score was sent to von Seyfried so late in March that he had time for only a single rehearsal with full orchestra. This is exactly what I thought the performance sounded like in March 29. Even so, the *Allgemeine Musikalische Zeitung* managed a favorable review: "Beethoven has again produced his opera *Fidelio* on the stage, with many alterations and abbreviations. An entire act has been omitted, but the piece has benefitted and pleased better."

A second performance was given on Thursday evening, April 10. I was disappointed with the musical and financial results. There was better drama in the new overture than in the entire opera, and the paucity of florins trickling down to the composer convinced him that he was being cheated in his percentage. I went straight to the director of the theater.

B. See here, von Braun! I'm dissatisfied with the way things are going.

V. Br. Patience, Beethoven. New operas take time. I've witnessed the slow and painful birth of many an all-time favorite. *Fidelio* will come into her own if we just give her time. Her audience grows with each new performance.

B. But each new performance is poorer than the one which preceded it. Their playing grows *worse* instead of better. The choruses need more rehearsals; they're still full of blunders. Seyfried *tries* hard, but what can *he* do with an orchestra of bungling fools? The woodwinds sound as though they had yet to have their first lesson in orchestral ensemble! They don't know the difference between *pianissimo* and *fortissimo*. I'd rather not have my music performed than to hear it so poorly played. There is *no* delight in composing when your intentions are completely disregarded. What's more, I can't help thinking that their mistakes are made *on purpose*!

V. Br. Nonsense! Who would *do* such a thing?

B. My enemies. The orchestra is *filled* with them!

V. Br. You imagine a vain thing. These men are *not* your enemies. They fear and detest your conducting, but they admire you as a musician. If they make mistakes in your score, it's probably because of the many changes you've made. Remember, only four months ago they learned to play the *original*. And now after changing most of the numbers, you expect these musicians to "unlearn" what they've learned and, with the benefit of only *three* performances, to render the new score unblemished. You ask the impossible!

B. Is it asking the impossible to have *played* well what I've taken the time to *write* well?

V. Br. Of course not. But you must be patient. With each new performance, the playing will improve, the audience will grow, and so will our share of the receipts.

B. That's my *other* complaint—receipts! The house was *full*, and yet my pockets remain *empty*. I believe the income was much higher than reported and that I'm cheated in my percentage!

V. Br. No one has cheated you. My employees are perfectly honest. Since *my* share is based upon the same earnings figure as *yours*, I would stand to lose considerably more than you in the event of fraud. The house was not as full as you think. Only the first ranks, stalls, and pit were occupied. Why don't you offer some cheaper seats in the upper ranks? These would greatly increase our profits.

B. I don't write for the galleries!

V. Br. No? My dear Sir, even *Mozart* wrote for the galleries.

By now, I was shouting.

B. That settles it! I'll not give the opera again! Give me back my score!

He rang for the heavy folio. I stuffed it under my arm and snorted from his office.

Thus *Fidelio* was withdrawn from public performance for a period of *eight years*! When I again took up the task of revising it, I had become *twice* the orchestral composer that I was in the Spring of 1806! I was then able to recast it into the form that is *solely responsible* for its present-day survival in the repertoire.

Some biographers *marvel* that I was not crushed by the collapse of my operatic dreams. Actually I was *glad* to be rid of *Leonore* for a while. She had caused months of painful suffering and in return had brought me nothing but a "crown of martyrdom." Now I was *free*—free to enjoy the glorious realm of instrumental composition! Gone were the restrictions of stage and script. I could be *myself*, speaking my *own* language and wallowing in the abstract reflections of *pure music*! My return "home" ushered in the most consistently sustained, if not the most *vitally creative* period of my Earthly career. For the next four years, I was a very happy boy!

If 1806 brought happiness to my *creative* life, it also catalyzed a barbarous frustration within my *personal* life. Brother Carl had become increasingly involved with a harlot named *Johanna Reiss.* Realizing the potential dangers of this relationship, I invited Carl to my apartment for some *inexpensive* brotherly advice. He came on the evening of May 18. We pulled our chairs close to a window, hoping better to enjoy the Spring sunset, a cool Danube breeze, and our new bottle of Grinzinger. Prior to Carl's love affair, I simply regarded him as my *proud, passionate,* and *presumptuous little brother.* Now, in the wake of his admitted cohabitations with Johanna, my psychologically malconditioned eyes saw in him only the unalterable image of an *ugly wretch.* His coarse red hair seemed coarser and redder. In place of the youthful glance of admiration that once shined from his eyes, there was the dull stare of bored politeness. His thick gray pockmarked face now suggested the bull-necked brutality of a hungry dog.

B. Carl, I want to make one final appeal to you regarding your affair of the heart. I do this not out of envy or maliciousness, but because of the love that I have for you and for our dear mother.

Ca. But, Ludwig, my feelings for this woman are a *personal* matter. You have no right to interfere.

B. As the oldest living Beethoven, I'm still responsible for the safety and well-being of my younger brothers.

Ca. This was true when we were children. But I'm now an adult of thirty-two years, and my private lif is no longer your concern.

B. You and Johann must profit from my sad experience. I have greatly suffered because of youthfully imprudent flirtations with Vienna's tribe of unchaste women. Heaven forbid that either of you should do the same.

Ca. But I'm not *flirting* with Johanna. I really *love* her!

B. Ridiculous! How can you love a girl who invites you into her bed before she marries you? To how many other men has she offered herself?

Ca. I can't help what she has done or hasn't done. All *I* know is that we are in love.

B. Why?

Ca. If you *must* have a reason . . . she carries my *unborn child of six months*!

B. God in heaven! You told me nothing of this!

Ca. Why should I?
B. Because I'm your brother, that's why!
Ca. Wait 'til you meet her, you'll love her as I do.
B. Never! I could have nothing but hatred for such a "Queen of the Night"!
Ca. How can you *hate* someone you've never met?
B. I don't need to meet her, I know exactly what she's like. Her sensuous eyes, her warm flesh, what a bitch! She'll suck her animal pleasures from your body like milk from a helpless cow. Then she'll flit from your arms to those of another, and you'll have nothing left*!* Nothing but a lifetime of hideous suffering and ineradicable memories. Come away from this woman, Carl. In God's name, have nothing more to do with her!
Ca. You still don't understand. We're in love, and we're going to be married.
B. Ye gods! Why must you *marry* the strumpet?
Ca. Because we're in love. Because we wish to make a home for our little child. Because Johanna's father offers an enticing dowry of 2,000 florins.
B. Ah! I might have known there was money at the foot of it.
Ca. Florins are a very practical wedding gift. They will buy a good beginning for our marriage.
I licked the wine from my lips.
B. Well, Carl, my heart aches for you. I see that you must learn from your *own* experience.
Ca. You should be glad—not sad.
B. Glad? My deafness grows worse, I need someone whom I can trust, along comes this professional whore and takes you from me.
Ca. Just wait, Ludwig. Soon *you* will marry. Then you'll realize that there's no such thing as a perfect girl. You'll look upon my little Johanna with friendlier eyes and see her in a different light.
B. I'll *never* see her except for what she is! When is this monstrous wedding to be?
Ca. On the twenty-fifth. A week from today at the Holy Trinity. Will you come?
B. I'll *be* there. I'll come not to greet a *sister*, but to say good-bye to my poor *brother*.

Carl's wedding should have been a day of bacchic revelries; instead I felt only shame and sorrow. Though Johanna *was* rather attractive, her voluptuous magnetism only increased the vehemence of my hatred. Thank God for my art! In *her* I was able to lose myself, to find myself, to go on living. The little fetus, who on this day attended the marriage of his parents, was born *three months later.* He turned out to be their only child, a son named *Karl,* an impossible nephew who figures prominently in every emotional crisis of my last decade on Earth!

Through Lichnowsky, I had gotten to know a tall, thin, artistic, intelligent, curly-haired, priestly faced nobleman. Dressed in a top hat and fur-lined cape, he was *Count Andreas Razumovsky,* the Russian ambassador to Austria. His elaborate salon was among the finest in Vienna. Being a good musician, he loved to "fiddle" in Mozart and Haydn quartets, which he had studied under "Papa" himself. In the fall of 1805, Razumovsky handed me a commission for three string quartets. He was to receive one year's performance rights, after which their ownership would revert to me. What a pleasure to return to this idiom. I began work immediately and, in spite of *Fidelio's* onslaughts, had all three quartets pretty well sketched by May 1806. The day after Carl's wedding, I grabbed my studies for the *First Razumovsky* and so completely immersed myself in its composition that within a few hours, all of life's jagged frustrations had faded from my consciousness.

For twelve weeks, I held my nose to the writing desk and derived genuine therapy from the flow of instrumental wonders that came from my pen. By the end of August I had completed the *First Razumovsky* and most of the other two. I had added a few bars to the *C Minor Symphony* and then had put it aside to complete its predecessor, the *Fourth Symphony in B-flat.* I had finished a set of piano variations and had sketched most of what turned out to be my only violin concerto!

For the summer of 1806, there was a slight change in routine. I did *not* move to the country. Lichnowsky was planning to spend autumn at his Gratz estate near Troppau and had invited me to come with him. This would serve as my annual vacation from Vienna.

After a few weeks at Grätz, the prince suggested that the two of us should make a three days' excursion to Count von Oppersdorff's castle near Ober-Glogau in Upper Silesia. Since I was profitably engaged in polishing my new symphony, in completing the *Razumovskys* and in composing the *Violin Concerto,* I begged Lichnowsky to make the trip by himself. This would circumvent a painful interruption in my work. The prince exclaimed beneath questioning brow, disappointed eyes, and wrinkled nose.

L. But Beethoven, it is because of *you* that I wish to make the trip.
B. Why?
L. Oppersdorff has planned a wonderful and rewarding surprise.
B. What *kind* of surprise? Is it something to eat, or something to drink? Or is it perhaps something to listen to?
L. I can't tell you. You'll have to come and find out for yourself.

Since Bonn's "Frau Fischer" days, old Beethoven has never been one to resist a surprise—least of all one planned for him by a *count.* Early next morning, Lichnowsky and I set out in his comfortable coach for Ober-Glogau. The day's journey was made under a cloudless blue sky that breathlessly magnified the falling hues of golden harvest fields, fruit-colored trees, and ripe red foothills.

I found Oppersdorff to be a dilettante of the highest order. Some fifty men in his service were hired predominantly on the basis of their musical aptitudes. With these capable musicians, he staffed a fine private orchestra, which in turn afforded me the "big surprise"—a *musical* one after all! On both evenings of our visit, they presented my *Second Symphony* in the best readings that I had yet heard. What a pleasure to have one's music performed *substantially as written*! I was so elated that I offered Oppersdorff the dedication of my new *Fourth Symphony*, together with a half year's performance rights.

I thoroughly enjoyed my vacation at Lichnowsky's summer home. The building was, of course, much smaller than his town palace but nonetheless huge by *any* standards. In place of stone and marble, there was stucco and wood. Rather than porcelain stoves, each room had an ornately carved wooden fireplace of just the right size. There were no expensive frescoes and tapestries; instead the walls were richly adorned in choice wooden panels so highly "beeswaxed" that they shimmered like frozen satin. All rooms, from my cozy bedroom-study to the stately dining hall, had floors and cross-beamed ceilings of fine wood. Instead of the Alserstrasse's careful courtyard and microscopically clipped gardens, there were acres of semi-wild woods and fields.

Each morning, coincident with my final bite of breakfast, I would fling myself into this glorious landscape and become totally lost in its rainbow of color. I'd walk, I'd run, I'd lie flat on the sun-warmed ground and stare through baring branches at cotton clouds floating on their sea of infinite blue. What *impossible beauty*! What *peace* and *sweetness*! What a lasting inspiration for the days ahead!

If any man from fumbling fiddler to plotting prince had called Beethoven a "cow," I would probably have crowned his head with an upside-down bowl of *hot porridge* or *something worse.* But truth of the matter, in these favorable surroundings, I *did* behave like a cow! As soon as I'd find some fresh green grass of edible length (difficult to do this time of year), I'd plunk down on my belly and "make like a cow." I loved the feel of warm coarse blades beneath my teeth. But unlike most contented cows, I produced *music* instead of *milk.* I'd chew and *sketch,* and chew and *orchestrate,* and chew and *grow and grow*! What a life!

Everything at Gratz was as natural and informal as its landscape. The servants dressed and came and went as they pleased. On each succeeding week, a *different* handful of them would assume total responsibility for the housekeeping and meals. Thus *most* of us were free *most* of the time, and since many of these men were capable instrumentalists, Lichnowsky's domain came alive with the sounds of beautiful chamber music. From a pyramid of cypress trees came a *Mozart trio,* from a clump of beech trees came a *Haydn or a Förster quartet.* On the steps at the main entrance, a countrified group of woodwinds gnawed at my *octet* while in the great hall, our host himself accompanied a fine vocal or instrumental soloist. Each evening at about 5:00 PM, a high-pitched dinner bell would call us from our varied musical delights. There was no formal dressing for *this* table; we came as we *were,* filled with the fresh smells of open country. Counting guests, servants, the prince and myself, there were never less than forty of us crowded around the huge oak dining table. Here we were cheerfully waited upon by a half dozen of our "equals," who in subsequent weeks would take *their* turns at being "aristocrats." Immediately after dinner, I would retire to my room and spend three or four hours ordering my musical thoughts at a magnificent Stein piano, which Lichnowsky had placed there *for my use.*!

Though difficult to believe, these happy and productive days were explosively concluded by a heinous appearance of the "Great Mogul." On the second evening of my ninth week at Gratz, Lichnowsky was entertaining a dozen French officers. After supper, these Frenchmen began coaxing and pestering me to play.

"A solo by Beethoven!"

"What better ending for our meal?"

"Yes! A performance by the great Beethoven!"

"Surely this new 'Mozart' is not one to hide his light under a bushel."

"Another bottle of champagne for the Maestro, if he will play for us!"

Somehow their entreaties struck me more like a *command* than a request. Who did they think I *was*, Haydn?

B. As a true artist, I am at the command of great audiences. I have no intention of performing the menial labor of fools!

They continued.

"We *are* a great audience!"

"And we *command* a performance."

"Perhaps you *are* an artist. But you're still a *Prussian*, and we conquered you at Jena."

"You're our *prisoner of war*!"

In an attempt at levity, Lichnowsky added the "straw" that broke the "Mogul's" back.

L. Come, Ludwig. You must *humor* our guests. Play for them. Surely you don't want these fine gentlemen to place you under house arrest!

I jumped to my feet, screaming at Lichnowsky:

B. Prince, I am the prisoner of *no* one, least of all, *you*! What *you* are, you are by accident of *birth*; what *I* am, I am through *myself*! There have been and will still be thousands of princes, there is only *one Beethoven*!

I turned to the officers:

B. And as for *you*, "fine gentlemen," it's a pity that I don't understand the art of war as well as I do the art of music. If such were the case, I'd conquer your little Bonaparte and take Paris in *one week*. Then we'd see *who* was the prisoner of *whom*!

I stumbled to my room, grabbed my scores, bolted from the castle, and stormed a mile through the dark to Troppau. There I took an extra post chaise for Vienna. The next morning, while climbing to my apartment, I was *still* breathing threats of *murder* and *hellfire*.

B. Damn the prince! Away with him! May the devil take *all* such pinheaded prinks. Let him *try* to arrest me, I'll drown him in *half notes*. Just because of a few favors, does he think he *owns* me? I'll *never* set eyes on him again!

I opened my door and there was "Lichnowsky." His grinning likeness beamed down at me from my bookshelf. I grabbed the life-size bust and, to the accompaniment of choice and final profanities, smashed it to pieces!

After a "fighting" sleep, I awakened to the cold purple of an early November sunset and to the sad realization that the "Great Mogul" had better swallow his pride once again. For the sake of his career, he'd better stay in the good graces of his *little prince.* But at least he could *begin* a gradual transfer of respect (and dependence) from *Lichnowsky* to *Rudolpf.* After all, an *archduke* should be worth ten princes *any* day!

Since I could no longer depend upon brother Carl to manage my business affairs, I thought it would be a good idea to arrange for a *single German publisher.* This should greatly simplify finances, correspondence, and record keeping. I bargained and bickered with *Breitkopf and Härtel,* but my negotiations came to naught. Giving up the idea, I went on wrangling with the whole pack of hellhounds for the balance of my marketing days. Frequently I would "play off" one publisher against another to my best possible advantage. Why not? Didn't each of these houses seek the optimum financial arrangement for its *own* cash box? Why shouldn't *I*? My conscience never bothered me when it came to matters of (so-called) "*business morality.*"

The balance of 1806 was devoted to finishing my *Violin Concerto* in time for *Franz Clement's* concert of December twenty-third in the *Theater-an-der-Wien.* It was the usual frustrating routine—plenty of diarrhea, but no time for rehearsals. Opus 61 was completed only *minutes* before the concert, and poor Clement had to sight-read his part without the benefit of a single rehearsal!

What do I now think of these latest compositions? The *Fourth Piano Concerto* is one of two Earthly piano concertos that I still perform. I find it the ideal companion piece to the *Emperor,* which comes three years later. My *Fourth Symphony* seems no more than a restful plateau between the *Eroica* and the *C Minor.* It was fun to write, required little planning, little suffering, has little to say! Today, I'm twice the violinist that I was on Earth. Consequently, I now find more enjoyment in the *Violin Concerto* than I did back in 1806, especially in its first movement. But only in the *Razumovskys* do I still hear really great music! The first of these quartets is comparable to the highest soundings of the *Eroica.* In fact, this *Razumovsky* is among my three favorites of the sixteen quartets that I composed on Earth. Here in the *F Major,* I first fathomed the unique power of four little "strings."

Their carefully disciplined lines were better able to translate my wordless thoughts into tones than had been either the freedom of *extempore playing* or the *shoutings of a great orchestra*! I knew that if I ever discovered something profound to say, the *string quartet* would be my idiom. I'd remember the *Razumovskys* and call upon my "fiddlers four."

How were these quartets received by my contemporaries? The only favorable comments were in the *Allgemeine Musikalische Zeitung*: "Three new, very long and difficult Beethoven string quartets, dedicated to the Russian Ambassador, *Count Razumovsky*, are also attracting the attention of all connoisseurs. The conception is profound and the construction excellent, but they are not easily comprehended . . . with the possible exception of the third in *C Major*, which cannot but appeal to intelligent lovers of music because of its originality, melody and harmonic power."

Notice how artfully they dodged the *F Major*. All *other* responses were *negative*. Schuppanzigh burst out laughing; he thought the *First Razumovsky* was some sort of *joke*! As soon as "Milord Falstaff" realized otherwise, he stopped laughing and started practicing. Then came the inevitable bitching about difficulties. As usual, I cut him down in the third person.

B. Does "Milord" *really* suppose I think of his pulsing little fiddle when the spirit speaks to me and I compose something? When Gyrowetz bought the quartets, he bemoaned his investment as a "sad waste of money." When Bernhard Romberg first tried his part to the *F Major's Allegretto vivace*, he literally trampled it underfoot for its "contemptible mystification." Radicati came to finger the manuscript for me, and when he reached the one-tone opening theme of this same *Allegretto vivace*, he stopped and stared at me from above a greasy sneer.

Rd. Surely you don't consider these works to be *music*?

I outstared him and then countered appropriately.

B. Don't worry, little fiddler. These quartets are not for *you*. They are music for a *later age*!

Chapter 14

The year 1807 was a happy little year. It had its ups and downs, but generally speaking, more *ups* than *downs.* My petition for a spring *Akademie* was denied, but I was strongly represented in private salons and in the *Liebhaber* concerts. A new theater management arrived and completely ignored my request for a subsidy. I fought with *Johann* over the repayment of a loan. My persecution complex reached permanently unconcealable proportions, but at least my bad hearing grew no worse! I exchanged an *old* factotum for a *new* one. Because of war conditions, I failed to negotiate a decent publishing arrangement in France, but in England, an ideal contract was worked out with the firm of *Muzio Clementi.* In 1807, I was commissioned to write my first *Mass*; its reception was a *disgrace*! In this year, I completed my best dramatic overture and also the definitive sketches for what turned out to be my most popular work: Beethoven's *Fifth.* Now some details of this happy little year.

In January 10, *Ignaz von Gleichenstein* replaced *Zmeskall* as my chief factotum and business manager. Within three months, he was handling my business correspondence, supervising my copyists, arranging for summers' lodgings, worrying over my finances, correcting my French, buying pens, and refurbishing my wardrobe. *Wow*!

Lichnowsky forgave my explosion of the preceding fall and arranged a private concert of my music. *Lobkowitz* followed suit with two Beethoven concerts in *his* palace, where there were performed my first four symphonies, the *Fourth Piano Concerto*, selections from *Fidelio*, and a brand-new dramatic overture based on Collin's *Coriolan*.

Cramer's great teacher, *Muzio Clementi*, came to Vienna for a visit. When our paths crossed, I was overwhelmed by his praises for my newest works. Then quite unexpectedly, he presented me with a business proposition:

Cl. Are you engaged with any publisher in London?
B. No.
Cl. Well, you *should* be. Your reputation there is fast approaching that of Haydn and Handel. Londoners are extremely interested in your new scores. But because of Napoleon, it's next to impossible to obtain copies from continental publishers. Why not give *me* the English rights to your music? Wouldn't you like Clementi and Co. to represent you there?
B. With all my heart!
Cl. Good! What have you ready?
B. I'll give you a list.

For British rights in my newest six works, I received two hundred pounds sterling!

Half the summer of 1807 was spent at *Baden*, the other half at *Heiligenstadt*. During these months, my "second period" creative efforts reached their peak. They bore fruit in three major compositions: *Symphony 5, Sympnony 6*, and my newly commissioned *Mass in C*. By October, the final sketches for both symphonies were completed, and I was very proud of my summer's work. In *Symphony 5*, I discovered that it *was* possible for Beethoven to write another orchestral piece big enough and bold enough to follow in the wake of the *Eroica*. *Symphony 6* proved to be my first "philosophical" composition. During this period, my "inner life" was feeling its first tremors of metaphysical insight. I sensed that there was far more to life than had ever met the eyes of the "Great Mogul." However, I could not express this extended view in *words*—only in *tones*. Why not portray my evolving thoughts within the convenient abstractions of *pure music*? This decision resulted in the opening movements of the *Pastoral*, my first truly "philosophical" utterance.

What *were* these "rare occasions" that took me out of myself and permitted me to see things clearly? They were of two distinct types. Foremost came the priceless hours that I spent in the countryside. No clipped avenues or trimmed Viennese parks would do. I had to savor the beauty of untouched nature and found the ideal spot in the rolling woods and meadows that cupped the cool valley between *Heiligenstadt* and *Nussdorf*. In this dancing thicket I'd pick a chair whose *seat* was the soft green turf and whose *back* was the trunk of a mighty elm. Thus enthroned, I divided my time between sketching new pieces and absorbing the countryside. Often I'd lie flat on my back and reach for the sky. The sun was beyond my grasp, but many were the little white clouds that I'd stop in their Olympian tracks and hold fast until they had become part of the Beethovenian realm. Such procedure never failed to refresh me in both body and mind.

My other enlightening experience arose from countless visits to a little tavern near *Mödling* on the outskirts of Vienna. There at the "Sign of the Three Ravens," a small band of seven totally unsophisticated musicians held forth regularly. In spite of their naïvely bad playing and their coarse peasant background, I soon discovered that there was little to teach *these* men in the art of *really enjoying music*. As a matter of fact, the *reverse* was true: I had much to learn from them. They confirmed my belief in the honesty and immortality of *true folk music* by introducing me to the unadulterated national dance tunes of Austria. These in turn produced an inexhaustible wellspring for my later compositions. We became great friends, and it wasn't long before these humble colleagues had taught me to *eat better*, to *drink better*, to *laugh* and *swear better*, to *smoke*. But even *they* couldn't teach old Beethoven how to *dance*. While everyone else danced to the zestful tunes of our rural septet, I sat there keeping time with snorts of laughter and by loudly tapping my feet and my glass of Hungarian red wine. The contagiously uninhibited spirit of *musical merrymaking* emanating from these children of nature was precisely the optimism that I hoped to capture in the *Scherzo* of the *Pastoral*.

In December, a number of Viennese dilettanti formed an organization called the "Concert of Music Lovers." They built a respectable orchestra consisting almost entirely of local amateurs. Only in the brass section was it necessary to sign more professional players. In the great hall of the university, they performed *twenty times* in less than *four months*! At three of these Liebhaber concerts, I was invited to conduct my newest orchestral pieces. This invitation came just at the psychological moment, at the very time when I thought Vienna had lost all interest in Beethoven and his career. We performed my second, third, and fourth symphonies, also my latest overtures.

The year 1807 ended with an eruption between Johann and myself. How different were these brothers of mine! Johann had none of Carl's short-statured ugliness or redheaded temper. He was a tall, dark, and almost handsome individual with a disposition that was usually good-humored and placable. A carefully parted crown of beautiful black hair tapered into thick sideburns, which descended the full length of his cheeks and met beneath his chin. We often joked about this little beard goatee that "tried but couldn't." Johann's usual defense for an unshaved chin was that he liked to have at least enough whiskers there to keep out the cold. His lips were drawn into a perpetual smile, which literally extended from ear to ear. Both brothers had somewhat questionable business ethics. Their philosophy seemed to be that money was the ultimate goal of a properly directed life and that such a desirable end would more than justify any means for attaining it. Their grasping greed could easily be blamed on the scratching poverty of our childhood. But even in *this* respect, my brothers were different. Carl's passion for money arose from his joy of spending it. Johann's desires were purely possessive and gradually evolved into unbelievable penuriousness.

As might be expected, my argument with Johann was over a financial matter. My journeys of the preceding year had cost me a great deal of money, and I was obliged to borrow heavily from Johann's modest savings. Now suddenly, at a great bargain, he had a chance to buy a registered apothecary shop in Linz. To complete the transaction, he needed the immediate return of his loan. Three days after Christmas, he burst into my theater apartment like a mother bear hunting her lost cub.

J. Ludwig, you must pay me my loan at once.

B. Impossible! I haven't the money.

J. Gleichenstein tells me that the *Industrie-Comptoir* owes you 1,500 florins. And besides, won't there be an *honorarium* from the *Liebhaber* concerts?

B. I'll never understand you, Johann. You do me a favor and then bite off my hand!

J. I'm *not* biting your hand. I simply need the money I lent you. With it I shall be able to go into business for myself. Such opportunities are now few and far between.

B. I get more respect and obedience from princes and archdukes than from my own brothers!

J. My request has nothing to do with respect or obed—

B. Then why do you and Carl seek revenge on your poor deaf brother. . . I, who have been like a father to both of you?

J. We seek *no* revenge, and this has nothing to do with Carl. It's a simple business proposition between the two of us. A year ago you came to me for money. What I had was immediately put at your disposal. Now *I* am in need of capital. I believe you have adequate funds, and I'm asking for the return of my loan. Such a request is neither disrespectful nor vengeful.

B. You make it sound so proper. But I still feel that I'm betrayed by my own brothers. Betrayed for the sake of a few florins! Carl tells me that I'm overly suspicious of my contemporaries and blames this on my competitive position and increasing deafness. Perhaps he's right . . . perhaps not. In either case, I wish you knew how important to me are the love and confidence of my brothers. But no, this is expecting too much; neither of you could understand. Go your way, Johann. I'll send you your *pound of flesh*, and God keep me from ever having to ask you for another benefaction!

Gleichenstein drew enough money against my contract with *Kunst-und Industrie-Comptoir* to settle the loan. With this amount, Johann completed the first payment on his *Vielguth house* shop, which was located in the main square of the *Hauptplatz*. He moved there on March 20, 1808, and by careful penny-pinching, managed to continue his payments for a full year. Then praise be Napoleon, Johann's scrimping ended once and for all. In April 1809, the French army entered Linz and brought with them huge contracts for medicaments. These products Johann dutifully supplied to the enemy's commissariat---and at a handsom profit for himself. He was thus able to pay off his shop, and lay the foundation for subsequent financial success.

Chapter 15

The final *Liebhaber* concert was given on March 27, 1808 in honor of Haydn's seventy-sixth birthday. All the elite of Vienna's nobility (including the "Great Mogul") stood at the door of the university's tall-windowed, high-ceilinged, richly frescoed hall. When old "Papa" finally arrived in Esterhazy's coach, we greeted him with shouts and cheers and drums and trumpets:

"Long live Haydn! Long live Papa Haydn!" He was carried into the hall with the pomp of a pope. As soon as he was seated in his chair of honor, the Concert of Music Lovers performed his *Creation*, this time with Italian text.

The 1807–08 season concluded with two additional Beethoven programs. On Monday evening, April 11, my *Sinfonia Eroica* opened *Sebastian Mayer's* annual benefit concert in the *Theater-an-der-Wien*. Two nights later, I offered my services to the *Charity Institute* for *their* concert in the *Burg Theater*. Here I conducted my *Fourth Symphony, Third Piano Concerto,* and *Coriolan Overture*. The concerto was neatly interpreted by *Friedrich Stein*. While such charity concerts contributed nothing to my personal finances, they *did* keep my name before the public—and I was grateful for this. But I still hoped and planned for an *Akademie*. Surely in the coming season I would be able to give a concert for my *own* benefit, and for this big day, I prepared some choice items—*two new symphonies* and the first *public performance* of my *Fourth Concerto.*

During the Spring of 1808, *Symphony 5* was fully orchestrated. The following summer, through another inspiring visit to *Heiligenstadt*, the same was done for the *Pastoral*. It was my plan to combine these symphonies with the *Mass in C* in the hopes of finding a publisher for the entire "package." I anticipated no trouble getting the symphonies into print, but at this time, the market was glutted with an incredible number of cheap masses which came to little more than wobbly exercises in thoroughbass. Compared to these, my initial attempt was good music and deserved a publisher. From June through September, I corresponded with *Breitkopf and Härtel*, trying to convince them of this fact. Although Industrie-Comptoir had become my major publisher, I still preferred Breitkopf and Härtel to all others. I preferred them because of their excellent editorial, engraving, and marketing services. In spite of my summer's careful negotiations, when Herr Härtel came to Vienna in September, he handed me one hundred gold ducats for the exclusive continental rights to the new symphonies. He took with him my latest cello sonata and the promise of two new piano trios, but left the *Mass in C* sitting quietly undisturbed on my writing desk. Not until 1812 did their house finally accept this work for publication.

It took me until *December* to finish the *trios*. They were first performed at Christmastime in *Countess Anna Marie Erdödy's* palatial residence over the *Schottentor*. Four years earlier, I had gotten to know this beautiful Hungarian as a neighbor of the *Pasqualatis*. She was an excellent pianist and a fine interpreter of my works. After a few months of mutual admiration, our relationship deepened to something *beyond* the purely musical. I stood at the threshold of another Beethovenian romance. As always, the same patterns emerged. My passionate desire for a wife and family locked horns in mortal combat with the "Great Mogul's" omnipotent career. Our emotional sharings ran the usual gamut from love to hatred, but without reaching either extreme of the scale. We fought—throwing bouquets and sharp words at one another, but never dishes or furniture. We loved—finding physical and intellectual attraction, but never did she mistake *me* for her "Prince Charming," nor I *her* for my "immortal beloved." Since absence *does* make the heart grow fonder, I decided to move into Erdödy's home upon my return to Vienna in the Fall of 1808 from a long summer at Heiligenstadt. Please notice that I said *into her home* and not *into her bed*! I still clung tenaciously to my postsyphilitic vow of chastity and was determined that the next woman whose bed I'd share would be my *wife*! Old Beethoven kept this promise and realized his dreams of sexual bliss only after a quiet sleep in a polished oak coffin at *Währing*.

While still at Erdody's, my life was suddenly brightened by the return of *Ferdinand Ries*! I jumped from my writing desk to give the boy a hearty welcome, but he stubbornly held me at arm's length.

R. This time, Maestro, I must be sure that there's no shaving soap!

We laughed ourselves into tears, then I ended his official welcome by throwing my half-eaten apple at his curly head.

B. Dear Ries, you can't know how glad I am to see you again . . . and you still look like an artist. Not even Bonaparte can make a soldier out of *my* best pupil! How long have you been in *Vienna*?
R. Since the end of August.
B. So? And you wait 'til *now* to come and see me?
R. I visited Pasqualati, and he told me you were spending summer with the *Grillparzer* family in the *Grinzingerstrasse*.
B. You could have made it to *Heiligenstadt*. You're just like all the rest—out of *sight*, out of *mind*!
R. Not at all! I stayed away to avoid the risk of coming between you and your summer's work. What *did* you finish at Heiligenstadt?
B. The second of two new symphonies. I hope to conduct them this winter in my own *Akademie*.
R. *Hope* to! Is there nothing definite?
B. Of course not! These plump-assed theater rabble go out of their way to make things difficult for me. I'll be lucky to hear from them two weeks before the concert. Then they'll bitch about my inadequate rehearsals!
R. Are these new symphonies anything like the size of the *Eroica*?
B. They're big . . and the *Fifth Symphony* makes a lot of noise. But I doubt if the première of any symphony could please me as much as the *Eroica*. I'll have to wait and hear for myself. Then I'll know.
R. How *is* your hearing?
B. Same old routine. It comes and goes. Thank God it seems to come when I need it the most!
R. Then you must be a happy Maestro.
B. Not exactly. I request a theater appointment, and am politely ignored. I try to plan an *Akademie*, only to be blocked every step of the way by jealous cabals of button-headed bastards who have no right to call themselves musicians. I cry for help, and even my

own brothers turn from me. I'm neglected and misunderstood. Now what were you saying about a "happy Maestro"?

R. Perhaps you'll not admit to "happiness," but at least Vienna has never treated you to the supreme insult of total indifference. She *always* provides you with a tribe of admiring friends and disciples. She absorbs your new compositions as fast as they're written and tries her best to perform them according to your wishes. A talent like yours will always create cliques of jealous contemporaries—poor devils who hang together more out of fear than hatred. But you would find this anywhere, not just in *Vienna*. You can't turn your back on such a great public. Why, the Viennese are as fond of your instrumental concerts as they are of Haydn's oratorios.

B. Bah! Is this why I must shed life's blood to arrange an *Akamedie*?

R. There's probably a good reason for the delay, something to do with the new management.

B. Well, new or old, if things don't soon improve, I'll leave this damn place and be off to Cassel!

R. But, Maestro—

B. I appreciate your concern, dear Ries. But the decision is mine alone. I'll think it over carefully. If I decide to leave, I'll not do so until I've put you back in the public's eye. Before the year is out, you'll be performing a new Beethoven concerto.

R. How about *Razumovsky* and his quartet? I've heard you concede his strings to be the finest in Europe.

B. Indeed they are, Ries. This quartet is one of my strongest inducements to stay in Vienna!

On November 15, *Joseph Härtl* signed me for a program in the *Theater-an-der-Wien*. It turned out to be another charity concert—the third in twelve months! I played my *C Minor Concerto* and conducted the *Eroica* and *Coriolan Overture*. Because of these charitable contributions (and my threat of a lawsuit), the pompous ass finally named a day for *Beethoven's Akademie*. I was to have the *Wiener Theater* for my own use on Thursday, December 22.

In time for the November fifteenth concert, my conducting technique had reached its final stage of Earthly evolution. I had come to believe that a conductor must use his entire body in order to successfully translate orchestral music from players to audience. The job seemed too big for the mere tips of one's fingers or the point of a baton. Accordingly, my podium mannerisms had become those of an impassioned *Italian orator.* "Beethoven the Conductor" was now a gesticulating, gyrating jack-in-the-box. The Wiener players of November fifteenth were not expecting such wild antics, nor were the choirboy and candlesticks that my impassioned left arm knocked to the floor. The musicians laughed like children, and we resumed our Scherzo only after I had given them a thorough dressing-down in the biting profanity that I had sharpened to perfection at the Sign of the Three Ravens.

On December twenty-second in the Wiener Theater, my *Akademie* began promptly at 6:30 PM and lasted *four hours*! This was twice as long as it should have been, considering the bitter cold hall. A squeaking ten degrees blew fresh white two-foot drifts across the dirty snowy cobbles of the Graben while the inside of the theater building could boast little above freezing. I stepped to the podium and acknowledged the polite but feeble applause of a practically empty house. It appeared that less than half the seats were occupied. Except for a handful of noblemen, the orchestra stalls were empty. I began the concert by conducting the first public performance of *Symphony 6.* Its opening movements affected me like a beautiful dream—they were indeed an "awakening of cheerful emotions upon arriving in the countryside." The coldness of a lean hall was exchanged for the sun-drenched fields of *Heiligenstadt.* Instead of the questioning glances of envious players, I saw the constant reassurance of mighty oaks. The pulsing of uncertain strings was totally outsung by the unmonotonous monotony of August wind through tall grass. The nervous sweat of a première was replaced by the scent-filled prayer of thankful fields under a late Spring rain. Before the last "bird call" of the "Scene by the Brook" had died away, I realized that old Beethoven had done it again. In a different (philosophical) way, he had equaled the opening movements of his *Eroica.* Here was true "music of the spheres," whose rustic tones sang the promise of entire countrysides of meadow, brook and forest. In composing the *Pastoral,* I was determined to be more concerned with the expression of *feeling* than with tone painting. This is exactly what happened in the first two movements—not so, the concluding three. By the time I reached these, I had put down my pencil and had picked up a palette and brush. After "painting over" my careful resolution to avoid tone painting, I went on from birds to rocks to clouds to rain to thunder and lightening to peasants to all the humorous scenes that I could remember from the *Three Ravens.* Is it any wonder that these movements are less "philosophical" than the opening two?

To conclude Part 1 of my *Akademie,* I played and conducted the first public performance of my *G Major Concerto.* No one could then have convinced me that *this* evening would bring to an end my Earthly career as a concert pianist! I felt that old "fast-gun Ludwig" could hold his own for at least another decade. But the demon of my bad hearing had other plans!

After intermission, Part 2 of the *Akademie* began with my conducting the now famous *C Minor (Fifth) Symphony.* Considering the rude laughter evoked by this first performance of its opening bars, I wonder that the work has survived at all. But it has. I'm told that after all these years of "*ta-ta-ta-tuming,*" it remains the best-known symphony on Earth! I'm often asked to what I attribute its popularity. My answer is always the same: "Its first movement has a good structure; its *Scherzo* was born of Mozart."

Since it became obvious that I would have to go on living with this opus, I have recently revised its second and fourth movements. On *my* side of the grave, each is now more palatable. If you're a dear Earthling who once enjoyed the *C Minor* but who has now outgrown its "five-one-ish-ness," my advice to you is wait and hear. Wait 'til you hear its liberated variations and its new fugal finale. With these changes, I believe that Beethoven's *Fifth* will once again find a place in your heart. It has in mine. *"Ta-ta-ta-tummm!"*

Chapter 16

The offer of an honorable position in Cassel gave me a lever with which I could move, if not the world, at least the purse strings of my wealthy Viennese friends. On the tenth of January, I had a little talk with *Countess Erdödy.*

B. I have decided! I'm definitely going to Cassel. I've had enough of Vienna with her pack of jealous wolves—childish Miserabiles who spend most of their time putting obstacles in my path.

E. Ludwig, you can't think of such a thing! Vienna is yours, and you are hers!

B. You sound like my pupil. If this were true, then how come she provides me with so many "loving friends" like *Salieri*? Have you heard what this low-life bastard did behind my back? He threatened to expell from his orchestra every musician who played for me at the *Theater auf der Wieden* on December twenty-second. What an unmitigated wretch! I hope he dies giving birth to an impossible stool!

E. Ludwig! You rave like a madman!

B. If I reacted otherwise to such treachery, then you should regard me as *less* than a man.

E. Granted you *have* enemies, all great artists do. But you have many wonderful friends and admirers who will stop at nothing to keep you here in Vienna.

B. So?
E. Why don't you draw up a formal list of conditions under which you will agree to remain here. I'll see that it gets to *Archduke Rudolph*, and unless I miss my guess, he'll make you a better offer than the *King of Westphalia*!

With the help of Gleichenstein, we prepared such a list. It was circulated among the nobility, and on February 26, 1809, I received an agreement that convinced me that I should remain in Vienna. Under its terms, Archduke Rudolph, Prince Lobkowitz, and Prince Kinsky bound themselves to pay me a lifetime annuity totaling 4,000 florins per year. It mentioned nothing concerning my request for the title of "Imperial Kapellmeister," nor did it guarantee me the use of the *Wiener Theater* each Palm Sunday for the rest of my life. But even so, its monetary rewards were inducement enough. By this time, I had also worked out a fine arrangement with *Breitkopf and Härtel* of Leipzig, and with *Artaria* of Vienna. These two houses had agreed to publish my new works simultaneously in their respective cities. And neither firm was the type that would quibble over prices. Each seemed willing to accept whatever new compositions I sent them and to pay what I asked. Was my lifelong dream of financial security and peace of mind finally becoming a reality? Perhaps now with such a promising purse, I could at last go shopping for a wife!

The Cassel episode ended with an unpleasant misunderstanding. Door- keeper Tiepke informed me that Gleichenstein had informed him that pupil Ries had attempted to secure the position at Westphalia for himself—and behind my back! You can imagine what effect this bit of news had upon the "Great Mogul." At that time, there were painfully few Viennese whom he felt he could trust. If not his own brothers, certainly his pupil was among the chosen few. And now, Ries too was a traitor! I cursed him with such vehemence as to bring on a serious ringing spell. I swore that I would not only never *play* for him, but I would never again *speak* to the wretch. For three weeks, I tore up his unopened letters and had Tiepke turn him from my door. Then on March 20, quite unexpectedly, we met at the Ridotto.

R. Maestro, you *must* tell me what has come between us!
B. You don't know?
R. If I did, would I ask?
B. As a friend of your father's, I took great pride in your ability and progress. With heartfelt love I embraced you as my very best pupil! Then what happens? On a beautiful sunny morning, I

wake up to find that you're just another grasping dungheap like all the rest. What in God's name made you think that you could ever fill a position which had been offered to *me*?

R. You don't understand the cond—

B. Suddenly I'm totally deaf, I can't hear a word you say.

R. Let me explain.

B. You might as well leave, Ries. It's finished between us.

R. How can you forget the old days? Your promises to my father?

B. Very well! If *you* won't leave, *I shall*!

I turned and walked away.

Next morning at Erdödy's, I heard a commotion outside my door that made me think that Napoleon had at last made it to the Krugerstrasse with his howitzers. I jumped from my desk and ran to the anteroom. There on the floor lay poor Tiepke. He had been fighting with *Ries*, who was determined to enter my apartment. Before I could say or do anything, my "former" pupil let go with a pent-up diatribe that seemed to last for an hour.

R. Now see here! I'm *not* going to let some stupid misunderstanding come between us. You'll hear me out if I have to throw *you* to the floor. I'm well aware that no ordinary mortal could ever hope to fill a position that had been offered the great Beethoven! Your accusation to the contrary is entirely unjust. I have many faults, but immodesty doesn't happen to be one of them. And what's more, *I did nothing behind your back*! On March first, Kapellmeister Reichardt came to *me*, not *I to him*! He informed me that you had definitely declined the Cassel post. Since I was your only pupil, he wondered if I would be willing to go there and accept the position at a smaller salary. I told Reichardt that he'd have my answer just as soon as I had gotten your advice. That was three weeks ago, and I'm now probably too late for the appointment. But this doesn't matter. What *does* bother me is your sudden hatred! If you can show me anything in my words or actions that has been deceitful, underhanded, or treacherous, then I'll gladly disappear from your life.

There was something humorous in Ries's outburst; there was something tragic in it. His words towered before me as a giant looking glass clearly reflecting my stupid pride, my insane suspicions, my petty jealousies. Did the sobering glimpse make a new man of me? Of course not! Ries turned out to be just another *Eulenspiegel* in which I perfectly fulfilled the old German proverb: "Man sees his own faults as little as a monkey or an owl recognizes his ugliness when looking into a mirror"!

Ries and I immediately went to Reichardt in an attempt to make good my mistake. But it was too late. The kapellmeister had learned through Waldburg that the position was filled.

On May 12, *Vienna* displayed her white flags to the enemy and began paying the price of surrender. From her capitulation until the armistice of July 12, she was forced to contribute millions of florins and mountains of food and supplies to the French cause. Without these, the enemy could never have waged her two months of bloody battles: Aspern, Esslingen, Wagram, Znaim. Since battles cost money, a natural, and expected, result of this summer was the terrible inflation that gripped our city. The cost of food and other necessities became exorbitant, copper coins disappeared from circulation, and a graduated French tax on Viennese rents added its staggering weight to an already impossible financial burden. What strange irony! I wait forty years for my purse to begin to swell. Along come an *annuity* and some decent sales figures that cause it to do so. I reach out to enjoy its roundness. Bang! The "Little Corporal" rides on the scene and promptly smashes it flat!

It's hard to imagine such a great city as ours surrendering in only three days. If I had been in Maximilian's position, Bonaparte would have had to pay a terrible price for each building in town. And if he *did* take the capital, he would have been good for little else, having spent five years' fighting and a million men for a pile of ashes! But unfortunately (or fortunately) for *Vienna*, I had specialized in *music* instead of *war*. The old burg had no "General van Beethoven" to protect her. She died a painless death on May 12 and then, as if this weren't enough, nineteen days later, gave up her *favorite son* in the death of *Franz Joseph Haydn*! A final touch of irony. Little Beethoven comes from *Bonn* to conquer *Vienna*. He works for seventeen years to enshrine his name among the immortals. At last an archduke whispers in his ear, "Congratulations boy, you've done it!" (Disregard this space--continue below.)

The "Great Mogul" jumps up from his desk to welcome his distinguished colleagues. Whom does he find? No one! *Mozart* is dead. *Haydn* is dead. *Albrechtsberger* is dead. All that remains is the crack-mirrored image of the *little boy from Bonn*!

Coincident with my moving to the Klepperstall, there was a slight raising of the French heel. Vienna's beautiful parks and gardens were again opened to the public. I behaved like an uncaged beast. For a full week, I did nothing but walk, exploring each blade and twig of the Prater, the Schwarzenberg Garten, the Augarten, the Schönbrunner Garten. Except for ten days with the *Brunsviks* in *Korompa*, this was the extent of my "life in the country" for 1809.

Musically speaking, this year represented a slowing down of my tempo. I gave but a single concert during the entire period. This was another charity program for Director Hartl in which I conducted *Symphony 3*. In return for these services, I did *not* receive a day in the *Wiener Theater* for my personal use. The year ended with a delightful Christmas present from *Franz Clement*. At his annual concert on *December 24*, he conducted my *Mount of Olives* in the best performance of this work I had ever heard. Not a small proportion of my composing time was devoted to preparing a course of study for the *archduke*. These plans turned out to be a synthesis of the theoretical works of *Carl Philipp Emanuel Bach*, *Kirnberger*, *Albrechtsberger*, *Fux*, and *Türk*. Regarding my composing, only a few worthy numbers were completed. Most important was my *Piano Concerto in E-flat*, the best and the last of my *Earthly* five. A close rival for first place was a new quartet in the same key. In 1933, I read *Schauffler's* sensitive and perceptive description of this opus, and since then have been unable to dissociate the two:

> This Tenth Quartet leads us back into the sunlight and begins to take on the October mellowness of old wine, of good tobacco, russet apples, burning leaves, and hillsides of ripe-fruited beeches turning a dull gold.

I was able to hear some of this same "October mellowness" in the *Emperor Concerto*, especially in its *Adagio*. Two piano sonatas and a fantasia were also finished at this time, but I did nothing in the direction of a new opera. How could I? The French had completely taken over our court theaters, which meant that we were again betrayed to the harlot of Italian opera. Dim prospects for the "meat and potatoes" of a poor old German. Nevertheless, by November, I was hard at work on some incidental music to Goethe's *Egmont*, this under a commission from *Härtl*.

Chapter 17

At no time in my Earthly life did I come upon such an overwhelming concentration of strong inducements to marry and settle down, as I did in the early days of 1810. Everything seemed ready and waiting—the time, the place, the money, the girl.

I had just completed a fertile decade of inspiring creative activity—ten years that carried me from the Lobkowitz quartets to the *Piano Sonata in F-sharp.* The intervening opuses encompassed six symphonies, an opera, a mass, five concertos, an oratorio, six overtures, more than twenty sonatas, a ballet, and chamber pieces including ten quartets. The happy story of these works was the story of steadily increasing creative ability. I had scaled "Mount *Eroica*" and then had gone on to prove that for me, such dizzy heights were *not* to be a once-in-a-lifetime proposition. Through these compositions, I had earned a secure place in the company of *Haydn* and *Mozart.* In spite of the threat of increasing deafness, I had found a successful way of life whose princely sponsorship had at last placed me on a sound financial footing.

Who *was* the lucky girl? She was *Fräulein Therese Malfatti,* the beautiful eighteen-year-old niece of my physician. Though I stood at the beginning of my fortieth year, I sensed in this sweet and bubbling intellectual the complete fulfillment of an "immortal beloved." Her physical charms were sheer perfection, sculptured in a doll-like, peach-colored loveliness. Her deep eyes were those of a French girl. They stared directly at you without a trace of uneasiness or bashfulness. In these eyes was the spirit of absolute truth that hid none of the volatility, the laughter, the unbelievable candor of her personality. Is it any wonder that *Therese* seemed to handle everything in her life with the carefree confidence of a happy little girl?

Gleichenstein was directly responsible for this latest of my romantic adventures.Through his love affair with Therese's younger sister, I had witnessed the complete transformation of his personality. Gone were those fears and uncertainties of earlier days. Now his entire life seemed to glow with the true optimism of perfected self-confidence. He attributed the miracle of it all to his little *Anna* and assured me that a similar treasure for *my* life could be found in the arms of sister *Therese.* I had but to make known my amorous intent and to claim her as my own. This I decided to do. Through the winter and early spring of 1810, Gleichenstein and I were constant visitors at the *Malfatti* home. Therese had a fine talent for music, and her rapid development in piano reminded me of *Giulietta Guicciardi.* After a few months, I suspected that my pupil had fallen in love with *me,* though I still wondered if at the last minute one of her parents would come between us as had *Giulietta's* father. But even in this matter, there seemed little room for doubt. The countless warm courtesies heaped upon me by her entire family, surely these were meant to encourage our engagement and eventual marriage.

You can't imagine what tremendous effect this lovemaking had upon the forty-year-old "Mogul." He suddenly felt like a boy of twenty who could smell flowers and green things that he'd never smelled before and could see stars and clouds and sunbeams that a few weeks earlier had passed my unnoticed. Though his work on *Egmont* slowed to a snail's pace, all was activity in the "production planning" department where he could now hear sounds beyond the *Eroica.* Regarding his romantic life, things moved so rapidly that he had to enlist the services of his entire Court. *Gleichenstein* was given 300 florins and sent to the haberdashery for shirt cloth and at least a doen neckties. Another 300 florins went to *Oliva,* who visited Lind the tailor in an attempt to update my wardrobe. *Zmeskall* was sent scuttling for a new mirror; I had broken two of my own in passionate tries for the impossibility of a close shave. Dear old *Wegeler* was commissioned to journey from Coblenz to Bonn in order to secure my baptismal certificate, a document essential for marriage. With the coming of spring, I began staggering like a somnambulist. When I *did* go to bed, instead of sleep, there came pink clouds filled with mouth-watering visions of little *Therese.* Poor Gleichenstein—he was going through the same enjoyable suffering. But we *both* preferred such awakening to the best of sleep.

By April, my visits to the *Malfattis* were like trips to heaven. I felt so happy with this family—as though they might heal the wounds inflicted upon my soul by wicked men. Even Therese's little dog, *Gigons,* treated me royally. He'd not leave my side from the time I arrived until I left. Often I had the pleasure of giving him his evening meal, and on several occasions, he accompanied me all the way home.

The affair ended, of course, like all the others, but not with the merciful swiftness and finality of most of them. On April 17, Therese and I attended a benefit concert featuring *Coriolan* and then went walking hand-in-hand among the Spring beauties of the *Prater.* Its hotbeds were wide open, and they soon brought us both under the magical spell of their dense perfume. Later that evening, we were alone in the Malfattis' drawing room, and I played the *Adagio sostenuto* from my *Moonlight Sonata.* These doleful sounds had brought to an end the *Guicciardi* affair, and now at last I wanted them to commemorate my victorious realization of love's dream.

As I played, *Therese* came and sat on the bench next to me with her soft hair tickling my right ear. The beautiful fragrance of her young body more tantalizing than all the flowers of Spring. Being part "Mogul" and part "wolf," I couldn't resist a physical expression of my love for this girl. At the conclusion of the *Adagio,* my right arm encircled her dainty waist and pulled her toward me. With unfortunate abruptness, I unleashed a torrent of kisses and caresses that for endless days and nights had been locked in my dreams. Therese jerked her heaving breasts from my grasp and stood by the bench. Neither of us spoke a word. Instead of the warm encouragement of passionate love, I saw in her tear-filled eyes the frightened stare of absolute shock and amazement! She sobbed like a child and ran from the room. *Gigons* looked up from his favorite spot on the sofa. Judging by the sleepy and puzzled expression in his face, even *he* didn't understand *Therese.* And he'd known her all his life. He followed me to the door where I bade him good-bye, let myself out, and then spent the rest of the night walking the streets. What had I *done*? I thought back upon those earliest of my Viennese flames. Each one seemed to admire the animal qualities of Beethoven's lovemaking, though several, like Giulietta Guicciardi, *did* consider his passionate displays a bit sudden. Could this be the case with *Therese*? Was she mistaking my serious intent for a mere flirtatious promiscuity? Gleichenstein's engagement to Anna was secure. This meant that he was established in the Malfattis' confidence and could well present my position. Next morning, I invited him to the *Klepperstall.* After we discussed the sad details of my indiscretion, I filled him with breakfast and then sped him off to *Therese* as my intermediary, my hope, my ambassador of goodwill.

Patiently I waited, hoping against hope that Therese would understand my true feelings and would open her arms to my love. Gleichenstein's advice: "Your burst of passion has deeply wounded this girl.You must be patient and give the wound time to heal.Write Therese a formal proposal of marriage which I shall then deliver personally."

This I *did.* Another month passed; still no reply!

By August first, even *I* had to admit that my marriage project had fallen through. I had done it again! Therese's admiration for Beethoven the artist; her respect for Beethoven, a friend of the family; her devotion to Beethoven, the companion of *Gleichenstein*—all these warm and welcome feelings I had mistaken as her love for Beethoven the man. I had sent her my very heart and soul in an envelope and had received not even the courtesy of a reply. I proceeded to rationalize the failure of just another Beethoven romance. All things turn out for the best. Had I married this girl, I would surely have wrecked *her* life and my *own.* Under the combined burdens of my career, growing deafness, my enemies, and the demands of a young wife, what could I possibly hope to achieve as a composer?

Ever since the Bonn-Breuning days, I had been an ardent admirer of *Johann Wolfgang von Goethe.* I now wished to finish the *Egmont* music as an act of love for our great poet. To emphasize my true motivation, I planned to accept no monetary reward from the theater directors. But in spite of these high ideals and good intentions, I made little progress with the composition. Oddly enough, my help came from Goethe himself. He sent me his own personal little angel to come, stand by side, and point the way.

On the afternoon of May 10, seated at my faithful old Erard in the Pasqualati apartment, I had just finished composing a Goethe song, when I was startled by the feel of two small hands on my shoulders. No one was more certain to get an explosive rise out of the "Great Mogul" than someone who surprised or interrupted him while composing. Turning on the bench, I had a beam in each eye, a fixed jaw, and a mouthful of boiling profanity. With these I intended to slay whoever stood behind me. What a surprise! There danced a lovely young girl who spoke to me even before I could change the cannibal expression on my face.

BB. My name is Brentano.

She needed no further introduction; her brother *Franz* was at this time numbered among my best friends. I had gotten to know him through *Razumovsky's* neighbors, the *Birkenstocks*, in whose home I was then a frequent and welcome guest. Joseph Melchior von Birkenstock had retired in 1803 and thenceforth devoted his full time to the enjoyment of art, science, music, and literature. At his lofty museum-home in the Erdbeergasse, he had created a *Breuning-like* musical culture that I found irresistible. Four years later, Joseph's daughter Antonie married Franz Brentano. Because of the father's poor health, the young couple soon returned from Frankfurt and took up residence in the Birkenstock house. They lived there two years before and after the old man's death, which occurred in October1809. I had often heard Franz boast about his beautiful and talented sister. Undoubtedly, this was she who now stood before me.

B. You must be *Elizabeth.*

BB. I am called *Bettina.*

B. Very well, Bettina . . . I've just made a beautiful song for you. Do you want to hear it?

BB. That's why I came.

B. Here, sit beside me.

As she positioned herself on the bench, I suddenly became aware of her extraordinary physical beauty. Soft brown hair in delicate disarray curled its way to her perfectly contoured shoulders. Her thin face had the boyish firmness of a *St. Joan.* It glowed not with the self-conscious blush of a maiden, but with the divine fire of unbounded love and enthusiasm. Like a Greek goddess her full lips pouted in a tempting reddish ripeness. Her round white breats struggled as if to completely free themselves from the daring U-shaped *décolletage* of her pink and white gown. But over and above this inventory of angelic charms was the penetrating intellectual splendor of her deep brown eyes, whose glowing immortality would challenge death himself. The memory of their impish loveliness was to span seventeen years and bring comfort to my last hour of Earthly consciousness.

Because of *Bettina's* unusual warmth and freshness, I was tempted to repeat the performance, which, only three weeks earlier, had sent *Therese Malfatti* running from me in tears and humiliation. Before

I could decide what to do, Bettina took my right hand into hers. Holding it tightly, she turned it over and raised my palm to her lips.

B. Now, *Bettina* . . . for such fine kissing games, I prefer to offer you my mouth.
BB. The lips of a *god* are not for little girls to kiss.
B. Enough of this! I'll have none of your idolatry . . . not from an *angel*!
BB. Truth is *never* idolatrous.
B. If you persist, I'll have to spank you on the spot.
BB. The pleasure would be mine. What spot?

For the first time in fifteen years, I felt myself blushing in the presence of a maid. The mischievousness and spontaneity of her replies were too much for old Beethoven. No words of mine could ever hope to tame the likes *of her.* I tried to swallow—tried to get my huge forefinger beneath the tight folds of my neck cloth. These failures only made me blush the more! At last I remembered my new composition and sought refuge in *it.*

B. Now for your song: *Kennst du das Land.*

As I sang, my neglected old voice sounded rasping and crumbly, but nonetheless passionate in its vibrating response to a newfound inspiration. At the end of the poem, I turned to Bettina.

B. These beautiful words of Goethe, they contain all the warmth and sunshine of Italy. This is what I see in your eyes. How do you like your little song?

She said nothing, but nodded her approval with burning cheeks and starry eyes. I sang the entire piece again, not once removing my gaze from her sparkling face.

B. Aha! You're a true artist, my dear. When a thing of beauty touches your soul, you respond with fire, not with tears. Would that every musician had such warmth and spirit for his audience! Did brother *Franz* send you to me?
BB. No, he advised me to stay away.
B. What?

BB. He told me that whatever day or time of day I came, my visit would be only an interruption to your work. . . that if you *did* open your door, it would be to throw a book at my head!

B. Well now . . . you must tell your brother that I'm not such an old bear after all! Why *have* you come, Bettina?

BB. I've come to tell you how truly great you are.

B. This is most unusual . . . and very kind.

BB. I'm not here to be kind, but honest. And there should be nothing unusual about such visits. Fie on those of us who sit idly by, mutely watching our great men live through their days, complacently accepting from them their priceless treasures as though they were our just deserts, and then offering in return not so much as a word of thanks. I for one *do* appreciate great artists whose divine magic becomes the very essence of our intellectual life. I believe in thanking them to their faces, not in waiting until it's too late and then carving some slushy sentiment into their headstone.

B. And what measure does my little angel use to discern greatness in old Beethoven?

BB. My ears! I apply them to your music, and at once my heart and soul are infinitely enriched by the gift of true happiness!

B. You find all this in my art?

BB. And more. When I hear your compositions, the world vanishes. I behold a true artist who stalks beyond the culture of mankind, so far ahead that I wonder if the rest of us will ever catch up.

B. Dear Bettina, if I thought you were merely another idolatress, then I *would* spank you and send you away. But when I search your eyes, I find in them what appears to be the warmth of true sincerity. Am I correct?

BB. I'm being honest with myself and with you.That's why I'm here.

B. Then my little angel *does* come from heaven. You can't imagine how much your words mean to me. There are those who say that I behave like a *musical Mogul*, that I surround myself with a clique of obedient followers whose constant praise is my daily sustenance. This is not true! I have too much a loathing for miserable egotists ever to become one myself. If I *appear* to be so, it's a case of mistaken identity. The battles I fight and the goals I seek for my art—these are mistaken as self-centered ambitions and personal quests.

BB. Having the deserved praise of your companions, why do my words mean so much to you?

B. I worry little about pleasing or not pleasing those who are close to me. The one who bothers *me* is that "big fellow" with a thousand eyes, that "*gentleman*" who occupies the five hundred seats of a hall, that "critical connoisseur" who sits in the shadows and waits to be pleased, that "corporate being" who could outlive me by ten centuries, that warm, cold, heavenly, damnable creature—my audience! What does *he* think? Twenty years ago, *Mozart* himself commissioned me to devote my life to composition. From his hands I received the torch and have attempted to run on with it. I look upon my composing as a sacred task and believe that I founded a new sensuous basis for the art. For me, passion is the very throne of music, and I try to breathe this spirit into each movement that I write. Passion has become the climate of my soul; there it blooms and does not run merely to weeds like the thoughts of others who call themselves composers. Now for twenty years I've studied my audience. I've watched him sitting there with shaded face and folded hands. I've wondered if he really appreciates my new combination of harmony, counterpoint, spirit, and love. Those close to me have both praised and damned my latest works . . . and I couldn't care less which they did. But what about *him*? What does *he* think? At last . . . today . . . through your spokesmanship, I find out his opinion. For this is what you are, my dear. You're neither my parent, nor child, nor sweetheart. You're not my teacher, my pupil, my servant, my publisher, my sponsoring prince. You are my public. You bring your love. You kiss my hand. You tell me that I'm achieving my dream. If I live for a hundred years, I shall not forget the kindness of your words, nor their positive confirmation which I read in your sparkling eyes. What can I do for you in return?

BB. Nothing that your music has not already done!

B. But this is too impersonal! You were very direct in your praise of my work. Now I must do something for *you*!

BB. Very well. Suppose you come home with me to the Birkenstock house. Brother Franz is having a large dinner party this evening. More than forty people are invited. Since he wagered that I couldn't get so much as my nose into your apartment, I can think of nothing that would make his chin drop faster or farther than for me (on the very day of my unspeakable adventure) to bring to our table the greatest composer on Earth!

B. I'll do it, Bettina! This will be my revenge. We'll walk into the dining hall arm in arm and sit down together as though we'd known each other for twenty years, all the while keeping a sharp eye on your brother's chin. First I must freshen up a bit.
I nodded in the direction of my bookcase.

B. While I'm shaving, why don't you help yourself to my books? Everything's there from Kant to Schiller.

As I filled the washbasin on my old pine table, I couldn't take my eyes off Bettina. Her girlish charms vibrated suggestively from the flirtatious cut of her pinkish gown. As she threaded her way across the room, I noticed that she was observing and carefully cataloguing each wild disorder that she passed: my disreputable night clothes strewn over the floor, the sack of straw on which I slept, my writing desk with its perilous piles of *Egmont* music, the broken serving spoon that I used for a candle snuffer, the broken candle snuffer that I used for a toothpick, the fine old *Amati* violin and *Zuaneri* cello that I had uncrated this very morning, my favorite easy chair with its shedding leather upholstery and lumpy cushion, and finally, that ultimate horror which stopped Bettina in her tracks and brought both hands to her cheeks, three old legless pianos stacked in the corner (one upon the other) like so many coffins. Lowering her right hand, she pointed toward the gravelike fixtures while turning her face in my direction:

BB. Who's buried in these?

I walked over and stood beside her, my face fully lathered by now.

B. A few boisterous melodies, my dear. You see, when I first came to Vienna, I would give away old pianos as they became worn. Soon I discovered that my newest instruments often became worse than some which I'd given away. So, I've taken to saving my old pianos. I collect them—just like Birkenstock with his engravings, coins, paintings, vases, and walking sticks.

BB. What is your present instrument?

B. An *Erard.* I've had the old beast since 1803, and now something must be done about her. I'm negotiating with Streicher for a new one. It's either this or replace her with one of those monsters in the corner.

At last, Bettina reached my books. She scanned the titles for several minutes before deciding upon Christian Sturm's *Betrachtungen der Werke Gottes in der Natur.* This took complete possession of her while I finished my shaving and dressing.

B. Well, Bettina, your escort is ready. Shall we leave?
BB. Surely not in that old coat . . . your elbows are out!
B. A coat is a coat! What's the difference, so long as there's a Beethoven inside?
BB. You must have something better than this.
B. I doubt it . . . but if it pleases you, we'll look and see.

I took Bettina by the hand and led her to an anteroom where the bulk of my topsy-turvy wardrobe was wrinkled into three old trunks. She immediately began a courageous search, going about her work as though she knew exactly what she was looking for. As she finished the first trunk, without success, I offered a few words of apology.

B. You know, Bettina, my apartment doesn't always look this bad. You must forgive the disarray. I moved in only two weeks ago, and I wasn't expecting company today.

At last she found a short blue jacket that seemed to meet with her approval. She held it up, examined it carefully, shook the dust from it.

BB. Here, this will make you a handsome fellow.

I donned the coat and we left my apartment. As we descended Pasqualati's stone steps, I couldn't help wondering what sort of little monster Bettina was. Think of it—this dainty figurine with fairy feet and angel eyes, I had known her for less than two hours and already she was telling me where to dine and what to wear. By the time we reached the street, I had decided (for the sake of my pride and the "Mogul's" reputation) to refuse her last-given command.

B. Wait here, Bettina. I forgot something.

I returned to my apartment, climbed out of the mandated blue spencer into the condemned brown swallowtail, and promptly rejoined my companion. Bettina put her hands on her hips and looked at me with real fire in her eyes.

BB. You're right, Herr "Mogul." You *have* forgotten something!
B. What's that, my dear?
BB. Your desire to do something nice for me!
B. I am. I'm helping you win your brother's wager.
BB. Not in that holey brown jacket! Why, in such a coat I wouldn't be seen with Napoleon himself!

Needless to say, I returned for the prescribed garb, and only *then* did we begin our long walk to Birkenstock's suburban house. (Such is the price of sociability and the power of a beautiful girl!)

Since there were nearly two hours until dinnertime, we decided to take the scenic route through the Prater and along the Donau canal. Our final trek to the Erdbeergasse was by way of Razumovsky's gardens, which had just exploded into the full-bloomed and bewildering beauty of a sudden Spring. As we walked, we talked of many things.

B. Do you think it strange, Bettina . . . strange that an old man of forty is not yet married?
BB. Not in the least. Not when that "old man" is the world's greatest musician!
B. But what does it mean to become musically great, when there's no one to share with me the pleasures of fame?
BB. Perhaps isolation is the preeminent ingredient of your success. A wife and family could fatally separate you from your work.
B. This is what I keep telling myself. But then I observe that most of my musician acquaintances are happily married and seem to derive their chief pleasures from their families.
BB. If their chief pleasure is their family, then it is not their art! This is my point. A lesser musician sacrifices less to the Muse. He receives less in return and must look elsewhere for his life's greatest joy.
B. You amaze me, Bettina. Young, beautiful . . . a little girl with the tongue of *Socrates*!
BB. In the presence of a Beethoven, anyone becomes philosophical.
B. You're sweet, my dear. And I agree with what you say. It is a great pleasure to sacrifice all to the Muse. But something is missing; I still feel the need for a wife. I've struggled long and hard to secure my place in music and have done so by my own strength. My finances have at last become stable: annuity payments from Rudolph and Lobkowitz, royalties from my publishers, even old

Clementi is settling his account. Now isn't it natural that conjugal love should be my next goal?

BB. Not necessarily. What makes you think so?

B. Over twenty years ago, I met the Mozarts. And I still remember the radiant happiness that existed between them. It was unconcealable---literally shining from their faces. And yet no man gave more of himself to his art, nor received greater joy from it.

BB. No doubt Mozart had an entirely different temperament from yours. Though a wife and family could be for him the beginning of all wisdom, they could be the opposite for you.

B. Some angel! Why can't you speak the words I want to hear?

BB. That would be too easy. I'd rather say those unkind things which (perhaps) ten years from now, you'll be glad you heard. What sort of girl are you looking for?

B. She must have a beautiful face, a kind heart and a true spirit. She must be sufficiently homespun to assume the entire burden of my domestic affairs, yet sublime enough to enjoy the companionship of a "Mogul." She must protect me from the emotional irritants of life, and with tear-free eyes send me off each morning into the world of my creative endeavors, where I've been taught since earliest youth to live and work through my waking hours.

BB. And at sunset when you journey home with frayed nerves, tired mind, and bended knee, what would you bring this little wife in return for all her love and devotion?

B. My love for her.

BB. And how is she to recognize this love? Where is she to find it?

B. In my music. . . . She must learn to look for it there.

BB. Where is the girl who can do this? Have you found her?

B. Not for certain. But I'm still looking. Had you asked me three weeks ago, I would have answered, 'Yes. . . .*Therese Malfatti* is her name.' Now, I'm not so sure.

BB. Well . . . if she doesn't come along, you have no reason to feel slighted. I doubt if any girl could offer you the love and joy you now find in your music.

B. This is reassuring, Bettina, but has Franz told you about my ears?

BB He mentioned that they give you some trouble.

B. And they grow worse. They threaten me with total deafness! If this should be my sad lot, can you imagine the terrible loneliness and isolation? The thought of facing such an ordeal by myself has turned me into an incorrigible flirt. You must watch out for me, Bettina. I'm constantly losing my heart to beautiful young girls like yourself. I've come to believe that only one such angel can save me from my fate.

BB. Nonsense! The power of your music could save you from *any* ill fate.

B. I wish I could believe this!

BB. What *does* Beethoven believe in? Are you a strongly religious man?

B. Not more than I can help. At the hour of my death, I shall probably fly back to the safe conformity of my Roman Catholic childhood. But in the meantime, my search for God continues through the heresy of freethinking. I find him in the most out-of-the-way places—in Persian, Greek, and Hindu literature, in Herder and von Hammer, in Kant, and especially in Schiller's *Die Sendung Moses*.

BB. Sounds like a real composite. What is this god of yours like?

B. He's a loving Father, a *personal* god. I find him in the world about me. His throne is the whole of nature. I have but to extend my hand, and there he is. Who needs a mediator between himself and such a god? Why call upon some saint, or virgin, or messiah, or prophet, or a dirty little priest? God is as near as the starry heavens above us, but his chief revelation of himself is in the glory of the countryside. If all else fails, the beauty of God in nature remains. Even in wintertime, his voice is heard from the sloping banks of silent snow, from the evergreen and from the quiet gray of sleeping trees.

BB. What about *Goethe*? You haven't mentioned him. Do *his* words speak to you of God?

B. Goethe's poems have great power over me, not only because of their contents, but because of their rhythm. They tune me up and stimulate me to composition, these poems that bear within themselves the mystery of the harmonies. Brother Franz tells me that you're a friend of Goethe's. Are you his little angel too?

BB. I hope that I am. How would you like to meet him for an exchange of artistic views?

B. This would be my pleasure. But what makes you think that our great national poet would be interested in the tone-centered ideas of a musician?

BB. He is interested in everything that has to do with art, truth, beauty, and moral progress. Besides, you are the one European who is clearly of his stature.

B. Bettina! A few more compliments like this and there'll be no room left in my belly for dinner.

BB. My words are for your heart, not your stomach!
B. My heart is such a rebel; it betrays me over and over again. But never my stomach. Friends often accuse it of being able to digest the impossible. This is why when a sincere compliment *does* come my way, I lose no time in swallowing it!

We arrived at Birkenstock's some fifteen minutes before the dinner hour. Bettina requested me to hide in the garden while she entered through the kitchen and made secret arrangements for an extra place at the table. In a few minutes, she rejoined me for a short bowling game on the garden's tender carpet of clipped May green. When dinner was finally served, the two of us entered as planned without being noticed until we had reached the table. There Bettina curtsied and offered me her hand. I bowed, kissed her dainty paw, and held her chair. During snatches of this passionate display, the two of us carefully observed and utterly enjoyed a remarkable performance by brother Franz and his chin.

For the next month, Bettina followed me around like a beautiful little shadow. She said that she was gathering information about me for her letter to Goethe, and everywhere that Beethoven went, Bettina was sure to go. We enjoyed countless walks and talks through the perfumed alleys of Schönbrunn. Together we attended the theater, the galleries, and Augarten concert, and even climbed to the top of St. Stephen's tower for a bird's-eye view of the city. All the while, my angel shadow was asking questions, taking notes. At last, in May 28, Bettina completed her letter to Goethe. When she read it to me the next morning, I was amazed by its beautiful spirit of genuine reverence that was epitomized by the closing exclamation:.

BB. If I understood him as I feel him, then I would know everything!

Bettina's letter also contained many of my own comments about music, art, and matters of the spirit. These were garbed in such clairvoyant and philosophical terms that I couldn't believe they were my own words.

B. Did I really say that?
BB. Exactly! I simply copied down your words.
B. Well then . . . I had a raptus.

After my striking out a few lines and adding a few, the letter was sent on its way. Twelve days later, Goethe replied. His letter contained the following invitation that was eventually to bring the two of us together in the summer of 1812 at Teplitz:

> Give Beethoven my heartiest greetings and tell him that I would willingly make sacrifices to have his acquaintance, when an exchange of thoughts and feelings would surely be beautifully profitable; mayhap you might persuade him to make a journey to *Karlsbad* whither I go nearly every year and would have the greatest leisure to listen to him and learn from him. To think of teaching him would be an insolence even in one with greater insight than mine, since he has the guiding light of his genius which frequently illumines his mind like a stroke of lightning, while we sit in darkness and scarcely suspect the direction from which daylight will break upon us.

Two days after reading me Goethe's reply, my little angel spread her wings and returned to Bohemia. What a sad coincidence! For within six weeks, my marriage project with Therese Malfatti was to collapse, and how willingly I would have transferred the totality of my love and devotion to Bettina Brentano. But such is life, or at least *my* life. This young lady, like all the rest, had *other* plans. In December, she became engaged to a poet named *Ludwig Joachim von Arnim*. They were married the following year.

Let me repeat a few of Bettina's choice words that came from her soul and were graciously attributed to my lips. These are the dearest and sweetest of the lot. They brought happiness and courage to my remaining years on Earth and even to the final tears of the Schwarzspanierhaus.

> When I open my eyes I must sigh, for what I see runs contrary to my religion, and I must despise the world which does not divine that music is a higher revelation than all wisdom and philosophy. It is the wine which inspires to new acts of creation; and I am the Bacchus who presses out for men this glorious wine and intoxicates their souls. Then when once more they are sober, they find they have fished all sorts of things out of the sea of tones and brought them along to the shore. . . . I have no anxiety whatever about my music; it can have no evil fate. He who truly understands it, must thereby go free from all the misery which others bear about with them!

Chapter 18

The first seven months of 1811 were relatively unproductive. Things were still busy in the editorial department where I prepared the *Emperor Concerto*, the *Gegenliebe Fantasia*, and the *Sonata Les Adieux* for Breitkopf and Härtel. But the only creative outburst occurred during three weeks of March, when I grabbed some sketches of the preceding year and molded them into my finest trio, the *Archduke*, Opus 97. I was especially pleased by the structural and harmonic contents of this "baby *Eroica*," where tones fell together as if by magic.

It seemed a good idea to contact Goethe before Bettina's sincere liaison had a chance to grow cold. Accordingly, on April 12, I wrote him the following note:

> Your Excellency!
>
> A friend of mine, who is a great admirer of yours (like myself), is making a hasty departure from here, and this urgent opportunity permits me but a moment of time to thank you for the many years I have known you (for I have known you since my childhood). That is so little for so much! . . . *Bettina Brentano* has assured me that you would receive me in a gracious, even a friendly way. But how could I think of such a reception, when I can approach you only with the greatest reverence and with an unutterably

> deep feeling for your glorious creations. . . . You will soon receive the music to *Egmont* through Breitkopf and Härtel; this glorious *Egmont* which through you I have thought over with the same warmth as when I first read it, and experienced it again by setting it to music. . . . I would very much like to have your judgment on it; also your criticism would be beneficial to me and my art, and would be accepted as gladly as the highest prase.
>
> Your Excellency's great admirer,
> Ludwig van Beethoven.

Goethe replied from Karlsbad on June 25:

> Your friendly letter, very esteemed Sir, was received through Herr Von Oliva, much to my pleasure. For the kindly feelings which it expresses towards me I am heartily grateful and I can assure you that I honestly reciprocate them, for I have never heard any of your works performed by expert artists or amateurs without wishing that I might sometime have the opportunity to admire you at the pianoforte and find delight in your extraordinary talents. Good Bettina Brentano surely deserves the friendly sympathy which you have extended to her. She speaks rapturously and most affectionately of you and counts the hours spent with you among the happiest of her life! . . . I shall probably find the music which you have designed for *Egmont* when I return home, and am thankful in advance . . . for I have heard it praised by several and plan to perform it in connection with the play mentioned on our stage this winter, when I hope thereby to give myself as well as your numerous admirers in our neighborhood a great treat! But I hope most of all correctly to have understood Herr Von Oliva, who has informed us that in the journey which you are contemplating, you will visit *Weimar*. I trust it will be at a time when the court as well as the entire musical public will be gathered together. I am sure that you would find worthy acceptance of your service and aims. But in this, nobody can be more interested than I, who with the wish that all may go well with you, commend myself to your kind thought and thank you most sincerely for all the goodness which you have created in us.

Thus were mutually confirmed our desires to meet. In thirteen months, we did so.

This year, winter clung to Spring with the strong-toothed tenacity of a February wolf. I had grown as weary of slushy streets and numbing cold as I had of my routine services to *Archduke Rudolph.* His piano lessons were no bother; I had merely to assign a sonata, a concerto, or a set of fugues that he would then completely master before playing them in my presence. My objection was to the endless sequence of dull compositional exercises that poured from his pen. These he would expect me to examine, correct, explain, and (ugh!) praise. It was all that I could do to keep from telling him (counterpoint after counterpoint, page after page, year after year) how far he remained from ever becoming a true composer. Old Albrechtsberger (after one or two lessons) would have thrown him through the nearest window. Not so, the Great Mogul. Carefully folding his tongue in his cheek, old Beethoven went on and on examining, correcting, explaining, and (ugh!) praising. My reasons for such insincerity were purely selfish. I had caught me an *archduke* and didn't want to let him go. His purse was big enough to match all the princes of Vienna and still have plenty over for me and my career.

By the middle of April, I began suffering from gnawing headaches that showed up with persistent regularity between my deaf spells and my ringing spells. Such ominous recurrence frightened me into visiting Dr. Malfatti, who, after a thorough examination, prescribed the waters of *Teplitz* for my summer vacation. Although I didn't arrive at the Bohemian spa until August 2, I was preceded there by Franz Oliva, who had obtained a cheerful room for me at the "Harp" in the Badgasse. For the most part, my first three weeks at Teplitz were devoted to restoring my health. I took the baths, went for long walks, got lots of rest. While I composed nothing new, I did manage to correct the final proofs for the *Mount of Olives* and send them on their long-awaited journey to Breitkopf and Härtel. Toward the end of August, I noticed a decided improvement in my health. The headaches were gone; my spells of colic, nearly so.

When Malfatti suggested Teplitz, he went into great details about its quiet solitude and beneficial isolation. Recalling the description of my lonely summer at Heiligenstadt, he told me to be sure to take along a good close friend whose presence should prevent any chances of another psychological breakdown like the one that tempted me to commit suicide in the Fall of 1802. Franz Oliva was the "good close friend" who volunteered. As things turned out, I could have managed without him, Teplitz being anything but an isolated spot. During my seven weeks' sojourn at the "Harp," I gathered about me a fine circle of friends, new and old, whose companionship I thoroughly enjoyed. Among my earlier acquaintances were Prince Lobkowitz, the Esterhazys, Pasqualati, Dr. Johann Kanka, Joseph von Varena, and Prince Ferdinand Kinsky, who at this time made a welcome payment on his arrears in my annuity. The new friends included a philosopher, a professor, a Berlin countess, a poet, a young Austrian lieutenant with his fiancée, and finally, the first two of my last three "Immortal Beloveds." These twin romances were begun too late in the summer; they amounted to little more than agreeable flirtations. After all, I was very busy preparing my incidental music for those mustachioed Hungarians of the Pesth theater.

In spite of my arrowlike flirtations at Teplitz, I returned to Vienna convinced, more than ever, that the joys of married life were to be mine in dreams alone. No doubt *Bettina* had been correct in her analysis of my romantic aspirations. And if such were to be my sad lot, then I certainly needed the best of factotums on the "home front." Who *was* the best? One by one, I considered all those who had served me in this capacity. *Gleichenstein*? He was now lost to the Malfattis. *Tiepke*? A doorman, nothing more. *Oliva*? A fine young chap, but more like a demanding friend than a servant. *Zmeskall*? Ah! Here was the man for the job. Dear old "Count Z.," my Glutton Count, my Music Count, Master of the Hungarian Vineyards, my Dinner Count, my Procurer of Quills, Lord of the Burgundian Wineries, the humblest of all my servants, and yet a man with a profound musical sense who could benevolently slap me down without challenging my "kingship." In spite of his dwindling physical vitality, he was the man for the job. I decided to gradually transfer to him my dependence upon *Oliva* and the others. *Zmeskall* would now be reinstated as the plenipotentiary of my realm. With open arms, I would again welcome his dear "*Zmeskallian Zmeskality*."

Upon returning to the Mölkerbastei, I was now famished for some good hard work. My intellectual demands for artistic achievement had reached orchestral proportions. Accordingly, I began sketching my seventh and eightth symphonies, also a few lines which, in twelve years, were to become the choral section of the *Ninth*.

During my penning of *Symphony 7th*'s merriment, I was fully convinced that my princes had let me down, that my cherished dream of financial independence had been one grand disillusionment. An unwarranted fear of imminent starvation was not the *only* dark cloud obstructing my view of the new score. The *Finanz-Patent* had made everyone covetous of his precious *florins of redemption*. Very few Viennese at this time were willing to invest in tickets of admission to a private concert. Another *Beethoven Akademie* was therefore out of the question. Even if I *had* been assured of a decent house, there was every indication that my neglected piano technique would prove inadequate for the occasion. I still felt "at home" when it came to improvising, or conducting, or transposing, or playing Bach from memory; but piano concertos in public? No! My hearing was precarious; I had too long enjoyed an exclusive devotion to composition, my fingers had learned to misbehave. If poor old Neefe could have then visited me, he would *never* have recognized that fine-playing mechanism that he had once so carefully trained. The torch had clearly passed from Beethoven's hand into the hands of his best pupils. And rightly so. For several years, the *Baroness Dorothea von Ertmann* had become my chief exponent in private concerts and salons. *Carl Czerny* was now commissioned to do the same for me in public. This meant that my final Earthly concerto was not presented to the *Viennese* by Beethoven himself but by young *Czerny*. He performed Opus 73 on Wednesday, February 11, for the benefit of the Society of Noble Ladies for Charity. Though my pupil gave the *Emperor* a brilliant reading, it was coldly received. This was neither *Czerny's* fault nor mine. The work was simply too heavy for the rest of the program—something like performing a *Wagnerian* opera between acts of the *Mikado*!

My search for a second operatic text was as frustrated as ever. Napoleon flexed his tiring muscles and aimed 500,000 men across the Niemen toward Moscow, his fatal decision transforming everyone's life plan into a grab bag of uncertainties. During the 1811-12 season, there was no Beethoven *Akademie*, but there were a dozen charity concerts in which my music was well represented.

What *was* behind the *Seventh Symphony*, this spirit of boot-slapping mirth, this personification of childlike joy, this uninhibited laughter of the gods? *Another love affair—the last of my "Immortal Beloveds."* I met the young lady quite by accident on February 11 at Czerny's concert. She combined the physical charm, if not the intellectual maturity, of Bettina Brentano with the musical aptitude and sensitivity of Therese Malfatti. A week later, I was invited to the celebration of her twentieth birthday. By Easter, we were really "going steady." By mid-June, I felt that the old ship had at last found its way into port. Only one cloud marred the horizon—she admitted being (for nearly two years) practically engaged to a young and successful merchant. I immediately asked her parents how *they* felt in the matter. Unbelievable though it sounds, her father took the attitude that his daughter knew exactly what she was doing—the marriage was hers and therefore the decision would be hers. By the time summer vacation arrived, we were thoroughly in love and planned to announce our marriage in the Fall.

Because of my favorable reaction to the baths of Teplitz a year earlier, Dr. Malfatti recommended that I go there again. Upon visiting his office, I foolishly brought up the matter of Therese. We wrangled for nearly an hour until at last the doctor shouted his conclusion that Therese had made the best choice of a husband *after all* and that I should look for *another* physician!

At any rate, I left Vienna for Prague on July second, accompanied by Oliva's friend Willisen. There I managed to collect sixty ducats on account from Kinsky and to spend a heavenly day with my "Immortal Beloved." Then came the parting of our ways—she to Karlsbad, I to Teplitz. Arriving there on the morning of July fifth, I could think of nothing or no one but "my angel, my all, my very self." To relieve the anxieties of heart and mind, I emptied my soul into the penciled scribblings of a three-part letter to this dearest of creatures. After all these years, Beethoven biographers have *yet* to trace the recipient of this message to my "ultimate Isolde." And I have no intention of helping them *now*!

During the four months from July to October, I labored strenuously to finish my *Eightth Symphony*. If the "Seventh" was able to *smile* and *tap his foot*, then the "Eighth" could *laugh* and *dance*. This "small one" is the "laughing-est" of the nine. Therefore it stands close to my heart and differs from the *Eroica* in *kind*, but not *degree*. The spirit of its joyful singing and dancing is undoubtedly the optimism of my final *Earthly* love affair.

July 19 began like any other day. There were the 6:00 AM baths, a brisk walk through the castle park, and a birdlike "health" breakfast consisting of broth, milk, zwieback, and fruit. Then I went straight to my piano where the night before I had left off "stretching" a neat little fugue for the finale of the *Eighth Symphony*. Sunshine now poured onto my music rack, and within minutes, I was completely lost to the world. At quarter past ten, someone "turned off the sun." I glanced toward the window to see what sort of nasty cloud would dare to interrupt my work. This was no cloud, but the shadow of a *god*. There, between me and the window, stood the "first poet" of our land—the *soul* of Germany, *Johann Wolfgang von Goethe*!

Only three days earlier, Lichnowsky told me that our great poet had arrived in Teplitz. I was planning to call on him just as soon as the "Eighth's" *Allegro vivace* could be set aside. But now, he did *me* the honor instead. I recognized him from the prince's description. An enormous man in a top hat, he looked about seven feet tall! He appeared much younger than the sixty-three years Lichnowsky had described. (I wished that I were as healthy and buoyant-looking at forty-one!) Beneath majestic brows was a pair of eyes the likes of which I had never seen—huge black saucers that absorbed the entire world and transformed it into poetry. Their regal stare was lightning cold, yet encompassed a burning love for all mankind. Under their spell, I stumbled to my feet. The hairline wrinkles of his forehead deepened into furrows as he spoke.

Go. Herr Beethoven, now comes your visit from Mephistopheles!

B. You mean to say that at last I'm face-to-face with the *devil*?

Fortunately, my barbed question brought a smile to Goethe's lips. Standing at arm's length, he grabbed my hands, shook them, raised them toward his face. I feared they would melt under his examining beam.

Go. So these are the strong hands which have consoled us for the loss of *Mozart*. They look exactly like the music sounds!
B. Your Excellency, I'm honored by your visit. But it is *I* who should have paid this respect to *you*!
Go. Dear Beethoven . . . which of us calls upon the other is unimportant. What really matters is that artists *do* get together, share their views, and draw inspiration from one another.
B. Would you care for some coffee?
Go. I don't believe so. *No* coffee could outflavor the waters of Teplitz.
B. *Mine* does . . . after I boil the *devil* out of it and little Mimi keeps some on for me all morning.

In a few minutes, we were seated knee to knee in opposite chairs, sipping my boiling brew. I couldn't resist an obvious question.

B. You *like* the coffee?

Go. Superb! I should not for a moment have doubted our Beethoven. Any man who builds a career in the wake of *Mozart* should be able to transform even the waters of a *spa* into delicious coffee!

Goethe continued to sit and sip—a cup in one hand and a saucer in the other. His huge eyes swallowed up the room. At last they settled on my music stand.

Go. What's this you're working on, a new symphony?
B. Number *eight*---the smallest of the set, but it contains enough optimism for a work three times its size.

I put down my cup, went to the keyboard, and improvised for an hour on themes from the first and last movements of the new symphony. This particular improvisation was unusually rewarding. It served as a measure of my artistic growth. Sitting opposite me was the very "personality" of German art—a *giant* whom I had worshipped like a god ever since my teenage enlightenment at the Breunings. I now played for him and was not in any way embarrassed or uncertain of my musical beliefs. Had our meeting occurred a dozen years earlier, I would have melted under the sheer weight of his personality. Not now! I felt comfortable and secure. Such feelings in the presence of a *Goethe* convinced me more than anything else that I had reached the true stature of an artist. Toward the end of my improvisation, he came and stood by the clavier, keeping time with his right hand as though it held an invisible baton. When I finished playing, I felt his huge hands on my shoulders. Turning and observing his sculptured features, I was reminded of a similar event that had occurred on my first visit to *Mozart*. The Maestro had responded with a *smile*; now the poet did so with *words*.

Go. Magnificent! I have never heard such an orderly explosion of concentrated thought. Your speech is as powerful as it is intense! For many years I've been tortured by the intolerable anthisisis of spirit and flesh. My dream has been to reconcile these two within the bosom of my creative activities. And now, strength for the days ahead, I hear such reconciliation within your music. My untrained ears would probably require many hearings to fully appreciate the new sounds of your symphony, but not so its message. The latter is pure and simple and optimistic. 'Tis the oration of a great philosopher who has reconciled his music with life's ultimate reality and who is still able to laugh. This laughter of yours brings me courage and much happiness!

I was impelled to repay Goethe's fine tribute with an encore. Remembering his modest claim to "untrained ears," I tried to think of something nice and classical. A minuet . . . why not a minuet? In fact, why not the very minuet I was now sketching for the *Eighth Symphony*? Without further delay, I swung 'round to the keyboard and launched my newest bit of three-four-fun. As I played, I couldn't help thinking how my jovial "cousins" at the Three Ravens would have reacted to this piece. Lo and behold, Goethe must have read my mind. After several bars, I felt the floor shake and turned to examine the cause. There at the center of the room was *Johann Wolfgang von Goethe*—poet, scientist, dramatist, philosopher, metaphysician—responding like a *peasant* to the music of *Beethoven*. What a sublime compliment—as dear to my heart as was his praise! There, like a graceful bear, danced my 250-pound guest, amidst a huge cloud of dust and sunshine.

After our "song and dance," we went arm-in-arm for an hour's walk in the Schlossgarten, hoping to arrive at the Silver Serpent in time for supper. As we stepped along, we talked of many things ranging from Napoleon's latest maneuvers to the "ultimate reality," which Goethe mentioned hearing in my new symphony.

Go. Does Vienna open her court to Beethoven?

B. Not the Emperor himself. But I've found a little core of princes whose sponsorship is more important to me than *any* court position.

Go. This is well for you to say. But you'll change your mind the very day you receive such a position.

B. I don't think so; I like being independent of court life.

Go. You've denounced the court . . . you hate your public. Who's left?

B. My friends are the great men of Earth like yourself—mighty spirits predestined by Fate to rouse the sleeping masses and jolt them into action.

Go. I'm flattered that you number me among such men.

B. You're there because of what you *are*, not because of what I *say*. There are many great poets, but there's only *one Goethe*. When I read *your* words, they go straight to my heart.

Go. Coming from Beethoven, this is indeed a compliment. I value it because of its sincerity. You must know that my appraisal of you and your work is much the same. After your personal performance, I conclude that I have never before observed an artist with greater power of concentration, more energy, or more inwardness. Your strong personality is filled to running over with confidence, hope, and indomitable power—the selfsame ingredients of your music. If you truly value my art, then you'll permit me the immodesty of claiming that in every respect, young man that you are, I recognize you as my equal!

B. Excepting a few words spoken to me twenty-five years ago by *Mozart*, you pay me the greatest compliment of my lifetime!

Go. Do you regard your artist's life an unhappy one?

B. When I live completely within my art, I'm the happiestof men. Beyond such confinement, I never seem to grasp the commercial side of life—always living in fear of poverty and starvation.

Just now, we approached a huge clump of dancing poplars, whose towering contours framed the orange and green spires of Teplitz. Grabbing Goethe's sleeve, I brought us to a halt. With my other hand, I pointed toward my stately friends.

B. You see those trees? They mean more to me than the companionship of *ordinary* men. I'm never happier than when I walk among them, and my ears permit me to hear their heavenly chorus. In all that I do, I'd like to become more and more like a tree. I always feel that they have something profound to tell me, and hope that (before I die) I might learn to speak their language.

Silently, Goethe stood for a long time, watching their dance and listening to their silvery speech. It was as though he too, perhaps for the first time, had become aware of their philosophical splendor.

We resumed walking, and during the next half hour, our conversation drifted from my bad hearing to literature, to music, to the possibility of my composing *Faust*, to theater, to wines, to Napoleon. By the time we entered the Silver Serpent, our discussions had turned to that "ultimate reality" that Goethe had mentioned hearing in my new symphony.

Years earlier, at Bonn, when Madame von Breuning was first consoling me for the loss of my mother, she advised me to cultivate a strong personal philosophy as the only safe weapon against that "old man with the scythe." She believed that all life was but a short prelude to death and that the chief philosophical responsibility of our days on Earth was to gather bits of love and wisdom that would bring peace and happiness to the hour of our death. Such a divine "bit" now fell to my soul from Goethe's lips, as we sipped our glasses of Würzburg.

Go. It is my belief, dear Beethoven, that any work of art, or science, or philosophy becomes truly great only if it can be brought face-to-face with death and still hold its own reality. For me, to die is to become, and the essence of all living is creation! I create without ceasing, and this is my only claim to immortality. One should believe in immortality. Each of us has a right to this belief. It satisfies the wants of our nature. There are many ways to define immortality of the soul. Some turn to religion, others to philosophy, or legend, or mythology. The path we take is irrelevant. What matters is that we do seek and find. For me, the eternal existence of my soul is proven from my idea of activity. If I work on incessantly till my death, nature is bound to give me another form of existence when the present one can no longer sustain my spirit.

The following afternoon, Goethe and I went riding together on a pleasure trip to *Bilin*. Next evening, I improvised again for the great poet. These were the final crossings of our Earthly paths.

My replacement for Malfatti was Dr. Jakob Staudenheim. He was not at all pleased with my three weeks at Teplitz and recommended that I now try the waters of Franzensbrunn. Since I had not yet heard from my "Immortal Beloved" and had every reason to believe that she was still in *Karlsbad*, I obtained medical permission to go *there* instead. What a disappointing twelve days! I continued suffering from colic, and there was no trace of "my angel, my all, my very self." In August 8, I took Staudenheim's advice and journeyed to *Franzensbrunn*. After four weeks of swimming, splashing, and drinking the waters of this spa, I could boast a small miracle—the first decent stool in over two years! In September fifteenth, I returned to Teplitz, and in another week found my health to be greatly improved.

Upon returning to Vienna, I looked for the open arms of my "Immortal Beloved," or at least for her reply to my Teplitz epistle. I found neither—nothing but an ominous brown envelope containing my original letter and a caustic note from the "other man" in her life. Twice in a single paragraph he referred to me as "music mad" and demanded that I have no further correspondence with his fiancée. I threw his two pages of drivel the same place where I had thrown my cover sheet to the *Eroica* and almost followed suit with the love letter. But as an afterthought, I decided to keep those pages as a permanent reminder to never again lose my heart over a girl. While on *Earth*, I never again did! It took me six years to choke down the bitter pill of irrevocable and profound loneliness. But once I did, there came to me nine years of glorious composition to complete my life on *Earth*!

Chapter 19

Now comes the last transition of Beethoven's Earthly days. It carries him from the second to his "final period" of creative activity and is anything but a smooth or enjoyable development. In fact, it amounts to a painful hiatus in composing that lasts for nearly six years.

After finishing Symphonies 7 and 8, I felt as though I had nothing more of importance to say. And I had never been one to compose for the mere purpose of repeating something that I had already spoken as eloquently as I knew how. Enter Johann Nepomuk Mälzel, with his world-famous "pyramid" now known as Mälzel's metronome. At first, I thought it was a stupid affair to think of tempo in such exacting terms. What could a ticking box possibly have to tell us about something as natural and immeasurable as the gentle swaying of underbrush beneath a playful breeze? But then, the more I thought about it, the less stupid it seemed. Didn't the Italian designations (such as *Allegro, Andante, Adagio con dolore, etc.)* mean ten different things to ten different people? Wasn't there a need for something more precise? Before too long, I was publically recommending the use of Mälzel's metronome and was pleased to send out my symphonic scores with a numerical designation for each movement.

It was this Mälzel who was responsible for what little (although trite) composing I managed to do during the barren period at hand.

Besides his metronome, he invented a huge music box, twelve feet high. On the turning of its cylinder, this Panharmonica could imitate all the sounds of a military band. Since at this time all I talked about was making a trip to London where I might follow in the financially rewarding footsteps of Georg Friedrich Handel, Mälzel proposed that I write a "battle piece" for his Panharmonica. He suggested further that it commemorate Wellington's current and decisive victory over the French at Vittoria and guaranteed that (with the aid of his unusual music box) the two of us could then make our fortunes in the British capital. . . .

During August and September, I sketched out the work's general plan. Thus, my *Battle Symphony* was finished in October, and Mälzel began transcribing it to his cylinder. He now shrewdly suggested that I arrange the work for full orchestra and parade it about Europe to celebrate the downfall of our French tyrant. He believed that the more popular it became as an orchestral piece, the greater would be our profits from his mechanical reproductions of it. This is exactly what I did. The *Battle of Vittoria* was performed at two charity concerts and at two Beethoven akademies. What unbelievable results! What irony. For twenty years, I had tried to seat myself on Mozart's throne. Neither my best playing nor my best composing could do the trick. To most Viennese, I was still the incomprehensible Rhinelander, the mad musician! Now suddenly, things changed. I jumped on the back of my poorest potboiler and rode it to the end of my wildest dream. Overnight (on the strength of less than nothing), I became "King Beethoven," the darling of Vienna!

Then suddenly a miracle occurred; I abandoned my commercial ways, rolled up my sleeves, wrinkled up my brow, girded up my sketchbook, and plowed headlong into the most glorious period of Beethoven's Earthly composing. Like the Second Period, this final sequence was ushered in by two piano compositions: the *Sonata in A* and the *Grosse Sonate für das Hammerklavier.* Most of my biographers are of the opinion that these pieces are transitional, that my Third Period begins after the *Hammerklavier.* As *I* hear it, this is simply not the case. These sonatas have their full share of Third Period. From the time of its composition until my death, I regarded the *Hammerklavier* as my greatest sonata. This was natural for I spent more time composing it than any other piano piece. Compared to its brothers and sisters, the *B-flat Major* is twice as long and twice as difficult. The mystical abyss of its *Adagio sostenuto* and the harsh, clattering speech of its enormous three-voiced *fugue* appeared to be the very means by which the old prodigal finally returned home and extricated himself from the hopeless morass of his composing doldrums. But (as you'll discover) death and rebirth usually brings a remarkable sharpening of perception, judgment, and objectivity. Today, the *Hammerklavier* seems too big and too much worked over. The *A Major* says a great deal more in half as many pages. Its opening *Allegretto* has a lot more tears-in-the-eye beauty than does its unwieldy counterpart in the *B-flat Major.* By comparison, its *fugue* is also better—more like those bygone peasant tunes whose contrapuntal blending had won me the approval of Mozart himself.

To sum up, the first and last movements of the *A Major* and the *Scherzo* from the *Hammerklavier* are now my favorite Earthly Beethoven piano pieces. No other Third Period music for this instrument can equal these numbers. In composing them, I reached that highest plateau of my artistic sensitivity on which were written my last and best compositions. In fact, by the end of 1818, I had sketched most of the first two movements of my final (Earthly) symphony.

That these years were a period of creative fertility is the last impression I wish to make. Actually, the sudden explosion of opuses occurred at the close of six barren years! My "second period" ended in 1812 with a magnificent outpouring of two worthy symphonies and my best (Earthly) pianoforte trio—all within fourteen months. Then it happened. Six years of creative paralysis! From 1813 to 1818, there were nothing but weeks of painful hackwork on *Fidelio* and a string of hopeless potboilers until, out of the clear blue, came my best piano music and the opening movements of my greatest symphony. Why? What caused the breakdown and (even more important) the joyous rebirth of my creative life? As I recount these Earthly years, a discussion of this question seems more pertinent than the careful detailing of day-by-day frustrations.

Was it a matter of money? In terms of florins and ducats, things add up to a pretty good argument. Brother Carl and his family fell into such dire financial straits that in order to help them, I was obliged to borrow 50 ducats from partner Mälzel. Through 1813 into the Spring of 1815, there were annuity payments from neither Lobkowitz nor from the Kinsky estate. To make matters worse, Carl needed another 1,500 florins in October 1814. My house rent was doubled. The "benevolent" Streichers spent enormous sums raising my wardrobe and lodgings to the level of respectability. Unfortunately, it was *my* money they spent. . . . "Count Z." found me a tailor-and-wife team to come and live in my anteroom at Pasqualati's. In spite of the husband's using this room for his tailor shop, I was required to pay them an exorbitant 900 florins for their modest performances as servant and cook. . . . I borrowed heavily from publisher Steiner, and remained in his debt for many months. The Austrian National Bank came into being and promptly called in the redemption certificates, exchanging them for silver florins on a two-and-a-half-for-one basis. Thus my annuity was further reduced from 3,400 florins to a mere 1,360 florins, whose purchasing powers were not unquestioned.

All this sad news roughly coincided with the lull in my creative writing; however, to support the arrival of "Period 3," there were some financial bright spots. Archduke Rudolph never faltered in his share of my annuity. The Lobkowitz payments were resumed in April 1815 as were those from the Kinsky estate, the latter being strictly a compromise (amounting to two-thirds of the original contract) and being resumed only upon my threat of a lawsuit. Thus reestablished, the annuity continued until my death. As Vienna's popular composer of the "great" (ugh!) *Battle Symphony*, Beethoven concerts became sellouts, and for the first time in my life, I had spare cash to invest. Can you believe it? The Great Mogul turns capitalist and becomes the proud owner of eight shares of the National Bank of Austria. What about this financial ebb and flow? Was it actually the cause of my professional breakdown and recovery? No! I'm convinced that it wasn't. There are too many exceptions to the pattern. Many of my best works were composed during periods of monetary drought.

There can be no thought that my composing break was caused by public indifference to Beethoven's music. Nor was it caused by such physical ailments as deafness, failing eyes, asthma, diarrhea, and colic. Each of these adversities was present and worse during Beethoven's most creative days, "period 3." Could musical famine have resulted from the ultimate collapse of my dreams for marriage? I think not. Many of my best works came into being as direct sublimations of frustrated amours. Could it have been my nineteen changes in residence within a span of six years? I don't believe so. I was every bit as much the rolling stone throughout my Third Period as I was during those six years that preceded it. Was it the death, departure, or alienation of many old friends that caused the barrenness of the period? Wrong again! Empty places were substantially filled in by new social and professional relationships. Could it have been the death of brother Carl (age forty-two) on November 16, 1815? Two days prior to his death, he executed an elaborate will that commended his soul to God, his body to the earth, and then went on disposing of things down to the last goat, peacock, and potted plant. In the midst of this detailed inventory, he appointed me guardian of his little son Karl, along with the boy's whorelike mother. On November twenty-eighth, I appealed to the Upper Austrian Landrecht to transfer Karl's guardianship exclusively to *me* on the basis of his mother's infidelity. On January 19, 1816, I was appointed sole legal guardian of my nephew. His "Queen of the Night" mother was obliged to apply solely to *me* as to "whether, how, and when" she could see her son. Naturally, this pronouncement resulted in endless quarrels between the two of us.

After summering at Heiligenstadt and Nussdorf, my physical health took a sudden turn for the better. Except for deafness and naughty intestines, I felt a rebounding youthful vitality breeze through my middle-aged hulk. After five dead years, a new Beethoven came to life in the sketchbooks. The glorious sounds of *Symphony 9* began to be. On the strength of their optimism, was there anything theGreat Mogul could not now do? Certainly the mere bringing up of a son would be no challenge to such regal power. Concluding that I could do more for Karl than anyone else on earth, I once again decided to bring him under my roof. Because of the smallness and drabness of the Landstrasse apartment, I moved into bright (if not cheerful) rooms in the Gärtnergasse. These accommodations had the added advantage of being near my nephew's school. By November first, I was ready for Karl, but still the little fellow remained with Giannatasio. My own indecision prevented his joining me at this time. I wondered whether Beethoven's domestic budget could survive the inevitable demands of a son. I wondered if my work on the *Hammerklavier* should be put aside in favor of completing two symphonies for the London Philharmonic. I wondered whether I should accept Giannatasio's offer to keep Karl at half price in order that I might visit London and claim there the Handelian nest egg assured me by Ries. Not knowing what to do, I did nothing!

At last on January 6, 1818, I wrote Giannatasio that I wished Karl to leave the institute and come live with me as of February first. In preparation for Karl's arrival, I added three members to my household: a housekeeper, a cook, and an instructor from the institute. Initially, things went perfectly in the Gärtnergasse—a veritable heaven on earth for Beethoven. Little Karl behaved like a son. Before long, he was calling me "Father" instead of "Uncle." I never thought of him as the descendant of the "Queen of the Night." It was as though he had sprung pure and undefiled from my brother's loins, not even stopping off in Johanna's womb. I saw him as the beloved grandson of my dear mother. As such, he became the perfect resolution of my lifelong craving for someone to love and cherish.We walked together, we played together—we even prayed together. Yes, twice a day, we knelt by his little bed and prayed! The Great Mogul and his son—we knelt there and prayed—prayed to a God that I wasn't sure even existed. At suppertime, when Karl would come running in from his games, I'd jump from my desk, fall to my knee, and open my arms to him. How boyishly he blushed as his warm little cheek met my face. How happy I was. There in my arms I held more than just a little nephew with curly black hair, dimpled chin, and sparkling prank-filled eyes. I held the promises of tomorrow—my reasons for completing the *Hammerklavier*, for composing more symphonies, for going to England—for conquering new worlds. It's easy to see why I clung to Karl like a trouser button. My all-consuming love for the boy forbade that I share him with anyone, least of all, his mother. Since Johanna was the logical and rightful person to assist me in caring for Karl, my antipathy toward her quickly developed into thick black hatred. Before brother Carl's death, I regarded his wife as a mere wicked and useless woman. But now that we openly vied for the guardianship of her son, she appeared to me as a vicious, monstrous, bloody whore, whose mere touch would pervert the boy's ways into a wasted ill-spent life. It became my chief ambition to permanently separate the two. Efforts in this direction caused me nine years of domestic hell, which, in turn, contributed to the six-year hiatus preceding the nine years of my final creative period on Earth.

Though all the negatives I've mentioned were no doubt contributing factors, the main cause of my prolonged inactivity (1813–1818) was the simple fact that after completing two new symphonies and the *Archduke Trio,* I had nothing more of comparable importance to say. Only another philosophical breakthrough could open the door to bigger and better compositions. Such breakthroughs are not easy to come by—can't be ordered up like so much brains and gravy. They must be searched out, waited upon, and paid for by the price of patient suffering.

The great music that ended "period 2" derived its inspiration from that same exultant self-confidence that had sustained me for so many years—the belief that my own strength was adequate for life's demands. Though I no longer felt that I had the power to overcome the "slings and arrows" that fate directed toward me, I did believe that my career (at least) was secured through the might of self-determination. But to *speak* more meant to *grow* more; the prerequisite for higher-level composing was the evolution of a new, deeper, more meaningful philosophy. What philosophy? Where was I to go for the magical key? Each time I asked this question of the divine Muse, she pointed toward me—toward my inner self. Apparently, this was the only place where I could now hope to find new sounds and deeper meaning for my music. But what a terrible price to pay—the complete withdrawal into my inner self. Why should the Great Mogul ever be asked to suffer such irrevocable and profound loneliness? Even so, to live without composing was to die! Having no choice and deciding to sample the "new life," I tiptoed into the world of my self. What a strange and exalted region! There the tones ran rich and deep. Before I knew it, the clatterings of the *Hammerklavier fugue* had come to paper. They frightened me, and I ran all the way home. Dare I return to this place? I dreaded the move. I hated to leave the familiar world of things and people. I clung to little Karl as though he were my last contact with humanity. What was I to do? Once again, I came before my Muse. I fell to my knees, clasped and raised my hands to her:

B. Tell me, dear soul. Must I return to this awful and lonely place?

Smiling grimly, her silence answered, "Yes!"

Chapter 20

My misgivings concerning the lower tribunal turned out to be amply justified. Although this den of plebes granted me the continued supervision of Karl's education, it suspended me from his general guardianship and permitted him to spend the first months of 1819 with his mother. On January eleventh, I was summoned before the magistrates and accused of committing an immoral and selfish act in trying to separate a twelve-year-old boy from his mother. My defense took the form of a long letter to the magistracy, a document that required three weeks of careful planning and polishing by Bernard (my lawyer) and myself. In this letter, I stated that I had never done a more beneficial or magnanimous act than when I took my nephew to myself and personally assumed charge of his education. I went on to proclaim the virtuousness of all my deeds, and the superiority of *my* educational plan for Karl over the one proposed by his mother. I blamed all interruptions in the boy's scholastic progress upon Johanna's treacherous and deceitful interferences and then proceeded (fault by fault) to dissect her personality and that of the dirty priest from Mödling who had sided with her against me.

Since I had no acceptable evidence to support my violent accusations, the court naturally discounted most of what I said. Karl remained with his mother. However, instead of sending him to public school, I decided to place him under the private tutorship of Johann von Kudlich. This fine teacher was conveniently situated in the Landstrasse institute and should guarantee my nephew at least the personal attention and direct supervision that I felt he needed. Since the time of my summer vacation had arrived, I conveniently placed Karl in this institute.There he remained for the most valuable months of his education.

The appellate court commanded the magistracy to file a complete report on its proceedings. To strengthen our position, Bernard and I spent two weeks preparing a huge seven-part memorial describing the history of the case from *my* point of view. Then with painful patience, we settled back and awaited their decision. Three days before receiving the ultimate decree, Bernard brought Karl for a visit. As usual, I fell to my knee and embraced the boy with mighty hugs and kisses:

B. Karl . . . just think! Soon it will all be over. You'll be my son, and we'll travel the world together. What fun we'll have—I with my music and you with your studies. Does this make you happy?

On my left cheek, he planted a timid little kiss, and because of my deafness, went searching for a "Conversation Book." While he searched, I added a question:

B. How are things going at Blöchlinger's?

His written reply:

Ka. I'M BEING A GOOD BOY AND WORKING HARD.

For a wonder, this is an accurate description of Karl's behavior over the long term.

Although most of 1819's productive hours were devoted to the *Missa Solemnis*, by the end of that year, only the *Kyrie*, the *Gloria*, and the *Credo* were substantially finished. Whenever I ventured to any extent into the fields of vocal or ecclesiastical music, I found it essential to codabble in that safe, sure realm of the instrumental. Accordingly, during these first two years of the *MIssa*, I continued to mold my *Ninth Symphony* and began sketches for what turned out to be my last three piano sonatas and a set of thirty-three pianoforte variations on that "cobbler's patch" of a little waltz by Diabelli.

During these months, my brother Johann's financial accomplishments reached a new high. He so "reeked" with unapplied funds that he decided to purchase the huge Wasserhof estate near Gneixendorf. Ironically (at this very time), *my* finances turned in the opposite direction. Because of Karl, I was obliged to borrow over 2,400 florins from Steiner. This I did on the strength of my promise that the "Lieutenant General" would be the first to publish a complete edition of my works. I also promised him to repay my debt in semi-annual installments of 600 florins.

With the extreme cultivation of inner self required to dig out the new sounds of "period 3," it's no wonder that my circle of friends began to narrow. How easy it was for the glamorous young Beethoven to dazzle total strangers into worshipping every finger of his pianistic ability. But now that he'd become an egg-throwing, profane, book-throwing, slanderous, dish-throwing, suspicious, chair-throwing, covetous, nonperforming, eccentric old composer, it was all that he could do to keep a few of his old friends, let alone make new ones. And besides, the only human beings he could tolerate were those obedient subjects who pledged unquestioned allegiance to the Great Mogul.

Who *were* the staunch courtiers remaining faithful to Beethoven in spite of Beethoven? The protecting Maecenas behind my little throne was and continued to be Cardinal Archduke Rudolph. During these years, my favorite pastime was publically to denounce the Emperor, his government, the police, and the church. To the painful embarrassment of close friends, this I would do at restaurants and in winehouses. Far from being whispered, my incriminatory denunciations were boomed out in the shrieking bark of a deaf man! Except for Rudolph's quiet (behind-the-scenes) ministrations, I'm sure that my scandalous behavior would have landed me in jail time and again. "Count Z" was the other genuine nobleman admitted to the ranks of my private club. Were it not for his growing spells of physical incapacitation, Zmeskall would certainly have remained my ultimate factotum. However, Count Z's failing health required me to name Anton Schindler as his successor. Umlauf stood by with his military baton in hand, ever ready to replace my deaf ears on the podium. Thanks to Steiner and Haslinger, I never had to look beyond my nose to find an eager publisher. Bernard and coguardian Peters were forever offering their expert advice concerning the problems of young Karl. Czerny came often to beg reinforcements—new sonatas and concertos for his instrument. When Stephan von Breuning and I are finally reunited, there remain but one year and a few days for the social entwinement of our Earthly lives.

An interesting happening closed out 1820 and provided me with yet another publisher. Things were so bleak and dreary in the Paternostergässchen that I found the little one-room music shop (the "foxhole") lighting its way with every available candle. As usual, the place was packed to the door with writers, musicians, artists, critics, and a few customers. Head down and armed with the most serious of Beethoven scowls, I boldly traversed the full twenty feet of storeroom in order to reach my favorite spot at the back counter. As soon as I was comfortably seated there, a handsome stranger approached and handed me his tablet. There in carefully formed letters was written:

> Eminent Maestro:
>
> My father and I have entered the field of music publishing—he in Berlin and I in Paris. Our firm is unique in that whatever we handle is presented simultaneously in these two great capitals. With something from *your* pen, our success is assured! Could we be of service to Beethoven's new *Mass*? Or perhaps in a complete edition of his works?
>
> Your sincere admirer,
> Moritz Schlesinger

I returned his note.

B. Now come, Schlesinger. What could you possibly want with my *Mass*? The blessed thing is neither kosher, nor is it circumcised.

Sl. Crumbs from *your* table are worth more than feasts at others.

B. What you say is very nice. I appreciate these words. But when it comes to business matters, I'm poorly informed and am therefore leery of Jews and Italians. They're bound to get the better of me with their fast talking and their little tricks.

Sl. The only tricks I know will be used to promote your music—not to deceive you.

B. You look like an honest man, Schlesinger. I welcome you as my newest agent.

I took a sketchbook from my left pocket and opened it to a blank page:

B. Here—write me your address so that I may contact you.

As Schlesinger wrote, I couldn't help noticing his handsome pipe.

B. Tell me. Where does one find such a pipe? I've seen few like it. I'll wager it really takes the bite out of tobacco. Where might I buy one?
Sl. It is a Parisian pipe. I'll see that you receive one.

My real acceptance of the Schlesingers occurred one week later at Mödling. I emerged from my study at 9:00 PM and told the cook exactly where to go and exactly what to do with her cold meal. Easing myself into a tattered gray coat (far worse than the one which Bettina had criticized), I headed for the Haupstrasse Inn. As I walked and breathed deeply of the refreshing green smells, there danced through my mind mouth-watering visions of thick-sliced veal, rich brown gravy, and fresh warm biscuits. By the time I entered the Last Rose, I could fairly taste the juicy contents of my dream. You can imagine my disappointment when told that there was no more veal to be served. Throwing my napkin at the waiter's stupid face, I stormed across the room with such clumsy wrath as to upset two trays and a serving table. I gave the door a splintering kick (completely severing its lower hinge) and went cursing into the street. Rather than compromise my sudden passion for veal, I decided to go to bed hungry.

After spending some thirty minutes storing away the fiery colors of a Mödling sunset, I arrived at my apartment. There in the Hauptstrasse stood a two-horsed open carriage, occupied by a pair of stately servants. Though their uniforms identified them as employees of the spa's hotel, they reminded me for all the world of Lichnowsky's lackeys who (years earlier) had first opened the gate of Vienna for Beethoven. The smaller of the two jumped down and began casting his words upon my deaf ears. I handed him a Conversation Book:

B. Here! You'll have to write, for I'm deaf as a stone.
L_2. Am I addressing Herr Beethoven?
B. I am Beethoven.
L_2. Good! We have come from the hotel to serve you a special supper. Will you show us to your quarters?

I peeked into the carriage. Sure enough, there were four serving trays and a dozen covered dishes. When our little procession reached my rooms, we couldn't find an uncluttered area big enough to accommodate the sumptuous spread. At last, one of the servants tapped me on the shoulder and directed my attention toward the spacious mahogany casing of my Broadwood. Before I realized what was happening, its top was lowered and covered with three folds of fine linen tablecloth. Candles on both sides of the music rack were lighted, and a high stool with a cushion brought me to exactly the right height. Then came the big surprise. In typical fairy-tale fashion, as silver covers were removed from the dishes, my eyes and tongue were met with the most deliciously elaborate serving of veal that I had ever seen or tasted!

B. What little "Messiah" is responsible for this?

The nearest servant pointed to a note attached to a bottle of champagne. With great excitement, I tore it open and read.

> Dear Beethoven,
>
> Please accept this little greeting as a token of the great admiration held for you by the Schlesingers. I'll be staying here at the hotel for a full week, and sincerely hope that you might spare me a few minutes of your time for a short visit.
>
> Hopefully your publisher,
> Moritz Schlesinger.

After sugarplum cake and coffee, this ideal supper was climaxed by additional surprises—two beautifully wrapped gifts (one short and round, the other long and thin) were handed me together with another note:

> May these bring you many happy hours of creative meditation. . . . M.S.

The first contained a large canister of fine Turkish tobacco; the second, a long-stemmed pipe exactly like the one I had admired at Steiner's.

After enjoying my surprise, I returned to the hotel, gave Schlesinger a hearty embrace, and promised him some Beethoven compositions in the very near future. I simply had to find out how he knew to send veal to a dying man at the precise moment in which the dying man was dying for the lack of veal. It so happened that Schlesinger had just arrived at Mödling and was walking along the Hauptstrasse to pay me a visit, when he witnessed my stormy exit from the Last Rose. Deciding that perhaps this was not the most expedient time to inquire of my health and future publishing plans, he stealthily entered the inn and determined the cause of my profane outburst. When he discovered how easy the matter would be to correct, he returned to the hotel and immediately arranged for my pleasant surprise.

I made good my promise. During the remaining years, Schlesinger was to receive my last three piano sonatas and two of the last five quartets. After all, I felt that any young chap who was shrewd enough to know that the direct way to Beethoven's heart was through Beethoven's stomach, was certainly shrewd enough to publish Beethoven's music!

Chapter 21

The years 1821 and 1822 were dominated by the *Missa Solemnis.* Its sketching and scoring absorbed most of my composing time during the period. I developed such a passion for revising and improving this particular score that had the work remained in my hands for another ten years, I would probably still not have considered it finished. To break the spell of its endless demands, I wrapped up a beautiful copy of the commemorative opus and sent it to Archduke Rudolph.

Counterbalancing the enormous energies required for pushing Beethoven's pencil through the dense texture of a High Mass, I returned once again to the instrument of my youth. Interspersed among battles with the *Missa,* my final Earthly piano pieces were composed. These included the last three of thirty-two sonatas, and my most ambitious set of variations, those structured on Diabelli's little waltz. For a wonder, I made good my promise to Schlesinger and sent him the three sonatas at 40 ducats each. During these years, there was even a little work done on *Symphony 9,* more at the subconscious level than in the sketchbooks. I also began toying with the idea of returning to the string quartet medium. A philosophical breakthrough had been achieved and was directly responsible for the newness of Third Period sounds. However, the ultimate expression of this higher order of consciousness required something more personal than full orchestra, and yet more sensitive than piano solo. A string quartet was the answer. With the hungry stare and wet lips of a little boy eying a freshly baked kuchen, I began lusting after the sublime intimacies and perfect balance of four strings—this after an absence of fourteen years! But what about money? Considering the vast expenditures of time required to bring these latest opuses into being, it was absolutely essential that I be well paid for my new quartets. After all (aside from an ever-eroding pension), composing was my sole source of income. I contacted Neate, Ries, Artaria, Schlesinger, and Steiner in an attempt to feel out the market for new Beethoven quartets. No one seemed the least bit optimistic about obtaining subscriptions. Then suddenly (as if by magic) on November 9, 1822, from faraway St. Petersburg, there came a letter that clearly settled the matter.

> Monsieur, I take the liberty of writing you, as one who is as much a passionate amateur in music as a great admirer of your talent, to ask if you will not consent to compose one, two or three new quartets for which labor I will be glad to pay you what you think proper. I will accept the dedication with gratitude. Would you let me know to what banker I should direct the sum that you wish to get? The instrument that I am cultivating is the violoncello. I await your answer with the liveliest impatience. . . . I beg you to accept the assurance of my great admiration and high regard.
>
> Prince Nicolas Galitzin.

On January twenty-fifth, I sent my reply. It was written above my signature by young Karl in what I proudly considered to be impeccable French for a mere boy of sixteen:

> Your Highness,
>
> I would not have failed to answer your letter of November 9th sooner, if the multitude of my affairs had not prevented me from writing you. It was with great pleasure that I found that Your Highness is interested in works of my creation. You wish to have some quartets; since I see that you are cultivating the violoncello, I will take care to give you satisfaction in this regard. Inasmuch as I am constrained to live by the products of my mind, I must take the liberty of setting the honorarium for each quartet at 50 ducats. If

> this is agreeable with Your Highness, I beg you to inform me soon and to direct this sum to the banker Hénikstein in Vienna. I bind myself to finish the first quartet by the end of February or at the latest by the middle of March. In expressing to you my real interest in your musical talent, I thank Your Highness for the regards that you have been willing to indicate in choosing me to increase (if it is possible) your love for music. I have the honor of being Your Highness's very humble servant, Louis van Beethoven.

Perhaps I should say a few words in defense of my business ethics, which at this time (in the eyes of the casual observer) will appear to have gone from bad to worse. As work on the *Missa* drew to a close, I promised the score simultaneously to four different publishers (actually accepting an advance from Peters) and then ended up by awarding it to still another! My reasons for such deceptive dealings were to obtain maximum cash from the opus and to use its rights as an inducement for some house to manage the first complete edition of my works at the comfortable fee of 10,000 florins. This sudden interest in money did not mean that I had acquired a taste for personal luxuries or for an easier way of living. Increased funds were needed merely to maintain the status quo. Continent-wide inflation had seriously diluted my pension. A six-week attack of rheumatic fever, the violent return of my diarrhea, and a stubborn case of jaundice led Dr. Staudenheim to prescribe costly summers at health resorts. Karl was now a high school boy, and his expenses at Blöchlinger's increased sharply. I had borrowed 3,000 florins from Steiner and 1,000 each from Artaria, Brentano, and brother Johann. These moneymongers not only requested the return of their loans, but now threatened to charge me interest! I realized that the sale of one or two of my bank shares would have put things on an even keel, but such action was out of the question. These fruits of my "popular" days had been put aside for Karl's future, and to touch them for my personal needs was unthinkable. Ironically, these could have been my most profitable years. Diabelli, Breitkopf and Härtel, Peters, Simrock, the Schlesingers, Artaria—everybody was clamoring for new Beethoven scores. I could have sold fifty times the number written. My finances remained precarious for no other reason than because of the high artistic ideals of "period 3," which curtailed production. I therefore plead innocent regarding the immorality of my business dealings.

I plead innocent on the grounds that Beethoven at least remained true to his art.

The summer of 1821 surprised me with a couple of unusual experiences that are now considerably more fun to talk about than they were to live through. On an early June morning, Kritz, the mover arrived at the Landstrasse suburb and began loading my possessions into his van. At ten o'clock, I shook his hand, bade him a safe journey to Unterdöbling, and promised to meet him there with further instructions.

As I walked the trail, the spell of growing things soon worked its magic upon Beethoven. I gesticulated along like a wild windmill—waving my arms, pencil in one hand and a sketchbook in the other. Before I realized what was happening, I had written my greatest march tune and on its buoyant strains had tramped my way to the very center of a little square, which coincidentally turned out to be . . . Unterdöbling!

The sudden consciousness that I had arrived among people brought to mind Karl's criticism of my eccentric street antics. I wheeled around to see if there were any urchins following in my wake. Sure enough, there were! Eight miniature soldiers, each replete with wooden musket and paper helmet. My deafness transformed their harmless, boyish smiles into grotesque, grinning mockery. I licked my parched lips and then screamed at them:

B. What little bastards you are! To hell with the lot of you! Take your brothers and sisters with you! And if there's room there, come back for your parents. . . . What's this world coming to? . . . Prickish little mosquitos who have nothing better to do than mimic the suffering of a deaf man. . . . To hell with you!

I walked to the center of the square and sat down on the mossy stones of a saint-studded fountain, helping myself to a convenient ladle. How delicious and cool the water tasted and felt. By now, I located the little army that had been scattered by my profanity. They had regrouped and taken refuge in what appeared to be a small fort. How unusual! What manner of people would provide such an elaborate plaything for their children at the very center of town? Was it a pile of rocks? Reinforcing my eyes with silver-rimmed spectacles, I discovered their encampment to be neither rocks nor a fort, but rather a disorderly maze of household furnishing. This called for closer inspection. My jaundiced face broke into a wide grin as I thought to myself: "So this is the type of bastard-citizen we have in Unterdöbling. For the sake of a little rent, they'd throw some poor devil out of house and home!"

As I approached the "fortress," its "soldiers" scattered again. That is, they all scattered except for one little towhead about six years of age. Sliding down the back of an old leather chair, he watched my every move with a pair of the biggest blue eyes I had ever seen. When I finally broke the spell of his stare and examined his splintery "fort," I discovered it to be none other than the life possessions of Ludwig van Beethoven, gathering dust in the main square of Unterdöbling. On the topmost box of clothes was a note from Kritz:

> Herr Beethoven,
>
> I waited two hours for you and then had to leave for Vienna. Would you please send my 30 florins to Herr Reed in the Klepperstall?
>
> M. Kritz

I could have cried. I could have taken vengeance upon the little blue-eyed soldier staring innocently at my puzzled face. But instead (once again) I took refuge in music. Fortunately, my legless Broadwood was sitting right side up, balanced upon two heavy cartons. I opened its lid and placed an old kitchen chair at the keyboard. As I seated myself, I turned toward the little private and commanded him in the deep authoritative voice of a "generalissimo":

B. So you think you're a soldier? . . . Very well! Let's see how you obey orders. When I start playing, I want you to march over there toward the fountain. When the music stops, you're to do an about-face and stand at attention. When the music resumes, you're to march back to me. Understand?

He nodded his head affirmatively and stood as erect as Gunga Din. This little game provided me an excuse for trying out my new march, the one whose composition had so filled my day's journey. Though I couldn't hear the actual tones, I'm sure that the next half hour contained the best improvisation of my Earthly career. Never had I been so completely caught up in the spirit of my own music. Though I did feel a bit like the Pied Piper of Hamelin, I wasn't actually surprised by the sociological reactions to this music. The little soldier carried out his instructions implicitly. As he repeated his maneuver, he was joined by a comrade, then by another. Soon all eight had joined in the march. Then came some older boys, and finally a half-dozen men who swelled our ranks by cymbals, two drums, a bugle, a trumpet, and a trombone. What a parade! Then suddenly the marchers stopped in their tracks and stared in the same direction.

Dropping my hands to my lap, I looked over my other shoulder to see what had caused the interruption. There, two doors down, a big red-faced man was shouting instructions from a second-story window. Apparently, his apartment was the one that Bernard had rented for me, and its owner was requesting the marchers to carry my belongings upstairs. This must have been the case, for when I resumed playing, this is exactly what they did! Each one, still marching in perfect step with the music, picked up something, carried it inside, and then marched back for another armful. In about ten minutes, everything was moved in except my piano and the two large crates supporting it. As soon as the march ended, these also were efficiently transported, leaving nothing for Beethoven to carry up but the kitchen chair from which he had directed his "army." I turned and examined the street to see if anything had been left behind. Nothing had been—nothing except that first little soldier. He sat there on the dusty curb, having something more to say. With a disarming smile and blue eyes bigger than ever, he seemed to be telling me that he'd thoroughly enjoyed himself and that he hoped we could do it all over again soon. I smiled down at him, winked, and handed him a tiny bag of chocolates that I had brought from Vienna in my coat pocket.

That evening at the Red Ox, after a gluttonous meal of boiled bacon and roasted capons, I treated my adult movers to a joyous bacchanalian feast. Unfortunately, I think I drank more than all my guests put together. I couldn't remember when I had laughed so much. I must have presented a gay old picture—sitting there drinking wine, drinking beer, eating hard-boiled eggs, and smoking my long-stemmed pipe.

It was about 3:00 AM when I finally staggered upstairs to my new apartment. The view of the night sky was so tempting that I pushed the feather-mattressed bed flush with the sill and plunked down crosswise with my head practically out of the window. What beautiful inspiration! A dainty new moon crested her way toward the Carpathians. How deliciously the clear summer night communicated with my upturned face. As I lay there breathing in all time and eternity,

I felt like the wisest of men. At this very moment, what couldn't I have told Socrates, Plato . . . Goethe? I seemed to understand all things!

As I thought back upon the day's happenings, it didn't seem strange to me that these peasants had reacted to my music in the way they did. You must realize that what I "heard" that day was not the silence of a deaf man, nor the crotchety technique of a rusty virtuoso. What I "heard" was the fully orchestrated *Alla Marcia*, which in three years would sing to heaven from the final movement of *Symphony 9.* To this day (in any decent performance of the *D-Minor*) you can hear the very sounds that inspired me on that unusual afternoon so long ago. Listen to this music carefully. . . . Start your feet going to its infectious rhythm. . . . And then ask yourself if you honestly wouldn't have done the same for old Beethoven had *you* been a resident of Unterdöbling in the summer of 1821, when the little parade marched by.

The following September, I migrated to Baden under Staudenheim's orders to take a full treatment of thirty baths and to replace the beer and wine in my diet by unlimited quantities of Johannes spring water. For me, such a cure was worse than the ailment. But at least my liver didn't think so. It responded favorably to the dull diet, and within four weeks, my sickly yellow was replaced by the golden tan of an open-field peasant.

All summer I had been working very hard on the *Missa*. My only diversion was to work very hard on the sonatas. Suddenly, on the morning of September seventeenth, I reached a breaking point. I felt that if I wrote one more note, my brain would explode! The best thing for me to do was to go for a long walk and completely forget about music. I donned the eternal gray coat that by now had truly reached beggarly proportions. Taking no chances of being caught up by some wayside inspiration, I even emptied its pockets of sketchbook and pencil.

It didn't matter which direction I took; I decided to follow my nose. After an hour or so of post route, I crossed through a dusty sun-crisped field, entered the refreshing cool of a thick pine forest, and then for miles and miles followed the deserted towpath of a little canal. Toward evening, I ended up at the canal's basin, which framed the picturesque hamlet of Ungerthor. Since I was famished and dead tired, I went looking for food and a coach back to Baden. As I searched from house to house, I couldn't find anyone but little children. Where was the adult population?

At the end of the block, I came to a flower-laden cottage with a half-open door. I entered its carefully hedged yard, walked up a sandy path, and peered inside. There I discovered a large cheerful parlor with beamed ceiling and floor, painted walls, fluffy curtains, and cozy furniture—but still no adult human being. I then walked to the side of the cottage and peered into its kitchen window. My nose had not deceived me. There on a cutting board were four loaves of fresh-baked bread. They smelled so delicious that I decided then and there to purchase one of them for my evening meal, and was prepared to offer a thousand florins and the dedication of my *MIssa.* As I stood there planning my next move, I sensed someone coming up behind me and was quite surprised when he turned out to be a policeman.

B. Officer! . . . You're just the man I was looking for. Could you tell me where I might find some decent food and public transportation to Baden?

The constable said something (which, of course, I didn't hear) and motioned for me to follow him. As we walked along, my thoughts bubbled over with tempting visions of tasty home cooking and a comfortable ride home. You can imagine my surprise when, after a dozen blocks, we came to an old stone building that looked more like a watchtower than a restaurant. As we climbed its eroded steps, I recognized it as the local jail. Convinced that my escort was bringing me here to make arrangements for the trip home, I turned and spoke in an attempt at levity:

B. So you're going to arrest Beethoven, are you?

He looked at me and said something, but there wasn't the trace of a smile. We walked down a long narrow corridor, turned left, and entered an enormous damp room, which was almost as poorly lighted as the corridor. In this room, there were three other policemen and one who appeared to be the "king of constables," seated at a large black desk. My companion took me by the arm and led me before the "king." For several minutes, I stood there in deaf silence while the two of them were discussing (presumably) my meal and trip home. At last the "chief of law and order" turned to me and spoke. I politely waved my hand in interruption.

B. You'll have to write what you say, for I am totally deaf.

He fumbled through his desk and came up with a dirty old envelope. On the back of it he wrote:

SP. HAVE YOU ANY IDENTIFICATION?
B. I am Beethoven!

His fat neck folded over his collar as he jerked his head toward me in a look of total disbelief. Still staring at me, he pointed again to his question. In somewhat stronger tones, I replied with a question of my own:

B. Would the sketches of a new Beethoven sonata convince you that I am Beethoven?

He nodded assent as my hand fell to the familiar spot in my ragged left pocket. . . . Empty! There was nothing in it but a crumbled zwieback. Now I remembered! In my determination to abandon music for a day, I had left the sketchbook at home on my bed in the Rathausgasse. I swallowed clumsily and resumed speaking:

B. I didn't bring my sketches today. . . . But you must believe me! I am Beethoven from Vienna. I'm visiting Baden under the advice of my physician, Dr. Staudenheim. What's the fuss about? All I want is some decent food and transportation home!

My interrogator picked up his brown envelope and wrote again:

SP. SINCE YOU HAVE NO IDENTIFICATION, WE CONCLUDE THAT YOU'RE A VAGABOND AND MUST PLACE YOU UNDER ARREST UNTIL YOU ARE EXAMINED BY THE COMMISSIONER OF POLICE.
B. I am Beethoven! . . . You'll do nothing of the kind!
SP. I AM "NAPOLEON" AND ORDER YOU TO GO PEACEABLY WITH THESE OFFICERS.

By the time I finished reading this last comment, I felt a policeman at each elbow. They "assisted" me away from "Napoleon's" desk and, in spite of my dragging heels, carried me swiftly toward a fearsome iron door. As we left the hearing room, I turned and (with burning face) shouted at the fat-necked chief, "You'll be sorry for this foolery. . . . Archduke Rudolph will hear of it, and so will the Emperor. . . . Then you'll have my foot up your ass!"

Two barred gates opened and closed. I found myself in a tiny cell containing a stone-soft bed, a small table, and a defiant three-legged stool. As soon as I realized what had happened, I unleashed a screaming hour of choice Beethoven profanity that must have convinced my captors that I was indeed a ragamuffin. No one paid the slightest attention to me—no one but an old white-bearded man in the opposite cell. By the looks of his toothless grin, he seemed to enjoy (and agree with) each syllable of my heinous damnings. Presently, even *he* grew tired listening and disappeared into the dimness of his cell. I stretched out on the unyielding cot to give my feet and voice a rest. Through a narrow slit of a window I could see the first stars of evening as they studded the bluish blackness of a clear September sky. It was now quite dark in my cell. The only light came from two yellow-flamed torches that were bracketed to the archway of the corridor. I sat there pondering the strange irony of my fate. The Great Mogul devotes his life to freeing music from its bondage, and now he himself is a prisoner. I wondered about the countless beggars who had spent a night upon this bed. I thought about Karl, about Schindler, about my present labors on the *Missa*. I wondered what Ries was doing at this very minute, probably in bed with his beautiful wife. What about London? If I went there, would they arrest me as a vagabond?

Suddenly I was back in Bonn, thoughtfully peering out of our narrow window in the Fischer house. The delightful sights and smells—they were all still there. I could even hear the voice of Father Rhine as he moved on quietly about his business, thinking his eternal thoughts, and reconciling all mankind to his gigantic soul. How beautiful were the green fields, gently sloping to the water's edge. On the opposite bank, sleeping behind their thickening shrouds of evening mist, were the willows, the fruit trees, the poplars. What a refreshing sight! I thought of the Breunings, of my bashful love for sweet Eleonore. How happy she must now be, married to Wegeler. Did they ever think of me? What would they say of my present predicament? This last question rekindled my indignation, and I walked toward the cell door with every intention of ripping it from its hinges.

Before my hands reached the bars, I noticed an increase of light in the corridor. It was caused by a handsome young guard who brought me an evening meal consisting of bread, jam, and a pitcher of cool milk. He entered the cell and leaned against the bars while I gulped down food and drink. This wasn't exactly what I had had in mind for supper, but it tasted too good for me to complain. I masked my busy jaws in a broad smile and tried to be tactful.

B. Look here, young man. Surely a fine chap like yourself will understand. I am Beethoven. I've never done anything wrong and have no business being here in jail. I've been working very hard on my greatest composition, and this morning I simply reached the point where I had to go for a long, long walk. When I go for a walk, I go for a walk. I don't first prepare a carefully certified statement identifying me as Beethoven! Your chief tells me that I must be examined by the commissioner. Very well! Bring him to me now, and we'll get the matter over with.

The handsome fellow left with my empty plate and pitcher. He immediately returned with a little note, which, by the light of his torch, I was able to read through the bars:

Guard. I AM NOW OFF DUTY AND WILL GO TO THE COMMISSIONER ON YOUR BEHALF.

This friendly declaration brought such peace of mind that I actually dozed for an hour. The return of his light awakened me to read another note. How different in tone from the first!

Guard. I JOURNEYED ALL THE WAY TO THE TAVERN ZUM SCHLEIFEN IN ORDER TO SPEAK WITH THE COMMISSIONER. HE SAID THAT HE WILL COME AND EXAMINE YOU IN THE MORNING.

B. Surely you don't expect Beethoven to spend the night here?

The tall officer shrugged his shoulders and walked away, taking his light with him.

This triggered another extended outburst from Beethoven. I cursed and screamed and tore the legs from the stool. With these I attacked the cell door. What a tragicomic picture! Mozart's successor, pounding out the ugliest tune of his career on a giant "glockenspiel," whose hammers were the legs of an old stool and whose bells were the bars of a prison door! At last my fortissimos were answered by my squat policeman, who came prepared with a note:

SP. WE MUST PUT AN END TO YOUR SCREAMING. SHORT OF RELEASING YOU, WHAT WOULD YOU HAVE ME DO?

B. This town is Ungerthor, is it not?

The little guard nodded.

B. Very well. I happen to know that Herzog, Musical Director in Wiener Neustadt, lives close by. He must be brought to identify me at once!

SP. IT IS NEARLY ELEVEN O'CLOCK!

B. I don't give a damn what time it is. I'll not spend the night in this rat hole!

My questionable pocket watch showed "twelve" when the commissioner and Herzog finally arrived. The latter grabbed the guard's torch and held it aloft as he entered my cell to complete what was to him an obviously distasteful examination. Herzog was an angry-looking man. His peaceful slumbers had been interrupted by a trip to jail for the specific purpose of refuting the mad claims of an impostor. His expression abruptly changed to one of joy and mirth as he discovered the turbulent jailbird to be none other than his old friend from the Paternostergässchen. Beethoven was also an angry-looking man. His innocent day's walk had been ridiculously terminated by imprisonment. However, the composer's expression (as well) changed to one of joy and mirth as he observed the comical proof of the Director's sudden extraction from bed. Nearly falling from his tousled head was an extraordinary brownielike nightcap, and below his partially buttoned coat hung at least six inches of telltale nightgown. We burst into laughter and met in a hearty embrace!

Herzog immediately took me from prison to his home, where I spent the rest of the night in his very best room. Next morning, something sad—Beethoven and his old gray coat finally parted their ways. At the foot of the bed, I discovered that my dauntless companion had been replaced by an entirely new outfit, complete from shirt to shoes. At breakfast, we were joined by the Burgomaster who nearly choked over his excessive apologies, and then offered me free transportation to Baden in nothing less than the magisterial coach!

Herzog and the little group of dignitaries accompanied me to the marketplace where the "royal" coach, its drivers, and team of four were waiting in the shade of the watchhouse. How like the Great

Mogul I must have appeared, as I sat there in the plush seat, chin high and eyes squinting defiantly from under my new silk hat. The Burgomaster concluded his apologies by making a short speech to the inquisitive crowd who had gathered about the coach. He must have said nice things about me, for while he spoke, a young peasant lady looked up with tears in her eyes and handed me a large wicker basket. I thanked her and placed it on the seat beside me, assuming it to be food for the trip home. The coach lurched forward; I waved good-bye. Within a few minutes, Ungerthor and its jail had disappeared behind green hills and a cloud of dust. After several miles, my thoughts turned to the lunch basket. I removed its serviette, and what do you think I found there? Two delicious loaves of fresh baked bread!

The following spring, I enjoyed my first, though indirect, contact with a young composer who was then struggling to establish a career in Vienna. Apparently, this gifted colleague preferred to admire me from afar, or perhaps he feared my direct judgment of his talent. At any rate, he took great care to deliver the first sample of his work when I was not at home. On the morning of April twenty-fifth, I discovered that my scoring of the *MIssa* was up to date. Whetting my appetite for further *suffering* in the "choral department," I decided to spend a few days on the *Diabelli Variations*. Armed with a new sketchbook and three sharp pencils, I stormed out of the Hauptstrasse_for an all-day's composing-walk. It was nearly 6:00 PM when I returned to the apartment and found Karl busily practicing at the Broadwood:

B. What's this? You'll be a pianist in spite of yourself!

He motioned for me to come and sit at his left on the bench. I carefully followed the printed page while he played. It turned out to be the Primo to a set of delightful variations for piano, four hands. The second time through, I joined my nephew by playing the Secondo.

B. Who *is* this gifted melodist?

I thumbed for the title page, but before I could open to it, Karl's hand darted out and held the score tightly against the music rack. His happy smile told me that he wished to surprise me. We played the entire set a third time; by now I could "hear" all the parts and enjoyed them immensely. At last Karl went for a slate, still greedily clutching the variations:

Ka. THE OLD WITCH TELLS ME THAT SHE ANSWERED THE DOOR TO A SHY YOUNG MAN WITH DARK CURLY HAIR AND STRANGE-LOOKING GLASSES. HE SAID THAT THE SCORE WAS A PRESENT FOR YOU AND THAT HE HOPED SOMEDAY TO GET YOUR OPINION OF IT. WHAT DO YOU THINK, UNCLE? IS IT GOOD MUSIC?

B. I hear a few unusual voice leadings and some weak developments, which I would have handled better. But with such a divine spark of melody, this man need apologize to no one!

Ka. MAY WE PLAY THEM AGAIN?

B. Yes. But first you must tell me who he is.

Karl opened the music to its title page, where I read, "Variations on a French Song, Dedicated to Herr Ludwig van Beethoven by his Worshipper and Admirer, Franz Schubert."

The time had come for *Fidelio*'s next wave of popularity. Naturally I was determined to ride its crest into the podium. Schindler (who by now had given up his study of law in order to be a violinist and full-time worshipper of Beethoven) objected strenuously:

Sc. MAESTRO, SURELY YOU DON'T INTEND TO CONDUCT!

B. And why not?

Sc. HAVE YOU FORGOTTEN A MONTH AGO, AT THE JOSEPHSTADT THEATER?

B. That was different. Consecration of the House was ruined by the alterations in Kotzebue's text. The words didn't fit the music; the music didn't fit the words. No conductor could have saved *that* day!

Sc. IT CLEARLY SHOWED THAT YOUR EARS WILL NOT PERMIT YOU TO CONDUCT LARGE BODIES OF PERFORMERS.

B. Nonsense! Consecration was an "occasional" piece; *Fidelio* is my favorite child! I've loved her since the day she was born, and know her backwards and forwards. If I were deaf *and* blind, she'd give me no trouble!

Sc. YOU MAKE A BIG MISTAKE.

B. There's nothing to worry about, "Papageno." If the singers get out of hand, Umlauf will be there breathing down my neck. He'll take care of them.

The revival of my opera on November third was a benefit performance for Wilhelmine Schröder. After my death, this young girl of seventeen was to become world-famous as Madame Schröder-Devrient, the greatest of all the "*Fidelio*s." My limited conducting for this event was at dress rehearsal on the afternoon of the third. We began with the overture, which went beautifully. Though I couldn't hear a note, I was able to keep things together by carefully watching for important entries, especially in the strings. When it was over (and as the curtain rose), I turned and looked at Schindler as if to say, "You see? . . . Things aren't going to be so bad." Then came the first duet. I slackened my beat, which, of course, the orchestra followed. Apparently the singers went on their merry way. In a few minutes, we had such confusion that Umlauf stopped the performance. As soon as I discovered what had happened, I turned and stared at the conductor. He kept his nose buried in the score. Not knowing what else to do, I tapped my baton on the music stand:

B. May we begin again? . . . From the beginning!

At the same scene by the jailor's lodge gate, an identical breakdown occurred. I looked to the right . . . to the left . . . onstage . . . into the orchestra. No one's eyes would meet mine. It was as though the players, the singers, and Umlauf (individually and collectively) were trying to say, "Go home, poor wretch. . . . We like your music, but we have no use for a deaf man!"

I felt a huge lump come into my parched throat; my knees trembled. With an unprecedented emotional composite (fear, suspicion, hatred, humiliation, self-pity), I stumbled over to Schindler, handing him my sketchbook and pencil:

B. Tell me! . . . What's wrong?

Using eight little words, this gaunt factotum reached out and "ever so gently" quartered my heart:

Sc. PLEASE DO NOT GO ON; MORE AT HOME.

Throughout a silent, melancholy meal, I stared at Schindler without seeing him. I was too busy contemplating my future. What would I experience as a nonparticipating musician? What would it be like to face a public who on the one hand appreciated my music, but on the other had little use for an old musician too crippled to play or conduct?

This dilemma caused me to seek help from my estranged brother:

B. Johann! Do you realize what this cruel blow means to me? . . . It was one thing to give up a fine career as pianist, but now I find that deafness has robbed me of my baton as well. What am I to do? . . . I no longer have *any* contact with my public. . . . How am I to find pleasure in music?

I handed Johann my sketchbook and pencil:

J. YOUR MUSIC BRINGS PLEASURE TO *OTHERS*; IT WILL BRING PLEASURE TO *YOU*! . . . IF YOU CAN NO LONGER PLAY OR CONDUCT IT, THEN YOU MUST FIND YOUR JOY IN COMPOSING IT. . . . VIENNA HAS GREAT RESPECT FOR YOU *AND* YOUR MUSIC.

B. Thanks, Johann. Thanks for refocusing my life's true goal. . . . We finite creatures with infinite spirits are born to suffer and to rejoice, and one could almost say that only the most excellent derive joy from suffering.

J. HOW DOES ONE FIND JOY THROUGH SUFFERING?

B. It is my belief that art is a way of communicating knowledge about reality. The more I suffer, the sharper my perception of this reality becomes . . . the more I have to *say* in my art . . . the more I *grow* as an artist.

J. IS DEAFNESS THE CAUSE OF YOUR SUFFERING?

B. No! . . . Deafness is merely a symbol of the isolation required for my composing. . . . It's probably a blessing in disguise. . . . For some inexplicable reason, I know that I have reached the final plateau of my career . . . that the songs I now sing will be my last.

J. YOU ARE WELL, AND MUSTN'T TALK OF DYING.

B. Within the next few years, wait and see. . . .This is why I come to you today. As death approaches and the fickle world turns completely from me, I must be assured that at least my brother will be there to close my eyes. . . . But don't worry, Johann. Apollo and the Muses will not yet deliver me into the hands of death. I still owe them so very much. Before my departure to the Elysian Fields, I must leave behind all that with which I'm inspired, and which I must complete. . . . Even so, dear Brother, it seems as though I have hardly begun to write.

Chapter 22

I come now to the story of *Symphony 9*—my last and greatest. The details of its composition and première are the main theme for the years 1823 and 1824.

You'll recall that Prince Galitzin had commissioned three string quartets at 50 ducats apiece. To compose these was my chief creative aspiration. What I now longed to say seemed best suited to the intimacies of this perfectly balanced medium. . . . However, *Symphony 9* was given priority over the quartets for the simple reason that its composition (and accompanying trip to London) promised far greater financial rewards than those offered by the prince. And at this time, I was desperately in need of cash to pay off my debts, also to provide for Karl's future and my own. I was determined to breathe into this symphony the best sonata-allegro, the best scherzo, and the best adagio ever composed for full orchestra by Beethoven. . . . Alas, this composition met with its full share of obstacles: I was still adding notes to the *MIssa,* my *Diabelli Variations* were not completed until April 1823, and my final piano sonata remained "in-process" throughout this time period. Financial difficulties were ever present: I still owed large sums to Franz Brentano, to Lind the tailor, and to Steiner. The latter threatened to sue me unless I either paid off my debt or assigned all future compositions to his firm. To raise cash, I sold one of my eight bank shares. The other seven were hidden away with the solemn resolution that I would endure starvation and even a return to jail rather than deprive Karl of his inheritance.

On the first day of 1823, Czerny's brilliant eleven-year-old pupil, Franz Liszt, made his pianistic debut. Schindler brought the boy and his father for a visit. It so happened that I was currently suffering from very sore eyes. Consequently, I composed using an improvised eye shade and with my desk flush against the window. This meant that my back was facing the door and that it was impossible for anyone to approach me frontally. Since I disliked being interrupted second only to being surprised, a visitor at this time was truly jeopardizing his pride, if not his life! Schindler and his guests were no exception. I jumped nearly a foot when he tapped me on the shoulder:

B. Damn it! Papageno! . . . Why do you disturb me? Go away until I finish my symphony!

Sc. YOUNG FRANZ LISZT AND HIS FATHER HAVE COME TO SEE YOU.

B. Who in the hell are *they*?

Sc. YOU REMEMBER! CARL CZERNY IS HIS TEACHER.

I pushed the eye shade higher on my forehead and gave the doorway a squinting examination. Sure enough, there stood a handsome young lad and a very distinguished gentleman. The latter stepped forward with courtly politeness, bowed, and then reached for Schindler's Conversation Book. As he wrote, I couldn't help noticing his marked pallor and trembling hand—no doubt the results of my sudden outburst:

FL. I HAVE OFTEN EXPRESSED THE WISH TO HERR VON SCHINDLER TO MAKE YOUR HIGH ACQUAINTANCE, AND AM REJOICED TO BE ABLE NOW TO DO SO. AS WE SHALL GIVE A CONCERT ON SUNDAY THE 13TH, WE MOST HUMBLY BEG YOU TO GIVE US YOUR HIGH PRESENCE.

B. Herr Liszt, I appreciate your respect and your invitation. But these days (with ears like mine) I attend very few concerts. There is little pleasure to be had in the act of watching others make beautiful music and hearing not a tone of it yourself. Someday when I'm not so busy, I'll have Czerny bring me your little son. But for the present, I must return to my scherzo.

Return I did, so abruptly that I didn't even notice the father and son leave my study. In a few minutes, Schindler tapped again, and I jumped another foot.:

B. What do you want *now*?
Sc. YOU WERE VERY RUDE TO OUR VISITORS. AND TO THINK THAT THEY BOTH WORSHIP YOU LIKE A GOD!
B. *Our* visitors? You mean *your* visitors! I can't remember inviting either of them. And when I need your opinion concerning the treatment of intruders in my own house, I'll *ask* you for it! ... Now *go away*!!

Ignaz Schuppanzigh returned to Vienna after spending seven years in Russia. In April 29, he came for an evening visit that occasioned an extraordinary bacchanal! Our celebration at the Swan Inn lasted until two o'clock in the morning. For seven hours we talked over old times and gorged ourselves on an endless supply of fish, fried oysters, Vöslauer, Melniker, and champagne. He was shocked by the totality of my deafness, couldn't get used to the idea of writing everything down. When I described my new symphony, old "Falstaff" seemed so anxious to hear it that I promised him that he would be the one to conduct its première. He was also excited about my "stringy" commission from Galitzin and promised to resume his quartet meetings within a few weeks. Toward the end of the bacchanalian feast, our dialogue became thoroughly wine-soaked. "Milord" couldn't understand how I managed to go on living without a wife. He wrote on my pad:

Sp. CZERNY KNOWS A WIDOW WHO LOVES BEETHOVEN AND WANTS TO MARRY HIM.
B. Frau Stramm, I suppose?

Schuppanzigh nodded his huge round face and the assortment of chins connected to it:

B. Forget the matter! She was his *mistress*, not his *wife*.

"Milord" grinned like the devil, and turned a satanic red as he wrote his next question:

Sp. WOULD YOU LIKE TO SLEEP WITH *MY* WIFE?

B. Be careful! I'm not as old as you think. These gray hairs are premature.

We laughed and joked until my boisterous profanity became too much even for Schuppanzigh. Our party was over. As we staggered from the Swan, I could hardly stand on my feet. My pregnant-looking "Falstafferel" accompanied me all the way home to the Oberepfarrgasse. There on the doorstep, I bade him good night with a most dubious farewell. What must the Obermayers have thought when they heard Johann's famous brother screaming in the night:

B. I wish you open bowels plus a handsome and convenient stool!

The very next morning, I had Czerny bring young Liszt to see me. How handsome he looked with his beaming face, his ever-changing expression, and his shoulder-length reddish-brown hair. The latter was combed straight as a whistle and was kept constantly in motion by the delicate movements of his head. I couldn't get over the young fellow's eyes—worshipful to be sure, but also extremely alert and keen. He never removed their intelligent gaze from my face. To break his apparent shy spell, I walked over, shook his hands, and held them up to examine their magnificent pianistic qualifications:

B. And where does a little boy get such big hands? With these, you must span an octave and a fifth!

He laughed in reply.

B. Come, play something for me. What have you prepared?

Czerny held up a slate.

Cz. He will play the Rondo in G by Ries.

As Liszt played, it was easy to read the enjoyment in his face, for he never took his eyes from mine. When he finished, I stroked his beautiful hair and inquired if he knew any Bach. Czerny replied on the slate:

Cz. He knows the entire *Well-Tempered Clavichord*. Which piece would you have him play?

B. Play the *C Minor Fugue.* I think it's my favorite.

Bach was as easy for him as the Rondo. At my request and without the slightest difficulty, he transposed the fugue into F-sharp Minor. I was so pleased with the results that I bent over and whispered in his right ear:

B. Devil of a fellow! . . . And such a rascal!

He then took the slate himself, wrote, and blushingly held it up for me to read:

Lz. MAY I NOW PLAY SOMETHING OF YOURS?

I nodded and smiled. After watching his hands carefully for a few minutes, I detected the first movement of my *C Major Concerto.* As its final measures were approached, I walked over and stood behind the prodigy, ready (in Mozartian fashion) to slap my hands on his shoulders. This I did, and followed it up with a kiss on his forehead. I then spoke a few words to the promising lad, which I sincerely hoped would mean as much to *him* as Mozart's words have meant to *me*:

B. Young man, you must wonder what a deaf old musician can possibly hear in your playing. But I must tell you. I have learned to hear with my eyes! And what they have just heard pleases me very much. Everything that Czerny tells me about you is true. I know that you're a very happy fellow because of the joy and happiness you bring to others. What more could one do than this? Now, off with you!

Johann had invited me to spend my vacation at his estate near Gneixendorf. But I preferred to remain closer to Vienna. The new symphony was literally "extracted" from the fields and pastures of Hetzendorf. Six years of clumsy sketches, which had refused to budge one way or another, suddenly melted and ran into beautiful music—this under the divine magic of pastoral inspiration, and in spite of my sore eyes and endless correspondence with Schindler over the *Missa* manuscript. By the end of the summer, my *Ninth Symphony* was completed, except for its *Choral Finale.* By the end of this same year, the choral movement of *Symphony 9* was pretty well sketched out. Even so, not until late February 1824 was the last note of my last symphony finally placed in score, an event that I felt "old man death" could well prevent happening.

In December of 1822, the London Philharmonic Society had remitted £50 in fulfillment of *their* part of our agreement. They did so in the good faith that a symphony would soon arrive and bring with it my guarantee of eighteen months' exclusive performance rights. At last on April 27, 1824, a copy of *Symphony 9* was sent to the Londoners. Sad to relate, six weeks before the score had begun its journey, I had already decided to give locally a Grand Musical Concert, which (in direct breach of contract) would feature this very symphony, as well as portions of the *Missa*. What an *honest* fellow I was becoming!

The date of my *backhanded* concert was set for May seventh, to begin at seven o'clock in the evening. The program would commence with a grand overture, to be followed by three sections from the *Missa*, and to conclude with *Symphony 9*. Two lovely enchantresses, Henriette Sontag and Karoline Unger, were named as soprano and alto soloists. Anton Haitzinger and Kurt Seipelt were chosen as tenor and bass. The orchestral conductor would be Schuppanzigh, and the entire performance placed in the hands of Herr Kapellmeister Umlauf.

With only eight days until curtain time, we all settled down to the serious business of rehearsing. Dirzka was in charge of choral practice. Schuppanzigh met daily with orchestral players in the rehearsal room of the Ridotto. The soloists were invited each morning to my Landstrasse apartment, where Umlauf and I carefully supervised their progress.

Our final rehearsal lasted until 2:00 PM, singing through all the parts with many repetitions and, for the first time, in tempo. Umlauf directed the singers, I pounded the Broadwood. Frequently in my excitement, I outpounded everyone in the room, only to be tapped on the shoulder and "shhh'ed" in the direction of a pianissimo by Herr Kapellmeister. Halfway through our third and still unsuccessful rendition of the *Allegro ma non tanto*, Henriette stopped singing. She came over and most invitingly plunked herself down on my bench. After depositing a dainty kiss on my right cheek, smoothing my hair, and staring me into a smile, the enchanting nymph picked up a slate and "spoke":

HS. WON'T YOU PLEASE BE A GOOD MAESTRO AND TAKE BACK SOME OF YOUR HIGH As?

B. There's nothing so high about these As. Any sweet young soprano like yourself should manage them perfectly well.

HS. NOT WHEN THEY'RE SO FAST!

B. When we sing of "Joy, thou daughter of Elysium," we can't mumble along in the slow tempo and the muddy range of a dirge! It is Schiller himself who calls for high As here.

HS. ROSSINI NEVER CONFRONTS US WITH SUCH TYRANNY!

B. Rossini is a potato peddler, I'm an artist! There's a difference. Let's try it again, my dear. Everything will be all right. Concentrate on the music, and don't worry about how high you are or how fast you're going.

Later in our practice session, Haitzinger was met with a crushing obstacle in his *Alla Marcia.* After a series of annoying reattempts, he grabbed my slate and registered his complaint:

Hz. YOUR ACCOMPANIMENT . . . IT'S TOO LOUD AND TOO INDEPENDENT OF MY PART. I CAN'T KEEP THE RHYTHMS SEPARATE.

I stared at him with great contempt.

B. Haitzinger, why don't you try biting your nose? I think you're a coward and a bastard! Something difficult comes up, and you run away. I know some little boys at Unterdöbling who march to this tune better than you sing to it. Come over here. . . . I'll show you how it's done.

All present gathered round the "Mogul" while he improvised for twenty minutes on the *Alla Marcia.* The poor tenor was then once again clamped in Beethoven's stare.

B. You see, Haitzinger? There's nothing to it. First you must really hear the accompaniment, get caught up in the spirit of what it says. . . . Then the vocal part is bound to fit. Let me show you.

From all of Beethoven's days on Earth, I'm sure this was his classic example of going out on a limb. The tree was very tall, the saw was very sharp. The only singing I had done in thirty-five years was the horrible screeching that usually accompanied my sketching and brought teeth-grinding complaints from all within earshot. And now with such a bad old voice, I blindly (and deafly) waded into the roughest section of the entire choral movement. I'm sure you know what happened next. It was very difficult to play this accompaniment and at the same time try to sing the tenor part. Twice I got off the track, but managed to jerk myself back on again. And then embarrassingly, at the very spot where Haitzinger had failed, I became so tongue-tied and finger-twisted that I could do nothing but stop singing, stop playing, and drop my hands in my lap. For a long silent minute, my eyes beamed from face to face, settling once again upon the frightened tenor.

B. Haitzinger! Who could have written such damned nonsense?

Instantaneously, all six of us cleared the air with an explosion of laughter. Then instead of Haitzinger presenting me with a hard-earned and well-deserved "I told you so," he erased the slate and stunned me with words of exceptional modesty:

Hz. NOW THAT I'VE REALLY HEARD THE ACCOMPANIMENT, I DO UNDERSTAND IT BETTER. I'D LIKE TO TRY SINGING THIS AGAIN.

We performed the *Alla Marcia* three times without a mishap. And I could see by our tenor's face that he'd caught the spirit of the music and the words.

Two days later, Karl came running home from the Ridotto, his eyes filled with tears. He gave me a big hug, and when he finally calmed down, I asked him what was the matter. Still with tears in his eyes, he told me that for the first time he had just heard Schuppanzigh's regiment of strings play the *Andante moderato,* that it was the most beautiful piece I had ever written, that he was grateful to me for including it in the symphony, and that hearing it played by the orchestra had made him proud to be my son. Can such a boy be bad? Perhaps he does waste time. Perhaps he does enjoy his trips to the Lusthaus. But there's good in any young man who has the sensitivity to respond to music in this way.

Duport had planned for two full rehearsals, but the second had to be canceled because of its conflict with ballet practice. This meant that Henriette and Karoline were present for only the single rehearsal of May sixth.

Next evening at concert time, every seat was taken except those in the Imperial box. Schindler and I had gone in person to invite the Imperial family, but they were to be out of town for two weeks starting May fourth, and my idolatrous Archduke was still at Olmütz. Though poor Count Zmeskall was now so invalided that he had to be carried to his seat in a sedan chair, I knew he'd be there. Nothing but a deathbed could keep old "Greedygut" from my first important concert in ten years. Nevertheless, during intermission I stepped into the parquet to shake his hands and to tell him how much his presence there really meant to me.

The first half of the program passed routinely enough. I was led onstage by Umlauf and Schuppanzigh; there was applause. The overture and hymns were received politely via more applause. The miracle of the evening occurred after intermission in the world première of *Symphony 9.*

As before, I entered stage with Umlauf and Schuppanzigh, the soloists having already seated themselves directly in front of the podium. Umlauf sat down to the left of the conductor's stand, having little to do until the choral section was reached. My chair and music rack (facing the orchestra) were to the right, within arm's reach of Fräulein Unger. As with earlier pieces this evening, I took the podium to conduct a few opening measures of the symphony's first movement, thereby establishing its tempo. For years I had planned a section such as this—an orchestral piece in which the instruments entered a few at a time, until a tutti was reached just before the first full statement of the main theme. I was so delighted with what was going on before me that the mere mechanics of the orchestration became like "music" to my deaf ears. Only by exerting the utmost willpower was I able to hand over my baton to Schuppanzigh in time for the recap of the *Sotto voce.* I returned to my designated chair and attempted to follow the orchestra in my copy of the score. Several times I was completely lost, and managed to get back "into step" only by watching for important entries. As I studied the tone lines and felt their strong vibrations through the floor, there was much in this opening movement that made me very proud: a fugal section that echoed the glories of the *Eroica,* the best balance I had yet achieved between strings and woodwinds, a rhythmic independence of voices that represented for me the efforts of a lifetime, interesting ritardandos occurring in just the right places, a delightful horn duet that was pure gold and finally, a cadence big enough and strong enough to sum up and conclude all that had gone before it. Surely when my Viennese heard these treasures, they would know that old Beethoven was not yet dead and gone—that he still had important things to say.

I returned to the podium to set the tempo for the *Scherzo* by conducting its first dozen notes. "Falstaff" nearly knocked the two of us down, getting himself into position in time for the *pianissimo* that immediately followed the opening *fortissimo*. I returned to my chair to watch (and revel in) the new and high-speed goings-on. I loved to "unhorse excellent riders," and there was no place I could better do this than in my *scherzos*. I put on my glasses and examined the musicians' faces—almost without exception, sweat on each brow. A broad grin crossed my face. It was not a sadistic grin evolving from the tense suffering of these poor musicians. I smiled rather at myself! To think that a broken-down, deaf, white-haired little old composer could be the cause of all this sweat. To think that I could be the reason for eighty men sitting galvanized to the edges of their chairs, straining every fiber of their beings in a superhuman effort to prevent the horrible (and humorous) breakdowns that had occurred two days ago from happening again this evening before the public. Not a single musician could return my stare; they were all too busy! I could tell by the sequence of ghostly pauses that we were approaching the *Ritmo di tre battute*, and decided to follow in the score. I was very proud of this particular section because, to the best of my knowledge, this was the first time in orchestral literature when the kettle drums were brought up from the basement and permitted (repeatedly) to interrupt the entire orchestra and sing a bold little song of their own. The section was of technical interest to me, but I expected it to mean little to my audience. How wrong I was!

I had tapped my way nearly to the *Ritmo di quattro battute*, when suddenly Karoline Unger pulled at my sleeve. I glanced a quick smile and a nod in her direction, then went on tapping. The little enchantress tugged again, this time much harder. I knew that something was wrong and glanced a harsh stare at what I hastily concluded was a bungling orchestra. Imagine my surprise. No bungle at all! By now the entire orchestra was standing—most were clapping, a few were tapping bows across their instruments. Before I could gather my senses, Schuppanzigh grabbed my arm and directed me toward the podium. There for the last time on Earth, the Great Mogul ascended his throne in public. He bowed once, twice . . . three times. The applause was unprecedented. People were everywhere—standing at their seats, on their seats, in the aisles. Most of the handclapping was not the refined concert-hall variety. It was that spontaneous, loud, raucous, over-the-head kind that we "peasants" engaged in so frequently at the Three Ravens. I took a fourth bow and stepped down from the platform. Still they clapped. As I returned to the podium, my vision suddenly dimmed. Was it blindness? A stroke like grandfather's? Neither! My glasses were so drenched with tears that I could no longer see through them. As I snatched them off, I thought to myself, what a strange turnabout. Through my entire career, I complained of audiences having too many tears and not enough applause. Now they gave me more plaudits than I could ever use, and I, Beethoven, supplied the tears!

Many a composer would be incensed at having his composition interrupted halfway through. Not Beethoven! He delighted in every second of the interruption, having brought from Bonn the unshakable Rhenish belief that nothing on Earth measured the responsiveness of others to his music as directly or convincingly as good, loud, boisterous applause. Such he preferred even to the ducats of princes or the gold medals of kings. As I stood there enjoying my most glorious hour, it wasn't simply a matter of petty vanity. True, I was still the Great Mogul. But I was also an artist as sincere and self-sacrificing toward my art as I knew how to be. For six years, I had given my soul and life's blood to the creation of these last symphonic works. I now presented them to my public, and miraculously they somehow knew to give me in return precisely what my heart desired. And they knew that by the spontaneous interruption of the composition itself, their applause would mean ten times more to me than had they politely waited until the end of the concert.

As I stood there soaking up this heavenly wine, the ovation told me many things. It said to me, "Dear old white-haired man, forgive us. We now clap entirely for you. Though we have gone whoring after the harlot of Italian opera, we have not forgotten you. Though we have long danced to the happy tunes of Rossini, we do remember our beloved Haydn and Mozart. We now see you as their spiritual heir, standing before us. We are surprised how little and old you are, but the spirit of your new composition is young enough to inspire our children's children. We realize that this might be the last time you will stand before us, and because of this, we must interrupt the music of the hour. We hope that our applause tells you in a way you'll understand: thank you . . . thank you for doing what you've done . . . thank you for being what you are . . . thank you from the bottom of our hearts!"

After this unmistakable embrace, Schuppanzigh began the beautiful *Adagio molto e cantabile*, my final set of variations for orchestra—the last and sincerest of them all. I only hoped that the audience would receive as much pleasure from hearing this theme, as I had gotten from working with it. In this nice slow tempo, the musicians were not so busy—no sweat-filled brows. I could glance at their faces and be glanced at in return. Though their busy instruments were silent to my ears, I could read the music in their faces. There were no looks of short-sighted jealousy, no questioning stares, no scowls complaining of more nonsense from the "mad musician." I saw men whose souls were deeply moved by the music they played—men whose eyes were not afraid to express love, understanding, respect, and appreciation.

We now reached the *Andante moderato.* Its quivering *Espressivo* for violins and violas made me think of Karl. This was the section that earlier in the week had sent him running to my arms for a tearful embrace. I stood up so that I could see over the music rack and behind the orchestra to the extreme right of the first row of tenors where my nephew and Schindler were sitting. Karl noticed me, though none of the players did. For the sake of the performance, Umlauf had warned the musicians to keep their eyes on Schuppanzigh and to ignore any and all conducting emanating from me. But this didn't matter. I knew what the little tune meant to Karl, and was determined this once to conduct it personally just for him. By watching the second violins, I could tell exactly where we were, and could hear the melody in my head. Gently I swayed back and forth to the broad rhythm of twenty bows sweeping across "silent" strings. I conducted with my carpenter's pencil, and for the first time began to suspect why the *Andante moderato* could mean so much to a sensitive boy. This then, would be my real gift to him—the lasting gift of Beethoven to his nephew. Long after our countless petty arguments and tearful reconciliations were forgotten, long after my bank shares had trickled through his fingers, long after we were both dead and gone, these little notes would remain. And any who truly heard their song would surely agree that here was the gift from a father who (in spite of his inadequacies and eccentricities) really loved his son. I could tell by watching Karl's face that he understood this. He was smiling and crying at the same time!

At the beginning of the final movement, I turned my chair around, and for the first time this evening studied audience reaction to *Symphony 9.* I wanted to watch them cringe at my sharpest orchestral dissonance since the *Eroica.* Next, I wanted to see if they recognized earlier themes as restated in an ingenious recap section used to introduce the *Joy Theme.* And finally, I was interested in their response to the *Joy Theme* itself, especially to its long initial statement in unison by cellos and basses alone. What would they think of the ensuing polyphonic development? The best (most natural) counterpoint I had written since the *Allegretto* of *Symphony 7*. After these observations, it was time to turn around and again face the orchestra. Following another fortissimo statement of my gratingly dissonant chord, the soloists and chorus were at last to stand up and sing. Needless to say, their vocal performance was a great success!

During my stay at Baden (in fact, through the rest of 1824) my sole creative project was the first of three quartets promised for so many months to Prince Galitzin. Excellent progress was made with the composition because I had few interruptions and even fewer guests at the spa.

Upon reaching my last two years of Earthly life, I felt as though I had achieved a great victory. The mountain was now fully climbed. As I inspected its craggy summit, there came to me the joyous realization that I need never again descend to the lowlands. You might as well ask, "What sort of achievement is this?" On the top of a mountain or otherwise, what good is an old musician who can neither hear, nor play, nor conduct? What sort of "victorious" life can boast neither wife nor child of its own? Certainly my attainment was not a financial one—nothing accumulated but a few bank shares, which I regarded as my nephew's personal property. Nor was my accomplishment in the sparkling realm of social conquest. Now that the glories of the Kärnthnerthor were a thing of the past, Karl's words and actions remained my sole criteria for measuring the feelings of mankind toward Beethoven. And already in his eyes and speech, I could read the growing coldness of pending teenage revolt. What then was this victory? A figment of my imagination? No, it was real enough—and (as with countless lesser victories) came about through the act of composition. After spending six months on the "First Galitzin," I could hear still newer sounds in Beethoven's music—a sort of spiritual and emotional unity that was never there before. Though all the world should crumble about me, nothing (save death itself) could now separate me from the serene happiness of the most precious gift on Earth—a creativeness approaching the divine! And best of all, there seemed to be no end to this, my new song!

Chapter 23

The year 1825 began with another invitation to visit England. It was written by Charles Neate on behalf of the Philharmonic Society of London and offered me £300 for conducting at least one Beethoven work at each concert of their coming season, and for writing a new symphony and concerto to be played during the season, but which was to remain my property. Neate estimated that £500 could be earned from a single concert of my own, and another £100 for a year's rights in the new quartets. He went on to confirm the arrival of *Symphony 9* and expressed his hope that I would come in time to conduct its première at their opening concert. I replied on January fifteenth, stating that I was well satisfied with the conditions made, however requesting that I be sent another £100 for traveling expenses. Two days later, their first rehearsal of *Symphony 9* took place, and in early February I received a second letter from Neate informing me that the Philharmonic was unable to change its original offer at the present time. He further stated that the new symphony would not be performed until the season's second concert of March twenty-first, in the hopes that I might still arrive in time. Karl, Johann, in fact, everyone in my Court advised me to go. Schuppanzigh even went so far as to volunteer his services as traveling companion. Nevertheless at this very time, I was choked by an ever-thickening smog of doubts, suspicions, and indecisions. I feared for my health and for Karl's future. I questioned the effect that my physically weakened condition would have upon the British. Things seemed too uncertain to make the trip at this time. I wrote the Society that perhaps I could come in the Fall, and this ended the matter.

You might wonder why my chief London correspondent was now Charles Neate instead of Ferdinand Ries. The explanation is simple. Ries was no longer in England. During the preceding year, he purchased an estate in Godesberg, near Bonn. How happy and proud old Franz must have been when his successful son returned home to live close by on the most beautiful tract of the entire Rhineland! My, how I would have loved such a property. But it now appeared that my destiny was not to be quite the way I wanted it. In January, I received a letter from Ries, informing me of his recent move and of his fortunate appointment as conductor of the Lower Rhenish Musical Festival. He wished to perform my *Ninth Smyphony* during these concerts and asked for an MS copy of it. I know he expected me to send it gratis, but my financial condition would not permit. Beneath the thin veneer of a weak Beethoven pun (We must satisfy our Nöthen through our Noten!), I requested 40 Louis dór for the new symphony, the *Missa*, and the new overture. Ries accepted my offer and conducted *Symphony 9* on May twenty-third, the second day of the festival. He later wrote me that there were 422 performers in the chorus and orchestra, that this work alone would have made me immortal, and that he wondered to what heights I would next lead them.

After promising the *Missa* to a half-dozen different publishers, it finally went to Schott and Sons on January eighteenth, along with my last symphony. I had also promised Schott my *Quartet in E-flat*, but did not send him this "First Galitzin" until after its première. On January twentieth, I was surprised to read in the *Theaterzeitung* that Schuppanzigh was offering a new series of quartet concerts at the Vereinssaal beim rotin Igel. What surprised me about "Milord's" notice was that he promised his subscribers a première performance of my "First Galitzin" on Sunday, January twenty-third, while there I stood with at least another month's work on this very opus! Herr "Falstaff" was immediately summoned to share with me a bottle of Seideler and a sobering side dish of cold, hard facts. I patiently explained to "the pregnant one" that my new quartet would probably not be finished until the end of February at which time it was my plan to have Linke give the première, and then hand it over to "Milord" for as many "Falstaffian" performances as his big fat heart desired. There followed a thorough discussion of the matter, and I ended up in promising Schuppanzigh the première after all, this with the understanding that the "Second Galitzin" (the *Quartet in A Minor*) would go first to Linke. At any rate, "Milord" found it necessary to substitute my *Opus 95 Quartet* for the unfinished "Galitzin" in his concert of January twety-third.

The *E-flat Quartet* was sent to Schuppanzigh only nine days before the second concert of his subscription series. Little wonder that the results were disappointing. Neither players nor public seemed to understand the "new" music, and when details of the fiasco reached my Conversation Book, I exploded and held "the fat one" directly responsible!

During Schuppanzigh's long stay in Russia, Joseph Böhm had taken "Milord's" place as first violinist with Holz, Weiss and Linke. Böhm was a professor of violin at the Vienna Conservatory and a member of the Imperial Orchestra. In my disappointment with Schuppanzigh, I now insisted that he once again step aside for Böhm, that my new quartet be scheduled for immediate reproduction under the professor's direction, and that I personally be permitted to supervise all rehearsals. This is exactly what happened. By the first week in April, the "E-flat" had received four performances under Böhm, and had met with public response that was at least encouraging!

Two of these rehearsals were attended by my publisher, and he was so impressed with the new quartet that he offered me 60 ducats for it. Nevertheless, I kept my promise to Schott, and sent him the score on April twenty-seventh, not failing to emphasize that he was receiving it for 10 ducats less than had been offered me by Steiner. In December 1824, Prince Galitzin had sent 50 ducats for this first quartet of his commission. I now thought it was high time that he receive *his* copy of the score, and mailed him one on April twentieth.

In March of this year, I came across an ideal candidate for my factotum. He was none other than Karl Holz with whom I became acquainted during his rehearsals under Böhm. For a young man of twenty-seven, he was an excellent violinist—naturally so, since he had studied under both Glöggl and Schuppanzigh. He had all the ingredients of a prime assistant: well-read, witty, a clever talker, an engaging personality, a cheerful companion, a man of firm convictions who (like Zmeskall) was not afraid to express them, well-informed in worldly affairs, good at figures, and the direct antithesis of my hesitating indecision. In short, he was another Count Waldstein, and it's no wonder that I was anxious for his friendship. I changed my factotum from Schindler to Karl Holz. Thus Holz became Factotum No. 1, and Schindler became Factotum No. 2.

Soon Holz was assisting me with correspondence and copywork, spying on Karl, advising me on financial matters, and even helping me choose the best publisher for a given opus. Though his independence of manner and speech made him less easy to contradict than Schindler, I sincerely admired this young musician. Where Waldstein had developed (literally) an appetite for young women, Holz cultivated a supreme passion for strong drink. This was the main distinction between the two men. If I should classify Schuppanzigh (or myself) as a one-bottle man and Zmeskall as a two-bottle man, then I must dub Holz as a three-bottle man, well on his way to becoming a four-bottle man. (With due respect for Shakespeare, here was a Dutchman who could outdrink an Englishman!) When I criticized Holz for his heavy drinking and for taking me on a constant round of inns and coffee houses, he said he was doing so for my benefit and that this was the only way he knew to break the terrible isolation of my existence, and to bring some cheerful thoughts into my life and music. I appreciated the young man's efforts, but he wasn't fooling me. I knew full well that his virtuous passion for wine would have developed quite independently of me and my problems—that Holz would have become a hard drinker whether or not he had ever gotten to know an old composer whose social life needed improving. By the end of 1825, this drinking companion had become Beethoven's chief factotum. In German, Holz means "wood." And since I was still a punster supreme, this man of wood was knighted into the "Realm" as "Best Mahogany" and "Best of Splinters." It would be grossly unfair to blame Holz in any way for my early death. I greatly enjoyed his companionship, and our drinking bouts were chiefly responsible for what little worldly happiness I found in the remaining days. But how could either of us have known? How could we have known that I was the possessor of a poor old liver that needed but slight encouragement to become malignant? No doubt our heavy drinking provided the encouragement. I died exactly two years from the day when I first went drinking with this "Best Splinter from the Cross of Christ."

My immediate composing project was to finish a second and third quartet for Galitzin. Not only would this provide me with a hundred gold ducats, but it would also enable me to go on working in a medium richly pregnant with endless and important things to say. In spite of these realizations, work on the "A Minor" was interrupted by a sick spell that began the third week of April. On this occasion, Staudenheim was unable to give me his attention, and I contacted Dr. Anton Braunhofer:

> My honored friend,
>
> I am feeling poorly and hope you will not deny me your help, since I am suffering great pain. Is it possible for you to visit me as early as today? This I beg of you from the bottom of my heart. With everlasting gratitude and respect, your Beethoven.

Braunhofer turned out to be an even worse "dictator" than Staudenheim. He diagnosed my ailment as a severe inflammation of the bowels, and came at me with such blunt forcefulness that I was actually frightened:

> No wine, no coffee, no spices of any kind. I'll arrange matters with the cook. . . . A sickness does not disappear in a day. I shall not trouble you much longer with medicine. But you must adhere to the diet; you'll not starve on it. . . . I'll wager that if you take a drink of spirits, you'll be lying weak and exhausted on your back in a few hours. . . . When you have been in Baden for a while, it will be better. Should there be a recurrence, let me know. . . . When are you going?

By May 7, I was sufficiently recovered to make the trip to Baden—my last vacation at the beloved spa. After two weeks of green country, fresh air, and natural milk, I was able to return to the "Second Galitzin" with renewed vigor and enjoyment. Even so, I was still plagued by servant trouble. Before the first week was out, my new housekeeper and cook were respectively (and contemptuously) referred to as the *old witch* and the *wench*!

During the spring of 1825, it became obvious that Karl was set upon leaving the University of Vienna. Rather than become a professor of languages, his greatest desire was to enter the Polytechnic Institute and, following Uncle Johann's example, receive training for a merchantile career. At first I would have none of it. My son, a huckster? Nonsense! But Karl begged and sobbed and pleaded, until he finally persuaded me to discuss the move with Johann, Peters, and Dr. Bach. All three gave their hearty approval, and encouraged me to do likewise. On Easter Monday, my nephew was enrolled at the Polytechnic, and the institute's vice-director, Dr. Reisser, was appointed coguardian in place of Peters. Since Karl's new school was on the opposite side of the city, it seemed expedient for him to move from my apartment in the Kletschka house. Accordingly, he took lodgings in the Alleegasse home of Matthias Schlemmer, who agreed to carefully supervise Karl's "after school" activities. Since the boy entered late in the term, it was necessary to provide him with a special tutor. You can imagine what all this did to the purse of an old composer—2,000 florins per year for room, board, and special tuition. But it was worth this price because Karl made good progress and, for the first time in his life, actually developed an enthusiasm for his work.

When I moved to Baden, I expected Karl to come and spend Sundays and holidays with me. He complained that regular visits took too much time from his studies, but I insisted. Naturally a conflict on this point soon developed. Why did I require such frequent visitations? When Karl came, he would run household errands, handle my correspondence, and negotiate financial transactions. But certainly he was not needed for the very things which Holz managed perfectly well. Why then? Why my inflexible insistence upon these visits? I think it was just another case of my paternal possessiveness rearing its ugly head. For me, Karl *was* humanity. Should he become an independent being and go his own way, then my sole nonmusical contact with mankind would be severed. The thought of this was unbearable. Hence my unwarranted treatment of a nineteen-year-old man!

We had not been separated for more than two weeks when I began to suspect Karl of everything imaginable. Through Reisser and Schlemmer, I tightened my prying controls to a strangling grip. Suspecting the boy of visiting his mother and other prostitutes, I instructed Schlemmer not to let him out of the house at night without a letter from me. I greatly reduced his spending money, and required a meticulous accounting of every kreutzer. It wasn't long before Karl began to weaken under the combined demands of his school and his uncle. During my summer at Baden, the independence of a grown-up nephew began asserting itself, and my letters to him swung violently between the extremes of unnatural tenderness and cruel reproach. An example of the first extreme would be:

> My precious son,
>
> Go no further. Come but to my arms; not a harsh word shall you hear. O God, do not rush away in your misery. You will be received as lovingly as ever. What to consider, what to do in the future, these things we will talk over affectionately. On my word of honor, no reproaches since they would now be of no value. Henceforth you may expect from me only the most loving care and help. Do but come! . . . Come to the faithful heart of your father, Beethoven.

Having heard from "Henry Jeckyll," let's see what "Mr. Hyde" had to say:

> Until now only conjecture, although someone assured me that there were again secret dealings between you and your mother. . . . Am I to experience once again the most abominable ingratitude? . . . No! If this bond is to be broken, so be it! But you will be despised by all impartial men who hear of this ingratitude. . . . Shall I get involved again in these vulgarities? . . . No, never again! . . . In God's name if the Pactum weighs upon you, I turn you over to Divine Providence. I have done my job, and upon this I can appear before the mightiest of all judges. Do not be afraid to come to me tomorrow. I can still presume (God grant) that nothing of this is true. For if it were, truly your unhappiness would be unending. . . . I am expecting you for sure, along with the "old witch."

And a week later:

> God is my witness. I dream only of being completely removed from you and from my wretched brother and this abominable family to which I am attached. God grant me my wish, for I cannot trust you anymore.
>
> Unfortunately your Father,
> or better,
> Not your Father!

When I left for Baden, I knew that my return to Vienna would not bring me again to the Kletschka house. Something had to be found within walking distance of Karl's new school so that the two of us could resume living together. For this reason, I terminated my lease with Frau Kletschka as of May first, moved the bulk of my possessions into Johann's apartment at the Obermeyer's, and took with me to Baden only the barest essentials.

In spite of a summer's searching by Karl and Holz, nothing suitable could be found really close to the institute. I ended up renting four rooms, a kitchen, and servants' quarters on the second floor of the Schwarspanierhaus—that huge four-story pile of gray stones which, twenty-one years earlier, had attracted my attention from the open windows of das Rothe Haus apartment that I then shared with Stephan von Breuning.

Since Breuning and his family were still living in "the Red House," it was apparent that our paths should soon cross. They did so on a beautiful August morning, ten days after my lease was signed for the new apartment. I had just entered the Alsergrund Glacis, when I spotted the Breunings walking some twenty paces in front of me. I quickened my step, tiptoed up behind them, and tapped Stephan on the shoulder. Remembering his delightful note at the *Fidelio* concert, this time, I was the first to extend a hand:

B. Stephan von Breuning! (I nodded to the wife.) Madame Breuning! . . . I know that you don't remember me, but I'm an old piano teacher from Bonn. I've just arrived here in the big city and thought perhaps these children of yours might be interested in some lessons. (I knelt down and embraced the two of them in a gentle hug.) And this is little Marie . . . and Gerhard, right?

The youngsters looked about eight or ten years of age, and since I had met them only twice before, they probably wondered who I was. Their father leaned over and told them, no doubt reminding them of my deafness. Marie responded with a finger in her mouth; Gerhard with a blush of the greatest admiration.

B. You think I'm a mean old man. . . . I'm really very kind! (I snipped little Marie on her nose.) I know your grandmother and love her dearly. She made a son of me when my own mother died. This makes me your father's brother, and means that you must call me "Uncle."

I stood up and spoke to the parents, while pointing toward the Schwarspanierhaus.

B. I've taken an apartment here in the Black Spaniard's House. How fortunate can I be? After all these years, moving next door to my best of boyhood friends!

During the rest of my summer at Baden, I must have made twenty visits to the capital. There were so many petty things to tend to. Each moving became more difficult than the one that preceded it, and this was the worst of them all. You can't imagine what help the Breunings were to me in every way—from the selecting of curtains to the moving of books, from the furnishing of my kitchen to the engagement of servants. Some eleven decades following this incident, a certain American comedian became quite famous with his invitation: "Come over for dinner; you bring the chicken." He must have gotten his idea from my visits to the Breunings. Two or three times a week they would invite me for supper at the Red House, and invariably I would take with me a big mess of fresh fish wrapped in a pink paper. It never occurred to me that perhaps other people were not as everlastingly fond of fish as I. At any rate, the poor souls would always tastefully prepare what I brought, and Beethoven days became fish days at the Breunings.

In spite of my moving troubles, I was able to complete Galitzin's commission before the end of the year. The "A Minor" was finished on August twenty-fifth, and immediately I began planning for its first performance. This was to be (as promised) a benefit concert for our cellist, Joseph Linke. However, wishing to avoid another embarrassing première such as was had by the "E-flat," I decided that the initial reading of the "A Minor" should be for a small select audience. Besides Karl and Holz, my little group of musical elite was to include Czerny, Böhm, Schuppanzigh, Weiss, Schlesinger, Haslinger, and that gentleman who had recently conducted the London première of *Symphony 9*, Sir George Smart. Small as this group was, my stuffed rooms at Baden would not accommodate them. And such a distinguished company should not be expected to travel far just to perform my latest quartet. What could be done? Schlesinger again saved the day. He was staying at the tavern zum Wilden Mann, and arranged with the innkeeper there to provide a room large enough for our purposes.

The *A Minor* was given twice on Friday, September ninth, and again the following Sunday. I came in from the country to personally direct these performances, and found the little room so hot and crowded that I was obliged to do so in my shirt sleeves. Schuppanzigh and his men were amazed at my compensatory ability to *hear with my eyes.*

Schlesinger was so impressed with the new quartet that he wished to buy it for 80 ducats. I accepted his offer on September tenth. When he heard that there was to be another "Galitzin," he repeated his proposition. He also commissioned three quintets, and offered to publish the first complete edition of my music! The young entrepreneur further requested an essay on orchestration and another on the art of fugue. When I asked him why he wanted these, he told me that just recently at the Paris Conservatoire, Luigi Cherubini was telling his students that Beethoven and Mozart were the greatest musical minds ever to live!

Following Sunday's private concert, all ten of us dined together at the "Wild Man." We were anxious to see how much our English guest could actually drink, and before long, the gay fellowship turned into a Sunday bacchanalia. Sir George Smart outdrank all of us—that is, all of us except "Sir" Karl Holz!

Five days later, Sir George came to visit me at Baden. Our conversation was in French. We discussed music, musicians, the future of opera, and the correct tempos of my various symphonic movements. Smart repeated his belief that I could carry away £1,000 from a single season in London. In remembrance of our visit, we exchanged gifts: a conductor's diamond pin for a composer's canon. I wrote the tiny "Ars longa vita brevis" in two minutes while waiting for the Vienna stagecoach.

The remaining weeks at Baden were devoted to the Third Galitzin. On October fifteenth, I returned to Vienna and moved into the Schwarspanierhaus, my final dwelling place on Earth. I had hoped to finish the new quartet during vacation, but as things turned out, its concluding double-bar was not drawn until November ninth. This was, of course, the first version of the "B-flat," that version in which the Great Fugue served as a finale. Following those private performances in September, the "Second Galitzin" had its first public hearing on November sixth in the Music Society's room at the "rother Igel." This also was a benefit concert for Herr Linke, and proved to be very successful.

My new apartment (like the one at Kletschkas') was too far from the Polytechnic for Karl to come and live with me. He remained with Schlemmer and still felt the need of a private tutor. This meant another 2,000 florins for his final year in school. Our relationship continued to degenerate. My suspicions, criticisms, and moral sermons kept even pace with his swiftly growing demands for greater independence. Brother Johann could see the writing on the wall, and advised me to turn my guardianship over to Dr. Bach, ridding myself of Karl once and for all. This, of course, I could never do!

Counterbalancing the hatred and grief that I experienced through Karl was a God-sent treasure of love and understanding from the Breunings. Stephan's position as Councillor in the War Department of the Austrian Government enabled their family to live in a sort of calm affluence, strongly reminiscent of the mother's home in Bonn. I enjoyed each visit to the Red House; however (even with all my fish), I felt as though our social scales were out of balance. I was forever visiting their apartment, and yet they never came to mine. Madame von Breuning would consistently turn down my dinner invitations and (usually) even those for coffee. Could it be that she disapproved of my bearish manners, or my broken furniture, or my roomful of dusty scores? Was it my composing outfit that frightened her away? (Worn slippers, baggy trousers, sometimes a shredded shirt with open collar and raveled rolled-up sleeves, but more often merely an undershirt, and in cold weather a Gauss-type "thinking cap," and an ancient dressing gown that must have been born in that fatal year when my late lamented gray coat first saw the light of day.) Or did she object to my constant spitting on the floor? Be this as it may, there was one Breuning who wasn't afraid to visit me. Starting about November, young Gerhard would come to my rooms for two or three visits a week. I grew very fond of the bright-eyed, dark-haired "page," and he was the last Earthling to be knighted into my Court. I dubbed him Hosenknopf ("trouser button") because he stuck so close to his father, and Ariel because he was so light on his feet. He would sit for hours at my Broadwood, practicing his Czerny and Pleyel. This bothered me little since I heard none of it. Occasionally I'd look over his shoulder to see how he was doing. Sometimes I'd criticize a passage, or correct the position of his hand. In a few months, I thought my charming page was far enough along to begin Clementi, and made him a present of the Gradus. Unlike other human beings, this little boy actually had the courage to accompany me in the streets. When the inevitable army of urchins gathered to do their mocking and their laughing and their hooting, did my Hosenknopf run on ahead (or to the other side of the street) and pretend not to know me? Never! He'd hold his head up high, take me by the hand, and act as if he personally were there to protect me from the cutting barbs of his insensitive playmates. But even more beautiful than this were his eyes. In them I could read an unmistakable combination of love, respect, and admiration, which I could no longer find in the face of my own "son."

Although the Third Galitzin was promised to Schlesinger, I sent it to Artaria for the simple reason that I believed this local house would more quickly bring the score to press. Early in January, Schuppanzigh and his men began rehearsing it. As I could have predicted, they were delighted with the tearful beauty of the *Cavatina*, but were frightened to death by the terrible difficulties of its *fugal finale*. Both players and publisher requested me to replace the *Great Fugue* with an easier, more conventional final movement. But for the present, I insisted that things stand as they were. Schuppanzigh gave the première on March twenty-first, and was reluctant to follow through with additional performances. However, Böhm and Mayseder were anxiously willing to do so.

Having completed my commissioned quartets, I felt like the "wild rider" who had just raced across that famous bridge, and was tempted to react to its imposing crossroads by sprinting off in ten different directions at the same time. Should I prepare for another akademie in the Kärnthnerthor by concentrating on Symphony 10 and a B-A-C-H overture? Should I compose the Requiem Mass commissioned (and partially paid for) by Johann Nepomuk Wolfmayer? Should I spend three to five years on Goethe's *Faust*, or try something simpler like Grillparzer's *Melusine*? Should I follow in the footsteps of Georg Friedrich Handel and try to compose a new oratorio for each remaining season? If so, should I start with Bernard's Der Sieg des Kreuzes for the Gesellschaft der Musikfreunde? Should I use a new text by Kuffner? Or should I continue my studies of ancient Hebrew music, and attempt to create a more authentic Saul than the one left us by Handel? As things worked out, the momentum was too great. I turned neither right nor left, but went galloping straight forward along the mellowing road of string quartets! Two more were to come from my pen: the first (in *C-sharp Minor*) would be the greatest composition of my Earthly career; the second (in *F Major*) would be the final composition of my Earthly career.

How is it that a fond parent of 138 children can point to one of them and pronounce him unquestionably the greatest of them all? Such a decision in favor of the "C-sharp Minor" lies beyond the mere mechanics of composition. Opus 131 is neither the longest nor the shortest nor the loudest nor the softest nor the slowest nor the fastest of my children. It is the greatest! It is the greatest because of what it has to say. After a casual exposure to the harshness and length of this work, you might well ask what's so great about it. It has its fugues, its adagios, its allegros, its variations, its scherzos, and a march. But so what? Aren't others of my offspring composed of the same clay? Isn't the "C-sharp Minor" just as scale-clad and key-centered as its brothers and sisters? The language of this quartet is no different from that which I had spoken for nearly a decade. As a matter of fact, basic themes were abstracted from Bach and Mozart, from my researches in early Hebrew music, and from younger compositions of my own, so much so that I scribbled across the title page, "Cribbed together variously from this and that." My comment scared the Schotts out of their wits. I promptly received a letter from them reminding me of their stipulation that the quartet must be an original one. Original! I wrote them back that nothing I had ever done was as funkelnagelneu as the "*C-sharp Minor.*" And this brings me to my point. How can an opus be structured from the same old blocks which I had used over and over again, and yet be called the newest and greatest of them all?

As I've said before, it is my belief that to create a work of art is to push back the boundaries of reality . . . perhaps an inch or two, perhaps a foot. And when a dedicated artist spends a lifetime doing this, on one rare day his push of an inch might suddenly become the unanticipated thrust of a mile! The first half of 1826 was my "rare day," and the new quartet, my forward "thrust." What made them so was the higher order of consciousness that dominated my life during these months. For practical purposes, I had finished with the world, and more than ever before, had retreated to the isolation of inner life. To be sure, the shaggy remnants of my dear old Court still hovered over me, doing my bidding and offering their encouragement. But all these fellow creatures—Holz, Schuppanzigh, Schindler, Rudolph, the Breunings, Lichnowsky, Johann, Haslinger—they moved about me like pale shadows, compared to the explosion of light going on in my soul. Within this mystical explosion were fused the sweet treasures of a lifetime: the words of Mozart and Goethe, the first sweet bloom of Eleonore, the inspiration of God in nature, the first performance of the *Eroica,* the concert of May seventh, the quiet serious beauty of my mother's eyes, the sparkle of Bettina, a final walk with Father, the proud hopes of Grandfather, my dreams for Karl, the serene peace of Father Rhine. And from this fusion came a beautiful insight into the reasons for human life and suffering. Had you visited the Schwarspanierhaus at this time and asked me to describe the new vision, I'm sure that my scraping tongue could have put but little of it into words. I probably would have told you that (like Mozart and Goethe) I too now believed in the immortality of man's soul. I believed in the dignity and inextinguishability of man's suffering, and that there was far more to human life than birth, training, position, money, recognition and death. Here my words would have ended. But my thoughts ran on for six months, those very months during which the "C-sharp Minor" was composed! This is why the new quartet is my greatest composition, and has so much to say.

Now that I've lived through the enlightenment of death and rebirth, I realize the full meaning of my mystical experience. Apparently some of this message did get through to the quartet, for at least one of my biographers (who played it and heard it for thirty years) was able (a century later) to translate my vision into words. Robert Haven Schauffler, in speaking of the opening *fugue*, said that it

> offers me, in a language far more veridical than any words, the illumination of the mystic vision. Its "twenty minutes of reality" communicates directly, without recourse to such awkward conventions as the worn counters of speech, the secrets of the universe. I feel myself a completely balanced and integrated being. . . . The past, present and future are made to form one pure ring of burning light.

And of the closing movement, Schauffler goes on to observe:

> Those painful, resolute footsteps of the *finale's* heroic march fall on the ear like heartening exhortations TO LIVE OUT THIS PHASE OF EXISTENCE FULLY AND COURAGEOUSLY IF WE WOULD DEVELOP THE MOMENTUM OF SPIRIT NECESSARY FOR THE NEXT.

The first half of 1826 was predominantly, though not entirely, filled with mystical bliss and the "C-sharp Minor." February was the exception. During this cold-footed month, there was a serious breakdown in my health. Abdominal and back pains became so sharp that I found locomotion next to impossible. Even my sore eyes flared up again. Dr. Braunhofer was called in and, as he had done the preceding year, recommended soup and quinine as necessary substitutes for the coffee and wine in my diet. When I asked him the reason for the constant pain in my right side, he said that it was probably an attack of rheumatism or gout. Would that his diagnosis had been correct!

I had no sooner recovered from February than my poor Broadwood was stricken critically ill. From keys to casters, it was ravaged by a terrible disorder that silenced most of its strings. In spite of my deafness, I had no choice but to send it to Graf for extensive repairs, the first time the two of us were separated since our beloved association began.

The *C-sharp Minor Quartet* was not delivered to Schott's agent until August twelfth. For it, I received 80 ducats and a passionate request for more new chamber pieces. In spite of the fast-moving efficiency of this house, my "greatest" composition was not published until three months after my death!

During the months of June and July, the relationship between Karl and myself rapidly disintegrated. I tightened my controls to the breaking point: reducing his allowance for the third time, constantly inquiring into his affairs at the institute, going to the school each afternoon to escort him home arm in arm, and insisting that Schlemmer be the watchdog of his evenings. Karl's response to these restrictions was typical of a twenty-year-old "boy." He did precisely the opposite of what I wished him to do. I screamed threats, curses, and accusations at him as though he were still a boy of twelve. As a direct result of this, he purchased a pistol and shot himself in the head! The bullet caused a bad flesh wound, but did not enter his skull.

Dr. Gottfried Dögl arrived in response to the mother's request. Since Karl was satisfied to leave things in Dögl's hands, he removed the bullet and dressed the wound. Though Holz reported regularly on the boy's condition, I myself did not visit him until six weeks later. The reason I stayed away so long was because of Karl's stated wish that I would never show myself again! My friends advised me to drop the guardianship, and Breuning offered to take it up in place of Reissner. They further recommended military service as the only possible way Karl could avoid the penal aspects of his foul deed. Breuning contacted Baron von Stutterheim, and persuaded the field marshal to give my nephew a cadetship in his regiment. On September twentieth, I made my first visit to the hospital and discussed with Karl the new plans we had made for him.

B. Karl, I've not come here to lecture, but to discuss our plans for your future. There'll be no more tirades from me. That bullet at Rauhenstein pierced my heart no less than your head. From now on, what you do with your life is *your* business. If you prefer billiards and prostitutes to the joy of self-sacrifice, so be it! But tell me. Why did you do such a terrible thing? Was it fear for your examinations?

Ka. IT WAS NOT THE EXAMINATIONS. I HAD UNTIL SEPTEMBER THIRD TO MAKE THEM UP. I WANTED TO DIE BECAUSE I WAS TIRED OF LIVING!

B. Life is God's gift! How can you tire of it in twenty years?

Ka. WITH ALL YOUR SPYING, MY LIFE IS WORSE THAN IMPRISONMENT.

B. As I promised, I'm not here to argue, but to discuss your future. I've talked things over with Bach and Breuning, with Schindler and Holz, even with your mother. They all agree that a military career would be the best for you. What do you think of the idea?

Ka. SUCH A CAREER WOULD BE FINE WITH ME. I WISH TO LEAVE VIENNA AS SOON AS POSSIBLE.

On September twenty-fifth, Karl left the hospital. Breuning arranged for him to take the oath of service, and to leave for Stutterheim's regiment, which is stationed in Iglau.

From the time of my nephew's shocking deed until his departure, nothing really creative was accomplished. To be sure, I tried to lose myself in music, but nothing happened beyond the mechanics of sketching. A new *finale* was begun for the Third Galitzin, and a few weak thoughts fell into shape for the *F-Major Quartet*, my last "Earthly" composition.

Since I felt like a father who had lost his only son, it was natural that I should dream of finding another. I didn't have to wait long. During Karl's stay in the hospital, little "Hosenknopf" visited me every single day. I could feel my broken heart reaching out to him, and so could he. How deeply touched I was by his reaction to what Karl had done. The very next day, he wrote on my tablet:

Ho. YOU MUST COME TO US FOR ALL YOUR MEALS SO THAT YOU WILL NOT BE ALONE.

Holz also sensed that I should not be left alone. Unfortunately, his response was less conducive to good health than young Breuning's. He invited me to one merrymaking after another—exactly what was needed for my broken spirit, but the last thing in the world that should have been directed toward my poor old liver in its then advancing stages of cirrhosis!

During the warm season, I stayed at Johann's estate at Gneixendorf. Though I hadn't been an overnight guest for fifteen years, and in spite of my inability to adjust to family life, I managed to show up each morning at the breakfast table with a hypocritical mask of friendly smiles to hide my negative feelings toward these people. Then out into the autumn fields I'd go—tramping, gesticulating, stopping, walking, dreaming, stumbling, staring but not seeing, and trying unsuccessfully to pretend that the Danube was Father Rhine. Here was old "King Lear" on the heath, hurrying to write down the last notes of his final compositions.

Afternoons were spent at the little writing desk in my room, busily transforming sketches into quartet music. Since there was still no Broadwood, I engaged in comical sequences of loud singing and incoherent muttering, wildly conducting with both hands, and noisily beating time with both feet. These unbuttoned performances were too much for the cook when she came to dust, sweep the floor, and make the bed. On the fifth day, I happened to turn around just as she burst into a laugh. This was enough. I ordered her out of the room for the duration of my visit. She had a little shadow of a helper named Michael Krenn, who was a stable boy and the son of one of Johann's vinedressers. When my screams drove the old woman from the room, naturally her shadow tried to follow. I reached out and grabbed him by the arm, dropping some twenty-kreutzer pieces into his hand: "Don't be afraid, young man. I wasn't shouting at *you*. How would you like to tend my needs for the rest of my visit? I'd rather have you running about me than twenty old snickering bitches like that cook!" Krenn accepted my offer, and came every day to look after things.

It seems strange, but my long association with Karl made me absolutely dependent upon the image of a young "son" following me about, and looking up to me. When Karl became too big, too independent, and too obnoxious to fill the part, "Hosenknopf" was called in to take his place. And now, during my absence from Vienna, Michael Krenn became "son number three." As my projected visit of one or two weeks grew into two months, Krenn became the only person in the entire household whom I trusted. When I lost my sketchbook full of *F Major Quartet*, he was the one to scramble across the "heath" and find it for me. When I wondered what these aloof people were saying about me at the dinner table, he was the faithful spy who would come to my room and write down their conversation. Is it any wonder that I tried to take Krenn with me when I finally returned to Vienna.

On October thirtieth, the tiny *F Major* was sent to Schlesinger—for "circumcised" ducats, a "circumcised" quartet! On November twenty-fifth, my new *finale* for the Third Galitzin was sent to Artaria. And thus ended Beethoven's composing career on Earth.

It was a sick old Beethoven who started for Vienna on December first. The food at Gneixendorf had been anything but to my taste. Lunches were so poor that I resorted exclusively to soft-boiled eggs, which in turn generated an enormous thirst for Johann's Nessmüller, Ofener, and Tokayer. Excessive wine drinking brought a violent return of diarrhea and caused my belly to become so swollen that from November on, I had to wear a bandage over it. During my last week at Gneixendorf, my appetite disappeared altogether. I began suffering from an unquenchable thirst, and from even sharper pains in my right side.

Upon leaving Gneixendorf in Johann's shaky calash, we got no farther than Kirchberg on the Wagram by late Friday afternoon. Our old driver warned that he could not go on with all three of us, for fear of breaking the axle. Johann decided to return to Gneixendorf the next morning.

My small room at the village tavern was the last word in inadequacy—damp, cold, gloomy, and no winter shutters. Without too much imagination, one could believe there was frost on the furniture, the only source of heat in the room being its miserable reading lamp. When I complained to the mustachioed innkeeper, he excused himself by assuring me that at this time of year, there were few visitors to Kirchberg.

Having no other way to keep warm, I went straight to bed. About two in the morning, I awakened with a violent thirst, a fever chill, and a dry hacking cough, which brought the taste of blood to my lips. Breathing became so difficult that I had to spend the rest of the night sitting up in a chair. I tore all the blankets from my bed and wrapped them around me. There I sat for five hours: coughing, shivering, sweating, sipping ice water, and waiting for the first signs of daybreak.

When Saturday morning finally dawned, I discovered that the only conveyance obtainable was an ancient and enormous hay wagon. There was no charge for its use since the owner lived in Vienna and would be grateful for having it delivered there. In spite of the empty rig's huge size, there was room on its box for only the driver. I was lifted into the back and sat facing the rear with my legs dangling behind. To keep from being bounced out altogether, I wound my left arm around the last upright beam of the four-wheeler's framework. With the other hand, I tried to keep winter's icy fingers from my throat by pinching together the gaping collar of my ragged lightweight coat. The entire day's journey was gloomy, dark, and foreboding. After several hours, the sky changed from gray to black, and stayed that way. It began to snow. The smelly lurching rackwagon made me sicker by the minute. Each nauseating vibration ran the full length of my spine, and then cut into my right side like the devil's own sword. The wind took off my old hat and sent it turning cartwheels among fuzzy flakes now deep enough to outline our tracks. I was too sick to bother stopping for it, and watched it come to rest in tall frozen grass on the bank. I wondered what the driver would have done had *I* blown from the wagon instead of my hat. Perhaps he would have stopped. Before long, the road became sheeted with ice. This caused the horses to steam and stagger and slip. A dozen times we lurched so violently that I thought the old wagon would completely overturn. We stopped at the coffee house by the Metzen Canal for a hot and much-needed cup. Entering the post road, I found it more heavily traveled. Instead of frozen crusts and dancing flakes, there were deep sloughs of slippery mud that slowed our pace to an unsteady walk. The driver's whip beat the horses' steaming flanks until I thought the poor beasts would drop dead in their tracks. We arrived at the Leopoldstadt suburb in late afternoon. A penetrating fog blowing up from the Danube was thick enough to completely obscure the steepled towers of our beloved skyline.

As the last weary steps of my painful journey were trod, I sat there on the back of the old wagon and thought. I thought of an earlier day, of my first visit to this great city. It was a long time ago, and yet it was not so long ago. What a difference between then and now. Forty years earlier, I came here on the breath of spring to see Mozart, to build my career, and to live. Today I arrived here on winter's wing—to suffer and to die!

Chapter 24

When the driver helped me down from the wagon, I felt as though my poor frozen legs weighed a hundred pounds each. It was all I could do to get upstairs and into bed. Alternating chills and fever lasted until morning. What frightened me most was my great difficulty in breathing, and the fact that I was again coughing blood—very much like my dear mother in her final days.

First thing next morning, I sent a note to Dr. Braunhofer, urgently requesting his services. He replied that he couldn't come because of his great distance from the Alsergrund Glacis. Great distance! My guess is that the man had a pretty good idea of what was going on in my right side and didn't wish to put himself in the position of doctoring a short-tempered old lion through his terminal illness. Next I wrote Dr. Staudenheim. He also refused to come.

On Monday morning, December fourth, Sali reported to the Schwarspanierhaus to resume her duties. She was the wonderful maid and housekeeper whom the Breunings had obtained for me in November of the preceding year. I sent her to Holz with a little note:

> Your Official Majesty,
>
> Immediately after my arrival which occurred a few days ago, I wrote you a letter but mislaid it. Then I became so unwell that I decided to stay in bed. . . . I shall be very glad

> if you come to see me. It should be less inconvenient for you now, since everyone has come back from Döbling to the city. . . . Finally I will just add . . . [There followed a four-measure canon on the words, "We all err, only each in his our way!"]
>
> As always your friend,
> Beethoven

Alarmed by Sali's report on my condition, Holz went immediately to the hospital in search of a doctor. Early next morning, the "Best of Splinters" came for a visit and reported that Dr. Andreas Wawruch, professor in the hospital, would see me before lunch.

I slept most of the morning, finally to be awakened by the new doctor. I tried to speak, but (having slept long and open-mouthed) my tongue felt like a hot, dry stone. The doctor had already written a note in my Conversation Book, which he now held up for me to read:

> ONE WHO GREATLY REVERES YOUR NAME WILL DO EVERYTHING POSSIBLE TO GIVE YOU SPEEDY RELIEF.
>
> PROFESSOR WAWRUCH

He concluded that I was suffering from pneumonia and, with his burning plasters, was able to cure my bloody cough and respiratory difficulties within three days.

By Thursday afternoon, I felt strong enough to get out of bed and walk about the apartment. I even did a little reading and writing. To be sure, I didn't go to work on Symphony 10 or Faust, but with Karl's help, I was able to dictate long overdue replies to those delightful letters from Wegeler and Eleonore.

Karl had no sooner returned from posting my letters than we became involved in a violent argument over his immediate financial requirements. Though there remained little more than 600 florins in my iron cash box, he requested half this sum to cover merely the cost of new uniforms. On top of this, there would be his transportation expenses to Iglau, and an exorbitant monthly allowance. I reminded him that I had to provide for my own requirements: doctors, medicine, food, rent, servants, and God knows what else. He told me to stop being so miserly, and to cash one of my bank shares. This brought an explosion . . . just like old times. But before I could really get myself "tuned up," he left the room and presumably went to his mother's. The fact that he had gone didn't matter. I raged on and on until bedtime. During the night, I nearly died from the most vicious choleric attack of my long illness. When Wawruch came next morning, he found me trembling, jaundiced from head to toe, and bent practically double from the demonic pain in my right side. It was so sharp that I could neither stretch out nor lie flat on my back, but sat there on that "straw sack" of a mattress, propped up by three pillows, and with my chin clamped against my knees. Wawruch also discovered my feet and ankles to be moderately swollen, the beginning of a dropsical condition that would cause me additional pain and suffering. During the next ten days, my spells of nocturnal suffocation continued, there was an increase of jaundice, and the doctor could actually feel hard nodules on my liver! Also the swelling worsened in my feet, and rapidly spread to my legs and belly. By Monday the eighteenth, there was such an enormous accumulation of water that Wawruch recommended immediate tapping as the only possible safeguard against the danger of bursting.

During this period of terrible suffering and inactivity, the faithful Sali remained in regular attendance. Johann arrived in Vienna on December twelfth. He came often to advise me concerning my diet and to discuss our nephew's pending military career. Even Karl himself began treating me with some respect. Apparently my symptoms were severe enough to convince him that I was really sick! He worked closely with Wawruch and carefully wrote all details of the doctor's recommendations. Since Holz was now married, Schindler once again became first and foremost factotum. Holz did manage occasional visits to look after the correction and publication of my final pieces, but it was dear dull "Papageno" who now stood constantly at my side. No doubt Stephan von Breuning would have stood there as well, except for the stubborn illness that plagued him through December and part of January. But even so, Stephan was well represented by little Gerhard, who never missed his daily visit to the Schwarspanierhaus. "Hosenknopf" would bring me soup from his mother's kitchen, practice awhile at the Broadwood, and then humorously relate each detail of his father's affairs. I'd usually end up reading to him from one of his favorite books.

There were a few other cheerful events to brighten these dark days. Two summers ago at Baden, a fine English musician and harp manufacturer named Johann Andreas Stumpff (no relation to my Broadwood's piano tuner) was brought for a visit by Haslinger.

During the course of our bacchanal, he raised the question of whom I considered to be the greatest of composers. Bending one knee to the floor, I emphatically replied:

B. Handel! . . . To him I bow the knee.

My new friend then wrote:

St. As you yourself, a peerless artist in the art of composition, exalt the merits of Handel so highly above all, you must certainly own the scores of his principal works.

B. I? . . . A poor devil like me? . . . How should I have gotten them? . . . I consider myself fortunate in having read through *The Messiah* and *Alexander's Feast*, to say nothing of owning the scores!

Apparently Stumpff made up his mind then and there to send me a complete edition of Handel, for this was my surprise two years later! On December fifteenth (almost the very day when those obnoxious aspects of my fatal illness first asserted themselves to the fullest) I received through this dear German-Englishman a gift from heaven—in forty huge and sturdy volumes, the complete works of George Frideric Handel!

During the months of suffering that led to my death, I was too ill to do any composing. Thus this precious gift was responsible for the sole pleasure and comfort afforded me by my art. "Hosenknopf" would bring to my bed one volume at a time, and prop it up against the wall. There I'd lie for hours on end, turning the pages, reading the tones, smiling, laughing, weeping, and proclaiming before Almighty God the greatness of this eternal composer, and the smallness of the rest of us! Caught up in Handel's mighty stream, I completely forgot the pain in my side, the numbness of my yellow feet, the swollen belly, the stablelike conditions of my sickroom. All that remained were sunshine, Gerhard's smile, and the glorious sounds of the greatest music ever written!

Karl also would come and stand by my bed—not to turn pages or tell stories or be read to, but (of all things) to teach me arithmetic! It was really humorous, suddenly to behold my little "son" in the role of "Herr Professor." How hard he worked, how poorly I learned. Our textbook was entitled, The Easiest Method of Teaching Arithmetic to Children in a Pleasant Way, Revised Edition in Two Parts. We got as far as the chapter on multiplication. Then my poor "professor" threw up his hands in despair, pronouncing me hopelessly illiterate in all things mathematical!

On December nineteenth, Staudenheim was called in to confirm Wawruch's decision. He agreed that my gigantic "belly" should be tapped at once, lest it burst of its own accord. I gave my consent, and Dr. Seibert, principal surgeon at the General Hospital, came early next morning to perform the operation. Those present (besides the doctors) were Karl, Johann, and Schindler. Seibert was a distinguished-looking man with handsome gray hair and a reddish face. I wondered to myself if his ruddy facial tone was but a reflection of the "bloody business" of his profession. But then (frighteningly) I remembered seeing not a few butchers with faces just as red as Seibert's. As he removed the bandage and placed his cool, comforting hand on my swollen abdomen, I tried my best to find some humor in the situation.

B. I've always wanted a child. Do you think they'll be twins, doctor?

There were smiles, but no one laughed. As the surgeon completed his preparations, Wawruch wrote,

Wr. WE ARE NOW READY TO BEGIN. THERE'LL BE A LITTLE PAIN, BUT IT WILL LAST ONLY A MINUTE. . . . WHY DON'T YOU GRAB HOLD OF THE BEDRAIL?

The pain was not little. An angry sword could have felt no worse! My nails dug a quarter of an inch into the wood. But no matter. Those two could have cut away half my body, and I would not have cried out. I was determined to set a brave example before my son and my brother.

As Seibert introduced a tube into the incision and twenty-five pounds of grayish-brown fluid spurted out, I continued with more grim humor:

B. Better from my belly than from my pen! . . . Professor, you remind me of Moses striking the rock with his staff!

Following the operation, my wound continued to drain . . . nearly 130 pounds in the afterflow! But at least the liquid became clearer. The strictest controls were now placed upon my diet. I was allowed soup, a little coffee, and small amounts of almond milk. Worst of all, for nine days I had to remain in a near-lying position, while my doctors decided whether or not a second operation would be necessary.

During the month of December, Karl inched ever so slowly toward his new career. His physical was passed, uniforms were purchased, he was introduced to the Field Marshal, he took the oath of service, his allowance was fixed, and transportation to Iglau was arranged. Finally on Tuesday morning, January second, he stood before my bed to say good-bye:

> DEAR FATHER—I'VE COME TO BID YOU FAREWELL. THE STAGECOACH LEAVES IN AN HOUR.

B. Good-bye, Karl. . . . I wish you a happy new career and a Happy New Year! . . . Both are starting together for you. Both are brand new! . . . I think this is a good omen.

Ka. IT SEEMS WRONG FOR ME TO LEAVE IN THE MIDST OF YOUR ILLNESS. . . . WOULD YOU PREFER THAT I STAY HERE UNTIL YOU FEEL BETTER?

B. Johann, Breuning, Bach . . . they all say that the sooner you begin your career, the better. . . . You must leave now, Karl. . . . I have no doubt that when we are separated from one another, a natural love and affection will develop between us—far more so, than when we were living and fighting under the same roof. . . . In case I'm not here when you return, remember my music. Listen to the *Andante moderato,* and at least I'll be with you in spirit!

Ka. YOU MUSTN'T TALK THIS WAY, FATHER. . . . AS SPRING COMES, I KNOW THAT YOUR HEALTH AND STRENGTH WILL BLOOM AGAIN. . . . NOR SHOULD YOU LIE THERE AND WORRY ABOUT ME, FOR I SHALL NEVER AGAIN VACILLATE FROM MY PURPOSE. I'M GLAD THE AFFAIR HAS ENDED THE WAY IT HAS, AND I SHALL NEVER REGRET MY DECISION FOR A MILITARY CAREER. . . . GOOD-BYE THEN. . . . THE HEART OF YOUR SON IS EVER GRATEFUL FOR ALL YOU HAVE DONE!

He kissed my forehead, I kissed his cheek, we shook hands. And this was the last we saw of each other on Earth.

By early January, my belly was as big as ever, and Wawruch began talking of a second operation. On Monday morning, January eighth, Seibert repeated the tapping, and this time drew off twice as much water as had spurted from the first incision! . . .

That afternoon (actually in tears) I begged Schindler and Johann to get me someone better acquainted with my constitution, someone who had known me longer: Staudenheim, Braunhofer, or (best of all) Malfatti. . . . Through the unremitting efforts of "Papageno," Dr. Johann Malfatti was at last persuaded to visit me. He came five days after the second tapping.

B. Miracle of miracles! Dear friend and great doctor! . . . Thank God you've come. . . . Without your help, I would surely die. . . . All these years . . . I can't believe you're here!

After shaking hands and without saying a word, he began his examination: taking my pulse and temperature, staring into my eyes, and carefully studying each square inch of my still-flattened and yellow abdomen. . . . Only then did he finally take up a Conversation Book and "speak":

Mf. YOU'LL LIVE. . . . YOU'RE TOO MUCH THE CANTANKEROUS OLD MAN TO DIE. . . . BUT I STILL DON'T OWE YOU THIS VISIT . . . NOT AFTER THE WAY YOU TREATED ME.

B. Our misunderstanding developed over your little Therese. I was very much in love with her . . . even went so far as to propose marriage. . . . Then I got the impression that as her uncle, you stood between us, betraying the confidence which I had placed in you as my physician. . . . But now I'm glad for what you did. All is forgiven. You saved Therese's life. . . ."Cantankerous" old musician that I am, I would have made a poor husband for *any* girl.

Mf. I CAN SEE WHY YOU WOULD SUSPECT ME OF DOING THIS. BUT ACTUALLY I SAID NOTHING TO HER OF YOUR PHYSICAL CONDITION. MY DISCOURAGEMENT OF THE MARRIAGE WAS BASED ENTIRELY UPON YOUR EXCLUSIVE DEVOTION TO MUSIC. I REALIZED THAT YOU WOULD HAVE LITTLE TIME FOR A WIFE, AND THAT THE RELATIONSHIP WOULD BE DOOMED TO FAILURE.

B. Good! . . . You were very wise. . . . And all is forgiven.

Mf. NOT QUITE. . . . WHAT DROVE ME FROM YOU WAS NOT OUR DISAGREEMENT OVER THERESE.

B. What then?

Mf. YOU GAVE ME THE DECIDED IMPRESSION THAT YOU BLAMED YOUR GROWING DEAFNESS NOT UPON YOUR OWN INDISCREET BEHAVIOR, BUT RATHER UPON MY PROFESSIONAL INCOMPETENCY!

B. And I also blamed God! But this doesn't give him the right to abandon me. . . . You must try to understand what it means for a musician to lose his hearing. . . . I had to strike back at someone, and you just happened to be sitting there at the time. . . . It was nothing personal. . . . Besides, if I really considered you incompetent, would I beg you to come to me now?

Mf. EVEN A DOCTOR HAS PERSONAL FEELINGS, AND SOMETIMES THEY COME BETWEEN HIMSELF AND HIS PATIENTS.

B. Then you've forgiven me?

Mf. (Malfatti clasped my hands in warm reassurance and nodded a comforting "Yes.") I'LL DO EVERYTHING I CAN FOR YOU, BUT WAWRUCH IS YOUR DOCTOR AND—

B. (I interrupted his writing.) Wawruch is an ass! I drink his bottles and bottles of medicine, and grow worse by the day!

Mf. WAWRUCH IS YOUR DOCTOR, AND I MUST LIVE IN HARMONY WITH MY COLLEAGUES. . . . IF I'M TO HELP YOU, IT MUST BE AS HIS ASSISTANT OR ELSE NOT AT ALL.

B. Why can't I quit him altogether, and put myself in your hands?

Mf. THIS WOULD VIOLATE THE ETHICS OF MY PROFESSION. . . . I'LL STILL COME TO YOU AT REGULAR INTERVALS, BUT WITH WAWRUCH'S APPROVAL.

This is exactly what happened for the remainder of my illness. Wawruch came once or twice a day; Malfatti, once or twice a week.

On Monday the fifteenth (through Malfatti's influence), there was a decided and tasteful improvement in my treatment. Instead of Wawruch's endless stream of strong medicines and bitter powders, I was given frozen fruit punch to drink, and they began rubbing my abdomen with ice-cold water. Having abstained from spirituous liquors for over a month, you can imagine how naturally I took to my new medicine. At first, two glasses a day; by the end of the week, I was drinking five times this amount. What wonderful results! . . .

Refreshed by the alcohol and ice, I relaxed and actually slept soundly again. Perspiring profusely, there was much less swelling in my belly. I grew cheerful and hopeful. The sketches for Symphony 10 were handed me from my desk. I'd scribble a few notes, doze off, dream that I'd finished the score, then wake up to discover that I hadn't, and would ask for another glass of punch. . . . There was no doubt in my mind that I would soon be completely restored by Malfatti's magic. . . . There was no doubt in my mind until Wednesday, January twenty-fourth. On this cruel, cold morning the cutting pain in my right side returned sharper than ever. It was accompanied by colic, loss of appetite, sore throat, hoarseness, and diarrhea. These maladies remained until my death, growing worse day by day. Malfatti attributed them to my overzealous use of his prescription and, on January twenty-fifth, gave strict orders that I be totally withdrawn from my precious tonic. Immediately I stopped perspiring, and my belly began to swell. Within a week, it was necessary for Seibert to return for the deliverance of a third "baby." . . .

His third tapping occurred on Friday morning, February second. Three days later, Malfatti concluded that his medicine was not having the desired effect. To prevent my body from swelling up again, he prescribed a sweat bath, using hayseed and birch leaves. This was supposed to induce a productive perspiration over the entire surface of my skin. It had the opposite effect. My recently dehydrated body soaked up moisture like a sponge, and became so filled with water that on the following Wednesday, a tube had to be reintroduced into the still unhealed puncture of the third operation.

During these days of terrible suffering, Schindler brought me cheerful greetings from my old friend "Count Z.," who was imprisoned in his own sickroom with a crippling gout. In response, I managed a little note to him:

> Dear Zmeskall,
>
> A thousand thanks for your sympathy. I do not despair. The most painful feature is the cessation of all activity. No evil without its good side. . . . May heaven grant you relief in your painful existence. Perhaps health is coming to both of us, and we shall meet again in friendly intimacy.
>
> Warm regards from your old sympathizing friend,
> Beethoven

The condition of my legs and abdomen continued to worsen, necessitating a final tapping on February 27th. The twenty-five days between my third and fourth operations were a period of great melancholy and suffering. During these weeks there were old friends like Schuppanzigh, Linke and Dolezalek who came and tried to cheer me up . . . but had little success. Moritz Lichnowsky thought he was entertaining me with his latest gossip of the theatres. Diabelli talked of new Beethoven compositions, but he wasn't deceiving anyone. As a gift he presented me with a print-picture of Haydn's birthplace. How proudly I showed it to Gerhard:

B. Look, I got this today! . . . See this little house, and in it such a great man was born.

Gleichenstein made several visits, and once brought with him his wife and son. The countess was Therese Malfatti's sister, and seemed terribly disappointed when I was unable to guess who she was. . . . None of these attempts could penetrate the gloom that now paralyzed my life. I had lost faith in my doctors. No one, not even Malfatti, could save me! I walked a narrow, dark, and lonely road. Before me stood the grim figure of death himself! I had no choice but to meet him face-to-face, and to feel at last the cold and dreaded grip of his tomb-white hands. Under normal conditions, I would have had no fear of him. But this wretched illness had separated me from my art! And without her standing beside me, my idle hands felt like those of a slingless David going out against Goliath! . . .

Not only was I suffering from the first complete absence of music from my life, but I also began once again to have real fears of starvation. The seven shares were not mine to spend, there remained only a few florins in the cash box, and (in spite of my three letters) I had heard nothing from the Philharmonic Society. . . . Nor was Karl any comfort during these days. He had completely abandoned me! Not a single letter did I receive from him. Breuning tried to explain away the boy's negligence by speculating that his attention was probably engrossed in the gaieties of carnival season at the military post. . . . Carnival season! . . . If only he had known what a few words would have meant to me at this time! . . . These were the darkest days of my life on Earth. . . .

After the fourth operation, Malfatti and Wawruch concluded and concurred that my liver was in such bad shape that nothing could make it any worse. Frozen punch was restored to my diet, and they even recommended that I drink some good old Rhine wine or genuine Moselle, but none of the heavy varieties of Hungarian Ofener. These fine unadulterated wines were not to be had at *any* price. However, the longer I thought about such a treat, the more convinced I was that some delicious wine from the homeland would, if not cure my disease, at least restore my strength. I wrote several letters to the Schotts, requesting them to send me a few bottles.

Financial worries continued to bother me as much as my physical suffering. I had still heard nothing from London. On March sixth and fourteenth respectively, second letters were sent to Smart and Moscheles, urging them to please help me so that I might be protected against want at least during this period of "living death." . . . On the very next day, I received a letter from Moscheles. He informed me that the Philharmonic Society wished to express their good will and lively sympathy by requesting my acceptance of £100 to provide the necessary comforts and conveniences during my illness. The money would be paid to my order by Mr. Rau of the house of Eskeles, either in separate sums or all at once if I so desired. . . . You can't imagine my joy! I folded my hands and practically dissolved in tears of gratitude! Over and over again I kept saying, "Thank God for these Londoners . . . thank God for the whole English nation. . . . God bless them and reward them all a thousandfold!" . . . While I contentedly slept that night, the excitement of the gift apparently caused one of my wounds to open. Next morning, I found myself lying in dripping-wet bedclothing. In fact, a large portion of the mighty tide had flowed halfway across the floor to form a steaming puddle in the middle of the room! . . . This proved that Beethoven could now deliver his own "babies." At any rate, from now on, I did my sleeping wrapped in oilcloth instead of undersheets and blankets.

Less than an hour after receiving Moscheles's letter, I was visited by Herr Rau. He wanted to know what proportion of the sum I wished to have delivered at once, and I begged him to send the entire amount. On Friday the sixteenth, it arrived—1,000 florins! . . . With the old cash box filled nearly to its lid, I felt once again like a happy little boy who could at least look forward to a few comfortable days! No longer did we economize on the amounts spent for fish, beef, and vegetables. We even invested in a new easy chair, one big enough to hold me and my belly. In this, I would sit for a half hour each day, while Sali and "Papageno" went about making up my bed.

On Sunday morning, Schindler took my dictation of a thank-you note to Moscheles:

> Vienna, March 18, 1827
> My dear good Moscheles,
>
> I can't describe to you in words with what feelings I read your letter of March 1st. The generosity with which the Philharmonic Society almost anticipated my petition has

> touched the innermost depths of my soul. I therefore beg of you, my dear Moscheles, to be the agent through which I transmit my sincerest thanks to the Philharmonic Society for their particular sympathy and help!
>
> I found myself obliged to collect at once the entire sum of 1,000 florins, as I was in the unpleasant position of being about to borrow money, which would have brought me new embarrassments. Concerning the concert which the Philharmonic Society has resolved to give for my benefit, I beg the Society not to abandon this noble purpose, and from the proceeds of the concert to deduct the 1,000 florins already sent to me. And if the Society is graciously disposed to send me the balance, I will pledge myself to return my heartiest thanks to the Society by binding myself to compose for it either a new symphony (which lies already sketched in my desk), or a new overture, or something else which the Society would like.
>
> May heaven very soon restore my health, and I shall prove to the generous Englishmen how greatly I appreciate their interest in my sad fate. Your noble act will never be forgotten, and I shall follow this with special thanks to Sir Smart and Mr. Stumpff. . . . Farewell!
>
> With kindest remembrances from your friend who highly esteems you,
>
> Ludwig van Beethoven

My plans for Smart and Stumpff were never carried through since there remained for me but one more week of life on Earth!

Most of the final week was spent sleeping. My disease acted somewhat like an anesthetic, in that I became less and less conscious of what was going on about me. . . . There are those who say that Franz Schubert paid me a visit. Perhaps he did, perhaps he didn't. If he did, then I'm afraid that I was very rude. I must have slept through the entire event. . . . I would have really liked to have met this young man. His "duet present" had provided happy hours for Karl and me. Also, I had recently "read through" some fifty of his songs, and couldn't believe Schindler when he told me that a Schubert of barely thirty years had already composed over five hundred of them! . . . Each setting, in its own way, revealed a natural beauty and textual sensitivity that betrayed an enormous musical talent! I wanted to examine his sonatas, symphonies, and operas. If they contained anything like the lyrical spell of his songs, then here at last would stand before me my musical heir! Here would be the young man to receive the spirit of Haydn and Mozart from the hands of Beethoven! . . .

Several events of the last days come to mind with vivid clarity. . . . There was a final letter to Stieglitz and Company, requesting payment of the 125 ducats still owed me by Prince Galitzin. . . . There were visits from Hummel, his wife, and his young pupil Ferdinand Hiller. Coming from Weimar and having just seen Goethe, they brought me all the latest news of our great poet. On their last visit, I can remember dear Madame Hummel taking her own fine handkerchief and several times drying the sweat from my forehead. . . . There was the afternoon when I awakened to find little Gerhard sitting beside my bed with tears in his eyes:

B. Hosenknopf! . . . What's the crying for? . . . You mustn't spend your time sitting here watching an old man die. . . . What's the matter?

I reached out and raised his chin with my forefinger. In reply to my questions, he pointed to the place in a Conversation Book where someone had written:

YOUR QUARTET WHICH SCHUPPANZIGH PLAYED YESTERDAY DID NOT PLEASE.

Holding his hand tightly, I offered him laconic reassurance:

B. Never mind. It will please them someday. . . . I write only what I know is best, and refuse to be swayed by passing judgments of the day. . . . I know that I'm an artist.

There were constant and loving ministrations by Schindler, Breuning, Johann, and Sali. They came and went so frequently that I couldn't keep track of them. I couldn't be sure who it was that stood beside me with a fresh blanket, a cool cloth, a sip of ice water, a spoonful of soup, or a taste of wine. I probably called them by the wrong names, but this didn't matter. Their sympathetic eyes told me that they understood and forgave me. . . . Several times they sat me up in bed and supported my shaky arm with a pillow, in order to get my signature on a document. I had to copy and sign Breuning's restatement of my will. Signatures were also needed on my January third letter to Bach, and on the statement that officially transferred Karl's guardianship from me to von Breuning.

Toward the end of the week, Wawruch and Johann came and together wrote a frightening admonition in the Conversation Book:

Wr. & J. WE THINK THE TIME HAS COME WHEN YOU SHOULD STRENGTHEN YOURSELF BY RECEIVING HOLY COMMUNION.

Were they serious? . . . Was this their way of admitting their belief that my end was near? . . . I tried to make light of their request.

B. For fifty years I've gotten along without it, why should I bother now?

Wr. & J. YOU WERE BROUGHT UP AS A CHILD OF THE CHURCH. BUT THE DEMANDS OF A BUSY LIFE HAVE MADE YOU CARELESS OF YOUR CHRISTIAN DUTIES.

B. If I've lived carelessly, then let me die that way.

Wr. & J. WON'T YOU LET US CALL THE PRIEST?

B. Why? . . . What hypocrisy! . . . Why should I end my life play-acting at something in which I don't believe?

Wr. & J. YOU MUST HAVE THE PRIEST. . . . YOU OWE AT LEAST THIS MUCH TO GOD AND TO YOUR FELLOWMEN.

B. If I haven't paid my debts by now, then I'm afraid they must go unpaid!

J. IF YOU RECONCILE YOURSELF WITH HEAVEN AND SHOW THE WORLD THAT YOU END YOUR LIFE AS A TRUE CHRISTIAN, THINGS WILL BE MUCH EASIER FOR KARL.

These words of Johann changed my mind. I glanced from him, to the doctor, and then back again. . . . At last I responded as they wished.

B. Have the priest called.

About an hour later, I received the viaticum in the presence of Johann, Therese, Breuning, and Schindler. Before the pale little priest departed, he gave my hands an edifying clasp while I looked up into his thin white face:

B. I thank you, ghostly Sir. I thank you for this last service. . . . You have brought me comfort.

He had no sooner left than my watchful foursome pressed closer than ever to my bed, and stared down at me like so many pious birds. Their pleased expressions seemed to say, "Good! . . . All is well with our Beethoven. No evil can now befall him."

Wishing that I could share their optimism, I studied their faces for a long time before speaking.

B. Well . . . if it does no good, it will do no harm. . . . Didn't I always say it would end this way? . . . Plaudite, amici, comoedia finita est.

After this classical Roman cadence, I sighed deeply, closed my eyes, and went sound asleep.

Whatever tricks my bad old liver was playing on my poor old brain, it let up long enough on Wednesday evening (March twenty-first) to permit me now a perfect recall of my final conversation with Anton Schindler:

B. Well, "Papageno" . . . it won't be long and I'll be going up there.

Sc. YOU MUSTN'T TALK THIS WAY. . . . T,ODAY IS THE BEGINNING OF SPRING. THIS COULD WELL MEAN A CHANGE IN YOUR CONDITION. . . . BE PATIENT AND DO NOT DESPAIR.

B. I've been lying here for four months! One must at last lose patience. . . . Have I shown you this tiny picture of Haydn's birthplace?

Sc. YES. I'VE SEEN IT SEVERAL TIMES.

B. See how little I can remember? . . . The end must really be near!

Sc. YOU SPEND A LOT OF TIME SLEEPING. . . . THIS IS WHY YOU'RE FORGETFUL.

B. Thanks, dear friend. . . . Thank you for your optimism. But I know that my day's work is now finished. . . . There is no physician who can help me, and I'll soon be going above!

Sc. PERHAPS YOU'RE RIGHT. . . . PERHAPS GOD DOES LET US KNOW WHEN OUR FINAL HOUR IS NEAR. . . . BUT I WISH YOU'D TELL ME YOUR SECRET. . . . I'M NOT A YOUNG MAN, AND IN A FEW DAYS OR YEARS I'LL FOLLOW IN YOUR PATH. . . . BUT WHEN *MY* HOUR COMES, I KNOW THAT I'LL BE FILLED WITH TEARS AND DREAD. . . . AND YOU? . . . YOU LIE THERE LIKE SOCRATES HIMSELF. . . . WHAT IS YOUR SECRET? . . . WHENCE COMES YOUR COURAGE? . . . EVEN WITH THE PROSPECTS OF MEETING THE GREAT UNKNOWN, YOU BEHAVE LIKE A GALLANT KNIGHT IN SHINING ARMOR. . . . WHAT IS YOUR PHILOSOPHY OF DEATH?

B. It's something which can't be totally expressed in words. . . . Perhaps Mozart comes closest when he sees death as the doorway to a new life. . . . Or Goethe, who plans to write until he breathes his last breath . . . this in the belief that nature will then provide him with the physical means for continuing his writing. . . . I share the faiths of these men. . . . I've always believed in my own strength and self-reliance. . . . Though I've not found the beauty of God in our church and its sacraments, I have discovered in nature and in art, the divine stampings of a Surpreme Being. And if this sweet God can so fill our lives with inexhaustible inspiration, then death as well must have a beauty of its own. And a thing of beauty is nothing to be feared. . . . In spite of my faults, I've been a good man and have tried to do good works.

Sc. BUT WHAT ABOUT THE REST OF US WHOSE WORKS ARE NOTHING COMPARED TO YOURS?

B. As a musician, I dare say you are a lesser man than I. But what a small stone is musical talent within the total glitter of man's crown! . . . In other matters, I can't compare with what you've done. . . . You've humbled yourself as a faithful servant, bearing endless troubles on my account. And from a Christian standpoint, this is a far greater thing than I have ever done!

In my long acquaintance with Anton Schindler, I had never observed in him anything like an emotional breakdown. Now was an exception. His poor thin frame shook with tears. Instinctively, I reached out my unsteady hand to comfort him. This made him cry all the more.

B. Now now, "Papageno." . . . You must concentrate on your own career, and learn to carry on without me. . . . Are you still giving your concert in two weeks?

He nodded "Yes," while blowing his huge nose so efficiently and proficiently that I imagined I could almost hear the explosion.

Sc. I'LL GIVE MY CONCERT, BUT WHAT WILL IT BE WITHOUT YOU?

B. When Hummel was here, I talked him into joining you for the event. His piano should help your receipts.

Schindler began writing some detailed comments about his concert. As he did so, I must have dozed off. . . . When I again raised my heavy lids and stared into the Conversation Book, all was crossed out except for one little question:

Sc. Do you feel sleepy?
B. I'm afraid I do.
Sc. Well then, good night.

On Saturday, March twenty-fourth, a case containing twelve bottles of Rüdesheimer Berg finally arrived from the Schotts. Schindler set several bottles beside my bed, and held one up for me to read the label. . . . There it was! At long last, my treasured taste of Father Rhine, vintage of 1806. . . . Nearly choking on a weak dry smile, I looked up into Schindler's face and whispered to him the last words I spoke on Earth:

"Pity . . . pity . . . too late!"

I cannot say whether those present had left the room, or whether my eyes had simply focused on the tempting gift, but my last vision of Earth was three bottles of wine. They transported my thoughts to the landscape of my childhood. They recalled the sweet vision of Mother's tears. The faces of young Karl and Breuning's "Hosenknopf" appeared in succession, and then in confused simultaneity. . . . Then came little Bettina with her sparkling eyes. I tried to form her words with my lips: "I am the Bacchus who presses out for men this glorious wine and intoxicates their souls!" A final vision of the Rhine, and the mystic wine faded from my sight.

Those present later informed me that there followed forty-eight hours of unconscious death struggle. Then my poor old body finally stopped breathing at five forty-five on Monday afternoon, March 26, 1827.

Part 2

BEETHOVEN NOW (1827–1950)

The Beginning of Second-Order Life

Chapter 25

A warm summer evening, a huge red sun still plainly visible through toothpick trees fencing the western slope of a long straight road, tall grass and bony shrubbery on the eastern side, crickets and tree frogs juggling into position for their evening concert, a wide two-lane road (smooth like macadam, only dark green with phosphorescent dividing lines). . . . For thirty minutes, absolute silence along the road. A gentle wind blows subtle rhythms through the skinny trees, but makes not a sound at its game. A soft, puffy bunny sticks its pink nose out of the underbrush, and points it due south into the breeze, which it attempts to decode. . . . Suddenly the brown rabbit's nose stops twitching. His ears point upward and seem to lengthen, as he jerks his head in the opposite direction. Something's coming down the road! It's moving fast and quietly, but neither fast enough nor quietly enough to sneak up on these brown ears. Not a man on horseback, not the Vienna post chaise. . . . It's an automobile! A sweet little, sleek little sports car at that. . . . Could this be 2010, and a beautiful country road on the coast of New Jersey?

As the underslung, wide-tracked, rust-colored, tan-topped two-seater speeds by, our retreating cottontail observes there to be nothing "ordinary" about it. The low-centered speedster is neither a Ferrari nor a Jaguar nor a Mercedes, but it radiates that pedigreed gleam and contour that would certainly place it among such a company. And yet there's something different about this pipeless sports. Cutting past at better than a hundred, there's not a sound except for the whisper of its tires. The light of sun and the shade of trees play hypnotic patterns across its gleaming hood. . . . Could this smooth bomb be powered electrically? . . .

The only occupant of our "spokey" sports is the driver. And a handsome young fellow is he, sitting there beneath curly black hair with the face and body of a teenage Adonis! He's dressed impeccably in a soft white shirt, a silver ascot and vest, dark trousers and a bright blue perfectly tailored sport jacket. His trousers are tight fitting. They reveal the neat waist and beautifully developed legs of a young athlete . . . something like those of a weightlifter who swims enough to round off square corners. Although his handsome face shines with a coppery heathful glow, its sad expression hovers between disappointment and anger. He keeps push-buttoning changes on the car radio. Suddenly three speakers blast into the middle of a masterful performance of the *Hammerklavier*'s *Fugue*. This does it! Off goes the radio! One thing is certain—our driver is no friend of Beethoven's. . . .

In something like twenty-five minutes, he leisurely chops down another fifty miles of smooth green road without meeting so much as one other car in either direction. The flashing countryside is extremely beautiful: no signboards, telegraph poles, or wayside shops. In fact, not even a home or building to mar the pastoral scene. We must be driving through some huge national park on an evening when it's closed to all but one visitor. . . . Suddenly, a crossroad sweeps into view, bringing with it the first trace of civilization: a rustic route sign with half-a-dozen clearly legible markings on it. Our driver slows to a stop, pulls out a map, compares it to the sign, and chooses a sharp left turn. In two minutes, he's once again speeding along miles of empty green highway, not unlike the road from which he has just turned. . . . With such a handsome girl-stopping physique, and like-talented sports car to call his own, and with such a beautiful evening and countryside to drive through, how can we explain the sad, angry look on this young man's face?

Our silent sports travels about ten miles east and then turns south again. . . . What's this? . . . It can't be! . . . It is! . . . A signboard! . . . There on the left is a huge artfully constructed wayside announcement. In letters two feet tall, it reads,

SEASIDE VILLAS
No.131–No.140
NEXT THIRTY MILES
ON THE LEFT

Though not yet dark enough to be put into use, the sign is obviously provided with elaborate means of illumination. There's no doubt about it, we have "driven into" the age of electricity! . . .

Spaced at three-mile intervals are sandy blacktop turnoffs leading to the advertised villas. On the left side at each turnoff is a fancy gadget about three feet tall, which could pass for a small mailbox or a large birdhouse. Each of these displays the easily read number of the corresponding seaside cottage. Our driver slows down at No. 137 and observes a bright red light on the top of its "birdhouse." A loud "Damn!" is followed by more elaborate curses, which audibly confirm an even angrier expression on the young man's face.

He clocks another three miles to the next turnoff, and then actually breaks into a smile at the sight of a green light above "No. 138." Entering the blacktop, he follows it about a mile to an orange-yellow beach that turns out to be wide, flat, and "drivable" like the one at Daytona, Florida. Where the road meets the sand, there's an arrow-shaped sign containing a "138" and pointing south. A falling sun of gold makes our sports look reddish brown as it skims along parallel to the ocean for half a mile, then pulls up in front of a cozy villa set picturesquely before a backdrop of sand dunes and tall grass. Its brick walls are painted blue, its tile roof is white, its door latch is on the outside, and has neither lock nor key! Our driver jumps out of his coupé, enters the cottage, makes a quick tour of inspection, then drives back to the "birdhouse" numbered 138. Oddly enough, part of the little structure *is* for receiving mail, but its upper half is an electronic device for registering guests at this particular villa. On the inside of its door are printed instructions:

> If the light on top is green, this means that Villa 138 has been housecleaned and is ready for guests. Please dial the number of days you intend to stay. If your visit is longer than one week, the maintenance crew will automatically come for housecleaning each seven days from the date of your arrival. Should you leave earlier than expected, please cancel your unused reservation by pushing the black button. Maximum stay at this Villa is sixty-three days.
>
> HAPPY VACATION
>
> IMPORTANT: If the light on top is red, this means that Villa 138 is already occupied or has not yet been readied for

> guests. Please note. If you desire information concerning the availability of Villas 101–200, push the red button and dial 1222-339.

Our young man dials a reservation for one night, and then speeds off in the same southerly direction, checking the red light atop No. 138 in his rearview mirrors. . . . Is some lucky girl to be his guest for the night?

During the next hour, a fading sky above our topless coupé takes off his coat of sunset hues, puts on a night-colored robe of dark blue purple, and contemplates his starry crown. . . . We turn right, enter a four-lane expressway, and speed inland at considerably better than a hundred. It is during our forty minutes on this divided road that we meet our first signs of traffic. We pass a huge black sedan going in our direction, and count the lights of several cars coming toward us. Not much traffic for an expressway! . . . A brightly illuminated sign advertising the accommodations of Chateau L'Arbre Fée de Bourlemont invites us to leave the speedway in five miles. This we do. Some twenty minutes of winding two-lane road lead us through rolling hills to the chateau's parking lot. . . . Whom have we come here to meet? . . .

L'Arbre Fée de Bourlemont is a rambling five-story U-shaped resort hotel constructed like a baby Versailles. Besides the well-shrubberied, hedged-in parking lot, its commodious "U" contains elaborate gardens, tempting paths, graceful sun decks, and an enormous swimming pool. Our hero walks directly toward the pool, as though there is no doubt in his mind that the person he comes to meet will be found there. He's not disappointed. By the green and blue lights directed on and through the water, we observe there to be only three people in swimming. At the shallow end, two small boys are roughhousing over an inflated hoop. On the ten-foot side, a white bathing cap is streaming its way across the width. Our sportsman takes his position on the inlaid walk at the edge of the pool, and waits for the cap to come up for air on the opposite side.

When it does, he shouts across the water: "Are you ready? . . . I'll clock your new record for a hundred feet!"

A beautiful arm at the left of the cap waves back.

"One, two, three . . . GO!"

Our swimmer skims along like a wake-cutting speedboat, and then (as she approaches) turns out to be a curvaceous mermaid who jumps out of the water with such disarming suddenness as to totally interrupt her handsome timekeeper's calculations and watch watching. As she unsnaps and pops off her cap, the loveliest blond hair imaginable falls into tempting bangs and irresistible ringlets. Her delectable teenage charms are abundantly revealed by the scantiest of "two pieces." She comes close enough to our friend for a hearty embrace, but the water on her body and the fine clothes on his prevent it from taking place. The two of them carefully lean toward each other. He places his hands on her firm little waist, and their lips meet in a kiss that is less than passionate but considerably more than a "Hi there!" The deepest blue eyes that ever stared, do so from beneath their dainty blond thatch:

JA. Paul! Are you still the same old fellow?
P. Yes, Judy. Seventeen-and-a-half years old, and *still* the same old fellow!

What a strange question! . . . What an unusual reply! . . . What could they possibly mean?

Paul helps his Judy into a thigh-high terry cloth robe, and the two of them walk toward the locker room entrance of the chateau.

JA. Were you able to get No. 137?
P. No. We'll have to settle for 138!
JA. That's not so bad. It's only a mile or two south of the light. And the beach is probably just as smooth.

They pass an ornately barbered hedge. Paul grabs Judy by the arm, pulls her to a stop, and points her in the direction of an adjoining grass plot.

P. Just think, Kitten, we first met by this little hedge three years ago almost to the very day!
JA. Yes, Boo. And if my father hadn't lost his ring of keys, you would have saved yourself the pangs and frustrations of falling in love with me.
P. Praise be your daddy's keys! . . . You looked so cute going along on your knees there in the grass. Even at thirteen and with ponytails, you were sexy.
JA. No one could be more surprised than I was. . . . Imagine coming around that hedge on your knees and suddenly finding yourself nose to nose with a handsome young knight of fourteen-and-a-half,

wearing swim trunks, and creeping along on his knees. Then by way of explanation and formal introduction hearing nothing more from him than, "Hi, Kitten!"

P. And to explain your unladylike behavior, there you were with big blue kitten eyes, and nothing more profound to say than,"Boo!"

JA. Oh well, it was a profitable nose-bumping. It produced two classical nicknames, one set of keys, and we've been in love ever since.

They kiss again and resume their walk, hand-in-hand. After a few meditative steps, Paul continues the conversation.

P. And our parents didn't even suspect.

JA. Not until last year, they didn't.

P. Now they'll probably never come to L'Arbre Fée for another Christmas vacation.... Do you think they'd explode if they knew we were here together?

JA. I don't think so, Boo. . . . They probably have an idea that we're spending a day here between quarters. . . . I believe that our parents have a mutual respect for the two of us; it's just that they consider us too young to be as seriously involved with each other as we already are.

P. Well, Kitten, far be it from me to doubt the wisdom of our parents, but I know we're in love, and this is the one thing in life that I *am* sure of.

JA. I too, Boo. . . . Here's the locker room. Where shall we have dinner?

P. How 'bout a table for two at the Boot and Saddle?

JA. Steak again?

P. Do you mind?

JA. Not really. . . . I like the Boot better than the main dining room, anyway. . . . See you in ten minutes.

The Boot and Saddle is a homey wood-burning, spit-turning steakhouse on the ground floor of the chateau. Paul stops at its bar for some dark foamy beer. He calls it by name: "A pitcher of Old Vienna, please." He drinks half a glass at the bar, then carries the rest with him to a small candle-lighted table by a window that commands a colorful view of the courtyard's illuminated fountains and gardens. He puts his elbow on the red checkered tablecloth, props his chin on his palm, stares out of the window, and becomes totally lost in thought. . . . Somehow, as if by impulse, Boo turns just in time to observe his Judy enter the room. What a symphony of beauty and rhythm she is! Poured into an above-the-knee, skin-tight, brass-buttoned single piece denim, the girlish quiver of her perfect body is now in some ways even more devastatingly revealed than it was in her less-than-brief swimsuit! Paul wonders what great master of seduction could have taught his little Kitten to perambulate the way she does. Her firm round hips move with a certain right-left rightness about them, which makes it impossible (when she walks) to think of anything under heaven except how delightfully she walks! Paul jumps up and holds Judy's chair. This gives him another chance to observe (from behind) those perfectly sculptured calves—muscular and yet feminine to the last smooth inch.

JA. You're a naughty boy, Boo.
P. Why, my dear?
JA. The way you stare at me.
P. Such beauty is meant to be stared at. You'd better get used to it!

To prove this point, Paul focuses his stare on the twin mounds of pink-and-white loveliness that breathe temptingly within the less-than-half-concealing neckline of Judy's dress. She counters with a sharp thunderbolt of her own, then tries to change the subject:

JA. Have you ordered yet?
P. No.
JA. Aren't you hungry?
P. How can you ask me a question like that?
JA. I mean, aren't you hungry for steak?
P. I was. . . . But now, I think I'd rather just sit here and watch you breathe.
JA. (*Judy reaches across the table and slaps the back of Paul's hand.*) You are a naughty boy. If you don't behave yourself, I won't go driving with you tonight. . . . Now let's order.

Before she can make her retreat, Paul grabs Judy's right hand, raises it to his lips, implants several kisses thereon, then gently releases his grip. He winks reassuringly at his Kitten, then nods to a waiter their readiness to order.

If these young people have in any way been adequately portrayed, then you must recognize them as the handsomest couple you have ever met. You must expect to see them today (possibly tomorrow) as the newest and greatest discovery of youthful beauty on stage, screen, or TV. . . . Under normal conditions, this would be the case. But the sociophysical context in which we must view our couple is not normal. . . . There's something strange about the "Boot and Saddle." As we glance from table to table, nowhere in the entire room do we find a person who does not have a youthful glow and bodily charm comparable to that which we have observed in Paul and Judy. . . . How can this be? . . . Including waiters and waitresses, how can the entire forty or fifty occupants of a dining room boast uniform physical perfection of such exceptional quality and degree?

While ordering dessert, our couple requests that a lunch basket be packed for them: club sandwiches, fruit, a thermos of coffee, some ice, and a bottle of champagne. Along with Judy's suitcase and Paul's suitcase, there's barely enough room for the large thermos-fitted basket in the compact trunk of the coupé. But there is! And with top still lowered, our young lovers whisk away in speedy silence for a ninety-minute drive through the warm breezes and starry dreams of a midsummer's night. Within a half hour, Boo's Kitten has curled up on his shoulder and is fast asleep. Though he knows she can't hear him above the wind-cutting sound of their sports, Paul whispers,

P. I love you, Darling.

Judy doesn't reply in words, but as her soft golden hair caresses her lover's nose, right cheek and ear, it seems to say,

JA. And I you, Boo.

During the entire drive, they pass but one other car and arrive at Villa 138 shortly after 12:00 PM. Several of its lights are on, as Paul had left them. They change into their swimsuits and go for an invigorating dip in a rolling surf, which feels like seventy degrees because of the cooling ocean breeze. Then splashing through baby breakers up to their knees, they walk hand-in-hand a mile and a half north to the quaint little lighthouse that seems to hold a sentimental value for the two of them. Like the villa, its door latch is on the outside. They enter and climb five stories of spiral stairs to the top of the stubby tower. From here, they survey miles of moonlight beach with its cresting whitecaps, pounding waves, and rolling dunes of tall dancing grass. After examining their domain, our lovers engage in a crushing embrace. Paul is totally disarmed by the sudden feel of Judy's warm (almost naked) body clamped firmly against his. She wriggles at the knowing explorations of his hands, but soon terminates these by involving her lover in an extremely thorough kiss:

P. My! . . . Kitten! . . . That's quite a kiss, compared to three years ago.

JA. I thought you'd appreciate something special to celebrate our "anniversary."

P. Just think! . . . Three years ago, this very night our parents were about to terminate their Christmas vacation. We climbed to the top of this tower, admitted to each other that we were in love, and appropriately confirmed our declaration with love's first kiss. . . . Pretty drastic developments for only one week's acquaintance!

JA. And with each passing year, my love for Boo has grown and deepened until it is now unquenchable!

P. As is mine for you. . . . But damn it, Judy! How much longer do we have to wait?

JA. It won't be long now, Boo. You've been very patient, and this makes me love you all the more. You're now seventeen-and-a-half. Before this time next year, your waiting will be over. You'll know fully who you are. You'll be a whole person at last . . . in total command of your past and future. . . . Perhaps by then, I too will be a whole person. No longer will the mysterious darkness of earlier lives cast doubts upon our love.

Whole persons! . . . What can Judy mean by this?

The electric clock on the light's control panel confirms the time, and our couple leaves the tower. They walk, run, hop, skip, and caress their way down the beach to Villa 138. After showering off the salt from their ocean swim, they dress in comfortable sweatshirts and shorts, then climb with their picnic basket to an adjoining dune several feet higher than the cottage roof. There in a cozy spot, spreading their warm beach blanket and cuddling up in each other's arms, they enjoy their sandwiches, coffee, and fruit. Then while sipping champagne and embracing the clear sky with its billions of silvery stars and three bright moons, Paul whispers into Judy's ear,

P. It's past midnight, Darling. Happy New Year!

JA. Same to you, Boo. . . . Happy 1827!

Chapter 26

Across Paul Rezler's face blows a chilling ocean breeze. The intent of its starlight journey is sufficient to awaken him from a sound sleep. There are still two bright moons above the horizon, providing ample light for Paul's half-open eyes to read the dial of his wristwatch—4:30 AM. He and Kitten have slept in each other's arms for nearly two hours! Because of the penetrating dampness of nighttime beach, Paul decides that he and his ladylove should climb down from their tree-high dune, and do the rest of their sleeping in the comfortable bedrooms of Villa 138. Carefully and quietly, he folds the soft blanket over his sleeping Judy. But as he attempts to pick up his precious cargo, she opens her bright shining eyes and starts giggling.

JA. Bless you, Boo! I was just dreaming that you were raping me, and now I awaken to find that you are. What a naughty, wonderful boy!

P. You're the naughty one! . . . Such utilitarianism never occurred to me. I was merely carrying you inside the cottage, where you'd be warm and comfortable. . . . But now that you mention it, I suppose this is as good a time and place as any to steal away your virginity.

Still wrapped in her blanket, Paul raises Judy higher until their lips meet in a searching kiss. At its conclusion, she reaches out and taps his nose with her forefinger, looking up at him with a glowing love and respect and admiration, which identify her as anything but a "naughty girl."

JA. Put me down, Boo. Come join me in our little cocoon. Let's look at these stars for a while, *then* we'll leave. . . . I've never seen them so clear and bright, too beautiful to simply walk away from.

Once again our friends cuddle up in their blanket. As they lie there pointing out familiar patterns in the sky, their conversation turns to matters astronomical.

P. I agree with you, Judy. It *is* a beautiful sight, but it's all so big that I feel small and of no consequence.

JA. You needn't, love. . . . Buried within our brains is a spiritual subelectron, the tiniest of all particles, and yet of greater significance than the entire display we see above us tonight.

P. But we have so much to do besides wait and wait and wait! . . . Will these precious subelectrons, these eternal souls of ours, never come into their own? . . . How long must we wait for the doorway of Second-Order life to open before us?

JA. Not much longer, Boo. The advent of our rebirth occurs somewhere between ten and eighteen years of age. . . . So you have at most six months to wait.

P. I can't stand it! . . . If only tomorrow would be our big day.

JA. Perhaps it will, perhaps it won't. . . . After all these years, I know we can last another few months. The fact that so many of our friends and classmates have already experienced rebirth is no doubt the cause of our impatience. Both my brothers were "reborn" during their fourteenth year, your brother when he was only ten, and even your little sister (three years ago) when she was twelve. Naturally this makes us feel terribly old and neglected. . . . But it shouldn't! . . . "Rebirth" is a tremendous adventure, and we should look forward to it. Though we stand to experience it an infinite number of times, only *once* are we the recipient *of it*, rather than a contributor *to it*!

P. How do you mean?

JA. In a few days or months, we shall inherit a set of spiritual patterns from First-Order life. During our present waiting period, though fully aware of who we *are*, we have no idea of who we *were*. There's something goose-pimply about this, Boo!

P. I'll say there is! And it doesn't make the waiting easier.

JA. But actually we have little to complain about. . . . What if we were a pair of Hundredth-Order teenagers, waiting to inherit the spiritual accumulations of ninety-nine prior lifetimes? Then we'd really have reason to wonder and worry.

P. Thank God we *are* Second Order!

JA. Exactly! . . . In most cases, the inheritance of a single order of life has less than a dominating influence over what follows. . . . Any day now, a pair of Earthlings will die out of their First-Order existence. Whether their bodies are carefully entombed in the crypt of a king or dumped namelessly into a pauper's grave is of no consequence. All that is "eternal" about them is faithfully recorded in their spiritual subelectrons, which are death-freed from their First-Order brains, and which have sufficient spiritual momentum to place them in orbit within the third subelectronic ring, setting the spherical boundary of our own Second-Order-MAJOR universe. After a few days in orbit, these spiritual particles are electromagnetically attracted into our brains, and become inseparably fused with our souls. The waiting is over. We are at last whole beings of the Second Order. And through the miracle of total recall, we shall have literally inherited the spiritual patterns of First-Order life!

P. And great teacher, how does knowing this make waiting any easier?

JA. Bless you, Boo! I don't mean to sound like a textbook, but I think we should remember that only once in all eternity are we called upon to suffer the anxieties of waiting and wondering about who we were.

P. I think I follow you, Kitten. You're emphasizing that only one time must we experience rebirth on the *receiving* end—from *this* side of the fence.

JA. Yes. And shouldn't this fact ease the burden of waiting?

P. It should. . . . But it doesn't seem to in *my* case.

JA. As soon as we've acquired our thousand years of First-Order patterns, we have only to settle down and build upon them the one thousand years of Second-Order life. Then when death and rebirth carry us into the Third Order, there'll be no waiting around to find out who we *are* and *were*! This will be done for us by a couple of Third-Order teenagers, eagerly absorbing what the totality of *our* lives will bring to *their* souls.

P. You're sweet, Judy. . . . All that you say is true, and I have no business being impatient. But what do you suggest might help us through the next few months?

JA. Forget about rebirth. Concentrate upon other things.

P. Like maybe what?

JA. Like the reassuring message (points upward) this beautiful sky has for our souls!

P. Tell me what he's saying, Judy.

JA. Tonight he's autobiographical . . . so proud of being a great big First-Second-Order universe that he sounds boastful. He reminds us that over 51 billion years ago, his present life cycle began its expansion from an invisible blob of subenergy, smaller than the point of a pin. Within a few hundred years, three spherical rings of subenergy had spun themselves free from this tiny mass core, and had established gravitational limits. Between the first and second of these subelectronic rings (those farthest from the core) lies our First-Order universe. (See sketch; subelectronic rings are specifically numbered.)

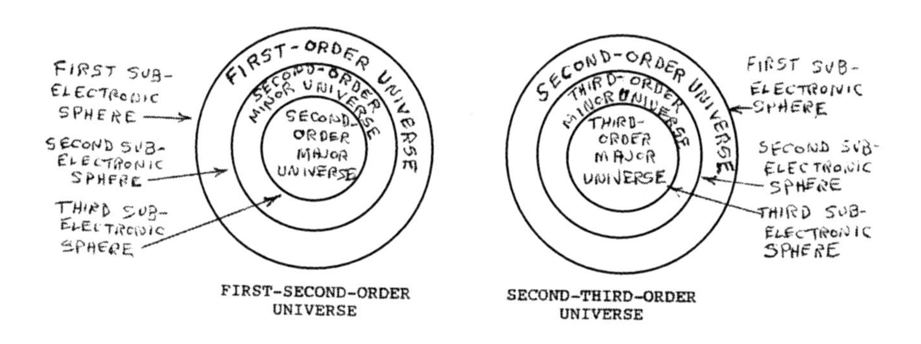

FIRST-SECOND-ORDER UNIVERSE

SECOND-THIRD-ORDER UNIVERSE

The second and third rings establish the boundaries of our Second-Order-Minor universe. And at the center of all this, extending from the third ring to the core itself, is our Second-Order-Major universe, whose sky smiles down upon us tonight. . . . For three million years these bounding rings continued to expand, racing from the mass core at better than the speed of light. As they did so, about half of the subelectrons comprising these rings lost sufficient velocity to fall from orbit and pass into the solid spaces of the three-part universe. Here they became the matter and energy from which all things were built, accounting for everything from particles of dust to circling galaxies . . . from starlight to the sound of music. . . .

Then during the fourth million years came the first colonization of our universe with plant, animal, and human life. During each succeeding million years, it became host to yet another life system, until today there are over 51 thousand space cultures living within this mighty frame.

P. Whoa, Kitten. . . . How is the personal account of a giant braggart supposed to make us feel more secure . . . or our waiting easier?

JA. There's more to his story, Boo. If you'll just listen. . . . He takes a deep breath and flexes his muscles. His proud smile breaks into a roar of conceited laughter, as he contemplates his life for the next 150 billion years. . . . The poor being is entitled to a little conceit. . . . But something unexpected happens. . . . His confidence melts into a look of genuine admiration . . . then tearful envy as he looks down upon two young lovers wrapped in a cozy gray blanket and staring up at him from a tiny sand dune on Aaron VP 33. He realizes that his expansion is not infinite! Following a mere 200 billion years of growth, he will enter the reverse pattern of his cycle. His subelectronic rings will begin to contract, and after 100 billion years of moving toward his mass core will (in the final 300 years) once again convert all the matter and energy of our three-part universe into an invisible speck of concentrated subelectrons moving in the Second-Order space of our parent Second-Third-Order universe. Immediately he will begin another cycle of expansion and contraction, continuing these repetitions for nearly 300 trillion years! . . . How could such a long-lived creature be envious of the likes of us? How could one whose body fills the heavens with stars and light turn jaundiced eyes upon a pair of minute Second-Order beings who will die out of their mortal bodies in less than 1,000 years? . . . He *is* jealous of us, Boo. . . . He's jealous because for all his size and extent, there's nothing immortal about him. At the end of his allotted time, he will be absorbed by the contracting first ring of our Second-Third-Order universe, and will completely lose his identity. . . . Yet within *us* dwells the secret of true immortality—a human soul, a spiritual subelectron whose infinite capacity for surviving death and experiencing rebirth can make the insignificant 300 trillion years of our immediate universe seem like the passing of a day. . . . With this in mind, seeing something above us as big as this sky, and yet knowing that we are greater than he, shouldn't we be able to stand a few weeks or months of waiting?

P. Yes, Kitten. You've gotten your point across. . . . I'll remember your story and try to be patient.

At approximately 8:00 AM on the first day of the new year, Paul is rudely awakened by a sprinkling of saltwater on his upturned face. There beside his bed stands Judy, clad in her less-than-modest swimsuit, and still dripping wet from an early morning swim. Paul closes the one eye he had opened and turns his face wallward, hoping Judy will take the hint. She doesn't. Finding her "water treatment" ineffective, she grabs Paul's sheet and gives it a mighty pull. This technique likewise must be abandoned, for it lays her handsome lover bare to the waist. She kneels beside the bed and whispers into his ear.

JA. Are you still the same old fellow?
P. (*Yawning, Paul stretches and turns toward his tormentor.*) Yes, Kitten. . . . If I weren't, do you think I'd be lying here trying to sleep through your kittenish pranks? . . . How about you? . . . Don't tell me you've—
JA. No, Boo! . . . I'm still the same Kitten, and I hate to awaken such a dear fellow. But if you plan to reach Valhalla by noon, we'd better be on our way.
P. I'll shower, then we'll leave.
JA. Not without another dip in the ocean. Come on down, the water's perfect!

Paul joins his love for a half hour of surfboarding. Then they shower, dress in comfortable walking clothes, return to L'Arbre Fée for a healthy breakfast, have a picnic lunch packed for them, then drive 150 miles inland to a range of beautiful green mountains known as the Nibelungen. These are not unlike the Great Smokies of eastern United States, and soon after entering the range, our couple turns off the main parkway at a sign marked, "Valhalla—Elevation 7,200 ft." On fifteen miles of smooth, narrow, upgrade road, they drive to within 2,000 feet of Valhalla's summit, and park their sleek sports in a stone-walled lot from which a dozen different foot trails beckon them to explore the mountain's crest.

At the entrance of each path is a wooden "mailbox," smaller than but similar to those guarding the villas. These boxes have three lights on their roofs: red means that the trail is occupied or reserved (please keep out), amber indicates that there are climbers on the trail but welcome aboard (the more the merrier), green signifies an empty trail (come climb me). Trail No. 7 displays a red light since Paul had phoned in a reservation from the chateau. He and Judy climb to within a few hundred feet of Valhalla's summit, then turn off on a little path of their own. Steep and narrow like the trail of a mountain goat, it leads to a throne of rock and moss just big enough for two. Here they sit, embrace, and (for an hour) silently dream about their future plans. The eternal wind sings its mournful song in accompaniment to endless pockets of gray-white fog that traverse Valhalla's peak like so many "lost souls." Warmth and light of noonday sun cause widening gaps in this funeral procession of ghostly passers-by . . . gaps big enough to bring to the eyes of our beach-blanketed king and queen inspiring views of the bright, silent valley below.

Paul kneels at the side of their "honored perch," removes a loose rock and (from a crevice behind it) takes out a small velvet-covered cubical box. Again cuddling beneath their blanket, they open the container and smile down upon a wedding-engagement set of sparkling diamond rings. The stones are modest in size, but certainly of rare gem quality. With a happy sigh, Judy breaks the long silence.

JA. Well, at least our treasure is still intact.

P. It better be! . . . These stones have been in the family for a dozen generations. . . . Do you think we're being overly sentimental with our buried treasure, our lighthouse, and our quarterly trips to Valhalla?

JA. No, Boo. Such little romantics make the waiting easier. . . . Eighteen months ago you placed beneath this stone the symbols of our formal engagement, and (hopefully) of our marriage. Each quarter since then, we've journeyed here believing that surely by our next visit, one or possibly both of us would become full Second-Order beings.

P. And here we are . . . another quarter comes and goes with no change in either of us!

JA. But with its coming and going it brings the expectations of a new quarter, along with the assurance that there aren't too many more of them to wait.

P. I'm beginning to wonder.

JA. There can't be! . . . In another six months, you'll crash the "eighteen-year" barrier. And only one in ten billion has to wait beyond eighteen years for rebirth.

P. Watch me be this unfortunate soul. . . . Do you mind if I smoke, Kitten?

JA. No way! I love the smell of your pipe, especially out-of-doors. . . . Did my little sermon last night help you at all?

P. It did, "Professor" Judy. . . . Thanks to you, I'll probably hold my impatience in tow. . . . There is something exciting about it all. We might as well sit back and enjoy the anticipation. . . . Just think what's going on in our Earthly minds right about now.

JA. This is what I meant last night. No matter who we are on Earth, we're so much more fortunate here in the Second Order. At least we know that human life offers its possessor the reassuring possibility of an infinite span, without ever once suffering the loss of one's accumulating spiritual identity. And further, when we finally die out of our present Major Order of life, we are guaranteed rebirth into either the Major or Minor physical reality of our Third-Order universe. With such positive assurance, death should have no sting for us!

P. If I were some poor uninformed Earthling, I don't think I'd have the courage to face death. . . . Imagine what it must be like! . . . Regardless of whether I was a primitive tribesman filled to my beaded neck with sun-god awareness, or a learned professor of theology rolling smooth-sounding metaphysics across my tongue, when that final hour began to breathe down my neck, I'd be scared out of my wits. . . . In spite of Earth's happy and persistent rumors of Christ's death and resurrection, I'd probably be the type who would stand before the empty tomb with its rolled-back stone and, even on Easter morning, have plenty of doubts about life beyond death!

JA. It's strange that Aaron (as Christ on Earth) has done so little to convince Earthlings of the potential immortality of their lives!

P. Someday when I meet him face-to-face, this is the first question I'm going to ask.

JA. We're taught that such a gospel is being withheld from Earthlings until their culture enters its Space Age.

P. Probably when Aaron does tell them the good news, they won't believe him anyway.

JA. Aaron . . . what a great man he must be!

P. Someday (in fact, many times) our lives will cross his path, and we'll sit down and talk with him as unassumingly as you and I now speak with each other.

JA. What must it be like to meet the founder of our very own space culture—the physical and spiritual Father of the Aaronian System?

P. Physically, he'll not look much different from us. No matter during which of our lifetimes we meet him, he's bound to occupy the same Order of physical body as ours. . . . But spiritually and intellectually, what a chasm of difference between us.

JA. Understandably so, Boo. . . . Just think . . . His spiritual subelectron (soul) carries within it the instant and total recall of nonillions of nonillions of ordinary lifetimes!

P. And following these countless lives, he entered his prophetic phase and has spent nearly 100,000 spiritual lifetimes in the founding and nurturing of the space culture that bears *his* name, and of which we are a part.

JA. This Aaronian stream is the 51,327th life system to be established within our immediate First-Second-Order universe. Although it is over 2,220,000 years old, there are only two other cultures younger than ours!

P. And it all began in the Milky Way galaxy of our First-Order universe on a tiny speck called Earth, a standard globe that had sustained plant and animal life for nearly 330 million years before Aaron stopped by to procreate his race of humans.

JA. A race of men and women which has been physically projected forward through 1,000 years of Second-Order life.

P. And from then on, each successive life has a span of almost exactly 1,000 years! . . . We have *Aaron* to thank for the reality of our eternal lives.

JA. I understand this perfectly well. . . . Aaron! . . . He's hard to believe!

P. And yet someday we'll meet him. . . . We'll meet him face-to-face . . . that physical and spiritual being responsible for building the entire system into which we were born, and through which we are called upon to live.

JA. But when that happy day first comes, I don't expect Aaron to "look down" upon me as the poor little person that I am.

P. I'm sure he won't, Judy. . . . When he stands there in all his authority, beckoning us to follow him, he won't be speaking to us as a master to a servant, as a god to a knee-bent worshiper, nor as a great lord and judge of our lives. I think it'll be more like having a friendly talk with an Eternal Teacher, or with one's own father who desires nothing more for each of his children than that we should choose what is best for our immediate lives, that we should make the most of our small but developing talents, and that we should continue to grow! This in the hope that one day (through an infinitude of deaths and rebirths) our lives, too, may enter their Prophetic phase . . . that very special relationship with God, wherein each of *us* will be called upon to experience "Fatherhood" in its ultimate glory, becoming (as Aaron has now become) the founder of our own space culture, a Wayshower, the author of a race of humans . . . our very own life stream.

JA. Do you think there's any chance that we'll meet him here in our Second-Order life?

P. I doubt this very much, Judy. . . . Since Aaron was last here from 1701 to 1733 (synchronized perfectly with Earth time), it would be most unusual for Him to visit the same Order of his culture twice during the lives of many of its inhabitants. . . . But then, we never know! That's what's so fascinating about it all. We might wake up next week to the glorious news that Aaron has been reborn in our midst for another thirty years!

JA. How wonderful this would be! . . . Just think, my parents were living during Aaron's last visit here. Though they had not yet met one another, each separately did manage a private consultation with Aaron, and each found in him predominantly the historical and spiritual personality of Jesus.

P. Naturally they would! . . . Had my parents been living during Aaron's visit, they too would have seen in him a great deal of the Christ. . . . When we first meet him, we'll probably do the same. Anyone this close to our First-Order life who has been raised in a Christian home, or who has cultivated a love (or even a modest respect) for the life and teachings of Jesus, is bound to feel the impact of this powerful facet of Aaron's spirit and personality. . . . Imagine looking into those very eyes whose spiritual subelectron faithfully records (besides the love and wisdom of countless lifetimes) a ninety-third visit on Earth, which was none other than the final twenty-one years in the life of Christ!

JA. I'd probably burst into tears. . . . Imagine! . . . Those eyes! . . . The spirit behind them. . . . That selfsame spirit which looked down from a cross, forgave his children for their blindness, and referred itself into God's keeping, thereby terminating a lifetime whose impact required the very calendars of Earth to throw away their accumulations of years, and begin a new accounting of things!

P. Dear Kitten, I hope that together we shall make our first pilgrimage to Aaron's feet . . . if not in this lifetime, then surely in the next.

JA. Perhaps we shall. . . . But even here we mustn't plan so far ahead. . . . As things now stand, we are both Christians simply because we were born of Christian parents. We both look forward to meeting Aaron and finding in him preeminently the reflection of Jesus. . . . I have an interest in art, and ever since my two weeks' session with Rembrandt last summer, I've had a strong desire to devote my Second-Order life to painting. My parents heartily approve, and hope that I shall follow their example by spending the first years of this life on my chosen career. Then (still with teenage physique and years of potential motherhood ahead of me) marry, settle down, and devote my remaining time to a husband, a family, a home, and to those routine assignments that may be required of me here in our Second Order. . . . By contrast, you have no particular passion for any career. You toy with the idea of architectural engineering not because you love it, but simply because it is the profession of your parents, who wish you to follow their example by marrying early and by marrying someone with whom you can share a common career besides a home and family. . . . But at present we have no common professional interest. . . . We are physically and spiritually in love with each other. Because of this, we find it impossible to think that anything could come between us and an early marriage. . . . Yet . . . who can tell? . . . We can't really plan our future until each of us has inherited his First-Order patterns from Earth. . . . Think what unusual conflicts could develop from our pending rebirths. . . . Suppose I were to absorb a spirit that would doubly reinforce my love for painting, while at the same time you inherited the unshakable conviction that all art and artists were a waste of time. . . . Suppose further that my rebirth would increase to a passion my love for the "Jesus" aspect of Aaron, while yours would bring you a genuine loathing of Christian ethics. . . . Just these two differences (professional and philosophical) could be more than enough to break apart the teenage love we now feel for each other.

P. This is the reason why our parents, our families, and even our friends advise us to slow down our love affair until after the "big day" has come for each of us.

JA. (*Returning the rings to Paul*) Here you are then, Boo. . . . Take our rings and put them back in their little "cave." Who knows? . . . Perhaps by the end of March when we come here again, we'll be able to use them.

P. That's right, Judy. . . . Meantime, let's go on up to the top of Valhalla and enjoy our lunch.

Paul returns his rings to their hiding place beneath the rock. He and Judy rejoin Trail No. 7, and follow it to the ample picnic accommodations at Valhalla's summit. After a feast of food and impressive scenery, they climb back down their mountain, reaching its parking lot a little before 7:00 PM. Since they're both due back at their dorms by the ten o'clock curfew, they are left with about two and a half hours to spend on Aaronian Vacation Planet No. 33. From the glove box of their sports, Paul takes out a leather-bound atlas entitled, The 6,000 Decomposition-Recomposition Chambers of Aaron VP 33. These D-R Chambers are shown on the maps by different sizes of dots. A small dot indicates a station having little more than the chamber itself; a large dot represents a chamber surrounded by some sort of museum, art center, or historical attraction. Of the two D-Rs closest by, they choose No. 621 whose large dot is described as a planetarium. This station seems the best choice because it is only 200 miles south of Valhalla; it can be quickly reached by expressway, and its colorful exhibits and informative demonstrations sound like a fitting climax to the astronomical-philosophical discussions of their short vacation. . . .

Paul and Judy arrive at D-R 621 about 8:30 PM. Since this gives them a little more than an hour to explore the planetarium, they decide against visiting its main auditorium in favor of viewing several of the many and varied Subsidiary exhibits. At a garage adjoining the principal building, our couple steps out of their rust-colored coupé. They remove their suitcases from its trunk, and turn the sports over to a handsome, neatly uniformed attendant who salutes, squints at a perforated card that Paul hands him, compares some numbers on the card to others stamped on the inside of the driver's door, salutes again, and without saying a word to Paul or Judy, drives the car inside. . . . In the lobby at the main entrance of the planetarium, they check their valises at a window marked "Baggage Transport, D-R Chamber No. 621," and then proceed to enjoy the educational displays.

The exhibit that makes the greatest impression is a full-colored twenty-minute motion picture, an animated cartoon entitled, The Adventures of Little Joe or How to Survive the Beginnings of Life in the Aaronian System. . . . To set the stage for Little Joe, the film portrays some of the very things Paul and Judy were talking about at their New Year's Eve party. It starts off with the point of a pin balancing our universe's invisible mass core, made visible for demonstration purposes. A calendar to the right of the pin identifies this situation as January, the year 1. Our blob of subenergy spins off a first subelectronic ring, then a second and finally (closest to the core) a third. These three rings are shown to be actually the impenetrable surfaces of three concentric spheres of subenergy, expanding concurrently at velocities far exceeding the speed of light! In fact, by the time our calendar shows the passing of only 300 years, our first subelectronic ring is three billion light years distant from the center of our universe, the second ring is two billion light years away, the third ring, one billion. These concentric spherical surfaces are shown to divide the totality of our immediate universe into three solid spaces entirely separate from one another! The outermost space is identified as our First-Order universe, the next is our Second-Order Minor universe, and that space closest to the center is our Second-Order Major universe. The entire structure is called our First-Second-Order Universe.

Suddenly our calendar indicates the year 3,000,000. All three spaces of our First-Second-Order universe are filled with matter and energy, but as yet no living creatures. Both components are shown to be the result of subelectrons losing velocity and falling from ring orbits in their respective subelectronic spheres. As such, they experience conversion into matter or energy. As matter, they become components of masses that vary in size from particles of dust to huge galaxies, filled with billions upon billions of stars, suns, moons, and planets the size of Earth.

Another reading of our calendar—the year is 3,500,000. By now, in all three spaces of our universe, there are nonillions of Earth-like planets that have been colonized with plant and animal life. These colonizations are simply transplants from other identical orders of the countless First-Second-Order universes (older than ours) circling in the vast Second-Order space of our parent Second-Third-Order universe.

Back to our calendar . . . the year is 3,851,000. At this time, there begins the first implantation of human life upon an Earth-like planet within our First-Order universe. During each succeeding million years, a new human culture is established by still another prophet until by the time our calendar reads 51,000,490,069 years, there exists within our immediate universe a total of 50,997 life systems. Our calendar flashes an important reading 100 years later—the year 51,000,490,169—important because in this year Earth is implanted with plant and animal life.

The next date shown is 51,330,375,520. This is the year in which Aaron comes to Earth, founding thereon his race of humans, the 51,327th life system to be established within our First-Second-Order universe. The number 51,332,594,011 is given as the year in which Aaron arrives on Earth as the twelve-year-old Jesus of Nazareth, thus fulfilling a 93rd visit to the First Order of his life system.

The final year to show on our calendar is 51,332,595,753—important not because it marks the moving of some great prophet through his life system, but because it brings us to the year 1750 AD, when "Little Joe" is reborn on Earth to fulfill the concluding segment of his required span of one thousand years of First-Order life. During the final ten minutes of our film, Little Joe dons the garb and personality of three different roles in the thoroughly convincing way that only the hero of an animated cartoon can manage to do. . . .

He first appears as a handsome French boy who has only modest talents, but a warm and delightful personality. Since he asks nothing more of life than to be as happy a man and as good a man as his father, he decides to become a mender of shoes, and is apprenticed at his father's modest shop in Reims. At eighteen, "good" Little Joe is a full-fledged cobbler. He thence divides his time vigorously between his shoes and a beautiful wife. She bears him (in succession) eight children, and then dies of "overexposure." Undaunted, Joe does not abandon himself to a life of self-pity and remorse. He assumes the full responsibility of his many shoes and his many children. Then finally (in 1820), he dies of "underexposure," having reached the ultimate three score years and ten of his thousand years of First Order life. With the death of this "good Joe," the world does not mourn the passing of any great genius. Aside from his children, his patrons and his friends, no one more than ten miles from Reims has ever heard of Little Joe. They don't even know that he was born into the world, much less that he's now died out of it! . . . But who mourns Little Joe (and who doesn't) is not what matters. . . . What really counts for him now is the quality of patterns that he has accumulated in his spiritual subelectron (soul) during his thousand years of First-Order life. If these "bits and pieces" provide vibrations that are sufficiently high, then his soul will be instantaneously attracted from the neutralized magnetic field of his dead First-Order brain to outside the Earth's galaxy, across some 50 billion light years of First-Order universe, through our second subelectronic ring, across 100 billion light years of Second-Order Minor universe, and into orbit among the subenergy of our third subelectronic ring. This immense journey is completed in negligible time . . . in far less than the smallest fraction of time required for Joe to breathe his last breath of life on Earth! . . . Within our third subelectronic ring, Joe's spiritual subelectron remains in orbit for several days. Having awaited its turn, it is then instantaneously summoned across billions of light years of our Second-Order Major universe into the just-matured (and activated) field of the brain of a handsome Aaronian student named Big Bill. This student is seventeen years old, and now attends school within the Aaronian Galaxy. . . . What a huge life system Little Joe now finds himself living within as Big Bill! Most of the planets inhabited by Aaronians are within the Aaronian galaxy. All are Earth-sized, having velocities of rotation and revolution that are practically identical to those of planet Earth. Thus (with minor adjustments made at the end of calendar years) each planet within the complex has a length of day, season, and year comparable to those of Earth. Of the 600 planets comprising the system proper, there are 351 located within the Aaronian galaxy. These include one Administrative Planet (Aaron AP) that houses the seat of government, the College of Counselors, Population Records and Control, the Cultural Archives, etc., plus 350 planets supporting Aaronian life within our Second-Order Major universe: 205 Cultural Planets (Aaron CPs) are those upon which day-to-day art, science, and applied disciplines constitute the prime activities of Second-Order-Major Aaronian life + 101 Supply Planets (Aaron SPs) supply the physical needs of Aaron's Second-Order Major system: food, clothing, building materials, transportation, etc. + 44 Educational Planets (Aaron EPs) open the door to elementary, secondary and college education for Aaronians, and as well the facilities for theoretical researches. Beyond the Aaronian galaxy (and each in a separate galaxy) are 249 Vacation Planets (Aaron VPs) whose entire surfaces are sparsely populated parks, filled with beautiful vacation lands and year-round resorts. These are the 600 planets that form the core of Aaron's life system within our Second-Order Major universe. Within them, good Little Joe (now as Big Bill) is called upon to live out his thousand years of Second-Order life.

The next role in which our hero appeares is that of "poor" Little Joe, a handsome German boy who was also born in 1750, but with an enormous talent for mathematics and science. Since he asks nothing more of life than to sit back and live happily ever after upon his family's huge accumulation of wealth, he decides not to follow his father's and grandfather's example as a merchant of textiles. Nor is he interested in developing his God-given talent for mathematics—a talent which his instructors assure him is that of another Sir Isaac Newton. Poor Little Joe never marries. He lives a long, fat, gluttonous life filled with wine, women, song, worldwide traveling, gout, seventy years, and a fatal heart attack to conclude his thousand years of First-Order life. Upon his death, the world does not mourn the passing of the great scientific genius this man could have been! Aside from a few jealous friends, a poor beautiful blind girl (and her large family) to whom he had given financial aid for more than a decade, and three young men who had received the entire cost of their education from his purse, no one even knows that poor Little Joe has been born into the world, much less that he's now died out of it. . . . During poor Joe's thousand years on Earth, his spiritual subelectron (soul) accumulates a variety of patterns: not all good, not all bad. Are they sufficiently positive to provide him with the joy of physical rebirth? . . . If so, into which Order of a second life will he be born? . . . As things turn out (considering his pitiable waste of a great talent, and in spite of his monetary kindness toward a few friends), Joe's soul doesn't have what it takes to be attracted all the way to our third subelectronic ring. The positive patterns of his spiritual subelectron are sufficient to carry it only as far as our second ring of subenergy wherein it goes into orbit. After waiting its turn, it is instantaneously attracted across billions of light years of our Second-Order Minor universe into the just-matured magnetic field of the brain of a handsome Aaronian student named Big John, who is nearly fifteen years old and who attends school in the Aaronian galaxy. . . . The Minor-Order life system in which our hero now finds himself living as Big John is (with respect to size and material accommodations) comparable to that Major-Order system in which we have just thumbnailed the career of Big Bill. Within the Aaronian galaxy of our Second-Order Minor universe, there are 342 Earth-sized planets comprising the central core of Aaron's system here. These include 1 Administrative Planet, 203 Cultural Planets, 96 Supply Planets, and 42 Educational Planets. Beyond the Aaronian galaxy (and each in a separate galaxy) are 248 Vacation Planets, which bring the entire core of Aaron's Second-Order Minor system to a total of 590 planets. Within this system, Little Joe (now as Big John) is called upon to live out his Second-Order life.

As things turn out, Big John has been sitting around with no particular vocational interest, and wondering what "on Aaron" he should do with his Second-Order life. Along comes poor Little Joe and the problem is solved. Though he did nothing on Earth to develop his talent for math and science, he brings with him into the life of Big John a mountain of latent leanings toward these disciplines. And Big John, frustrated and not a little frightened at finding himself in a Minor Order of life (providing no guarantee of rebirth), supplies the necessary motivation to put these long-neglected aptitudes to work . . .

A final role for our versatile actor is that of "bad" Little Joe, a handsome English lad who was also born in 1750 to be a natural leader of men. But instead of using his convincing administrative ability to benefit himself and his countrymen, he unwisely turns toward a life of crime. His final seventy years on Earth include the masterminding of six armed robberies, the committing of rape and murder, the perpetration of fraud and blackmail, kidnaping, high treason, and finally, death at the hands of an angry mob. As a coarse cutting rope chokes the final breath of life from bad Little Joe, the crowd cheers and all that could have been eternal about this man takes its flight. . . . Where does it go? . . . What happens to "bad" little subelectrons? You'll find out at the conclusion of our review.

At this point, the film really projects its message. . . . A man's soul contains the physical seed of its own judgment. In the case of good Little Joe, we find a spiritual subelectron whose talents are slight, but whose accumulation of positive patterns over successive lives is enormous. This soul goes straight to the "heaven" of Second-Order-Major life. Instead of eternal rest or pearly gates or streets of gold, it finds there the suffering hustle of a new and demanding life—but a life of 1,000 years, which carries with it the heavenly guarantee of eventual rebirth into our Third Order. . . . Not so with the spirit of poor Little Joe. During his successive lives on Earth, he had made little positive use of the great gifts that were heaped upon him. His spirit continues to live—but in only the Minor Order of a second life. For nearly 1,000 years (as Big John), he must now walk the path of his Second-Order life in the purgatorial gloom of penitence, doubt, and fear. When he again comes face-to-face with the grim reaper, will he or will he NOT experience rebirth into our Third Order? . . . Search as he may, there's no answer to this question—there's no comfort for his new life comparable to that guarantee of rebirth, whose warm sunshine fills each day of Big Bill's Second-Order experience.... What of bad Little Joe? . . . For him, there's no "heaven"—no "purgatory." Following a sequence of lives, his spiritual subelectron is now so filled with negative patterns that instead of being attracted toward the center of our First-Second-Order universe, it moves outward and into orbit within our first subelectronic ring. Here his spirit finds neither the hell of eternal thirst nor the hell of eternal fire, but the hell of *nonbeing*. Not that his soul itself is destroyed. All spiritual subelectrons are immortal and indestructible—even bad Little Joe's. But the life patterns recorded within one's soul (whether they be the spiritual accumulations of a single lifetime or of ten million lifetimes) are neither immortal nor indestructible. At the instant of death when one's spirit has become predominantly negative, it is no longer attracted toward the center of its immediate universe for a physical rebirth into the next higher order of life. Instead, it journeys outward until it reaches the first subelectronic ring of a First-Second-Order universe, where it goes into orbit and where the *totality* of its life patterns are completely erased from its infinite capacity of total recall. It is as though the life (or succession of lives) recorded therein had never existed! There's nothing wrong with the spiritual subelectron itself. It starts all over again—recording the patterns of some newborn First-Order being. . . . Bad Little Joe receives the just rewards of his sinful ways—the ultimate punishment. What could have become the endless recordings of an immortal life, now suffers the complete loss of its identity—the cruel and wasteful hellfire of nonexistence.

At the conclusion of Little Joe, Paul and Judy spend the last ten minutes of their vacation walking together in the softly moonlit terrace and gardens of the planetarium.

P. Thanks for everything, Judy. . . . Thanks for being patient with my impatience. . . . Because of your efforts and those of Little Joe, I should find the next few months easier to bear.

JA. And thanks to you, Paul. . . . Thanks for being bold enough and man enough to fall in love with me—and for admitting this love even before you know the full story of your "total self." Just think what wonderful surprises our next visit here might hold for the two of us. . . . Good-bye, Darling.

They embrace in a final outburst of love and kisses—a beautiful expression of young love whose genuine establishment and whose permanence would seem absolutely defiant of any change, regardless of the unknown patterns that would soon be entering their lives from Earth. Their passionate caresses seem to say, "Come on, Little Joe! We're ready for you now!"

In the basement of the planetarium, our couple arrives at the D-R Chamber some thirty minutes before their ten o'clock curfew. They pick up their valises and then approach a formidable computer-like console, where they dial for Judy, "Aaronian Galaxy-Educational Planet #21 D-R Chamber #884." A few lights on the panel above the console start to blink in response to their dialing. Judy grabs her baggage and steps into a cubicle that would easily pass for an ordinary elevator. As its doors close, she turns toward Paul and they wave good-bye. For a few seconds, more lights flash. The blinking stops and the doors open to reveal an empty D-R Chamber—not a trace of Judy or her suitcases! Paul dials "Aaron EP #10 D-R Chamber #42," steps into the chamber, puts down his valises, turns, presses a button, and as double doors of the stainless steel compartment smoothly and quietly close, observes a farewell glimpse of Aaron VP 33. The doors scarcely meet when they start opening again, and Paul notices a sudden change in the lighting appointments and color of the chamber's interior. Yet within this brief time span, a miraculous microsecond occurs, a microsecond in which Paul and his suitcases are converted from matter and energy into subenergy, are attracted across eight billion light-years of time and space—from VP 33 to EP 10 in the Aaronian galaxy—and are there recomposed into precisely the same structures that had just departed the vacation planet. A miracle of transportation—and all that Paul notices is a slight change in the color of his surroundings, a change from silver white to pale blue.

D-R Chamber 42 is in the basement of a transportation center, where Paul signs out another coupé. He drives twenty miles through peaceful rolling country which, especially in the moonlight, looks no different from the surface of the beautiful vacation planet he has just left. Then at the crest of a hill, he looks down into a valley and enjoys a sparkling sight entirely different from anything on VP 33. Sloping with Athenian simplicity toward a shimmering lake is a complex of thirty Doric structures, looking like the Acropolis itself. Such would be the envy of any university campus on Earth, and yet it is only a secondary school—one of thousands of secondary schools located on Aaron EP 10. Here Paul is enrolled as a pre-engineering student with a major in architecture. . . . The inspiring view soon passes from sight behind a silhouette of purple trees and twisting highway. At the bottom of the hill, Paul turns right at a sign marked, "Lakemont Secondary Center 3,021." Since no automobiles are permitted on campus, all driving is underground in brightly illuminated, white-tiled tunnels. After "tunneling" for about three miles, our driver reaches the school's transportation center located beneath its administration building. Here he signs in his coupé, takes an elevator to the ground floor, and walks across campus to his Parthenon-like dorm. His student quarters are on the fifth floor of a gable-roofed structure made entirely of white marble with an encircling double row of Doric columns, a portico in the front and back, and a wide colonnade on each side. For several minutes, Paul stands out front, stroking his chin in philosophical contemplation. His eyes feel the cold white of the columns, the silver white of the frieze, and the blue white of the stars.

P. Don't you wish you knew my secret, little temple? . . . I'll share her with you. . . . She comes from beyond those stars. . . . I'm in love with a beautiful artist, and she's in love with me!

As Rezler checks in at the desk, the cheerful white-haired face of a kind old clerk smiles benevolently.

Ki. Three past ten! . . . You just made it, young man. . . . Another two minutes, and I'd slap you down with a demerit!
P. Not *you*, Pop Kircher. . . . You're too fine a fellow to give some poor moonstruck boy a demerit for being moonstruck!
Ki. I guess I wouldn't, Rezler. But you're not supposed to know this. . . . Get on up to bed 'fore I change my mind. . . .

Paul steps to the right of the desk, where he deposits himself and his suitcases in a tiny elevator. He presses his floor and complains audibly as the red numbers slowly flash from 1 to 5:

P. Damn it! . . . It's taking me longer to ride five stories in this little box than it took me to cross eight billion light-years of outer space!

Chapter 27

Paul enters his three-room quarters at the end of corridor 5H. He drops his suitcases at the foot of his bed, then searches the rooms for his seventeen-year-old dorm companion, Ray Culbertson. Not finding him, he complains audibly: "I might have known old Culby wouldn't be here. . . . That's the trouble with athletes—they're always taking showers!"

The next day, Tuesday, January 2nd is not a regular school day. The students' sole responsibility is to show up in the administration building at their appointed times and register for the new quarter beginning January 3rd. Since Paul and Ray are both scheduled for 10:00 AM, they feel free to stay awake as long as they wish. While students on the fifth floor are required to be in by 10:00 PM, there's no particular time for "lights out." The boys prepare an evening snack of cheese, crackers, and tea. Then they stretch across their beds and talk until after midnight:

RC. Well, how was your vacation, Paul?
P. Perfect as usual. . . . Couldn't be otherwise with *that* girl!
RC. How far did you and Judy go this time?
P. Love and kisses—that's all. . . .You know me better than this!
RC. I know you well, Paul—but I don't understand you. . . . How can you love Judy as much as you do, and be satisfied with love and kisses?

P. I concentrate on her other virtues, and try to forget all that "mighty meatiness" until after we're married.

RC. You mean to say that a girl her age has other virtues?

P. Definitely! . . . She sensed that I was filled with self-pity emanating from my seventeen-and-a-half years without rebirth. In order to help me, she turned into a delightful "professor of philosophy," so filling me with patience, self-confidence, and gratitude, that now instead of dreading another quarter's waiting and uncertainty, I rather look forward to its expectation!

RC. This is too much, Rezzi—I can't believe it! . . . If I were as much in love with a girl as you are with Judy, I'd be going at her on all fours, instead of supinely resting beneath some banyan tree and quietly philosophizing about the life to come.

P. This sounds like Culby doesn't trust himself.

RC I don't! . . . I wish I could. . . . If I were as sure of myself as you are with yourself, then I too would be" head over heels" in love!

P. Be glad you're not, Ray. . . . I think you're very wise in heeding the wisdom of our ancestors. By not falling in love until after rebirth, you're saving yourself a lot of worry and grief.

RC. I don't know. . . . Your love for Judy seems like the happiest thing in your life!

P. It is! . . . But I'm constantly worried about what will be my lot from Earth. Among our own acquaintances who have fallen in love before their rebirths, think how often these premature affairs have ended in disappointment. Take, for example, my grandfather—and your own father! . . . I hate to admit that such things happen, but what if I did inherit some weird string of patterns that would come between me and my love for this girl. . . . What then? . . . I don't think I could go on living!

RC. I know what you mean, Paul. I've not lost my heart to a girl, but I am in love with my work. Coming in "second" once, and "third" twice at last year's Olympics, I believe I stand a good chance of becoming a track champion. . . . And yet—what of my Earthly patterns? . . . What if I inherit something that violently conflicts with my chosen career? . . . What could I do?

P. As regards my profession, since I can either take engineering or leave it, it's hard for me to realize that anyone this side of rebirth can become as involved in a career as you have. . . . Actually, you're no different from me and my Judy. . . . You have every right to be as frustrated as I am!

RC. We might as well be optimistic, Rezzi. . . . Until something happens, let's assume that your rebirth will deepen your love for Judy, and that mine will enhance my athletic career.

P. Now you sound like my "little girl professor"—the very thing she would advise us to do. . . . There's something strange about our predicament—almost humorous. . . . What if I were to inherit the vivid patterns of an expert Parisian whore with a passionate hunger for the bodies of handsome young men?

RC. I don't think there's much chance of this happening here in the Major Order, but if it did, I'd sure kick you the hell out of my bedroom!

P. We'll probably both be surprised by what few changes rebirth will bring to our present life plans. . . . So there's no use worrying about it or even joking about it. Maybe by morning it will all be over for the two of us, and we'll be sitting here laughing about our former concerns, and gleefully describing to each other who we *are* in terms of who we *were*!

Chapter 28

On the afternoon of January 29, Paul receives great news in a letter from his Judy:

January 28, 1827

Dearest Boo,

Good news from EP 21! . . . It's happened; it's finally happened! . . . I'm now a full Second-Order being! My rebirth occurred this very morning (of all places) in church, while sitting there with my brothers and parents. It came to me like the pealing of bells . . . a stroke of pure light, which has made everything clear and beautiful. Rebirth is the greatest experience of life, well worth the long years of agonized waiting. Soon you too, dear Paul, will know what I mean. And I can hardly wait to share with you the joy and happiness of the experience.

I'm writing you instead of calling, because I know that you couldn't resist asking me a lot of questions . . . questions which I shall delight in answering upon our next visit to Valhalla. But we've so long romanticized the event of our rebirths, that to discuss them initially anywhere but on our sacred mountain would seem to me like cheating.

And so good-bye, dear Boo. Good-bye until we meet again at L'Arbre Fée on the evening of March 28th. Please don't phone or try to see me until then. . . . Let it suffice to say that I'm now ten times the Christian, ten times the artist, and ten times the girl that I was yesterday. Because of the resolution of my uncertainties, I'm also ten times more in love with you than ever before. . . . I send you my heart of happiness, praying for your patience and for your imminent rebirth!

Love and kisses,
Judy

Chapter 29

On Saturday afternoon, February 10, Paul journeys to Aaron SP 71 for his visit with Judy's family. As requested, he arrives at D-R 2021 by three o'clock. In the station's parking lot, he recognizes Mrs. Adams's prize possession—a huge shiny black Daimler-like sedan. Though intended to be owner-driven, its enormous tread and 155 inches of wheelbase make the silent, smooth car look for all the world like the Queen's limousine. Through its wide three-wiper windshield, Paul spies a tuft of bright-red hair sticking up above the car's ship-sized ebony steering wheel. The handsome close-cropped hair belongs to Fred Adams, Judy's younger brother.

P. Freddy! . . . Don't tell me you're out driving "Big Zipper" all by yourself?

F. I am. . . . Poor Mom couldn't help it this time. She's busy with the dinner, and Dad has his car on a visit to the Rosenbergs. . . . Throw your bag in the back, and let's go!

P. (*This Paul does, and off they go.*) You didn't have to meet me. I could have signed out a little coupé, and driven to your farm myself.

F. You know Mother. . . . She's convinced that being a good hostess begins with picking up a guest at the station, and ends with dropping him off there.

P. Well, what do you think of your little sister? Is she now a happy girl?
F. Very much so, Paul. . . . It seems as though everything she's inherited from Earth dovetails perfectly with her Second-Order plans.
P. What can you tell me about her?
F. Not much. . . . Last week at her "rebirthday party," everyone pumped the devil out of her, only to discover that she was a twenty-seven-year-old French girl, who died giving birth to her third child, and that she's now more than ever an artist, a Christian, and in love with you!
P. Nothing more?
F. Nothing!
P. She told me almost this much in a letter.
F. You're the cause of her secrecy. . . . She insists on your being the first to know the details of her past life, and apparently plans to share these with you on the very first day you "arrive" from Earth!
P. I hope I'll inherit a genuine involvement in some worthwhile goal, something I can really share with Judy, and something that will mean a lot more to me than any of my present studies do. . . . Profession, profession, profession—this is all that matters to anyone!
F. Not true, Paul. . . . I like you for what you are, and Judy loves you for what you are. . . . Choose any job you wish—our feelings toward you won't change!
P. Thanks, Freddy! It's a real comfort to know this. . . . I hope I'll inherit a genuine involvement in some worthwhile goal.

Fred carefully moors his mother's big black boat, an operation made doubly difficult by the prior docking of a little red convertible.

P. Isn't that your dad's car?
F. Yes. He must be home early. (*Fred pivots in several directions, then finally points a stubby forefinger toward the main barn.*) There's Dad—stomping around in his eternal vegetable garden. Why don't you run down and have a talk with him? . . . I'll go help Mom with the dinner, and we'll let you know when things are ready.
P. I'll do that, Fred. Thanks again for the ride.

SA. (*The father's boyish features brighten to a sparkle, as he discovers Paul approaching.*) Hi there, city boy! . . . Come on—take your shirt off and give the old man a little help.

P. Will do, Mr. Adams.

Their hands meet in a friendly shake, and as usual, Paul winces under the force of the older man's firm grasp.

SA. I s'pose you think I'm crazy with all this digging and puttering around.

P. Not at all, Sir. . . . Someday I hope to do a little farming myself. . . .Congratulations on this new little daughter of yours. . . . What's it like, suddenly to be the father of a French girl?

SA. Actually I don't really know, Paul. . . . I think she plans to wait until *your* rebirth. Then the two of you can join us for a sort of "mutual surprise" party.

P. I'm *so* in love with Judy!

SA. I admire her as well, not just because she's my daughter. . . . I admire the wonderful person she is. And in some strange way, her rebirth has actually deepened this admiration. . . . In all matters, I have a tremendous respect for her judgment. This is why I think so much of *you*. . . . Someone could hand me a hundred-page listing of The Virtues and Attributes of Paul Rezler. Yet nothing in it could tell me so much good about you, as the mere fact that this little girl of mine tends to claim you as her own.

P. Thanks, Mr. Adams. This means a lot to me.

SA. Good! Then take off your jacket, and let's get at these beets and carrots.

For one full hour, Stewart Adams and Paul Rezler go digging together, enjoying the rejuvenating sounds and smells of Aaronian soil. A bell rings from the porch of the farmhouse. Paul caps his eyes with his left hand, and can just make out the white shirt on Fred's waving arm.

SA. We can stop now, boy. . . . You've earned your dinner!

Rezler tries to keep his promise to young Adams—his promise to avoid another argument with the father over his daughter's future. He succeeds only as far as dessert.

P. You know, I've been wanting to tell you folks the main reason for my coming here this evening.

EA. You've come to enjoy the unique pleasure of our company, and the rare delicacies of my "blue-ribbon" cooking.

P. Right, Mrs. Adams, I have! . . . But I've also come to clarify my deep and abiding feelings for Judy.

SA.(*Mr Adams interrupts.*) We know exactly how you feel about Judy. But you are not yet a full Second-Order being! . . . When you know who you really are, and there are no resulting conflicts, *then* we'll all get together for a good planning session.

P. Until then, I'm going to go back to Lakemont, put my nose in those books, and keep it there until my wretched waiting period is over!

F. Good idea, Paul. . . . I'll drive you to town.

EA. (*Mrs. Adams has different plans.*) No you don't, Freddy. *I'll* drive Paul to the station. . . . There are a few things I wish to talk over with this young man. . . . Why don't you and your dad get out there and tidy up the kitchen?

SA. (*Mr. A handsomely submits.*) Yes, Betty. You two run along. . . . Fred and I will take care of things here.

As Elizabeth Adams handles the "Big Zipper" with a certain air of authority, Paul wonders what it is that she seems so anxious to tell him:

EA. You know, Paul . . . Judy and I have kept a little secret from the rest of our family. I now wish to share it with you, because I think it will make your waiting easier. . . . It is simply this: Judy is completely and unreservedly in love with you! She was before her rebirth, and now (after it) she is even more so. She lives in constant fear that you might inherit something from Earth which would come between the two of you. And yet her love for you is so great that she wants you to feel free to leave her in case your Earthly spirit demands such freedom! . . . I think knowing this, will ease the absorption of your own First-Order life, and should help you plan your future.

P. I'm sure it will, Mrs. A.. . . This secret is the dearest thing we two can share in our present life. I treasure it above all Second-Order blessings, short of Judy herself. And I promise you that I shall betray neither it nor her, no matter what my First-Order life may bring.

EA. And dear Paul, when that big day of yours finally rolls around, you must pay us an immediate visit! Don't call or write, just "come as you are." . . . Bring your entire family. We'll send for Judy, and have the happiest "rebirthday party" that ever resounded on SP 71.

P. Thanks, Sweet Cat. I'll do this. . . . And thanks for the ride. . . . It was a real "lift" in more ways than one!

Chapter 30

From February 10, until the end of the quarter, nothing much occurs in the life of Paul Rezler except a string of schooldays at Lakemont. There are conventional showers on the fifth floor, but no trips to the dorm's pool. On alternate weekends, there continue to be regular CP 25 visits with Paul's family: his parents, his nineteen-year-old brother, and his fifteen-year-old pigtailed sister. But there are no more Friday evening phone conversations with Judy Adams. There are final exams on March 26, 27, and 28, but neither hide nor hair nor hint nor trace of rebirth in the life of our hero.

By far, the happiest thought of this quarter is the end of it—March 28, the evening of Paul's long-anticipated rendezvous with his beloved Judy. What will it be like to finally come face-to-face and arm-in-arm with a "fully arrived" Second-Order sweetheart?

Paul's concluding final is over on Wednesday afternoon at three thirty. Ray's exams last until five thirty, and since Paul wishes to leave before this time, he scribbles a few lines on his roommate's desk calendar:

> Dear Culby,
>
> I'm off to the land of fun and games. Wish me well! . . . There's not much chance of my returning to Lakemont as

an old married man, but with a little luck, perhaps I can at least return to you as one who is happily engaged.

Rezzi

Paul enters the parking lot of Chateau L'Arbre Fée de Bourlemont at 6:00 PM on a clear, cool fall evening. This time, even though its blue and green lights are going full blast, the pool is deserted. A pungent tobacco smell of burning leaves hovers over the courtyard like a friendly old man whose billowy pipe smiles the assurance of a short, mild winter. Paul enters the chateau's main lobby where his famished eyes are magnetically attracted to the gold-spun tresses of his "immortal beloved." She's sitting on a typical hotel-sized couch with her back to the main entrance which Paul has just used. He goes up behind her and plants a dainty kiss in the perfect part of her sweet-smelling hair:

P. Rise and walk, Kitten.
JA. Paul! . . . You wonderful boy! You're a half hour early.

He takes her by the hand, and they go for a moonrise stroll, naturally gravitating to the careful hedge that marks the spot of their original meeting. Here they embrace mightily in a three months' backlog of kisses and caresses.

P. Do you suppose there's any chance of my Kitten telling me a few of her Earthly secrets, right here and now?
JA. I love you and I'm proud of you. That's all I'll tell you tonight. Tomorrow at Valhalla, you'll hear my entire story, but nothing more until then. We've sentimentalized over that dear old rock for too long a time to ignore it completely, now that our waiting is nearly over. Where are we sleeping tonight?
P. This time I *was* able to get Villa 137. I phoned in our reservation way back on March fifth and confirmed it only yesterday.

Our young couple returns to the chateau for a leisurely steak dinner at the Boot and Saddle. As before, they have a lunch packed for them and then head off in their sports for a top-down (though this time, scarf on and cap on) moonlight drive to the shore. Arriving at No. 137 shortly after 10:00 PM, they find the beach too cold for a nighttime swim. Instead, dressed in shorts and heavy sweatshirts, they go walking barefooted in the surf, down to their lighthouse and back. The salt air is almost too fresh and invigorating; Paul can taste it on his lips and tongue. As our lovers go splashing along, the foam and spray from pounding breakers are clearly visible in the blue-white light of double moons. They embrace often, but seldom speak. Only once during the entire evening does Paul tempt his Judy to break her avowed secrecy. This occurs while they are standing in the light of their tower, surveying ten miles of moonlit seascape. Paul suddenly leans down, kisses Judy's left ear, and then whispers into it:

P. Tell me, Darling. . . . What's it *really* like to die?
JA. (*Her eyes look up and meet his in a compassion of burning love.*) Tomorrow, Boo. . . . Tomorrow!

They return to their villa, eat their lunch, build a cozy fire, cuddle up in a comfortable love seat, and spend a silent, thoughtful hour watching countless changing patterns intensifying, then fading, only to sparkle up again over the burning logs.

Next morning, Paul and Judy return to L'Arbre Fée for breakfast and supplies. Then heading for Valhalla, the farther they drive, the more beautiful the fall coloring becomes. Not until evening do the lovers finally seat themselves on their uncomfortable throne. Paul unearths his heirloom ring and moves it toward Judy's left hand, which he gently traces with careful kisses.

P. Let me place this on your finger now before I hear the story of your Earthly days. This will prove that my love does not require the confirmation of an earlier life!
JA. No. Not now, Paul. We've waited all these months; another quarter won't matter. Let me tell you my story. Next vacation (amid snow and ice and wintry blast), we'll come here and listen to yours. If the both of them confirm our mutual love, then I'll be glad to wear your ring. If yours further shows that you can be happy and grow as an artist, then, with the full support of our parents, we'll plan for an early marriage and productive lives together.
P. I suppose you're right, Kitten. Now what have you to say for yourself?
JA. First of all, Boo, this business of death, rebirth, and total recall of earlier days . . . it's every bit as wonderful and awe-inspiring as we've been told. I know of nothing that will so thoroughly

convince you of the immortality and real worth of human life. It clearly explains the reasons for our living, our suffering, our growing and our having fun. On Earth, my final chunk of First-Order reincarnation, rounding out a total of 1,012 years, was as Jeanette Ribeau. For this I was born in 1803 on my father's farm near Vaucouleurs and was the third in a family of four children. Jean, my older brother, became a priest; Paul, my younger brother, a farmer. Sister Marie, a year older than I, was the one to whom I really attached myself. We came and went everywhere together like a couple of twins. Then suddenly, sadly, at only ten years of age, Marie died of consumption. I was lost, didn't know where to turn. . . . So constantly was she on my mind that by my twelfth year, our family physician warned us that my mental stability was being severely threatened by morbid thoughts concerning her death. He advised that I be removed from the immediate surroundings where I had spent so much time with little Marie. Accordingly, for six months I was sent to live with my aunt and uncle on their farm near Domremy. Here, quite naturally, I became familiar with the glorious and priceless story of La Pucelle, the "Maid of Orleans," Joan of Arc. I roamed the very fields where Joan played when she was a little girl. I knelt and prayed in the very garden where she knelt and prayed . . . and first heard her "voices." Before long, the mighty impact of her short life and her great victory over it began to penetrate the gloom of my sister's death. Bitterness and fear melted away, and I no longer felt deprived. Though I still couldn't explain death, it ceased to be an unfathomable pit of darkness and became a friendly doorway, simply because La Pucelle, at nineteen years of age, had boldly ridden through it with her chin high, a faint smile on her pale face, and with the sparkle of irrevocable victory shining in her bright eyes.

Toward the end of my stay at Domremy, I too was hearing voices. They were not those of St. Michael, St. Marguerite, or St. Catherine come down to speak with a "Child of God" or with the "Daughter of France." Nor were they the pitiable hallucinations of a full-blown psychotic. They were the silent voices of the woods and forests and sky, echoing in my ears through the faint, shimmering song of vesper bells. They told me to be not afraid of death, to be confident, to no longer mourn my sister's passing, to gather vivid memories of the pastoral beauties about me, and to return to my father's house, cheerfully accepting whatever life should bring my way.

P. These voices, Kitten . . . did you see them, or just hear their echo?

JA. I neither saw nor heard them as living beings. But I sensed their presence through unusual (almost frightening) bursts of consciousness and perception.

P. What happened next?

JA. I tried to do what the voices bade me and returned to my father's house. In 1822, I married Jacques Morel, a boy whom I had known since our childhood together at Vaucouleurs. You can imagine my delight when Jacques's brother, then living in Rheims, arranged for our wedding to be held there in the very cathedral where Joan had her Dauphin crowned King of France! We returned to Vaucouleurs and settled down on a generous tract of my father's farm that was given us as a wedding present. In 1823, our first son was born, and in 1825, a daughter. On the twenty-first of this past January, I brought our second son into the world. He was a healthy baby, and his birth seemed normal enough. However, on the following Tuesday morning, I woke up with a chill and a terrifying numbness on my left side. That afternoon, I lost consciousness and apparently died soon thereafter. Having completed 1,012 years of First-Order life, two days later, on Sunday morning, January twenty-eighth, rebirth came to Jeanette Ribeau, and the life-patterns of this innocent country girl, this happy wife, this little mother of three, became one and inseparable with the Second-Order spirit of your very own Kitten.

I said nothing about this to my family until we returned home from church. Then when I told them, you should have heard their explosion of mirth! They had a big party for me the following Saturday, and it seemed as though all my friends were there except *you*, dear Boo. How they coaxed and pumped and pleaded for my story! In response to their entreaties, I told them little, insisting that you would be first to hear the details.

P. From the standpoint of Jeanette Ribeau, what do you think of Second-Order life?

JA. I find it a disappointment in only two respects: it saddens me to leave behind a poor husband with three little children, and I'm sorry to find myself in a world that contains no Joan of Arc. But with a little effort, I can rationalize myself out of both these complaints into the total acceptance of a challenging new life.

As for Jacques, at least he now has a farm of his own, and I have no doubt that before long, he'll find himself a new wife and mother for our own children. As for Joan, since she died out of our Second Order way back in 1612, there's nothing I can do to bring about our loving embrace!

P. But in other respects, are you a happy girl?

JA. Extremely so, Boo! Especially in my love for art and for you. All those beautiful landscapes surrounding Vaucouleurs, Rheims, and Domremy now come vividly to mind with the impact of total recall! Bringing with them all their shadows and lights and colors, they literally compel me to put such visions on canvas.

Suddenly it's cold. An ominous wind begins to sing. They realize how close to winter they are. Will it snow? Was it foolish to come and spend such a night on such a mountain? No matter, it's too dark now to make their descent. They've come to the mountain, and here they must stay until morning. Thank goodness they had the foresight to bring their sleeping bags, which they now place behind the stone seat. Into their cocoons they go. Nothing exposed except their fur-lined faces, Judy's left arm, and Paul's right. Hand-in-hand they bid each other good night, and Paul watches in amazement as sleep and moonlight caress the beautiful face of his Kitten, now a definite artist and a full Second-Order being!

Soon Paul too is asleep. The fire dies away, and its ghost rises to heaven in a thin trail of restless smoke. Everything is dead or asleep. The mountain is cold, quiet, and dark. Not entirely dark—there's the light of two moons. Not entirely quiet—there's the clitter . . . clutter . . . tick . . . tack . . . of falling leaves. . . . Then a third and largest moon joins its companions. The games of these three bring to Valhalla practically the light of day. How clearly we can see our sleeping lovers; their hands no longer touch. A tiny oak leaf descends a moonbeam path. Where will its journey end? Down and up and down again it comes. Up and over their throne it flies. Down and to rest on the back of Paul Rezler's hand. Will it awaken him? . . . Let's watch and see.

The sleeping hand is turned palm down, flat against Valhalla. The prankish leaf flitters and flutters and tickles. . . . Ah! The hand begins to move. Its fingertips turn inward, raising the palm like a mighty claw. Is this the hand of Paul Rezler? . . . It clutches the soil, digging two inches into a blanket of fallen spruce needles. Is this the tentacle of some grasping monster, or is it the hand of Paul Rezler? It pounds Valhalla, trying to awaken some deeply hidden spirit within. Now the fingers move flexibly, as if finding their way along some ghostly keyboard. Is this the hand of Paul Rezler, or is it the hand of a pianist?

Although in a nightmare, Paul reaches out for help. When his hand finds Judy's, he grasps her with the same death grip he'd held upon the mountain. She wakens with a start:

JA. Paul! What's the matter? Are you dreaming?
P. My God! My God! Judy! It's happened! It's all over! God in heaven!
JA. What, Darling? Your rebirth?
P. Yes! Miracle of miracles! At last the waiting is over, and what a surprise I have for you!
JA. Wonderful! Tell me about it.
P. Not now, I can't! Sing me something.
JA. Sing? . . . What?
P. Anything! . . . Just to hear the sound of a human voice!
JA. I'm so excited I can't remember any songs!
P. Who ever heard of a French girl without songs? Sing me something from Vaucouleurs.

Judy takes a deep breath. Her voice quivers in the cold might air, but she does manage to sing all three verses of the Fairy Tree Song—a soul-moving air that she had learned on her visit to Domremy. At its conclusion, Judy looks into her lover's face, finding huge tears in each of his eyes.

JA. Darling, you're crying!
P. How beautiful! . . . To hear your voice—it brings me such sweet music! . . . What time is it, Judy?
JA. Twelve eighteen.
P. Then March 30, 1827, is my rebirthday.
JA. Many happy returns! . . . Kiss me, Boo.

Seated once again on their blanketed stone, they engage in a long and passionate exchange. Judy is first to speak.

JA. Tell me, Boo. . . . Tell me about yourself.
P. Not now, Judy.

Paul attempts to offer an excuse, but Judy lovingly silences him with her palm. She stares directly into his brightly illuminated eyes.

JA. That's all right, Darling. . . . You needn't tell me anything until you're ready. . . . In those sparkling eyes, I can read all I need to know.

P. Oh? . . . And what do you see there?

JA. I see dedication, determination, sacrifice, and love. I can't tell whether you're an artist, but I know that the spirit behind your eyes has found the miracle of "joy through suffering." And this is precisely what I see and admire in the eyes of dear old Rembrandt.

P. You're very perceptive, my love. Some twenty years ago, I knew another little girl who was much like you. She too would stare into my eyes and read things there. Then she'd write the most flowery words imaginable, and tell me that they came from me!

JA. Words like what?

P. Well . . . words like "I am the Bacchus who presses out for men this glorious wine and intoxicates their souls."

Chapter 31

Thus we come to the final part of Beethoven's story—a story that brings us to the year 1950 and which, unlike most, transcends the deceptive barriers of death and grave. Dying and rising up again was as simple as going to sleep and being awakened by the playful antics of an oak leaf. As in the case of Jeanette Ribeau, death came to Beethoven amidst a spell of unconsciousness. He was no more aware of death's actual approach than was she. But when touched by death's grim scythe, the effect was complete and ultimate—like the throwing of a switch. All that was "eternal" about Beethoven took its flight from Earth at 5:45 PM on March 26, 1827. What remained behind for Dr. Wagner to dissect was no more Beethoven than was his watch, his gold medal, his Hammerklavier piano, or his old gray coat. The *real* Beethoven—his spiritual subelectron—passed instantaneously from the neutralized magnetic field of his deceased First-Order brain to the third subelectronic ring of our First-Second-Order universe. Here it remained in orbit until rebirth. During this time, he was his spiritual subelectron, and this invisible speck of subenergy was all that existed of Beethoven and his preceding fifteen Earthly lives. Having no brain within this speck, there were no thoughts of what he was or where he was going. Nor were there any fears of death. All that remained was a total consciousness of sixteen Earthly lives that had concluded with a perfect awareness of Beethoven's Earthly experiences from the hour of his birth to the hour of his death!

Without a physical brain, there were no new thoughts—nor could he focus his attention on any particular First-Order patterns. Then it suddenly happens. He awakens and finds himself living in the body of a brand new animal, a young man named Paul Rezler.

Since Judy had never heard Bettina's words, she has no idea of the particular Bacchus I was referring to. Still staring into Paul's eyes, her lips melt in a soft smile:

JA. Such a man sounds like an artist to me. I do hope so! . . . Think how happy this could make the sharing of our second lives!

P. Dear Kitten, except for the interrogators and my counselor on Aaron AP, you'll be the first Aaronian to know who I was. And I'll tell you my big old secret here on top of Valhalla. . . . But for a month or two, I think it best that I remain totally anonymous—even from you and our immediate families.

JA. Serves me right! . . . My just reward for keeping *you* in suspense for eight weeks. But do tell me one thing. Are you now an artist?

P. I was an artist during my final Earthly span, and this I shall continue to be with all my strength and vigor!

JA. Good! Then there's nothing to come between us.

P. Nothing except perhaps my art itself!

JA. What do you mean, Boo?

P. During my final Earthly span, I was so completely devoted to my muse that there was no time for anything else!

JA. No wife?

P. No wife, no children. . . . An incorrigible old bachelor, with nothing but his career to make him happy.

JA. But this was on *Earth*, during a lifetime which you thought ended in the grave. Now you know better. With all eternity to grow, surely you'll find time for your art *and* your Kitten.

P. I hope so, Darling. . . . When I'm certain of this, on that very day, I'll come after you with my wedding ring.

JA. But until then, we're at least engaged, aren't we?

P. I don't know. . . . Perhaps this isn't fair to you.

JA. In what way, Paul?

P. If I can't give you first place in my life, then I'm not worthy of your love!

JA. Oh, I don't know. . . . Why must I have first place? Why can't I be shared on an equal basis with your art?

P. If I remain anything like I was during my concluding Earthly days, then nothing or no one can be shared with my art. Perhaps

Paul Rezler will supply the needed leavening, perhaps not. I just don't know!

JA. Then what are we to do?

P. Wait, I guess. Wait and see if a career-dominated old fool can change his spots in time for Second-Order life.

JA. But there's no need to change. I probably have the same spots myself. Because I too am an artist, I'll have no trouble understanding your devotion to your career. This only makes me admire and love you the more!

P. Perhaps so. . . . But I still feel that you deserve *more* from a husband than my art might permit me to give. Let me find myself. . . . Perhaps in the light of "eternal" life, I shall be able to embrace my art in a more balanced way. If I can, then I'll ask you to be my wife; if not, then I'd rather see you in the arms of another!

JA. This sounds fair enough, Paul. . . . In the meantime, let's consider ourselves formally engaged!

P. But what if it takes me a hundred years to put my house in order?

JA. Don't worry. I'm sure this is exactly what my father would hope for. A century isn't so long a time, considering our current span of a thousand years. By then, coincidentally, I'll be the same age my mother was when she gave birth to me. Give me your ring, Boo. I'll wear it for a hundred years. If you haven't married me by then, I'll return here to Valhalla on midnight, March 30, 1927, and give you back your ring. If you're not here to receive it personally, then I'll place it in its tomb, shed my final tears over you, and be off to marry another!

For the second time this evening, Paul withdraws his ring from its case and now places it on Judy's finger.

P. With this ring, my dear, I pledge you my eternal love. If I'm to marry, you will be my wife; if not, then at least you'll be the prime inspiration for anything great I might do in Second-Order life!

Following our engagement kiss, the moonlight reflects tears in Judy's eyes.

P. Why the Kitten tears?

JA. Because I'm at once happy and very proud of you. . . . But please, Boo, as soon as you possibly can, let me in on the secret of your recent identity. I'll never betray your trust, and I have no doubt that knowing this will make the waiting both easier to understand and easier to endure.

P. This I'll do, my love!

After another kiss, she playfully tweaks my nose good night.

JA. Well, once again—happy rebirthday! I'll turn in now because I'm sure you want to be alone with your thoughts of Earth. There's nothing more dramatic than those first few hours of *total recall*!

P. Thanks, Kitten. I fully agree with you.

With love (and still more kisses), I tuck Judy back into her sleeping bag, then sit there and stare admiringly as she dozes off. Continuing my adoration, I'm tempted to reach down and waken her—to tell her everything! But a more cautious judgment stays my hand. Before she can know my secret, I must better know *myself,* and to what extent the Great Mogul will now dominate the life and environment of Paul Rezler!

Suddenly I feel like walking about and observing a moonlit Valhalla through Beethoven's eyes, but it's too bone-chilling cold—too cold even to sit on our blanketed rock and study the stars. The modest fire has completely died out, and I don't wish to rebuild it for fear of disturbing Judy's sleep with its snapping and crackling. I return to the warm comfort of my sleeping bag, and for several hours lie there absolutely reveling in the quiet sounds of wind and falling leaves. Just think—one week earlier, Beethoven was living between a pair of poor old ears that heard neither the fortissimos of an orchestra, the crash of thunder, nor the arm's length firing of a cannon. And yet tonight (over and above the wind and leaves), he hears the tiny ticking of Judy's wristwatch.

As I lay there, my racing brain delights in sampling the spiritual highlights of Beethoven's Earthly days via the miracle of TOTAL RECALL! What fun it is once again to behold the face of my grandfather, to feel his huge forefinger beneath my infant chin, to hear his sour comment on my total lack of physical charm, to see again my dear First-Order mother, to return to Neefe for another lesson, to relive each precious moment of my first visit with Mozart, to recall my pianistic triumphs one by one, to renew my acquaintance with Lichnowsky, with Lobkowitz, with young Liszt, with old Goethe, to conduct the orchestras of Vienna, to feel little Karl hopping on my knee. . . . Then came the tears. Oh God, how dark and ugly! The death of my mother, the first realities of deafness, the frustrations of *Fidelio,* the battles over Karl, the painful degeneration of my physical body, the months of death agony at the Schwarspanierhaus, the final offer of wine from Schindler's shaky teaspoon. . . . The joys and the tears—they all mingle together and sing me the song of a great musician. To this melody, Paul Rezler goes to sleep. He goes to sleep with moons and wind overhead, with Judy at his side, and with the spirit of a new Beethoven within him, anxiously awaiting the morning!

Chapter 32

Next morning, I awaken to Judy's staring at *my* sleeping face:

P. Kitten! . . . How long have you been sitting here?
JA. I've been awake for over an hour. You were sleeping so soundly that I couldn't bear to disturb you. I went for a half- hour's walk, built a fire, and then returned here to study my sleeping artist.
P. Any conclusions?
JA. Only that I love you, and wish that you weren't so secretive about your affairs.
P. If it weren't for my secrecy, then I'd never be able to give you nice surprises.

Four eggs and a modest supply of bacon prove to be an adequate breakfast only because there are five sandwiches and some fruit remaining from our snack of the night before. Devouring these morsels with "mountain" appetites, we discuss our plans for the immediate future.

JA. I suppose your rebirth will cut short our vacation.
P. I'm afraid it will, Judy. I'd like to get home this evening so that I can make my visit to Aaron AP on Saturday. If my counselor should recommend a change in schools, things could be arranged in time for the new quarter on Monday.

JA. Rather convenient, I'd say!

P. Naturally! All it took was careful planning, some grunting, some altitude, and the inspiration of *your* rebirth. By the way, Big Cat invited me to your farm for a wild party on the very day of my rebirth. I'm sure the purpose of it is for me to tell my complete story so that our plans can be resolved and, hopefully, our engagement announced. But as things now stand, I can't yet reveal my identity. So give her a big kiss for me, and tell her to keep the soup warm. I'll come for our party just as soon as I can make it.

JA. I'll tell her, Boo. How shall we spend today?

P. On Earth, next to the divine Muse, my greatest friends were inhabitants of the woods—rocks, trees, birds . . . green things. During three horrible months on my deathbed, I wished above all else that I might spend a final day among these delights. But neither the weather nor my big old rock of a belly would permit this luxury. All I could do was lie there and try to remember how things used to be. Also, there was never time in the First Order for me to see or hear the beauties of a pounding ocean. So if you don't mind, Kitten, I'd like to divide this day between tramping over Valhalla and wading in the surf back at our villa. It would now give me great pleasure to behold these wonders through the mind's eye of my First-Order life!

JA. I can well believe this. When do we start?

P. The sooner the better!

Thus begins the first accomplishment in the second life of Ludwig van Beethoven. He spends nearly four hours descending the slopes of Valhalla. As he does so, his "entire body" breathes in the sound of every bird, the fiery path of each falling leaf, the subtle motions of bare beckoning trees, the playful ripples of sun-sparked dancing brooks, and the quiet voyages of clouds across their sky-blue sea. Just like old times, except now when he reaches for his sketchbook, it's not there. And instead of a patient Ferdinand Ries trailing behind him, there follows in his wake a tired, breathless, panting Judy Adams. As she tries to keep pace, she wonders what sort of mountain-devouring monster her poor, innocent lover has now become.

Paul and Judy reach their cottage at the entrance of Trail No. 7 by early afternoon, and eat such a big lunch that it becomes the final meal of their vacation. They go to the seashore and spend two hours walking the surf, and another two hours kissing and caressing before a cozy log fire in the parlor of the villa.

At 9:00 PM, our lovers jump into their sports and head for the nearest D-R Chamber. For a half hour, they drive with the top back, enjoying the wind and stars. Then suddenly it's too cold to proceed further with only the sky for a roof. Paul pulls over and closes the coupé's tight-fitting top. In the absolute quiet of the little car's interior, they begin their first serious conversation since breakfast.

JA. You know, Boo . . . I don't think you'd better see me again until you're ready to tell me who you are.

P. Why not, Kitten?

JA. I'm a better detective than you think. You'd be surprised what I've discovered about you, just by following you around for a day.

P. A great deal, I'm sure. . . . Like maybe what?

JA. Well, for one thing, artist tall or artist small, you're the greatest lover of nature Earth has ever produced!

P. Why do you say this, my dear?

JA. Many an artist would stop in his tracks to admire a beautiful tree. But you . . . you lie flat on your back and stare up through its branches! Who among us doesn't enjoy the song of a brook? But my big old devotee stretches flat on his belly and paddles in the water with his hands and ears. We all love the cheerful message of birds. But how many of us break into tears at the sight and sound of them? There's no doubt about it, you've become the spirit of nature itself!

P. Congratulations, subtle sleuth! Your observations are as keen as they are correct! . . . But why should I keep my love of nature a secret from you? This is all you've learned?

JA. Not quite. You're a powerful, proud, bombastic, self-confident Germanic artist, who spits in the presence of a lady!

P. I can see how you've observed the spitting aspect of me. And I apologize for my ungentlemanly acquisition. But in God's name, how the rest of it?

JA. Nothing involved. . . . I can tell by the new and ungraceful way you walk: chin high, nose in the air, hands behind your back . . . a proud peacock if I've ever seen one! And your driving . . . it's ten times more aggressive than it was yesterday!

P. Very clever! But why a German peacock?

JA. Twice you lost your temper today: first when you slipped on Valhalla's mud and went ankle deep into the little brook, and a second time, when you tried unsuccessfully to pass that speeding roadster. On both occasions, I heard a tremendous rolling of German profanity. I couldn't understand the exact words, but I had no trouble placing their national origin.

P. You're too much detective for me. I'll not spend another vacation with Judy Adams until I'm ready to tell her my whole story!

JA. Precisely what I suggested, my love.

At the D-R Chamber, good-bye kisses are mixed with tears—no doubt for the simple reason that this time there is no specific date set for their next embrace. Judy returns to SP 71 to spend the rest of the weekend on her parents' farm. I journey to CP 25 for a first visit with my Second-Order family as Ludwig van Beethoven.

I arrive at Dogwood at eleven thirty. Except for two table lamps, the house is entirely dark; except for soft piano music coming from sister Regina's phonograph, it is perfectly quiet. No doubt about it. The family has retired for the evening.

Immediately I gravitate to the kitchen, where my famished belly is rewarded with coffee and big slices of Mother's delicious apple cake. Quietly I climb the stairs to my bedroom. Tiptoeing into the bath that separates my brother's room from mine, I carefully close his door before flicking on the lights. Deciding in favor of a warm shower, I wriggle out of my clothes and return to the bathroom. Something truly wonderful stops me in my tracks. It's the sight of my nude Second-Order body, viewed in a full-length mirror, and for the first time through Beethoven's eyes! What a miracle of transformation—yet how simple, how logical, how natural!

Gone are the mop of unruly gray-white hair, the pockmarked yellow face with its spreading nose and frightening jaw, the distended belly scarred by Seibert's handiwork, and those short and shapeless tree-trunk legs, which brought me a foot below normal height. In place of this First-Order hulk of physical dilapidations, I now behold a strong face whose healthful glow, whose coppery features, and whose curly black hair would put even young Waldstein to shame. Still studying the mirror, there comes a frightening thought. On Earth, I was sickly, small, poor, ugly, and deaf. From midtwenties until the grave, my sexual and biological energies were *totally* deflected into piano and composition. Now, as Paul Rezler, I am neither sickly, nor small, nor poor, nor ugly, nor deaf! Having nothing to sublimate, does this mean that my present life services to art will be inferior to those fanatic devotions rendered the Muse on Earth? Will the comforts and conveniences of Paul Rezler dilute Beethoven into Second-Order mediocrity? Or will the Great Mogul rise again and stamp out everything in my life but music?

Finishing my shower, I slide back the curtain, and there stands nineteen-year-old brother Freeman in bathrobe and slippers. As usual for bedtime, he has his long brown hair combed straight forward so that it almost touches his arched eyebrows. With a quizzical expression, he stares me down from head to toe:

Fr. Paul! . . . What are you doing home so early in the weekend? Have you and Judy had an argument?
P. Argument, hell! We're engaged!
Fr. Engaged? I thought you weren't going to make it formal until . . . Don't tell me you're . . . ?
P. That's right, Freeman, it's all over. Happened right there in the middle of our vacation. Now at last I'm a Second-Order adult like the rest of our family!
Fr. Congratulations, Paul! Will you be going to Aaron AP tomorrow?
P. That's why I'm home early.
Fr. Wait 'til I tell the folks. Put on your robe and come downstairs, I'll get the celebration started.
P. Don't bother, Freeman, it'll keep until morning.

My words fall on deaf ears. I finish drying, don my plaid robe, and comb my hair. Then when I open the door to my bedroom, there stands our whole family, waiting in line. First comes a big kiss from Mother, then a hug and handshake from Dad, and finally my fifteen-year-old sister knocks me into a chair, throws herself in my lap, and gives me a big passionate kiss that is ten times what I would expect from such a proper brunette pigtailed young lady.

P. Regina! Who taught *you* to kiss that way?
Rg. One of my many boyfriends. . . . I'm practicing up for when I really fall in love.
P. Well, you'd better stop practicing or I'll be an uncle before you're a married woman!

I turn Gina over on my lap and am about to give her a good spanking, when Mother grabs my sleeve.

PM. This is what she deserves, Paul. But first things first. . . . Let's all go down to the kitchen where we'll hear your story and toast your "arrival" with apple cake and coffee.

As I trail our family down the circular stairs and through the hall, Beethoven's eyes make some interesting and lustful observations about his "new" mother and sister. What they behold is neither a mother nor a sister, but two beautiful girls! Hard for Beethoven to believe, but such is human aging in Second-Order life. Each person's body attains a physical maturity of eighteen to twenty-one years. Then for an approximately 900 years, there's no change at all! Following this period of glorious health and constancy, there come the final hundred years of day-by-day physical obsolescence, comparable to those that terminate life on Earth!

We reach the kitchen just in time for me to hear a sad complaint from Freeman.

Fr. Guess what, Mom! Some hungry wolf has eaten half our apple cake. Now there's not enough for five servings!

P. (*I avoid Mother's stare and start toward the cellar.*) Wait here! I'll be right back.

Since earliest boyhood, I never thought of the rambling basement of our home as anything more than a wonderful place for hide-and-seek. Now suddenly it takes on the charm and glitter of a freshly trimmed Christmas tree! For there in its wine bin are row after row upon row of tempting bottles, whose dusty labels bring supreme joy to the heart of Beethoven. What wonderful names! What dear old friends: Ofener, Rüdesheimer, Nessmüller, Melniker, Erlauer, Vöslauer, Adelsberger, Ruster, and a dozen brands I'd never heard of. I grab four bottles and return to the kitchen.

P. If I'd known we were going to have a party, I wouldn't have been so hard on the apple cake. But since I'm guest of honor and since it's *my* rebirthday, don't you think I should be the one to select the refreshments?

Father sides with me.

PF. By all means, Paul. But I can see where we'll be getting a lock and key for our wine cellar. It looks as though we've inherited a prime alcoholic from the First Order!

P. Not really, Dad. I'm no drinker at all, compared to some of my old friends.

PF. Then how come the four bottles?

P. One for me, and three for you folks!

PF. No drinker, eh? A week ago, you had no taste for anything stronger than coffee. Now you plan to down one of my best bottles of Nessmüller without any help from anyone!

Mother slices a plate of fresh nutbread, and the five of us saunter into the living room—I with my bottle, and each of them with a mere glass of Melniker. During the next half hour, I completely absorb the stated amount of Nessmüller, requisitioned for Paul Rezler by Beethoven!

At the time of my rebirth, Robert F. Rezler is a man of fifty years. Like Mother, he would pass for a mere teenager, although he wears a trim little mustache that makes him look a shade older than would otherwise be the case. It is no doubt from him that I inherit my healthy head of curly black hair. As we seat ourselves in the living room, it is this handsome young father who opens the conversation.

PF. Now Paul, suppose you tell us your big story. Who is our new mystery son? After all this waiting, you must be some sort of king or prince!

P. Actually Dad, you're not far from the truth. In a way, I *am* a king . . . a Great Mogul to be exact.

PF. Well come on! What are the details?

P. I can't share my story with anyone, until I've had time to think through my present and future plans.

PM. (*Mother interrupts Dad's interrogation.*) Were you so prominent on Earth that you must now be secretive from even your own family?

P. I don't know, Mom. Perhaps so. . . . As soon as I meet my counselor and get to know him, he'll advise me (in the light of past and future careers) how secretive I should remain.

Rg. (*Gina chimes in.*) Come on, Paul! You can give us a little hint.

P. Let it suffice to say that I'm now an artist of considerable merit and reputation!

PF. (*Dad's expression quickly sours.*) I knew as much! As fate would have it, you just *had* to be some sort of artist so you could run off and marry Judy. Well, I've got a surprise for you. (*His strong features modulate into a warm smile.*) I'm glad! . . . I think Judy is a terrific girl with as inspiring a personality as you'll find in Second-Order life. The fact that your mutual affection was so great and so natural that you fell in love before either of you had experienced rebirth, this confirms a true foundation for a happy marriage. My sole basis for opposing your youthful romance was the probability that the two of you would end up having no interest in a common career. And this would be to miss half the joy of married life. Neither you, your brother, nor your sister tested unusually high in any particular Second-Order talent. Mother and I encouraged the three of you to study architectural engineering, not so much because it is our chosen profession, but because we wished to avoid the possibility of your entering Second-Order adulthood without anything definite to do. And this could well be your dangerous lot should you inherit no career incentives from Earth. As things have worked out, neither Gina nor Freeman have absorbed Earthly careers, which they would prefer to engineering. Probably, for want of something better to do, they will follow their parents' example. But I guess this will not be the case with you, Paul.

P. No, Father, definitely not! What's come my way from Earth is so powerful a thing that I'm sure it will dominate my entire Second-Order life— no doubt the Third and Fourth as well!

PF. Wonderful! This means that you and Judy now share a common interest *besides* the love which you have for each other. Premaritally, I could require nothing more of you! When's the wedding going to be? Before, during, or after your college days?

P. Ironically, Dad; I'm not so sure there's going to *be* a wedding!

PF. What? . . . Don't be ridiculous! What's holding you back?

P. The very art you're so glad I inherited!

PF. How can a common professional interest hold you back? Don't you still love the girl?

P. I love her more than any human being I have ever known. But now there's the chance that I'll love my art more than I love my Judy!

PF. Bah! No one's *that* serious about his career. Didn't you have a wife and family on Earth?

P. No. My art was my wife, my child . . . everything! When I finally had to assume the guardianship of a nephew, the resulting conflicts nearly killed the both of us.

PM. (*At this point, Mother interrupts with her usual optimism.*) Never mind, Paul. Your attitude toward art was no doubt a reflection of typical First-Order feelings about the mortality of human life! The old case of "Art is long; life is short." You probably felt there were millions of things to be done and no time in which to do them. No wonder the Muse crowded all lesser joys from your life. But now, given time, I have no doubt that your philosophical views will change. Within a year or two, or ten, you'll suddenly wake up to the joyful realization that there's plenty of time for your art and your Judy!

P. I hope you're right, Mom. But for the present, knowing my former self as I know my former self, it seems like a long and difficult resolution!

Rg. (*Gina takes a turn.*) What about Judy? It doesn't seem fair to keep her waiting for years and years until you finally resolve your personal problems!

P. On the contrary, her parents have conditioned her to prefer waiting. From the cradle up, she's heard nothing but career first, then marriage. She told me she'd wait until my hundredth rebirthday before even thinking about marrying someone else.

Fr. Let's hope it doesn't take you a hundred years to revise your philosophy and resolve your problems. When exactly *was* your rebirthday?

P. Early this morning . . . a few minutes past midnight.

Fr. March 30, 1827 . . . we'll put you down for future celebrations.

PM. (*A smiling promise from my beautiful young mother.*) No doubt you'll be making a trip to Aaron AP tomorrow.

P. I thought I would. It's mighty convenient having rebirth come precisely between quarters!

Fr. Do you think you'll need a full term of transitional studies at Lakemont before entering college?

P. I'll certainly need something. I hope my AP adviser can help me with my indecisions.

Fr. I'm sure he will, as one of 350 ruling mentors appointed by Aaron himself back in 1733. He'll study your problems and tell you exactly what to do about them.

Father puts down his empty wine glass, yawns, stands up, leaves the room. All have gone except Gina and me. Suddenly, there comes a painful pinch on the back of my left thigh.

P. What the hell was that for?

Rg. For being a bad boy and spitting in our parlor. If Mom had seen you, then *you'd* be the one to get the spanking. I could hardly believe my eyes, but since Mom's departure, I saw you spit twice on her best carpet!

I could blame this little habit directly upon Beethoven, but Gina would never have believed me!

Chapter 33

Next morning, I'm up at 5:00 AM. I repack my valise, get my breakfast, and tiptoe from the house at six o'clock. As I walk toward the garage, I suddenly hear Gina's girlish voice chirping from her side window:

Rg. Good luck, Paul! Hurry back and tell us everything!
P. Thanks, Sis. I hope I can!

Only "Class A" D-R Chambers provide transportation to Aaron AP. The nearest "A" station is a two-hour drive from Dogwood. Using Freeman's roadster, as I speed along the empty highway, vivid recollections of nephew Karl descend upon me with the same impact as the preceding night's bottle of Nessmüller. How I miss the boy! How I wish I could tell him what I now know of life! I wonder if he's getting along with Baron Von Stutterheim? Did he attend my funeral? Is he at all proud of his uncle? Will he succeed in a military career? How will his finances turn out? Will he marry and continue the name of "Beethoven" on Earth?

At eight-fifteen, I am "recomposed" in the Aaron AP D-R Chamber, located in the basement of the huge registration building. This multistory labyrinth is in the shape of a regular decagon with mile-long sides, ten floors below ground level and seventy above. As I follow signs along twisting corridors to a particular bank of elevators,

I suddenly have the strange feeling that I'm being shadowed! I imagine that I hear footsteps, yet on three separate occasions, my sudden stopping and turning around reveals no one. The final sign points to a dozen elevators and reads, "Preliminary Registration-40th Floor." Arriving on this floor, I quickly enter a phone booth from which there is a clear view of the elevators. The one on which I rode was empty. If I *am* being followed, the culprit will probably step from the next car! Presently a double door from the adjacent elevator opens and out come two beautiful blondes—definitely not the cloak-and-dagger type. How silly! I'm being so secretive about my precious identity that now I imagine people are following me around just to discover who I am. Even so, as I leave the elevator and start toward Preliminary Registration Headquarters, my suspicious eye scans the elevator dials and carefully observes that a car *has* stopped on the thirty-ninth floor—a car which then immediately returns to "one." (Elevators—what a wonderful invention! How Milord Schuppanzigh would have appreciated one of these at the Pasqualati house or at the Schwarspanierhaus!)

Upon entering room 4000, an oldish-looking receptionist greets me with a pleasant smile, which she then promptly folds into a mask of stern features. Handing me a card, she motions for me to fill in its blanks at one of the unoccupied desks. This I do, carefully pondering information requested by the first three lines:

(1) FIRST-ORDER NAME: <u>Ludwig van Beethoven</u>
(2) SECOND-ORDER NAME: <u>Paul Rezler</u>
(3) NAME DESIRED FOR SECOND-ORDER REGISTRATION: <u>Ludwig van Beethoven</u>

Patiently I waited until others in the room had filled out their cards and left. Then (encouraged by absolute privacy) I walk timidly to the receptionist and hand her my card. Her reaction is entirely different from that directed toward the other registrants. The smile returns, and with extended hand, she practically rises to attention.

Rc. Congratulations, young man! I'm indeed honored! Although in the course of my job each year I welcome thousands of new arrivals through this door, rarely do I have the privilege of greeting such a great man. On behalf of Aaron and his College of Counselors, let me be the first to welcome you to the Major Order of second life!

B. Thank you! Where do I go from here?

Rc. (*She finishes typing a few more words, unzips a yellow card from her typewriter, and hands it to me.*) Present this card to the receptionist in room 6000. There the official authentication of your First-Order life will be made.

B. Authentication?

Rc. Yes. It would never do for us to have some impostor parading in our midst as Beethoven!

At the first audible mention of my Earthly name, something attracts my attention across the empty room to the opaque glass door where I had entered twenty minutes earlier. Apparently it had been held open an inch or two, and now closes itself coincidentally with the jerking disappearance of an ominous shadow on the other side of its less than semitransparent ripples. Now try to tell me that I'm not being followed! I mumble a few quick words to the receptionist, something like "I can see what you mean."

Nodding a final thanks in her direction, I run to the door as quickly as possible and bolt clumsily into the hall. Who do I find there? Neither friend nor family nor phantom. Just a twisting, quiet, empty corridor!

On the sixtieth floor, a young lady shows me to a room containing two handsome medical technicians and an apparatus not unlike a giant X-ray machine. Its business end, which resembles a hair dryer, is placed over the top of my head, and my chair is swiveled into such a position that I might comfortably view a large TV-type screen. After glancing at my card, both young men come over and shake my hand. One is a wiry Oriental who focuses the sparkling beam of his black eyes directly on mine as he speaks.

Y. Congratulations, Herr Beethoven! Welcome to heaven.

B. This *must* be heaven! Even a Chinese appreciates Beethoven.

Y. On Earth, I was a negro. I arrived here knowing nothing of Western music, but it wasn't long before the bold spirit of your works completely won my heart!

B. This is a great compliment. Will you accept the dedication of my next piece?

Y. I certainly will—a real pleasure. Here's my card.

On the dainty two-by-three, I read:

Kevin Yee, MD, LLD, PhD, Etc.
Electroanalytic Specialist
College of Counselors
Aaron AP

Y. (*Yee continues.*) With this little gadget, we actually peer into your spiritual subelectron. Using the Second-Order property of total recall, we can establish your First-Order identity beyond the shadow of a doubt. And in the case of Beethoven, this should be easy to do.

B. Suppose I *were* an imposter. What would prevent me from sitting here, thinking of "Beethoven" with my Second-Order brain, and passing off these identifying thoughts as First-Order recall?

Y. That's easy. Contemporary images could never be mistaken for the smooth continuity of Earthly patterns. And besides, this machine is so rigged that only genuine First-Order recall appears on our screen in color and with sound. Present-life thoughts would show up as disconnected frames in silent black-and-white. Now let's concentrate on some First-Order events that will confirm your identity.

B. What kind do you suggest?

Y. Through composite spiritual analyses of those admiring contemporaries who have preceded you here, we now have a vivid portrait of the ugly little man you used to be. Why not give us a picture or two of Beethoven viewing Beethoven in a mirror? Throw in a few concerts, some official signatures, a pastoral scene, a bit of enlightening dialogue—this should be enough.

B. The conversations will be in German.

Y. Ayars and I speak *ten* languages. German is one of them.

For fifteen minutes beneath the buzzing helmet, I conjure up selected patterns from First-Order life. Then the humming stops and, still under the mechanism, I join my two companions in viewing scenes from "Beethoven," which flash across our screen with clear sound and brilliant color. Naturally the first picture is a conversation between little Beethoven and his mother. We are discussing my newest assignment from Herr Neefe, and what a pleasure it is once again to actually see her dear face, to hear her sad, sweet voice. Next comes a dialogue between Mozart and his aspiring student. As the door to the great musician's apartment opens, my sixteen-year-old voice is heard to ask, "Herr Mozart?"

The richly adorned Maestro smiles as he looks directly into my eyes (hence directly into *our* eyes):

M. Yes indeed! . . . And what young devil have we here?
B. Not a devil, Sir. I am Beethoven. I have come from Bonn to see you.
M. Oh yes! Just last week I received a post from your elector. He introduced you and included some fine commendations from Herr Neefe and my friend Waldstein. Come in! I must hear you.

As the scene shifts, I notice my two observers smiling and nodding at one another. Suddenly we ascend a polished marble staircase and enter a palatial drawing room. A tall, thin, priestly man walks toward us and extends his hand:

L. Herr Beethoven, I'm Prince Lichnowsky and I welcome you to Vienna.

Then (without warning) we go from the sublime to the comical. There follow half-a-dozen mirrored and temperamental scenes of poor Beethoven's bloody and unsuccessful attempts to shave himself. How strange it is to look upon a face that *was,* but now is no more! Behind this gruesome mask, I spent my days on Earth. Now it is but dust in a grave, yet the spirit behind it is more alive than ever! My serious thoughts are in no way communicated to the technicians; both have laughed their way to tears over my weird antics. The Beethoven within me is tempted to ask them what's so goddamn funny, but Rezler takes a wiser course. He bursts out laughing at himself. A final sequence features the hands of Beethoven. How short and strong and hairy they are! We see them composing bits of the *Pastoral,* they become rain-soaked while sketching the up-and-down contours of the *Appassionata,* they claw Bonaparte's name from Opus 55's title page, they pound out some final arpeggios of the *Moonlight,* they carefully print the title page for Symphony 9, they conduct a portion of Symphony 3 (My doctor-friends wince at the raggedy sounds of the little orchestra.), and finally, they turn pages at the *Kärnthnerthor* concert of May 7, where we observe admiring glances on the faces of players, but our screen is silent. There are no sounds for *us* because there were none for our poor deaf Beethoven!

Yee removes my headpiece while his associate turns off the machine. The two of them slap my back, and we again shake hands. They present me with an important-looking diploma:

Y. Here! . . . Here's the official authentication of your Certificate of Identity. There's no doubt in our minds who you are. May we again congratulate you? As Aaronians, we're proud to welcome such a great Earthling into our culture!

B. Thank you! I trust the two of you will keep my secret. I'm not sure that it's in the best interest of my career to reveal Beethoven's professional identity at this moment.

Y. We understand. Keeping secrets is an important part of our job. Good luck to you, Herr Beethoven.

B. Do I meet my counselor now?

Y. First comes the Personality Data Sheet. On the basis of your answers to its questions, an advisor will be chosen for you. Suite 2812 is now reserved for you. Present your certificate to our receptionist on the twenty-eighth floor. She'll give you the Data Sheet.

Suite 2812 is assigned to me for the balance of my visit to the Administrative Planet. By Lakemont standards it is considerably smaller than dormitory accommodations, having only a bedroom, a study, and a private bath. Immediately I go to work on the questionnaire, and it takes me until one o'clock to complete its twenty pages. These twenty pages summarize my entire 991 years of life on Earth. The first 934 years included five lives as women and ten lives as men. Then came my final 57 years on Earth as Beethoven; the essence of these years occupied fifteen pages of the summary.

Upon my presenting this packet to the receptionist, she rushes it off to the AP central computer for analysis.

Rc. The information you've supplied here will determine your counselor.

B. How long will this take?

Rc. At least two hours.

B. Then what happens?

Rc. We contact your new counselor, then he contacts you!

B. You mean he phones?

Rc. Sometimes he phones. Usually he comes for a get-acquainted visit.

B. I hope I'll be as lucky as George Rezler, my father.

Rc. In what respect?

B. None other than Robert Carrick was appointed his adviser.

Rc. This *is* unusual. Only a handful out of a million Earthlings are assigned the mentorship of a *ruling* counselor. Such men are so busy with the administrative problems of an entire planet that they have little time for personal counseling. But don't worry. Each has appointed several thousand assistant advisers, who do nothing *but* counsel. They'll find just the right man to solve whatever problems you have.

B. Should I wait for him here in 2812?

Rc. Yes. If I were you, I'd return to my suite by four o'clock and wait for his phone call. In the meantime, since you haven't had lunch, why don't you go up to the seventieth floor and enjoy our wonderful restaurant with its spellbinding view?

B. Thanks! I think I will. And how about a little visit to Population Records?

Rc. Why not? That's where most new arrivals are anxious to go. The Records Building is only ten miles from this one, and can be reached in a few minutes by going to level -8 and taking Subway Express 41. Just make sure you're back by four o'clock.

Like the Registration Building (and all other administrative buildings for that matter), Population Records is in the shape of a giant regular decagon. I arrive at the eighty-story center at 1:45 PM, and spend two fascinating hours determining which of Beethoven's old friends and loved ones have preceded him here. From the immediate family, only Mother and Grandfather are present in the Major Order of second life. Of the great Earthly musicians, we number among us: Bach, Handel, Mozart, Förster, and Haydn. Even my former teachers, Neefe and Albrechtsberger, are now Major-Order Aaronians. Among old friends, there's no trace of Waldstein, but Lichnowsky and Lobkowitz are very much alive and in our midst.

To prevent Second-Order adult life from becoming one continuous wasteful spree of Earthly reunions and reminiscences, such matters are placed entirely in the hands of Reunion Control, another of the countless decagonal centers on Aaron AP. Through this administrative unit, reunions are brought about only by the mutual consent of *both* parties. They are also carefully planned to provide the least possible interruption in the daily routines of the Second-Order lives involved. For example, if I were now interested in meeting my Earthly mother, I would fill out one of three types of cards:

> Type A - Urgent! I must see you immediately. My present life's plan requires this meeting, even at your inconvenience!
> Type B - For my sincere pleasure, I request a meeting with you at your earliest convenience.
> Type C - If you are interested, I should like to meet with you, but only at your complete convenience.

The card would be sent to Reunion Control, and they would notify Mother as to the urgency of my request. If agreeable to her, our get-together would then be arranged, and each of us would be notified as to when and where. While at the Records Building, I fill out type A cards for Aaron, Mother, and Mozart; type B for Grandfather, Bach, Handel, Förster, and Haydn; also a type C for Neefe, Albrechtsberger, Lichnowsky, and Lobkowitz. With the exception of Aaron's, I send none of the cards to Reunion Control for processing. I place them in my pocket for *future* use because I have no idea how long it might be necessary for me to keep my First-Order identity a complete secret.

As promised, I return to Suite 2812 by four o'clock, but its phone doesn't ring until nearly five! When it finally does, my tone of voice reflects an obvious impatience. The other voice sounds apologetic and excited.

B. Hello!
Ro. Herr Beethoven?
B. Speaking!
Ro. This is Hal Robinson, your duly appointed counselor.
B. Where are you calling from—outer space?
Ro. No, I'm downstairs in the lobby. May I come up for a little chat?
B. By all means—I'm anxious to meet you!

Presently the door opens and in comes a bouncing, wiry youth with sandy hair and a freckled reddish complexion. He looks like an Earthling of twenty-five, but since he is an Aaronian, his slightly receding hairline could belong to a man considerably older. As we shake hands, he is first to speak.

Ro. I must apologize for not being one of Aaron's original appointees. Though I'm not a personal disciple of our great Master, I think you'll find me an ideal counselor for Ludwig van Beethoven. My assumption is based on the fact that during the past century, I have successfully guided some rather prodigious Earthly musicians into well-adjusted Second-Order lives.

B. Who, may I ask?

Ro. You'll find out soon enough. I'm planning a little surprise for you this evening; that's why it took me so long to get here. I judge by your questionnaire that there are quite a few problems for us to discuss.

B. You probably think I baby myself.

Ro. Not at all! Anyone who takes as big a professional step forward as you've taken in First-Order life usually has a difficult time adjusting his Earthly patterns to the Second Order. What do you feel will be the main obstacle to your happiness?

B. I'm very proud of the love and talent for music which I've inherited from Earth. But at the mere threshold of a new life, I can't stand the feeling that my Second-Order battle is already fought and won—won entirely by the blood and toil of an Earthly Beethoven!

Ro. Is this why you propose keeping your First-Order identity a secret?

B. Yes. I *must* feel that whatever respect and admiration might come to me from my Aaronian colleagues will result from what I do with Beethoven's talent here in Second-Order life, and not from what I did with it on Earth.

Ro. Very interesting! One of your great predecessors reached the same conclusion for *his* life.

B. Does he still conceal *his* Earthly identity?

Ro. No. But he did until he was sure that his contemporaries respected his talent, and not just his First-Order reputation.

B. This is exactly what I mean!

We then enter a beautiful little auditorium of about four hundred seats. As we walk down its main aisle, I observe a concert grand and three chairs onstage. The lid of the piano is propped open six inches. One chair supports a glimmering violin, the other a stately cello.

B. It looks as though we'll be hearing a trio this evening.

Ro. We shall indeed, Herr Beethoven. Your *B-flat* to be exact.

B. To think that the *B-flat* has actually preceded me here to "heaven."

Ro. It certainly has, as have all your principal works from the first trios and sonatas through the final symphonies!

B. This no doubt is through the total recall of deceased performers and conductors of my music.

Ro. Correct! And in spite of our meticulous cross-referencing, there are probably a few wrong notes in each score. One of your first obligations to our present culture is for you to select those Earthly works of Beethoven which you deem worthy of survival here on Aaron, and to carefully edit them, perhaps even *revise* them to your complete satisfaction. These considered pieces will then become the sole block of Earthly Beethoven to be forwarded into higher orders of our system.

B. Wonderful! Now that I have ears again, I shall enjoy this task. Who plays for us this evening?

Ro. You, my dear Beethoven. You and a couple of fine Aaronian musicians.

B. Don't be silly. You promise to keep my secret, and now you send me before an audience.

Ro. Not an ordinary audience. To celebrate your rebirth, I've called together the 350 governing counselors of our Second-Order-Major planets. All but a dozen of them were able to come, and should walk through those doors in a few minutes. Each of these men will be as responsible as I in keeping your secret. Besides, you'll be playing behind a semitransparent curtain that fully emits the *sound* of you, but little more than the *silhouette* of you.

B. How about my fellow performers? They'll see my face.

Ro. They will, and this is according to plan. The effectiveness of my counseling requires them to know who you are. But don't worry, your secret will be as safe with them as it is with me. Are you not afraid of such an astute audience?

B. No. Fear is one thing I've never felt on a concert platform. And now with ears that *hear,* it is furthest from my feelings.

Ro. I thought you might be a little timid about playing in public, since you haven't done so for some time.

B. Not at all. In fact, I can hardly wait to put my new hands and ears to a keyboard. I feel that my piano technique is now as good as the best that it was on Earth; no better, but every bit as good. And as for the *B-flat,* my total recall of First-Order life now brings it more clearly to mind than Beethoven's "memory" could ever have done, even on that March afternoon sixteen years ago when I sketched its final bar! How strange it is that you've selected this piece for my Aaronian debut. Thirteen springs ago (way back in 1814), two performances of this very trio constituted my final public appearance as a pianist. Tonight I begin all over again with the same composition!

Ro. But now your playing will not be marred by deafness, nor by lack of practice.

B. I know. And this realization makes me as happy as a bridegroom! . . . During that second concert, I was convinced that Beethoven would never again perform in public. There were tears in my eyes. Had Jesus himself been in the audience that night, I'm sure he would have seen my tears. He would have heard the jangled poundings of a poor deaf man, and in loving sympathy would have come and placed his hand on my shoulder. After looking into my eyes and discerning their insufficient faith for anything like a miracle, he would have said, "Fear not, poor Beethoven. Though the time has come for you to say good-bye to your beloved instrument, the day shall soon arrive when you will take it up anew in the Kingdom of Heaven. With surer hands and with ears that hear, you will again play your way into the souls of men!"

I would have smiled (perhaps even laughed) while my reply would have done little more than betray a pitiable lack of faith: "Thank you, gentle Rabbi. . . . Thank you for trying to reassure me. Perhaps your words would bring comfort to a young child, but they are of little help to an old Beethoven. I'm convinced that I shall concertize no more, neither in this world nor the next."

Then with a shrug of the shoulders, I would have turned my back on the very man and on the very words that I should have most wanted to hear and to believe. And yet tonight in the simple act of playing this trio, I confirm here on Aaron a logical continuity which on Earth would have seemed too miraculous for Beethoven to accept as the natural reward of his growth and suffering!

Ro. And the time of your miracle is at hand. . . . Those doors will be opening any minute. We'd better get backstage. I'm going to give you a dress suit to put on.

While I don my formal attir, Robinson closes the semitransparent curtain he'd been talking about and turns up the auditorium lights so that we can pretty well make out its rows of bluish seats.

Ro. Don't worry, Rezler. Later when I raise the stage lights and lower those in the hall, your audience will *still* not be able to see you as clearly as we shall now observe them. As soon as you're ready, let's sit here on the piano bench and watch them come in.

We swing the bench at right angles to the keyboard and perch ourselves there like a couple of master spies in an observation tower. But I can't resist pivoting toward the huge twelve feet of ebony concert grand and running my fingers lightly over its keys. Directly above the ivories in three-inch gilded letters, I read the manufacturer's name: "SPANGLERSDORF." On Earth, I had never *heard of* such an instrument, nor *heard* such an instrument. Its key action is light but full—perfectly responsive! And its beautiful singing tone is unlike anything I had ever thought possible. I ripple over a few scales and arpeggios. What delight! All the hickory-stick training and discipline of young Beethoven now command the fingers of Paul Rezler with that same self-confidence, which thirty-five years earlier had burst open the musical doors of Vienna. My attention turns to the *Archduke*. First come eight measures of the blithe and lucid opening subject of the *Allegro moderato*, then a few measures from its broadly modeled second movement, then some deep and quiet organ harmonics that begin the *Andante cantabile's* theme. These are soon interrupted by Robinson's hand on my shoulder:

Ro. Shhh! You'd better stop playing now. Here comes your audience!
B. Where should I sit?
Ro. Go stand there in the right wing. As soon as I finish introducing you to our counselors, come to the center of the stage and take your first bow of Second-Order life. And remember, when the lights go on behind this tricky curtain, all we out front will be able to see is the mere outline of you. The secret of your identity should be perfectly safe regarding general audiences, following tonight's performance.

My counselor steps to the right of the stage, carefully puts his nose to the edge of the curtain, and peers into the audience. When he satisfies himself that all who are coming have come, he signals for the auditorium doors to be locked (my first truly "captive" audience), and then motions to two young men in the left wing, one of whom turns up the stage lights. Judging by the formal attire of these young men, I assume them to be the musicians with whom I'm to play. I nod to them; they nod and wave back. By now, Robinson has reached the center of the stage in full view of the mass of Aaronian counselors. He clears his throat, and I clear mine. Then standing there in the shadows and feeling tense with anticipation, I hear through the curtain a noble speech indeed—the official welcoming of Beethoven into Second-Order life!

Ro. Great counselors and fine gentlemen, it is a pleasure for me to welcome you to this concert. For nearly a hundred years, I have specialized in counseling Second-Order musicians--955 of them to be exact. And now, a unique privilege and responsibility. Today I have been assigned the mentorship of one of the two or three greatest composers ever to come here from Earth. Throughout the entire history of our culture, this is only the twelfth time that a meeting of ruling counselors has been called to honor the arrival of an Earthling musician. And yet I'm sure you'll be more than pleased with what you're about to hear. We have few composers, even in our Second-Order- Major culture, whose musicianship is on a par with that of *this* young man. For over thirty years, his best compositions have found their way to us, deeply enriching our musical lives. And now tonight, we welcome the man himself! He was born on Earth at Bonn in 1770. There he received his unshakable training in music and self-discipline. In his early twenties, he moved to Vienna, where he spent the rest of his life sacrificing all things to the divine Muse. This past Monday when he said good-bye to the reality of life on Earth, he did so as the greatest contemporary musician of Europe! His faith in himself and his divine optimism were strong enough even to carry him through a dozen years of total deafness and, consequently, the almost complete degeneration of his once fine piano technique.

We are now privileged to witness a great moment in this man's career. Here and now for the first time in Second-Order life, he places his new hands on a keyboard. His joy could well bring tears to our eyes, as he discovers in these new hands not the shriveled-up technique of a poor old deaf man, but precisely the optimum skill which he had developed as a young Earthling and with which he then conquered the city of Vienna! If his technique doesn't sound exceptional to *our* ears, we must remember that only yesterday was his rebirthday, and that he hasn't had the benefit of a single hour's practice as a Second-Order musician.

> Like many of our great reborn, this young man hopes to earn our respect by what he does *here* in Second-Order life, and not because of the things he did on Earth. For this reason (at least for the present), he wishes to keep his new identity a secret. He asks that we refrain from mentioning his rebirth beyond these walls in order to facilitate the keeping of his secret. He further requests your indulgence in permitting him to play for us behind the semitransparent anonymity of this curtain. Thirteen years ago, he last performed in public by playing the piano part of his own *Trio in B-flat.* Then the black shroud of total deafness closed over his career and separated him from his admiring public. Tonight he returns. He returns to us with a performance of this same trio! Gentlemen, may I present to you the composer of the *B-flat Trio,* the composer of the *Eroica Symphony,* the composer of *Fidelio,* the composer of the *Fifth Symphony,* the composer of the *Missa Solemnis* and *Choral Symphony,* the composer of the *Moonlight Sonata.* . . . Gentlemen, may I present to you Herr Ludwig van Beethoven!

As I stand there in the left wing, my apparent co-performers motion for me to come onstage. As I approach the center, I'm greeted with a thunderous explosion of unmistakenly genuine applause! My deep bow only brings the audience to their feet in a standing ovation. On and on they go for what seems like ten minutes of clapping, shouting, and wild bravos. A rush of hot tears now stains my face. I bow again while my two companions come onstage. I'm surprised! They come with neither music nor music rack. Both are tall, handsome, and young. The one who takes up the violin has a huge mass of reddish-brown hair, with a handsome mustache and goatee to match. His eyes are deep and penetrating (almost frightening), the kind that Judy Adams would love to look into. His lips are thin and sensitive, more like those of a flutist than a violinist. As we move behind the curtain, I whisper to our violinist:

B. No music?
Violin. For such a beautiful piece, I'm sure we can manage without a score. Give us an "A."

Seating myself at the keyboard, I sound the "A" while making a few careful observations of our cellist. His eyes also are deep and penetrating. (Do all Second-Order musicians develop such frightening stares?) Like the violinist, our cellist has very thick hair, but it is dark and close-cropped. His stern face is clean-shaven. His gaunt features look as though (under just the right conditions) they could break into a warm and friendly smile. But obviously a concert stage and the cello part to the *Archduke* are not the right conditions. As soon as the strings are tuned, I "conduct" a few silent measures to set the tempo. Then the three of us launch our way into the opening *Allegro moderato.* After thirteen years of absolute silence, it's impossible to convey the full effect these first few moments of glorious sounds have upon my mind and soul! The strings (and even the piano) sing more beautifully than anything I had ever heard. I'm so pleased with the sounds and structures of the first two movements that I decide here and now not to change one note of them! But it's the delightful *Andante cantabile* that truly reaches my heart. I'm not alone in this respect; for when we reach the final unearthly ecstasies of its expressive *Coda,* I turn toward my string players just in time to detect admiring smiles on their faces and appreciative tears in their eyes. As we're about to pounce uninterruptedly on the painful and shabby realities of the *Rondo-finale,* both fiddlers hold out their bows and stop the performance! They react to my questioning beam by pointing to the ghostly curtain. I glance in the direction of their pointing and am surprised to find that in response to the *Trio*'s third movement, our counselors are presenting me with another standing ovation, this one accompanied by absolute and reverent silence. The three of us sit there wondering what to do next, until (fortunately) Hal Robinson's head pokes itself in at the left of the curtain and solves our problem for us:

Ro. Go ahead! They want you to play the *Andante* all over again!

Exactly what we do, only this time we go on and attach the ugly little misfit of a *Finale.* As we suffer our way through its "sounding brass," I resolve that my first creative act of Second-Order life will be to provide the *Archduke* with a new and better-integrated closing movement!

At the conclusion of the *Trio,* the audience calls for the three of us, and then for Beethoven alone. Robinson then requests me to improvise on a theme:

B. What kind of theme?

Ro. Anything. How about a peasant tune? Something that will display Beethoven's improvisatory powers that we've been hearing so much about!

Diabelli's ridiculous little waltz tune comes to mind. As my string players go out front to join the rest of the audience, I raise the lid of my Spanglersdorf to wide-open position. Then I sit down and for a solid hour lose myself in brilliant improvisation on that dry little cobbler's patch of a theme. At the conclusion of my tricks and games, there are more wild rounds of applause. Then Robinson adjourns the meeting of counselors.

Beneath the fifth-floor stage is a tiny lounge where I'm told to go and wait for my advisor. This little room would be completely empty if one were to remove its rows of leather chairs and its wall-length mirrors. Here I'm promptly joined by the rest of our "trio," and the three of us sit down and talk a little shop while we're waiting for Robinson.

B. You young rascals are the greatest string players I've ever heard!

Cello. (*As he replies, the cellist's somber face breaks into precisely the warm smile that I had predicted it was capable of breaking into.*) Not exactly *young*. I'm eighty-three and my friend here is ninety-one.

B. But you look and play like young rascals. That's what's important! When old Schuppanzigh and Linke get here to "heaven," I must send them to you for lessons.

Cello. (*Still smiling, the cellist accepts my proposition.*) By all means! If they come to us upon *your* recommendation, I'm sure they're worthy of our time.

At last our violinist has something to say, breaking into the conversation with a complete change in topic.

Violin. By the way, who do you consider the greatest of Earthly composers?

B. Handel! . . . To him I bow my knee. He was unquestionably the ablest composer ever to live on Earth.

Violin. (*The violinist's handsome reddish mane seems to swell as he fixes his mighty eyes on mine.*) Not Bach?

B. No, Handel!

The two glance and smile at each other in such a curious way that I'm prompted to ask them a question that somehow I had failed to ask earlier in the evening: "Incidentally, who *are* you fellows?"

Their unexpected replies cause me to do something that I had never done in all my fifty-seven Earthly years as Beethoven or in my seventeen years on Aaron—I faint! . . . Unreservedly and flat on my face, I faint completely out of the picture! What little musician newly arrived from Earth wouldn't do the same under such conditions? Here I am, having just played with and for a perfectly harmless-looking cellist and an (almost) perfectly harmless-looking violinist. I ask them quite simply: "Who *are* you fellows?"

And their respective answers:

Cello. I'm Georg Friedrich Handel!

Violin. And my name is Bach . . . Johann Sebastian Bach!

Chapter 34

I regain consciousness to the acrid scent of smelling salts and discover that my friends have apparently lifted me from the floor of the cozy lounge into an uncomfortable couch formed from two of its chairs. The blood pounding back into my head makes me suspect that I'm blushing like a little girl. And yet the sight of these two greatest musical spirits ever to inhabit the Earth, the sight of them both staring down at me is practically enough to make me faint all over again. I offer an apology:

B. You must forgive me for acting like a child. This is the first time I've ever fainted. It's just that the two of you have always been such gods and constant inspiration to me on Earth, that when I now suddenly behold you face to face, each garbed in a handsome young body . . . it's just too much of a surprise, that's all!

Ba. (*As Bach replies, the expression on his face mellows slightly.*) We can understand how you feel. Perhaps Robinson should have better prepared you for our first meeting.

Ha. (*Then it's Handel who puts on a sober countenance.*) You probably wonder why your new counselor's first act is to bring the three of us together.

B. As a matter of fact, I do!

Ha. You must realize that he is *our* counselor as well. He has aided us both in adjusting to Second-Order life, and we know that he'll be able to do the same for you. Yet he's smart enough to discern that the initial advice given to a young Beethoven on the threshold of a new life stands a better chance of being heeded if it comes from the lips of a Bach or a Handel rather than from those of a new counselor whom he hadn't even heard of this time yesterday. I think Robinson's plan is to lead Bach and myself into a discussion of how we resolved our Second-Order problems, this in the belief that the history of *our* resolutions may be of help to *you*.

B. What other great men does Robinson counsel?

Ha. He specializes in musicians; you'll soon learn their names. . . . Speaking of Robinson, I wonder what's keeping him.

Ba. This *is* strange. He told me that he'd meet with us here in the lounge immediately following the concert.

He no sooner speaks these words than our counselor appears in the doorway, pale and breathless, as though he'd been running from a ghost. Bach booms out a question and a comment.

Ba. Where in god's name have *you* been? . . . You're soaking wet!

Ro. (*Instead of answering Bach, Robinson focuses his attention upon me.*) Herr Beethoven, I fear something terrible has happened.

B. What?! (*We all jump to our feet.*)

Ro. I fear there's been a security leak.

B. Oh no!

Ro. It's the first time such a thing has happened in all my years of counseling.

B. What makes you think it has?

Ro. During your performance, I sat at the foot of the stage with my chair facing the audience. This gave me an excellent view of the auditorium, including its three-story stained glass windows. Since we've been having some trouble with our air-conditioning unit, all five of these windows were opened at the top. While you were improvising on Diabelli's theme, the storm outside grew much worse. There were frequent and bright flashes of lightning. Suddenly, in one of these flashes, I thought I detected the outline of a man's face peering into the hall from the top of the farthest window. How could this be? What sort of winged devil (or angel) could stand there peering into a window eight stories above the ground? As the flashes continued, I thought I could see even the outline of a rain hat and a turned-up collar. How could I find out for sure? I decided to try to make our phantom go away. Then at least the absence of his shadow would confirm that he was there in the first place. This is what I did.

During your improvisation, I tiptoed back the right aisle to the quiet pulley that operates the top sash of the fifth window. I closed it and immediately opened it. In fact, I did this twice. Then I returned to my chair and carefully observed the open panes in subsequent flashes of lightning. There was no silhouette in any of them. After the concert and after shaking hands with most of the departing counselors, I went immediately to the stage manager and told him what I had seen. He said that it was quite possible for someone to have peered into the hall through an eighth-story window since an elaborate scaffolding had been erected there to facilitate repairs. I went outside myself and, in all that rain, climbed to the top of the fifth window. Through it, I observed a perfect view of the stage, and I'm sure I could have heard anything going on inside. There's no doubt in my mind, Herr Beethoven, your concert and my speech were both overheard by some mysterious intruder. And I'll be damned if I can figure out his reason for doing so!

B. Well, we won't worry about him for now.

Ro. But I feel terrible about this. After promising you "perfect security conditions"—

B. The fault is mine. Ever since my arrival here, I've had the feeling that someone has been following me. But I said nothing about it to you. If I had, I'm sure you would have taken the necessary additional precautions. I'll not give the bastard another thought until I find out who he is and what he wants. Let's get on with our evening. (*For the first time since we'd met, I observe Bach's face break into a huge smile.*)

Ba. Hal, you should have been here fifteen minutes ago. When Georg and I first introduced ourselves to young Ludwig, he fainted flat on his face!

Ro. Oh no! . . . This makes a perfect zero for my score. (*By now, Robinson has seated himself. He reaches over and puts his palm on my knee.*) Young man, I'm afraid you're going to think that I'm nothing but one big bundle of inadequacies.

B. Not at all! My adverse reactions to your careful plans are certainly no fault of yours.

Ro. How kind! I appreciate your saying this.
B. What remains for this evening?
Ro. Since Bach and Handel have both made adjustments to Second-Order life, which are in many respects identical to those which you must now make, I thought it would be a good idea for the three of you to sit down and talk things over.
B. Fine! Let's begin.
Ro. But not here! Why not over a stein of good beer? The St. Stephen's is only a short distance, and it's as close as Aaron AP comes to an authentic Viennese beer hall.
Ha. (*Handel interjects a question.*) What makes you think we're beer drinkers?
Ro. I know you are, all three of you! And besides, I'm sure that Beethoven will enjoy this as a genuine reminiscence of the old Order.
Ba. (*As we stand up and head for the door, Bach grabs my right arm in his strong fist and halts the entire procession.*) Just one minute! I'm not so sure that I *care* to go drinking with this fellow. He just told me that he thinks Handel is the greatest composer who ever lived.

I had not yet learned to read the sparkle in Bach's eyes, and mistake him for being deadly serious.

B. You must understand, Maestro. I had no idea who you were. A few months before my death, Stumpff made me a gift of the complete edition of Handel's music. The last Earthly pleasure I received from my art was to lie there in bed and completely drown my sorrows in the glorious sounds that flowed from these pages . . . past my deafness . . . into my soul. . . . Considering this divine music, is it any wonder that I champion Handel as the greatest of us all? Had my treasured gift (instead of *his* works) been a complete edition of Bach, I would no doubt be proclaiming *you* as first and foremost! Even so, were it not for your mighty *klavier fugues*, I could never have played my way into the salons of Vienna! The entire success of my Earthly career rests squarely upon the works of your hands. Could I really be less worshipful of *you* than of *Handel*?
Ba. (*By now, Bach's hand has slipped down from its hold upon my right arm.*) Dear brother, you take me too seriously. I was only having some fun with your staunch judgment. The careers of Handel and myself have become so closely entwined that to compliment

one of us is to praise us both! And besides, after the kindness you showed my one surviving daughter, there can be no doubt in my mind as to the genuine respect you have for *me.*

B. You heard about this little deed?

Ba. When a great First-Order musician uses his art to raise money for a poor daughter of Bach, such news soon reaches us here in "heaven." Your kindness brought tears to my eyes, and I vowed that someday, in some way, I would try to pay you back. Let's begin by having a beer together. Come on! It's only ten- thirty, and St. Stephen's is beckoning.

Inside the beer hall, I observe five bigger-than-life colored portraits of five Earthly musicians: Bach, Mozart, Handel, Haydn, and as I live and breathe, BEETHOVEN! How strange it is to behold the body that I *was,* to see it more clearly than I did when it was *mine.* Who *is* this artist who better understands Beethoven than Beethoven? Ah, no wonder! Down in the left-hand corner of each glimmering study is scrawled the painter's name: Rembrandt van Rijn. How I wish Judy were here. Now I see why she worships the man.

Retiring to one of several private rooms in the back, we order strong cheese, bread, ham, and a dozen tall beakers of Pilzner. Over this delicious spread, we discuss two main items. First comes Paul Rezler with his *zero* musical background, a simple case of Beethoven bringing everything to *me.* Next comes a discussion of how Second-Order musicians are organized into professional firms like lawyers and accountants, thereby providing them with a measure of corporate immortality. A typical musical firm is composed of a dozen juniors and seniors, a handful of principals, two or three partners, and a managing partner.

Ha. (*Handel then adds.*) The undergirding personality of a given composer is the integrating device and the lifeblood of the firm itself. The entire success of the operation depends upon bringing this *personality* to life, keeping him alive, and sending him before the public to perform and conduct his own works and the works of others.

B. (*My response is a question.*) Who actually goes onstage?

Ha. Usually the partners, occasionally a principal.

B. But how can different artistic temperaments ever be integrated? How can such a personal thing as the creation of art works be achieved as a collaboration? I can't imagine the day when

Beethoven will sit himself down at the composer's desk and meekly collaborate with *any* musician in *any* way!

Ha. I know. At first I felt this way myself. But it's amazing how one's attitude can change.

B. Why should it? Why do we need corporate composers? What's wrong with an individual artist going directly to his public, just as we did on Earth?

Ha. Nothing's wrong with it. It's just that Aaronian musicians have developed a different way of doing things, a way that works best for our Second-Order culture.

B. You say "best," why is it best?

Ha. As on Earth, we Aaronians love our heroes. But heroes are expensive. Often it takes a lifetime of toil and suffering to bring one into existence. Then along comes "death" and snatches him from us. We attempt to avoid this wasteful situation by creating *corporate* heroes!

B. I still can't believe they exist. Being true to the feelings of Beethoven that are now within me, I can't imagine myself collaborating with other artists, especially at the creative level!

Ha. Someday you will. Wait and see. Think how a musical partnership would have changed your Earthly career! Instead of struggling for twenty years to convince the Viennese that you (and you alone) were the true successor to Mozart, suppose you had spent the time building up a little corporate BEETHOVEN. Instead of beating down every formidable pianist who crossed your path, suppose you had selected two or three promising young men and had carefully trained them in your manner of playing and improvising. Suppose you had taught someone your technique of conducting and had permitted two or three others to learn your composing procedures from raw sketch to finished score. Suppose further that you designed a handsome mask and a convincing hairpiece and that for the next thirty years instead of you alone going before the Viennese, as the "big I," all six or eight of you would have taken turns appearing behind the mask and beneath the hair. Under these conditions, think how different things would have been. When your public career was crushed by deafness, BEETHOVEN would have gone right on performing and conducting. When you grew too ill to compose, BEETHOVEN would have forged ahead with as mighty a hand as ever at the composer's desk. And now that your Earthy self is dead, BEETHOVEN would still be composing, conducting, and playing the piano for your beloved Viennese. And these happy people would not even know you had died, nor that the founding spirit behind their revered musician had passed from them! . . . Even more important, of all the treasures you've left on Earth, none would now give you greater pleasure than this true artistic child, this corporate being, this BEETHOVEN! True, as the decades run their course, he might evolve into something entirely different from what you'd have intended; but isn't this half the fun of parenthood?

B. If I could have done these things on Earth, my name would have been Socrates or Jesus, but not Beethoven. On a crowded little planet where there's such *lust* for fame and power, such *greed* for dollars and ducats, and such petty rivalries and jealousies among men, I doubt if a corporate artist could survive *childbirth*, much less outlive his *parent*!

Ba. I agree with you, Ludwig. This is why we *do* have corporate artists on Aaron, and why we *don't* have them on Earth!

During this long dialogue, Handel and I do the talking while Bach and Robinson do the eating, the drinking, and the listening. I'm especially conscious of how carefully (with "psychological" ears) Robinson listens to each of my questions and answers. He's probably learning more about me *now* than from all his subsequent study of my questionnaire. There's a pause in the serious conversation, while Handel and I put away our share of the bread and goodies. By the time we finish, Bach and Robinson are on their third stein of beer, and have lighted up huge long-stemmed pipes identical to the one given me by Schlesinger.

B. Where on Earth did you get these?

Ro. (*While Bach hands me his lighted pipe, Robinson explains.*) We *didn't* get them on Earth. They are luxury products of the Aaronian culture and have set us *each* back ten dollars!

Sure enough, beautifully carved into the hot bowl are the initials, "JSB." Robinson continues.

Ro. Since the St. Stephen's is our favorite meeting place, we keep them here to enjoy on our visits. Marie knows just when to bring them; we end every snack with a smoke.

Ba. (*As I return Bach's pipe, he makes a kind offer.*) Let me buy you one. It will have your initials on it, and will always be here when you come.

B. I accept, and shall regard this as an absolute achievement. Imagine being in Second-Order life only two days, and *already* Beethoven has received a gift from J. S. Bach!

Soon Handel and I reach the "beer stage," and our conversation returns to my future plans.

B. How many of these corporate monsters *are* there?

Ha. Monsters? . . . You mean musicians! . . . We now have seventy-five, and according to Aaron himself, we should set 205 as our eventual goal—*one* for each Cultural Planet.

B. Seventy-five! I don't think I can name more than two or three.

Ha. Naturally! You've had no interest in music. I suppose YAABDHN is one of the two or three.

B. Yes. I've enjoyed his music since elementary school. It's so much fun to dance to.

Ha. This is the reason for its popularity among young people. Of course, you realize that his music is strictly Eastern, but I'm glad to say that his tremendous flair for textural rhythms has produced many things more important than dance pieces. YAABDHN is among the oldest of our corporate musicians, the *third* to be exact. Though the founding partner died over a thousand years ago, his spiritual descendants are still very much alive in our midst. In fact, their firm is producing the most popular music of our present-day Second-Order culture.

B. Isn't there a BACH, a HANDEL, and I think even a BEETHOVEN?

Ha. Yes. . . . Let me fill you in on the total breakdown. As I said before, there are now seventy-five professional firms, each representing a *separate* cultural planet. Thirty-two of these are characteristically Eastern. I imagine their scales and tone-combinations would sound unbearably Oriental to Beethoven's ears. Western and African styles are represented by the other forty-three firms. These include a dozen whose output is essentially melodic, eleven whose music is textural, eight whose works are predominantly rhythmic, and nine whose changing styles defy categorizing.

B. That makes forty. Who are the *other* three?

Ha. The remaining three are those most recently established, and are Aaron's only corporate musicians to be directly inspired by men of Earth.

B. BACH, HANDEL, AND BEETHOVEN?
Ha. Not quite. . . . There's a BEETHOVEN, A MOZART, AND A BACH-HANDEL!
B. How are these formed in the first place?
Ha. Instead of your musical talent coming to you from Earth, suppose it had originated *entirely* in the Second Order, your heritage as Paul Rezler. You now wish to devote your life to composing. What doors are open to you? Just one. By studying and teaching and accumulating degrees, you must rise to the level of assistant, associate, or full professor in one of our 484 music schools. Only *then* would your compositions be performed by student groups, and heard by other composer-teachers. If the pieces are good enough, they might attract the attention of several colleagues, and thence become the basis for a professorial partnership. There are many of these around. Most music schools support a dozen of them at any given time. Next would come ten, twenty, perhaps thirty years of learning to collaborate with your partners and principals. It's unlikely that the *original* staff would remain the same. *Old* colleagues would leave, *new* forces would join the ranks. . . . At last the big day arrives! You launch your first season's tour of our cultural planets; something which you could *never* have done as an individual composer, conductor, or pianist! A careful record is kept of your firm's activities. After three seasons, a revealing tally is made of its popularity points as measured within the Aaronian system. If the count is sufficiently high, your group would be granted full professional status, would be assigned a home planet, and would become our culture's seventy-sixth corporate musician. If the points are too low (which is usually the case), you and your associates would have to return to an educational planet and be granted another three seasons' tour, only after spending ten more years in profitable work, study, and teaching!
B. But since I *am* Beethoven, surely I don't have to go through all this!
Ha. That's right, you don't. Your situation is almost identical to mine. My best compositions preceded me here through the "total recall" of friends, performers, and singers who died before *I* did.

A few of the pieces became so popular that they were performed throughout our cultural planets by all the corporate musicians in our Western group. The resulting storehouse of untapped popularity points prompted a dozen musicians from EP 11 to put together a HANDEL. After only a two-season tour, it was officially incorporated in 1745 as our seventy-third Professional Musician. When I arrived here in 1759, it was going full blast with six juniors, six seniors, six principals, two partners, and a nice big managing partner's chair sitting there waiting for *me*. But somehow I couldn't claim it. I preferred to work my way up, to earn their respect through Second-Order endeavors, and *not* by exploiting my First-Order reputation.

B. This is *exactly* the way I feel! What did you do?

Ha. Since my Second-Order ambition was to become a carpenter, I had music credit deficiencies to say the least. These were made up during a five-quarter extension of secondary school, and during eight years of study at the University of EP 11.

B. You went there because of HANDEL's founding partners?

Ha. Precisely! What better way to meet them than to attend the school where both were still teaching on a part-time basis?

B. Then what happened?

Ha. In 1768, I was appointed to HANDEL as a junior. Six years later, I was named a principal, and after two years in this capacity, decided to reveal my true identity. This I did in 1776, and was *immediately* promoted to managing partner of the firm.

B. This sounds like a good way for me to deal with BEETHOVEN. . . . Herr Bach, how did you approach *your* corporate self?

Ba. I had no such problem. When I arrived here in 1750, there was a very popular HANDEL composing, conducting, and performing throughout our culture. But there was not the *sign* of a BACH. I therefore decided to *create* one, following the procedures just outlined by Georg. . . . First I had to translate my Second-Order interest in merchandising into a total commitment for music. This I did during two final years of secondary school in which I prepared ten volumes of my best Earthly compositions. With these, because their Baroque sounds were suggestive of the popular HANDEL, I had *no* trouble creating an interest in my project among the professors at the University of EP 5 during my six years of study there. In 1758, I was named an associate professor, and eight of us (at EP 5) spent the next three years organizing a BACH. In 1761 we launched our interplanetary tour; and even before the end of the first year; we knew that BACH had failed. It failed because the public interpreted our music to be but a careful imitation of their beloved HANDEL. What could we do? . . . We decided to return to EP 5 and spend a decade modifying our style to a complete independence from its great contemporary firm. But this was not necessary. A strange and wonderful thing happened!

Late in 1761, the firm of HANDEL began a selfless promotion of our BACH. This was all it took. Within two years, we were popular enough to receive our charter as Aaron's seventy-fourth corporate musician with myself as its managing partner. I felt terribly indebted to the HANDEL firm and went to them often, requesting that BACH be dissolved and absorbed into their organization. They told me that nothing could be done in the matter unless Handel *himself* would approve the merger. For this I waited thirteen years for my personal development. In 1776, when I finally revealed myself as Bach, Handel joyfully accepted my proposal. But *only* on the condition that the new firm be known as BACH-HANDEL, and that *each* of us be named a managing partner. Exactly what happened! In 1777, the old firms were dissolved and BACH-HANDEL became Aaron's seventy-third corporate musician.

B. That leaves MOZART and BEETHOVEN. . . . What *about* MOZART? I'm especially interested in this firm, because I'd like to meet its managing partner. Back in Vienna, he promised me some lessons, you know. Perhaps now I can collect!

Ro. (*This question brings Robinson into the dialogue.*) You might have to wait some time before meeting Mozart. He has yet to identify himself with his firm. In 1785, MOZART became our new seventy-fourth corporation. Six years later, the great Maestro arrived in our midst, but (for personal reasons) has not to this day assumed the responsibilities of his spiritual child.

B. Why not?

Ro. That's hard to say. Someday you'll know. . . . In 1815, a young chap entered MOZART as a junior. Five years later, he was named principal, and in 1823 suddenly revealed himself as Franz Joseph Haydn! Pending the arrival of Mozart himself, the delighted administrators immediately named him "managing partner, pro tem."

B. Haydn! . . . Dear old "Papa"! . . . I can hardly wait to meet *him*, as well. This leaves BEETHOVEN. What can I learn about *my* firm?

Ro. It was founded in 1810 as our most recent corporate musician, the charter being drawn up by a group of professors from the University of EP 20.

B. EP 20? Ye gods! That's where Judy Adams goes to school!

Ro. Ah . . . the girl next door!

B. She's the girl of my dreams. I think I know where *I'll* be going to college!

Ro. I think you'll be going there for more reasons than Judy.

B. Such as?

Ro. Such as two of your great old teachers being on the faculty there.

B. Albrechtsberger?

Ro. He *and* Neefe!

B. My God! Then this *is* the place for me. . . . Are these men on the staff of BEETHOVEN?

Ro. No, neither of them. Though they were both instrumental in getting your firm started there.

B. Who is guiding BEETHOVEN at the present time?

Ro. A strange young chap who appeared at the university in 1822, and after only two years' study was admitted to BEETHOVEN as a junior upon the strongest possible recommendations from both Neefe and Albrechtsberger!

B. Who *is* he?

Ro. No one knows. . . . His outstanding aggressiveness and compulsive devotion to the firm were so unusual that in only three years, just this January, he was named managing partner, pending your arrival. His strong personality is so much like yours that many suspected that he *was* you; that upon being named "manager," he would reveal himself as the true Beethoven. But no, his identity is *still* a complete mystery, and so is the reason for his unheard-of devotion to BEETHOVEN!

B. I bet *I'll* find out who he is!

Ro. Now that we've talked things over, what are your immediate plans?

B. Thanks to you gentlemen (and your provocative beer-drinking), my plans are now definite. I'll be following very much the path of my friend Handel, here. Since I've put down roots at Lakemont, I think I'll stay there and work off my Second-Order musical deficiencies. As soon as I've done this, I'll be off to the University of EP 20 for another round with Albrechtsberger. It'll be fun to see if he's changed at *all*.

This caustic remark (exploding from the Great Mogul within me) brings astonished smiles to the faces of my friends. In spite of their questioning glances, I continue.

B. Upon my old teachers' recommendations, I *know* that I'll be admitted to BEETHOVEN. Once in the firm, I'll rise to partnership in *no* time. Then I'll tell that pro-tem boss who *I* am, and demand that he do the same!

The deep sincerity in Bach's eyes stares into my soul and cuts through my pompous remarks as though they had been made by a little child.

Ba. When you first take up music here (especially at Lakemont and during your early days at the university), I know that things will seem to be going slowly for you. To help you over this period, may I suggest that you use the time to prepare your catalogue of revised First-Order works that you intend to use *here*, and which you will not be ashamed to have forwarded into higher orders of our culture. Even though you don't publically reveal your identity, BEETHOVEN will be most anxious to receive the list and will send only these compositions into the Third Order as representing your Earthly career.

B. How will they be distinguished from what I create during *this* lifetime?

Ba. Your First-Order works should be signed "Beethoven I"; those of *this* order, "Beethoven II." The production of your professional firm will, of course, be identified as "BEETHOVEN."

B. This is a good idea, Herr Bach. I should enjoy reworking the best of my early music. Such a creative task will ease the pain of returning to piano practice, to harmony and counterpoint, and to the endless books of rules.

Having finished our beer and pipes, we all stand up and stretch. Robinson informs us that it's 2:00 AM, and time to adjourn our meeting. As I shake hands with my new friends, each in turn makes a delightful parting comment.

Ro. Well, now that you've met your new counselor, I hope you're not entirely disappointed. I think we'll get along just fine, and I'm very proud to have you on my list. . . . Since it's so late, you might as well leave here from the basement of St. Stephen's—it has an elaborate D-R Chamber all its own, one more reason why we like this place for our meetings.

B. How about my old clothes back in the Registration Building?

Ro. I'll send them to you immediately. And don't forget, you do the same with your formal. Simply drop it in a clothes bag and mark it "Aaron AP, 3115 Registration Building."

Ha. It's been a real pleasure meeting you, Herr Beethoven. I know that our paths will frequently cross, and I look forward to hearing from you, both musically and socially.

Ba. (*Best of all was a parting comment from Bach.*) I'm pleased to have met such a great admirer of Handel. I'll forgive you this, though I'll never forget your kindness to my little girl. If at any time you should need a helping hand (and have no objection to its being a musical hand), you have only to call upon J. S. Bach. I'll drop whatever I'm doing and come to your side! . . . I'm sure my "partner" here will do the same. And you can always reach us through Robinson.

When I finally arrive at Dogwood, it's four o'clock Sunday morning. This time there's no shower. In fact, I can just make it up the stairs, and into bed.

When I awaken Sunday afternoon, there's beautiful little Gina standing at the foot of my bed in a short, tight robe with her dreamy brown eyes, her sweeping locks, her glowing face, her graceful hips, and her creamy round calves *all* combining to make me forget she's my sister.

Rg. Hi there, big Brother! Are you going to sleep all day?

B. Not with a beautiful sister stomping into my room.

Rg. Quick, what happened? Can you tell me who you *are* now?

B. Not yet, Gina, but someday.

Rg. Oh well! Here, I brought you a little breakfast.

As I sit up in bed, she places her thin wooden tray in my lap, and I gently kiss the back of her right hand.

B. Thanks, Sis. This is very sweet of you!

She leaves the room, and I start my leisurely breakfast. Next to the tray is Sunday's paper. Quite casually, I turn to its first page.

POW! What a shock! I'm so startled that I upset most of the breakfast and tumble out of bed. From my mouth pours a cesspool of Earthly profanity. My heart stops beating and starts pounding. What gives? It's that first page of the morning paper, *that's* what gives! The entire page is devoted to a picture and less than a dozen words in headline print! The picture is an enormous blowup of Kloeber's grisly portrait of my Earthly self. And the words above and below the picture:

HAPPY REBIRTHDAY

HERR LUDWIG VAN BEETHOVEN

. . . . . .

<<<IMAGE>>>

. . . . . .

WELCOME TO OUR MAJOR CULTURE

Chapter 35

There is no doubt in my mind that Robinson and his fellow counselors (and of course, Bach and Handel) can be trusted. I'm further convinced that the shadow at the door, the steps in the corridor, and the phantom face, *all* belong to the same man; the very one who is responsible for what I now see in the paper. As my fumbling hands tear open the second page, I expect the *worst.* But I'm pleasantly surprised. The full-page article congratulates Beethoven on his rebirth, welcomes him to the Major Order, then proceeds to detail the history of his Earthly days. It makes no mention of Paul Rezler, Hal Robinson, the concert, my desire to remain anonymous, or any of the other little secrets that could be known by my phantom follower. *Why*? . . .Why does the article oblige me by stopping where it does?

On the next page, another article catches my eye. Its heading: "Open Letter to Beethoven from BEETHOVEN. . . . When news of Beethoven's arrival reached us here, we immediately contacted Richard Grant, twenty-two-year-old musical dynamo who manages the BEETHOVEN firm. He expressed genuine happiness with the glad tidings and gave us an open letter to Herr Beethoven." Then came a picture of Mr. Grant, followed by his letter:

> Congratulations, Herr Beethoven! . . . Welcome to your new life. . . . We at BEETHOVEN have been *living* for this happy

> day! We extend to you our hand of warm fellowship and hope that you'll join us tomorrow, if not sooner. . . . When the great Handel arrived in our midst (before revealing *his* identity), he thought he had to spend seventeen years proving the worth of his Second-Order musicianship. Of course, no such thing was necessary. And it's certainly not needed in *your* case! . . . So please come and provide BEETHOVEN with his true guiding light. . . . The office of the managing partner beckons you. Our entire staff eagerly awaits your arrival. . . . The pay is excellent, but our cooperative spirit is even better!
>
> Sincerely yours, BEETHOVEN

Concluding that my secret is still safe, I feel my blood pressure, heartbeat, pulse, and what-have-you return to normal. Thus relaxed, I spend a leisurely half hour studying the letter and especially the picture of Richard Grant. Who can he *be*—this handsome young musician with the deep-set eyes, the firm chin, the broad shoulders, and the friendly nose? Could *he* be the culprit who's been following me around? Does he (or will he soon) know more about me than his letter would indicate? Puzzled by this turn of events, I spend the rest of the afternoon moping in our living room. My contemplative reverie convinces Dad that I've been drinking . . . and too much at that. All he can get from me is that I plan to return to Lakemont for another quarter or two.

Immediately following dinner, I pack, bid the family good-bye, and leave for school. How anxious I am to see Culbertson again. What surprises I have for *him*.

As usual, down the hall Ray is very busy showering. I take a minute to admire his soap-blinded hulk, then go on about my business. On our way to the bedroom, I break the good news:

B. Guess what, Culby!
RC. What?
B. I've gone and done it!
RC. What?
B. I'm engaged to Judy Adams.
RC. Don't *tell* me!
B. And that's not all!
RC. You didn't get yourself reborn?

B. Yep! . . . Engaged and reborn in one mighty weekend!
RC. I'll be damned! . . . Congratulations, Paul! Come on, tell me everything.

By now we've reached our room. As soon as we're comfortably spread out, I elaborate on the details. How proud I am to discuss the beautiful Judy Adams, who now wears my ring. Then (without divulging my secret), I inform Culbertson of my artistic inheritance, and of the fact that I'll be transferring to our music department for the new quarter.

RC. Music department! . . . You? . . . I can't believe it!
B. What's so terrible about this?
RC. I send you away a perfectly good fellow, a he-man architect, a real guy. And what happens? Two days later, you come back as some stupid Beethoven!

It's a good thing Culby isn't looking at my face when he says this. Its expression would certainly have betrayed my secret. Fortunately, his back is toward me as he reaches across his bed and grabs the morning paper. He throws its first section at my head.

RC. Have you seen *this*?

I stare at Kloeber's portrait and the editorial, pretending to study them for the first time. After a polite silence, my roommate continues.

RC. Imagine absorbing *that* into your spiritual subelectron!
B. I should be this lucky.
RC. Well, you came close, same weekend!

To throw Culby off my trail, I spend thirty minutes weaving a fancy fabrication. By the time I'm finished, he thinks I was a fat Viennese piano teacher named Schuppanzigh, who had a fat little wife and three fat little children. He also hears that on several occasions I had the honor of meeting the great Beethoven. This prevents Ray from suspecting my true identity, but he does associate the weekend of *my* rebirth with that of Beethoven's. And for our remaining days at Lakemont (to my teeth-grating chagrin), he's forever calling me by the resulting nickname: "How's Beethoven this morning? . . . Am I having lunch with Beethoven today? . . . Don't work too hard there,

Beethoven. . . ." And halfway across the filled lunchroom, "Hey, Beethoven, pass me the salt!" Nothing I can do or say will stop the flow of "Beethovens" from Culbertson. I simply grin and bear them, thinking how much fun I'll have on that day when I can at last tell him who I *really* am!

Several times I try to feel out his obvious resentment for musicians and artists:

RC. Oh, I don't know. They just don't seem like real men to me. There's something inherently "sissyish" about them.

B. Like what?

RC. I can't put it into words . . . they're just effeminate, that's all.

B. What's so damn masculine about an athlete? Just because you swim across a pool and run around a track, this doesn't make you any better man than those of us who pound keyboards, play strings, or sing songs! In fact, the physical training of a really good singer is more demanding than anything you've ever known. And just wait, young fellow. Wait for *your* big day. You might inherit something far less male than the demanding career of a good musician!

On Monday, April 2, we register for the new quarter. You should see the look on my Lakemont counselor's face when I tell him that I wish to transfer to music.

LC. Now? . . . At this late date? . . . Only one more quarter and you'd graduate with a top credit in engineering prep.

B. I know. But there's the little matter of my rebirth. It's changed *everything*!

LC. (*The handsome old Negro with thick eyebrows and silver-rimmed spectacles fingers carefully through my secondary-school records.*) Just look at this, Paul. In the music division of the Junior School Aptitude Test, you ranked only 614 out of 630 freshmen, almost the bottom of the lot! And as a freshman here in the senior school, you showed even *less* aptitude for music: 582 out of 585! Since you're one of the best engineering students we have, don't you think you should postpone music until at *least* the Third Order?

B. Under normal conditions I'd agree with you, Mr. Lawson. But rebirth has brought an enormous change in my life. I must now transfer to music; there's no doubt in my mind about this.

LC. Very well, Paul. I realize life happens this way, but it seems like such a waste of well-spent time. First comes another aptitude test, *then* we'll see how we can best change things.

For ten minutes, Mr. Lawson works with his schedules and folders. Then he hands me a little packet of cards.

LC. Here you are, boy. They're all yours. For a senior to make such a complete change, we'll need three days of tests from you. These cards show when and where you're to report. Good luck, Paul! I'll see you back here again on Friday at nine.

When I return to my counselor on April 6, he has Dr. Forbes (principal of the music school) with him. They're both smiling, so things can't be too bad. Lawson is first to speak.

LC. Paul. You know Dr. Forbes here.

I nod that I do, and we shake hands.

LC. The two of us just reviewed your exam papers and were tremendously impressed by the genuine musical talent you've inherited from Earth. We both agree that you should transfer to music, but in order to prepare an adequate course of study, we *must* know your college plans. Which university do you prefer to attend?

B. My definite choice is the University of EP 20.

Fo. (*This brings Forbes into the dialogue.*) EP 20 for *music*? That's more of an *art* school!

B. How about its M93 College?

Fo. You'd *never* get in there.

B. Why not?

Fo. It's become a highly specialized little school whose main purpose is to prepare juniors for entering BEETHOVEN!

B. (*The mention of BEETHOVEN requires another evasive fib from Beethoven.*) I *still* wish to go there and join my fiancée.

Fo. Ah, the ulterior motive! Perhaps we *can* arrange things.

Opening an M93 catalogue, the two wise men put their heads (and scratch pads) together for half an hour. Finally, Mr. Lawson presents their verdict.

LC. Paul, because of M93's stiff requirements and because they admit freshmen only in October, we recommend at *least* six quarters of preparatory studies here at Lakemont. . . . Possibly *ten* quarters.

B. Ridiculous! I can be ready for them by *this* October! Put me down for two quarters.

Fo. (*Surprise, excitement, and even a little anger sound in Forbes's voice.*) Their entrance exams are merciless! In two quarters, we could *never* prepare you for them.

I'm tempted to unleash a fit of Beethovenian wrath, but I remember Bach's words warning me that the prime cost of my secret would be the initial slow pace of things here at school. I further recall his advice as to how I might take up the inevitable slack inherent in the early days of Second-Order music. Think how much "Beethoven I" can be revised during a year and a half at Lakemont!

B. Very well, gentlemen. Put me down for six quarters. I guess I'm too anxious—the old case of wanting to fly before knowing how to walk.

Thus begin my final months of secondary school. In Beethoven's story, they carry us forward from April 9, 1827, to September 26, 1828. Of the various major and minor courses available at M93, I choose two majors and begin preparing myself for them. They are, of course, piano and composition. My preparation for composition is entirely theoretical: harmony and counterpoint reminiscent of Albrechtsberger's discipline. In piano, my chief studies are the Mozart and Beethoven sonatas. Consequently, I begin with the sonatas in making my Second-Order revision of Beethoven's Earthly works. Of the famous "thirty-two," I'm able to salvage only eighteen. These and a revised *Archduke* stand ready for publication as "Beethoven I" by the time graduation day rolls around.

The final days at Lakemont bring with them several other activities besides studying and revising. There are no passionate dates with Judy, just a few letters and phone calls. A big shock occurs on the morning of July 2, 1827—Stephan von Breuning has arrived. Imagine! Stephan, here in the Second Order! He outlived me by only three months. How I'd love to see him! Think what he could tell me about Karl, about Johann, about my funeral.

In September 1827, my entire family moves to CP 55, where Mother and Dad are appointed senior assistants in the architectural firm of Reed, Levin & Kosoff. As soon as they reach principal status, they hope to transfer to CP 25 and move back into Dogwood. No doubt my parents decide upon this firm because it agrees to take on both Gina *and* Freeman as junior assistants. For them, promotion to senior status would, of course, require their completing six to eight years of college work in architectural engineering. But at least this valuable experience should enable them to observe our parents in action and to decide once and for all whether architecture is to be their Second-Order profession.

By far, the greatest surprise is what happens to Ray Culbertson. After all his tirade regarding the femininity of art and artists, wouldn't you know that he'd find his spiritual rebirth to involve the patterns of a dainty, sweet, and talented Parisian ballerina, who had danced over Europe for thirty years! On separate plateaus of her career, she was ballet mistress at three different opera houses. Now suddenly, she and he-man Culby are one! What a strange combination of conflicting patterns they make. As his handsome body dances through our apartment (from tops of chairs, to tops of desks, to the couch and back again, turning somersaults, midair backflips, and swan dives, executing every step known to modern ballet and a few unknown to it), I can't help feel the impact of the determined spirit within it. My dear friend, who only yesterday belittled male artists, and was determined to become a he-man athlete of Olympic standards, is today a he-man artist of equal determination. He amuses me no end as he goes dancing along gracefully, constantly reiterating his enlightened declaration that there's nothing more masculine in all Second-Order life than a good he-man primo *ballerino*!

Chapter 36

On the last two days of September 1828, I report to M93 on EP 20 and sit for my entrance exams. Its campus is small for a college and consists of only three twelve-story stone and marble structures. These are set down on beautifully spacious grounds, sprinkled with poplars, willows, lovers' paths, and fish ponds. One building, the largest, accommodates the entire student body. Another, the smallest, does the same for the faculty. The third is the college building itself, and consists of recitation rooms, lecture halls, soundproof practice cubicles, offices, and an assortment of auditoriums. Though M93 is small, one can't forget that it's part of an enormous institution—the University of EP 20. As such, it is only one of 9,047 campuses and the ninety-third of ninety-five music schools spread out over EP 20.

The examinations are given in the college building, whose corridors and test rooms become jammed with 322 confused and frightened-looking applicants. From this motley group will be selected the 150 members of the new freshman class. It's hard to describe my net response to the situation. As Paul Rezler, I'm scared to death; as Beethoven, I'm perfectly calm.

Monday's tests are general exams in which we are proctored as groups. They have objective and subjective questions, covering everything from music history through harmony and counterpoint to orchestration. On Tuesday, the situation is quite the opposite: individual students examined by individual teachers. Prospective pianists are divided into four groups: pre-BEETHOVEN (major or minor) and non-BEETHOVEN (major or minor). Since I've signed for pre-BEETHOVEN with a major in piano, it's only natural that for my examiner I be saddled with the sternest-looking of the four young professors of piano. He never introduces himself, nor changes the serious expression on his face. His sparse comments are little more than directions for continuing. The deadly gleam in his eye gives me the uncomfortable feeling of having seen it somewhere before. First I'm asked to play scales and arpeggios. Next he turns pages for my interpretation of Mozart's *Fantasia* and *Sonata in C Minor.* Then he proceeds to do the same for my own *Sonata in A* (Opus 101), and doesn't seem at all impressed when I close the score and play it entirely from memory! To test my sight reading, he comes up with some horrible things by Clementi. For score reading, as fate would have it, he chooses my favorite Beethoven symphony and seems, for the first time, observably impressed by my ability to read and interpret *Sinfonia Eroica* at any page where he opens it. My examiner's face assumes its former cast in plenty of time for his final comment: "This will do, Mr. Rezler. You'll hear from us."

Prospective composers are divided into the same four groups. This places me in pre-BEETHOVEN with a major in composition as well. Consequently, in the afternoon session, I'm presided over by the same type of examiner: a handsome nameless brute, but one with even fewer words, sterner face, and more piercing eyes. After a brief examination in harmony, counterpoint, and orchestration, he dismisses me with words identical to those of his morning colleague.

I return to Lakemont and on Friday the third, receive notification from M93. The Rezler in me is afraid to open it, the Beethoven within rips it open. It contains good news indeed: "Your official notification: You are hereby granted full admission to the pre-BEETHOVEN division as a piano and composition major."

What great news! I can hardly wait till bright and early Monday morning!

Chapter 37

Following Monday's registration at M93, Dr. Albrechtsberger addresses those of us admitted to the pre-BEETHOVEN division. His mind is filled with vital statistics, and he seems to take sadistic delight in throwing these at our heads:

Al. Ladies and gentlemen, it is a pleasure to stand here and welcome the cream of our new crop. Out of 150 freshmen, you are the chosen 55 to be enrolled in the highest division of our academic program. However, I should like to make one thing very clear. While junior assistants are appointed to BEETHOVEN solely from *our* graduating class, the appointment of these juniors is by no means the sole purpose of M93. As for BEETHOVEN, it's the old story of many being called and only a few chosen. Among you 55 sitting before me, we have 5 majors in conducting, 16 in composition, 26 in piano, and 8 in piano *and* composition. Based on historical data, I would estimate that when your final exams roll around (eight years from now), about two of you will have survived in conducting, and about a dozen each in piano and composition. I tell you this not to discourage you, but to encourage each one of you to accept the realities of our academic world relevant to your personal career. Failure to remain in pre-BEETHOVEN does *not* mean failure at M93. We have many fine courses leading to excellent professional fields

> having nothing to do with BEETHOVEN. What I'm trying to say is quite simple. Should the time come when you must transfer to another division, please don't feel that we have failed you or that you have failed us. Such transfers are normal, and we expect them. Whether or not they apply specifically to you, we are proud to have you aboard.

Considering the intimacy of M93's tiny campus, you'd think I'd make many new friends during my eight years here. I don't, at least not among the fifty-five students in my division. All these young people are gifted and aggressive, in most cases as gifted and aggressive as *I* am. A good example of this is Victor Dimos, my new composition-major roommate. He works so hard and is so hell-bent on appointment to BEETHOVEN that I can feel my entire First-Order self running from him—running for the same reason that it ran from Neefe's superior ability as an organist. After rooming with Dimos for eight years, I'm no closer to him than I was at the end of our first week together. This certainly tells me something about Beethoven and his social adjustment. As Paul Rezler, I can make friends with almost anyone; as the Great Mogul, I have to be certain that the potential acquaintance is not a musician—at least not a musician whose talent threatens my own!

There are exceptions to this observation. Changing roommates from Culby to Dimos leaves a terrible void in my social life. I attempt to fill this vacuum by cultivating the acquaintance of a young man newly arrived in the Second Order. This young man is Kieth Kracsun, who comes to M93 in 1831. We meet at the Student Union, and I'm immediately attracted by his sensitivity and his genuine modesty. In December of 1832, he invites me to an all-Schubert concert given on CP 74 by MOZART. How I revel in the delightful sounds: *Ballet Music from Rosamunde, Symphony VII in C,* and *Symphony VIII in B minor.*

After the concert, we return to M93 and spend an hour walking its moonlit campus, discussing the evening's music. When Kracsun is absolutely certain of my approval of what we had heard, he admits to being none other than Franz Peter Schubert!

B. You young devil! . . . What are you doing here in pre-BEETHOVEN?
FS. Each of us is a branch of *some* tree, and for me that tree is Beethoven.
B. I can see why you'd come here to school, but why aim for our professional firm?

FS. My ultimate goal is to found a SCHUBERT. This requires my PhD, which I would far rather achieve through three years of BEETHOVEN and one year of graduate study, than through three years of graduate study.

B. Then you intend to use BEETHOVEN as part of your schooling?

FS. Yes! . . . But you *must* keep my secret. If this had been known to the faculty, I would never have gotten my appointment here.

B. Your plans are safe with me. . . . I'm *so* glad you told me who you are. To know a real musician; this means a lot to me during these schooldays. But tell me, Schubert, how can such a born lyricist as yourself now settle down to the harsh dictates and stern pedantries of Dr. Albrechtsberger?

FS. Actually, I find this easy to do. On Earth, I had always felt lacking in contrapuntal discipline. Only two weeks before my death (in an attempt to remedy this), I arranged for theory lessons from Herr Sechter. Now I study with even *greater* teachers. I'm thoroughly enjoying myself!

B. Another thing. *You* lived in Vienna, did you ever meet Herr Beethoven?

FS. I once visited his abode to make him a present of a little Schubert duet. But I didn't have the courage to wait and meet him, or to get his opinion of it.

At the sound of these modest words, I can hardly resist embracing the young man, telling him my Earthly name, and confessing that the guileless warmth of his treasured duet was directly responsible for many of the few really *happy* hours I had shared with my nephew. But rather than betray my own secret, I continue the present conversation:

B. Was this your *only* visit to Beethoven?

FS. No. When I heard of the Master's serious illness, I went to see him at the Schwarspanierhaus. But I was too late. The poor dying man was unable to speak. He didn't even know that I was in the room, that I stood there in silence beside his bed, that my tears came as much from veneration as from pity!

B. Then what happened?

FS. Ten days later, I was one of thirty-eight torchbearers who stood beside his grave.

B. Who were some of the others?

FS. Hummel, Czerny, Linke, Seyfried, Kreutzer, Schuppanzigh . . .

Upon hearing these names, I can feel tears coming into my eyes. Lest they should give me away, I interrupt Schubert's roster with another question:

B. What was the funeral like?
FS. Fitting for a king! All Vienna did him honor. The city's schools were closed. Even the military were called out to check the throng of thousands who jammed in front of the Schwarspanierhaus and then followed in procession to the cemetery at Währing. Why are you so interested in Beethoven's funeral?
B. No particular reason. Since I hope to stay on at BEETHOVEN, I thought perhaps the more I learned about his Earthly days, the better.

During our five years together at M93, Schubert and I are constant companions. Often I'm tempted to reveal my Earthly identity; but for the sake of my *own* adjustment to BEETHOVEN, I never do. Many evenings we spend in a practice room where Schubert sings me his song-cycles, and plays for me his sonatas, impromptus, and Moments Musicals. My undisputed favorite is the *Impromptu in G-flat*; I request it at all our meetings and never tire of its divine message, whose boyish insights reveal about as much of life as *any* of the old-man metaphysics from Beethoven's *C-sharp Minor Quartet*. Bit by bit, Kracsun fills me in on the history of his Earthly days. I marvel at Schubert's youthful will to create. How could he have done so *much* in a mere thirty-one years, in a drab life completely void of musical and monetary recognition?

Another close acquaintance is Marcie Sbalzato, who starts at M93 the same year as *I* do. In the pre-BEETHOVEN division of my class, she is one of only *three* girls, and I can't help noticing her excellent pianistic ability. Realizing that a girl cannot represent BEETHOVEN in public, Marcie does *not* aspire to the career of concert pianist. She wishes to become a *recording* artist for the firm; hence her insatiable appetite for Beethoven sonatas.

One afternoon in the spring of our second year at M93, I'm sitting in a practice room playing my Earthly version of the *Waldstein*. Without letting me hear the door open and close, Marcie tiptoes into the cubicle and, with the impudent grace of Bettina Brantano, plunks herself down on the bench beside me. To say that she's prettier than Judy, or not as pretty, would be like trying to compare two perfect rosebuds on the same bush:

MS. You're Paul Rezler, aren't you?
B. Yes. . . . And you're Marcie?
MS. Marcie Sbalzato. I've long admired your playing, especially when performing the Beethoven sonatas. Will you do me a favor?
B. Anything, Marcie. Just to keep you sitting here this way.
MS. Would you help me with my interpretations of the Beethoven sonatas?
B. I'm sure our teacher could do this for you.
MS. Herr Neefe has mastered the notes and so have I. . . . But *you* have mastered the *spirit* of Beethoven.
B. What a beautiful compliment!
MS. And this is what *I* must do. Will you help me?
B. Be glad to, my dear.

My assistance to Marcie soon exceeds the bounds of piano lessons. Before long, we're holding hands, walking arm-in-arm, following each piano lesson with an hour of genuine lovemaking. By the end of the year, our petting parties are fewer, but frequently become all-night affairs. In a purely physical sense, we are as totally intimate as any young couple can be. The promised joys of Aaronian sex (doubling their Earthly counterparts both as to intensity and duration) are no longer mysteries to either of us. We understand each other perfectly, realizing that our love is strictly animal, but something without which we could not survive the intellectual burden of eight years' intensive musical training. And because of certain Second-Order techniques, unwanted pregnancy is no problem.

By the standards of some Earthly cultures, our *affaire d'amour* would be judged illegal, unlawful, immoral, illicit, sinful. On Aaron, it is none of these. It is a simple act of love, neither good nor bad, but under the circumstances, necessary. I should emphasize that here in the Second Order, sexual drive has twice the potency it has on Earth. It is not a matter to be toyed with by some flabby moral code, a thing to be dusted off and put aside for future use. Sex is part of the eternal here and now. God be praised that it *is*!

Judy Adams and I are to have no further dates until I can reveal the entire story of my past. She prefers our romance to go quietly to sleep rather than be wide awake and frustrated. Thus I'm expelled from her arms for a period of six to twelve years, possibly longer. Along comes Marcie Sbalzato—young, vivacious, and equally vibrant with Second-Order desires. She has definite ideas as to the man of her dreams and openly admits that Paul Rezler is *not* this man. Yet she has no idea if or when she'll find him . . . possibly in six years . . . possibly not at all! Under these conditions, what could be more natural than a physical love between the two of *us*? When I am able to return to my Judy and tell her the story of Beethoven, I'll tell her the *entire* story, including Marcie's chapter. I'm sure she'll understand.

My eight years at M93 are nothing short of a backbreaking grind. How could they be otherwise, with a major in piano *and* composition? Neefe is still the old taskmaster, but not so much so as Albrechtsberger. In piano, my main studies are pianistic material from BACH-HANDEL, Bach I, Bach II, Mozart, and Beethoven. There are frequent concerts involving each student about once a week. In composition, my studies consist of harmony, figured bass, orchestration, score reading, and (especially) counterpoint. There are tons of exercises, but no student compositions until the eighth year.

With clocklike precision, Victor Dimos (my industrious roommate) visits his family on the first weekend of each month. Enjoying his absence to the fullest, I usually invite Culby for an overnight vacation. Ray has followed me here to EP 20, where he majors in dancing and dramatics at D52. Each time he visits, I reaffirm my promise that as soon as I'm named a principal at BEETHOVEN, I'll see to it that we compose him an entire ballet for his own use. This he assures me is all he'll need to become a primo ballerino.

Throughout these eight years, I continue to receive cards from Reunion Control. Each week without fail, there's another invitation from Richard Grant to come to BEETHOVEN and identify myself. There are several cards from Mother, Lichnowsky, and Lobkowitz, but *none* from Grandfather or Breuning. To my astonishment, I receive urgent requests from two faithful old members of Beethoven's "Court:" Zmeskall and Schuppanzigh. I should like to have answered all these, but silence continues to be my sole response.

More are required than the companionship of Franz Schubert, the coquettishness of Marcie Sbalzato, and a few visits from Ray Culbertson if the free and demanding spirit of Beethoven is to submit itself to eight years of college training. There must be some genuine musical projects in operation. There are--two of them. The first is Bach-inspired: the selection, correction, and revision of those Earthly works to be published here (and in subsequent orders) as "Beethoven I." To the sonatas and *Archduke*, I now add seven of the nine symphonies, three out of five piano concertos, the violin concerto, and *Fidelio*. Oddly enough, the most extensive revising occurs in *Symphony 5*: its second movement gets three new variations, and the texture of its finale is much improved. During all this work, I make frequent trips to St. Stephen's in order to enjoy my new pipe and, of course, the musical companionship of Bach and Handel. Without their encouraging comments and advice (and without these two great musicians knowing me as the Beethoven I really am), I could never have survived the galling routine of my daily tasks! Making good his promise, Handel accepts Zmeskall as a private student of cello; Bach does the same for Schuppanzigh on the violin. Indirectly, the students send me their profound thanks, professing that only through Beethoven could Second-Order life have brought them such great teachers. From their masters I receive glowing progress reports and can hardly wait to hear my old friends play again.

The other musical project I like to refer to as my Goethe plan. It develops during these college days out of my sincere conviction that sooner or later, Beethoven *must* revolt against BEETHOVEN. Why not? When I arrived on Earth, I found composers to be nothing but lowly servants of the nobility. As soon as I sprouted my Mogul's wings, I challenged the status quo, moving "above the salt" and proving *one* Beethoven worth *ten* kings! Now I enter another system that grates against my ego. Composers are organized into *corporate beings* who have no direct contact with their public. This seems unnatural to me. When I grow my wings again, perhaps I'll change it all. Why not? What's so sacred about 10,000 years of Second-Order corporate music that it can't be changed by Beethoven? But the accepted practice of 205 cultural planets is quite a Goliath for one little David to bring down. I'll need something in my "sling" besides an Earthly reputation. Hence, the Goethe plan. Our great poet arrives on Aaron in 1832 and sends me not so much as a Type C card from Reunion Control. Oh well, probably an oversight.

Apparently Goethe has no qualms about his Second-Order worth. He immediately joins GOETHE and accepts the position of managing partner. Within two years, a complete and revised version of *Faust* is published by Goethe I. I pounce on it like a hungry wolf, devouring it from cover to cover. There's no doubt in my mind. This is the stone for my sling. As planned on Earth, *Faust* will now become my second opera. I'll start sketching it here at M93 and spend ten years on it if necessary. Later, after I've joined our firm, if things don't go the way I think they should, I'll revolt! I'll go straight to Goethe, tell him who I am and what I've done. I know he'll give our opera his blessings, for who (other than Beethoven) can better prepare a setting of *Faust*? Thus armed, I'll make war on the corporate giants. I'll take careful aim, sending my music straight to the hearts of the Aaronian public. The Goliaths will come tumbling down, and long will live Beethoven II.

About the middle of July 1835, I come to the startling realization that I have less than one year left at M93, less than one year to prepare for final exams, and to qualify for admission to BEETHOVEN as a junior assistant. This sobering observation brings some changes in the daily routine.

For the first time in seven years, my theoretical studies amount to actual composing instead of teacher-directed discussions, class exercises, and homework. Each comp major in the pre-BEETHOVEN division must submit a full-length orchestral piece in the style of second- or third-period Beethoven. Since the work is considered an integral part of our final exam, and since it is no doubt an important criterion for admission to BEETHOVEN, I decide to give the project everything I have. I shall prepare not only a genuine Beethoven symphony, but also a mighty string quartet in the style of the "Galitzins"! This resolution dampens most of my social activities. I hardly know that Schubert and Marcie are alive while Dimos (poor devil) becomes less than a stick of furniture. My Goethe plan is reduced to a few sketches here and there while revision of my Earthly music stops altogether. This latter now presents quite a library: eighteen piano sonatas, the *Archduke*, seven symphonies, four concertos and an opera. In July 17, I pack the entire caboodle in a case and head for my musical advisers at St. Stephen's. Only Bach is present, but his elaborate praise of my revisions (one by one) certainly compensates for his partner's absence. He offers to take them himself to Richard Grant, corroborating their genuineness and their composer's approval for publication as "Beethoven I." This he does, and I forget about the matter until reading a startling announcement on the music page of December sixth's Sunday paper:

BEETHOVEN PRESENTS CHRISTMAS PRESENT

> The firm of BEETHOVEN will present a music festival featuring the entire list of Earthly compositions so far approved for Aaronian publication as "Beethoven I." This event comprises eight concerts from December 26th through January 3rd, excluding December 31st.

Needless to say, Schubert and I plan to attend the festival together. The initial concert is on Saturday evening and begins with a few introductory comments by BEETHOVEN's strong man:

Gr. Ladies and gentlemen, as acting manager of BEETHOVEN, let me welcome you to this series of concerts. Our great Master has been living among us since 1827. During this period of almost nine years, he has edited (and in most cases revised) thirty-one of his Earthly compositions. To date, these alone have been authorized for publication within our Aaronian system and are precisely the works you will hear during our festival. Within a few months, their scores will be available to students, amateurs, and professional musicians through the house of Berghoff & Brunn, publishers for BEETHOVEN. I have no doubt that somewhere in our vast interplanetary TV audience, or perhaps in this very hall, Beethoven himself sits and watches and listens. I would direct a comment specifically to him from all of us associated with his professional firm. It is simply this. During the five months we have studied your revised opuses and prepared for these concerts, each one of us has been greatly impressed by your profound Second-Order musicianship. There is no need for you to further prove your worth to any of us. We long for your inspiring presence and leadership, begging you to join us today rather than tomorrow, tomorrow rather than the day after. Each day you stay away, our firm suffers another twenty-four hours' loss of maximum spiritual and musical growth. You alone, great musician, are the answer to our prayers. And now, the festival! . . . May I present our own corporate BEETHOVEN, who begins tonight's concert by playing his newly revised version of the ever-popular *Sonata quasi una Fantasia in C-sharp Minor*. . . . Herr BEETHOVEN!

The stage is so huge that its gilded front curtain dwarfs a gargantuan concert grand poised in front of it. As Richard Grant exits to the right, BEETHOVEN ENTERS on the left and acknowledges a boom of enthusiastic applause. Though dressed in contemporary formal attire, this physical representation of a corporate being depicts my Earthly self with the same startling penetration that I had observed in the Rembrandt portrait. Obviously the work of a makeup artist, his very physical body has the same distortion as the "Great Mogul's": gorilla shoulders and chest, short thick legs, clumsy walk, proud chin-high stance, and awkward bow. Everything from his collar up is strictly Beethoven: unruly hair, high forehead, massive cheeks and chin, thick jaw, deep-set eyes, threatening stare—the peasant face of a determined man set for battle! He seats himself at the piano and begins the *Moonlight Sonata.* I can tell at once that at least this BEETHOVEN-ite has been studying more than pictures of my Earthly face and body. Everything about his playing is Beethoven: phrasing, accents, rubato, tempo, dynamics, nuance, emotional content. . . . Having a corporation represent me at the keyboard gives me a chance to examine audience response more closely than ever before. Until now, I had never realized the full emotional impact of this opening movement. As I look around, there are many tears (even on Schubert's face), accompanied by not a few "oohs" and "ahhs" and "mmms" whispered beneath the simple melody and harmonies of the *Adagio sostenuto.* As those final chords die away, the entire audience rises in a silent ovation and remains standing until BEETHOVEN begins again with the *adagio*! Following this sonata, the endless span of golden curtain is raised to reveal a 120-piece orchestra, tuned and waiting for its conductor. The piano is pushed to one side, and a podium moved forward. Another BEETHOVEN (I can tell he's a different man.) takes his place and conducts my revised *Symphony 3.* Every trick that I had ever learned about conducting, this man knows and uses to perfection. Once again I'm sitting there in the audience, watching *me* outperform *myself.* Following intermission, the concert concludes with the *G Major Concerto* and *Symphony 5.*

Schubert and I arrive early for Sunday's concert. To kill time, I borrow his opera glasses, prop my elbows on the balcony railing, and carefully study glamorous couples arriving on the first floor. Before long, my pleasant pastime is jolted to an abrupt conclusion. I practically fall off the balcony at the sight of what I see! There, entering the parquet circle on the arm of a gentleman is none other than Judy Adams! During the concert's first half, I hear little of the *Sonata in E* or the *Archduke.* My mind is too filled with Judy to admit the sounds of the music. As I sit there staring at her beautiful shoulders and the golden sunset of her hair, I wonder how far her relationship with this man has gone. Has it paralleled mine with Marcie Sbalzato? Are Judy's Second-Order patience and dedication really as strong as she says? Have I neglected her for too long? I think perhaps I have, especially when I observe her companion helping adjust her stole and then keeping his arm about her shoulders for the remainder of the *Archduke.* The time has come when I must tell Judy everything!

At intermission, I carefully watch as the first floor thins out. Her companion leaves for a smoke; Judy remains in her seat. I know exactly what I'll do. I'll go boldly down the center aisle, pop myself into her friend's chair, and almost before she realizes who I am, give Judy a great big passionate tongue-to-tongue kiss. Then I'll know whether she still loves me!

This is what I do. And her uninhibited response is thoroughly convincing.

JA. Paul! Where did you come from?
B. The balcony.
JA. You're still a nice boy. . . . That's the first decent Christmas present you've given me in seven years! What's my great secretive artist doing at a BEETHOVEN festival?
B. One of my best college chums is a musician; he asked me to come here with him. . . . What's my beautiful artist doing at a BEETHOVEN festival?
JA. I'm here with Dave Donovan, a great admirer of Beethoven.
B. I see! . . . Are you two going steady?
JA. Don't be silly, Boo. You know I'm engaged to you.
B. Looking down from the balcony, I find this difficult to believe.
JA. Paul! . . . You've got to understand my position. When I promise you that I won't fall in love with another man until your hundredth rebirthday or until you break our engagement, I mean just this! Not that I won't look at another man or enjoy the companionship of men.
B. All right, Kitten. If that's all Donovan is to you, we'll forget the matter. But why can't I, your true fiancé, accompany you to these affairs? Wouldn't this be better than some compromising boyfriend?
JA. We've been over this before, Darling; nothing's changed. I'm as much in love with you as ever, but I simply can't stand being in your arms without knowing who you are. Just imagine, you've been going to college for seven years and haven't been able to tell me where or why. Our only correspondence has been through Reunion Control. This isn't natural, Boo. A few secrets have every right to exist between friends, but not between lovers. As soon as you can tell me your full story, from that day on, if you wish, I'll date no one else but you.

B. Then we'd better send Donovan home now because I've made up my mind to tell you everything! I thought perhaps on Thursday we could—

Our dialogue is interrupted by a pat on my shoulder. I look up, and there's Donovan himself!

DD. Say! . . . What are *you* doing sitting in on my date?
B. Just reminding her that she's engaged to me, that's all. There's something important I'd like to talk over with you, Dave. Would you come to the foyer with me for a few minutes?
DD. I guess I can, though I hate to miss what's coming up. The *Pastoral* is my favorite Beethoven symphony. Will you excuse us, Judy?
JA. Yes. But I hope the two of you don't forget that I'm sitting here all alone: poor, defenseless, and frightened.
DD. Don't worry, little girl. . . . *One* of us will see you home!

We climb to the second-floor lobby. As soon as we seat ourselves, Donovan pops a question that makes me gulp and gasp for breath:

DD. Do you think you'll ever write another symphony as great as the *Pastoral*?
B. (*To recover some semblance of balance, I pretend I didn't hear.*) What was that, Dave?
DD. The *Pastoral*. . . . Do you think you'll ever write another symphony as great as this?
B. What are you talking about?
DD. Your music, Herr Beethoven.
B. And what makes you think I'm Beethoven?
DD. When Judy told me of your rebirth and what a great artist you were, I decided to follow you to Aaron AP and find out how great.
B. Then *you're* the bastard who spied on me!
DD. Yes.
B. And who gave you the right to do this?
DD. No one! I did so because of my love for Judy Adams. She told me that on Earth you were an extremely dedicated artist and that you feared that perhaps this dedication might eventually come between the two of you and prevent your marriage. If this happens, then I know she'll marry me.
B. So?

DD. So this is why I followed you and stuck my nose into your affairs, affairs which are mine in so far as they affect Judy's future.

B. Suppose I do master the Beethoven within me and that our marriage does come off?

DD. Then I'll settle for someone else, but still hope to remain good friends of the two of you.

B. Did you give that story to the papers?

DD. Yes. I wanted to put myself in a good bargaining position with you.

B. Bargaining! . . . Don't you mean blackmail?

DD. No! Nothing of the kind. . . . Just a little bargain for the sake of Judy's happiness.

B. What are your terms?

DD. I realize that you wish to remain anonymous. Fine! We'll keep Beethoven's identity a secret, provided that you're fair in your dealings with Judy and me.

B. And what do you mean by fair?

DD. That you don't keep us waiting a hundred years until Beethoven finally decides whether he can share his Second-Order life with a woman!

B. I've just spent seven years adjusting to the difficult requirements of BEETHOVEN for acceptance as a junior.

DD. How far must you rise in BEETHOVEN before revealing your identity?

B. I'd say a principal, certainly not all the way to a partner. When I've been a principal for one year, I'll tell them who I am!

DD. Good! Then this is how long we'll wait. At that time, you must either marry Judy, or break your engagement. Agreed?

B. Agreed! You know, Dave, I never did think my arrangement with Judy was fair. I'm actually glad you know what you know and did what you did. I'm glad for *her* sake. . . . Have you told anyone else?

DD. Just one man, and the secret is safe with him.

B. Who's this?

DD. Before long you'll know who he is and why I told him. But not now. . . . What is it you wish to discuss with me?

B. Oddly enough, it has to do with Judy. I've decided to tell her everything.

DD. Good! She deserves your complete confidence. I guess this means you'll be dating again.

B. Yes it does. And I'd like to begin with the BEETHOVEN festival!

DD. Say no more! We'll trade seats, and that's all there is to that. But remember our bargain—one year as principal, and then you must decide.

B. I'll not forget. And I'm even going to throw in a new Beethoven sonata to seal our agreement.

DD. My own Beethoven sonata—I can't believe it!

B. Neither can I, Dave. . . . I swore that if I ever discovered the identity of my phantom follower, I'd punch him square in the nose. Now that I know who you are, I shake your hand, thank you for what you did, and promise you a sonata!

For the remainder of the festival, I continue to share a room with Schubert while Judy and Dave keep separate quarters at the Aldridge Hotel. Donovan and I trade seats, which naturally results in his becoming a good friend of Kieth Kracsun. What a deceptive little circle we make! Donovan knows that I'm Beethoven; Schubert doesn't. I know that Kracsun is Schubert; Donovan doesn't.

Because of New Year's Eve, there is no concert on Thursday. For this reason, I suggest to Judy that we return to Valhalla where I can tell her my story and we can exchange an Oakmont blizzard for a day of summer sunshine. We arrive on our peak at high noon and plunk ourselves down full length in the warm, tall grass, whose swaying carpet is bordered on three sides by boulders. With hands folded behind our heads, we stare up at the cloudless blue and for long, inspiring minutes listen to the eternal wisdom of the wordless conversation between our mountain and the sky. Our hands touch, we snuggle closer.

B. Just think, Darling. . . . Almost nine years ago, we were lying here together when a leaf from one of those very oaks came tickling down and awakened me to my rebirth.

JA. And now, finally, I'm to hear your story. . . . Tell me, Boo. Who is this staring at me through the grass?

B. First I must confess my sordid involvement in a collegiate love affair.

JA. Another woman? . . . What a bad Boo you are. . . . And all the while I thought you were devoting yourself to art and celibacy.

B. To art and a beautiful pianist.

JA. That's all right, Paul. I don't hold this against you. . . . We've been taught enough about the hygiene of Second-Order males for me to know that I've been neglecting you terribly. But pray tell, have you come to love this girl more than you love me?

B. Never, Kitten! . . . My love for Marcie is a passing glitter, a purely physical delight, but something without which neither of us would be graduating from M93. My love for you is a rhapsody of flesh and spirit, a rich palette waiting for the hand of Rembrandt, the theme of a great symphony, the smiling face of a beautiful child, the clear warm sky of a summer evening looking for its stars. Had it not been for our cruel separation, I would have had no extraneous affairs. Am I forgiven?

JA. How does one forgive the sun for shining, the rain for raining? There's nothing to forgive, Paul. Now tell me who you are.

B. What do you think of the music we've been hearing at our festival?

JA. I think it's great art. . . . The more of it I hear, the better I'm convinced that its composer is a man of Rembrandt's stature. But, Boo, you don't answer my question by—

B. Its composer is a strange little man. He hates people, but loves humanity. He hears the voice of God in nature. He serves his art as La Pucelle serves France. He's a spoiled child in all things but suffering. He fears the loss of his identity, but not death. He lies under trees and stares through their branches. He dabbles in brooks and cries at the song of a bird. He swears at passing sports cars. . . . On top of a warm mountain, he stares through tall grass at the surprised little face of his immortal beloved.

JA. Paul! I can't believe it!

B. It's true!

JA. I think I'm going to cry.

B. Why, Darling? . . . You should be *proud* of me.

JA. I am, but . . .

Judy dissolves into tears. Tears which I wipe away with a passionate sweep of tender kisses. For a long time we lie there, hardly breathing, silent in each other's arms. My own little kitten becomes the first Aaronian girl to be loved by Beethoven and to *know* that she is being loved by Beethoven.

Not until we return to our coupé and are speeding toward the D-R chamber does our conversation resume.

JA. I think what frightens me, Paul, is the vast disparity that now exists between us. . . . Before rebirth, we were just two young lovers dreaming about our future. Now suddenly I'm an *aspiring* artist, you're an *accomplished* artist. And there's a world of difference between these two, a difference which I fear will separate us all the more.

B. Outwardly, I may be an accomplished artist, but within I'm still Paul Rezler, wondering how I shall exist under the demands of a Beethoven. . . . You have no idea of the artistic fervor and discipline he requires of himself. For him, the act of composing is so intense that it becomes a mystical experience.

JA. This is what I mean, Boo. . . . You've already accomplished what I fear to hope for in ten lifetimes—the stature of a Rembrandt! What will this do to our relationship?

B. I don't know, Judy. If old Beethoven has his way, there'll be time in this life only for music. . . . But I'm hoping that Paul Rezler will supply the needed leavening . . . will transform the Great Mogul from a lonely artist into a happy man, a man whose balanced life finds love for music *and* for you!

JA. Suppose Rezler can't do this!

B. Then I'll personally deliver you into the waiting arms of Dave Donovan.

JA. Poor Dave. If he only knew who you were. . . . He worships the music of Beethoven.

B. Dave knows who I am.

JA. He does? . . . Why did you tell him?

B. I didn't. When I went to register on Aaron AP, he followed me there and spied on me like a thief in the night.

JA. You must hate him for this.

B. Actually I don't, Judy. . . . He's kept my secret well, and as I now understand it, his spying was motivated entirely by his love for you.

JA. How do you mean?

B. The keeping of my secret provides him with sufficient leverage to strike a bargain over our mutual amour.

JA. Oh? I like the way you fellows plan my entire future. I think I'll foil the both of you and marry someone else.

B. Really, Judy, we do this only for your happiness.

JA. And what have you decided?

B. Dave will honor our engagement as it now stands, but not for a hundred years! By the time I'm a principal at BEETHOVEN, I should know whether I can survive as a musician within our major culture. If I can, good. We'll be married! If not, then we'll send you off to Donovan . . .

JA. I must say, you two have certainly thought things through! . . . Thanks for letting me in on your plans.

B. We mean only well to you.

JA. I know, Boo. And I really appreciate your concern. . . . I guess we'll just have to wait and see how things work out for Herr Beethoven. In the meantime, are we dating again?

B. I hope so, my dear. . . . But be sure to keep in touch with old Donovan, just in case.

JA. I don't suppose I should tell Mother and Dad who you are?

B. Don't tell anyone, Judy. Not until I reach my goal at BEETHOVEN. After that, I don't care *who* knows.

JA. They'll be so proud of you, I can hardly wait.

B. Someday soon we'll tell them, and I'll come to your farm for that long-overdue celebration.

JA. Yes, Boo. I mean, yes, Herr Beethoven . . .

From January through April, Judy and I have occasional weekend dates. She talks constantly of her musical paintings, but I'm never permitted to see them. . . . Then comes a two-month hiatus in our romance, caused by my final exams at M93.

The first barrage of tests is given during the week of June 13. Only candidates for admission to BEETHOVEN participate. And the frightening thing about it all is that after eight years of intensive study and practice, acceptance or rejection now depends almost entirely upon the results of a single week! None remain of the original five candidates for a conducting position. Of sixteen composers, twenty-six pianists, and eight pianist-composers, there are now only twelve students taking their exams in piano and fourteen in composition. Besides myself, these include Marcie Sbalzato and my bristling old roommate, Victor Dimos. In piano, the tests cover sight reading, transposition, spot accompaniments, improvisation, and the playing from memory of six Bach fugues, three Beethoven sonatas, and (with orchestra) the opening movement of my G Major Concerto. In composition, we're faced with timed writings of all kinds, score reading, and rapid-fire orchestrations. To satisfy the requirement of an original composition in the style of Beethoven, I submit my A-flat Quartet and another of the remaining symphonies. The symphony is performed by our own student orchestra on Thursday afternoon.

The quartet is played by Albrechtsberger and three other professors on Friday morning.

During all these performances and tests, the constant physical presence of Richard Grant weighs down upon us like some mighty god, busily gathering information to pass judgment on our souls. He looks just like his pictures, except that now his chestnut hair is combed forward toward one eye, giving him the appearance of young Adolf Hitler, senza mustache! He has a vigorous, wiry walk, and it's easy to tell when he approaches because he's forever jiggling a handful of change in his right pocket. (I assume this is what he's jiggling.) A mountain of nervous energy, he's like a man constantly running, not so much toward a distant goal, as from something in his past. During the entire week he remains aloof, listening and writing in his notebook, but never speaking to any of the candidates. At last, on Friday afternoon, we're called in one by one for a brief interview.

Grant sits behind Albrechtsberger's huge mahogany desk and puffs on a handsome pipe whose smoke fills the small office with a saccharine (almost sickening) smell. When my turn comes, our eyes meet for a long, long minute before he finally addresses me:

Gr. So you'd like to enter the BEETHOVEN firm?

B. Yes indeed!

Gr. Why?

B. Because of all the corporate musicians in our Major culture, this one appeals most to me.

Gr. Why?

B. Oh . . . something about the personality of Beethoven himself.

Gr. Good! This personality is the very spirit of our firm. It holds us together and gives us a sense of direction. But have you any idea of the heavy demands it places upon each one of us?

B. I suppose it's nothing short of total commitment.

Gr. Correct! . . . And if you were to marry, would your prime allegiance be to your family or to BEETHOVEN?

B. First BEETHOVEN, then my private affairs.

Gr. I notice that you're one of three remaining candidates who has prepared for both piano *and* composition. If you had to choose between these two, which would be your choice?

B. Composition! I could survive without piano playing, but *never* without composing!

Gr. This is all very interesting, Rezler. . . . I hope we'll have some good news for you.

The final exams for graduation from M93 last three days, beginning Friday the twenty-fourth and ending Tuesday the twenty-eighth of June. These seem like child's play. After writing my final counterpoints for Albrechtsberger, I turn them in and we shake hands.

Al. I've enjoyed having you in class, Rezler. At first, I had my doubts as to whether you belonged here in the BEETHOVEN division. But you soon changed my mind on this score. As a teacher of prep BEETHOVEN, I see many good students come and go. Some are accepted by our firm, most are refused. Some capture a portion of the spirit of Beethoven, others are no closer to the man than they were when they came here. In this respect, I consider you an exceptional student. And I don't base my opinion on your symphony. We produce many young graduates who can stomp around in the orchestra like Beethoven. But seldom do we find someone who actually penetrates the spiritual development of our composer. This is what I believe you've done—not in the symphony, but in your magnificent quartet! . . . On the basis of the *A-flat*, I have given Mr. Grant my strongest recommendation that he employ you at BEETHOVEN as a junior composer!

My lips quiver, my eyes well up with tears. . . . If only I could tell him who I really am!

B. Bless you, Dr. Albrechtsberger. . . . Your recommendation is all that I'll need. . . . God bless you!

The next ten days contain two huge installments of good news. The first arrives on the morning of July fourth: the official notice of my commencement. I have satisfied the Master's requirements and am to be graduated from M93 with the highest honors. The second occurs as part of our graduation exercises. One-hundred-thirty-seven Master's Degrees and eighteen Doctor's Degrees are awarded. Then comes a speech by Mr. Grant, a few fatal words which those of us in the BEETHOVEN division have been waiting eight long years to hear:

Gr. Dean Borg, administrators, faculty, parents, and distinguished graduates. . . . This year, the firm of BEETHOVEN is able to absorb five young masters into its ranks as junior assistants. In our piano department, the awards go to Mr. Ches Bergman and Ms. Marcie Sbalzato. Our composing division welcomes the talents of Victor Dimos, Paul Rezler, and Maurice Sopolov. Will these graduates please come forward for their BEETHOVEN certificates and their letters of instruction.

As we cross the platform, shake hands with our new boss, and bow to the loud applause, I can't help thinking of those eighteen of us who received no appointment. How heavy their hearts must be. It makes me wish that BEETHOVEN were ten times as large so that he could absorb our entire graduating division instead of just five seniors!

In recognition of my graduation and appointment to BEETHOVEN, our family decides on the spur of the moment to return to Dogwood and spend the week of July tenth celebrating. This means that on Saturday morning, I'm very busy packing my belongings into D-R transport cases. Since Dimos left with his folks immediately following commencement, I'm all alone in the apartment. At about noon, there's a knock at the door. Answering it, I find Professor Neefe.

N. Good morning! . . . Do you need a little help packing?
B. Professor! . . . It's good of you to come! But I know you're not here to help me pack.
N. That's right. I've come to congratulate you on your appointment and to ask you some questions.
B. Well here, sit down! . . . I'll move these boxes.
N. Tell me, Rezler. Do you know a certain Dave Donovan?
B. Yes. I consider him a good friend.
N. In that case, would you be terribly angry if I told you something he told me about you?
B. Like what?
N. Like your First-Order identity . . . who you really are.
B. God in heaven! . . . Neefe! . . . Dear old Neefe!

I grab his hands, pull him out of his chair, and embrace him in a genuine Beethoven bear hug. My right cheek touches his left, as tears stream down my face. You'd think I were embracing my own father.

B. I can't believe it! . . . Dear Neefe! . . . After eight years, you're my first reunion with an Earthly acquaintance. . . . Go sit down again. I'll bring you something.

I run to my dresser, where a sparkling bottle of Nessmüller smiles at me. Then I snatch two wine glasses from my drinking shelf.

B. This is a little graduation present from Dad, and I can think of no one I'd rather share it with than Bonn's great organist . . . my first real music teacher.

N. How wonderful! I haven't tasted Nessmüller since the Rhine days. I give you the "career of Beethoven." May it be as successful here as on Earth! I'm so proud of you, Ludwig. . . . Just think! My own little assistant becomes one of the two or three greatest musicians on Earth! . . . And then here in the Second Order, he returns to me for more lessons. How proud your family must be! The Breunings, Mozart . . . have you seen none of these?

B. No one. You're the first of the old acquaintances to go drinking with Beethoven here in heaven. I can't wait to see them all, especially my mother! As soon as I'm named principal, I'll reveal my identity to everyone, I'll embrace the lot of them! . . . How long have you known my secret, Neefe?

N. For eight years . . . since you first came here to M93.

B. Why did Donovan tell you?
(Correction made. Please disregard this space.)

N. Both Albrechtsberger and myself had turned you down on the basis of your entrance exams. Donovan appeared this same day and inquired as to whether we had admitted you. Imagine how I felt when he told me the stupid mistake we had made. Our little school is founded for the purpose of promoting the musical spirit of Beethoven. Along comes Beethoven, and we turn him away. Donovan explained to me what you were trying to do and the reason for your secrecy. He insisted that I tell no one else of your Earthly identity. I went to Albrechtsberger and convinced him there was an error in my records, that in Paul Rezler I was losing the best pianist of the new crop. He looked over your exam papers again and declared that he could never admit you to pre-BEETHOVEN in composition. I begged him to do so on the grounds that if you were that poor a composer, you would soon be transferring to piano and as such would become my sole responsibility. Reluctantly he agreed, and this is how you were admitted to M93.

B. Have you told anyone my secret?

N. Not a soul. All that you've done here, you've done on the strength of your ability. Your talent (not a First-Order reputation) has won for you a highest honors diploma and an appointment to BEETHOVEN!

B. God bless you, Neefe! If you had betrayed my secret, all would have been lost. I have you to thank for the success of eight years' work!

N. You have Donovan to thank.

B. Donovan as well. Let me refill your glass. . . . I give you Dave Donovan. May he live a long and happy life! . . .

Chapter 38

On July 3, 1835, Judy Adams completes her eight years' work at A707 of the University of EP 20. She earns a master's degree in fine arts with a teaching certificate and finds her college days both happy and productive because they are spent among students and a faculty who best understand the life, spirit, and works of Rembrandt van Rijn. In fact, during each summer of this period, the great painter continues to offer his six-week master class for graduate students at A707. Also, starting in 1833 and recurring in alternate summers, he teaches a six-week class there for amateurs.

Although Judy's love and respect for Rembrandt are as great as those of any student at her school, she considers herself unworthy of his professional firm and never applies for membership in the pre-REMBRANDT division. Following graduation, she takes a full year's vacation to do nothing but paint. This she does in a tiny cabin studio high in the Schlessbern mountains near the charming Swiss-like mountain town of Bernette, a noted artists' colony on VP 17. Judy's return to A707 is scheduled for October 3, 1836, the very day when my junior duties at BEETHOVEN are to begin. Since I'm free for the first time this summer, I decide to join her at the colony. This will give me an opportunity to make up for the long years of our separation . . . and also the chance to do some serious composing.

I arrive at Bernette on July eighteenth at noon. Judy meets me for lunch in the dining room of the Stolevsky Hotel. After our meal, we climb to the modest cabin that she has registered for my summer's use. I find it unpretentious to say the least: a sleep room, a work room, and a tiny bath. But it has the distinction of being one of only three cabins in the entire group that boasts a piano and easel beneath its skylight. For this I'm indeed grateful.

For eleven weeks, our hardworking routine is unchanging, but the two of us enjoy every minute of it! Each morning at sunrise, we meet for breakfast at the social center. Then, sunny or cloudy, into the open fields we go our separate ways: Judy to paint and I to compose. After dinner, we go for an arm-in-arm sunset walk and traditionally end up at my cabin for a few hours of improvising, dreaming, stargazing, and very polite lovemaking. Occasionally, Judy will spend an entire night at my cabin or I at hers. Although under these circumstances we share the same double bed, as unEarth-like as it may sound, we do *not* cohabit! Conditions that encouraged Marcie and me to do so are not now present. And free love is by no means the guiding light of Second-Order life.

It never ceases to amaze me, the total lack of change that death and rebirth have wrought in my creative habits! I still carry sketchbooks in my left coat pocket and stubby pencils in the right. In this final year when I set my sights on a new Beethoven symphony and quartet, all the old Viennese work habits return and force me out into the woods to do my sketching. No wonder I enjoy my summer with Judy at Bernette. It's like reliving all the fresh green inspiration of Mödling and Heiligenstadt rolled into one.

On Friday morning, September 30, Judy and I meet to discuss our summer's wares. Hers include two magnificent paintings of the Mozart and Beethoven of Earth. For long minutes (and without comment) I carefully examine each picture. y devastating scrutiny finally exceeds the bounds of Judy's patience. When she can no longer stand my silent glancing back and forth between the two, she interrupts.

JA. Come on, Boo! Say something! . . . I realize that silence is golden, but I can't stand not knowing what you think. After all, it isn't every day that my works are appraised by Beethoven himself!

B. All right, Judy, I'll say something. And I hope it doesn't make a conceited kitten out of you. Based upon a lifetime of dedication to art, it's my sincere conviction that the quality of your painting is indistinguishable from that of your Master. And I don't mean this at the mere imitative level. . . . Anyone who worships

Rembrandt as you do and applies himself as you've done should eventually achieve the balance, the light, and the rippling strokes that are characteristic of the Master's present style. But you've gone beyond this, Judy. You've acquired the technique and the creative spirit of the man! I see this especially in your Mozart and in your Beethoven. Have you shown these to Rembrandt?

JA. Heavens no! . . . Nothing I've done is yet worthy of his time. Do you really like the musicians' portraits?

B. Very much!

JA. Good! . . . I've had them framed in the hopes that you'll accept them as a gift.

B. I certainly will. We'll keep these in our family for at least a hundred years, then bequeath them to our own children. It should be fun to compare them to what you're doing in *1936*.

JA. Suppose you fill me in on what you and Faust have been doing this summer.

B. Goethe's revision of his play has resulted in a close-knit drama of four acts. These are so masterfully woven together and so perfectly suited to the stage that I've decided to avoid even the slightest tampering with their underlying structure.

For nearly two hours, I play, sing, and discuss the themes of Act 1. Then I improvise upon them for another hour. Judy's reactions are entirely favorable. She makes no attempt to conceal the genuine warmth of her emotional responses and frequently interrupts my music with her applause. This means as much to me (I'm sure) as my optimistic judgment of the paintings had meant to her. At the conclusion of my improvisation, Judy throws herself in my lap, and we engage in a long and passionate embrace—an embrace inspired not so much by our pending farewell as by the sudden realization that each of us has discovered in the other a mature and dedicated artist!

The time has arrived for another surprise. At her request, I play each movement of the *Moonlight Sonata*. As I do so, she unveils the corresponding canvas and directs me to "read it" from left to right. I had expected glimmering pastoral scenes. No matter what the particular landscapes might be, I had resolved to reconcile them with the scenes I had had in mind when composing the sonata, and to tell my young "Rembrandt" that her paintings had caught precisely the spirit of the music. Imagine my shock and disappointment when they turn out to be utter abstractions—geometric patterns and formless blobs of color that could possibly delineate the rasping sounds and meaningless ramblings of contemporary Aaronian music, but certainly not the restrained emotions of the *Moonlight Sonata*. At the end of our duet for piano and paintbrush, I try to force a kind and sympathetic expression on my face. This doesn't fool Judy for a minute; she has learned to read my eyes.

JA. That's all right, Boo. . . . At first sight, I don't expect you to understand what I'm trying to do.
B. I was looking for a picture . . . something definite.
JA. It is a picture . . . a picture of music. . . . And music is *not* definite.
B. But when I play my sonata, it says something to *me*.
JA. And it says something to *me*, something entirely different. . . . If you performed it for an audience of five hundred, it would say five hundred different things at the same time. Such is the real power of great music. And if a painting is to portray this power, it too must be thoroughly abstract.
B. Then you're not just dabbling in modern art for the sake of dabbling.
JA. Modern, ancient, classical, contemporary—these words have little relevance for me. I paint the way I must in order to say what I have to say! Normally I would evolve from the technique of Rembrandt . . . but when it comes to the portraiture of music, here I feel the need for *total* abstraction.
B. But what relates *your* abstractions to *mine*?
JA. Many things: color, form, motion, rhythm, sequential patterns, background contrasts, to name a few. I don't expect you to notice all these relationships at first, but I do hope you'll feel that at least a parallel exists between the tone colors of each movement and the color toning of its related canvas. Play them again, Paul. But this time, try to think and hear in terms of color.

I do as Judy requests and, strange as it may seem, actually begin to feel that a slight aesthetic relationship *does* exist between her canvases and the movements of my sonata! Our heated discussions resume, only to be interrupted by the stroke of four o'clock. It's time to say good-bye again, but not another indefinite good-bye. As Judy begins her first year of graduate studies and I begin my first year at BEETHOVEN, the two of us can at least look forward to the joy and inspiration of regular weekend dates.

BEETHOVEN was chartered in 1810 and was named the official corporate composer of CP 75. Naturally he chose downtown Altburg for the location of his principal studio, where he moved into the thirty-second floor of the May Building. This placed him at the very center of the musical capital of his assigned cultural planet. Within walking distance of these headquarters are no fewer than six symphony halls and four opera houses, not to mention a hundred smaller stages suitable for chamber music and for solo performances. Altburg contains CP 75's chief recording enterprise and its main studios for broadcasting musical events throughout the planet. It is also the home of half a dozen music publishers, from which BEETHOVEN selects the largest to represent his firm. This is the house of Berghoff and Brunn, the only one of the group that has interplanetary facilities. It is hoped that this organization will be named exclusive publishers for Beethoven I and Beethoven II as well. Directly opposite the May Building is the huge DeWitt apartment complex in which BEETHOVEN reserves a sufficient number of single, double, and family-size units to accommodate those of his staff who prefer living in town.

Upon arriving in Altburg, the first thing I do is call Ray Culbertson to see if there's any chance of his coming there to share an apartment with me. I learn that he has completed his undergraduate studies at D52, but unfortunately has been apprenticed to the Headmire Ballet Company on CP 21 for his three years of in-service training. Because of extensive road engagements, it is not possible for him to transfer to one of the Altburg theaters. We wish each other good luck, and I reiterate my promise concerning his BEETHOVEN ballet. To me, this is a great disappointment, for I would have really enjoyed the cheering companionship of my old Lakemont friend. But rather than risk another three years with a musical roommate like Victor Dimos, I sign for a private apartment in the DeWitt complex.

At eight thirty on the morning of October third, I pay my first official visit to BEETHOVEN. Upon leaving the elevator, I find myself in a rather long, narrow hall whose bare walls, low ceiling, and thick carpeting are all pale green. At the end of the corridor is a double door made of thick transparent glass. The right-hand pane contains the single word BEETHOVEN, embossed in black and gold. Above the entrance is a huge gilded reproduction of the life mask of my Earthly self. As I enter the reception room, I'm not a bit surprised to find Dimos already sitting there. He jumps up, shakes my hand, and introduces me to Ms. Mary Banks, the firm's beautiful young receptionist. Within a few minutes, we are joined by our other composer, Maurice Sopolov, and by our two new pianists: Marcie Sbalzato and Ches Bergman. Ms. Banks rings for the boss:

MB. Mr. Grant, everyone's here.
Gr. I'll be right out, Mary.

Enter Richard Grant, looking all the more like young Adolf Hitler, and still jangling coins in his right trouser pocket.

Gr. Welcome to BEETHOVEN, class of '36. Come on, I'll show you around.

The five of us are given a complete tour of BEETHOVEN's facilities in the May Building. These occupy the entire thirty-second floor and include two large staff rooms for junior and senior assistants, two smaller staff rooms for executive meetings, fifteen soundproofed practice studios, twice this number of soundproofed composing rooms, a musical library, a general library, a recording studio, a secretarial or business office, and finally, mahogany row: three dozen private offices for principals and for future partners.

We are introduced to all the staff, which at this time includes two junior conductors, a senior conductor, a principal conductor, five junior pianists (besides Marcie and Ches), four senior pianists, five principal pianists, a pianist partner (Artur Lesch, one of the three founding partners of the firm), fourteen junior composers (besides Dimos, Sopolov, and myself), ten senior composers, twelve principal composers, and three composing partners (Walter Abel and Jon Floyd, the other two founders of BEETHOVEN), and of course, Richard Grant, who serves as managing partner until that day I choose to reveal my true musical identity. In addition to the professional staff, our firm employs a business manager (Roy Kreps), two secretaries, and a secretary-receptionist (Mary Banks).

After these introductions, our grand tour ends at a gray metallic door that proudly displays the words:

HERR LUDWIG VAN BEETHOVEN, MANAGING PARTNER

Behind this door comes the biggest surprise of all, the throne room of BEETHOVEN, the ultimate spot of the thirty-second floor, furnished, ready and waiting for the reborn being of my Earthly soul. With chin-dropping amazement, I discover it to be neither an executive office nor a studio nor a practice room, but an exact reproduction of my dear old workroom in the Schwarspanierhaus! Gone are the dirt, the disorder, the squalor, the vermin, and the unmistakable sickroom smells of stagnant urine and enema-induced excrement. But everything else is here, just as it was on Earth: double-sashed casements (actually requiring a considerable modification of two of the May Building's windows), dainty white curtains waiting to be blown and torn by the wind, a pair of mahogany bookcases containing all the old favorites from Plutarch's Lives to beginning arithmetic, a bust of Brutus, a writing desk complete with bells and quills, an inkstand, a candle snuffer, a comfortable lounging couch (in place of the old straw bed), a five years' supply of sketch books, a box of carpenter's pencils, and (most temptingly) the "twenty-fifth century" version of a concert grand by Broadwood. Though fully aware of the presence of Mr. Grant, my four classmates, and of my compulsion to remain anonymous, I boldly seat myself at the Broadwood and (with the authoritative air of a nondeaf Beethoven) pound out the scherzo from my *Hammerklavier*. By the time I'm finished, the room is filled with staff members. Subsequent to their loud applause, Richard Grant is first to speak.

Gr. Congratulations, Rezler! . . . You play with genuine gusto . . . fire in the Beethoven tradition. I thought we signed you on as a composer/pianist.

B. You did!

Gr. Maybe we were wrong. . . . What do you say we transfer you entirely to our *concert* division?

B. Forgive me. I was carried away. When I saw the instrument you've provided for Beethoven himself, something came over me. . . . I just *had* to try it!

Gr. The pleasure was ours. Would that you *were* Beethoven. . . . Think how happy this would make the lot of us! Our little staff would become like a mighty army of ten thousand men. No victory would pass beyond our reach. There's nothing we couldn't do. If only he'd come in as you've just done . . . come in, sit down, and go to work.

B. Someday, I'm sure he will. How did you get to be managing partner pro tem?

Gr. Based on the technology I was able to stuff into my weary brain during three years at M93, our partners were not interested in hiring me. But when I told them the secret of my Earthly name and why I wanted to be here, they signed me on at once and, in little more than two years, promoted me to managing partner pro tem! They alone know my First-Order identity, and it shall remain a secret until the day Beethoven arrives in our midst. . . . So my contribution to the firm is more a thing of spirit than of music, a spirit which according to our partners is greatly needed during these lean years of watching and waiting. Since becoming a partner, my chief purpose has been to make our organization absolutely irresistible to Beethoven! Obviously I've failed. . . . He's been living on Aaron since 1827, and we have yet to hear the pounding of his fist upon our door. But at least I've tried. To the best of my knowledge, I've made things as tempting as possible. This is why our chief executive office is not an office at all, but a quaint old room from the Schwarspanierhaus. This is why our firm, unlike many of its contemporaries, has the luxury of a summer's quarters, which I'm now taking you to see. . . . We maintain this music camp not for the sake of our present staff. I don't suppose there's a single one of us who couldn't well do without it. But when Beethoven shows up, how different the story will be. Remember . . . he'll no longer be deaf. But he'll bring all of his composing habits with him. When he composes, he sketches; and when he sketches, he walks; and when he walks, he walks out-of-doors! Can you imagine the effect of his violent walking, stopping, and arm swinging here in downtown Altburg? . . . I'm sure he wouldn't worry about the questioning stares of strangers, but how could he manage with a pair of ears that would now admit all the hubbub of busy city streets? . . . No. . . . He wouldn't stay *here*. . . . He'd take his little sketchbook and go walking until he found some rocks and trees and quiet countryside where his outer ear would be obliged to admit only the sounds of nature and blend them with the glorious tones of new compositions singing in his soul!

B. I totally agree with your reasoning.

Gr. When our dear Beethoven settles down to compose, he'll lose no time heading for the country. Just as soon as he does, most of our staff will want to follow him. This is the reason for our elaborate facilities at Oakmont 12. To a casual passerby, they'd look like just another productive dairy farm, but wait till you see what we have here. The main farmhouse has sleeping and dining accommodations for thirty-five. Another building houses practice rooms, composing rooms, a small auditorium with recording equipment, a library, and a staffroom. There are twenty-five one-room work cottages widely scattered over two square miles of green rolling pasture. A delightful mountain stream cuts a sparkling diagonal across the land and at one end is dammed into a tiny mirror lake. But best of all, emanating from the farm are a dozen different mountain trails cutting through countryside, which is as much like the environs of Mödling and Heiligenstadt as any which can be found here on CP 75. This is why I recommended a farm near Oakmont 12 for our summer retreat, not because the town is at all like Vienna or Mödling or Heiligenstadt, but because its surrounding terrain provides us with a typical Beethoven stomping ground. Oakmont is very pleased to have us here. They've given us practically unlimited use of their main concert hall, the Evansville Center for the Performing Arts. Last fall, when planning our weeklong BEETHOVEN festival, we were not able to obtain a full week's booking at any of the Altburg theaters. But here at Oakmont, no trouble at all. . . . Well, now it's our turn at the D-R chamber. I've dialed 2341, and this will take us directly to the basement of our farmhouse. Naturally, our private chamber there is nothing as elaborate as this. In fact, its magnetic field is so limited that it has the capacity to translate only between Oakmont 12 and the May Building. . . . All right, Ms. Sbalzato. Ladies first! . . . We'll meet you there in ten-second intervals.

Our summer retreat turns out to be even more wonderful than Grant's elaborate description of it. We have a delicious lunch at the farmhouse dining room and then spend most of the afternoon exploring the many pastoral delights of an early autumn countryside.

At their staff meeting one week later, my colleagues vote to accept Judy's painting as the official portrait of the First-Order identity of their chief executive. They prefer her Beethoven to all the others excepting Rembrandt's original, which apparently is to remain at St. Stephen's. Her Mozart graces my wall at DeWitt's, where its life-bright countenance serves as a constant remembrance of the great Earthly musician I once knew and of the beautiful gifted artist who painted it!

In spite of the Great Mogul patterns that I forged on Earth, I find my three years as a BEETHOVEN junior composer not only bearable but actually enjoyable. For the first time in my Second-Order experience, I am now a salaried employee. Think of what this means. . . . Here in the Second Order, each major culture functions within a perfectly balanced economic system. For all the necessities of life (goods and services), supply is keyed precisely to demand. Each person is accorded free of charge the material necessities for an unbelievably high standard of living. At present, it takes 101 supply planets going full blast to provide material goods required by the six hundred planets of our life system. But all material needs of every Aaronian are satisfied by a rich assortment of quality products and professional services. Food, clothing, shelter, transportation, education, entertainment—for everyone, the requirements of a happy material life are in abundant supply and are freely available. Such ideal conditions can and will happen in any human culture where growth of population is kept in balance with the capacity of that culture to produce the necessary goods and services.

Question: With all this profound abundance of cost-free goods and services, who needs a salary? Answer: We *all* do! To add the sparkle of individuality to our material lives, we have had to utilize some sort of monetary basis. Contrary to popular belief, there *is* a need for money here in heaven. Since 1803, the dollar has been our unit of exchange; and at the present time, it is used throughout Aaron's Second-Order culture.

This raises another question: since we've planted the root of all evil here in our midst, doesn't this imply that we Aaronians must thereby suffer from the same combination of greed, lust, imbalance, and warfare that plagues the men of Earth? Fortunately, the answer is *no.* We've learned to use money in a more intelligent way than it is used by Earthlings. It is our servant, and not our master. We've arranged an equitable system of pay scales so that no person need choose a particular job simply because it pays more than another. Our medical men are doctors because they love healing, not a set of economic advantages they would hope to gain over men in other professions. Our business executives become presidents of companies because they have a flair for assuming managerial responsibilities, not because they aspire to become millionaires.

Here in the mainstream of our Major culture, there are no monetary advantages between one profession and another. Doctors, lawyers, ministers, teachers, musicians, tradesmen, farmers, executives—we *all* function within the bounds of a common five-part salary scale. The five plateaus are called by different names in different professions, but regardless of what they're called, they have fixed terms of service and offer uniform salaries. The first two terms are of three years each and constitute an apprentice-type internship. Pay is fixed at three hundred dollars and six hundred dollars per month, respectively. Today (1950), the amounts are the same as they were back in 1836. At BEETHOVEN, these plateaus are, of course, our junior and senior assistantships. In each profession, there comes next a six-year transitional term, paying nine hundred dollars per month. At the end of this period, an individual either reaches or does *not* reach full professional status. This is why I feel rather secure following my appointment to BEETHOVEN. I'm practically guaranteed a tenure of twelve years with the firm. The crucial moment will arrive when I complete my six years as a principal. On the strength of Beethoven's musical abilities, will they or will they *not* promote me to the partnership status of our fourth plateau? Until I know the answer to this question, I'm determined to keep the secret of my identity. Should they refuse to name me as a partner, then at least I'll have the satisfaction of informing them precisely whom they have spat from their organization!

Although Richard Grant holds the title of managing partner at BEETHOVEN, his position is strictly pro tem and carries with it the standard fourth-plateau salary of twelve hundred dollars per month. Should I decide to claim my throne, I would immediately replace Grant as the firm's chief executive. Only my title of managing partner would be the real thing and would earn me a top salary of fifteen hundred dollars per month! Thus, you see from junior to chief partner, there is a monthly pay differential of only twelve hundred dollars. After a dozen years of successful employment, every Aaronian settles down at the twelve-hundred-dollar mark with only a three hundred dollars' difference between *his* pay and that of his boss.

My first three years at BEETHOVEN are happy ones because of the paydays they contain. They are happy for other reasons as well. The staff with whom I work are sympathetic, understanding, and helpful. Though our senior and principal composers are exceptionally talented, *all* of them seem to remember their recent experiences as juniors. Promotions haven't gone to their heads; when working with us beginners, they are neither snobbish nor condescending. My initial assignments at BEETHOVEN are, of course, horribly routine: analyses and syntheses of works by various individual and corporate composers, the solution of minor problems in contrapuntal fluidity, countless bits of orchestration, textural expansions, and the supervision of Subsidiary rehearsals. I could never have stood the monotonous grind had it not been for the companion suffering of my fellow juniors and for the excellent private progress I was now making at the creative level with my secretive endeavors in Act 2 of *Faust.* And most important during these years are the wonderful weekend dates with Judy. Without her constant and reassuring love, I'm sure old Beethoven would have broken through at the seams and ruined everything!

For the summer of 1837, my three weeks' vacation runs from the first to the twenty-third of July. Judy's six weeks with Rembrandt extend from June twelfth to July twenty-first. Aside from weekends, this prohibits an extended vacation at Bernette like the one we had enjoyed the preceding summer. I spend my three weeks at A707 where I'm able to see Judy a few minutes here and there when she's not "turning cartwheels" for the great Rembrandt. Her intense reaction to the Master is nothing short of phenomenal, like a beautiful seedling set out for the first time in the reviving sun and showers of spring.

On Earth, as a young man anticipating the challenge of a musical career, this is probably how I would have responded to six weeks' pupilage under Bach or Handel or Mozart. How differently things might have turned out had Mozart been able to make good his promise of lessons! Under the guiding light of such a divine creator, I would have received an inspirational and spiritual revelation not unlike that which presently descends upon Judy. What strange mystery now keeps our beloved Mozart from us? He lives in our midst, the greatest singer of us all, and yet he is silent! . . . Why? . . . Will we *never* meet again? . . . If we do, I have no doubt that his beautiful soul will inspire me as much *here* as it did on Earth.

I return to Altburg on Sunday the twenty-third and, on Monday after work, receive an excited phone call from Judy.

JA. Boo! It's happened!
B. What?
JA. I'm too excited to tell you!
B. Then hang up and call back in an hour!
JA. You're mean!
B. All right, Judy. . . . Take a deep breath. Hold it for ten minutes. Then tell me what's happened.
JA. Rembrandt! . . . He's invited me back for next summer!
B. *Next* summer? . . . I thought he didn't have another amateur class until '39.
JA. He doesn't! I'm invited to join his *master* class, some thirty-five graduate students.

B. This doesn't surprise me one bit! I told you that you're no amateur. When will it be held?

JA. Roughly the same six weeks as this year's amateur class—June eleventh through July twentieth.

B. Good! I'll try to get my vacation in August next time. Then we can enjoy three solid weeks together at Bernette.

For the summer of 1838, my vacation materializes exactly as planned. I arrive at Bernette's Gerber Inn on August fourth and spend a lonely weekend awaiting Judy's arrival there in time for Sunday's supper. Although I don't expect her until 6:00 PM, I enter the little white-curtained dining room at four thirty and select a cozy table for two. There I sit for an hour, smoking my pipe and sipping a bottle of cool white wine.

By five thirty, the room is filled with happy people and smiling faces. The "smilingest," roundest, reddest face of all belongs to an old Santa Claus of a man with bushy eyebrows, twinkling eyes, cherry nose, long white hair, snowy mustache, portentous belly, and thick legs. All that's missing is the beard. He pounds his huge fist on the bar and accordingly is handed a flagon of rum. He leans over and speaks a few words to the innkeeper, who responds by sending him in my direction. As he approaches, there's something about the nobility of his countenance that causes me to rise to my feet:

Rb. Young man, may I have a few words with you?

B. Please do. I'm just sitting here waiting for my fiancée.

Rb. Don't worry. I'll leave before Judy arrives.

B. You know Judy?

Rb. Yes. . . . Very well.

B. You must be her . . . don't tell me you're—

Rb. Rembrandt! I answer to the name of Rembrandt. And I'm here to tell you some wonderful things about your Judy.

B. Well, come . . . sit down!

Rb. Go ahead. Say it! You were going to tell me to take the weight off my feet.

B. Not at all! I was going to tell you that Judy worships the ground on which you stand!

As we seat ourselves, Rembrandt fixes the mighty beam of his eyes upon mine, and for the duration of our talk, never once removes his stare. Its penetrative power reminds me of the Earthly Goethe.

Rb. I've had many students here (and even a few on Earth) who sing praises to my art. But Judy is not just another drooling child. Let me tell you, Rezler, she's an artist! And that's the greatest compliment I can pay anyone.

B. I thought you might react this way. Two summers ago, she showed me a series of her paintings. I was amazed at how much they glimmered with the same spirit as yours.

Rb. You mean those landscapes and portraits?

B. Yes. Twenty of them.

Rb. These are not the basis of my judgment. I find them nothing but the careful strokes of an admirer, another little Rembrandt. Most of my students can do this.

B. What *is* the basis of your opinion?

Rb. Three paintings—a certain piano sonata by Beethoven.

B. You mean those blobs and scratches?

Rb. Far from blobs and scratches. They're the founding of a brand new school of art.

B. What's so new about abstract paintings? We've had them here on Aaron for ten thousand years.

Rb. I'm not praising abstract art for the sake of abstract art. Heaven forbid! . . . Every hundred years or so, our corporate artists swing through another cycle: classical, romantic, semiabstract, hopelessly abstract, nonsensically abstract, hypocritically abstract. . . . Then (praise God) they return to the classical for a clean bill of health. During my entire Second-Order career, I've planted my feet firmly among the semiabstractionists, and here I shall remain. Though most of the younger generation swishes by on both sides, I'll not budge an inch. And my unwillingness to change is not due to stubbornness. . . . To me, the semiabstract is all that's worth putting on canvas. Our pure classicists and romanticists are fighting a losing battle against colored photography. And our total abstractionists are a bunch of lazy fools, too weak to learn the craft of their art.

B. This makes Judy's sonata the work of a lazy fool.

Rb. Not at all! She has blazed a new trail, broken away from the beaten path of meaningless cyclical change.

B. How? Her musical paintings look no better than the work of any other abstractionist.

Rb. At first sight, I feared so myself. But then I studied them more carefully. I looked and I listened. The paintings gave color to the music, the music gave form to the paintings. Each complemented the other. I'm convinced that this young lady has founded a new branch of art.

B. But there are many musical paintings, no doubt a few done to this very composition.

Rb. Any that I've seen have been filled with romantic distortions: sunsets, angels, clouds, mystical surfs, ethereal gardens—weak-kneed attempts to paint a specific program on music that often claims as its sole virtue the *lack* of a specific program!

B. And in Judy's case?

Rb. Judy knows better. She recognizes great music for what it really is—a personal invitation for a soul-rewarding journey into the land of pure abstraction. And to paint such scenes (also to avoid the pitfall of programing), she fills her canvases with the balanced beauty of geometric patterns and careful abstractions.

B. But you don't *approve* of abstract painting.

Rb. Not for its *own* sake. But thanks to Judy's contribution (the wedding of music and art), abstract painting now has a reason for being, a soul, a set of legitimate structural bounds within which to practice its unlimited freedom. Because of her gift to us all, I'm now prepared to offer your fiancee a principalship at our firm.

B. A principal? . . . At REMBRANDT?

Rb. Yes. A principal in charge of musical paintings, the first pure abstractions ever to come from our studio.

B. Does Judy know this?

Rb. Not yet. I think *you* should be the one to tell her.

B. She'll faint at the news!

Rb. All the more reason—better in your arms than in mine. She tells me you'll be spending three weeks here together. Suppose you talk the matter over, and let me know her decision before the end of August. I realize she's in the midst of a doctoral program, but perhaps a place at REMBRANDT will mean more to her than two more years at A707.

B. I'm *sure* it will! And I thank you, Herr Rembrandt. I thank you for making me the bearer of such good news.

Rb. She's dedicated and entirely too modest. It'll take some real talking to convince her, but I think you're the man for the job.

B. I'll do my best.

Rb. I'd better leave now, Rezler. . . . Judy's due in ten minutes, and she mustn't see me here. I want my invitation to come from *your* lips, and to be a complete surprise.

We stand and shake hands, Rembrandt still gazing into my eyes. His stare becomes even more penetrating.

Rb. You know, young man. There's something strange about you.
B. What's that, Sir?
Rb. Judy tells me you were born on Earth a hundred years after my death there. Today is the first we've met on Aaron, and yet I have the unmistakable feeling that I've done your portrait. How can this be?
B. You mistake me for someone else.
Rb. Then I must be aging more rapidly than I realize. When I paint a man's portrait, I study his eyes; when I study his eyes, they reveal his soul; when I view a man's soul, I rarely forget what I see. . . . Your eyes seem to reveal a spirit that I've studied carefully and respected greatly. . . . Yet you tell me I've never done your portrait. Oh well . . . poor old Rembrandt! . . . Take good care of that little girl. She's a real artist and deserves all the encouragement you can give her. Good-bye, Rezler.

Our Santa Claus man with the deep eyes and huge spirit returns his flagon to the bar and leaves the café with surprising speed. As I sit there sipping wine and waiting for Judy, a feeling of guilt brings warm tears to my eyes. I had deceived a great artist. My quest for "secrecy at any price" had led me to deceive Judy's idol. How wretched of me! From sketches and portraits of my Earthly self, Rembrandt had painted the Beethoven that hangs on the wall at St. Stephen's and which gives me prideful pleasure each time I see it there. While working on this picture, he had penetrated the Earthly spirit of Beethoven. And now behind the eyes of Paul Rezler (as Judy has done), he perceives the presence of this very spirit! And I (because of my eternal secret) am obliged to deny the accuracy of his perception. Oh God, I hope how soon I can go to him with the truth—go to him, shake his hand, pat his back, commend him on those years that have only sharpened his artistic awareness, and tell him that it *was* Beethoven he had painted and that this is the spirit he now reads in the eyes of Rezler!

For three wonderful weeks, Judy and I are together at Bernette. We occupy the same two cabins we had enjoyed in the summer of '36. She works diligently on a set of musical paintings for the revised *Waldstein Sonata* while I completely lose myself in further sketches for Act 2 of *Faust*. We spend many an evening hour discussing

Rembrandt's offer. At first, Judy won't believe my story, but ultimately she accepts unconditionally. She abandons her doctoral program and joins the staff of her beloved teacher on October 1, 1838. As a full-fledged principal, her salary exceeds mine by six hundred dollars a month! She knows this bothers the Beethoven in me and therefore gloats over it to no end. I name Judy the official "musical painter" of all the revised opuses of Beethoven I, and this set of pieces becomes the initial project of the "musical painting department" at REMBRANDT. There are to be one, two, or three abstractions for each separate movement. For *Fidelio* (and eventually for *Faust*), she plans several hundred large canvases in the glowing semiabstract style of her teacher. From now on, the high point of most of our weekend dates is a visit to Judy's official studio at Bernette, where I play the "accompaniment" for her latest paintings in process.

On October 7, 1839, our entire class of '36 is promoted to the rank of senior assistant; there are neither transfers nor dropouts. Marcie Sbalzato continues to make great progress both as pianist and as lover—her advancement as official recording artist being directly proportional to the growth of her amorous control over Richard Grant. Poor Grant! Marcie practically charms the pants off him, and there's nothing he can do about it.

Our new crop of juniors includes none other than Franz Schubert! Although I'm the only staff member who knows who this Kieth Kracsun really *is* and that he plans to stay with us only three years, his secrets are safe with me. It's a pleasure to know that at least one other BEETHOVEN-ite is concealing a notable First-Order identity behind a mask of Second-Order flesh. Signing for a larger apartment at DeWitt's, I persuade young Schubert to come and be my roommate. We get along famously. His constant boyish pranks are reminiscent of dear old Culby's, yet (hard to believe) he balances these off with a set of rigorous work habits more stringent than even those of Victor Dimos! Never have I seen anyone more totally committed to the act of composition. At school, Kracsun once told me that as Franz Schubert, he would often sleep with his glasses on, this as an inducement to go straight to his writing table in the morning without any loss of composing time. I laughed uproariously and commended him for his cute little exaggeration and fib. Now that I see firsthand how young Schubert really does work, I'm convinced that his glasses-to-bed story is neither a fib nor an exaggeration.

My three years as a senior assistant are happy ones. I genuinely enjoy my close association with Schubert. My weekends with Judy are a constant inspiration. Her folks are still notably enjoying their nonprofessional assignment down on the farm, still waiting to give me my welcoming party as a full Second-Order being. The Rezlers are as immersed as ever in their professional careers of architectural engineering. Freeman and Gina complete their undergraduate studies at the University of EP 7 and, in the spring of 1838, return to Reed, Levin & Kosoff as senior assistants. In the fall of '39, the entire family is transferred to a branch office of their firm on CP 25. This enables them once again to take up permanent residence at our beloved Dogwood, where occasionally I now find time for one of those happy old weekends at home. Though the family is at last resigned to my being a musician, and though they know of my appointment to BEETHOVEN, I'm quite certain that none of them suspect who I really am.

During these years (through Population Control), I receive my weekly card from Richard Grant, inviting Beethoven to come join the firm. There are several cards from my old pupil and patron, Archduke Rudolph. There are a few from Mother, especially at Christmas and Easter and on my birthday. The big surprise comes when I suddenly receive a card from that other "mother" of mine—dear, sweet Madame von Breuning. Equally surprising is a series of cards from my friend and admiring pupil, Ferdinand Ries. Just think—while young Ries is now in our midst, the old father still keeps his "watch on the Rhine."

My work as a senior composer is enjoyable, if not creative. I get along well with our new crop of juniors while at the same time, our "bossmen" principals treat us with encouraging respect. I begin to feel that "professional growth of staff" is more than just a high-sounding phrase. Perhaps there *can* be a spiritual communion among artists, perhaps it *is* possible to avoid the paralysis of creative isolation, perhaps the advantages of constructive criticism *can* be brought to play on a composition before it has reached its final state of affairs, perhaps the" Great Mogul" *can* be subdued in the name of communal creation. . . . During these months, my optimism concerning BEETHOVEN reaches its peak. I marvel at the uniform quality of our output: twelve symphonies, twelve sonatas, eight concertos, and six quartets—*all* as good "third-period" Beethoven as I myself could write. We have truly penetrated the spirit of my Earthly endeavors!

When the romantic tinglings of Schumann, Chopin, and Liszt come trickling in from Aaron AP, our staff is naturally interested in the new sounds. Many would have BEETHOVEN speed off in their direction, but Grant wisely opposes this decision. He advises us to maintain the status quo until Beethoven himself arrives to pass judgment on the newly emerging romantic movement. To keep our ship on even keel (its rudder firm), he proposes another block of six symphonies. And away we sail!

I still find time for some work on Act 2 of *Faust.* And with the revision of twelve Earthly quartets, I finally complete my restatement of Beethoven I. These pieces are sent to Judy for painting and to Grant for playing and publishing. They inspire another complete performance of my First-Order music, this time a ten-day festival held at Oakmont in the Spring of 1842. At these concerts, twenty-seven of REMBRANDT's paintings are flashed on a huge screen during performances of their related sonatas. There is no longer any doubt in my mind concerning the magnitude of Judy's original contribution.

At the end of the three-year period, Kieth Kracsun resigns as I knew he would. He returns to M93 to complete his year's requirement for the PhD. From there, he plans to enter the University of EP 50 and start work on a SCHUBERT of his own. We shake hands, and I wish him well. But not even *now* do I reveal the identity of his admiring old roommate!

On October 3, 1842, I am promoted to the full status of principal composer. During this six-year term, I'm to discover that all is *not* sunshine and sweetness at BEETHOVEN. There are to be storm clouds on the horizon of my Second-Order life. The wall of my disillusionment is to crumble and fall. But at least there's one good thing accruing from my principalship. My salary is at last on a par with Judy's. This should put an end to her cute little nose-in-the-air boasting—always bragging about how good painters are worth more than good composers!

Chapter 39

There are advantages concerning my principalship besides salary. The day-to-day assignments are far less routine; in many respects, they are actually creative and bring with them interesting responsibilities. As a principal, I find genuine pleasure in working with our junior and senior composers. I enjoy watching their progress. And the Great Mogul within me reacts favorably to the wide-eyed respect these younger musicians obviously direct toward their superiors. The greatest advantage of all is the comforting realization that I have begun the final phase of my secret- keeping. At the conclusion of these six years, I shall at *last* receive BEETHOVEN's rating for which I have worked so hard and waited so long. Our firm has the policy of promoting no one from principal to partner until Beethoven himself is on hand to approve such appointments. This means that until I declare my true identity, *no* one will be kept on our staff beyond his initial twelve years of service. Each principal is sent on his way with the blessings of BEETHOVEN and with the firm's professional rating of one to five points. One point means that the candidate's services have been unsatisfactory; two points, that his work has been satisfactory but that he's not recommended for partnership status; three points, a borderline case, the firm is neither for nor against his promotion, it's up to Beethoven; four points, a strong recommendation for partnership, subject to Beethoven's approval; five points, a partnership rating, with or without the sanctions of

Beethoven. Thus, a five or four-point rating becomes the main objective of my Second-Order life. Until I receive it, my conscience will not permit me to take a stand among Aaronians as Ludwig van Beethoven.

At the conclusion of my first year's principalship (almost to the hour), Dave Donovan shows up as I knew he would. In anticipation of his visit, I had completed my first piano sonata as Beethoven II, a typical third-period work, which is now known as the *Donovan Sonata.* I take him to dinner, then the two of us climb to BEETHOVEN's empty quarters in the May Building. There we enter a practice room where I perform Dave's sonata and offer him one or two autograph copies of the score. He expresses genuine delight with the dedication and (rather wisely, I think) likens it to a cross between my Earthly opuses 101 and 109. He plays some Chopin and Schumann, telling me that this is his favorite piano music next to third-period Beethoven. Then he tries a few pages of the *Donovan Sonata,* and his eyes register such sparkling approval that I conclude this to be the best possible time to take up our serious business.

B. I suppose you've come to discuss our mutual plans for my fiancée.

DD. Yes, Paul. I've come to remind you of your promise. You agreed that after one full year as a BEETHOVEN principal, you would either marry Judy or break off your engagement. Which is it to be?

B. At the time we reached our agreement, Dave, I had no idea of the five-point evaluative system employed by our firm. I must remain anonymous until the end of my principalship, when I will hear their unbiased judgment of me as Paul Rezler, not as Beethoven.

DD. And how long will this take?

B. Five more years.

DD. That's all right, Paul. Your secret is safe with me. I'll not tell a soul, provided you keep *your* promise.

B. And what does this mean?

DD. It means that you must then either marry Judy or break your engagement with her and permit one who truly loves her to take your place in her heart.

B. Actually, Dave, I can't do *either* of these things. I'm too busy with my music to marry Judy, and I'm too much in love with her to break our engagement!

DD. Then I'll not keep *my* part of the bargain. By this time tomorrow, all Aaron will know the true identity of Paul Rezler, principal at BEETHOVEN!

B. You wouldn't do this, Dave.

DD. I would indeed! You're not being fair to Judy or to me.

B. Do me one favor.

DD. What's that?

B. Let Judy decide. I'm sure she understands what I'm up against here at the firm. If she thinks I'm being unfair to her or to you, then we'll consider our engagement broken, and the two of you are free to marry.

DD. This sounds reasonable.

B. But remember . . . if under the circumstances she thinks I am being fair, then I ask you to wait another five years. By then I'll surely know which path my life is to take.

DD. I'll have a talk with her, Paul. We'll see what she says.

B. Thank you, Dave. . . . Here, don't forget your sonata.

Two days later, I receive a note from Judy.

October 3, 1843

Dear Paul,

This evening I had dinner with Dave Donovan. He told me of your conversation . . . especially the part where you mentioned being too busy to marry, and yet too much in love with me to break our engagement. He considered this a gross violation of our agreement and wanted to know if I concurred. . . . I told Dave that at present I'm so busy with my responsibilities at REMBRANDT, that I wouldn't have time to marry *anyone*. . . . I begged him to keep your secret another five years, and to give me a like period of time for the continuation of my work. (I have a feeling they'll be naming me a partner before long!) . . . Dave agreed to wait and also to keep your secret. This seemed unselfishly kind of him, and accordingly (during the years of waiting) I promised to date him on alternate weekends, leaving the others for you. . . . He was pleased, and we parted friends. . . . I hope you understand, dear Boo. . . . I cherish

my weekends with you, and yet I must be fair to Dave. . . . This seems a small price to pay for his keeping our secret.
Until next weekend.

Your loving Kitten,
Judy

The advantages of being a principal are far outweighed by an accumulation of disadvantages, reaching such heights that I wonder if their crushing weight will not drive me from our firm before my five remaining years are up. Now that my hardworking Franz Schubert is gone and I'm once again alone at DeWitt's, I find the hours that I spend there both dreary and uninspired. Though I try to pretend that I'm grateful to Donovan for his compromising agreement, I can feel the Beethoven within me developing a genuine hatred for him. Why should I have to share my love for Judy with *any* man? In October 1844, my little Rembrandt is named a full partner at her firm. While I'm sincerely happy for Judy's good fortune, the ease of her promotion and her indisputable Second-Order recognition as an artist can't help but raise within me a feeling of deep and gnawing inferiority. Four years to wait and I *still* have no guarantee of an acceptable point rating. Without such, I shall fly from BEETHOVEN, having no intention of climbing upon the back of my Earthly reputation in order to claim the managing partnership of a professional firm.

Of my incessant secrecy, I grow more tired by the day. Will I *never* be able to throw off this yoke and fly to the arms of my Earthly loved ones? There are still cards from Mother and Ferdinand Ries—even a few from Ries's father, from Cherubini, and from dear sweet Eleanore von Breuning (to think that in three short years, their daughter will join her mother here, leaving poor old Wegeler to walk the face of Earth alone). For the first time, I receive a card from the great Goethe. What does he want with me?

Not the least cause of my growing frustration is the decision of our firm to write a *Faust* of its own! I have some serious talks on the matter with Richard Grant, suggesting that perhaps we should await the arrival of Beethoven before starting something as big and important as an opera. But nothing can sway his decision, and I'm placed in the embarrassing position of being in direct competition with my own firm! Our staff continues to pour out excellent third-period Beethoven—as good as any I have ever written. To make matters worse, their *Faust* booms toward completion with a speed and quality that frightens me. As fate would have it, there I am, spending daylight hours on BEETHOVEN's *Faust,* and then weary evenings on a secretive *Faust* of my own. With the completed revision of Beethoven I, I thought my progress on Beethoven II's opera would be nothing short of phenomenal. Far from it. I'm so thoroughly bogged down in the operatic chores of each day that I have little or no creative energy left for more composing after hours.

Besides the burden of a double-barreled *Faust,* there descends upon my shoulders the worrisome matter of corporate rating sheets. For the first time (as a principal), I'm now concerned with the number of quality points and popularity points earned by our firm during each quarterly period. When composing on Earth, my sole responsibility was to myself. If a composition pleased me, this was all that was necessary—I knew that someday it would please others. Not so with the corporate composer here on Aaron. Instead of art for art's sake, we have art for the pleasure and enrichment of the public. If an artist corporation is to survive within *our* culture, it must exceed the minimal standards of quality and popularity that are set, measured, controlled, and from time to time, revised by the Administrative Department of Fine Arts on Aaron AP.

To get BEETHOVEN born in the first place, professors Lesch, Abel, and Floyd had to earn in excess of three hundred quality points and a hundred popularity points during six successive quarters. At M93, they were able to do this for three full years and thence were granted a charter on September 12, 1810. Ever since this date, they've been living from one quarter to the next, and their lord and master has been the almighty AP rating sheet! Quality points are awarded by a fine arts committee that bases its judgment primarily upon the supervisory activities of attending concerts, listening to recordings and studying the latest musical scores. After three years of operation (in order to retain its charter), a corporate musician must not fall below a five hundred minimum for any continuous period exceeding eighteen months. Since 1812, the quality of BEETHOVEN's output has consistently exceeded eight hundred points! Popularity is measured by a computer center at the Department of Fine Arts. It keeps a careful sales record of sheet music, scores, concert tickets, and recordings credited to each corporate musician. It also runs popularity polls based on a firm's TV appearances and on attendance at whatever charity concerts the corporation might give. Most artistic entities are required to maintain a popularity rating of between three hundred and five hundred points. BEETHOVEN's vital statistic hovers impressively at the seven hundred mark!

There is little to worry about until one day (six weeks following my promotion to principal), Fine Arts blatantly tells us that we're not doing our share in the popularity department. They accuse us of relying too heavily upon the spirit, works, and reputation of the Earthly Beethoven. He is the one who earns our points for us, and not we ourselves! Accordingly (to our dumbstricken amazement), we are informed that commencing in 1850, a new minimum rating of nine hundred popularity points will be imposed upon our firm. Nine hundred points! As of 1845, the highest quarterly we've ever received is a mere 760. What are we to do? I have no doubt that this is why Richard Grant launches us in the direction of a monumental *Faust*. But will one great opera be enough to do the trick? I'm not so sure. Along with twenty other principals, I'm forced to do my daily work beneath the shrouded specter threat of insufficient points and corporate dissolution. Is it any wonder that I'm frustrated? On Earth I toiled for the sole pleasure of the divine Muse. Now I must work with one eye on the score and the other on our quarterly rating sheet. . . . God in heaven!

At a gala party on April 10, 1847, our entire staff celebrates the formal engagement of Marcie Sbalzato and Richard Grant. Six months later, the two of them are married, and their honeymoon is a record for brevity—five days at VP 200, and they're back again on the job. I'm truly happy for Marcie—our managing partner is just the kind of man she was looking for. But in a way, I'm jealous of her. Each time she wriggles through our staff room, the voice of Beethoven's envy can almost be heard through my hypocritical smile: "Aha! There goes little Marcie Grant . . . a partner-to-be if I ever saw one!"

Like all periods of suffering, BEETHOVEN's six-year principalship finally grinds to an end. It does so on the morning of my evaluation day, October 4, 1848. I'm too excited for breakfast. Instead, I stand at my apartment window for at least an hour, studying the rain-filled fog as it repeatedly wraps and unwraps the top floors of the May Building in a mysterious gray. Time and again I glance down at the wet streets below. Reflecting puddles on the asphalt stare back at me like huge expressionless eyes, telling me nothing. But one thing is certain. The days of my masquerade are over! At last BEETHOVEN must judge Beethoven. If my rating is favorable, the Great Mogul will immediately claim his throne; if not, then he'll snort and stomp from their presence—never again to return. Whatever the outcome, I'll have no further use for my smiling, congenial, friendly, warmhearted, patient, forgiving Paul Rezler veneer. From this day on, I shall face boldly the remainder of my Second-Order life, regardless of what it may bring. This I'll do with the strong hand, the steady eye, and the indefatigable will of Ludwig van Beethoven. In place of breakfast, I pour an overgenerous glass of Seideler and toast the Mozart on my wall. My waiting and hiding are over. I feel ten times taller than Rezler. The burning spirit of the Rhine courses through my veins; the proud confidence of Grandfather shines from my eyes. I'm now so much again the little giant from Bonn that in letting myself out of the apartment, I knock over two chairs and a lamp!

At 9:00 AM, our little "class of '36" (still intact) assembles in the principals' staff room. The five of us sit there like innocent lambs before the mighty slaughter of BEETHOVEN's judgment. One by one, a smiling Mary Banks summons each of us to Grant's office, where we're to be apprised of the firm's final evaluation of our twelve years' service. The entire class is to be dismissed this day—those with a rating of three to five points with the possibility of being recalled when Beethoven appears; those below three points, without this possibility. If I'm given a four or a five, it's my plan to hire the lot of us; if not, then I don't care who goes where or why! Marcie is first to be called and, as the rest of us predicted, receives a glowing five points from her little husband. Bergman, Dimos, and Sopolov are then summoned in turn, each receiving a four. At last comes our new "managing partner." I used to grow uncontrollably angry when Archduke Rudolph kept me waiting longer than ten minutes for a lesson. Imagine now the boiling Beethoven within me after twelve years of waiting! I can hear my own breathing as I enter Grant's office. Will they give me a five, or only a four?

Gr. Ah, Rezler! . . . Come in! . . . The last, if not the best.
B. Oh?
Gr. Sit down. Paul, I'll have you know that we partners spent more time mulling over *your* records than those of the other four put together.
B. How come?
Gr. We find your collaborative musicianship very difficult to appraise.
B. Why?
Gr. Because it's combined with such a strong self-will.
B. And what's so bad about self-will?

Gr. Nothing . . . from the standpoint of an individual composer. But as a *corporate* artist, BEETHOVEN's chief concern is how well the members of his staff work together. And a strong self-will is the greatest single detriment to effective collaboration.

B. For twelve years I've worked with underlings and overlings alike! . . . What are you talking about?

Gr. For six years perhaps . . . but not for twelve.

B. I still don't know what you mean.

Gr. Ever since you assumed your principalship, our records show that it's been largely a matter of others collaborating with *you.* To keep peace on our staff, most of us have had to bow their knees to you!

B. All that I've done has been for the good of our firm. When it comes to third-period Beethoven, my musical judgment is sure, definite, correct, and final!

Gr. We know this is how you feel. It frightens us, and is the basis for our negative judgment.

B. Well, I'm sorry I frighten you, Grant, but let me tell you one thing. A handful of strong-willed, self-esteemed, frightening musicians is worth more to BEETHOVEN than a whole staff of weak-kneed, polite little people!

Gr. This is not for *you* to judge.

B. What are you trying to tell me?

Gr. Your dedication is unquestionable. Your musicianship is satisfactory, but we cannot recommend you to BEETHOVEN.

B. This sounds like two points to me.

Gr. That's what it is. For the sake of our staff and BEETHOVEN's future, the best we can give you is a rating of two.

B. God in heaven, Grant! In the name of all that we're trying to do here, I *beg* you to reconsider this stupid judgment.

Gr. We've carefully evaluated your growth and capabilities for six months. . . . There's nothing to reconsider.

B. Then it's final?

Gr. Yes . . . but don't go away like some angry bear. There are a hundred-one challenging careers you can build upon the twelve years you've spent here.

B. Don't worry about me finding a challenging career. I might just kick the hell out of you and your polite little BEETHOVEN.

Gr. Go to it, Rezler! Constructive competition is something we all welcome. But I don't think your particular artistic temperament can adjust to *any* firm.

B. Who needs a *firm*? If you've worked for one, you've worked for them all. I'm finished with the lot of them!

Gr. Good! Now you're on the right track. . . . As an individual artist, you won't be able to compete with BEETHOVEN, but you'll be much happier.

B. Come into Beethoven's room for a minute. . . . I have a surprise for you.

The two of us enter my "old quarters at the Schwarspanierhaus," where I go immediately to Judy's picture of me and take it from the wall. As I place it (face up) on Beethoven's writing desk and comfortably seat myself in his chair, a pained expression flashes from Grant's eyes. It seems to say, "Surely you're not going to take our picture with you!" He slaps his hand on my shoulder and is first to speak.

Gr. I say, Rezler . . . I wish you'd use some other chair. We're saving this one for Beethoven!

B. Then you'd better enjoy these sixty seconds. It's probably the only time you'll ever see Beethoven sitting here!

Gr. (*Grant gulps enormously and turns white. His grip on my shoulder tightens.*) Are you trying to tell me—

I interrupt his question by taking up a pen and scribbling in Beethoven's own handwriting across the one light patch in the background of Judy's canvas:

Man, help thyself!

Ludwig van Beethoven
October 4, 1848

Still hovering over my shoulder, Grant reads and worships each word that I write. I can almost hear the beating of his heart as my pen scratches the date.

Gr. *Well, in God's name, old Beethoven! . . . Let me be the first to shake your hand!*

B. (*I return Judy's picture to the wall and walk toward the door where we do shake hands.*) What a pity, Grant. This could have been a greeting . . . the beginning of a new experience for *all* of us! But your stupid judgment has turned it into a farewell.

Gr. Quite right . . . a farewell to Rezler, and a hearty welcome to Beethoven!

B. But this can't be! When you sent Rezler away, you sent Beethoven with him.

Gr. You're wrong! . . . The young man we discharged with a rating of two was a strong-willed chap whose staunch musicianship would neither bend nor sway to the suggestions of our staff. He was unable to freely collaborate, to subordinate himself, to give and take, to question his own musical values, to adjust to the relative obscurity of staff membership. . . . In short, he is a potential leader of men, and as such we now hire him back as our managing partner and give him a rating of five times five!

B. These are clever words, Grant . . . but they're too late. The damage is done. While on Earth, I developed an ego the size of this building. A Great Mogul estimate of my own musical worth, which now (even with Rezler's help) absolutely forbids me to accept the indignity of a two-point rating. My pride has been hurt, and (for Beethoven) this is a declaration of war. . . . I actually feel sorry for the lot of you. You're so wrapped up with your credits, degrees, quality points, standard procedures, popularity scores, deadlines, staff meetings, rating sheets, and corporate policies, that not *one* of you can recognize a real musician when he comes and works under your noses for twelve years! But I'll not pity you for long. I regard this corporation as my mortal enemy, and no good soldier can afford compassion toward those whom he intends to defeat.

Gr. You make a big mistake, Herr Beethoven.

B. It is *you* who made the big mistake. I'm simply reacting to it!

Gr. Perhaps so. . . . You know, I too have a surprise to reveal this day.

B. I hope it's more enjoyable than the shock of my two points.

Gr. I think it is. You'll remember that I promised to reveal my true identity on the selfsame day that Beethoven would come before us here in the May Building. I can now do so.

B. Have I ever *heard* of you?

Gr. Yes indeed!

B. How do you know?

Gr. Because you dedicated your best composition to me.

B. Baron von Stutterheim?

Gr. No.

B. Galitzin?

Gr. No.

B. Archduke Rudolph?
Gr. No. . . . I'll give you a hint.

Grant seats himself at the Broadwood and begins playing the *Funeral March* from my *Third Symphont.*

B. The *Eroica*! . . . *Sinfonia Bonaparte*! . . . Ye gods! . . . Napoleon?
Gr. Correct! . . . Will you join me?

I sit down beside him, and the two of us perform the entire second movement. By the time we finish, the room is filled with juniors, seniors, principals, and partners. Grant jumps up from the piano and requests that we assemble in the main staff room. When everyone is seated, he takes his place at the lectern.

Gr. Esteemed staff and colleagues. . . . Our treasured BEETHOVEN was founded thirty-eight years ago. If he survives for another thirty-eight thousand years, October 4, 1848, will be the most important hour of his history. What a kind stroke of fate that our entire staff is on hand to observe it! Actually, we are all present in order to say good-bye to the class of '36. But this is not what's important about today. What is? Dear friends, on this day we have discovered Ludwig van Beethoven in our midst! It should be an occasion for great rejoicing and celebration, but it is an hour of sadness and remorse. Why? Because the day of our discovery is to be the day of our greatest loss! He came to us twelve years ago among the class of '36 and now plans to leave with them. He plans to leave because we gave him a rating of two instead of a four or a five. . . . Suppose we hear the story of our gross insult from his own lips. Then see if *any* of us can change his intent. Ladies and gentlemen, I give you the spirit of our firm. Herr Beethoven . . . our old friend, Paul Rezler!

All present stand and applaud.

B. Esteemed staff and *former* colleagues. The decision is final. I must now abandon the pleasure of your company. Nothing you can do or say will change my intent! As Paul Rezler, I would react to this day like a poor, sad-eyed dog . . . beaten and kicked by his master. I'd clinch my two points between sagging jaws and slink from your presence, never to return. . . . But as Beethoven, there is nothing to which I can react as an abused dog! When I'm slapped in the face, I *must* fight back. Had I received a rating of four or five, I would have stayed on as your managing partner, and together we would have accomplished great things within the framework of corporate music. With only two points, I can *never* return here to work. Nor can I become your chief partner! To this position, I recommend Napoleon Bonaparte . . . the Little Corporal . . . our old friend, Richard Grant.

As soon as our staff recovers from the open-mouthed shock of a second revelation, there is a standing ovation for Grant. He bows deeply, then I continue.

B. Only minutes ago I learned the truth about Grant, and I'm as surprised as you are. Though to be perfectly honest, ever since my early days as a junior, I've detected no small amount of the emperor in our fearless leader! Ten thousand credits in composition couldn't alter this.

Some polite laughter is heard—the kind that shows there are others in the room who agree with me.

B. On an individual basis, I would like to remain the friend of each of you. It could never be otherwise between Beethoven and a group of dedicated musicians. I don't hold my two-point rating against any of you, personally. I blame the inhumanity of the corporation itself, and it's this which I intend to strike down. On Earth, I discovered the lot of the professional musician to be that of a pitiable lackey. Most were convinced that no change could be made in the situation. Yet when I came to Vienna, I was not afraid to challenge the status quo. . . . Here on Aaron (within our cultural planets), I find the professional musician sadly reduced to a corporate cog! Based upon ten thousand years of Aaron's musical history, most of you probably consider this cultural blot as an inevitable and irreversible fact of life. . . . I do not! Once again, I challenge the status quo. On Earth, I freed the professional musician from servility; here I shall free him from corporate impersonality. And I begin by doing battle against the very firm that bears my name. I shall perform *myself* before the Aaronian public. They'll know it is *I*, and not someone masquerading as Beethoven! I shall prepare a *Faust* of my own and (with Goethe's blessings) shall present it directly to my public. It will be an opera by Beethoven, and not the clammy collaboration of thirty-five little BEETHOVEN-ites. As soon as the public learns the joy of responding *directly* to a musician and his art, they'll have done with these ridiculous corporate subsitutes! My advice to you, Herr Bonaparte, stop sending me those weekly cards. I shall *never* return to your side! And my advice to *you*, little BEETHOVEN-ites . . . gather round your general—prepare for battle. Gird up your halves and quarters and eighths. Gird up your staves and tapes and clefs and computers. Beethoven declares war upon BEETHOVEN! . . . May the best musician win! . . . Good-bye to all of you!

Without further ado, I step from the home of BEETHOVEN, having no intention of returning there again. As the double glass door closes behind me and I make my way down the soft green hall, I have the unmistakable feeling that I'm being followed. Believing it to be Grant with an armful of apologies, I neither stop nor turn. I push the elevator button and wait impatiently as the sound of October wind whistles and moans in the shaft behind the door. Footsteps come closer, and someone touches me on the shoulder. As I wheel around, my face is guised in Beethoven's angry sneer.

B. Marcie! . . . I thought we *said* good-bye.
MS. We did, Herr Beethoven. But I must ask you a question.
B. I know what it is . . . but ask anyway.
MS. Did you say anything to my husband about our affaire d'amour?
B. As Beethoven, I would gladly tell him that his little wife is a "Queen of the Night" and that I know so from personal experience. As Rezler, I have too much love and respect for you to tell him *anything*. No, Marcie. Your secret is safe. I told him nothing, nor shall I do so.
MS. (*Her huge moist eyes turn warm and penetrating.*) Thank you, Paul. . . . God bless you!

Before I realize what's happening, my blunt farewell to BEETHOVEN is thoroughly humanized by a warm embrace and a tender kiss.

B. Thank you, Mrs. Bonaparte. Good luck with your recordings!

As Marcie's perfect roundness curves its way down the hall, I'm tempted to follow after her, to renounce my plan for battle, to become BEETHOVEN's managing partner. A sliding open of the elevator door interrupts these thoughts of reconciliation, and I quickly banish them.

Back in my apartment, I pour another huge glass of Seideler. As I drink and reexamine Mozart's picture, the spirit behind the eyes (a combination of Mozart's and Judy's) seems to nod in thorough approval at what I had just done. For another spell, I stand by my window and examine the tremendous changes wrought by three short hours. There is no rain-filled fog. The streets below are dry, and the top of the May Building is outlined in crisp blue. All is clear and bright. I now know exactly what I'm to do with my Second-Order life. *At no time since rebirth have I felt the spirit of Beethoven more explosively alive within me!*

Chapter 40

As you might well guess, Thursday morning's paper contains the entire story. A huge headline warns: BEETHOVEN AND BONAPARTE GIRD FOR BATTLE. Other subheadings on the first page read:

> BEETHOVEN Dismisses Beethoven with Only Two Points!
> Beethoven Conceals Identity for Twelve Years
> Bonaparte Known Only to Firm's Founders
> Who Is This Paul Rezler?
> Richard and Marcie Grant: the Bonapartes
> Beethoven Challenges BEETHOVEN Single-Handed
> Can One Rhinelander Change Ten Thousand Years of Aaronian Music?

On the second page are several pictures of the Grants and of Paul Rezler. I half expect such coverage in the *Altburg Morning News*, but am really surprised to find an equivalent spread in the morning edition of the *Aaronian Interplanetary*. Now everyone knows who I am: Mother, Grandfather, Culbertson (Remember how he called me "Beethoven"?), my family, Judy's family, Lobkowitz, Lichnowsky, the Breunings, Schubert, Zmeskall, Albrechtsberger, Schuppanzigh, Rudolph, the Rieses, Cherubini, Goethe—everyone! Let old Donovan try to threaten us now. Had I received a four or a five and claimed my position as manager, I would have flown to the arms of all these loved ones. But with a slap in the face of only two points, Beethoven lacks the humility to accept defeat. I can't *bear* to face these people until I've won my victory over corporate music!

I decide that complete isolation is the best course for me to follow while preparing for battle. Judy helps me arrange things and becomes my sole contact with humanity. On dear old VP 33 (in her own name), she signs out a villa for twelve full months, and only she knows that this is to be my hideout. Cottages facing the beach are available for a maximum of sixty-three days. I'm therefore obliged to make my secretive quarters at Villa 139B, half a mile inland. Even so, I'm within walking distance of our lighthouse and our favorite beach.

As things turn out, my self-imposed exile lasts for two years instead of only one. This is the time required for me to complete my own setting of *Faust* and also a string of piano pieces including three sonatas, three trios, and a concerto. Thus armed, it is my intent to conquer the city of Altburg, and thence the entire world of Aaronian music. These days are days of sweat and toil and happiness. Death, rebirth, and twelve years of apprenticeship have only sharpened my will to create. Without exception, the resulting compositions are my best third-period Beethoven!

Thus for two years, Judy continues to alternate her weekend dating between Donovan and myself. Every other Saturday she shows up around noon with another two weeks' supply of food and clothing. Thanks to her loving care, the secret of my Second-Order whereabouts remains absolute. Although Judy is perfectly reconciled to the reign of corporate art and artists throughout our cultural planets, she never starts an argument with me on the subject. She doesn't discourage me from what I'm trying to do to BEETHOVEN (and indirectly to REMBRANDT), nor does she actually encourage me. She's neutral on the matter. But those big blue eyes seem to say, "Never mind, Paul. . . . Someday you'll see things the way the rest of us do. You'll realize that corporate artists are our friends, and not our enemies."

By now, poor old Donovan has lost much of his steam. Without the threat he once held over my head, there's little he can do but sit back and wait for Judy and me to make up our minds. Dave must truly love my little kitten. He tells her that if it's what she really wants, he'll wait another fifty years for a definite yes or no.

On December 1, 1848, Donovan and two other pianist-partners found the firm of CHOPIN. Their charter makes them the official corporate musician of CP 90. For Dave, this is indeed a stroke of good fortune. I know of *no* man who thinks more highly of Chopin nor plays him better than he. As to their firm, something quite unusual happens. They scarcely take on their first crop of junior pianists and composers, when POW! . . . Chopin himself is born into their midst. He arrives on Aaron in October 1849, and ten months later accepts the position of managing partner at CHOPIN. No doubt through Dave's influence, the great Maestro becomes instantly enthusiastic about musical canvases. He appoints REMBRANDT as the official "portrait painter" for his music. And thus the two of us are the first Aaronians to have our compositions professionally interpreted on canvas. Today, the practice is quite common.

Now that my identity is known throughout our Second Order, it is no longer necessary for friends and family to reach me through Population Control. Letters that are sent to me in care of BEETHOVEN are forwarded to Ms. Adams at REMBRANDT, and thence find their way to my desk via Judy's semimonthly visits. I shall quote a few of these incoming and outgoing notes to give some idea of the rapport (or lack of it) that manifests itself in the correspondence of these hardworking, isolated days. Each visit by my little mail carrier brings several letters from Bonaparte. Characteristic of them all would be the one dated October 4, 1849:

> Great Maestro, Spirit of the Rhine:
>
> One year ago today, you stamped from our presence, vowing never to return. Since that hour, we have been a company in deep mourning, a ship without a captain, a body without a soul. After one full year, would you not now reconsider?
>
> You've no doubt heard of the tremendous reception accorded our *Faust* (two months ago) at its première. This opera is filled with the spirit of your Third Period. It came into being through your efforts, and those of your browbeaten co-principals. . . . Thanks to *Faust*, our popularity rating is now comfortably in excess of the required nine hundred points. The opera has been signed for a full year's engagement at Altburg's Rhonda House. Both Tempo and Blackburn are interested in recording it. Why don't you come to us now, in time to conduct these performances?
>
> Wouldn't it be easier for you to accept the responsibilities of our managing partner than to try to

change the entire structure of Aaronian music? The door of the Schwarspanierhaus stands open wide! All of us are eager to welcome our beloved Maestro!

Yours to command,
Bonaparte

Determined in my course, I reply to none of the emperor's entreaties. Nor do I answer several little notes from Schubert and Culby, each expressing surprise and dismay at my long-kept secret. I do reply to a short letter from my old pupil Ferdinand Ries:

October 10, 1848

Dear Rezler . . . Dear Beethoven:

Congratulations! . . . At last we know who you are! And what a handsome young chap! I'm sending these words through BEETHOVEN, and hoping they reach you. How much better to write directly, a notable improvement over Population Control.

I could have predicted you would react to corporate music the way you have. The individual spirit and determination of our Beethoven could *not* do otherwise. Though you're one man against a hundred corporations, I'm certain you'll win over them. But how about your musical court? Surely you'll need some of the old friends hovering around you. You'll need them as much as they need you! As you go stamping through the mountains with sketchbook in hand, wouldn't it be nice once again to have old Ries trailing behind? I'll do your every bidding: transcriptions, orchestrations, copy work, business correspondence, finances, *all* in return for a lesson here and there. . . . Just like old times. . . . Have you forgiven me my little prank? Will you still not play for me?

A few years spent in your musical Court, and I'll be ready to launch my own career (just as on Earth)! Please say that I may come. I know I can be of help.

Always your admiring pupil,
Ferdinand Ries

October 22, 1848

Dear Ries,

Only yesterday I received your loving letter. The complete survival of your charm, your personality and your sensitivity brings tears to my eyes. You can't *know* how much your continued faith in me means at a time like this. Of course I have forgiven your little prank; of course I shall play for you again. And you're absolutely correct, I *do* need my little Court about me. Without their help and encouragement, I shall never be able to accomplish my Second-Order mission. But wait, dear Ries; the time has not yet come. I must take the first few steps alone, fight the first few battles myself. Then I shall receive you with open arms.

Your brother in arms,
Beethoven

On January 6, 1849, I receive a beautiful letter from Madame von Breuning. It brings me up to date on all the family affairs, especially those of their most recent arrival—dear, good Wegeler. They are planning a clanwide reunion for the first week in August at the White Lamb Chateau on VP 7. Madame begs me to join them there for at least part of the festivities. In a return letter, I thank her for still including me among the family. I explain why it's not now possible for me to attend, and beg to be invited to the next-scheduled reunion.

By far, the dearest letter of all is from my Earthly mother. No sooner do I open it than I begin to cry:

March 3, 1849

Dearest Ludwig, my great son:

Ever since the story of your twelve years at BEETHOVEN broke the news and I had a chance to see those handsome pictures of Paul Rezler, I've been eager to clasp you in my arms. Though all else has changed, the eyes have not; they're still my Ludwig. In them, I see the same little boy who used to go riding on my knee and on my shoulder. Do you remember how I would hold you above my head? Those sparkling eyes, they're still the same! . . .

Believe it or not, your grandfather and I are on good terms because of you. The two of us have followed every step of your Earthly career, and our common admiration for you has drawn us together. Can you imagine how happy we were with the founding of BEETHOVEN in 1810? We could hardly believe that the little boy who sat on our piano bench in the Bonngasse, and who wept bitterly under his father's discipline, was now the greatest musician on Earth, who was sending us proud symphonies for our hearts' enjoyment some twenty years before he himself would arrive to conduct them!

Not all has been joy and happiness with our poor old family. Neither your father nor brother Carl has appeared in the Major Aaronian system. God grant that they are alive, happy and growing within our Minor universe and that we shall all meet again in the Third Order. Just yesterday, your reborn brother Johann came to see me for the first time, and (of all things) he's now passionately interested in the career of a violinist. He says he's going to pester you until you write him a concerto for his own use! . . . Death and rebirth are a strange transition. Who would have thought that anything could induce our Johann to exchange his chemicals and moneybags for a violin?

We are all proud of you, dear Ludwig . . . not only because of your music. We are proud of your victory over deafness, and of your headstrong attempts to do what was right for your little son, Karl. Johann brings us good news of the boy, which I know will interest you. In 1832, he resigned from the army and married Caroline Naske. He became a farm administrator and is now a frontier commissioner. He's the proud father of four beautiful daughters and a wiry ten-year-old son named Ludwig! Regarding finances, he shouldn't have to worry. Johann left him an estate of over 2,000 florins! . . .

As for your long silence, I know you've had good reason. I shall be patient. But could you drop me just a line? Let me know that you love me still. . . . Please, Ludwig!

When the time is right, I shall plan a reunion for what's left of our Earthly clan. We shall flock to you like tender sheep about a loving shepherd. For you, dear son, are the root and cornerstone of our First-Order family. Though you neither married nor had children of your own, *you* are the father of us all. No other can take your place in our hearts!

I shall not write again until I hear from you.

Your proud and loving mother

Before the tears on the back of my hand have time to dry, I take up a pen and scribble my reply.

March 10, 1849

Dearest Soul . . . Mother!

Please do never question the love which I have in my heart for you. Neither ten thousand rebirths nor ten thousand happy marriages could in any way dull the image of this love. All that keeps me from flying to your arms is the weight of a Second-Order obligation which is now placed solely and squarely upon my shoulders. In the hour of my first victory over the injustices of Aaronian music, I shall come to you, dear Mother . . . and we shall have our reunion.

It is wonderful to know that you and Grandfather have overcome your ancient differences . . . and even more wonderful to hear of my little Karl's good fortune. I love him as if he *were* my own son, and now to think he's the father of five! . . . Tell Johann that I'm indeed proud to welcome another musician into our family . . . especially a violinist! Someday soon he shall have that concerto, and for his very own use.

But sweet soul, you are wrong about one thing. When our happy reunion day finally comes, *you*(not I) will be the loving shepherd about which the rest of us shall flock. You are the spiritual foundation of our Earthly days, no one else. . . . Each time Father's cruel tactics would beat me to tears, I'd run to your knee and bury my wet face in your lap. When the crying stopped and I could look up into your eyes, it was the strength of *your* spirit that sent me back to music . . . nothing else.

When I returned from Mozart to face the imminent reality of your approaching death, as your hands turned cold in mine and your sweet eyes closed forever, a strong voice from within the calm of your soul told me that our separation was not forever, but for a short time only. Even from beyond the grave, your gentle love would watch over me and somehow find delight in whatever Earthly victories I might achieve.

Young Ries was convinced that my musical inspiration came solely from nature's song of the forest. But he was wrong. . . . Beyond the sounds of wind and birds and trees and stream, I heard your voice. It inspired me, sustained me and beckoned me on. . . . When old Schindler marveled at my quiet calm in the face of death, he attributed it to some creative force within me. But he was wrong. It was the memory of your last hours which gave me strength. You, dear Mother, are the cornerstone of our First-Order family. No other can take your place in our hearts!

I am now called to my biggest musical battle of two lifetimes. Though never before have I doubted my strength and ability to achieve an artistic goal, I now have need of your prayers. The odds are strongly in favor of the enemy, but I shall fight long and hard! . . . At the first little smile of victory, I shall fly to your arms!

Your loving son,
Ludwig

My period of total isolation comes to an end on September 27, 1850. On this fair and optimistic Friday, I finally vacate my villa and move back to Altburg. I do this so that I can meet the enemy face-to-face. If I'm to wage war against BEETHOVEN, I must go to *him*; he'll never come to me. . . . The return to Altburg reminds me of my boyhood return to Vienna, but there are differences. The present trip requires three seconds of D-R Chamber instead of three days of post chaise. In 1792, I was provided a handful of recommendations from Neefe, Waldstein, and the Elector; in 1850, I have no recommendations from anyone! But I'm armed with the Earthly reputation of Beethoven! To Vienna, I carried sonatas and trios; to Altburg I bring sonatas, trios, a piano concerto, and *Faust*. I purposely sign for an apartment at DeWitt's; the closer to my foe, the better! Naturally, my rooms are not among those reserved for BEETHOVEN's staff. But I choose them to be strategically located on the thirty-fifth floor, directly opposite the May Building!

My first plan of attack is to visit Goethe and obtain his official blessings upon the latest version of *Faust*. Then in the clattering arena of popularity points, I hope to meet the corporate version head-on with my own, and to defeat it! . . . On Monday morning, I phone Goethe at his professional firm. We arrange an appointment for Tuesday afternoon at 3:00 PM.

The corporate GOETHE is located on the top three floors of the Bevlin Fine Arts building, which is situated in the heart of the Shadylane theater district of CP 22. Shadylane is the "Broadway" of this particular cultural planet—the very center of its legitimate stage. I no sooner arrive than the great poet enters their reception room, introduces himself, shakes my hand, and conducts me to his private office. Except for an inordinate number of potted plants, the cozy room is not unlike our partners' offices at BEETHOVEN.

Go. This is a great honor for me, Herr Beethoven . . . your coming to my little room.

B. Then the pattern swings full cycle . . . exactly how I felt when you first visited me at Teplitz.

Go. Do you remember that day? This reminds me. . . here. . . pull up a chair. I have a surprise for you.

B. Don't tell me you're going to make me coffee?

Go. No. I never did learn how to boil up that black Beethoven brew. But this is something I know you'll enjoy. (*He steps to a corner cabinet and takes from it a bottle and two wine glasses.*)

B. Damn! I shall never live down my reputation for winebibbing. . . . Würzburg! . . . Where did you ever find Würzburg?

Go. Renée's . . . Michelle Renée's on SP 10. They can supply any wine ever made on Earth, or here in "heaven." When I heard of your visit, I had them send us a bottle just for the occasion.

B. (*As Goethe pours, I study his handsome young face and body.*) Isn't it strange, your Excellency? In spite of my personal experience with death and rebirth, as I entered this building, I expected to find you precisely as you were on Earth: a huge tall man with a kingly brow, a long nose, and the brightest eyes that ever revealed a man's soul. But here you are, a handsome chap, clad impeccably in the cut of the hour. Not the *trace* of a big old belly, draped in a brass-buttoned swallowtail.

Go. I know what you mean, Herr Beethoven. As Paul Rezler, you're not exactly the broad-shouldered, pockmarked, square-jawed, hairy-handed, small-giant musician which I knew on Earth. But do you know something? . . . The eyes . . . the eyes are the same. Their shape and color are different, but the spirit behind them is definitely Beethoven's!

B. Now you sound like my mother . . . or like Rembrandt van Rijn.

Go. You know Rembrandt?

B. Yes. My fiancée is a pupil of his. Through her I met him once, and he related an observation identical to yours.

Go. It's true. The spirit of an Earthling *does* begin to show through the eyes of his Second-Order body. And in those of young Rezler, I behold the power of Beethoven! Here, let me fill your glass.

As he tilts the bottle again, his eyes glean the two large folios I had placed on the corner of his desk.

Go. And these I presume are your personal setting of my new *Faust*.

B. Yes. . . . I've brought them for your approval and your blessing.

Opening to the title page, Goethe reads aloud:

FAUST
An Opera in Four Acts by
Beethoven II

Opus 5

Based upon Goethe's Revised Play
and
Dedicated to Our Mutual Angel
Bettina Brentano

The poet smiles coolly as he closes the first volume and lifts it to the rack of a small piano by the window.

Go. So your dedication is to our little Bettina. Strange about this girl . . . I thought that she of all people would blaze a path of pure intellectualism to the very center of our Major culture. But there's not a trace of her. . . . Oh well, I have no doubt that we'll eventually hear from her. Come play me some themes from *your* setting. I'm anxious to compare them with those of your firm.

B. What do you think of our corporate *Faust*?

Go. I think it's the greatest music I've ever heard! That's why I tried to contact you through Population Control. I wanted to give you and your firm my heartfelt congratulations.

B. You'll like my personal version even better. At least it's pure Beethoven, and not the conglomerated confusion of a bunch of underlings. What's a piano doing here in the studio of our great poet?

Go. At present I'm collaborating with three different composers, each on a separate opera. If I'm not careful, I'll be entering my next life as a librettist instead of a poet or dramatist. Let's hear *your* themes.

I perform the Overture and the Prelude to Act IV. Then for nearly two hours, I play all the important melodies in sequence while Goethe reads his text and turns pages. At the conclusion of my *Faust*, he slaps me on the back and repeatedly shouts, "Bravo!"

B. Now, dear poet, tell me. Isn't this better than a corporation can do?

Go. Your corporate *Faust* is the greatest music I have ever heard. What you just played is as good. . . . I can't say more.

B. But this is not enough, Your Excellency. I've come for your rejection of the corporate version and for your official acceptance of mine. Only then shall I be able to proceed with my plan.

Go. Your plan to overthrow our happy status quo?

B. My plan to set things right between deserving artists and the Aaronian public.

Go. But dear Beethoven, this is only the Second Order. Things are beautifully right between our corporate artists and their public. I could ask for nothing more.

B. If you *have* a fault, great poet, it's your willingness to accept things as they are—to be tossed about and helplessly molded by the whims of other men . . . weak men who have no right to impose their stifling systems upon the creative efforts of others. On Earth, Herr Goethe, you were too much of the court; here you're too much the well-oiled gear of a smooth-running machine. Join forces with *me*, soul of our fatherland. Give me the golden streams of your thoughts and words, and I shall set them to music. Together, alone, we'll show these Aaronians what they've been missing!

Go. To accept things as they are, I count this a virtue, not a fault. It is a mark of intelligence, not weakness. In my own experience, I've known revolutionaries great and small . . . and I don't wish to be numbered among them. For the most part, they are wasters of time and talent. They spend so much of themselves changing things that their ultimate contribution is reduced to a clap of thunder or a passing wind. Much of what I accomplished on Earth was achieved because I accepted things as they were at Weimar. Here on Aaron, I'll do my best by accepting the corporate way of life. If things are entirely different in the Third Order, I'm prepared to change again.

B. But what of the present state of affairs? . . . Things are *not* right here! We must change them.

Go. By not right, you mean not the same as on Earth. . . . But who's to say this is not right?

B. Are you honestly satisfied with conditions here at GOETHE?

Go. Extremely so! I find them an enormous improvement over my Earthly lot, like one soothing balm, one giant incentive to my creative Muse. . . . Gone is the paralytic isolation of the lonely poet. Gone is the stranglehold of the big I. Gone is the lack of communion with other artists. In their place, I find an inspiring criticism and a helpful recognition of my creative thoughts while still cast in the soft clay of their prenatal state.

B. Doesn't it bother you to rub elbows with a bunch of little juniors and seniors who, in many cases, are as talented as you yourself?

Go. As talented, and often *more* so. . . . No. This doesn't bother me at all. I enjoy being surrounded by talented people. . . . When a young chap hovers over me with ten times my present endowment, I welcome him. The beauty of his gift only inspires me to work ten times harder.

B. But if your staff reeks with those who write better than you, this means that your managing partnership is justified on the basis of an Earthly reputation!

Go. Spirit, not reputation. Now I see the trouble with our Beethoven. He thinks that what he forged on Earth and brought with him into *this* life is solely a talent—an ability to play and conduct . . . a disciplined composing technology . . . a gift that now must be developed and proven superior to that of every other musician. . . . But dear Soul, this is not important. Talent is relative at best. On

Earth, you were among the greatest of all musicians; here, the dilution of your Second-Order musicianship might place you among the least. What does it matter? In the Third Order, your pendulum could well swing back again.

B. If Beethoven is now among the least, then he has no right being managing partner over those whose talents are greater than his!

Go. Talents, talents . . . bah! . . . You count them like an old miser with his bag of coins. The Beethoven you bring from Earth is more than a musical talent. He is a spirit, and what a spirit he is! . . . I don't doubt that some of your little juniors can shovel counterpoints around as well as you; your principals and partners can grind out authentic third-period pieces. . . . But who among them can bring the *spirit* of Beethoven to your firm? No one! Only *you* can do this, my friend.

B. And who needs the spirit of Beethoven? They seem to manage perfectly well without it!

Go. You'll never realize how poorly they manage without it, until you permit them to manage with it! Go claim your throne, dear Beethoven. This is the chief moral obligation of your new life. Perhaps a few of your staff have burrowed and calculated their way to playing or conducting or composing better than you. So what? Show me one of them who, though deaf, can hear the spirit of God in nature. Show me one of them who finds joy through suffering. Show me one of them who renounces the pleasure of wife and child for the sake of music. Show me one of them who is totally dedicated to the Muse. Show me one of them who is half the spirit of our Beethoven!

B. You make the title of managing partner sound like a noble cause!

Go. It is! The noblest calling of Second-Order art. You must go to your staff, dear Maestro. Let them love you for the overwhelming spirit you are, not for the super talent you think you must become. Remember—talents rise and fall, but spirits grow and grow!

B. I see that I shall never convert you to my cause. . . . Very well! But have I at least your blessings upon my *Faust*?

Go. Yes indeed! Upon yours and upon BEETHOVEN's. Like a parent of two fine children, I love them both!

B. Then farewell, Herr Goethe. I go to do battle against a foul system that imprisons the two of us. And as I raise my sword, remember—it is your lack of *freedom* that I strike down . . . not you!

Go. GOETHE is my body, I am his soul. You cannot pierce my flesh without grieving my spirit. Here on Aaron, I'm a corporate artist. If you challenge the existence of corporate art, then you're at war with me.

B. God forbid! To think that it should come to this. . . . But say what you will, dear Goethe. In my heart, for you there shall never be anything but great love and deep respect. . . . Some of your admirers worship you as a poet or dramatist, others revere you as a philosopher or (perhaps) a librettist. . . . But for me, you're a prophet, a First-Order prophet, the only such to cross my path on Earth!

Go. And why do you say this?

B. Have you forgotten that sun-filled windy day at Teplitz?

Go. That time we went walking among the poplars and sipping Würzburg at the Silver Serpent?

B. Yes. But it's not the walking or the sipping that makes you my First-Order prophet. It's what you said there. Words spoken by a poor Earthly creature like myself, yet words which clearly perceived the miracle of life and death and rebirth. Do you remember them?

Go. Ah yes . . . I remember: "It is my belief, dear Beethoven, that any work of art or science or philosophy becomes TRULY great only if it can be brought face-to-face with death, and still hold its own reality. For me, to die is to BECOME. And the essence of all living is CREATION. I create without ceasing, and this is my ONLY claim to immortality. One should BELIEVE in immortality. Each of us has a RIGHT to this belief. It satisfies the wants of our nature. . . . There are many ways to DEFINE immortality of the soul. Some turn to religion . . . others to philosophy, or legend, or mythology. The path we take is irrelevant. What matters is that we DO seek and find. To me, the eternal existence of my soul is proved from my idea of ACTIVITY. If I work on INCESSANTLY till my death, nature is BOUND to give me another form of existence when the present one can no longer SUSTAIN MY SPIRIT! . . .

Chapter 41

Now comes an important turning point in my history. Though profoundly altering the remaining years, it transports us only seventeen months along the way, from October 1850 to February 1852. Fresh from GOETHE's office, I spend most of October contacting Altburg's publishers, recording studios, and concert managers. Without exception, the magic of my Earthly name opens chief administrative doors at these firms. I'm received in the glorious tradition of the "Great Mogul," praised for my five newest pieces (*Faust* not more than the others), and congratulated for the great Aaronian enterprise that now bears my name. And that's as far as it goes!

Everyone's interested in publishing my new compositions as the initial works of Beethoven II, partner at BEETHOVEN. No one's interested in them as the music of Ludwig van Beethoven, revolutionary from the Rhine! Each of the Altburg studios would turn somersaults for the chance to record BEETHOVEN. Not one of them is interested in my personal recordings. Through Bonaparte and his staff, each concert manager is more than eager to bring my new music before the Aaronian public, to stage my opera. None will touch these works to help me set Beethoven against BEETHOVEN. In short, I'm absolutely alone in my dreams of conquest! Altburg stands firmly behind Bonaparte, his underlings, and the established artistic system of our culture.

One solid year is spent visiting a hundred musical capitals on eighty-three different cultural planets. Everywhere, my reception is the same. I'm welcomed, honored, respected, wined, and dined. But not a single musical entrepreneur shows the slightest interest in my revolutionary plot! None will even take it seriously. Without exception, they tell me to go home to BEETHOVEN, and there claim the pleasures and responsibilities that are rightfully mine.

On November 3, 1851, I return to my apartment at DeWitt's, convinced that if my initial battle is ever to be fought, it must be waged here on home ground. For one week, I knock on the same old doors. This time around (far from being wined or dined), I'm treated with impatience and contempt. Unanimously, the applied musicians of Altburg tell me to join my colleagues at BEETHOVEN, or else suffer the consequences.

My choice is quite clear. I can return to the May Building as managing partner (Bonaparte still sends me his weekly invitations). This would be my only access to the vast audiences of Aaron's cultural planets. Or I can transfer to an educational planet, obtain my PhD, and settle down as a professor of music. This would permit me to compose and perform exactly what I wish to compose and perform without corporate assistance or controls. But (by comparison) my audience would be horribly restricted—a mere handful of theoretical musicians who live and practice their intellectual snobbery on that particular EP.

To put things simply, after thirteen months of knocking on countless doors and having not one open to the revolutionary plan of the Great Mogul, I realize the obvious truth that no man (not even Beethoven) can grasp in his hands the entire structure of Second-Order music and mold it to his own liking! Nor can I accept either of the alternate plans open to me: I'll never return to BEETHOVEN, and I can't bear the thought of full-time teaching! What can I do? Where shall I turn?

Years earlier (at Heiligenstadt), when the unlimited frustrations of life first beat upon me, I considered suicide as a logical answer and a tempting possibility. Now I know better. Having passed through death and rebirth, I realize that a man can kill his own body, but never his soul. Ending my life would probably remove me to the Minor universe of our Third Order; there to face the same problems I'm facing now, but without the Major Order's comforting guarantee of another rebirth.

Seeing no way out of my dilemma, I react to life's innate cursedness in the same way my old father did at Bonn. I sit me down (in my rent-free apartment at DeWitt's) and take up the bottle in earnest! Since I no longer have a salary, I can't afford the luxury-item cost of Goethe's delicious Würzburg. But the perfect balance of supply and demand within our Major economy is enough to keep an infinite stream of German, Hungarian, and Austrian wines flowing to my thirsty lips.

Because of the favor my silence has done for Marcie and her marriage, she becomes my little spy at BEETHOVEN. At the end of each month (through Judy Adams), Marcie reveals the latest news of our firm. I learn that her husband has abandoned all immediate hope that I shall return. (Commencing with the new year, his unanswered weekly letters cease to arrive.) He and the founders name an initial batch of twenty-three partners. Included among them are Ches Bergman and Victor Dimos from my old class of '36. Mrs. Bonaparte (as I knew would be the case) is named partner in charge of recordings. The firm begins work on a huge block of twenty-seven symphonies, eighteen quartets, and nine piano concertos. Each fall (starting in 1852), it plans to première one new symphony, paired off with either a quartet or a concerto. This twenty-seven-year monument is to represent the firm's ultimate tribute to the third-period style of my Earthly endeavors. For 1880, they plan their first evolution from the standards that I set for them on Earth—hopefully under my leadership, otherwise without it.

All this talk about BEETHOVEN symphonies inspires me to write another of my own. If it's evolution they want, I'll give them something to worry about—Symphony 1 by Beethoven II, Opus 6. Alas! I'm so filled with jealousy, hatred, and disappointment that my new-sounding sketches amount to little more than fragments—bold beginnings of something great that might have been!

As these wasted days fade and die, I drink more and more, sketch less and less. Soon I'm outdrinking my old father and grandmother put together. Poor Rezler! His strong young body is no match for such an inheritance. How can it possibly cope with the gargantuan alcoholic appetite of a "mad musician" who spent his last seven years on Earth, drinking himself to death? My body reacts to Beethoven's intemperance by losing consciousness. This it does with alarming frequency. Throughout December, I awaken on my parlor floor more often than in bed. During January, it's the same story, but a bleaker chapter still. I drink constantly, compose nothing, and (on three separate occasions) regain consciousness at places considerably removed from my living room at DeWitt's. The first "awakening" occurs in the middle of a wintry night by a frozen pond in front of the May Building. A watchman nudges me with his billy to see if I'm still alive. One whiff of my sad breath convinces him that I've not yet attained the dignified state of a corpse. He helps me back to my apartment.

A second "awakening" occurs (of all places) at the doorway to my Schwarspanierhaus room. I have never turned in my staff key to Bonaparte. Apparently I find my way to the thirty-second floor, admit myself to BEETHOVEN's quarters, and make it as far as the managing partner's door. Here I collapse, this time to be awakened in the wee hours of the morning by the ticklish handle of a mop! The mop belongs to one of two beautiful cleaning women, who stare down at me in sympathetic amazement. Because of my state of total inebriation, their shocked expressions strike my funny bone. For long minutes, I roar at them in the humorless laughter of a drunkard! At last I'm able to speak.

B. Would you beautiful ladies please help me to my feet?
CL 1. Just who are you, young man?
B. I am Beethoven, trying to get into my room here. . . Who are *you* folks?
CL 2. I'm Cinderella, and this is my fairy godmother. We'll help you to the elevator.
B. No! . . . Wait! . . . I *must* get in here! . . . Please help me.

For no good reason, I start laughing again. The two ladies decide that I'm as harmless as I am helpless and hopeless. They open the door to my study, turn on the lights, and point me in the direction of the big black Broadwood. I start walking toward my piano and just this side of its bench fall flat on the soft green carpet! The next thing I see is an over-the-shoulder view of my hall at DeWitt's. I'm being carried to my room again by the same officer who (two weeks earlier) had saved me from freezing to death. He throws me across my bed, loosens my tie and collar, then speaks a few words of gentle warning before he turns and leaves: "The next time I find you in this condition, I'm going to look up your name and report you to your counselor. If he's worth his salt, he'll take your drinking privileges away from you. . . . Sleep tight, buddy."

My third "awakening" (on February ninth) is the last and the best. The shock of it turns the tide of my Second-Order life. It puts an end to my loitering and shows me a clear new path. This time I'm lying in bed, licking my cardboard lips with a wooden tongue. Slowly my eyes bring things into focus. There at the tip of my fingers is a dear, sweet, beautiful face—a face I haven't seen for twenty years:

B. Big Cat! . . . Where am I? . . . What are *you* doing here!?

Chapter 42

Judy's mother still displays all the charm of a beautiful teenager. Her face is bright and sparkling, her perfect red hair is unchanged in its soft beauty. Answering my questions, she smiles warmly.

EA. I've come to see if you're awake yet. You've been sleeping in my daughter's bed.
B. Really, Mrs. A., tell me. . . . Where am I, and how did *you* get here?
EA. After two decades, we grew a little impatient waiting for your rebirthday party. So we kidnapped you and brought you here.
B. You mean I'm down on the farm?
EA. Yes. Don't you recognize Judy's room? There's the window over the back porch, and that's the old elm you shinnied down that time when Mr. A. came home three hours earlier than expected.
B. Ye gods! Then I'm *not* dreaming! . . . But how did I get here on SP 71?
EA. What's the last thing you remember?
B. I was drinking. . . . You must be ashamed of me, Big Cat, but since last November, I've done little else. It seems that I was drinking beer and wine—a barrel of each, I fear.
EA. Exactly! That's what the innkeeper said you were doing.
B. And where was this?
EA. At the Red Rose—a little tavern on the outskirts of Oakmont 12.
B. What was I doing at Oakmont?

EA. No one knows. You showed up there last Saturday afternoon, started drinking, and kept things going for several hours in the grand style. Then you slumped over at your table, presumably asleep. Toward closing time, the proprietor discovered that far from dozing, you had lost consciousness. Unable to bring you around, he had you taken to the Oakmont Medical Center. There the doctors lost no time in diagnosing your malady. They momentarily restored you to consciousness, then injected a double dose of withdrawal serum that has kept you sleeping until just now. This medicine should obviate your alcoholic tendencies for at least two weeks. By that time, we hope to have discovered and removed the cause of your heavy drinking.

B. Then your name shall be called "Wonderful" instead of "Big Cat." But tell me, Mrs. Adams, how did I get here?

EA. When the attendants searched your clothing, they found no identification except a little picture of Judy with her old phone number scribbled on the back. They called here, and from their description, I detected who you were and told them I would come at once. Doctors Stutz and Waxman both agreed that a change in scenery and some good home cooking would do you the most good. They were delighted when I suggested bringing you here to our farm. Does this explain why you are where you are, and how you find yourself in Judy's bed?

B. Yes, Sweet, it does. And I thank you for your kind ministrations. . . . But I fear they are wasted on a poor lost soul!

EA. Nonsense, Herr Beethoven! Why do you say this?

B. You've named the reason squarely—old Beethoven! . . . Through him I've inherited an iron-willed inflexibility . . . a deadheaded determination to pursue an impossible goal.

EA. You mean your battle against corporate music?

B. Yes.

EA. And you feel this is now hopeless?

B. Yes.

EA. Then abandon it! Choose another goal, go another direction.

B. For Rezler this would be easy to do; for Beethoven it's impossible!

EA. Don't you think it's about time you have a little talk with your counselor?

B. I should have seen him long ago, but I couldn't convince Beethoven of this. My inherited mania for a musical victory squeezed all rationality from my thinking and planning and living!

EA. Would you be pleased to have Robinson come here to the farm?
B. Of course! How did Mr. A. react when you told him I was here?
EA. He was very surprised. And when I described your condition, he immediately suggested bringing Robinson for a visit.
B. Was he angry about my heavy drinking?
EA. Heavens no! This is only proof of your need for help. He really laughed when I reminded him of our long-promised rebirthday celebration. "Horribly ironic," he said. "We wait twenty-five years for a party, and now it has to be a perfectly dry one!"
B. Will Judy come for the occasion?
EA. I haven't seen her since last October. . . . I thought you lovers were dating every other weekend.
B. We were, until I began drinking my way into the Third Order! I told her that I was starting my greatest symphony and didn't want to see anyone until it was finished. Well . . . that was three months ago, and look at me now!
EA. What about the symphony?
B. It's still my greatest . . . still the most passionate . . . still unwritten . . . still singing its soul to heaven from the bottom of my final bottle . . . that bottle which I never seem quite able to reach! . . . Is Judy coming?
EA. She'd be here now, except for Rembrandt.
B. Rembrandt! . . . What's he to do with our party?
EA. He requested a brief meeting with Judy. He was once an overnight guest here. Did you ever meet him?
B. Yes, believe it or not, over a flagon of rum. He told me that Judy was a great artist, then looked me squarely in the eye and fairly called the Beethoven hiding within me!
EA. Did you admit who you were?
B. No. . . . Like some villainous coward, for my own selfish reasons, I denied the penetrating sureness of his keen perception. I insisted that he had never painted me, and sent him away highly confused.
EA. But now he knows who Paul Rezler is!
B. Yes. And I'm ashamed of my deception.
EA. Don't worry. He's forgiven you.
B. I don't know. In the disciplined eye of his greatness, I now feel very small. Do you think there's a chance that I might go to him and apologize?

EA. I don't see why not. Judy's coming here later today. She plans to return to Rembrandt in the morning. Perhaps you can arrange to go with her.

B. I hope so. If only he can be made to understand the reason for my secrecy, then he'll forgive me.

EA. In the meantime, how about a nice farm breakfast?

B. Griddlecakes? Your "famous fifty" with eggs, bacon, and coffee?

EA. That's the kind.

B. Wonderful! I was hoping you'd ask. My poor belly feels like I haven't fed it for three months!

EA. With all the drinking, you probably haven't.

B. It's amazing, Big Cat. That shot of medicine is really powerful! My appetite has returned, yet I have no craving for drink.

EA. This will last for about two weeks. Then watch out for the bottle. I hope by that time we'll have you converted to flapjacks.

B. To flapjacks and to good, clean living!

EA. Right! While I get things started, why don't you shower and shave? You can use Fred's bathroom and help yourself to his wardrobe. What you had on at the medical center wasn't worth salvaging.

Following my "breakfast-lunch," I have an uncontrollable desire to go walking over the farm. A fresh blanket of snow draws me into the open with the same urgency that old Vienna's streets used to call Beethoven from his composing into the cold air and inspiration of a winter's walk. From Fred's closet I further abstract a topcoat, gloves, scarf, boots, and a woolly hat. At the front door, I give Big Cat a polite little kiss on the tip of her nose. She wishes me a happy voyage and promises to call me with her dinner bell in several hours when Robinson and Mr. A. are expected to arrive. As I walk through the snow, all the beautiful sights and sounds are trying to tell me something. They seem to be saying, "Take heart, Beethoven. . . . In spite of the snow and cold wind, the winter of your new life is over. . . . Arise . . . grow . . . be happy yet again in the genuine creativeness of a new spring!"

There are 8,233,035 Subsidiary Cultural Planets . . . 21,485 Pre-Cultural Planets. . . . As I walk through the snow, my mind recalls many of the startling facts Paul Rezler has learned about these SCPs and PCPs, as well as other preparations Aaron has made to facilitate the adjustment of Earthlings to Second-Order life. The purpose of my walking meditation is to try to rationalize old Beethoven into accepting physical transfer to a Subsidiary cultural planet as the only possible solution to his dilemma. There's no hope of changing the entire structure of Second-Order music to suit him. As things now stand, nothing or no one could convince him to return to BEETHOVEN, or to settle down on a campus and act like a professor of music. Nor is strong drink the answer to his problem. Such a path leads only in the direction of his father and his grandmother. No doubt about it, Robinson will recommend an SCP for Beethoven. And my job now is to convince the "big I" within me that there's nothing at all calamitous about such a recommendation.

The planned death and spiritual absorption of a Subsidiary being for the specific purpose of enhancing the intellectual and spiritual growth of a Second-Order Major Aaronian would no doubt seem like an immoral act to any person who is not properly oriented into the philosophy behind such a procedure. One must understand that the prime reason for the very existence of these Subsidiary beings is to come to the aid of Aaronians who are having difficulty adjusting to the realities of Major Second-Order life. And such an Aaronian is Beethoven.

My mind recalls an entire sequence of important schoolboy facts that now help me see the proper relationship between Aaron's Major system and its countless Subsidiary cultures within the Minor Order. Our immediate First-Second-Order universe consists of three concentric spheres. The innermost of these is the solid space known as our Second-Order Major universe. Within this space, 51,329 prophets have established and given their names to Second-Order Major components of completely independent life systems. The 51,327th of these is the Major-Order component founded by our own Prophet, Aaron. Three hundred fifty-one of the six hundred planets comprising his system proper are within the Aaronian galaxy. (These include the Administrative Planet, 205 Cultural Planets, 101 Supply Planets, and 44 Educational Planets.) Beyond these are 249 Vacation Planets scattered among different galaxies of our Second-Order-Major universe. Upon these six hundred planets dwell the Aaronians, a race of Second-Order beings fathered by the same Prophet who procreated human life on Earth. To the spiritual subelectrons of these Aaronians, the spirits of Earthlings (freed by death) are electromagnetically attracted. Such is the destiny of Earthly souls who acquire a predominance of positive patterns, enabling them to reach the MAJOR ORDER of a second life. The very purpose of this plateau of Aaron's system is to provide each Earthling born into it an opportunity for maximum growth, leading hopefully to death and rebirth into the MAJOR ORDER of a third life within our Prophet's planetary structure. Because of the vast diversity existing among First-Order humans, it's impossible to design a single culture to which all of them will happily adjust. As ideally as our present plateau is structured, only about 60 percent of us manage to spend the entirety of our Second-Order days within its bounds. What about Beethoven and the other 40 percent?

For these poor souls, 8,233,035 Subsidiary Cultural Planets (most within separate galaxies, all within the Second-Order MINOR universe) have been carefully selected and sown with plants, animals, and humans whose life spans (like those of Earthlings) are usually less than a hundred years. From this unbelievable array of Subsidiary cultures, Beethoven and his companion 40 percent are able to select precisely those situations conducive to their maximum Second-Order growth. Transfer to an SCP is serious business, and in each case involves the death and spiritual absorption of a Subsidiary being whose place in life is then secretively occupied by the particular Aaronian effecting the transfer. Such use of human life sounds cruel and selfish, unless one realizes that this tiny harvest is the sole reason for planting huge crops of Subsidiary beings.

Continuing my walk through the snow and still busily snooping for spring, I try to imagine what a Subsidiary transfer could mean for Beethoven. The first problem is one of selection. From 8,233,035 SCPs, we must choose one to set me down upon where I'll be able to grow at *least* as productively as I once grew on Earth. After discussions with Robinson, I'll be asked to submit extensive data for computer analysis at the Subsidiary Transfer Center on Aaron AP. The ideal planet for Beethoven will then be selected and, unless I'm mistaken, will present conditions much like those which I left behind on Earth. From the Population set of this planet, a Subsidiary musician will be carefully chosen—the very man whom I'm to replace within his own culture. Soon after his selection, Mr X will be whisked from his surroundings, anesthetized, sped to the nearest D-R Chamber (whose existence and location on his planet are known only to the Aaronians), and transported to a special Aaron AP subelectronics lab within whose facility he will come to a painless death by the instantaneous transfer of his spiritual subelectron to my brain.

Though I'll still be only a Second-Order being, as of this instant, my spiritual composite will be tripartite: besides the talents developed and the memories recorded as Paul Rezler, I shall have at my disposal the total talents and spiritual patterns of Beethoven and Mr. X. By use of subelectronics, the entire surface of my body will be transformed identically to that of Mr. X, and I'll take my place among his family and friends without their ever knowing that a transfer has been made! I'm tempted to feel sorry for Mr. X, considering it unfair that his independent life should be snuffed out for the sake of my growth and my happiness. But then I stop and think for a moment.

The life of only one Subsidiary being in fifty million is used in this way. All the others must live out their days without really knowing why they were born, or what is the meaning of life and death or the joy of anticipating rebirth. Like typical First-Order beings (upon reaching the age of twelve to eighteen years), their spiritual subelectrons do not develop the capacity for attracting spirits of a lower order. In fact, the reverse is true. At the conclusion of Subsidiary life, their souls are attracted to the FIRST SUBELECTRONIC RING of our FIRST-SECOND-ORDER UNIVERSE, thence to be reborn as FIRST-ORDER infants on Earth or some other planet of the 51,329 LIFE SYSTEMS functioning within galaxies of our FIRST-ORDER UNIVERSE. While these former Subsidiary beings live through their normal (naturally procreated) First-Order and Second-Order lives, they have no recollection of the Subsidiary patterns recorded within their souls. Only upon rebirth into the THIRD ORDER of their particular life stream will they become conscious (through total recall) of the Subsidiary lives they have lived.

No. . . . Mr. X is not the one to feel sorry for. By taking up a new life within Paul Rezler, he gains much and loses nothing. The scheme of things continues exactly as it had before his translation, except that now he faces the equivalence of a Second-Order life among First-Order beings. Combining the physical stamina and intelligence of Rezler with the drive and power of Beethoven, how can he not now succeed at any musical task he sets himself to do? And why feel sorry for a successful man?

The wind is cold, but the sun is bright; and I've pretty well convinced old Beethoven to join Rezler in sharing things with Mr. X. Translation will benefit the three of us, and it's certainly more promising than wine and beer and self-pity. As I stand there viewing clumps of the small garden that will soon become Mr. A.'s spring planting, the sound of Big Cat's dinner bell rides the wind past my ear—Robinson has arrived! Spring has at last come to the dragging winter of my Second-Order life!

After dinner, Robinson and I are sitting opposite each other—alone in Mr. A.'s study. The time has come for our serious discussion:

Ro. Well, Rezler . . . by now you must think I'm not much of a counselor.
B. Why?
Ro. You've been through hell, and I haven't raised a finger to help you.
B. The fault is mine. I've never called upon you.
Ro. How nice of you to look at things this way. Would that others on my list did the same.
B. It makes sense. How can you be expected to come when no one calls you?
Ro. You'd be surprised. Counselors are expected to see and do all things! But you know, Paul . . . from my own experience, I've learned to stay away from a given problem until I'm called in by the individual himself, or by a very close friend.
B. And in my case?
Ro. Mr. Adams. He came personally and described your dire condition as reported by his wife.
B. Were you surprised?
Ro. Not really. Ever since I read of your decision to set Beethoven against BEETHOVEN, I knew you were in for a rough time. Whatever made you think you could change our whole structure of corporate music?
B. On Earth, I had no trouble changing things. Why not here?
Ro. German music and that of a six-hundred-planet culture aren't quite the same thing!
B. As I now well know!
Ro. Why weren't you happy at BEETHOVEN?
B. The old ego, I suppose. . . . For Beethoven to "play soldier," he must be generalissimo, and no one else.
Ro. Then what's holding you back? If you're not BEETHOVEN's top general, I'd like to know who is. Think of the freedom you'd have there. Apart from supervising production, you'd be entirely on your own. You could compose all the new music your heart desires, have it performed and recorded by experts, then use it to plot the future course of your firm. Why not claim your generalship at BEETHOVEN?
B. No. . . . I shall never return there! Had I earned the position, yes! But not as a gift of respect for the Earthly Beethoven.

Ro. I'm sorry you feel this way. How about a professional career? Think how they'd welcome you at EP 20, . . . especially at M93.

B. No thanks. I couldn't stand the formalities of supervising teachers!

Ro. There's only one alternative left.

B. SCP, here I come!

Ro. Exactly! Do you think we can sell Beethoven on a Subsidiary transfer?

B. It seems like the cowardly way to win a battle, but at least it's better than the past three months. Just before you arrived, I was walking across the farm. As I walked, I did some careful talking to old Beethoven. I think I've convinced him that a Subsidiary life is the only constructive path remaining for him here in the Second Order.

Ro. Good! This makes *my* job a lot easier. . . . But you're wrong in one respect—there's nothing cowardly about translation to a Subsidiary culture. Aaron would never have established 8,231,000 Subsidiary populational systems just to accommodate a bunch of cowards. They're there to provide essential growth opportunities for the nearly 40 percent of us who can't adjust to Second-Order life within our system proper. And people who can't adjust aren't necessarily cowards. What sort of culture do you think will best suit our Beethoven?

B. I think what he most needs is to take up things once again where he left them on Earth.

Ro. You mean toward the end of his Third Period?

B. Yes. . . . But this time without the illness, the deafness, the poverty . . . the responsibility of a wayward son! Combine his best musicianship with a set of decent conditions, and you'll have the most prolific Beethoven ever to pick up a pen. All the potential greatness that sang through his Earthly soul will at last be realized in tones!

Ro. This sounds like we should go looking for a Vienna of about 1820.

B. Wonderful! Will you have trouble finding one?

Ro. We shouldn't. Not with a million of them sitting out there. The big problem will be to select *precisely* the Vienna best suited to Beethoven.

B. How do you mean?

Ro. Well, for example, consider the one little item of cultural growth rate. Shall we choose an 1820 Vienna on a slow-paced planet that will hardly reach its 1850s by the year 2000? . . . Or would Beethoven prefer an 1820 Vienna on a fast-moving planet that will be far into its space age by 1900?

B. That's hard to say.

Ro. Damn right it's hard to say! Such problems are the reason for our extensive questionnaire. Only Beethoven and a lot of careful thinking can supply the answers.

B. Is this the famous five-hundred-page deal?

Ro. Actually, it's now closer to six hundred pages.

B. It'll take me a month to fill out!

Ro. Some people *do* spend a month on it. But considering what's at stake, this is well and good.

B. I suppose it's a job for Aaron AP.

Ro. Not necessarily. Let me send you one here. You can be filling it out while you're enjoying "Spring and recovery" on the farm.

B. Do you think Mrs. A. would mind?

Ro. I'm sure she wouldn't. The way her husband talks, they plan to keep you here for at least a month.

B. Good! Then this is what I'll do. How long should it all take?

Ro. You mean the entire transfer?

B. Yes.

Ro. Oh, I'd say about six or eight weeks. . . . If your questionnaire is in my hands by the end of February, it should take us another month to get things set up. With any luck at all, we'll have you back in old Vienna before April.

B. I can't believe it! A real chance to be Beethoven again. . . . A chance for my talent to win me an honest place among musicians, not some highly respected spot earned by the glitter of an Earthly reputation. I should have come to you long ago!

Ro. No! The time wasn't right. . . . There were some important things you had to find out for yourself. That's why I didn't come to you. (*In his typical "very busy" manner, Robinson stands up and offers me his hand.*)

B. Surely you're not leaving?

Ro. I must. I've got two other appointments lurking. Yours was strictly an emergency, you know.

B. Well, thank God you came, Robinson. A half hour with you has saved an old musician's life.

Ro. Not really, Herr Beethoven. You and Rezler had everything worked out before I got here. But I'm glad I came. No culture can afford to lose its great musicians. . . . I'll drop your questionnaire in the mail today, then we'll get together next month and prepare Beethoven for his new home.

No sooner had Robinson left than Judy phones from Phillipsburg's D-R, informing us that she'll arrive within the hour. When she does so, the two of us go for a cozy walk across the moonlit snow. She is very anxious to discuss my recent decision in favor of Subsidiary transfer.

B. Be honest, Judy. What do you really think of Subsidiary life?
JA. I think it's the most wonderful gift Aaron has left to his children. Without such provision, there are many of us who would find it impossible to cope with Second-Order life.
B. Specifically, in my case . . . do you think I'm being a coward?
JA. By no means, Paul. No one's a coward who's had the patience and strength to bear what you've borne for the past twenty-five years. I knew from the beginning that not even Beethoven could change the entire structure of Aaronian music. Yet you had to find this out for yourself. Now the learning and the suffering are over, and the great musician within you will begin to grow once more.
B. Then you're not angry with me?
JA. I'm happy for you. All I'm angry about is the past three months. I had no idea things had broken down and that you were suffering so. . . . You should have called me to your side. What good am I if I can't be of help during the hours of your greatest need?
B. The way I felt, I couldn't face anyone. Not even you. . . . But tell me, Judy, how will this affect our engagement? I realize that you're duty-bound to remain here at REMBRANDT. It's impossible for you to *leave*; it's impossible for me to *stay*. I'm off to the ancient culture of a distant planet for God knows how many years. And it doesn't seem fair to leave you sitting here, waiting and wondering.
JA. There's nothing unfair about it, Boo. I'll not be just sitting here. I'll be growing, and so will you. Each of us in an environment best suited to his needs. And as soon as you've mastered Beethoven, we'll know what to do about our proposed marriage.
B. And what if I *never* get him to settle down?
JA. We'll follow our original plan. I'll wait until 1927—your hundredth rebirthday. If we're not by then man and wife, I'll

return your ring to our throne on Valhalla, and we'll consider our long and happy engagement finally broken.

B. You're sure this is what you want?

JA. Yes, Paul. This is exactly what I want.

B. Very well, my dear. . . . So *be* it!

Chapter 43

On March 12, I receive a call from Robinson. I'm to report to Aaron AP on Thursday the eighteenth for a three-day discussion of and a one-day visit to the "1820 Vienna," which has been selected for me. I see detailed films and am exposed to countless bits of information concerning my prospective SCP. Especially informative are my discussions with Robinson.

Ro. Based upon your questionnaire, we think we've picked the ideal Vienna for your new home, and precisely the right musician for you to "absorb."

B. Quick! Tell me about them.

Ro. The planet is known to us as SCP 7,900,111. It is known to its inhabitants as "Earth" (as is the case with nearly eight million of our SCPs).

B. What about its music and its musicians?

Ro. Hold your horses. We'll get to this little compartment soon enough. First, some general background. You indicated your need for a Vienna of about 1820, one that would stay that way for twenty to thirty years.

B. Yes. This will give me time to get my bearings—to begin growing once again in the tradition of the Earthly Beethoven.

Ro. Fine! Then we've found just the Vienna for you. From now until March 1876, the world culture of SCP 7,900,111 is scheduled to creep along at a snail's pace, covering in twenty-four years only ten years of Earth's history from 1820 to 1830. This delays the close of what might well be another of Germany's period of greatest cultural glory and permits you to bask long and lovingly in the brightest sunshine of her classical humanism.

B. Ah . . . third-period Beethoven!

Ro. Precisely! The best works of your mature style are a musical representation of the ultimate flowering of Germany's classical humanistic tradition.

B. Twenty-four years of mature Beethoven. . . . This is perfect! Exactly the assignment I need to get me back on my feet. It's especially good since it fairly coincides with BEETHOVEN's plans here on Aaron for the next twenty-seven years.

Ro. You mean your firm's final tribute to the Earthly Beethoven?

B. Yes. They plan the premiere of a new third-period symphony for each of the next twenty-seven years. These they hope to pair off with new quartets or piano concertos. By 1880, this will amount to a monument of twenty-seven symphonies, eighteen quartets, and nine piano concertos—all in the tradition of my final Earthly style.

Ro. Then what?

B. Since I refuse to accept my position at their helm, Bonaparte plans to inspire them along some path of gradual evolution. He and his partners . . . God only knows where it will lead!

Ro. So you're going to parallel what your firm is doing here.

B. Better than parallel! I intend to *triple* their efforts on Beethoven's behalf. I'll show them what a man can do when he's given a personal relationship with his public and a talent slightly better than his fellows. I've set my goal as three times BEETHOVEN's tribute to Beethoven. I don't know what else I'll be able to do, but I'm planning on eighty-one symphonies, fifty-four quartets, and twenty-seven concertos . . . all by 1876!

Ro. Why so many?

B. To plant the foundation of my artistic growth and to win conclusively my battle with the corporate BEETHOVEN.

Ro. Won't it be difficult for such a versatile spirit as your Muse to create in the same style through so many works for so many years?

B. How do you mean?

Ro. Until 1876, you must not go more than a few measures beyond that spirit of late cassical humanism that you reached on Earth.

B. Have no fear. There's plenty for me to say without evolving into a later style.

Ro. Good! This is the prime restriction placed upon your composing for the next twenty-four years. The music of your chosen SCP is not to reach its Age of Romanticism until after 1876!

B. But wouldn't you say that third-period Beethoven *is* an expression of Romanticism?

Ro. Not in the out-and-out sense of say, Schubert, Schumann, Mendelssohn, Chopin, or Liszt. These men are pure romanticists. Their compositions are 99 percent Sehnsucht—each bar yearns for the unattainable, each melody pleads for the irrevocable, each harmony melts into fanciful dreams. For them, feeling is everything! The human heart is the key to their music.

B. Does it not also unlock the door to my *Ninth Symphony*, my *Missa*, and my last quartets?

Ro. Certainly! I don't wish to imply that your music is lacking in feeling or imagination. But beneath it all is the great spirit of the Classicists.

B. Bah! . . . To me, the classicist is a timid soul who follows his books of rules, formulas, and established patterns as though they were the one true road to heaven. Surely in your judgment, I've gotten beyond this state of affairs.

Ro. You have indeed. Your greatest works remind me of a giant classical cathedral, filled with the warmth and spirit of true Romanticism, yet admitting none of the self-doubts or inherent weaknesses of the undisciplined romantic soul.

B. A kind of classical romanticist?

Ro. Exactly! And this is the spirit in which you must compose for the next twenty-four years.

B. Then what?

Ro. Perhaps by then you'll be ready to return to Major-Order life among the Aaronians.

B. And if I'm not?

Ro. Wait and see.

B. It's not my purpose to seek a permanent shelter in which to live. Just enough time to put down my roots and start growing again. I feel that I've abandoned the mainstream of Aaronian life—an admission that corporate art is too much for my soul to bear. But I must prove that I'm at least strong enough to endure once more the artistic challenges of "life on Earth."

Ro. Such demands could well run counter to your maximum artistic growth.

B. Good enough! At least I'll have the feeling that I'm not running away from everything in Second-Order life. Now come on, Robinson, tell me about my new home. What's the music really like? Who are the chief musicians? What about this "Mr. X" I'm soon to become?

Ro. All right. But first, more general background, a little of your SCP's recent history. The Germany into which you are translating has just evolved from a mosaic of more than two thousand political subdivisions, ranging in size and power from large secular principalities to small village-size territories ruled by imperial knights. The French Revolution and Duvalian Wars have done more than anything else to integrate this maze into a present-day total of thirty-seven states. The larger of these states include Bavaria, Württemberg, Baden, Mecklenberg, and Saxe-Weimar. But the two most powerful (and those which vie for political leadership of Germany) are, of course, Austria and Prussia. Because of this rivalry, your new homeland is still torn by southern Catholicism versus northern Lutheranism. The House of Kreps rules Austria through the Court of Vienna; the Klinebergs rule over Prussia and have their court at Berlin. Both states had joined together in their "people's war" of liberation in which the French emperor Duval was defeated at Leipzig and thence driven all the way to Paris, where he was obliged to abdicate his throne. But now that the French invader has been expelled, the War of Liberation has lost much of its impetus. The Germans have ceased to be Germans and have gone back to being Austrians, Prussians, Hannoverians, Bavarians—each clinging to his individual sovereign prince for the peace and security he needs.

B. Then there's little hope for democracy in my new homeland.

Ro. I'm afraid so. Running true to form, the Germans' love for monarchical authority stands head and shoulders above their desire for liberty and human rights. Austria, under Joseph IV, is the real power over the Germany to which you translate.

B. What of Prussia?

Ro. At present, she is strictly subservient to the Court of Vienna.

B. And how long will this last?

Ro. Probably at least for the duration of your classical humanistic period. Even so, Prussia has had a notable reawakening. Her peasantry has been emancipated from serfdom. Her Municipal Act has laid the foundation for modern local government. She builds a system of national education, culminating in the founding of a National University at Berlin. Her middle class grows in number, in education, and in wealth. Although three-fourths of her population still live in the country, her newly acquired territories in Westphalia and along the Rhine show probable signs of future economic greatness. Her "industrial revolution" is delayed by the lack of suitable trade routes, by poor communications, by a scarcity of capital investments, and (chiefly) by the deadening effect of unbelievable customs barriers! She attempts to lessen these barriers by abolishing internal dues and by reducing shipping tolls on the Rhine.

B. Then Prussia is growing toward the industrial and political leadership of Germany!

Ro. Yes! The East-West division of her provinces practically demands that she become the leading force in German unification. Considering the well-trained and disciplined Junkers within her civil service and officers' corps, I have little doubt as to the eventual outcome . . .

B. And this new German state . . . what if it ends up a democracy?

Ro. Not a chance! The Germans have yet to be weaned from their strong diet of princely absolutism; they've never cultivated a genuine taste for human rights, democratic ideology, popular sovereignty.

B. I'm not so sure about this!

Ro. You should be! Old Beethoven was typical.

B. I resent that, Robinson. Beethoven was no such thing. He used to dream of becoming the citizen of a worldwide democracy . . . of moving far beyond the narrow confines of a single fatherland, ruled over by one little king.

Ro. So you've been reading Schiller.

B. I've read Schiller, but my views are my own. I believe in world citizenship, common brotherhood, universal peace, individualism, and the supremacy of art and science over politics.

Ro. This is exactly what I mean. Like most Germans, you think politics is a dirty word! You give lip service to world democracy, but aren't willing to pay the price for it.

B. What price?

Ro. The price of doing battle. Show me the German who would sacrifice his life for the sake of human rights.

B. There are many such.

Ro. I doubt this. Most of you view politics either with suspicion or with complete indifference. Now that your War of Liberation is over, you seem perfectly willing to return to your former bourgeois state of affairs, bowing to princely absolutism as though it were the will of God!

B. Democracy, monarchy—what's the difference? One political state is as good or as bad as another. What we German artists hope to build is a true Kulturnation—a state devoted entirely to the realm of poetry, art, music, philosophy, and metaphysics!

Ro. But this is impossible!

B. Why?

Ro. Because nations (like people) can't live in complete isolation from their neighbors. Germany is surrounded by political states. Regardless of her spiritual preference for art and science, she too must eventually become a political unit.

B. When the time comes, she will. Why worry about it?

Ro. German romanticism is a dangerous road to German nationalism.

B. Romanticism is as wide as Europe itself! What's so dangerous about the German variety?

Ro. If your new Fatherland follows the path of her more advanced predecessors, I fear that Romanticism will become for her an all-embracing way of life. As such, it will influence not only her music, art, and literature, but also her science, her economics, and perhaps even her politics.

B. What if it does? The more poetic and aesthetic a thing becomes, the more real it is. If German politics is romanticized, so much the better. This will deliver it from the realm of mechanization and materialism. It will become a sentimental thing, filled with life and emotion. Then you'll see how seriously we Germans can take our politics.

Ro. This is what I fear most!

B. What?

Ro. Such a blend of emotion and politics will give rise to the God-almighty leader, and away you'll go as a nation!

B. There's nothing wrong with a Great Mogul . . . a Führer. . . . So long as his spirit is aesthetically true, he will cast an emotional spell, and our Kulturnation will follow him like a mighty army.

Ro. Exactly . . . to its doom!

B. You worry needlessly, Robinson. People hunger for an exemplary individual to rally around, much like a family of planets has need for its sun. Without being the absolute center of my own little Court, I could never have achieved as a musician. The Earthly Beethoven was a monstrous dictator, yet no great evil came of this.

Ro. Art can survive her little tyrants, but not politics. Wait and see, Herr Beethoven. Following 1876, your new Fatherland is keyed to duplicate the Germany of Earth. Unless I miss my guess, you'll soon have your fill of tyrannical leaders. I won't be at all surprised to hear you knocking at our gates, begging to assume the responsibilities of the corporation that bears your name.

B. I doubt if things go *this* far, but we'll see. . . . Tell me about the music and musicians of my new Vienna.

Ro. You'll find music, literature, the stage, poetry, and philosophy much the same as they were on Earth during the 1820s. All the great artists creating in these fields have sprung from the ranks of bourgeois society. As such, their lives and works portray the very spirit of dedication, duty, self-sacrifice, and secularization that has characterized the best of the classical humanistic tradition on Earth.

B. Have they their "Schiller" and "Goethe" figures?

Ro. By all means. Georg Westphal was their "Schiller"; he returned here to Aaron just three years ago.

B. In other words, their "Schiller" is dead.

Ro. Correct. Paul Muchnik is their "Goethe," who is very much alive and producing at the present time.

B. Have they no "Beethoven"?

Ro. No! That will be *your* job. But they do have a "Mozart" who has practically evolved into a "second-period Beethoven."

B. What's his name?

Ro. Howard Black, known on your SCP as Roth von Collins.

B. Will I meet him?

Ro. I'll say you will. He's going to be our main springboard for launching your new "Beethoven" career.

B. And who is this new "Beethoven" I'm to become?

Ro. We've picked out an ideal eighteen-year-old for you. His name is Mason Voskamp.

B. Is he a native Rhinelander?

Ro. No. He was born and bred in Vienna and is 100 percent Austrian. He has done no composing of consequence, but he's a fine violinist and is on the regular staff of the Burgtheater Orchestra.

B. He's single, of course.

Ro. Yes. According to our records, he's not even romantically involved. You'll find him very close to the composite specifications of your questionnaire: eighteen, single, living with his parents, one more year at the conservatory, an orchestral musician, at the threshold of a promising musical career, which has yet to take a specific direction.

B. Good! When do we go spying on this young fellow?

Ro. On Sunday. We'll spend the entire day in old "Vienna," and we'll attend an afternoon concert at the Burg. This will give us a chance to observe your new self as your chief contemporary in action.

B. Is von Collins also a member of the orchestra?

Ro. No. He'll be conducting, and will appear as piano soloist.

On Sunday morning, March 21, I'm scheduled to meet Robinson at the Subsidiary Transfer Center. I'm to be there at 6:00 AM, and as I ride along in the speeding subway, my mind recalls certain earlier trips to Vienna. How different, and yet how much the same. Those of 1787 and 1792 were made in a clumsy mail coach, requiring days of smelly lurching and bumping. Today's journey is by D-R Chamber. It requires the turning of a dial, the pressing of a button, and no time at all! On the earlier trips, I was a monstrously ambitious "two-gunner" who felt like a green little boy from the farm; today I'm a world-famous musician who feels like a green little boy from the farm. At six fifteen (to disguise ourselves), Robinson and I don the early nineteenth-century garb of English gentlemen. I question my mentor's choice:

B. Englishmen? . . . In Vienna?

Ro. Yes. This will be our excuse for two strangers suddenly appearing at the Burgtheater from out of nowhere.

B. How's that?

Ro. I'm "Lloyd Smith" and you're "Harold Banes." We're from London, and we're traveling the continent interviewing potential string players for the Philharmonic.

B. I see. . . . This gives me a reason for making conversation with young Voskamp.

Ro. That's right. We consider it absolutely essential for an Aaronian to come face-to-face with his "future self" before effecting a transfer.

B. Sounds spooky.

Ro. You'll enjoy it—a traumatic experience if you've ever had one. At present, your SCP contains 241 carefully concealed D-R Chambers. For obvious reasons, we can't provide you with a list of these. Here are the addresses of the three located in your new homeland: one in Vienna, one in Graz, and one in Linz. You should memorize these, then destroy the slip. As you use other D-Rs, you'll automatically become familiar with their locations. Now as to identification. As you know (unless waived by the College of Counselors itself), each Major-Order Aaronian visiting or actually living upon an SCP is required to exhibit his Second-Order status in a way that is clearly discernible to other Aaronians on the same planet. Throughout our Prophet's system, the standard symbol used for this purpose is a gold and ruby ring (of countless different designs), worn on the fourth finger of the right hand. Let's try yours on for size.

It's no surprise to me that the fit is perfect; ring-finger measurements were supplied in my questionnaire. At the center of the beautiful stone (plainly visible through its face) is a blackish-purple A from the Aaronian alphabet.

B. *A* stands for "Aaron." Do you mean to say, Robinson, that this *A* is actually invisible to the First-Order beings among whom I'll be living?

Ro. Precisely! If as Beethoven you had examined such a ring on Earth, you too would have found not the trace of an *A*. The wavelengths reflected by this particular shade of blackish purple are to First-Order eyeballs indistinguishable from the wavelengths reflected by the color of the stone itself. If a Subsidiary citizen of your planet should examine this ring, he would observe nothing but a clear red stone; if a Second or higher-order being did the same, he would immediately spot the Aaronian *A* . . .

Convincingly bedecked in British raiment, we each take up suitcases filled with more of the same and translate to my new planet. Our "Viennese" D-R Chamber is hidden in the subbasement of the Waldmüller Kaffehaus located in the heart of the Graben. There in a tiny room containing the chamber, Robinson strokes his chin approvingly.

Ro. Ah, we've arrived. See that red number, 139?

B. What are we waiting for?

Ro. Easy! Don't forget that D-R processes are carefully hidden from the Subsidiary population. On the other side of this door, you'll probably find a room disguised to look like some sort of storage bin, with the door itself passing for part of the wall, and with all the D-R apparatus carefully concealed beneath its floor.

B. So?

Ro. So we can't simply go walking through the wall. One never knows who might be on the other side.

B. And that's what this button's for?

Ro. Correct. We push it, and wait for the local operator to open the door from *his* side.

B. And who might this be?

Ro. Here in "Vienna," our center is manned by Kurt Zweig and his wife. To the local population, they are merely the proprietors of a kaffehaus; but to us Aaronians, they are Paul and Georgia Fearon, an elderly couple from CP 37, here to fulfill the twenty years of their supplementary assignments.

B. Instead of twenty years of farming, like the Adamses.

Ro. That's right. Nearly two-thirds of our Aaronians translate to SCPs while serving their subordinate years.

B. Why so many?

Ro. How better can Aaron AP direct the affairs of its Subsidiary planets than through the mass translation of Aaronians?

B. How many of us are now here on assignment?

Ro. Counting yourself, there are at present 98,807 Aaronians here for psycho-spiritual redevelopment. These are the ones for whom the very planet exists!

B. Correct! Then there are 1,201,055 of us here, satisfying the twenty or more years of our subordinate assignments.

Ro. These Aaronians help mold the destiny of SCP 7,900,111 and cause it to move in the precise direction designated by our Administrative planet.

B. Over a million Aaronians . . . each with a ruby ring?

Ro. Yes. You'll have no trouble identifying them.

B. Damn this door! Shouldn't we push the button again?

Ro. Once is enough. The signal is on and will stay on until we're admitted. Remember, the Zweigs are busy people. They might both be in the midst of a conversation with little "Earthlings" who do not have ruby rings. They can't always respond to our instant beck and call. If the waiting grows wearisome, our only recourse is to return to Aaron, then come back later in the day. You realize it's impossible to transfer from this chamber to—look! . . . There's the admit signal! Herr Zweig is on his way!

In about two minutes, the heavy door slides open; on the other side is Frau Zweig, who graciously curtsies to us both.

FZ. Welcome to our SCP, gentlemen. You're just in time for lunch. I'm known here as Frau Agnes Zweig. My husband and I operate the Waldmüller Kaffehaus, which conceals "Vienna's" only D-R Chamber. What might be *your* names?

Ro. I'm Counselor Robinson from Aaron AP, and this is Paul Rezler. We've come to spend the day on your little planet.

FZ. Will you be needing a room?

Ro. Actually not. But since we're supposed to be visiting here from "London" and we'll be contacting a few musicians in the city, I guess we should have accommodations.

FZ. Good! I'll see that you're registered in room 32, and have your bags sent there.

Ro. (*Robinson reaches for Frau Zweig's right hand. He holds it out for me to see.*) Excuse me, Agnes, my young friend here can't believe there are enough ruby rings to go around.

FZ. Oh yes. We each have one. You'll have no trouble spotting a fellow Aaronian. See the big *A*?

B. Yes indeed. . . . But it's still hard to believe.

Frau Zweig closes the "wall" in front of the D-R Chamber, and we walk to the opposite side of what looks like an ordinary wine cellar. There she opens the "wall" at another spot, revealing a dingy narrow strip of stairway. Inside this opening, she points to two small sections of wooden molding:

FZ. You push here to open the door from inside; it automatically closes in thirty seconds. Pushing *this* piece opens the D-R Chamber, provided either Kurt or I have thrown the switch on our anklets.

Ro. I forgot to tell Rezler about these bits of ornamentation. May we show him yours?

FZ. You just want an excuse to peek at my poor old legs.

Ro. That's right, Agnes.

She removes her anklet and hands it to me. Robinson points to tiny knobs on the inner surface of the ornamental circlet.

Ro. See the electrodes? When we pushed that button in the D-R Chamber, these minute plates were activated, producing an almost negligible shock on the ankles of both Frau Zweig and her husband.

B. So this is how they know to answer their door?

Ro. Yes. And to be effective, at least *one* of them must remain within a mile of the kaffehaus at all times.

FZ. (*Our hostess readorns herself and again directs us toward the narrow stairs.*) Well, gentlemen. . . . Here's your doorway to old "Vienna." Be careful. The steps and corridor are very narrow; they are hidden within the walls of the building. After turning left, you'll notice eight illuminated numerals spaced at equal distances. These designate private rooms at the back of our inn. Number 7 is now ready for you; I've closed its curtain. Even so, before entering the sliding panel, I advise you to examine things through its one-way mirror. We can't be too careful about our secret. My husband will stop by to take your order. He'll want to meet both of you.

We follow Frau Zweig's instructions to the letter (or should I say, number), and sure enough, in about five minutes, Kurt Zweig enters our private accomodation through the parting of its wine-red opaque curtain. A towel over his left forearm gives him that typical headwaiter look.

KZ. Robinson! . . . This is a pleasure! I haven't seen you in over ten years! . . . Who's this young fellow?

Ro. One of our Aaronian musicians . . . name of Paul Rezler.

KZ. Paul Rezler? . . . You mean Herr Beethoven.

Ro. So you know!

KZ. Yes. We get little bits of news, here and there. I can still remember that headline about "Beethoven declaring war on BEETHOVEN." Well . . . that's one battle you'll lose, young man. But cheer up. There are plenty of others for you to win.

KZ. (*Herr Zweig crushes my fingers in a truly Rembrandtish handshake.*) It's a pleasure to welcome you, Herr Beethoven. What does it feel like to be "back home" again?

B. I can't believe what's waiting for me on the other side of that curtain: the same old world I knew and loved . . . the dear environment in which I grew. . . . It's as though I were born and then reborn for no other purpose than to pass through this door. You can't *imagine* the limitless hopes and dreams that await me on the other side.

KZ. My wife tells me that you've come for only one day.

B. Yes. But I plan to translate here in a week or so.

KZ. Wonderful! Then I have no doubt that our city will continue to be the musical capital of this world. Agnes and I are passionately fond of compositions in the Beethoven tradition—music such as is now being approached here by von Collins. Do you plan to follow in this path?

B. That's my plan . . . for twenty years, perhaps.

KZ. Good! A dream come true! Throughout the remainder of our Subsidiary assignments, my wife and I will both keep our ears cocked in your direction. Now for the sake of appearances, I'd better serve you gentlemen something. What will you have?

Ro. You order for us, Rezler. . . . It's been some time since you've visited a kaffehaus.

B. (*I glance down Zweig's noonday menu and can almost feel a boyish sparkle in my eyes.*)

That should be easy. We'll have *Linzer Torte, Mein Lieblingshonigkuchen, Apfelstrudel* . . . and to wash it all down . . . *Kaffee mit Doppelschlag*!

KZ. Fine! And I'll bring you each ten gold ducats. Can't go very far here on Aaronian dollars, you know.

While Zweig fills our order, his sudden comment about ducats inspires me to discuss monetary matters with my counselor:

B. You know, Robinson, it's going to seem strange once again having to pay money for everything. But I'll get used to it. The old rat-race will make a better man of me . . . a better musician.

Ro. If you care to earn and pay your way here, that's *your* business, but Beethoven's finances should never again be as frustrating as on Earth.

B. How do you mean?

Ro. Starting the first of April, your regular monthly salary of twelve hundred dollars will be credited to your account on Aaron AP. Any time you wish, you may draw "Viennese" ducats against that balance here at the Waldmüller Kaffehaus. Considering the favorable rate of exchange, this salary automatically assures you of great relative wealth for the duration of your SCP experience.

B. And if I don't care to *use* the money?

Ro. Many Aaronians don't. As I said before, it's your decision, but at least you know it's here in case of an emergency.

B. What if one of us should inadvertently divulge the hiding place of a D-R Chamber to members of the local citizenry? Then what?

Ro. Each D-R is expertly packed with extremely high explosives. In the event that a chamber is discovered by Subsidiary beings, the Aaronian operators responsible for that particular unit are morally obligated to completely destroy it, even at the cost of their own Second-Order lives! Should you or I be so disrespectful of Aaronian law as to bring a Subsidiary being to the subbasement of this building, then either Zweig or his wife would throw a switch on their anklet and reduce the entire block to a pile of dust.

B. I can't imagine that one of us would do such a thing, but it's nice to know there are safeguards. What are our plans until concert time?

Ro. It's now half past twelve; the Burg concert begins at three, and I know you're dying to go walking in the "Graben." Suppose right after lunch you go for your walk, and I'll make it my business to see von Collins. Through him, we'll get seats close enough to young Voskamp that you'll be able to form a genuine musical appraisal of your future self. During intermission or after the concert, I want you to strike up an acquaintance with the fellow. Remember to introduce yourself as Harold Banes, representing the London Philharmonic. One way or another, you're to have dinner with him, spend the evening with him . . . try to meet his family. I'll wait for you here in room 32. There's no hurry—stay as late as you wish. Considering the time differential, we should have little trouble arriving on Aaron at a convenient hour.

B. And Von Collins . . . am I to meet him today?

Ro. By all means. I'd like you to have an hour together before the concert. Plan to be at the Burgtheater by two o'clock. I'll see that Collins is there.

B. You're not going to tell him who I am, are you?

Ro. You mean, Beethoven?

B. Yes.

Ro. Why not?

B. That would make things as bad for me here as at Altburg; I'd be worshiped because of an Earthly reputation.

Ro. Not at all! . . . Except for Collins and the Zweigs, not a soul on this planet will know that Beethoven has arrived. Only two years remain of the thirty-six years in Collins's subordinate assignment. He was scheduled for an understudy six months before you decided to come here. The few little things he will do to get your career started, he would have done for *any* Aaronian successor—Beethoven or otherwise.

B. You mean things like accepting me as a pupil?

Ro. Accepting you as a pupil, sponsoring you in a concert or two, promoting your first compositions, finding you a publisher. . . . Then for the rest of your musical days here, you're entirely on your own. Beethoven's local achievements will be a true measure of his professional worth . . . not of his Earthly reputation.

B. Good! . . . This is exactly what I've dreamed of.. . . . We'll meet at the Burg then, at two o'clock.

After our feast of sweets and coffee, I exit from the Waldmüller Inn to inhale my first few breaths of a new life. How strange it seems once again to be alive and well in the "Graben" . . . to be the potential giant of a Second-Order musician among tiny quasi-Earthlings. Unfair odds, but it can't be helped; this is what it takes to get Beethoven growing again. How utterly nostalgic are the sights and sounds and smells of all the old familiar streets! From "St. Stephen's" to the "Swan," each building is "back in place" again. Just as before, there are horses and buggies instead of cars and trucks. I'm surprised at the loud noises of the city. Only the ears of a deaf Beethoven could have managed to compose among such clickety-clackety distractions. I can see that from now on, I'll be heading for the country with my little sketchbooks, not for downtown Vienna. As I go strutting along the cobbles in my thin British veneer, the handsome toning of Paul Rezler's Second-Order body shows through with remarkable clarity and attracts admiring stares from dozens of First-Order belles—even a few glances from members of the same sex. It's actually embarrassing thus to be physically superior to all those about me. When I next go walking on these streets, I shall have climbed into Voskamp's shell, and this should at least put an end to my embarrassment. Poor souls—how much they remind me of the population of Earth, busily flitting about in their broken-down bodies: stuffed and puffed in the middle from overeating and at the same time wrinkled and crinkled at the edges from malnutrition. In the entire Graben, I can't find a single physique past thirty-five that doesn't look "weary of life, but afraid to die." What a pity! Unhappy or (at best) briefly happy people who are born and who die without ever achieving a real confirmation of the infinite span of human life. Only a core of beings imported by Aaron from another system can be effectively used within our Second-Order Minor universe. How can these dear ones bear the stress and anxiety of human life without knowing what I now know? How I'd love to share with them the secret of my ruby ring. But if I did, they wouldn't believe me anyway.

I enter the Burgtheater at the stroke of two, at which time my counselor introduces me to Von Collins. I had half expected a gay little man in the lacy tradition of Mozart. But my chief contemporary turns out to be a serious, square-headed, big-boned, hairy peasant whose face and body remind me of pictures I have seen of the Earthly Schumann. As we shake hands, there is a mutual examination of ruby rings.

Co. This is a real surprise, Herr Beethoven. I knew that one day soon I'd be breaking in my immediate successor, but I had no idea he would be Beethoven himself. Robinson tells me that your translation is planned to absorb young Voskamp.

B. Yes. . . . What's he like?

Co. A very fine musician, an excellent violinist. Before my scheduled departure from this planet, I was going to recommend him to the post of concertmaster here at the Burg. But now I have no doubt that Beethoven has other plans for his new "self." Will you be switching him from violin to piano?

B. I don't know. . . . If Beethoven was a better pianist than Voskamp is a violinist, the answer is yes. . . . Otherwise, no. I'll have to wait and see. Robinson tells me that you've introduced several of my compositions here.

Co. Yes. Since my thirty-six-year subordinate assignment has been to bridge the gap between Mozart and second-period Beethoven, I was obviously the one to present a few of the more important compositions by each of these masters. Besides creating 105 pieces of my own in the Mozart-Beethoven tradition, I've taken credit for thirty-one Mozart compositions and twenty-nine of yours, which include Symphonies 3, 5, 6 and 7; the Violin Concerto; *Fidelio*; Piano Concertos 1, 3, and 4; eleven piano sonatas; and nine chamber pieces. Within the next two years,

I'm scheduled to introduce some new Aaronian "pupil," who (in turn) is supposed to evolve from von Collins into a "third-period Beethoven." This he will do under my tutelage by "composing" your *Missa Solemnis*, your *Fifth Concerto*, your *Eight* and *Ninth Symphonies*, and your last five quartets.

B. How unusual! This would put me in the position of recomposing my own best music.

Co. This *is* unusual. But it's a rare day when an artist of Beethoven's creative stature requests to relive a portion of his Earthly life within one of our Subsidiary cultures.

B. Since this is what I plan to do, why don't I change the name of Voskamp to that of Beethoven?

Co. Easier said than done. It's actually very difficult to translate an Aaronian name to a Subsidiary planet. The painful process is restricted exclusively to a handful of prophets, religious leaders, and philosophers whose lives on Earth have become the bases for important spiritual insights.

B. That's all right. . . . Beethoven, Rezler, Voskamp—it doesn't matter to me what it's called. The important thing is that for more than twenty years I'll be creating music in the style of my own Third Period, and I'll have the chance to bring it before a vast public that is preplanned to remain in the spirit of classical humanism for a like number of years. This will get me back on the right path, and this is all that will. When I show up in a week or so as Mason Voskamp, I take it you'll accept me as your pupil.

Co. I certainly will, then we'll make our plans. Having done some graduate work at M93 and EP 20, it has long been my dream to meet Herr Beethoven . . . perhaps receive a lesson from him. And now look what happens! Within a week, I'm to pretend I'm a teacher of the great Maestro himself.

I don't believe I have ever enjoyed a concert as much as this one. For our purposes, the seats are perfect: first row and an arm's length from the violin section. Collins begins the program by conducting his most recent symphony, No. 37 in D. This work is really one of his, but reminds me of an interesting hybridism of my own Third and Seventh Symphonies. As an original composition, there's not much to it; as an example of second-period Beethoven, it's a fine piece of writing. His conducting has a "Neefean" quality about it: precise, symmetric, restrained, perfect! My new sponsor then seats himself at the piano to conduct and perform his Twelfth Concerto. Although this opus is also a Collins original, it contains much of the same "sad laughter" that haunts the passages of my own *Concerto in G.* His playing is clear and beautiful in the Mozartian tradition. It often brings tears to my eyes—to think that Beethoven's life and work on Earth could so greatly influence the life and work of another musician on another planet in another universe!

During the performance of these two numbers, my attention is divided equally between the music and a handsome young violinist who sits within "touching" distance of my seat. There (practically at my knee) bows the young fiddler whom we've come to spy upon—Mason Voskamp! Because of the orchestral overtones, it's not possible for me to accurately appraise his individual playing, but I can tell that "Vos" is a young man who really loves his violin. He's taller and thinner than I had expected—almost "Lincolnesque." His hands are huge and packed with well-disciplined fingers that seem to have the added length of an extra joint or two. His face is strong and well-proportioned: cheerful blue eyes, a shock of blond hair parted neatly and combed toward his right eye, a pink complexion that is more the glow of health than a blush or the fever of hard work. How strange it is to sit there and examine the young musician I will soon become. I ponder the many ways in which my accumulation of two lives could influence his. I try to contemplate how the absorption of his spirit might possibly modify the determined path and self-centered schemes of the "Great Mogul." Could this busy little violinist make changes in Beethoven which Paul Rezler has been unable to effect?

Apparently, he feels the weight of my stare. Between movements of the symphony, he turns his face toward mine, and our eyes meet for the first time. Something unusual happens. Neither of us looks away. He smiles and nods politely, but never takes his eyes from mine. Our souls seem to speak to one another. It's almost as though he knows that I'm Beethoven and that I've come to lay claim upon his life. Of course, it's my imagination, but he actually seems to nod his approval of my plan.

At intermission, Robinson goes backstage to discuss some things with von Collins. Before Voskamp can leave his chair, I lean forward and tap him on the shoulder.

B. I say, young man . . . may I have a word with you?

V. Yes, Sir. I noticed you staring at me while I was playing. Are you a musician?

B. Of sorts. . . . My name is Harold Banes; I'm here representing the London Philharmonic.
V. Are you alone?
B. No. My associate, Lloyd Smith, is with me. He's gone to have a word with your conductor. The two of us are traveling Europe, recruiting young talent for our orchestra.
V. Surely you won't tempt our beloved Maestro from our midst.
B. Von Collins? No. He's too well established here for that. He belongs in Vienna.
V. Good! For a moment, I thought you'd come to steal away our soul.
B. Prophetic words, young man. But no, we're here in search of talents yet unrecognized. A talent such as yours, perhaps. . . . What's your name?
V. Forgive my bad manners. I'm Mason Voskamp, student at the Vienna Conservatory. This is my third year with the Burgtheater Orchestra.
B. Would you consider coming to London?
V. If the pay is better, yes!
B. Rather mercenary, aren't you?
V. Not really. Seven years ago, my dear mother was struck down by a speeding coach within one block of the Privy Court Chancellery. She recovered from her head injury, but has been totally blind ever since. Our family physician insists that a trip to Leipzig and an operation by Dr. Lüdenscheid at his clinic there would completely restore her sight. All that's holding us back is the necessary money for the venture. I hope this explains my lust for florins.
B. It certainly does . . . and a noble lust it is. Perhaps we can work something out. May I take you to dinner this evening?
V. Fine! Then I shall play for you.
B. Exactly what I was hoping. I'll meet you backstage after the concert.
V. Agreed! Now if you'll excuse me, Mr. Banes, I must get a breath of air before our performance resumes. We're about to play my favorite Collins symphony.

Think of it! Voskamp's favorite Collins symphony is none other than my own beloved *Pastoral.*

Robinson returns to his seat only minutes before the concert resumes. Somehow he finds time for a brief whispered interrogation:

Ro. Well? Did you strike up an acquaintance with Herr Voskamp?
B. Better than expected. We're to have dinner together, then he's to play for me.
Ro. Good! What do you think of him?
B. So far, so good!
Ro. If he meets with your ultimate approval, be sure to tell him that Herr Zweig will be contacting him.

The concert ends at five thirty. Briefly I introduce my "future self" to "Lloyd Smith," who then makes his departure under the guise of "urgent business." Vos and I have dinner together at the Gemütlich Kaffehaus in the suburb of Grinzing, where the young man's home is located. During our meal, Vos tells me about his family. He is an only child who lives with his mother and father in a modest apartment of the Hildebrandtstrasse. He has one more year at the local conservatory, after which he hopes to become a concert violinist—possibly a concertmaster or conductor. The family is poor, but they manage to put aside every spare florin for the mother's proposed eye operation. Voskamp senior is a fiddler at the Opera House. His income has always been low—so much so that he would prefer his son to be a "thief and murderer" rather than follow in his own musical footsteps. Not so the mother. She is very proud of her musician husband and prays that her son will continue the career he has begun.

After dinner, we visit Voskamp's home, where I meet both of his parents. Strangely, Herr Voskamp reminds me of my own Earthly father. Except for the mother's vacant stare of blindness, she is an unbelievable likeness of Madame Von Breuning. In both cases, it's "love at first sight," and I'm more than eager to accept the two of them as my newest "parents." In spite of the modesty of their third-floor apartment, its living room is typically musician-like: bare floors, uncomfortable chairs, a writing desk, a worn sofa, too many music racks, and a fine old Stein clavier. I accompany Vos in my *Kreutzer Sonata* and in my *Violin Concerto*—two works that on this planet are attributed to the respected pen of Roth von Collins. What great fun it is once again to play this music to an appreciative audience. At the conclusion of the concerto's first movement, I interrupt our performance with loud applause and a hearty embrace for young Voskamp. Before I realize what's happening, I clumsily blurt out a reference to my Earthly career:

B. Wonderful, Vos! You're a veritable Schuppanzigh!
V. Schuppanzigh? . . . This sounds like a disease of the foot!
B. (*To this comment, I respond with an explosion of coarse laughter—the kind that used to identify me at the Swan.*) Far from it, Vos. Milord Schuppanzigh is my favorite fiddler. And in your playing just now, I hear the budding mastery of one who will soon overtake him. I'm very pleased with what I hear!

After our performance, the four of us discuss possible plans whereby Vos will come to London for a "tryout" season. Since his pay would be three times greater than at the Burg, the father is all for it. A pitiable sad look crosses Frau Voskamp's countenance as she tries to imagine a long and lonely winter of separation from her son. She reaches for my hands and face; I kneel before her. After "seeing" me with her delicate fingers, her lips quiver, and soft tears descend from each of her closed eyelids.

Mrs. V. I can tell you are a great artist, young man. I hear it in your playing; I "see" it in your face and hands. . . . I beg of you, Harold Banes, do what you can for my dear son. Though his talent is smaller than yours, the love of great music truly dwells within him. He is a good boy, and is deserving of your help.
B. This I'll gladly do, Frau Voskamp. . . . Using whatever powers there are within me, I'll try to help your worthy son. Believe me, I shall.

I bid my prospective parents good night and go walking with Vos under the fresh spring stars. As we walk and discuss our future plans, I decide definitely in favor of the translation. This "musician's" violinist is the perfect Subsidiary being for old Beethoven.

B. I greatly admire your playing, Voskamp. You combine the virtuosity of a young man with the sensitivity and feeling of a much older player. I'm sure the Philharmonic will be pleased.
V. And I greatly admire *your* playing. There's something unusual about it.
B. How do you mean?
V. It lies on a higher plane than most. I've heard Collins play the "A Major," and tonight your interpretation reminded me of his.
B. In what way?

V. It wasn't like an ordinary accompaniment. You seem to have made a deep study of the work . . . almost as though you had composed it.

B. (*My companion's keen perception makes me gulp for breath.*) Thank you, Voskamp. . . . This is a fine compliment.

V. Great playing like yours and our Maestro's speaks a language of the spirit. It reaches my very soul.

B. You amaze me, Vos. Most young fiddlers your age are too busy with their scraping and scratching to admit they *have* a soul. Exactly what *is* the "soul" of a man?

V. My "soul" is what there is about me that's real. . . . Somehow I know it will outlive the few years we spend here called "life on Earth."

B. You really believe this?

V. I must, Banes. Otherwise there'd be no reason for the existence of all the treasures we know and love. Music, art, science—everything points in the direction of a plan much bigger than our brief experience here.

B. I wish more people shared your optimism.

V. If they did, then we'd have artists instead of suicides!

B. Keep talking, Voskamp. Maybe you'll convert me.

V. How can you walk under a sky such as this and doubt? . . . Just look at those stars; listen to what they're saying. Their message is the same as that of beautiful music. If I could understand the words of their cool tongue, then I'd know the meaning of all things. Since I am what I am, a tiny musician, all I can do is work and grow and hope—hope that *someday* I'll understand the joyous impact of their prophecy.

B. You do amaze me. . . . If you talk this way to some beautiful girl, she'll marry you on the spot!

V. I yearn to share these feelings with a sweetheart . . . but first comes my career and my dear mother. I must do something for her eyes. Do you really think there's a chance for me with the Philharmonic?

B. I'm sure there is. Anyone with your determination is bound to succeed. Someday soon, I know you'll have that operation for your mother. Wait and see. In the meantime, here are a few ducats left from our meal. Please accept them on her behalf.

V. Thank you, Banes. Why are you so kind to me?

B. I too had a mother whom I loved as you love yours. I lived for the day when I would earn the money to do some little kindnesses for her. But her cruel death robbed me of this chance. Is it any wonder that a small benevolence directed toward a sweet mother such as yours now brings me great pleasure?

V. I see. . . . Well, it's no less appreciated. . . . Here, you might as well take this hansom back to town. It's quite a walk, and I'm afraid I've kept you very late. When will I hear from you about the Londoners?

B. In a week or so, I'll contact you through Herr Zweig at the Waldmüller Kaffehaus. He'll arrange for a meeting between us.

V. Fine! . . . And thank you for the memorable accompaniment.

B. The pleasure was mine. Good-bye, Vos. . . . I'm sure we'll meet again soon.

V. I hope so. Say, you've given me all your money. How will you pay the driver?

B. Don't worry about that. I still have a few ducats at the Waldmüller. Good-bye, Vos.

V. Good-bye.

Bouncing along in the little cab, I feel tears on my cheeks. Why? Why should thoughts of a struggling young musician and his family bring tears to the eyes of Beethoven? They are tears of admiration. Voskamp is only an eighteen-year-old First-Order Subsidiary being, and yet (like Judy Adams) he has learned to read the eternal message of the stars and to interpret their optimism as the guiding force in his own life. What a profitable evening this has been for Beethoven. He has made up his mind. He will translate to SCP 7,900,111; and he'll be honored to do so as Mason Voskamp.

Robinson and I arrive at the Subsidiary Transfer Center by 8:30 PM, Aaronian standard time. It's still Sunday, March twenty-first, although I feel as though I've been away for a week. The date of my translation is set for Tuesday morning, March thirtieth at 7:00 AM. This means (considering the difference in time) the Zweigs must arrange for Voskamp to be in their D-R Chamber by noon of that day.

I return to the Adams farm for what could be my final week of Second-Order life in the Major Aaronian system. Judy takes leave of REMBRANDT in order that we might spend these joyful spring days together: working, dreaming, and planning. She is very busy with two landscapes of an important new series while I find myself completely absorbed in the happiness of fruitful symphonic sketching. Except for the altitude and precipitous footbridge, we're both reminded of our wonderful summer at Bernette, high in the mighty Schlessberns.

During this week on the farm, I also manage to write letters of farewell to Beethoven's close friends and loved ones who have arrived within the same order of Aaron's system. These include notes to Lobkowitz, Lichnowsky, Wegeler and the Breunings, Zmeskall, Schuppanzigh, Archduke Rudolph, and the Rieses. Without exception, I tell them of my planned translation to SCP 7,900,111. I want personally to inform them of the event before they read about it in the interplanetary news. Regardless of my passionate desire for reunions with these dear friends, I beg them (each and every one) not to come for a visit until Beethoven has built up some sort of victory to counteract his bitter defeat at the hands of corporate art. The tearful tone of all these notes is epitomized by the pleading sentiment of the "compound" letter that I send to the three surviving members of my Earthly family:

March 23, 1852

Dearest Mother,
Noble Grandfather,
Kind Brother Johann:

As each of you has probably suspected from the start, I have not been able to adjust the corporate structure of Aaronian music to the dictates of Beethoven's Earthly Muse. Here in our Major-Order culture, I am unable to continue the growth which was begun on Earth. I tried, and I failed. This failure has caused me great suffering and many tears. . . . The love which I have for each of you and my love for Miss Judy Adams—only these have nurtured me through the dark days of my pilgrimage. Without such undergirding love, I would have surely died. . . . I long to clasp each one of you to my breast, to feel you once more close to my heart. But I must do this as a victorious Beethoven, not as some poor little student whose shaking knees still betray the folly of his Second-Order ways. Where shall I find a victorious Beethoven? . . . Not here! I must seek him out in a Subsidiary culture, in the old Vienna he knew and loved. Only there can he once more live and grow toward a musicianship which is worthy of your love and respect . . .

One week from today, I'm scheduled for a translation to SCP 7,900,111. There I shall again sing the song of my true life's plan . . . take up the thread of my being, where it was cruelly severed twenty-five years ago. As young Mason Voskamp, I shall quickly evolve into the proud and creative artist you knew and loved on Earth. Just as soon as I can once more hold my head high among musicians, we shall observe the happy hour of our long-awaited reunion. Until that joyous moment, I *beg* of you not to come to your Beethoven. . . . For he is but half his former self, and cannot bear the gaze of your loving eyes.

Sooner than you think, dear Johann, I shall send you the concerto which you requested. It's hard to believe that my astute moneymonger of a brother has inherited the clean white spirit of a musician! Let us all continue to keep young Karl in our thoughts and prayers, that he may live a happy and productive life, thence join the four of us here in the Major Order. How I love the boy! He is still a "son" to me.

Wish me well as I begin my new journey. The past twenty-five years have been but a prelude to next Tuesday morning.

Your ever-loving
Son,
Grandson,
and Brother Ludwig.

News of my translation appears on the first page of Saturday evening's *Interplanetary*. Because of this, I'm not surprised that "guests" begin to arrive the very next morning. By Monday afternoon, all the Adamses and the Rezlers have joined Judy and me on the farm. Our long-delayed interfamily reunion finally does take place. It's especially wonderful to embrace the Rezlers once again. I haven't seen any of them since our Christmas celebration at Dogwood in 1848. Though Mother and Dad have fulfilled their Second-Order parental responsibilities, they still have the glow and vigor of handsome teenagers on fire with the creative demands of their full-partner status at Reed, Levin & Kosoff. Their practice carries them to hundreds of regular and Subsidiary planets of our system. Even so, they are able to make their principal residence on CP 25 at Dogwood.

Gina and Freeman both follow in the precise footsteps of our parents. They have completed their senior assistantships with the firm, are both now married, and have taken twenty-year leaves of absence for the rearing of their Second-Order families. Freeman is now the proud father of a two-year-old son, and Gina (as Mrs. Fred Rothfuss) is expecting her first child in three months. All the Rezlers seem well adjusted to my being Herr Beethoven. Gina especially has a profound respect for my Earthly inheritance; she practically worships the musician artist within me. Although my attendance at M93 convinced my family that I preferred music to architecture, not one of them suspected me of being the great Maestro until the famous "Beethoven vs. BEETHOVEN" article appeared in the Aaronian papers. Now the entire clan gathers to witness my translation.

We arrive on Aaron AP at 6:00 AM on March 30 and are met there by Robinson.

Ro. Herr Beethoven! . . . What a fine big family you bring with you . . . all here to say good-bye to Paul Rezler, and hello to Mason Voskamp. Well, we won't disappoint them. Your translation is scheduled for thirty-three minutes from now, so you'd better start your "good-bye-ing" right away. Incidentally, there are some other friends who have come to see you off. They're waiting for you in room 16, down the hall.

As I approach the designated room, my heart pounds in anticipation. Could it be that Mother, Grandfather, and Johann have come to see me in spite of my letter? Out of love for Beethoven, have the dear old members of my Earthly Court taken it upon themselves to dishonor my request? Would the opening of this door bring me face-to-face with the reborn spirits of Breuning, Lichnowsky, Ries, Zmeskall, Wegeler, Schuppanzigh, Lobkowitz, and my Archduke—send them crashing into my arms at a time when my soul is not yet ready to receive them? My fears are unwarranted. The bright little room contains not a single face unfamiliar to Paul Rezler. First comes Ray Culbertson. Dear old Culby! We shake hands and practically embrace one another. I reiterate my promise concerning his Beethoven ballet, and pledge to start work on it just as soon as I feel at home on my new "subordinate" legs. Next come the Grants. Marcie gives me a dainty kiss on my cheek; "King Richard" offers me his hand. As I make them a little farewell speech, the words come slowly and I can feel my throat tightening:

B. In a sense, I'm actually grateful for what you've done here in the name of BEETHOVEN. It's a pity that I can't be part of it. . . . Even so, I must regard your corporation as my mortal enemy. In the only way I know how, I go to do battle against him. . . . Let's hope that some good music will come of it all.

Neefe and Albrechtsberger are both there. My voice falters and my eyes dim with tears, as I say good-bye to these distinguished teachers:

B. Farewell, great masters of music. . . . I go to build upon what you've taught me here and on Earth. Whatever success or victory I might achieve belongs no less to you than to Beethoven. (*Next in line for a handshake is another roommate of mine.*) I'm glad you've come, Franz Schubert. This tells me that you've forgiven me my secrecy and my hypocrisy. . . . The good news and great music I hear from you and your firm make me very happy and proud. I wish you the best of good luck with your musical future and ask you to do the same for me . . .

Finally I'm greeted by those greatest of Earth's composers, Bach and Handel.

B. How wonderful of you to take the time to bid me farewell! You were the first musicians I met when I arrived here, and now you've come to say good-bye. Your Earthly careers did more than any others to inspire Beethoven's services to the Muse. Now, I sincerely hope that my Subsidiary career may do the same for musicians here on Aaron. . . . This is the true story of how artistic dedication is passed on from one generation to the next, eternal and immortal!

Suddenly, the room is filled with Judy's family and mine. Everybody is shaking hands with everybody—a joyous occasion altogether! Then comes Robinson, who interrupts the festivities.

Ro. Five more minutes, Rezler. . . . You'd better finish your handshaking and come along with me.

After a few more good-byes and a passionate embrace with Judy, I go with my counselor to a special soul-transference chamber in the subbasement of the Subsidiary Transfer Center. The huge white lab, crammed with apparatus, is not unlike an operating room. There are three technicians, an anesthesiologist, and two physicians in charge of the spiritual transplant. At seven fifteen, we are contacted by the Zweigs who inform us that Voskamp (anesthetized through a glass of wine) has been placed in their D-R Chamber, awaiting his physical transfer to Aaron AP. Within a few minutes, the young man's sleeping body arrives and is wheeled into a small cubicle next to the one in which I'm lying. At seven twenty-five, I'm put to sleep and awaken within ten minutes to find the spiritual transplant completed.

From head to toe, my body has been subelectronically disguised to be identical to that of Voskamp. My "soul" has reached the optimum composite available to it in the Second Order. It is now a tripartite spiritual subelectron, carrying within it a total recall of the fifty-seven years of Beethoven's days on Earth and a total recall of Voskamp's eighteen years on SCP 7,900,111. These patterns are inseparably fused with a limited recall of Rezler's forty-two years of life in the Aaronian system. The spiritual patterns of both Beethoven and Rezler are now conditioned to having those of Voskamp predominate. Though Vos is quite a handsome fellow by Earthly standards, Beethoven and Rezler stand entranced by the comparative imperfections (if not ugliness) of their new "body." In a full-length mirror, I'm still contemplating the nude image of my subelectronic disguise, when Robinson enters the cubicle.

Ro. Guten Morgen, Herr Voskamp!

B. Guten Morgen! . . . I can't believe it, Robinson. I see it with my own eyes, but I *still* can't believe it!

Ro. Naturally! For a while, it will seem to you as though Voskamp has absorbed Beethoven and Rezler instead of the reverse being true. This is because of your disguise and your plan to take up the thread of his life where he left off living it. But remember, what you see there is the living body of Paul Rezler. Beneath the subelectronic alterations of that skin of yours, still dwell the extrasense perceptions, the higher intelligence, and the greater sexuality of a Second-Order being. All these noble traits must be substantially concealed from the former Earthlings among whom you will now live. Be especially careful of your total recall of Voskamp's life. To reveal an excess of these patterns would make your fellow Subsidiaries suspicious to say the least.

B. And poor old Vos . . . is he now a corpse?

Ro. Yes. Do you wish to see him?
B. May I?
Ro. That's the usual first request of most of us who have made a spiritual absorption. Here, put these on. . . . They are Voskamp's clothes, or should I say, your clothes. And now you should start wearing your ring.

Robinson and I enter the adjoining cubicle, where a sheet is pulled down to reveal the dead body of Mason Voskamp. To Beethoven and Rezler, it's just another corpse; but to Voskamp, can you imagine the traumatic effect of such a sight? How shocking it is to view the still-warm temple that I had occupied for eighteen years on a Subsidiary planet!

B. What happens to this body?
Ro. We preserve it exactly as it is now, until you decide to make your permanent exit from SCP 7,900,111. When that time comes, we'll plan an event that will look like your "death" there, and this body will provide us with a "Voskamp" for burial.
B. In other words, it will someday be buried as my body!
Ro. Precisely! When Rezler finally decides to return to Aaron, we can't have Voskamp suddenly disappearing into thin air. This body and your simulated death there will put an end to the matter. Ever so gradually, we age your corpse a few wrinkles and a few gray hairs at a time. As soon as you bring about your permanent transfer back to Aaron, we'll withdraw this little body from cold storage, apply some final "ageing" modifications to it, and ship it off to take your place in a Subsidiary grave. . . . Go say good-bye to your family and friends, this time as Herr Voskamp. Won't they be surprised!

Next come fifteen minutes of cheerful handshaking and tearful embracing. These conclude with a final five minutes spent alone with Judy.

B. Shame on you, young lady, kissing a total stranger this way. What will Paul Rezler do when he finds out?

Judy tries to laugh, but her attempt dissolves into tears. How beautiful she is! Mason Voskamp has never seen such a girl, let alone held one in his arms. Those big blue eyes, always irresistible. But now, filled with tears, they're absolutely entrancing!

B. Never mind, dear Sweet. . . . This transfer is but a temporary thing. I'll return here long before the expiration of our engagement. Voskamp and I will bring old Beethoven to his knees. We'll whip him into shape, just wait and see. As soon as we get him growing again, he'll be more than fit to take his place in Major-Order life. He'll cast off his Subsidiary garb and return to your arms as one man, one spirit, one love! . . . Good-bye, Judy.

Chapter 44

As I exit from the Kaffehaus and hurry along the Graben on my way to the Burgtheater, Rezler's promise to Judy pounds its way to the forefront of my consciousness: I will master the Beethoven within me. . . . I will return to Major-Order life. . . . I will become her loving husband and fellow artist—all this, long before 1927.

Our rehearsal begins at two o'clock sharp and ends at four thirty. As I sit there next to the concertmaster and follow Collins's conducting through three symphonies, I'm amazed at the tremendous violin technique I have inherited through the spiritual absorption of young Voskamp. Never did I think I would live to see or hear Beethoven's fingers behave so well over a set of four little strings! Whether or not my career will resume in the fields of piano, conducting, and composing, I cannot yet say. But one thing is certain—for my Second-Order days, I will not put down the violin that Vos has so masterfully taken up.

Following our practice session, Von Collins invites me to his private dressing room at the theater. As soon as he closes and locks the door, we shake hands, and he carefully examines my new ruby ring.

Co. Ah, then you *are* Herr Beethoven!

B. Yes, Maestro . . . eager to spring from your pedagogy into my new career.

Co. This you should do. But you know, Vos . . . it's really hard to believe. Only yesterday you were a bashful young fellow, hoping to become our new concertmaster here at the Burg; today you're the very spirit of great music . . . the Master of us all!

B. Not really, Collins. I'm a tired old musician who's finally gotten himself reborn into a new chance to begin again. Here, on Beethoven's own terms, I should be able to grow to my absolute musical capacity . . . a tempting goal that I fell far short of on Earth. All I need is a little push from you to get me started.

Co. This I'll be glad to do, but you must first let me know in which direction to push. Now that you've experienced Voskamp's technique firsthand, do you intend to continue with the violin?

B. Definitely! Vos is as good a violinist as Beethoven was pianist. His technique is far too fine for me now to permit it to wither and die. I'll do whatever I can as pianist and conductor, but I *must* continue in his path of fiddler par excellence!

Co. Good! This is what I wanted to know. Klempberg is retiring at the close of the season; I'll recommend you for his chair. Before the year is out, we'll see that our Vienna begins to feel your presence in her midst. Mason Voskamp: Concertmaster at the Burg, graduating senior at the Conservatory, and Roth von Collins's private student of piano and composition!

My musical progenitor makes good his promise, and more. His "death" (return to the Aaronian system proper) is scheduled for April 1854. During the intervening two years, Collins does exactly the right things to get my career started. In June 1852, I'm named concertmaster of the Burgtheater Orchestra. The following November, our Maestro has a sudden (and convenient) attack of influenza. He requests me to conduct in his stead. Fortunately, the program is an all-Beethoven affair, consisting of Symphonies 3, 5, and 6—these are known locally as Symphonies 20, 27, and 31 by Roth von Collins. On June 17, 1853 (to celebrate my graduation from the conservatory), I'm presented as soloist in my teacher's Third Violin Concerto, which just happens to be the *Concerto in D* by Ludwig van Beethoven. But the biggest event of all (that which opens the doors and heart of this second Vienna to my new career) is a four-day akademie, featuring "Roth von Collins and his talented pupil, Mason Voskamp." This grand musical concert occurs during the third week of January 1854, and is especially memorable since it contains my teacher's last public appearances as pianist and conductor. The four evenings are really packed with symphonic music. Collins plays (and I conduct) two of his piano concertos. He conducts six of his own symphonies, and also his *Concerto in D* with myself as violin soloist. It is during this event that our tiny planet is treated to world premières of three of the best compositions from Beethoven's Earthly list: the *Fifth Piano Concerto, Symphony 8*, and *Symphony 9*. For these three works, I am featured as pianist and conductor. They are not credited to von Collins, but are listed as the First Piano Concerto, Symphony 1, and Symphony 2 by Mason Voskamp. The hall veritably explodes with comments concerning how precisely the "pupil" has evolved from his "teacher." These premières afford me no less than twelve standing ovations! The names of Collins and Voskamp are now revered interchangeably; the Great Mogul beams and swaggers to his throne; little Beethoven is once more the "darling" of Vienna.

Schoenbern and Kietzing of Vienna are von Collins's chief publishers. When they observe the quality and public reception of my "first three opuses," they offer like professional services to me on a fee-plus-royalty basis. Collins is present at the signing of my contract. Both partners laugh and joke and accuse him of having considerably more than a pedagogical finger in this latest of "musical pies."

On Tuesday night, April 4, my teacher and sponsor "dies" suddenly in his sleep. His "body" is discovered the next morning, and for his funeral on Friday, all the schools of Vienna are closed. The "death" of Collins creates a terrible musical void, and (just as we had planned) the entire city looks to young Voskamp to rise and fill the vacuum. Thus in two short years, I'm once again at the helm of German music. An admiring public, a chance to perform and conduct, an eager publisher—all the ingredients are present to inspire Beethoven to do the mountain of growing he was unable to do on Earth.

These two years of miracles are hopefully and quietly lived through in such a way as not to incur the suspicions of my new parents. Even so, I'm amazed at how matter-of-factly the two of them accept the elevation of their son to the very throne of music. Mother says that she knew all along I would receive the appointment of concertmaster. With my improved salary at the Burg, and with my first payments from Schoenbern and Kietzing, Father completely forgets that he was ever opposed to my following a musical career. Neither parent is one bit surprised at my becoming a pupil of Von Collins, and to *his* genius, they both attribute my sudden success as pianist and composer. Apparently, in their minds, there's nothing unusual about a typical conservatory student of piano and harmony exercises suddenly sprouting into a great pianist and composer. All it takes is a wave or two from a super Maestro's magic wand!

Through both these years, my twelve-hundred-dollars-a-month salary accumulates in my account; I'm determined not to touch a penny of it. By Christmas 1853, we've saved enough money to make Mother's eye operation an imminent reality. However, before we complete our plans for Leipszig, the real miracle of my new subordinate life occurs. After supper on the evening of January 10, 1854, Mother complains of a terrible headache and of a knifelike pain in each eye. We call in our family physician, Dr. Reddenbaugh. The kind old man gives her a sedative and sends her to bed. Seven hours later, she wakes up screaming—not in pain, but with joy! Her headache is gone, and she can now see the flickering gas lamps of the Hildebrandtstrasse. Again, I run for our doctor. Following a brief examination by candlelight, he confirms the good news that Father and I each held in our hearts, but were afraid to share.

Mother is no longer blind! After nine years of total darkness, her sight returns as suddenly as it had vanished. Reddenbaugh calls it a miracle. We break out our best bottles of Grinzinger and begin a predawn celebration of the good news. Our neighbors below lose no time in joining us. They, in turn, inform other friends nearby. Soon there are a "hundred" people crowded into our modest apartment—laughing, clinking glasses, and dancing to the joyous tunes of a little band that springs from nowhere. By sunrise, we have thoroughly celebrated the great, good light that has suddenly dawned upon the Voskamp family.

During my two years as Collins's pupil, our living room at the Hildebrandtstrasse is gradually transformed into a "typical" Beethoven study. To the bare floors, Stein clavier, worn sofa, uncomfortable chairs, and creaky music racks are added a writing desk, an ink stand, a pile of messy scores, assorted candle snuffers, a set of handbells, sketchbooks, scattered coins, scraps of paper, proof sheets, crumbs, dust, and Judy's masterful portrait of the Earthly Mozart. Thus the parlor of our own home becomes the Great Mogul's first official throne room on SCP 7,900,111; and my new parents become his first obedient courtiers. Father is all too happy to handle the details of our promising financial affairs, and to serve as my official concert agent. Mother is constantly at hand, making things run smoothly with her patient smile and her sparkling new eyes.

Following the "death" of my teacher, there begins a period of twenty-two glorious and creative years. All the musical dreams that my Earthly career failed to achieve do become reality here and now. The years 1854 and 1855 are spent predominantly upon the development and redevelopment of my instrumental capabilities. The interpretative powers of Voskamp's violin technique are vastly improved under the watchful eye of Beethoven. My own Earthly piano technique is once more brought to that successful "two-gun" level of the early Vienna days. To keep doors open for my performances, I join with four fellow graduates of the conservatory, forming the Roth von Collins Quartet—a memorial to my "late" great teacher. I reserve the chair of first violinist for myself (after all, it's Voskamp's association with Collins that attracts Viennese attention to our quartet in the first place). Mark Schu is named second violinist, Paul Nesbitt is violist, and Joseph Kovsky is our cellist. Karl Seibert, the oldest of our company, is named manager of the quartet and has the responsibility of arranging concerts and of sitting in as first violinist whenever I decide to perform with the group as pianist. Dear Seibert . . . what a big round fellow he is! The size of his body and the proficiency of his playing both remind me of Herr Schuppanzigh. Because of his fine musicianship and his managerial position with our quartet, he is permitted to join my parents as the third official member of Beethoven's new Court. I can't resist referring to him in the third person as "Milord" and "Herr Schuppanzigh." Like Vos, he inquires as to the meaning of my strange nomenclature. When I tell him that these are his official nicknames borrowed from a great violinist I once knew, he smiles warmly and gets on with the business at hand.

As I just said, most of these two years are devoted to concertizing. But something has to be done in the composing department to convince Schoenbern and Kietzing that I'm indeed a worthy successor to von Collins. Why not use those Earthly Beethoven works that Collins's successor is prescheduled to "compose" here? This is exactly what I do. In one mighty succession (and with only a few minor changes here and there), I send my publisher the *Missa Solemnis* and the last five quartets.

During these months, our Collins Quartet performs eighty-seven concerts in thirty-three different Viennese salons. I'm piano soloist in ten readings of my *E-flat Concerto.* I conduct three local performances of the *Missa*, and four each of Beethoven's last two symphonies (which are becoming very popular here as Voskamp's first two symphonies). Thus, by the end of 1855 (at least in the city of "Vienna"), my reputation is well established as pianist, violinist, composer, and conductor!

Now for twenty years, the busy routine of my professional life broadens, widens, and deepens. The old tree bears fruit beyond my wildest dreams. The intellectual capacity and Second-Order vitality of Rezler combine with the youthful ambitions of Voskamp and with the musicianship and dogged determination of Beethoven to produce one truly great artist! For two decades, there is little to my story apart from the music itself!

You'll recall that (during this same period) the corporate BEETHOVEN plans a tribute to the Earthly Beethoven, consisting of a sequence of twenty-seven symphonies, eighteen quartets, and nine piano concertos. My original Subsidiary ambition was to produce three times each of these numbers of works during the same number of years, thereby establishing my irrevocable victory over the corporate BEETHOVEN. Before too many years, I see myself falling miles short of this impossible goal; however, Rezler and Voskamp *are* able to convince Beethoven that there's nothing at all disgraceful or humiliating about this, so long as the pieces produced are top-quality third-period Beethoven. By 1876, I have composed a series of eighteen symphonies, seven piano concertos, three violin concertos, fifteen quartets, three piano quintets, three piano trios, ten piano sonatas, five violin sonatas, one opera, and three sets of ballet pieces. Without exception, each of these works is in the tradition of the very best of my mature Earthly style. The opera is Beethoven's ultimate statement and expansion of *Faust*, based upon our Subsidiary "Goethe's" superb treatment of the epic poem. All three violin concertos are sent to brother Johann; he uses them to establish his virtuoso career within our Major Aaronian system. Culby does the same for his dancing career by use of the three ballets that I send to him.

My failure to produce eighty-one symphonies, fifty-four quartets, and twenty-seven piano concertos is due in part to the high quality of the pieces I *do* compose, and in part to the unrealistic bounds of such an impossible goal. It is also due to an interesting artistic involvement with Judy Adams, which takes place during these years of "traveling back and forth." In spite of my busy musician's life, I manage about one weekend each month with my dear Kitten. Since her parents are still teaching on EP 40 and don't return permanently to their farm until 1873, this delightful old home serves as an artistic meeting place for our monthly weekend dates. (Dogwood won't do since my parents are very busy there, entertaining either clients or grandchildren; the studios at REMBRANDT won't do since Beethoven still abhors anything that reminds him of corporate art.) As an excuse for these occasional weekend disappearances, I tell my Subsidiary parents that I'm "off to the country" for some sketching. In reality, I make my way to the Waldmüller, thence to Aaron AP, and to Judy's farm. (Incidentally, in 1864, the Zweigs are replaced by Karl and Edith Hoffman as the new proprietors of our local D-R Kaffehaus.) My artistic project involving Judy is, of course, an extension of her dream of combining abstract painting with pure music. She comes to the conclusion that the composer and the painter must each go halfway. In other words, to achieve a genuine fusion of these media, each artist must create with the other in mind. It's not enough for the composer simply to write any music he pleases, and then for the artist to try to fit the emotional content of her tone painting within the spatial boundaries of her canvas. My new assignment is to create a series of single movements—no titles, just opus numbers. They may be scored for any instrumental grouping, but each individual piece must maintain a single predominant mood from beginning to end. These single moods will then contribute immeasurably to the unity and coherence of the related paintings.

Between 1855 and 1875, I compose a total of 177 individual movements: 90 for orchestra, 42 for string quartet, 12 for piano and orchestra, 9 for violin and orchestra, and 24 for piano solo. The joyous task of creating these individual mood pieces is the other reason for my falling short of Beethoven's preplanned challenge against BEETHOVEN. Although our collaboration requires me to study many of Judy's separate paintings along the way, it is not until the summer of 1876 that I'm absolutely struck down by the total impact of our joint labor of love!

Throughout these years, our third-floor living room in the Hildebrandtstrasse continues to be Beethoven's chief headquarters. When our late-hour interactions become too much for my parents, Beethoven's Court simply takes up and moves two blocks down the street to the Gemütlich Kaffehaus. There our socializing often continues until the wee hours of the morning. As on Earth, most of my serious composing (sketching) is done during summer vacations, which begin early in May and last until mid-October. Transportation is still very poor in my new Germany. We have no decent roads in the outskirts, not even paved sidewalks. Not until 1872 is our first railroad established between Nürnberg and Fürth. For this reason, most of my vacationing is done within close proximity to Vienna. Wiener Neustadt, Baden, Sankt Pölten, Linz, Salzburg, and Bad Ischl become my favorite summer retreats. Only twice do I venture as far as

Bonn and the Black Forest; the time-consuming onerousness of these journeys outweighs even the joy of visiting such dear and inspiring places.

At no time during this period does my Court reach the size or nobility of its characteristic dimensions on Earth. It boasts neither count nor prince, much less an archduke. Besides my parents and "Milord," it consists entirely of private students of piano or violin. Of all these pupils, only one reaches factotum proportions—Axel Oberhausen. Everything about this handsome curlyheaded eighteen-year-old reminds me so much of my favorite Earthly student, that I "knight" him into my realm as Sir Ferdinand Ries.

My concertizing centers mainly in Austria and Germany—the chief reason again being poor transportation. Without exception, Voskamp's public performances are keyed to the musical activities of the Roth von Collins Quartet. Where they go, I go and vice versa.

In the summer of 1860, the first Voskamp festival occurs on our planet. Unfortunately, the four-evening affair is not staged in my own city, but in faraway Berlin. Prior to this event, I had visited the Prussian capital twice and had found their imperial orchestra to have excellent discipline, balance, and control—but not the last word in youthful spirit. But this was before the advent of their new conductor—Arturo Sabatini, a young musician whose meteoric career required only six years to rise from the ranks of Italian opera to the permanent conductorship at Berlin. I had heard so many wonderful things about this fine artist that I very much wanted to attend the festival. Should I interrupt the summer's sketching and vacationing to do so? On June 4, a note arrives from Berlin that settles things in favor of the interruption:

May 28, 1860

Herr Mason Voskamp
Composer of our Century

Dear Maestro,

Have you heard about the Voskamp festival which we are planning in our city for the week of July 16th? We are performing here because the entire Prussian Court will be in the Capital during the last two weeks of July. It gives me great pleasure to include in these concerts every symphonic piece you have composed to date: all four symphonies, both piano concertos, the violin concerto, and your superb ballet music.

But what is a Voskamp festival without Voskamp? . . . Could you possibly find time midst your summer's composing to come and enjoy the great music which you've already given us? If you care to perform in any of the concertos, fine! If not, then come and enjoy the music and our stalwart appreciation of its creator. In either case, would you please consider being the guest of honor at our home? This for as long as you wish to stay.

Sincerely and affectionately,
Arturo Sabatini

When we meet, I'm not a bit surprised to discover a bright Aaronian *A* sparkling from the Maestro's right hand. A Second-Order talent—this explains his phenomenal rise to power. He locks the door to his study and, with tears streaming down his cheeks, gives me a typically warm Italian embrace.

Sa. Maestro, Maestro! . . . Dear Beethoven! . . . To think that after all these years, I should clasp you in my arms.

B. An Earthling! . . . In a universe this size, you'd think I could get away from you people. But no, you follow me everywhere! . . . Who *are* you, anyway?

Sa. I'm Roy Debbs, a negro music student from EP 10, here under the absorption of Arturo Sabatini. On Earth, you knew me as Maria Luigi Carlo Zenobia Salvatore Cherubini.

B. Cherubini! . . . In God's name, how wonderful! (*I return the embrace and the tears.*) Dear Cherubini. . . . What are you doing here?

Sa. As Roy Debbs, I was born with a fantastic Second-Order memory and an exceptional capacity for hearing tone lines. At only six years of age, I was examined before the College of Counselors. They speculated that both my talents were equivalent to high Third Order and strongly recommended that I devote my present life to orchestral conducting. When my rebirthday finally arrived and brought me a "Cherubini," I naturally accepted their recommendation.

B. But you're an opera composer, not a conductor.

Sa. Cherubini's talent for opera is but a small stream, compared to the "ocean" of Debbs's conducting. . . . No, this life at least will be devoted to the baton.

B. But what are you doing here?

Sa. Through Cherubini, I've inherited an enormous love for the music of Beethoven and Mozart. Since Mozart has failed to materialize, you are the prime object of my artistic affection. I ask little more of this life than to follow you around and conduct your music. If you remain on this planet, I shall stay also. If you return to BEETHOVEN, I shall apply there for a conducting position. . . . I hope you can *adjust* to having a "shadow."

B. Adjust? You do me a great honor! But you mustn't subordinate your career to mine.

Sa. There's nothing "subordinate" in the interpretation of your scores. You breathe into them the spirit of life and fire. My joy and challenge is to bring these qualities undiminished to the ears of our public.

During my ten days with Sabatini, I do not participate in the festival. I'm so completely overwhelmed by his conducting, that I can't do more than sit and watch and listen. His masterful technique affects me the same way that Neefe's organ playing affected my Earthly career—namely, as of the week of these concerts, I lose all desire to pick up my baton again. Perhaps in the Third or Fourth Order, but not here! Not in a tiny universe filled with Arturo Sabatini. To this day, I have yet to observe any comparable master of the podium.

At the conclusion of this festival, following the plaudits I share with Sabatini and his soloists, I'm standing alone outside the conductor's dressing room, when along come the Bonapartes—Richard and Marcie Grant. Using Voskamp's brows, I give the handsome couple an almost "Beethovenian" scowl.

B. Whatever you want, the answer is no!

Gr. Easy, Rezler. We're not asking you to return to BEETHOVEN.

B. That's nice; I'd refuse if you did.

Gr. We've been here for the entire festival. Allowing for your "1860" orchestra, we think these pieces are the greatest Beethoven we've ever heard.

B. So?

Gr. So we'd like your permission to take them with us to our Major system.

B. Certainly not! They're mine, and you have no right to them.
Gr. But ours is the only firm authorized to première your compositions before the Aaronian public!
B. They have other music; let them do without mine.
MG. (*Now it's Marcie's turn. She smiles convincingly as she reaches for my sleeve.*) Come on, Paul. Don't be stubborn! Think what these compositions will mean to your old friends and loved ones. Won't you do this for me, as a remembrance of our schooldays together?
B. No, Marcie, not even for *you.* You're a great pianist and a wonderful girl, but I can't oblige you in this matter.
MG. Why not?
B. You've built your precious corporation and carefully walled me out of it. Very well! . . . I know where I'm not wanted. Go your way, and let me go mine!
MG. But your music belongs to all Aaronians, not just the fortunate inhabitants of this planet.
B. My answer is no, I have nothing more to say to you.
MG. Won't you reconsider?
B. Good night!
MG. Please?
B. Good night to you!
MG. Come on, Rezler.
B. GOOD NIGHT TO YOU BOTH!

With sad countenances reflecting slight blushes of anger, my Aaronian visitors turn and leave. At the same time, a crisp feeling of satisfaction rises within Beethoven. His first little victory over corporate art, and he enjoys every second of it!

As victories go, this one is indeed short-lived. Within a month, Robinson intercedes for the Grants and convinces me that I'm doing a very selfish thing. If it weren't for these Subsidiary beings, SCP 7,900,111 wouldn't even be here for the sheltered nurturing of my preciously coveted talents. This Subsidiary culture has provided for all of Beethoven's artistic needs. The least he can do is share with all humanity the fruits of his present life.

Thus the BEETHOVEN firm sees to the premiering, publication, and distribution (within our Major system) of everything I compose between 1852 and 1876. They include even those works I wrote during (and immediately following) my apprenticeship days at their studio: the *Donovan Sonata,* Three Altburg Trios, Three Altburg Sonatas, and the Altburg Concerto. The only works *not* subjected to their sweeping program are the individual "mood movements," which I compose for Judy's paintings. These aren't even performed on my own planet. In fact, no one knows about them except Judy and myself. We plan to give their première at a grand Beethoven-Adams festival within our Major culture during the summer of '76. Thanks to the efforts of BEETHOVEN, my music becomes very popular throughout the Major Aaronian planets. Regarding our firm, I'm especially glad about one thing. Starting with the year 1859, they are able to offer an apprenticeship to each qualified member of M93's graduating classes who applies for one. What an improvement over my college days when twenty-three graduates in the BEETHOVEN division requested appointments, and only five of us received them! Of course, only a few of these many juniors survive to reach partnership status. But because of the great demand for "little Beethovens" on other planets throughout our SCPs, these faithful apprentices at least have interesting assignments to translate to, once they are booted from our firm. Because of my conforming actions, I again receive regular letters from Richard Grant. The "Little Corporal" constantly praises my new music, referring to it as the "chief and guiding light" of all his firm's composing activities. He boasts unendingly of my latest compositions' popularity. But he never goes so far as to invite me "home" again. He knows better than this.

During these years, I receive news of many interesting rebirths, among them the romantic composer, Robert Schumann; my "other" piano pupil, Carl Czerny; my spindly old factotum, Anton Schindler. All three of these recent Earthlings immediately send me cards through Reunion Control. I answer them with a polite no, as I had all the other friends, family, and admirers who preceded them. I'm still not enough of a "Beethoven" to hold my head up high and move freely among these people.

There is a single and notable exception to this lack of response; in fact, the pattern is exactly reversed! In 1858, I hear through brother Johann that our nephew Karl has arrived. Since his present address is published in the Interplanetary News, I immediately get off to him (via the Waldmüller) a big passionate tear-filled letter. Using that same dominating "Uncle Mogul" tone of the good old days, I invite him to "fly to my loving arms at once." Is it any wonder that the poor soul "flies" in the exact opposite direction! Through Johann, Karl writes me of his abiding love, but then (alas!) declares that he must do considerable growing before he feels secure enough to come face-to-face with his great father-uncle. How's *this* for a switch?

In June 1876, I offer the necessary excuses and sneak away from my SCP. I join Judy on Aaron AP to make plans for our long-awaited Beethoven-Adams festival. The huge string of concerts occupies eighteen (not all consecutive) evenings, starting June 5 and ending June 30. The affair is held on our Administrative planet not because of Beethoven's music or Judy's paintings. It is staged there because the College of Counselors wishes to give their official recognition to what they believe is a genuinely new art form within our Second-Order culture. As Rembrandt observed, there's nothing new about artists painting what they hear in a musical composition. What he admired in Judy was the particular and sensitive way in which she related abstract paintings to pure music—neither imposing a set program upon the other. But even *this* was not recognized by our counselors as a new art form. What makes the big difference now? It's all a matter of control, they say—artistic control of the media. As I mentioned earlier, each of my 177 individual movements carefully maintains a single mood from beginning to end. (Among the separate pieces, these moods vary from somber to gay to quiet to frightening to melancholy to cheerful.) Each has a distinctly predominating tempo: slow or moderate or fast. To each of these fixed sets of musical conditions, Judy composes a series of majestic abstractions. Her average requirement so far is about a dozen canvases per movement. (Several have as few as three; others as many as thirty-six.) Where a given movement is performed, its related paintings are displayed; where a set of paintings are viewed, the related music is heard. Now, whence comes the sudden burst of artistic control? Judy and I talked this matter over for hours on end. We agreed that it was not enough merely to display the paintings at a concert hall, or to throw their image upon a screen during performances. We had to discover some procedure whereby each audience eyeball would be focused on precisely the right spot of precisely the right painting at precisely the right time. We tried showing motion picture sequences of the paintings during performances of the music. This gave us wonderful control over color, lighting, and fractional viewing, but raised a serious problem of synchronizing music with the film, thus placing horrible restrictions upon tempo. Our experiments soon evolved into a colored slide technique that permitted all the advantages of motion pictures without their chief disadvantage. Each separate movement is now related to a block of Judy's paintings through hundreds of carefully made transparencies. These are flashed on a stagewide screen during performances, assuring adequate viewing by all. The musicians are free to perform at their own desired tempo while a musically oriented projectionist fills the hall with each specific frame as its particular number is reached in the score.

During our Beethoven-Adams festival, I perform in only nine of the movements: six times as pianist and three times as violinist. I'm too busy watching and listening to desire greater participation. Among the performers and conductors, Grant's BEETHOVEN is, of course, well represented. At my request, Sabatini is there to conduct many of the orchestral numbers. Even our old friend Donovan (on leave from CHOPIN) has his fingers in the show. He performs fifteen of the individual movements for piano solo.

On Saturday morning, July first, Robinson comes to congratulate me for my part in the festival. But this isn't his prime reason for visiting. During 1873, we had met frequently at the Waldmüller Kaffehaus. On each of these occasions, he'd bring me additional examples of Earthling music appearing between 1830 and 1873. He advised me to study the scores carefully as an aid in deciding my musical future on SCP 7,900,111. Now, on this Saturday morning at my apartment on Aaron AP, he comes to inquire of my decision:

Ro. Well, Herr Beethoven, what's on your next page?

B. I'm still on the musical fence, Herr Robinson. My big problem is that I can't specifically decide whether to return permanently to our Major culture, or to remain for a while longer in my dear old Vienna.

Ro. I should think that after the great victory of the past few weeks, you'd be more than ready to accept full-time Major life.

B. Perhaps. . . . But I'm still not sure.

Ro. Well, one thing is sure. For as long as you stay on the SCP, your composing days in the style of third-period Beethoven are finished. You can do all the piano or violin playing you wish, but if you compose further, it must not be in the voice of classical humanism. Your SCP has only twenty-four years to close the gap between its 1830 culture and whatever the culture of Earth will be by 1900. How far into Romanticism (and beyond) Earth's music will then be is anyone's guess. From your study of my scores, have you not yet discovered an Earthling romanticist into whom you could evolve?

B. Only one.

Ro. Richard Wagner?
B. Yes.
Ro. I thought so. Is it his very latest music that inspires your decision?
B. Notably, *Tristan und Isolde* and *Die Meistersinger von Nürnberg* . . . especially *Tristan.*
Ro. Why?
B. I hear in it a bold and honest voice, speaking of human passion as no other composer of Earth has yet done. . . . *Tristan* evolves from a rich heritage of German music; it's not some childish attempt to be modern or different. Quite naturally, it represents a complete break from the traditional methods of the lyric stage. Within its pages, the optimum spirit of chromaticism is raised to the level of genuine art. I'd be *proud* to follow in the path of music having such poetic charm and such a passionate hold on the reality of human emotions.
Ro. Good, then the matter is settled. If you remain here, you'll claim your rightful place at the helm of BEETHOVEN; if you continue as Voskamp, you'll evolve into a "Richard Wagner." Correct?
B. Except for one thing.
Ro. What?
B. At present, I'm not interested in operatic composing. Judy and I are having too much fun with our pure music and abstract art!
Ro. Then I don't know what the answer is.
B. Don't worry. I suppose I'll go on as Vos for a few more years. I'll not do any composing, but I'll certainly keep my eye and ear on Earth's musical scene. I've been listening carefully to Johannes Brahms . . . especially his *Concerto in D Minor* for piano and orchestra. Perhaps *he'll* be my answer, instead of Wagner.
Ro. You're probably doing the wise thing. Once you've "buried" Voskamp, that chapter in your life is forever closed. I'm sure you'll make the right decision. So take your time. But remember, no more third-period Beethoven!
B. Yes, Professor. I'll concentrate entirely upon performing.

On the evening of this same Saturday, Judy and I suffer the sweet sadness of another farewell date. I've been away from my Subsidiary planet (supposedly composing in the environs of "Salzburg") for over a month, and I don't want any of my Court to get suspicious.

B. Guess who came to see me this morning, Judy.
JA. Robinson?

B. Yes. How did you know?

JA. I spotted him several times during our festival, and just thought he was about due for a visit. Won't he be retiring soon?

B. I asked him that. He said he'd be quitting in another ten or fifteen years, but not until he gets me straightened out!

JA. What *does* he advise you to do now?

B. He thinks that in the light of our present artistic triumph, I should be returning here to Major-Order life.

JA. So do I. That settles it! Let's bury Voskamp and live happily ever after.

B. Not so fast! An artistic breakthrough is one thing, and Beethoven's adjusting to corporate art is another. I'm still not sure he belongs here. At least back in his old Vienna, I know he can live and create as on Earth.

JA. That "old Vienna" of yours will be changing now.

B. True. But it's still a far cry from "corporate" art.

As Judy asks another question, her blue eyes playfully brighten like those of a little girl. Except for the Beethoven and Rezler within me, her sheer physical invitingness would be too much for old Vos.

JA. Tell me, Dear, now that our festival has come and gone, aren't you proud of what our love has created?

B. Neither here nor on Earth have I ever enjoyed fathering works of art so much as these. It's almost as though we were married and had brought into being a tidy little family of 177.

JA. You're right, Boo. They *are* like our own children.

B. And I'm very proud of them. They represent something fresh and new. Something that very few of our big old stuffy corporate artists have been able to achieve. For all their finances and commercial power, for all their computers and calculations, for all their market analyses and perpetual existences, think how few of them have been able to contribute a genuinely new art form to our culture. Most of them are unduly long on mass production and imitation, but pitiably short on original creativity.

JA. Then haven't we achieved the victory you've been waiting for? Haven't we clearly reached an artistic goal yet unattained by your corporate BEETHOVEN? Haven't you now proven to yourself that you can successfully collaborate with another artist? If you can work with *me*, then why not with your fellow musicians at BEETHOVEN?

B. Working with a sweet young painter whom I love and working with a bunch of competitive, equally talented musicians whom I don't love, these are entirely different matters! No, Judy. I think I'd better return to my nice little "Vienna" for a few more years. Should Romanticism bloom into something less bearable than even corporate composers, then I *shall* retranslate to our Major culture and promptly accept my managing partnership. Otherwise, my future course remains almost as clouded as it was in 1827.

JA. There's another possibility, Boo. Since I've achieved most of what I'd hoped to accomplish at REMBRANDT, perhaps *I* shall translate to SCP 7,900,111. There we can be married and spend the remainder of our Second-Order days composing, painting, and procreating. We can still vacation in the Major Order. And I'll have the supreme pleasure of presenting you with a few children who, if not as aesthetically charming as the 177 we've already had, should be at least as lovable!

Chapter 45

Between the summer of our festival and the fall of 1879 are three quietly sleeping years—at least for Beethoven the composer. But from the standpoint of his personal life, they are neither quiet nor asleep.

Upon returning from Aaron AP, about the first thing I do is resign from my position as concertmaster at the Burgtheater. Although I enjoy being on the "inside" of our orchestra (so to speak), I find that this chair takes too much time from Voskamp's other musical activities. Besides, my income from concerts and my quarterly royalty checks from Schoenbern and Kietzing are more than adequate for my family's financial needs.

In fact, there's so much spare cash lying around that (in the summer of '78) I decide to buy the Hildebrandtstrasse house in which my parents have rented an apartment since the inception of their marriage. Our family continues to occupy the third floor as we rent the two apartments below and convert our new cellar to a music storage room. Although the building is held in my name, all rent money is turned over to my parents. Since neither Beethoven nor Rezler nor Voskamp ever owned a piece of property, this first acquisition of real estate provides a prominent feather in my new cap. It can't compare to Gneixendorf, but at least it's a home of my own. Would that I could show it to brother Johann.

During these three years, my concert tours still center about the performing activities of our Roth von Collins Quartet. Each season is stuffed to the breaking point with public appearances, but geographically speaking, none of the tours is very extensive; none goes beyond Germany and Austria. Next to Vienna, my favorite music center now is Berlin; I can't resist the inspired conducting and the masterful orchestra of Arturo Sabatini.

In accordance with Robinson's instructions, I do no further composing until my evolutionary path is decided. In fact, I no longer spend summers in the country; I just sit there on my third-floor throne and study the MS scores that my counselor continues to send me. Those which absorb most of my time and admiration are *Symphony 1* and *Symphony 2* by Brahms and *Der Ring des Nibelungen* by Wagner, but I can't for the "lives" of me decide which of these composers to represent through the Romantic age swiftly dawning upon our SCP. In the summer of '79, I have a meeting with Robinson and confidently declare that I wish to represent both Brahms and Wagner. He takes my request before the College of Counselors, and their reply is a firm, flat no! In order to properly parallel our First-Order culture, there must be two separate composers. In this way, the inhabitants of SCP 7,900,111 will have the same choice as their counterparts on Earth; they may join the Wagner camp with its "music of the future," or they may side with Brahms as a vote for the conservative faction in music. Which then am I to be, a Brahms or a Wagner?

Throughout these three years, the constitution of my Court remains practically unchanged. Mother and Father are as active as ever; to a great extent, they have replaced my Earthly need for factotums. In fact, old "Schuppanzigh" of a Seibert is still chief liaison between myself and the Collins Quartet. He begs constantly for new chamber pieces in spite of the fifteen quartets I have written specifically for our group. Oberhausen continues to behave exactly like my curly-headed Ries; he follows me everywhere, hoping to absorb whatever piano lessons might fall from my wings. Through Voskamp, I seem to have inherited a genuine pleasure in private teaching, and at no time do I have fewer than six violin students and ten piano students (besides Oberhausen). Except for the obvious internal bumps that result from choosing Beethoven's future path, all goes smoothly and quietly for Voskamp and his Court. All goes smoothly and quietly until a tiny seedling decides to plant herself at the core of my life—to plant herself there, to grow into a mighty tree, and to lift up the totality of my being into her skyward branches, molding it into something far bigger and better than Beethoven or Rezler or Voskamp would have thought possible.

My introduction to this unbelievable sprout comes as an informal note from my friend and associate, Vladimir Kassmann, Professor of Piano at the Vienna Conservatory:

September 20, 1876

Dear Vos,

Someone most unusual has just crossed my path . . . a genuine musical prodigy! Surely after all these years, you know that I'm not one to use this word lightly. Aside from Collins and yourself, this is the only person to whom I've applied the term in over thirty years of teaching. I realize your violent distaste for gifted young musicians, but I ask you to make an exception in her case. She is Anna Rosecranz, whose delightful family I got to know through her older brother, Albert. Neither parent is musical. Her father owns and operates the Rosecranz Shop, where he is regarded by many as Vienna's finest tailor. He is the third generation of their family to devote himself to this enterprise, and he puts together garments with the same love and skill that you compose great symphonies. The family is well-to-do and has made considerable financial contributions to our music school.

Though music is not the Rosecranz profession, one must certainly believe it to be the doorway to their heaven. They have staunchly resisted the current trend, which has set all Vienna to dancing stupid little waltzes. Realizing that this is but "music of the hour," they cling wisely to the genuine art works of Collins and yourself. It has been the parents' fondest dream that Albert might be the first of their family to enter our profession and perhaps follow in your footsteps. After the young man spent a full year at our school, the faculty had no choice but to inform him that his musical talent was very modest and that the best he could hope for was a minor position in the artistic world. This sad news almost killed the mother and father, but young Albert (still your great admirer) has adjusted admirably to the realities of life, and plans to devote himself to the family's trade. Naturally, the parents turned their attention to little Anna. Perhaps *she* could inherit their dreams. . . . Three years ago, they obtained for her the best private teachers in Vienna. She showed no aptitude in composition, and only a modest talent for piano and violin. Then suddenly, this past summer, a miracle occurred. Almost overnight, she developed a profound skill for both piano and violin . . . as if some weighty mental block had been lifted aside, permitting her to see the light. Her teachers were so impressed by the sudden change that they brought her to me.

Anna Rosecranz is still too young to be admitted to the conservatory. We've committed ourselves to do so in three years, but in the meantime, I wonder if you could take her under your wing. Do this as a personal favor for me, Vos. I promise she'll not disappoint you in the least. Let me know when to send her.

Sincerely,
Vlad

My reply goes out immediately.

September 22

Dear Vlad,

I don't know quite how to react to this latest discovery of yours. Of course I'll see her since you request me to do so, but I can't promise you anything. I'm glad you remember my aversion to gifted young musicians. Such antipathy does not spring from jealousy on my part. Perhaps on the surface it looks as though it does, but you know me better than this. My repugnance for gifted young musicians springs from the simple observation that the older they become, the less gifted they seem to be. They explode on the musical scene like a brilliant display of fireworks, then comes the light of day and you can't find a trace of them. They have no roots. That's it, Vlad—no roots! In the burning heat of our long day, they wither and die; they die for lack of moisture; they've sent nothing of themselves down into the soil. They were too busy exploding across the night sky!

This child represents quite a change in our established procedure. Thus far, you have prepared students for me; now you ask me to prepare one for you. . . . Oh well, perhaps Anna *is* an exception to the rules of our game. Send her to me any evening next week; I'll be glad to hear her play, and I'll try not to frighten her.

Your old devourer of prodigies,
Voskamp

On the following Wednesday evening, I return from a long walk that has taken me halfway to Mödling and back. I had been walking most of the day as a counterirritant to a particularly severe attack of "Brahms-Wagner indecision," which had plagued me for the better part of two weeks! By the time I arrive home (about 10:00 PM), I have quite forgotten my sociomusical invitation extended to Anna Rosecranz through Vladimir Kassmann. Opening the door to Beethoven's study, I'm in such a musical daze that I stand there staring at Mother Voskamp for nearly a minute, before I realize who she is or that she's speaking to me:

B. I'm sorry, Mother, what's that you're saying?
Mrs. V. Herr Rosecranz has brought his beautiful daughter Anna for a visit. She plays the piano and violin equally well, with great skill and fine musicianship. We've been waiting nearly two hours for you to come and hear her.

Joseph Rosecranz and I shake hands, and I apologize for being so late. As I do so, my attention gravitates toward the klavier on whose bench Anna is seated and above whose music rack her brown bright eyes stare at me with a lightning bolt of inquisitiveness. Her hair is a soft-spun silk of pure gold. When she bounces to her feet, I'm surprised at the shortness of her stature (the top of her head scarcely comes to my chest) and by the youthfulness of her charming face (the delightful dimples and tan freshness of a thirteen-year-old). But those eyes . . . there's something in them that almost startles me—something besides their youthful brightness . . . something hinting that we've met before. I remember Kassmann's description of the sudden and recent bursting forth of her musical talent. This past summer, could Anna have been absorbed by the arrival of a Second-Order being, someone whom I *did* know on Earth? I reach for her right hand under the pretense of examining its musical capabilities. What I'm really looking for is a ruby Aaronian ring. Not the trace of one! Whatever magic accounts for the sparkle of the little girl's eyes, I'm convinced that she's not the translation of an Aaronian and that we've never met before. I place a dainty kiss in her palm. She blushes and smiles toward her father as I comment:

B. This is a real pleasure, Anna. I've been wanting to meet you ever since Professor Kassmann told me what a fine and beautiful musician you are. What have you brought to play for me . . . some Voskamp?

AR. No.

B. No? . . . That's strange! . . . Am I not your favorite composer?

AR. No, Sir.

I glance at the father; now *he's* the one who's blushing. Looking back at Anna, I gently raise her chin with my forefinger.

B. Then why do you come to me for lessons? If you can't respect me as a composer, I'm sure you'll not like me as a teacher.

HR. (*By now, Herr Rosecranz can no longer contain his impatience.*) Anna! . . . You're being very rude. I know that you admire Herr Voskamp's music. You and Albert both do!

B. (*I interrupt the father's interruption.*) Yes, Anna. At least your brother respects what I do.

AR. (*By now, Anna's face glows with enthusiasm.*) Please, Sir. I have great respect for your music. . . . It's just that I like Collins better!

B. So *Collins* is your favorite! Good, he's mine too. I ask you a stupid question, you give me an honest answer. You're an exceptional young lady, indeed. But this is fine, Anna. I studied with Collins when I was just a boy, and I've tried to pattern my early pieces after his. You know, compositions are like children—they don't just come from nowhere. They have parents as we do. And the main parent of my music has been your idol, Herr Collins. So if you like *him* so much, perhaps someday you'll appreciate what *I'm* doing.

AR. I appreciate your music *now*; it is very great and seems to tell the same story as Collins. It's just that you use bigger words than he does, and take more time to paint the same pictures.

B. All right, young lady. Let me hear you play some Collins.

Like a graceful doll, Anna bounces onto the bench and plays from memory a Collins sonata, which happens to be the Mozart *Sonata in C*. As she plays, I stand behind her, look over her shoulders, and listen to the greatest pianistic interpretation I have ever heard at the hands of a thirteen-year-old. The maturity of her musicianship is every bit as great as her teachers and my friend Vlad have proclaimed. Allowing for the smallness of her hands and for a few rough spots in the phrasing, I immediately place her among the ten greatest pianists I have had the pleasure of hearing on Earth or here within the Aaronian system. Her playing of Mozart is truly that of a creative artist—miles beyond the mere attainments of correct notes, careful memorization, and proper tone control. Her scales are liquid smooth—like those of Cramer. I find myself double-checking her right hand again . . . no ruby ring!

At the conclusion of her sonata, a memorable Earthly experience of mine repeats itself with amazing accuracy—except that now the actors and the roles have changed. Now *I* am the revered Maestro, and little Anna is the hopeful musician-to-be. At the sounding of the final tones, I place my hands on her shoulders. She looks up into my eyes that are filled with tears of profound respect. I smile, but not a word is spoken. The totality of what I feel and have to say is clearly written across my face. Little Anna reads the message, smiles back, and sheds a few tears of her own. She realizes that her musicianship has conquered me completely. Poor Herr Rosecranz knows nothing of this clear, unspoken language that can pass from the eyes of one musician to those of another, when two such artists are not afraid to be honest with each other. He pulls gently at my sleeve.

HR. Well, Maestro, what do you think of our little Anna? Is her playing in any way worthy of your teaching?

B. It is indeed, Herr Rosecranz. But I fear there is little for me to teach this daughter of yours.

Mrs. V. (*Mother crosses in front of us and offers Anna a sweet.*) You play superbly, my dear . . . as well as my son has ever played.

Anna licks the chocolate from her dainty lips, and I hand her my violin.

B. Now let's see what a naughty little girl you really are. Let's see how your fingers behave over four strings and a bow. Do they cast the same spell as they do over a keyboard?

AR. (*Our star performer tucks my instrument under her chin and holds it in perfect balance. Her huge brown eyes stare me to silence.*) Maestro, would you accompany me in a Collins sonata?

B. No. This time we'll hear some Voskamp.

B. (*I reach for a set of proof sheets on my music cabinet.*) Here, Anna, is my newest violin sonata. It's not yet gotten into print, and this will give me a chance to test your sight reading. I don't expect you to play it in tempo; we'll go slowly, but try to keep a uniform beat.

AR. (*Anna glances through her part with all-seeing eyes, then smiles back at me.*) Please, Herr Voskamp. Let's try the piece in tempo. I think I can manage.

B. You *are* a bad little girl! . . . Very well. . . . But remember, one mistake and there'll be no more chocolates for Anna . . .

We play through all five movements of my brand-new *Sonata in D.* We play them at their proper tempos, and the only mistakes made are in *my* part, not in Anna's. At the conclusion of the *Presto Fugue Finale,* there are lots of tears and kisses for our little musician—tears, kisses, and a handful of chocolates!

It's nearly midnight by the time we finish our playing and Mother's light supper of sausage, cheese, and kaffee. Slowly and carefully, I light my long-stemmed pipe before answering Herr Rosecranz's thrice-asked question.

B. Yes, Sir! I'll be glad to accept your daughter as my student. But this dear Mother you see here taught me long ago that an honest admission is the best thing in the world for a man's soul. Therefore I must confess something. I must confess that there is little for me to teach Anna Rosecranz . . . in piano *or* violin. She is a genuine master of both.

B. (*Having answered the father's question, I turn my attention to our performer.*) It's true, Anna. On both instruments, you play as well as I. There is little for you to learn from me. Why do you want me for a teacher?

AR. Dear Maestro, it is not my ambition to play as well as you or as well as some other great musician. I sense that I *do* have a talent for music, and it's my joy and obligation to develop this talent to the best of my ability. . . . Whether it be greater or less than another musician's is not important.

HR. (*Again, her father interrupts, this time with considerable excitement.*) And for the development of Anna's talent, there is no surer inspiration than to come occasionally into the presence of a great practicing musician—not some bearded professor of music hiding behind his careful and proper degrees, but a creative artist such as *yourself* . . . one whose daily life is the very spirit of music. Neither my daughter nor I would suggest that your busy schedule be interrupted by regular lessons for a little girl. But we *do* hope that you might assign her sufficient pieces for a month or two, and when she has mastered them as best she can, permit her to play them for you and to benefit from whatever words of wisdom or criticism that might fall from your lips. Such an arrangement would be a dream come true—the answer to our prayers.

AR. (*By now, Anna is leaning against me, tugging at my sleeve.*) And I will no longer be just a little girl. I'll be Anna Rosecranz, PUPIL OF VOSKAMP!

B. (*These words, a perfect conclusion for the evening, blur my vision with tears.*) Very well, my dear. Here are six of my latest sonatas—three for piano and three for violin. As soon as you whip them into shape, I want you to pay me another visit. Please come in the evening, as you did this time. And if being my pupil is an inspiration to you, then consider yourself inspired. For I now welcome you into Voskamp's Court as the "Little Princess." "Princess Anna," my favorite student of piano and violin.

Thus, it is that Anna Rosecranz enters the life of Beethoven. She becomes my pupil at the very time when my chief interest is teaching. I do no composing and little touring because I'm in the process of choosing between Brahms or Wagner—an almost full-time occupation.

Of course, Judy Adams is still the girl I love. Since 1852, I've been making annual visits to Aaron AP for the specific purpose of applying successive installments of aging to my subelectronic Voskamp disguise. Although in reality I still have the virile physique of a teenager, on the surface I'm every inch a man of forty-two. And what possible interest could a little girl of thirteen have in the gray hairs and wrinkles of a middle-aged musician? Or do I underestimate the powerful and natural attraction that can exist between a man and woman when they share a common musical pursuit, perhaps even powerful enough to span an age-difference of thirty years!

Of course, Judy is still my little Kitten. Throughout these "Brahms-Wagner" years, we spend a weekend together almost once each month. But I notice that my lessons for Anna are strictly on the increase. By mid-1878, she comes two or three times a week, and I'm a frequent guest at the Rosecranz home. In January of '79, she makes her formal Viennese debut as the sixteen-year-old pupil of Mason Voskamp. The two of us appear together in this concert, each performing a piano concerto and a violin concerto. My friend Sabatini comes all the way from Berlin to do the conducting. Could I possibly enjoy being with Anna Rosecranz as much as I enjoy the companionship of Judy Adams? Could the Beethoven and Rezler within me ever exchange their love of a Kitten for that of a Princess?

Of course, I prefer Judy to Anna. From an animal point of view, what Second-Order male wouldn't prefer the body of a Second-Order girl to the fast-fading beauty of a First-Order teenager? But at least for the present (and in their own way), Anna's physical attributes are as enticing as Judy's. The little musician's eyes are filled with love and music. Her entire face, from golden curls to rounded chin, radiates a natural charm that is overwhelming. From what I can see, her dainty body has suddenly bloomed into a thing of great rhythmic beauty—still thin, though perfectly proportioned. Each time we meet, I find myself wishing more and more that I might climb out of my Voskamp disguise and show Anna what a handsome young fellow I really am.

Of course, I'm in love with Judy. But how else can I describe my feelings for Anna? Those delightful concert tours the two of us make to Graz, Innsbruck, and Salzburg; our joyous vacation among the mountain people of Tyrol; our promenades through the Chinese salons at Schönbrunn; our countless evenings at the theater; our visit to the famous Lipizzaner of the Spanische Hofreitschule; our frightening ski trip to Mürzzuschlag; and the many times we go dancing the Walzer, the Almstanz, the Trestertanz, and the Steirischer Wischtanz.

Of course, I'll soon be making my permanent return to the Aaronian system, there to become the proud husband of Ms. Judy Adams. This is one future event of which I'm perfectly sure. I'm perfectly sure of it until that eventful Sunday, October 19, 1879. Since my regular date with Judy is not until the following weekend, I decide to spend the day with Anna Rosecranz. What a shocking surprise comes my way before the setting sun puts an end to this fair Sabbath.

Anna and I devote the entire morning to horseback riding and walking in the Prater, where we absorb the priceless beauty of a perfect fall day. She has packed a delicious basket of rye bread, ham, cheese, and sausage. It is our plan to find some rustic tavern in the suburbs that happens to be serving Heurige; there to settle down for the afternoon, eating our tasty lunch and enjoying the unbelievable inspiration of this year's new wine. By some strange coincidence, our search for the Heurigen takes us to the suburb of Grinzing. Above the entrance to the Gemütlich Tavern is a huge branch of fir—no doubt about it, our quest has ended. When a tavern displays either a branch of fir or ivy above its door, this means that it has on hand a supply of new wine. What makes Heurige so delicious is its mild taste, being not yet fully fermented. But none of us "professional Viennese wine drinkers" ever treats this daintily innocent drink with anything less than a careful sipping respect; it is extremely potent.

Anna and I spend the afternoon sitting opposite one another in a secluded wooden corner of the Gemütlich. We hold hands across the table. We stare into each other's eyes, reading the dreams to be found there. We nibble our lunch and sip the delightful Heurige. The scent of fall leaves and sweet grapes fills the entire room; our ears are sung to by the soft, simple music of three violins, a guitar, and an accordion; slowly but surely, the new wine works its magic upon our souls. Beethoven, Rezler, and Voskamp are finally in perfect agreement. This is the girl of their dreams. This is the long-awaited materialization of the "Immortal Beloved". This is the one and only whom they would marry to love, whom they would love to marry! As naturally as the rising of a sun, our lips gently touch in the positive confirmation of love's ultimate kiss. For this instant . . . for this eternity . . . all time and space become totally irrelevant. There are no longer two musicians sitting at the table—only one. Should either of us leave, there would be no one there at all. Though hardly necessary, we exchange a few words, redundantly echoing what our hearts have already spoken to one another.

B. Dear Anna, I'm so hopelessly in love with you. But then it's easy for an old man to fall in love with a sweet young girl. What I'm wondering is . . . that kiss . . . could it actually mean that you're in love with *me*?

AR. Yes, Darling. I've been so since that evening in your study when we first met.

Our hands touch again. This time, the clasp is firmer.

B. How wonderful! . . . Anna, will you marry me?

AR. (*Her reply is sealed by another kiss, almost as lingering as the first.*) Yes, Vos. . . . And I know that our life together will be filled with the sound of beautiful music.

Chapter 46

News of my engagement to Anna Rosecranz swirls among my Subsidiary friends and musicians like grains of sand in a mighty windstorm. It seems as though all Vienna is gossiping about the sudden love affair between its middle-aged composer and its beautiful young prodigy of the century. Most of the idle talk is harmless, optimistic . . . complimentary. A little of it is on the dark side: "No! . . . Two accomplished musicians in one family? This would *never* do! Professional jealousy! . . . Such a marriage couldn't last more than two or three years. Wait and see!"

Mother and Father are delighted with the news; they were half afraid that (at forty-five) I wouldn't be marrying anyone more companionable than my precious Muse. Voskamp's entire Court rejoices in the proposed marriage of their "Great Mogul" and in the resulting elevation of their revered "Princess" to the rank of "Queen." Following the crest of this wave of good news, I'm surrounded by smiling faces and happy people. Only *I* am not happy; only *my* face is not smiling. Why? Because I'm simultaneously engaged to the two most wonderful girls in our First-Second-Order universe, and I don't know what to do about it!

I can't go to Anna for help; she wouldn't know what I was talking about. I can dump my problem in Judy's lap; she, no doubt, would find the answer. This childhood sweetheart, this "Kitten" of my dreams, this sensitive and creative artist, this inspiration of a lifetime, why not tell her the full story and let her decide which path our lives are to take.

On Wednesday evening (three days subsequent to my proposal of marriage), I stop by the Waldmüller Kaffehaus, stealthily make my way to its subbasement, and there phone Judy concerning the momentousness of our approaching weekend date. She's really impressed when I tell her that its importance entails a return visit to Valhalla:

JA. Boo! This is wonderful! . . . You've finally decided to resume your role in Major life, and you're going to set the date of our wedding!

B. Not so fast, love; maybe yes, maybe no. . . . The outcome of our mountain climb will be largely the result of *your* decisions, not mine.

I phone Administrative Control-VP 33 to inquire about weather conditions on our mountain: Spring has set in, all trails are free of snow. Since this is the case, I reserve a cabin for Saturday and Sunday nights at the foot of Trail No. 7.

As in the past, Judy and I meet at Chateau L'Arbre Fée de Bourlemont for a meal and provisions. From here we drive to Valhalla, arriving at our cabin at 4:00 PM. Our original plan was to spend the remainder of Saturday resting, dreaming, loving, discussing future artistic collaborations. Not a word of my shattering announcement was to be spoken until Sunday at the top of Valhalla. But all this is changed by a last-minute telephone check on weather conditions. They forecast rain and severe fog throughout the area, starting Sunday afternoon. For this reason, we begin our climb at once, deciding to spend Saturday night on the summit. Over our backs, we each carry a share of the provisions and a sleeping bag, the latter having been stored at our cabin for the use of its occupants.

As we climb the reserved trail, few words pass between us. We are too much overcome by the sight and sound of Valhalla giving birth to another Spring. The afternoon sun is still bright enough to work its contrasting magic of sparkling light and cool shadows over the new green carpet of our mountain's slope. A pair of owls trill briefly at one another, then stop abruptly as though someone even wiser than *they* had bluntly informed them that it was much too early for their song of the night. The air is clear and fresh with the cleansing smell of busy streams. From its God-appointed place on the mountainside, each stately pine beckons us on with the serene patience and quiet wisdom known only among trees. A tiny red fox scampers across our path, barking his toothy displeasure at the human intruders.

At the end of our climb, we are both surprised by the natural changes wrought in the pastoral surroundings of our tiny sanctuary. Only the sandstone seat and its mossy covering are still the same; everything else has grown taller, greener, and thicker. From our rock, there is no longer a view of the valley below; there is even less sky to enjoy. The one remaining open space is the clearing behind our throne—that very spot where (fifty-two years earlier) the fluttering descent of an oak leaf had awakened me to Second-Order life. Here we spread our sleeping bags, build a cozy fire, enjoy our modest supper. For a final time, from the base of our lovers' throne, I remove the velvet box containing Paul Rezler's diamond ring. This I hand to Judy as we seat ourselves on the sleeping bags. Then as night and the first-born stars of spring replace the fading purple light of day, there passes between us the conversation of a lifetime:

JA. Paul! . . . After all these years, you hand me this ring, but the handing is accompanied by neither kiss nor embrace. What does it mean? The ring is warm and smiling; it tells me that our wedding is near. Your eyes are cold and sad; they speak a different story. Our childhood love is now tempered by the maturity of artistic dedication. . . . Can such a sweet and abiding thing be reduced to mere vertices in another human triangle? . . . Who *is* this other girl? Is she some Tenth-Order creature? Only such could love you more than I. . . . Is she the spirit of music, that fugitive from Earth, here again to dominate the life of Beethoven? Is she another Marcie Sbalzato? Surely the mortal rippling of human flesh is no match for the shared creativeness of two artists in love. Tell me, Paul. Who *is* this other girl?

B. Her name is Anna Rosecranz, and she's far from being just another Marcie. Nor is she some devastating blonde from the Tenth Order. She's a cute little First-Order Subsidiary being who cheerfully walks through her days without the slightest notion of that meaningful eternity that comforts and directs *our* lives.

JA. Why are you so in love with her?

B. Like you, dear Judy, she's an artist. And when she takes up the magic wand of her art and waves it over my life, I become as a little child in the hands of a master parent. . . . This, even though

Voskamp is now a man of forty-five and she, a mere "slip" of not quite seventeen.

JA. Will she someday paint *your* music?

B. She's not a painter. She's a musician . . . a great and equal master of piano and violin.

JA. Then the matter's settled, Boo. Here are your rings. . . . Go marry your little musician. I'll spend the remainder of *my* second life being a painter for CHOPIN, the wife of Donovan, and the mother of his children.

B. But Judy, things aren't this simple. My heart is equally divided between the two of you. I love Anna because she's an artist who understands the spirit of Beethoven; I love you for the same reason. . . . I love Anna because she uses her talent to interpret my music, so do you.

JA. Perhaps there's room in your heart for both of us, but not in your bed. You must now decide, Boo. You must decide which of us is to be the inspiration of Beethoven's present life.

B. You're right, Judy. The day has come when I must choose my Second-Order hausfrau. (*As I continue talking, I return both rings to Judy's hand.*) This time next week, I shall at last become the loving husband of a sweet girl. But who is she to be? Mrs. Judy van Beethoven, or Mrs. Anna Voskamp? In God's name, Kitten, help me decide.

JA. Very well, Paul. Let's talk about these two girls in your life. First of all, Anna is a musician, so are you. Has there ever been a time in Beethoven's life when he was truly happy collaborating with another musician of almost equal talent?

B. Never at the creative level. On this rarefied peak, it has always had to be Beethoven—sole . . . complete unto himself . . . the Great Mogul . . . a divine force sharing his self-forged throne with no other man. This is precisely why I was unable to adjust to corporate art within our Major culture.

JA. Then perhaps you're asking too much of Beethoven, expecting him now to settle down as the happy husband of a truly creative musician. As such, you can no longer be "sole," complete unto yourself, the Great Mogul.

B. When you speak this way, Judy, the Beethoven within me begins to doubt the plausibility of his love for Anna.

JA. But there can be no doubt about *our* collaboration . . . *our* love. By working and growing together, we've produced a genuinely new art form, recognized throughout our Major culture.

B. And far from being jealous of you, my dear, I have nothing but profound respect for your growth as an artist. . . .

JA. How about this Rosecranz? Is she not Jewish?

B. Her father's side is Jewish; the mother is Roman Catholic.

JA. Might not that ancient (though mild) anti-Semitism of our Beethoven rise in ultimate revolt against such a marriage?

B. I doubt this, Judy. Through Anna, I've begun to recognize the living and moral grandeur of Jewish ethics . . . the ideal sensitivity of Jewish tradition.

JA. Perhaps *you* have, but how about your new Germany? Will it recognize these great Jewish virtues, or will it swing in a downhill course that could alienate Herr Beethoven from his own countrymen?

B. I don't know. Only if such a stupid thing could happen on Earth.

JA. Consider the two of *us* from a purely sexual standpoint. At present, Anna is young and beautiful and seventeen. But she is a First-Order Subsidiary being. In forty short years, she'll be an old woman of fifty-seven—an old woman married to a young and vibrant Beethoven whose Second-Order body would still respond to centuries of happy sexuality could it but lie within the caressing arms of a like-minded and like-talented female . . . specifically within the arms of Judy Adams!

B. I see what you mean, Love. There is real truth in what you say. Such premature deprivation could drive a wedge between Beethoven and his Anna.

JA. And even worse, Paul, have you considered what it would be like being married to a First-Order wife and begetting First-Order children? As much as you would come to love them all, you could never share with them the divine comfort emanating from our Second-Order understanding of a person's permanent place in eternity. Should one of them lie dying in your arms, even then, you could not share the great secret, the great comfort of your life.

B. This does it, Judy, you've convinced me. My rightful place is at *your* side, in *your* arms. Beethoven's love for Anna is true, and I shall never deny this. But it came into being mostly because of my long and continued absences from you. I shall now return to Major life, become your devoted husband, and take up my rightful place at BEETHOVEN.

JA. Have you grown enough for all this?

B. Yes, Judy, I have.

JA. What about Anna?
B. Early this week, I'll arrange for Voskamp's "death." I know this will be painful for my little musician, but she's young. She'll adjust to a new life and a new love.
JA. Are you sure, Boo?
B. I'm sure she will. She'll do very well in spite of my departure—more than likely, because of it. This doesn't give your parents much time. Can they arrange for our wedding by next Saturday?
JA. You know Mom, Boo. She's been preparing our wedding for twenty years! There's no problem here. The problem is between you and me. Should there *be* a wedding next Saturday?
B. What do you mean, Judy?
JA. I'm not sure what I mean. Here, put your head in my lap. Let's enjoy Valhalla's stars and moons; this will give me some time to think things over.

Judy's soft caresses on my forehead combine with cool breezes of the mountain to form an irresistible lullaby. In a few minutes, I'm sound asleep. When I awaken, the sky is filled with the magical brightness of triple moonlight. Thus transformed, Judy's face is an almost florid sculpture of indescribable beauty (and sadness). There are tears running down both of her cheeks.

B. Judy! . . . You're crying! . . . Does it make you *this* sad to become Frau van Beethoven?
JA. No, Boo. . . . The tears are from a little girl who is *not* to become Frau van Beethoven.
B. Kitten! . . . What are you saying?
JA. You *must* return to your SCP and to the arms of your Anna.
B. Why? . . . Don't you love me anymore?
JA. I love you as much as life itself.
B. Then forget Anna and my SCP.
JA. This I would dearly love to do, but true marriage is never born of selfishness.
B. What do you mean?
JA. In talking you into marrying me, I was thinking mainly of myself and my *own* happiness.
B. You were thinking of *us* and *our* happiness!
JA. No, Boo. . . . Deep in my soul, I realize that successful marriages between two *like* artists are the greatest marriages of all.

B. But we *are* like artists. Our collaborations have been the same as our own children . . . you said so yourself.

JA. By "like artists," I don't mean a painter and a musician. I'm thinking of two musicians, two painters, two writers, two scientists, two teachers.

B. But Judy, we just agreed that there's liable to arise a dly professional jealousy between two married musicians when one of them is Beethoven.

JA. Possibly, but not necessarily. . . . Anna could well be sensitive enough to prevent this from happening, and your marriage to her would then be ideally creative. Such perfectly suited couples are among the happiest of Aaronians, and I don't want to be the girl who keeps Beethoven from enjoying the ultimate of Second-Order life.

B. But Darling . . . you've been so loyal to me all these years; I can't just turn and walk away!

JA. You can, and you *must* for the sake of our future happiness. Had Rembrandt been young enough to become my husband, I would gladly have terminated *our* romance in exchange for his love and the prospects of an exceptional marriage. Now you must do the same for Anna. Someday, perhaps in the Third Order . . . the Tenth Order . . . the Thousandth Order, we will both be creative musicians. Then watch me fly to your arms and become Frau van Beethoven! . . . Our love is an *eternal* thing, Paul. It can't be quenched by a few deaths and rebirths, nor by the tiny passing of centuries. Wait and see. . . . Someday, we *will* be man and wife, sharing in parenthood, and (no less) in the supreme joy of a common intellectual creativeness.

B. I hope so, Judy. . . . But what will you do in the meantime?

JA. I'll live and grow and be creative in the life at hand.

B. You and Donovan?

JA. Yes, Boo. He's a dear fellow who's been very patient, kind, and loving. Although we share no common art, I know the two of us will be very happy.

B. Will you continue to paint my music?

JA. Of course, Boo. The only sad thing about *our* collaboration is that you'll not be able to share it with Anna and your Subsidiary loved ones. But even in secret and probably at a reduced rate, I hope we at least continue what we've begun.

B. Then this is your final decision?

JA. Yes, Darling. Here are your rings; they belong to Anna, now.

B. And those tears of yours?

JA. On my favorite mountain . . . in the arms of my dearest love . . . I experience the saddest evening of two lifetimes. For this occasion, there must be tears. But they are not tears of self-pity. They are tears of love, of sacrifice, and of rejoicing in the happiness you will find with Anna.

We stand for a melting embrace in the moonlight of our mountain—a final and passionate kiss between Second-Order lovers.

B. Judy! . . . Is this *really* what you want?

JA. Yes, Paul. For *you* at least, this is really what I want. Good night, Love . . . and tomorrow . . . good-bye.

Chapter 47

Judy's decision for our lives returns me to a Subsidiary cultural planet that is literally exploding with change. During a period of only twenty-four years, it is scheduled to experience seventy years of Earth's history—roughly a period from 1830 to 1900. Subsequent to the turn of the century, SCP 7,900,111 is to remain a "current culture"; in other words, never more than one year behind the events of Earth.

The Austria to which I now return has just afforded me twenty years of unbelievably happy marriage to an unbelievably great musician. The story of these twenty years is the story of a changing Beethoven—a Beethoven filled with outgoing love; a Beethoven made humble, if not yet wise; a Beethoven who begins to see himself as he really is. In other words, a Beethoven whose life promises ultimate transformation through the miracle of Anna Rosecranz!

Anna and I are married on Saturday morning, November 1, 1879. At the request of her mother, the ceremony takes place in St. Stephen's Cathedral. Also because of Frau Rosecranz, many a quaint marriage custom is graciously transplanted from the Austrian countryside to the Voskamp hearth in the Hildebrandtstrasse. The first gift to arrive is a live calf upon which other wedding presents are to be hung. Early Saturday morning when Seibert, Oberhausen, and I approach the Rosecranz house, we find its door locked—a symbol of family opposition that the bridegroom must overcome. This I do by climbing through a second-story window. After the ceremony when everyone gathers at the Voskamps', there are two guards at the door from whom Anna must get permission to enter. One offers her a wooden knife, and the other a piece of bread. In the front yard is a blue and gold Protzwagen, decorated with fall leaves plus a selection of fine cheeses. There are also three barrels of wine and all sorts of goodies to blend tastefully with the cheese. On the staircase, a band of fifteen spirited musicians (all former Voskamp students) gathers to play endless rounds of country dances. Until late afternoon, the entire building is filled with hundreds of friends and wedding guests, all happily eating, drinking, singing, or dancing. Late that evening, the festivities finally end with a torchlight procession and a huge feast of roast kid and wine. This, Anna and I are not there to enjoy. At 5:00 PM, amid handfuls of rice and good wishes, we leave by private coach for Tulln, where at the Marburg Inn we've made reservations for a first night of wedded bliss.

During our journey in the airtight coach, as we cuddle beneath its warm blanket and as Anna's soft hair tickles my right cheek, I'm reminded of another starlight drive on another planet with another sweet girl on my shoulder. Dear Judy. . . . Has she made the right decision? What if my little Subsidiary wife should suddenly die, say, within a year or two? There would then be no reason for my continuing as Voskamp, and even less reason for returning to our Major culture. By then, Judy would certainly have committed herself to the role of Mrs. Donovan. Have we done the right thing? Anna clearly senses my preoccupation with outer space:

AR. Come, Darling. Back to earth. . . . You must tell me your starry thoughts.

B. Would that I could! Forgive me, Anna. Daydreaming has long been a weakness of mine, and there are no words for such thoughts. It shan't happen again, not now that I've a little wife to dream about.

Our lips meet in a huge warm kiss, and I no longer question Judy's decision.

During my early youth as Paul Rezler, I had read and been taught all sorts of interesting things about the differences between First and Second-Order sexuality. Many First-Order women, the books said, have difficulty adjusting to the sexual demands of a First-Order male, let alone to the hypervirility of a Second-Order husband. Should one of us establish a marital relationship with a Subsidiary woman, they went on to say, we must expect to repress some 50 percent of our normal animal desires, perhaps even more. This statistic is foremost in my mind during these first nights of bed sharing. But it well might not have been. I soon discover that as far as Anna is concerned, there is no need to repress anything. She's as fine a sex partner as she is musician, and as a musician, she's strictly Second-Order. In every way, she's comparable to Marcie Sbalzato, and even to my wildest dreams involving Judy. With such perfect physical compatibility between us, we should expect our first visit from the "stork" in nine months flat! But not so fast. First our marriage must give birth to a genuine sharing of music between us, then children. From Aaron, I bring a supply of little red pills that I take regularly. As soon as our careers are jointly resolved, the pills will go, and I know that our "stork" will be busily engaged!

Though Anna is now old enough and more than proficient enough to enter the Vienna Conservatory, she has no intentions of doing so. She plans instead to devote her full time to being my wife and a professional musician. Our honeymoon lasts for six months and turns out to be one long and magnificent concert tour that takes us to the principal cities of Europe. It's as though Voskamp wishes to show everyone on "earth" what a fine young musician he now has for a wife. For this tour (since it's not centered about the Collins Quartet), I temporarily lay aside my aversion to conducting. Beethoven's musicianly fear of a comparison to Sabatini is overcome by his desire to conduct for Anna. With each major orchestra, our programs consist of late Voskamp symphonies and four Voskamp concertos. In two of the concertos, I appear as piano and violin soloist; in the other pair (under *my* conductorship), Anna does the same. To complete our honeymoon tour, my wife and I (for the first time) set foot in the "New World." Before sellout crowds, we perform our series of concerts with the orchestras of New York City and Boston.

Our grand tour ends in April 23, with the docking of the Graz at Rotterdam. There to meet our ship is my ever-faithful "Ries"—Axel Oberhausen. Coming aboard, his handshake is a warm greeting; his eyes are the sure spirit of love. But his cold gray face is the very sadness of our winter's separation. We embrace.

B. Dear "Ries," how wonderful to see you. But you needn't have come all the way to the coast. To find you at the Vienna coach would have been welcome enough. . . . How is everyone?

R. Dear Vos . . . sweet Anna . . . I bring you sad news indeed.
B. The Steiners . . . have they not vacated their apartment?
R. Yes, on the tenth, as planned. They were even kind enough to help the Rosecranzes and me prepare things for you and Anna to move in.
B. Then what is so sad? Has everyone died?
R. This is not far from the truth, dear Maestro.
B. God in heaven, Oberhausen! Of whom do we speak?
R. Your mother, your father, and our dear Seibert. . . . All three have gone to their reward!

From knees down, my body stiffens with the freezing jolt of sudden shock. I can feel my face bleach, my heart pound to recapture the beats it has skipped. The cold hand of unanticipated reality clutches the back of my neck. After dizzy moments of near fainting, my breath at last returns in scrapes and scratches. The three of us are seated in deck chairs before I'm able to reply.

B. How, "Ries" . . . how did it happen?
R. During the night of April second, your mother woke up with a terrible pain in her head. By morning, her blindness had returned. Three doctors were summoned and concluded that she'd suffered a slight stroke.
B. Affecting her eyes?
R. This they agreed upon. During the next night . . . Saturday night . . . your father heard a slight gurgling coming from her bed. He sat up and listened carefully. She seemed to be resting quietly, so he went back to sleep.
B. And the next morning, she was dead?
R. Exactly, another stroke! But even in *this*, there is something for which to be grateful.
B. Like what?
R. The dear soul was spared the tears of having to greet your return with the tragedy of her blindness—a now permanent affliction, according to all three doctors.
B. But sixty-eight years . . . what a short life for such an angel!
R. Longer than many of our parents enjoy.
R. (*"Ries" pauses to clasp Anna's hand.*) And besides . . . look at this angel who has come to take your mother's place.
B. Thanks, Axel. You are a brother to me. But what of Father? How did he die?

R. He fretted terribly that you were not here to comfort him. But he seemed to understand that writing you would in no wise bring you home in time for the funeral.

B. Did the poor old man go to pieces?

R. He spent all Tuesday afternoon, standing by the Voskamp plot at the Zentralfriedhof. No one could get him to leave, nor would he permit the gravedigger to shovel that first cruel clump of earth. At suppertime, a dozen of us went to carry him home, by force if need be. The poor soul studied each of our faces. He looked so old and frail, stooping there in the deserting sun, so helpless. At last he fell to his knees, covered his face with his hands, and sobbed the saddest words I've ever heard.

B. Poor Father. . . . What did he say?

R. "Go ahead," he said. "Go ahead and cover her with your monstrous stones and your foul-smelling clay. She's asleep now, and the likes of you can do her no harm!"

B. My God! Then what happened?

R. We got him home, all right, but he wouldn't touch his supper. It was two in the morning before he finally dozed off.

B. Was he no better when he awakened?

R. Next morning, he was his old self again . . . talked of nothing but you and Anna, and of the countless little preparations we must effect in the apartment below . . . all in time for your return to the Hildebrandtstrasse.

B. Did someone stay with him?

R. Through Thursday night. By Friday, he appeared so cheerfully optimistic that further vigilance seemed unnecessary. On Saturday morning, he was not to be found anywhere!

B. Where had he gone?

R. His bed had not been slept in, and he had quite disappeared.

B. Then what?

R. On Tuesday afternoon, Herr Voskamp's body was discovered on the banks of the Danube . . . not far from Krems.

B. But suicide is so unlike my father.

R. Exactly what we said. Perhaps in his mourning state, he wandered off, confused . . . stepped too close to the water's edge.

B. This is what I prefer to think . . . not suicide. In all his seventy years, he showed no signs of cowardice. He'd not be one to flee from the death of my mother.

R. Exactly right! Well, Vos . . . here you have the news of my sad mission—not a joyous trip to welcome you home, but the cruel blow of death's own messenger. I've leased a private coach. If you'll do me the honor, this should make the trip to Vienna less burdensome.

B. Thank you, Ries, I'm indeed grateful for your kindness. On the way home, I'll try to compose myself. How much better than arriving in a complete state of shock! You mentioned our Seibert, what on earth happened to him?

R. Poor old "Schuppanzigh." On the weekend of March twenty-seventh, he visited his brother at Berndorf. Late Monday night, his horse returned home without its rider. We feared the worst; and sure enough, on Wednesday morning, Seibert's body was found in a ditch about halfway between Baden and Mödling.

B. The roughrider! I told him he was too old for horseback. . . . Thrown from the saddle?

R. Yes. His neck was broken.

B. It seems as though you could have written me of all this terrible news. And yet . . . what good would it have done?

R. In no case could you have arrived in time to stand at the open grave. And moreover, this way you can remember your loved ones as they *were*.

B. I appreciate your wisdom, Ries. My honeymoon with Anna will always remain the happiest memory of Voskamp's life. And thanks to you, it will be a memory untouched by ravages of the Grim Reaper.

Upon our arrival at the Hildebrandtstrasse, Anna and I promptly move into the second-floor apartment (those rooms vacated by the Steiners) as planned. In spite of the elaborate preparations made by our friends and loved ones, we spend considerable time putting our new quarters in order. We further decide to indulge in the luxury of two apartments. Those rooms on the second floor will be used strictly for private Lebensraum (living space): no musicians, no pupils; those on the third floor will continue to serve as Voskamps' Court work rooms, practice rooms, storage space. There must be little remaining in that former apartment to remind me of the sad and sudden departure of my dear parents.

On Sunday morning, May 2, Anna and I attend church and candlelighting services at St. Stephen's Cathedral. We then journey to the Central Friedhof with flowers for the new graves. Anna returns home, leaving me there alone with my thoughts and tears and meditations. The fingers of spring search gently through the new green grass; there is nothing but a mound of brown to crown the head of each new grave. The almost warm wind sings clearly of winter's final song; beneath that clay, there is no singing, no end of winter's darkness. The sky moves swiftly about its important business; down below, nothing moves, nothing is important. I stand where my father stood not a month ago, and I weep bitter tears on the very spot where he wept bitterly. Poor Voskamp weeps long and hard; he weeps until the Beethoven within him at last begins to smile. Beethoven, smile? Yes! This is the ultimate miracle of rebirth; this is the true reward of having lived a regenerative life. To be reborn is never again to yield death or grave his greedy victory. I smile at the loss of these dear ones. Though I would love to have had them a while longer, their death is but a positive confirmation of our eventual reunion. These dear parents. . . . How strange! . . . They remain just long enough to see their old son happily married and then they journey on. Dear souls! If only I could have told them my secret, how much brighter their last hours would have been. Oh well, one day they'll know the reason for my smile.

June begins with the making of promises. Since I now plan in the fall to bring out my first block of "Brahms" on SCP 7,900,111, I promise Schoenbern and Kietzing a five-year pile of new music that will be Voskamp's first significant evolution in thirty years. Since I know that Anna will be deeply affected by this "latest Voskamp," I promise her the surprise of a lifetime. Realizing the importance of keeping the Collins group alive and happy (the backbone basis of any successful musical Court must always and of necessity be an excellent string quartet), I meet with Schu, Nesbitt, and Kovsky, promising them (by fall) a replacement for our dear and lamented "Schuppanzigh." This is doubly important since I now plan to do most of my concert touring with Anna, and the group will need the stabilizing influence of a more permanent first violinist than either Seibert or I had recently been.

My little wife and I spend the entire summer (through October 18) at Bad Ischl. During these months, I prepare my list of Brahms's opuses. For piano and voice, there is an album of fifty songs. These (like all the Brahms) are selected for our SCP by Subsidiary Control, and (without exception) I find no reason to doubt their choice. Since as Beethoven, I never contributed much toward German Lieder, the pieces of this set hold a great fascination for me—particularly as to their melodic beauty, their quasi-symphonic blending of parts, and their frugal but significant harmonic evolution. Anna spends much of her time singing these songs to my accompaniment, and by the end of summer we sincerely appreciate most of them. In the piano solo department, there is an album of ten pieces to be published "as is." There are also two sets of variations and three piano sonatas. The *Variations and Fugue on a Theme of Handel,* with the sole exception of Bach's *Goldberg* set, are the finest Earthly compositions in this form that I have yet had the privilege of hearing or playing. I can't decide which offers me the greatest pleasure—performing them myself, or listening while Anna plays them. The *Pianoforte Variations on a Theme of Paganini* at first seemed to rub against my grain—too much technique and not enough music. But as I hear Anna perform them, and (not to be outdone by my industrious wife) as I begin seriously practicing them myself, they seem suddenly to stretch and sparkle with the true light of Brahmsian inspiration. By fall, my piano technique has greatly benefited from their study, and I rank them but a few short steps beneath the summit of the Handel group. Of the three piano sonatas, only the third (in F Minor) is to be published on my SCP exactly as Brahms wrote it. The other two undergo a considerable revision by Beethoven, so much so that the "C Major" begins to sound like a second *Grosse Sonate für das Hammerklavier.* But in spite of my superimposition of "Beethovenisms," Anna cares little for these sonatas; she considers them "too big to be beautiful."

In the category of chamber music, there is the *Cello Sonata in E Minor* with its superb and characteristic piano part. There are three quartets for piano, violin, viola, and cello; of these, the first two are accepted note for note as written by Brahms. The third has its opening and closing allegros fittingly decomposed and recomposed in the Voskamp tradition. The list concludes with a pair of especially fine string sextets, a piano quintet, and three string quartets—these latter I'm tempted to revise, but for lack of time, decide to spend the precious summer hours elsewhere on my Brahmsian block. Anna is thoroughly pleased with her husband's "new" chamber pieces, and the two of us can hardly wait to perform them with our dear Hildebrandtstrasse colleagues.

There are four major symphonic opuses: *Piano Concerto in D Minor, Symphony No. 1 in C Minor, Symphony No. 2 in D,* and *Violin Concerto in D.* After much score reading and discussion, Anna and I agree that these works are indeed a worthy evolution from the best pieces composed by Collins and Voskamp. (What a tribute to Herr Brahms!) We further agree to make them the basis of our concertizing in the immediate future.

Concluding my first block of Brahms are two large choral works. *A German Requiem* and *Song of Destiny.* To their revision and polishing are devoted most of the summer's working hours at Bad Ischl. By fall, I'm thoroughly pleased with the results—a pair of good choral pieces, worthy to stand beside the very best pages of the *Missa Solemnis.*

The only dark spot in my new Subsidiary life with Anna is the total absence of friends, family, and loved ones from our Major culture. There are phone calls and short visits to Aaron, but these aren't enough to satisfy my deep longing. If only someone from "back home" could come here to my SCP and live out the days of his subordinate assignment, here in my new Vienna, here in the Hildebrandtstrasse, then how complete and how perfect would be the happiness of my new life.

In pursuit of this dream, I leave Anna at Bad Ischl during the first week of August and sneak away to Aaron EP4, where my Earthly brother Johann is taking part in a Beethoven festival. Perhaps he would enter my Court as Seibert's replacement and become the new first violinist of our Collins Quartet. During the festival, Johann performs three Beethoven concertos on three successive evenings. What a masterful violinist he turns out to be, and how proud I am of this former "landowner!"

At the conclusion of his third appearance (on Friday the sixth), I go backstage to introduce myself. This takes considerable doing since Johann has never seen me in my aging Voskamp disguise. It requires a piano improvisation and careful reminiscences of the Gneixendorf days to finally convince him who I am. Then comes an explosion of hugs and kisses and tears, fitting to commemorate the long-awaited reunion of Earthly brothers:

B. Dear Johann! . . . Little Brother! . . . How godly good it is once again to hold you in my arms . . . and such a great violinist you've turned out to be!

J. Dear Ludwig! . . . Big Brother! . . . I can't believe it's really you. . . . It seems as though you've gone on to some higher life and that only your great ghost has stopped off here to brighten our Second-Order days.

B. But I *am* here, Johann, and I can't believe my eyes or ears.

J. Seeing is believing . . . and so is hearing.

B. But you . . . my old moneymonger of a brother. To think that the likes of *you* could actually learn to fiddle away his time!

J. Always the punster! But I *have* learned to fiddle, and it's a lot more profitable than selling chemicals.

B. To what do you attribute your artistic success?

J. To you! . . . To being your brother! I have no illusions regarding my career. People don't pack the halls to hear Johann van Beethoven; they come to hear Johann (brother of Ludwig) van Beethoven!

B. Then you *do* owe me some small piece of your present career.

J. I owe it *all* to you!

B. This is not true, Johann, but very kind of you to say. Will you do me a favor?

J. Anything, Ludwig. You have only to name it.

B. I am now at the threshold of the happiest and most productive days I have ever lived. All the wonderful things I dreamed of having here in the Major Order (but could not have) are now unbelievably mine within the province of Subsidiary life. At my side is the perfect helpmate for Beethoven—a beautiful little girl who is as much an angel as she is musician, and whose face and eyes hold the inspiration for a thousand compositions. I am now free from the scourge of deafness and from the curse of financial insecurity. I have benefited from a thorough study of Brahms, which affords me a superb new garb for my greatest compositions. I have an eager publisher, a tiny but devoted Court, a group of industrious students, and an intelligent public that clamors to hear my concerts.

J. With all this, you need no favor from me.

B. But I do, Johann.

J. What?

B. To make my heaven complete, all that's needed is for an Earthling loved one to come and live out the days of his subordinate assignment within the midst of my ideal circle of Subsidiary musicians.

J. I'll be glad to do this, Ludwig. Side by side for twenty years, we'll grow as "brothers in music." I'll have a chance to snoop into your newest concertos while they're still being written.

B. And you'll be first violinist in the planet's best quartet trying over my greatest chamber pieces before their pages have dried.

J. Fine! Put me down for the first two decades of the twentieth century.

B. Twentieth century! You must come with me now . . . this Fall! I can't wait twenty years for your translation. I need you *now* . . . not in 1900!

J. That's impossible.

B. Why?

J. At present, my career is progressing too smoothly to be interrupted.

B. In what way?

J. I don't have a Court in the sense that my famous brother does, but I do have a core of admiring friends, twenty promising students, and a genuine musical public on EP4.

B. You'll have all this and more on my SCP.

J. But here there's a chance of my being admitted to BEETHOVEN. Several times their auditors have attended my concerts, and I've received very favorable reports.

B. There's more than a chance of your being admitted if you'll come with me now. We'll spend our twenty years together on SCP 7,900,111, and then we'll both retranslate to Aaron in 1900. I'll claim my managing partnership at BEETHOVEN, and I'll see to it that you're admitted as a full partner. How does that sound?

J. Wonderful . . . except for one thing.

B. What now?

J. My wife and I are the parents of three children, ranging in age from four to nine. Translating prior to 1900 would be unfair to them.

B. Damn! There goes the perfect plan. It seems as though there's always something to stand between me and complete happiness. Oh well. If you come in 1900, then we'll return to our BEETHOVEN in 1920.

J. You needn't wait twenty years. I've a better plan.

B. What?

J. Among my best students, there's a young chap who—

B. Don't be silly, Johann. I've got plenty of good violinists of my own. What I'm looking for is someone from my Earthly experience who will now come and stand beside Beethoven during his years of greatest musical change and growth—not just another violinist.

J. Perhaps this young fellow will qualify. You must hear him before you leave.

B. Why?

J. Wait and see.

B. When does he play?

J. He's second violinist in the Headley Quartet, which gives regular Sunday afternoon concerts at the Arcross Studio. This group specializes in your chamber music, and considering who their guest of honor will be, I see no reason why they can't meet tomorrow morning.

B. At their studio?

J. No. At my home, 3634 Eberton Way.

B. I'll be there at nine.

J. Good! So will they.

On Saturday morning at eight thirty, I arrive at my brother's house. Already, there are sounds of the beloved *C-sharp Minor* issuing from Johann's parlor. He introduces me to his wife and children, then leads the way to his living room. As we enter, the quartet of young men stops playing and jumps to its feet. After brief introductions, they resume their seats and their performance of my old (still new-sounding) Opus 131, beginning again with its opening fugue. My, how this glorious music brings back those final days of Earthly searching. How extremely close I was to discovering what I now know to be true—the absolute immortality of the human spirit!

While they play, I listen very carefully to Max Barth, the young second fiddler in whom Johann thinks I might be interested. I study his tones, his phrasing, his bowing, his ensemble. I study his face unremittingly; it soon breaks into the sweat of self-consciousness. I study his eyes; they are filled with sensitivity and, quite often, with tears. Have we not met before? Who *is* this lad?

At the conclusion of the *C-sharp Minor*, they launch an immediate performance of *Quartet No. 15 in D* by Beethoven II—that ultimate tribute of mine to my own third-period Earthly style. Although I would have been perfectly pleased to sit through their rendition of this newer work, Johann pulls at my sleeve and motions for me to follow him. Once in the hall, he closes the living room door behind us. We can still hear the music, but the players are well beyond the range of our whispered conversation.

J. Tell me, Ludwig, what do you think of young Barth?

B. He's a fair musician, but by Second-Order standards, there's nothing exceptional about him.

J. Last night, I had a long talk with the boy; he's willing to translate to your SCP.

B. But Johann, what good is this? Subsidiary beings as they are, several of my present students can play circles around your Barth.

J. You wanted an Earthling acquaintance who would translate to your Subsidiary world.

B. Ah! . . . Then we *have* met. I thought so! The expression of the eyes; this gives them away every time. Who *is* he? A former student?

J. Much closer than this.

B. Quick, Johann . . . tell me! Who *is* he?

J. For over fifteen years, you called him your own son.

B. God in heaven! . . . Karl! . . . Karl! . . . KARL!!

I burst into Johann's parlor, screaming the name of my former nephew. When I finally reach him, I'm practically on all fours, having upset a chair, a coffee table, a set of dishes, and two music racks. Three-fourths of the quartet flees for its life, leaving my poor wide-eyed Barth standing there alone with trembling knees. We clamp together in a huge father-son embrace, both of us laughing and crying at the same time:

B. Karl! . . . Dear Son! . . . I can't believe it, the two of us together again. Now there are no imperfections in God's creation, for even death has not kept you permanently from my arms.

Ka. Dear Uncle. . . . Father! . . . This moment brings me great happiness, but I'm not yet sure that I've grown enough to come and take my place at your side.

B. You have . . . you *have*, Karl! Never among Second-Order musicians have I heard a greater violinist than yourself! You play with the feeling of a true artist, and I'm very proud of you, my boy.

Ka. In the tradition of your Earthly example, I've *tried* to grow, Father . . . honestly I have.

B. Bless you, Karl.

Ka. My musical talent is nothing to brag about, but I *do* wish to make the most of it. Uncle Johann encourages me, and has been my teacher for eighteen years.

B. Uncle Johann is very wise. This is exactly what you should do for a career.

Ka. Your life on Earth has taught me something very important.

B. What's that?

Ka. Dedication. True happiness springs only from a complete dedication to something. And in this spirit, I have taken up the violin.

B. Then my dreams for you have come true. This is exactly what I was trying to teach you on Earth. You must have thought that my sole purpose there was to make your life miserable; but this was not the case, I assure you. In my poor misguided way, I was only trying to teach you something you now know. What a handsome fellow you've turned out to be. How old are you, Karl?

Ka. I was reborn in 1858 at thirteen years of age; I'm now thirty-five.

B. Have you become a Second-Order husband?

Ka. No, not yet. I'm still waiting for my First-Order wife to arrive here.

B. Caroline Naske?

Ka. Yes. What a dear soul she is! After her rebirth, if things are still companionable between us, we shall become a Second-Order husband and wife.

B. Unusual. . . . But this does happen. She bore you quite a family.

Ka. Four daughters and a son.

B. A son, Ludwig. What about him? Has he married?

Ka. Yes, in 1865. News of the Beethovens doesn't reach this Order as pronouncedly as it did when you were at their helm, but I hear that Ludwig is now married and has a son who bears my name.

B. Good. Then there's still hope for us "Earthly Beethovens." What of *your* translation? Johann tells me that you're willing to come to my SCP.

Ka. I might as well, perhaps it will be twenty years before Caroline joins me here. By then, my Subsidiary assignment will be out of the way, and I'll be a lot better musician for having spent two decades with my mean old uncle!

B. I'm not your mean old uncle anymore, Karl. If I sound mean and old, it's because you remember me as I *was*. If I look mean and old, it's because of my Subsidiary disguise as a Voskamp of forty-two years. But beneath these subelectrons is Paul Rezler—as handsome, as kind, and as understanding a young chap as has ever graced the planets of our Second-Order. Rezler has succeeded in taming 50 percent of your old Mogul uncle, and the other half has been amply taken care of by a dear teenaged wife named Anna Rosecranz. Wait until you meet her, Karl; you'll love her as I do. She is a truly great musician—a pianist and violinist of unbelievable stature. You'll learn as much from her as from me.

Ka. Then you promise there'll be no "ruling tyranny" over my personal life?

B. Absolutely! If you have a mind to do so, you can rape every pretty girl in the Prater. As far as I'm concerned, my sole jurisdiction over you begins and ends with the responsibility for your maximum musical development. Between Anna and myself, we can provide this for you.

Ka. Good! Then I shall translate as soon as possible.

B. You'll be glad you did, Karl. Everything that should have developed between us on Earth will now come true. For twenty years, we'll travel the extent of that little planet as man to man, as musician to musician, each inspiring the other, each growing because of the other. Then we'll return here together . . . the two of us. We'll take up our permanent places at BEETHOVEN. Hand in hand, we two shall direct the future course of that firm that now bears our Earthly name.

Ka. This is wonderful, Father. But it sounds as though you're doing everything for me; and I, nothing for you.

B. On the contrary. The next twenty years should contain the dearest memories of my Second-Order life. In 1900, I plan to return here; and without your loving presence on my SCP, there would be no one with whom to share these best of Subsidiary memories. No, Karl. Don't worry about how little you do for me. If anything, I'll end up owing much to you.

Ka. That settles it then. Have you anyone in mind through whom I should effect my transfer?

B. Definitely. A twenty-four-year-old master performer named Kurt Bardy. He's been my pupil since 1877 and, during the past three years, has made such progress on the violin (especially in chamber playing), that his technique is now every bit the equal of Anna's and mine.

Ka. He's free of amorous attachments, of course.

B. Not quite, being happily married and the father of two.

Ka. Then he's out of the question. It's impossible for me to become maritally involved with anyone until I've had a chance to talk things over with my dear Caroline.

B. But Caroline might not even be reborn into our Major Order.

Ka. Possibly not. If such should be the case, *then* would be time enough for me to consider marrying another girl. Who else is there? Surely you have another pupil, a handsome young bachelor through whom I could translate.

B. Yes I do. His name is Cabot Roscher. He's been my violin student for one year. He's brilliant, single, handsome, and twenty-two; but he's not half the musician Bardy is.

Ka. That's all right. I'd rather be half the musician than half a person. Besides, when I combine my Second-Order talent with that of Roscher, and when the two of us receive daily help and guidance from our "Uncle Ludwig," I have no doubt that we will eventually equal and surpass the musicianship of Herr Bardy.

B. Very well, Karl . . . Cabot Roscher it is! Have your counselor contact me through the Waldmüller Kaffehaus; I'll be glad to help him with the details. We'll be looking for you and Herr Roscher's ruby ring in about two months.

Ka. That's right, dear Uncle. By mid-October, the two of us will again go walking in the Graben; and this time, there'll be no tribe of "hooting imps" to embarrass me.

In October 18, Anna and I return to our Hildebrandtstrasse home, where we hold Court through January 1, 1881. Without children of her own, Anna finds relatively little housekeeping associated with our second-floor living quarters; she is able to spend most of her daylight hours working diligently at her husband's side, upstairs in our third-floor music department. By the end of 1880, without exception, each of my piano or violin students is now a pupil of Herr *and* Frau Voskamp. I'm amazed at how well we seem to complement one another as teachers. My little musician wife also proves herself indispensable to our editing department, where she works hand in hand with Oberhausen and me in preparing our new crop of "Brahms" scores for Schoenbern and Kietzing.

Karl "arrives" on November 2, 1880, and it doesn't take Anna long to notice my increased interest in (and preference for) Cabot Roscher. In the light of Kurt Bardy's still considerable margin of superiority, she finds this difficult to understand. As I begin preparing my new favorite pupil for the position of first violinist with the Collins Quartet, Anna commences a similar campaign for young Bardy. Thus are sown the seeds of what will presently become the first musical argument within our otherwise perfectly tranquil marriage.

Since Anna and I feel that neither of our protégés is yet adequate to serve as first violinist of our beloved quartet, we spend a good many happy hours occupying this "first chair" ourselves—on practically an alternating basis. With the Collins group, we participate in no less than thirty-six Viennese concerts during these twelve weeks. Most of them are devoted to premiering, performing, and reperforming my new "Brahms" chamber pieces. We both give solo concerts featuring the "new" piano pieces, and for the first time, Arturo Sabatini brings his great Berlin orchestra all the way to Vienna in order to present world premières of Voskamp's orchestral "Brahms": *Symphony No. 1, Symphony No. 2, Piano Concerto in D Minor, Violin Concerto in D, A German Requiem,* and *Song of Destiny.* All this "new" music is well received by the Viennese, though several important critics (notably Ralph Knepper of Berlin and our own Karl Herschl) embarrassingly lament the passing of my former style.

January 2 through May 15, 1881, is devoted to another grand tour. As on our honeymoon, this traveling takes us through most of Europe and to the United States. During these months, Anna and I perform with thirty-seven major orchestras. Our programs are devoted mainly to the new "Brahms," wherein the symphonies and especially the violin concerto are widely applauded. Our chief disappointment is in the relatively poor reception of the piano concerto. Though its careful pages contain much great music, they sing their song well over the heads (and ears) of most of our audiences. We feel that it's the Voskamps who are being applauded, *not* the concerto.

From May through October, we summer in Switzerland. During these delightful months, I compose nothing new! Instead, I carefully study the great Brahms pieces that have just been credited to Voskamp's pen. How else am I to effect a genuine Beethoven evolution from the style of this formidable Earthling? Strange indeed! What an unusual parallel. On Earth, Brahms studies Beethoven in order to write good Brahms; here in "heaven," Beethoven studies Brahms in order to write good Beethovenian Brahms!

The first months of our marriage set a creative-artistic-domestic routine, which is followed uninterruptedly for ten years. Summers are spent at Swiss and Austrian retreats. The first three are devoted to studying my block of "Brahms"; the remaining are used to compose a sequence of Brahms-like pieces of my own. These include the following credits to Voskamp's list: two symphonies, a piano concerto, a violin concerto, four string quartets, two piano quintets, a piano trio, two string sextets, a violin sonata, two piano sonatas, two sets of piano variations, three albums of lieder, and sixteen piano pieces published on my SCP as *Klavierstüke.* Running true to Beethoven, my song cycles are a poor substitute for genuine Brahms; but nevertheless, they find their way into print. All the other pieces are good music from the standpoint of what they're trying to do, namely, extend through Beethoven the production of Brahms on my particular SCP. Though hard to believe, none of this music sounds like the curious hybrid one might expect, nor is it merely imitative. It rings with the romantic melodies and the precise structures so characteristic of that Earthling poet-peasant whose creative technique inspires and (in a sense) fathers it all. These compositions are a disappointment to me in one respect. Through my study of Brahms, I had hoped to evolve a new and genuine Beethovenian style. Such does not occur. I succeed in writing good "Brahms" and nothing more.

As of 1880, within our Major culture, BEETHOVEN finally completes its ultimate tribute to my third-period Earthly style: twenty-seven symphonies, eighteen quartets, and nine piano concertos. By then, had it received no helpful suggestions from me, the firm was going to make its own evolution into its own fourth-period style. But such bold independence is not required; my creative adventure into the Classical-Romantic world of Johannes Brahms is ample inducement for Beethoven's namesake corporation to follow along the same path. Bonaparte considers my "decision for Brahms" to be prima facie evidence of the precise direction in which I would have led our organization had I become its managing partner. Throughout our cultural planets, the corporate BEETHOVEN accordingly publishes, promotes, records, and performs all the revised and nonrevised Brahms that appears under Voskamp's name on SCP 7,900,111. They do the same for the decade of original pieces that I compose in the style of Brahms. And finally, they go to work on a huge block of Brahms-like compositions of their own. To help them in this latter task, they absorb a group of two partners, three principals, and five juniors, which were granted the BRAHMS charter in 1876. This auxiliary corporation plans to remain with BEETHOVEN until Brahms himself arrives and decides what it should do.

January through May of each of these ten years is devoted to concert-giving. Most of our performances (especially premières) are in Vienna itself. We make frequent appearances under Sabatini in Berlin. Only three out of the ten seasons are extensive enough (in terms of miles traveled) to be called European tours. Even so, by 1890, there is wide acceptance of my new "Brahms" style. This is due partly to Anna's playing and mine, but predominantly to the extensive tours and superb conducting of Arturo Sabatini.

Late fall and early winter of each year are spent holding Court in the Hildebrandtstrasse. Although the unfolding beauty of an ideal marriage does manage to fill the huge vacuum left by the death of Voskamp's parents, Anna cannot replace Beethoven's need for a "Court." Even as a happily married man, I must have the comforting assurance of my tiny throne in order to function as a creative artist. I still need to be "king of the clique"—a leader of admiring followers, the "Great Mogul," if I'm to compose and perform at the optimum level.

During Vienna's epidemic of the winter of 1881, my Court is totally depleted by the death of Axel Oberhausen, whose flu turns suddenly to pneumonia. This dear young "Ries" of mine is as sadly mourned by Anna as by myself. Though he was only thirty-nine, my wife considered his interpretations of Voskamp's piano music to be as good as any she had ever heard. To fill the vacancy created by the passing of this beloved factotum-student, Anna and I carefully study our current crop of thirteen private piano pupils. One is from the Paris Conservatory, two are from Berlin, the other ten are local graduates. Within a month, we narrow our choice to a pair of brilliant twenty-three-year-olds: Ralph Gay and Victor Pepusch, both recent graduates of the Vienna Conservatory. In the fall of 1882 (just in time for the convening of Court), both young pianists are elevated to the full status of inner-circle courtiers. The pianistic progress and eager factotum services of these ambitious musicians remind me so much of Oberhausen that I'm tempted to dub them "Ries II" and "Ries III," but such numerical ordering would certainly raise questions. Therefore, Gay's official nickname becomes "Czerny," and I begin referring to Pepusch as "Ries." Just as on Earth, my new "Czerny" and "Ries" vie for first place in the heart of their teacher. And just as on Earth, the professional growth that explodes from the artistic competition of these young men is truly remarkable. With the passing of years, I'm almost sorry that I nicknamed them as I did. The personal warmth and sparkling humor of an exuberant Gay reminds me more of Ries than anyone else, and the serious plodding of Pepusch is typical of the Earthly Czerny. But once assigned, their given names remain unchanged throughout the years of our professional association!

Since the very day of nephew Karl's translation to my SCP, I can hardly wait to promote him to Seibert's former chair in the Collins Quartet. Here he will achieve maximum growth as a Second-Order violinist, and our careers should run parallel for twenty productive years. Though Kurt Bardy would be my logical choice for the position, I, of course, decide in favor of Cabot Roscher, who has been "absorbed" by my nephew and duly "knighted" as "Sir Karl." Roscher is an excellent violinist, but he lacks the natural talent and "violin personality" of young Bardy. It is my hope that in absorbing Roscher, my nephew will bring to him the genuine maturity of a Second-Order musician and will end up being at least the equal of Herr Bardy.

In the fall of 1882, upon our return from a refreshing summer at Thun, we hold our first meeting of Voskamp's Court. Without the slightest hint to Anna, and without consulting her, I proudly announce Roscher's appointment to the position of first violinist with our Collins group. There are rounds of applause for my nephew, but at least from Anna and Bardy, the congratulations filter through long, sad faces. After several hours of planning the current season, Court is adjourned for the day. To my surprise, when I go downstairs, I find that our guest for the noonday meal is Bardy and not my nephew. The three of us seat ourselves at the table and immediately begin talking instead of eating. It's almost as though the food were incidental—an excuse for our sitting down together. Anna is first to speak.

AR. Mason, there's something I wish to talk over with you.
B. I wonder if I can guess what it is.
AR. I'm sure you can.
B. Let me try. . . . It has something to do with my appointment of Herr Roscher to his new position.
AR. It does!
B. And what's that?
AR. In making this appointment, I think you're being grossly unfair to Kurt Bardy.
B. In making this appointment, I don't care *how* you think I'm being to Herr Bardy. The decision is mine, and it's final. That's all there is to it!
AR. But surely you must know that Kurt here is the better violinist of the two.
B. I know nothing of the kind. If I thought so, then *he* would have the appointment instead of Cabot.
AR. (*By now, Anna is in tears.*) Mason . . . as a personal favor . . . for the sake of our Divine Muse . . . I beg you to reconsider.
B. There's nothing to reconsider; my decision is final. If Kurt were any kind of a man, *he* would have brought his wishes directly to me instead of hiding behind your skirt.

KB. (*Bardy jumps to his feet.*) Sir, I have *no* wishes in the matter. Your decision is final, and I hide behind *no* one's skirt.

B. Then perhaps you'd better leave!

AR. Mason! . . . I'll not have you talk this way to our guest!

B. *Your* guest, not mine!

KB. (*Bardy takes a deep breath in order to compose himself. When he resumes talking, his voice is warm and friendly—the exact opposite of my shameful shrieks.*) Herr Voskamp, I come to this table to pay my respects to both of you and to say good-bye, not to seek advantages behind your back. No matter what my musical career might hold for me, the years in which I've known the Voskamps will always be the crowning glory of my life. Not only are you the greatest musicians that I shall ever know, but your creative marriage sets the perfect standard for me to dream of achieving in higher orders. I would have dearly loved to remain in your Court, but I accept your wise decision favoring Roscher. I accept it without question. Because of your kind recommendations, there is a professorship open to me at the conservatory. There I shall be able to teach, to solo, to play in chamber groups . . . in short, to continue my career.

I'm completely overcome by the nobility of Bardy's voice and attitude. Now there are tears in *my* eyes. How I wish that Karl had absorbed *this* young man. I can hardly resist throwing my arms around him.

B. Bardy . . . forgive my shouting at you. It's because you *are* such a master violinist that my choice was so difficult. Why not stay on in our Court? We'll make room for you.

KB. Thank you, Maestro. I appreciate your invitation, but for the sake of my playing, I must find a spot in a chamber group.

B. That's what I mean. We'll give you Mark Schu's chair. He's an old man now; it's high time that he retire.

KB. Schu *is* an old man, but he's also a great musician. And the reward of his greatness should not be some gold-watch request for his retirement. No . . . I thank you for your offer. I'll be glad to accept Schu's chair when *he* decides to retire, not when someone decides for him.

B. I marvel at your unselfishness, Bardy; you are a fine fellow. Someday when Schu retires of his own volition, we'll repeat our offer to you.

KB. Good! I'll be glad to accept. Until then, I bid you good-bye. . . . Good-bye to my dear inspiring teachers!

Our greatest violin student bows and leaves the room. Only after long minutes do Anna and I take up our untouched food. With tears in our eyes and with quivery lips, we're a sad picture indeed. At last, Anna speaks.

AR. I don't know, Vos. . . . Considering your preferential treatment, you'd think Roscher were our own son, or at least part of the family.
B. In a sense he is, Anna. He is like a *son* to me.

During concert seasons of this first decade of our married life, Anna and I share enough music (appearing alternately as pianist and violinist) to fill her days completely. During our regular fall-winter sessions at Court, Anna divides her time between second-floor duties as a housewife and third-floor responsibilities as a musician. With an artistically favored ratio of three to one, here again is plenty of music between us to keep her happy and bright. This is not true of our first three summers in the country, where about all we have time to share is a big fluffy feather bed. I'm so busy sketching and studying Brahms that I'm hardly aware of Anna's presence. The poor girl has little to do but become restlessly rested. Suddenly, early in the summer of '83, she sneaks up to my "composing rock" on the outskirts of Thun. I'm actually surprised by the determined look on her face:

B. Anna! . . . What's the matter?
AR. I've got a complaint, dear Husband.
B. I can see that, dear wife . . . but what?
AR. I feel as though we're sharing nothing at all!
B. Don't be silly, Anna. Not one couple in ten thousand shares as much of their lives as we do.
AR. Concerts and teaching . . . yes. But we share nothing at the creative level.
B. What do you mean?
AR. I want you to teach me composition.
B. Why?
AR. Since apparently we're not to have children of our own, I must feel that at least in some way, I'm sharing a creative act with my husband!

B. But composition isn't something to be shared. It's a private thing . . . a personal thing.

AR. It needn't be. Teach me what you're doing in those little sketchbooks of yours. Show me your creative secrets. Then I won't feel so barren without children.

B. Don't worry about children. They'll be along in a few years, I promise you.

AR. Even so . . . I still want to share your composing with you . . . your supreme creative act.

B. Dear Anna . . . one is *born* to compose; I can't teach you this. I can expose you to the accepted rules and practices of melody, harmony, counterpoint, form, and orchestration; but I can't teach you to compose. *No* one can!

AR. Then teach me the rules; your dedicated life will inspire the rest. Someday you'll be glad you have a composer for a wife; you'll want me to help you, and I'll be able to do so. Besides, long after our physical children are born, grown, and flown, we'll *still* be having our musical babies. When other marriages as old as ours have long since folded their hands and closed their eyes in anticipation of death, ours will still be young and smiling and creating. . . . Who could ask more from life than this?

Anna's request brims with such wide-eyed determination that I start her lessons at once. As in piano and violin, her results are phenomenal. By the summer of '87, she has left the "rules" behind and is snooping through my sketchbooks—offering suggestions and help, but never once getting in my way . . . never once offending the dwindling "Mogul" within me. How ironic! At BEETHOVEN, I grew to hate every form of creative collaboration. But here on my SCP with my own little wife, I begin to enjoy (actually profit by) collaboration with a giant composer whose profound gifts unfold so gently, so naturally, so unobtrusively that I'm hardly aware of them. Nor do I realize the growing dependence of my entire creative process upon her suggestions, her inspiration, her actual participation. While I'm composing my first block of "Brahms-like" pieces, it seems as though Anna actually knows what I'm trying to do. When a stubborn Beethovenesque phrase refuses to be "tempered" into Brahms, my little wife is always there, always knows *exactly* what to substitute for it. As I face the final decade of the nineteenth century, I have little doubt that Beethoven will achieve (through Brahms) a genuine fourth-period style of his own. My optimism springs not only from the unquenchable faith that Beethoven has in himself, but (even more so) from his growing realization of the great, good wife who stands at his side. Here are examples of her *invaluable* comments:

> Use a pedal-point here.
> Not so dissonant a chord at this point.
> Pure melody would perfectly end this section.
> Please, *not so sustained*!
> Too many notes in the melody.
> Avoid *more* of this rhythm.
> *Two-voice* counterpoint would be adequate.
> Too much for the brass, here!
> This use of strings is *perfect*!

During the first years of Karl's translation, he and I meet regularly at the Waldmüller Kaffehaus to discuss his present musical development, his future plans, and the old times we suffered through together on Earth. He never ceases to be amazed at the tremendous changes (for the better) wrought in his Uncle Mogul by the simple advents of death, rebirth, and marriage. Karl is glad that he's come to my SCP and has joined my Court. He especially loves my "Brahms-styled" chamber pieces and feels that through the Collins Quartet, he's learning to appreciate the very soul of this music.

At Waldmüller's, we also keep up with the latest news from the Major Aaronian system and put through regular phone calls to our Second-Order families and loved ones. In 1883, we learn that Richard Wagner has arrived in our Major culture. (I send for a copy of his *Parsifal* and obtain such profound enjoyment from studying its pages that I'm led once again to question my decision for a Brahmsian path.) Three years later, we read of the rebirth (within our Major system) of Franz Liszt—that bright-eyed, talented youth who visited the deaf Beethoven so many long years ago. In 1887, I'm not one bit surprised to learn that the two of them (former son-in-law and father-in-law) have gotten together to jointly manage the WAGNER firm, which was founded in 1875 as the official corporate composer of CP 82. With these musicians at the helm of WAGNER, BEETHOVEN's corporate hands will now probably be filled with a Brahms-Wagner clash that could well turn out to be more than they'd bargained for—especially as WAGNER literally explodes with music of the "New Germans," who are determined to flood our CPs with the mighty romantic tide of their musico-dramatic scores. Even on my little

SCP, the Brahms-Wagner struggle emerges and involves me squarely within it, though for the life of me, I can't see why there isn't plenty of room for *both* of them to exist (and to be enjoyed) side by side.

Opposite Voskamp in this competition for artistic survival is a "Wagner figure" named Ernst Koch. He is really a Second-Order musician, Heinrich Liebling, who translates to our SCP in 1875 from (of all things) a principalship at BEETHOVEN. Staunchly on my side throughout this battle is Arturo Sabatini. He conducts my new "Brahms" music everywhere he goes, and thanks to *his* baton, I know that Herr Koch will never achieve a complete "Wagnerian" victory within our Subsidiary culture.

One year from the date of my marriage to Anna Rosecranz, Judy Adams becomes Mrs. David Donovan, and I can't resist the invitation to attend her wedding. My little white lie to Anna informs her that "urgent business with a potential foreign publisher" is to begin on this particular Monday and that our haggling will probably last from morning till night. Anna is all too happy to stay at home and agrees not to wait up for me.

The wedding is held in a tiny wooden church not twenty miles from the Adams farm on SP 71. My drive out from Phillipsburg is in one of those magnificent sports coupés whose silent power and smooth handling remind me of at least one thing I've been missing by living for so many years in a "horse-and-buggy" Subsidiary culture. The spring morning is so perfect (and contrasts so favorably with the Vienna winter I've left behind) that I drive along, top down, inhaling as much of the sweet smells and sunshine as my lungs will hold.

I arrive at the church at ten forty-five—fifteen minutes before the ceremony is to begin. For some reason, I expect to find hundreds of people there, not the mere two dozen who actually show up. Among these is Judy's mother, dear old "Big Cat." There's a space next to where she's sitting in the second pew. This I politely occupy while commencing our whispered conversation:

B. Pardon, Madame . . . may I sit here next to you?
EA. Yes Sir . . . though I don't believe we've met.
B. We have indeed, Madame. By all rights, it is I who should be marrying your daughter this morning.
EA. Paul! . . . Is it really you?
B. It is, Big Cat. How have you been?
EA. I've been well . . . though I began to think I'd never live to see this day.

B. Judy's wedding?
EA. Yes. If you hadn't married your Anna, I'm sure Judy would still be waiting for you. How *are* things, Paul? Are you happy?
B. Very much so, Big Cat. I wouldn't have thought that marrying a musician could be so important to Beethoven, but you know . . . it really is!
EA. Good! Then you've done the right thing. Though in a way, I'm sorry. There was something very sweet and proper about your childhood romance with my daughter. I'm sorry that you're not now man and wife.
B. It was Judy's decision; she insisted that I do what I did.
EA. That's what she tells me. Oh well, Paul, things like this have a way of working out for the best. There's always the Third Order . . . the Fourth, the Fifth. . . . Someday I *know* you two will be married; I'll yet be your mother-in-law.
B. (*Once again, I lean toward Mrs. Adams and whisper.*) Dave's best man . . . he wouldn't happen to be Chopin, would he?
EA. Yes. Dave's boss, Frédéric Chopin. I'll see that you meet him.
B. Wonderful! But please, as "Mason Voskamp," not "Beethoven."

At the conclusion of the ceremony, there are rounds of picture snapping, bride kissing, and handshaking. I'm introduced to Chopin as "Mason Voskamp, a musician of sorts, and old friend of the family." We then drive to the Adamses' farm, where a delightful reception is catered by Claude René—Phillipsburg's finest chef. He and his associates overlook nothing in what amounts to perfect French cuisine. Champagne bottles pop like toy guns, and our glasses are never permitted to fall much below their brim. At the long, narrow luncheon table, our minister and Chopin are seated at opposite ends; halfway between are the bride and groom; directly opposite them are their parents and myself. In other words, I'm able to talk with Judy and Dave without being overheard by Chopin. A serious episode in our conversation begins toward the end of the meal. Judy reaches across the table, touching my hand, and smiling as she questions me (for the first time) regarding my marriage:

JA. Tell us, Paul, how are things going with you and Anna? Is your little wife expecting yet?
B. Not yet, Judy. I've decided that we should first share our music . . . then children.

JA. Is she turning out to be as great a musician as you thought she would?

B. Greater than my fondest wishes. I still can't believe that she's only a First-Order Subsidiary being. She seems to be more the spirit of music than Beethoven himself. No matter which path I choose for her, she flowers like a magnificent plant. There's no end to her potential growth. If she weren't my own wife, I think I'd be jealous of her talent.

JA. Then you have no regrets about your Subsidiary transfer?

B. None! Well . . . none except my permanent separation from you, dear Judy. Ask Dave here; even your new husband knows how much I've always loved you . . . and always will!

DD. (*David responds to this comment.*) Judy could never forget your love for her, Paul, nor could I. I shall try to be as worthy a husband to her as you are to your new wife.

B. I'm sure you will, Dave. . . . My only other regret is the fact that Anna is a Subsidiary being. Can you imagine loving someone as much as I love my Anna, and not being able to share with her that wonderful secret of time and space and life and death and rebirth . . . that greatest of all mysteries whose solution we Second-Order beings take for granted . . . the immortality of the human soul! Last summer I lost both my Subsidiary parents. Anna grieves for them terribly, and yet I'm unable to offer her any hope beyond those wretched condolences we had to be satisfied with as Earthlings. If only I could share with her the basis of our faith and hope.

JA. (*Judy's eyes burn with sincerity as she offers me encouragement.*) You can, Boo. Not in *words*, but through your *music*. The message of your music is the basis for our faith and hope. Anna is a great musician; she'll hear what you have to say to her through your compositions.

B. I hope you're right, Judy.

JA. I know I am; wait and see. . . . And we must continue our collaboration as well. Just because I'm Mrs. Donovan doesn't mean that I can no longer paint your compositions.

B. I hope it doesn't. What do you say, Dave?

DD. By all means! I never feel that I'm contributing more to Judy's happiness than when I'm performing your music for her paintings. Please do keep sending them. Are you planning any "mood movements" for the near future?

B. At present, I'm awfully busy with my studies of Brahms. But I hope eventually to compose a series of *Klavierstücke*. These should be sufficiently unified to serve as "mood movements," and I'll see that copies of them are sent to you.

DD. Wonderful! Then Judy can go right on painting Beethoven and Chopin. What do you think of our Chopin?

B. I can't get over the resemblance to his Earthly self. It's almost as though he translated from Earth to our Aaronian culture.

DD. I know. We're always accusing him of this. He only laughs and insists that his poor old tubercular body would have been the last thing on Earth he would bring here to heaven. Look! . . . Monsieur Chopin stands at his place.

Ch. (*The Maestro taps his glass for our attention.*) Ladies and gentlemen! May I propose a toast to our bride and groom. . . . In the Bible, our Lord speaks of going to prepare a place for us. In a very real sense, this is exactly what these two wonderful people have done for me. As a founding partner of CHOPIN, Dave Donovan not only discovered an outlet for his own fine talent, but he provided the ideal spot for me to take up my Second-Order life with the least amount of personal adjustment, and with a minimum loss of time. Besides a place to work, there had to be a reason for my composing still more piano pieces. In her collaboration with the great Beethoven, Judy Adams provided this for me. She and her former fiancé created a new art form—a wedding of music and painting that is ideally suited to my artistic expression and pianistic style. In short, along with Chopin's spirit, his art has experienced a genuine rebirth and has been called to creative tasks, which it could *never* have achieved on Earth. I propose a toast to this new husband and wife, who are in some respects like Second-Order parents to me, in other respects like the noblest children I could ever hope to have, but in either case, great artists who are directly responsible for the joyous realization of all my Second-Order dreams. Mr. and Mrs. Donovan, we wish you unbounded happiness, which is but a small fraction of the true inspiration your lives and love bring constantly to others!

(*Loud cries of "Hear! Hear!" go up from everyone at the table. When our applauding and toasting are finished, Chopin continues.*) Considering a wedding present, I wanted something personal for these dear ones. For many years now, Judy has subjugated her art to that of music—first the music, then her paintings. In commemorating this happy day, I decided to reverse the procedure. At my request, Judy provided me with three different sets of paintings, each set with its own unifying mood. To these, I composed three preludes that no one has yet heard and which (with your kind indulgence) I should now like to perform for you. Here are the scores, Dave, if you'll please assist with the projector.

Everyone applauds and rises from the table, following Chopin into the Adams parlor. Here the Maestro's own piano has been placed for the occasion. For nearly thirty minutes, Dave projects his wife's art onto a suitable screen, while my ears are treated to the greatest piano playing I have ever heard: greater than Liszt's, greater than Mozart's, greater than Anna's, greater than Beethoven's, yet I'm not jealous of the man. His soul and that of the piano are as one. His technique is perfect . . . never boisterous. His mastery is so pure and polished that it leaves no room for jealousy, only heartfelt admiration. His preludes are masterpieces of melody and structure, perfect soundings of the inspired beauty that shines from Judy's paintings. When the music ends, we are all filled with joyful emotion and request a repeat performance of the Chopin Preludes.

Following Chopin's musicale, we all return to the table for wedding cake, coffe and more champagne. Dave is next to stand and offer a toast.

DD. We come here today to honor my marriage to this creative artist and wonderful girl. The occasion has been graciously and adequately toasted by Monsieur Chopin. Rather than drink to the happiness of my own marriage, I propose a toast to our friends and loved ones at this table, to those who make possible the realization of this day. I give you Judy's parents . . . my parents . . . our friends . . . our teachers . . . the memory of Rembrandt . . . our fellow corporate artists . . . and especially I would drink to the pair of exceptional musicians seated here. To Frédéric Chopin, whose Earthly life inspired the corporation that now gives meaning, purpose, and direction to all that I do . . . and to Mason Voskamp, that great artist whose creative spirit is now revered among the gods of Earth, my new wife's former suitor whose music inspired them to create the art form we have just enjoyed, that greatest of Earthlings who is still reluctant to dwell among us, that fellow musician who married Anna Rosecranz one year ago today, that symbol of truth, freedom and total dedication . . . Ludwig van Beethoven!

As I feared would be the case, Dave's toast to all of us has the effect of a toast to me. I'm angry and grateful at the same time. Somehow, within my Voskamp disguise, I feel safe and secure. Everyone present (even the Adamses) crowds by for a welcoming handshake. Chopin is speechless; his huge eyes are filled with a crying happiness as his hands clasp mine and as he kisses me on each cheek. Suddenly, it's Beethoven who stands at the table, offering a toast:

B. Unlike my esteemed colleague, I would have us drink to our newlyweds. For many years, of all Second-Order beings, Ms. Judy Adams has been closest to my heart. In fact, she still is! Dave here has been the proverbial "second man" in our little triangle. And yet I now raise my glass to them both and propose that we drink to their future. Why? Because our particular triangle resolved happily, and for the best of all concerned. I now find myself married to an ideal musician. This has come to pass through Judy's own recommendation. Somehow she sensed that what Beethoven most needed (more than a wife, more than an artist-wife) was a musician wife. And through such a wife, the very Beethoven within me has at last begun to adjust to the rigors of Second-Order life. For example, if I had heard our Chopin's performance, say, two years ago, I would have cursed and damned my way from the room, jealously vowing never again to play the piano or to compose for it. But there have been changes in the "Great Mogul," changes for the better. Just now, I hear the greatest piano playing ever to cross my path. And how do I react? . . . I'm filled with undying admiration for our great "Poet of the Piano." I concede that my Second-Order talent could never be the equal of his. And yet I'm not jealous of the man. I only wish that my little Anna had been here to witness his superb artistry. Then she would know why her husband's interest in *Klavierstücke* is now suddenly renewed. So I say to you, dear friends, this Judy whom we toast is no ordinary girl. No ordinary girl would selflessly direct her own childhood lover into the arms of another woman specifically to enhance his musical and artistic development. May we drink to her happiness and to that of her husband. Ladies and gentlemen, I give you the

Donovans. . . . May their marriage be a long and happy one, filled with dedication and children—"children" artistic and otherwise!

"Hear! Hear!"

"Hear! Hear!"

"Hear! Hear!"

With the arrival of 1890 and the celebration of Anna's twenty-seventh birthday, I conclude that our musical life together is ideally established and that it's high time I throw away my bottle of red pills. This I do, and as I could have predicted, our old friend "Herr Stork" pays us a visit within a little more than nine months. Ah, the miracle of Second-Order fertility! Our firstborn is a little son whom I proudly request that we name "Karl." Anna agrees, though she can find no one on either side of our family who bears this name. She seems so completely to thrive on motherhood that I decide to provide her with a family of three, spaced at two-year intervals. Accordingly, a second son is born to us on May 5, 1893. Anna requests that we name him "Wolfgang," after her grandfather. Our third child is a darling daughter whom we name "Maria." She is born April 10, 1895.

Because of this child-rearing decade, Anna is much less active in my musical affairs than she was during the first ten years of our marriage. She realizes by now that it's absolutely essential for me to get away from the city for my "composing seasons" at our favorite retreats in Austria and Switzerland. Since our children are still too young for vacations, Anna dutifully stays home with them each summer while I merrily "head for the hills" with my sketchbooks. For a wonder, two compromises are made in our routine. Instead of five months in the country, I shorten my stays to three, returning each year by September first. And Anna manages regularly to spend the last two weeks of August with me when her parents visit our Hildebrandtstrasse nursery for baby-sitting purposes.

During these summers from 1890 through 1896, I prepare sketches for four symphonies, two piano concertos, a violin concerto, two piano sonatas, three piano trios, two string quartets, a piano quintet, a violin sonata, and thirty-six "mood movements" (for Judy) all in the style of Brahms. The mood pieces consist of three groups of a dozen each: twelve are for full orchestra, twelve for string quartet, and (due more to Chopin than Brahms) twelve are for piano solo. Since these thirty-six single movements seem incomplete without their respective paintings, and since with their paintings they would not be in conformance with "Earthly" developments on my particular

SCP, I decide not to perform or publish them within my Subsidiary culture. I can't, however, resist sharing them with Anna. Without exception, she loves them all and considers them the best things I've yet done in my new Voskamp style. She can't understand my reluctance to première this music, though of course, she respects my wishes in the matter. If only I could share with her Judy's contribution to these movements, then she'd really appreciate their significance and my desire to avoid using them apart from their paintings.

Each early September when I return to the Hildebrandtstrasse, none of my "new music" has reached beyond its sketchbook stage. I'm now so respectfully dependent upon Anna's musical judgments and recommendations that I refuse to transform sketches into finished pieces without the help of her uncanny artistic perception. And because of her growing ability as a composer and my admitted dependence upon her, the original compositions of these years are twice the authentic "Brahms" they would otherwise be.

On the evening of April 8, 1892, "Karl" and I stop by the Waldmüller for our first routine visit in over a month. I'm surprised to find there an urgent call from Judy Donovan. I phone her new home, and Dave tells me of the sudden death of Judy's mother, three weeks earlier. He also informs me that since the mother's passing, Judy has been staying with her father at the farm and that she wanted me to call her there. This I promptly do, and poor Judy sobs disarmingly at the sound of my voice, just as though she were still my little "Kitten." She tells me that her father has taken this death very badly and begs me to come for a visit. She seems to think that a little talk with me would do him more good than anything else.

That night, I make some sort of excuse to Anna and, early Saturday morning, sneak away from my SCP to spend the afternoon with Judy and her father. I find the old man dozing in his wheelchair. When Judy awakens him, he "unbends" into a combination of smiles and tears, offering me a weak, shaky handshake, something I thought I'd never receive from Mr. A.:

SA. Paul! . . . I knew you'd come. I . . . I'm so glad you married my Judy; she deserves a man . . . a man like you.

JA. (*Judy smiles and whispers into my ear.*) Never mind Dad, Boo. He's always getting you and Dave mixed up.

SA. (*At last, Mr. A. lets go of my hand.*) But you know, Paul . . . I'm afraid. . . . Now that my wife is gone, I'm really afraid."

B. Afraid of what, Dad?

SA. Of death . . . that's what!

B. But why? He's nothing to fear. We've all been through his mysterious and shrouded portals once; a second time should make us masters of the journey, not frightened travelers. There's no dark monster hiding there, no enemy of man's soul, no victorious grave, no eternal night. Just a kind old man who sings us to sleep and in a few short hours, awakens us again. We have no more reason to fear him than a tree has reason to fear the loss of her leaves . . . than thunder to be afraid of lightning . . . than our sun to fear the night. . . . As Major-Order beings, our rebirth is assured. What is there to fear?

SA. I fear the unkind tricks this "kind old man" of yours plays upon us.

B. Tricks? What tricks?

SA. I should have been the first to go, but instead, he comes and snatches away my Elizabeth.

B. What a comfort this should be to you. To think that someone so dear to us is waiting for you there in the Third-Order, perhaps this very hour is planning the joy of your reunion.

SA. But Paul, this is what I fear! What if there *is* no reunion? . . . What if my rebirth is Minor Order and hers is Major? How am I to wait a thousand years for the chance to hold her again in my arms?

B. This does sound fearsome, but it shouldn't. A thousand years, what is *this* to fear? A thousand years, a million years, a trillion years . . . what's the difference? Compared to the eternity of our souls, all time is but the ticking of a clock. Let the years be afraid of *us*, not us of them. Have no fear, Dad; the planned reunion of two loving hearts is more than a match for any extended sequence of centuries. Don't be afraid; your memories of Elizabeth are imperishable! You will be together again, and such a joyous thought should make even the waiting a pleasure.

The old man hangs his head for long minutes. I begin to fear that my words of encouragement have somehow hurt his feelings. At last, through heart-rending tears, his eyes are raised to mine.

SA. Paul, how ashamed of your old father you must now be. For hundreds of years I minister to the spiritual needs of others . . . poor souls who must have thought my faith worth imitating. . . . And now . . . when life and death make their demands upon me, where is this model faith? I seem to have nothing left but tears and self-pity. Forgive me, my son. . . . Forgive me.

B. Greatness such as yours, dear Father, is so filled with loving service to others that it is completely void of any superficial deed or thought that could require the forgiveness of anyone!

Mr. A. seems pleased with my reassurance; he half smiles, then calmly dozes off again.

Following the death of Judy's mother, I make it my business to contact the Donovans on a weekly basis and inquire about Mr. A.'s health. I don't wish to repeat the experience of hearing about *his* death some three weeks after it has occurred. For over a year, Mr. A.'s condition remains much the same. He's not quite so despondent about his wife's passing, but for the most part, he just sits there in his chair and dreams about the joy of their eventual reunion.

On May 12, 1893, my phone call confirms a sad change in the old man's condition. Two days earlier, he had suffered another stroke and since then has had intermittent spells of unconsciousness. Judy is now with him at the farm, and Dave tells me that he plans to join her there on Monday and to stay until the end finally comes. He encourages me to do the same and emphasizes what a great comfort my visitation would be for Judy.

Since it's nearly that time of year when I take my composing leave from Anna and our Court, I announce my plans (this particular spring) to depart for the country earlier than usual. Anna asks no questions, and we bid each other good-bye on Monday morning, May 15. My stay with Judy and Dave lasts exactly four weeks until June 12, the day of Stewart Adams's funeral. During these days, I have no profound philosophical discussions with either of the Donovans, and Mr. A. isn't even aware of my visit; but somehow, my presence seems to be a comfort to Judy . . . and this is what really counts.

I spend most of my time walking through glorious spring colors, sketching the third orchestral "mood movement" in my current series of twelve for Judy's brush. This piece is to be a humble monument to the loving memory of her Second-Order parents, a *Funeral March* worthy of succeeding its ancestral counterpart in my *Sinfonia Eroica*. The sketching is finished on June first, and the following Tuesday (three days before her father's death), I'm able to hand Judy my completed score. She responds with a tearful smile and a loving kiss, a kiss whose warm and passionate duration seems considerably more than an expression of gratitude. Dear Kitten! Could it be that she's still in love with me?

Funeral services are held in the same little church where twelve and a half years earlier, Judy and Dave were married. During his retired years, Stewart Adams spoke often of his death and expressed a keen desire thence to be buried in his own little garden. For this reason (upon the death of her mother), Judy had the garden turned into a family plot. Here Mr. A.'s body is to be interred.

The hearse and its accompanying limousines (including the one in which Judy, Dave, and I are riding) return from the church at 2:00 PM. As we pull into the circular drive, I get the surprise of my second lifetime! During our time-consuming trip to the church and back, a number of people have grouped themselves on three sides of a hundred-man orchestra that has assembled itself under a makeshift canopy directly before the open grave awaiting the body of our dear one. Additional spectators line the full length of the path that leads from the garage to Mr. A.'s former vegetable garden. As his coffin is removed from the hearse, the orchestra begins playing my *Eroica* Funeral March. My squinting eyes and gratified ears inform me at once that our conductor is none other than Sabatini himself! Suspecting some sort of monstrous plot, I grab Judy's wrist and pull her to the crowd-concealing side of our limousine. I'm practically in tears as I shout at her in a rasping whisper.

B. Judy! . . . This is nonsense! . . . I'm not going down there, and that's all there is to it!

JA. Why, Boo?

B. God knows who's standing there on that hillside . . . perhaps my Earthly mother . . . perhaps my old grandfather . . . perhaps Schindler . . . the Breunings . . . Archduke Rudolph . . . my entire Earthly Court, God knows who! And I'm not yet ready to meet these people.

JA. They're not here to meet *you,* my dear.

B. The hell they're not! I can spot a musical audience a mile away, and there *is* one to the last man and woman. They make a sacrilege of your own father's funeral.

JA. In what way?

B. They come to worship *Beethoven,* not the memory of Stewart Adams. Well, I'll have nothing to do with their stupid affair! . . . Good-bye, Judy!

JA. Paul! Wait! You really don't understand why they're here.

B. No? Suppose you tell me, my dear.

JA. They're here to help you honor the memory of my parents.

B. Hah! Don't make me laugh. They're here to gawk and stare at me! . . . What help do I need from a mob to honor your parents? My monument to them both was raised a week ago when I handed you that finished score.

JA. What you handed me, dear Boo, was a book filled with silent scratches and dots. For these to commemorate my parents, they must be translated into sounds. This requires an orchestra, and an orchestra requires an audience. Each musician sitting there, each person standing on that hillside has given of his time in coming here. They're not here so much to spy on their beloved Beethoven as they are to help Beethoven and his new Funeral March to truly honor the death and rebirth of my parents! Come, Paul, you mustn't turn them down. Do this for me! Join our procession . . . walk with us to the graveside . . . accept Sabatini's baton . . . and bring to life the great music you have just composed in honor of my parents—music which these musicians have sweated over, toiled over, and practiced to perfection. Do this for me, Boo . . . and for my parents.

B. I will, Judy. Forgive me. . . . I thought I had old Beethoven cut down to proper size, but I guess I haven't at all. The Great Mogul still looms so large at times that I can't see anything beyond his shadow. May I join you and Dave?

And so with Judy at his right hand, Beethoven joins in the procession and marches to the tune of his Earthly dirge. Slowly, in six-inch steps, we echo the solemn beat of the *Eroica*'s march. Down past the smokehouse with its crisp inviting smell, down past the grain bin that (in spite of us) continues its skyward prayer, down past the springhouse whose quiet waterwheel sings independently, down past the cool stream whose wooden bridge echoes the solemnity of our heavy steps, down, down . . . down. We enter the garden. We stand beside the grave. The coffin is placed directly above Earth's hungry mouth, which will soon feed upon it. The *Eroica* stops its sad lament. Our minister pays his final tribute to Judy's father. The heads of most spectators are still bowed as Sabatini hands me his baton, and I take my place before the magnificent orchestra. What a pleasure to conduct these superb musicians—Second-Order masters . . . all!

The rich full sounds of my new Funeral March are as deep and meaningful as I had dreamed them. They are the song of a Beethoven who has indeed grown ninety years beyond the *Eroica*. Glorious music fills the entire valley; it rises to heaven. I can't tell what Maestro Sabatini really thinks of my conducting; his face is like a kind mask. I can't tell what my players feel toward the music; they play each note perfectly, but their eyes tell me nothing. I can't even tell what my audience thinks; I'm afraid to look into their faces. I can't know the approval or disapproval of Mr. and Mrs. Adams; only God and Third-Order life can measure this. But Judy approves, and this is my soul's reward. All I hear is the music; all I see is her face. And through this face with its tear-stained cheeks, its reassuring warmth, its sparkling eyes, the spirit of my dear Kitten offers me greater thanks than I could ever deserve from anyone!

Between these two deaths, there is an important change in our Collins Quartet. In time for the 1892 season (and of his own volition), our second violinist, Mark Schu¸ retires from the group. Anna and I practically fall over one another in offering the position to Kurt Bardy. He cheerfully accepts, and (though I don't admit it to Anna) I'm as happy as a schoolboy in welcoming this great violinist back into Voskamp's Court. He and my "Karl" get along beautifully. There doesn't seem to be the slightest professional rivalry between them, yet my nephew learns more from young Bardy than from Anna and me put together! Two other changes follow in quick succession. In 1895, our violist, Paul Nesbitt, steps down, offering the position to his son Claude. A year later, our cellist does the same, passing that chair to his son, Jacob Kovsky. By 1900, they are the finest group of four strings I have ever heard. It's hard for me to believe that "Karl" is the only Second-Order musician among them. Their blending is so perfect and sensitive that I seriously doubt if my former "Earth" (at least at the beginning of its twentieth century) could find the equivalent to their playing anywhere!

In the fall of 1893, I stop at the Waldmüller for my weekly checkup on Aaronian goings-on. There I find a note from my dear old counselor, Hal Robinson, who requests that I meet him at the Kaffehaus on Monday evening, October 23, at 8:00 PM. I confirm our appointment by phoning his office on Aaron AP. Three nights later at the stroke of eight, I'm sitting there in booth no. 5 concealed by drawn curtains, when Robinson enters "ghostlike" from the dark passageway behind its sliding mirror. I'm dumbfounded by the tremendous physical changes that have occurred in the poor old man. He looks every bit his age, and then some! When he smiles, his face cracks; when he speaks, his dry old voice does the same.

Ro. Rezler! . . . How have you and Voskamp been getting along with old Beethoven?

B. Quite well. Better than you might expect.

Ro. Kind of a silly question; I knew you were! A man's life is judged by the fruit it bears; and what you've been sending back to Aaron is "prime stock" indeed.

B. You really think so?

Ro. Of course! Your new life and works are contributing as much to our BEETHOVEN, as had you dwelt among us as his managing partner! When the firm completed its homage to your Third Period, it didn't know which way to turn. And suddenly, there you were, gracefully pointing their way toward the path of Brahms.

B. Have they been happy and productive within the Brahms idiom?

Ro. No less than *you* have. In fact, there's now considerable talk that your firm will one day absorb BRAHMS as a kind of "operating division."

B. Johannes will have something to say about this!

Ro. That's all they're waiting for—an "OK" from him.

B. Are you expecting him soon?

Ro. Nothing definite on this. According to our latest reports, he's still in very good health; but after all, he's now "sixty." . . . Anything could happen. How's your marriage working out? Have you actually adjusted Beethoven to the demands of matrimony?

B. Perfectly! If you admire my present career, you must thank Anna for it. If I've succeeded in doing things here which I could never have done in the Major Order, then I've done so because of Anna, not in spite of her. And, Robinson, I *have* done things here that amaze the Beethoven within me. My marriage is truly ideal . . . a continuous honeymoon romanticized through the spirit of great art. I hear Chopin play; I'm not jealous. I hear Sabatini conduct; I'm filled with admiration. And the greatest miracle of *all*: when Beethoven now composes, he and his Anna sit down together at the composing desk. Think of it! Beethoven collaborating with another composer!

Ro. This *is* a miracle. I'm glad, Paul. I'm glad your marriage is working out ideally. You deserve this; you've waited and suffered long. You deserve a wife like Anna. Since you're so happy here, I don't suppose you ever give thought to returning to the Major Order.

B. I do, Hal. I think about it quite often. But so long as my little Anna is alive, it's out of the question. I realize that I'm growing older . . . that my Second-Order loved ones are doing the same. But I can't leave my Anna . . . not for any reason.

Ro. So be it, Rezler. You're not the first Aaronian to spend his Second-Order life on a Subsidiary planet, you won't be the last. The important thing is that our Beethoven is alive, and well and growing! . . . Speaking of growing older, that's why I've come to see you.

B. Counselors don't grow older; they grow wiser!

Ro. Hopefully wiser, definitely older. This is the reason for my visit, Paul. On December thirty-first, I'll be stepping down. In the meantime, I'm attempting to get around and say good-bye to all my faithful and aspiring assignees. So this is it, I've come to wish you well, Herr Beethoven!

B. I can't believe it, Robinson. You were here in the Second-Order when I arrived; it seems as though you should be here when I depart.

Ro. No indeed; I'll be waiting for you on the other side. Here's a photo of my successor, Ernst Hergenroeder. As of January first, he'll be your new counselor. I have no doubt that he'll be paying you a visit soon, and I want you to recognize him. Well, good-bye, Paul. I'm certainly glad things are working out so well for you and Beethoven. Our entire culture is the better for it!

B. Good-bye, Hal. Thanks for your patience and understanding. . . . Thanks especially for sending me here to heaven.

We shake hands, and this is the final time our eyes are to meet in Second-Order life.

On November 13, 1896, I'm on Aaron AP for another annual modification of my Voskamp disguise. Since Vos is now sixty-two years of age, Dr. Hartmann inquires as to how much longer I intend to remain in Subsidiary life. My reply is simple and direct, but indefinite:

B. So long, doctor, as my little Anna goes on living. That's how long.

Hm. And how old is Anna now?

B. She's thirty-three.

Hm. This means you could be staying for another fifty years!

B. Possibly.

Hm. Then we'd better start grooming Herr Voskamp as a "superman."

B. You mean, no more aging?

Hm. That's right. . . . Don't worry, there'll be nothing suspicious about this. Subsidiary beings are well accustomed to having

> occasional "men of genius" come and live among them for well over a hundred years—never looking much beyond their sixties! They can't explain such a phenomenon, but they accept it. . . . Herr Voskamp certainly qualifies as a man of genius. So think no more of it. Come back in about ten years, and I'll give you another gray hair or two.

Thus the stage is set for Voskamp's indefinite sojourn on SCP 7,900,111. On the occasion of this same visit to Dr. Hartmann, I call upon the Donovans and deliver into Judy's hand my recently completed block of thirty-six Brahmsian "mood movements." The only one in the group she has heard is "No. 3" for orchestra—that Funeral March dedicated to the memory of her Second-Order parents. Dave and I take turns in performing the others at the piano. Judy responds with tears, an almost frightening enthusiasm, and finally, with a huge kiss for Beethoven, which apparently has the approval of her husband. She blesses the music as containing enough true inspiration to keep her painting for ten full years!

In April 1897, I hear of the death of Johannes Brahms and of his rebirth into our Major Order. Rumor has it that he does not intend to head up his own BRAHMS at present; instead, he plans to prepare for a partnership at BEETHOVEN. Because of the Maestro's death, I now decide to bring out my final block of "his" music on my SCP. To this cause are devoted the summers of 1897 and 1898. Many of these great pieces are to be published as is under the name of Voskamp; others are to be considerably revised. In either case, there is no room in the project for Anna. To explain my sudden disuse of her services, I tell my little "musician mate" that I'm working out yet another step in the evolution of my style, and that I want her to be completely surprised by it.

By the end of the second summer, the extended list concludes with two symphonies, a piano concerto, a clarinet quintet, and a double concerto for violin, cello, and orchestra.

During the last two weeks of August 1898, when Anna comes to visit me at Luzern, I dump all my "Brahms' latest" squarely into her musical lap and ask her if she can find there any trace of a new Voskamp plateau, any specific direction our composing collaboration should now take. She answers that definitely she can, that three particular pieces point in exactly the direction we should go. When I ask her which ones, she dares me to name my favorite three. I think for a few minutes and then spiel them off:

B. The *Symphony in E Minor* is certainly my favorite. In it, I've struck the perfect balance between Classicist and Romanticist; the work is pure gold, the highest form of art. Its opening movement contains the best symphonic development since Collins's E-flat Major. Its *Andante modrato's* journey into the Phrygian mode is shot through from beginning to end with an exotic flavor all its own—this in addition to containing an inspired and sustained cello melody that is the greatest theme I have ever composed. Its closing passacaglia is an architectural masterpiece whose resourceful variations are the best ever to come from my pen. My second favorite is the *Piano Concerto in B-flat*, whose opening horn theme is almost on a par with the symphony's cello theme. Third on my list would be the *Quintet in B Minor*. Never have I been able to give the clarinet anything of such profound importance to say; never have I heard it sing so beautifully, or blend so perfectly with other instruments. These, Anna, are my favorite three—no doubt entirely different from yours.

AR. Indeed not, Mason. As God lives, these are my three as well. They are the greatest music I've ever heard, and they frighten me.

B. Don't be silly, Anna. How does great music frighten you?

AR. These pieces clearly set the standard for our future collaboration, and at the same time, they dare us to follow in their path.

B. How do you mean?

AR. I fear that even in putting our heads together, we shall seldom attain such a high standard of creative perfection!

Poor Anna! If she knew that her Voskamp hadn't even written these scores, then she'd really have something to worry about!

During these years, there are no extensive five-month concert tours lasting from January to May. I can't bear to be away from Anna and the children for so long a time. Until Maria's fifth birthday, Anna gives up the concert stage for the sake of being a full-time mother. Knowing what concertizing means to my little wife, I certainly admire her for making this sacrifice. Voskamp's concerts are limited to frequent performances in Vienna, a few in Berlin. Over half the local appearances are with the Collins Quartet. How I love to perform with this group (by playing an additional instrument), especially now that my former nephew is its official first violinist! This gives me a chance to keep a professional eye (and ear) on the boy; and believe me, he's fast approaching the ideal musicianship of Kurt Bardy, even Anna admits this. Most of what we play is, of course, chosen from my new "Brahmsian" list.

My days at Court are constantly brightened by the presence of "nephew Karl" and by Voskamp's close proximity to his lovely wife and three children. Contrary to Earthly belief, a wife and family provide me with greater (not less) dedication to music. What a foolish First-Order myth—that Beethoven could not adequately have served his Muse and a family. . . . Or was it? Perhaps my Second-Order spiritual and physical endowments do make a difference, and Anna is certainly no ordinary helpmate!

In both my sons, especially Wolfgang, we detect a genuine musical talent. In their sixth year, Anna starts each of them on piano and violin. Realizing that these boys are descendants of the great Beethoven, I immediately plan a musical career for them. Surprisingly, Anna is firmly against such a plan. She insists that it's far too early to exclude the possibility of their entering other professions—a very wise decision, but it sounds strange emanating from one of two parents who are (above all else) successful musicians!

Now comes the first genuine frustration of my Subsidiary life—a cruel hiatus in my original composing, which lasts from the fall of 1898 until Shrove Tuesday, 1903. The cause of it is exactly as Anna had predicted, those three great "Brahms": the *Symphony in E Minor*, the *Piano Concerto in B-flat*, and the *Quintet in B Minor*. They have set a standard of perfection that neither of us (working separately or together) is able to achieve. We try constantly, but without success. During these four dark years, nearly everything is given up for the sake of our composing: teaching is held to a minimum, there are no Voskamp concerts, Court sessions are short but not sweet, summers in the country are a thing of the past. In spite of all this, nothing comes; we are not able to rise to the impossible standard set for us by Johannes Brahms. But on we go, the two of us—hammering our determined little heads against the uncompromising stone wall of our three model compositions.

The most crushing blow of all occurs on the morning of May 10, 1902. He comes knocking at our Hildebrandtstrasse door when no one's there to answer it but myself. Anna and the children are visiting her parents for the weekend. There in the hall, I'm overwhelmed by the most penetrating eyes I've seen since those of J. S. Bach. They stare at me from under thick red eyebrows, from between combed red sideburns, from above a saucy red mustache. Needless to say, the crowning glory of all this redness is a huge head of thick red hair. Before Voskamp or Rezler can squelch it, and before my visitor speaks a word, the mild anti-Semitism of old Beethoven whispers "Jew" to itself. I'm vividly reminded of my ancient visit to Mozart, as the handsome young chap struggles to speak past the dryness in his throat:

SK. Herr Voskamp?
B. Yes indeed! And what young devil have we here?
SK. Not a devil, Sir. . . . My name is Sigmund Kapell. I've come all the way from Hamburg to see you, and I bring you a letter from Maestro Sabatini.
B. (*I open the letter and quickly scan its contents.*) Well, young man. . . . What have you brought with you?
SK. A symphony, a quartet, and a piano concerto.
B. Ah, a composer! And you want me to get these performed for you . . . right?
SK. Not necessarily. . . . I've come to study with you.
B. Composition?
SK. Yes.
B. But I'm a composer, not a teacher of composition.
SK. Then let me be your first student . . . your only student!
B. Why?
SK. Because I come not just to study with you; I come to evolve *from* you—precisely as you did from Roth von Collins. Your latest compositions have inspired my soul. I've mastered their content; I've learned to speak their language. And now I come to be born of you.
B. Let me see those pieces.

For over two hours I read through the scores of young Kapell—the most humiliating two hours of my entire Subsidiary life! Half a dozen times I glance at the young man's right hand . . . no ruby ring! Beyond the shadow of a doubt, here is a young Subsidiary composer who outcomposes Beethoven and his gifted wife put together! For over three years, Anna and I have tried to compose a worthy sequel to the "best of Brahms." We are unsuccessful. Then along comes this red-haired monster who *does* succeed! His symphony is a worthy child of the *E Minor.* His piano concerto is really super-Brahms, head and shoulders above the *B-flat* (if you can imagine such a thing). And his quartet is among the greatest of chamber pieces—more than worthy of the *B Minor.*

Here is an innocent Subsidiary musician who actually achieves what Anna and I have been dreaming about! How do I react to this Sigmund Kapell? Voskamp and Rezler would warmly clasp him to their breast, welcome him to our Court, beg him to teach them the secret of his mastery. . . . But not old Beethoven, and Beethoven is still at the helm of my professional life. The Great Mogul has done a lot of growing, but not *this* much! He can accept pianists and conductors greater than himself; he can remain happily married to his musician equal. But never can he concede a Subsidiary composer greater than himself! The Great Mogul takes charge of things, and my treatment of young Kapell is atrocious:

B. These compositions of yours are good music; they are good because of what *I* have put into them, not because of something *you* have done. If you would become a student of mine, you must prove yourself a composer, not a mimic.
SK. But Sir . . . mimicry is the one true basis for a genuine evolution!
B. It's also an excuse for plagiarizing the original works of others.
SK. I don't profess to be original as yet.
B. Good . . . because you're not!
SK. What would you have me do?
B. Leave your imitations with me; I wish to discuss them with Frau Voskamp. Go write me another symphony, another quartet, another concerto. And I want them to be *yours*, not mine! If they show a creative spirit of your *own*, I'll accept you as my student; otherwise, I have no time for you.
SK. This is the only way?
B. The only way! Good day, Herr Kapell.
SK. Good day, Herr Voskamp, and thank you for your time.

I seal the young man's scores in three large envelopes, then lock them in a drawer. Why should I show them to Anna? This would be like admitting defeat. Why should I accept him as a student? This would be like training someone to use my own sword—someone who would then cut me down! Out of sight, out of mind. To hell with Kapell! I hope that I shall never see him again.

As 1902 dies, so dies my hope ever to evolve from Brahms's "immortal three." I convince Anna that what we need most in our lives is a total rest from composition. Our rest cure takes the form of a complete absorption in the present season's Viennese Carnival! From New Year's Eve until Shrove Tuesday, we waltz by night and sleep by day. It seems as though we attend a thousand balls. We dance in homes, we dance in restaurants, we dance at masquerades, we dance in ballrooms. The "dancingest" evening of all is our night at the Opera House. For this grand occasion, all the ladies (hundreds of them) are replete with white ball gown, train, and tiara. Their partners are, of course, in black evening dress, white tie, and tails. We dance and waltz and gyrate and spin—all to the tunes of Strauss. As we rotate constantly to the left, the building itself begins to dance.

About halfway through the Opera House Ball, I'm tapped on the shoulder by none other than Kurt Bardy, who proceeds to dance with my wife! What a handsome young couple they make. I'm tempted to strip off my old gray "Voskamp" and go dancing with Anna as Paul Rezler!

While I'm standing there watching, another young man taps me on the shoulder. This distinguished chap waves a red Aaronian ring beneath my nose! As he does so, I recognize him as my new counselor, Ernst Hergenroeder. The two of us saunter toward a punch bowl, where we stand and talk for half an hour. He tells me of Robinson's "death." He sneaks me a plump questionnaire that I'm to fill out and mail within a week. He informs me that 1910 is the absolute cutoff for my current Brahms idiom. If I remain here beyond this date, I must again suffer the pangs of musical evolution! We shake hands, then he artfully disappears into the flowing crowd.

It takes me another half hour to relocate my Anna. When I do, I'm surprised to find that she's still dancing. But not with Kurt Bardy. Now she waltzes with a red-haired master of the dance, with a red-haired master of composition. . . . Goddamn! As I live and breathe . . . like a couple of old school chums . . . laughing, talking, and dancing together . . . there in each other's arms are Anna Voskamp and Sigmund Kapell!

Chapter 48

From the way Anna and Sigmund were dancing together, I could easily predict the next significant event in my Subsidiary life. Sure enough, on the afternoon of the very day following the Grand Ball, Anna sprints into our third-floor music room with a huge folio score in her arms. Through cheerful breathlessness, she smiles radiantly.

B. Ah, here comes my little Anna with a special delivery . . . something by Sigmund Kapell, no doubt.
AR. Yes. . . . How did you know?
B. I saw you dancing in his arms last night and knew at once that the red-faced bastard was planning to reach me through you . . . to further *his* career through *my* reputation and *your* naïveness. Well, I'll have nothing to do with him or his music, and you can tell him that for me.
AR. But, Darling, you close your eyes on the very door for which we've been searching for nearly five years!
B. Kapell is no door. He's one huge ape of a mimic, who plans to use *us* to his own advantage.
AR. I'm sure you misunderstand his intentions. He does mimic your latest style and he's the first to admit this, but he does so out of respect and admiration, not deceit! He wishes only to become your student and to evolve from you, much in the same way that you were born of Von Collins.

B. Well, he'll never become *my* student, and that ends the matter.
AR. But this is the chance we've been waiting for!
B. Chance? What chance?
AR. For months on end, we've tried to evolve a productive style from the ethereal standards set by your *E Minor Symphony*, your *B-flat Concerto*, your *B Minor Quintet*. Nothing has happened! And now comes a young man who *has* mastered the very technique we aspire to. By accepting Kapell as your pupil, we'll learn from him the precise things we most need to know!
B. Pupil! You're asking me to accept him as our teacher!
AR. Pupil, teacher . . . what's the difference? Each learns from the other!
B. In either case, Anna, I'll have none of him. He's cast some magical spell over you!
AR. Kapell hasn't, but his *music* has. Just listen to this *Symphony in E-flat* that he has composed at your request. It's as great as your *E Minor* and is dedicated to us both.
B. I don't wish to hear it! Now *please* let me get back to my sketching.
AR. Very well, Mason, but may I examine the other scores he's given you?
B. (*Unlocking and opening my cabinet drawer, I hand Anna the three sealed envelopes that contain Kapell's introductory "masterpieces."*) Here . . . I've sealed them up because I don't think they're worth bothering about. Study them if you wish. Become his teacher, his pupil . . . both, but *please* don't involve me in the matter!

This is exactly what Anna does. She studies his scores and within a week convinces herself that young Kapell is indeed our musical messiah sent by God to deliver us from our composing doldrums. She becomes his proud teacher of composition, and (as she predicted) immediately starts learning from him. She freely opens the door of our Court to her pupil, though of course, not that door to the Great Mogul's sanctum sanctorum. They do most of their work down the hall in Anna's studio. When I leave my room, I hear them playing and discussing fragments of compositions. I hear his cheerful, husky voice towering over that of my wife. I hear them humming and singing together. I hear the heavy pacing of his footsteps. But something dark and childish within Beethoven's soul refuses to recognize the reality of this great musician in our midst. Since he doesn't fit the precise pattern of obedient and less-talented "courtier," my prideful eye sees nothing but a ghostly shadow of the man. Though our professional paths come daily within a foot or two of crossing, not a single word passes between us in over twenty months!

During these months, I witness the extensive depletion of my Court personnel. There are still four young graduate students of piano and three of violin, but these are now chiefly Anna's responsibility. Everyone else is gone! Karl has completed his twenty-year "visit" as Cabot Roscher and has returned to Major-Order life, ten times the musician he was when he first entered my Court. Because of family commitments and responsibilities, brother Johann is unable to take Karl's place at my side. Once again, I haven't a single Earthling with whom to share the joys and sorrows of Subsidiary life! Being without a competent first violinist, my faithful old companion (the Collins Quartet) finally calls it a day. Each player goes his separate way, even the worshipful and dedicated Kurt Bardy! Our two great pianists, Ralph Gay and Victor Pepusch, launch highly successful concert careers and marriages of their own. Gone are their smiling faces, their eager solicitudes; and without this "Czerny" and "Ries," the quiet corners of my "throne room" now seem dark and foreboding to say the least!

Because of my loneliness, or was it in spite of it, I achieve one of the best musical victories of my hundred-eighty years. Fresh from our weeks of dancing, more determined than ever because of Anna's persistent infatuation with Kapell, I throw myself unreservedly upon a new set of sketches. At last they give way to my creative efforts. Starting off as the finest thoughts of Beethoven, they melt down and transform themselves into genuine Brahmsian inspirations of like degree. These in turn take root and grow to undreamed-of greatness—a symphony and a piano concerto well beyond the new and impossible standards that Anna and I have set for ourselves! Where did this music come from? I did not have Anna to help me. She and Kapell were working in the other room down the hall. I finally decided that in my desperate attempt to compose the ultimate symphony, I had unconsciously tapped into the ethereal spirits of these two great musicians, even though physically I was not with them. I concluded that this phenomenon was the work of God's angels. No other reason could be surmised by my limited mind. The work of spiritual forces is often known to produce miracles. With thoughts of humility, grateful appreciation, and complete faith, perhaps we three could receive help from these spiritual guides. Sigmund Kapell's musicianship would undoubtedly increase the outcome. I knew now that the Great Mogul must change his narrow ideas and agree with Anna's wise advice:

accept this rejected colleague not only as a student and teacher, but also promote him to a full-fledged partner! Just think, all three of us working together in joyful cocreation! As Christ has said, "When two or more people are gathered in mutual intention, we can join you and amplify your light and energy immensely."

The Great Mogul now takes a big step. I open my door to Sigmund Kapell! It occurs on Sunday morning, January 8, 1905. At about 10:00 AM, I hear my "silent partner" ascending the stairs on his way to Anna's study. With all the abandon of a bosom friend, I fling open my door and invite the musician in, just as though this were an established morning ritual of at least twenty months' duration.

B. Young man, come in here a minute. I have a few things to talk over with you.

SK. Maestro! . . . I can't believe my ears. . . . You're inviting *me* into your study? . . . There must be some mistake!

B. There *has* been a mistake, a stupid one, and I'm the one who's made it. I now intend to rectify my childish misjudgment of you.

SK. Maestro! . . . Are you accepting me as a student of composition?

B. Certainly not! I'm accepting you as a partner . . . a coworker . . . a fellow composer . . . a cocreator. That is, I'm accepting you if you'll have the likes of me!

SK. To work at your right hand is the very center of my life's dream.

B. Good! Have a chair, Kapell. Let me make you some coffee. . . . Double cream?

SK. No thanks. . . . Black!

Brewing my strong and stimulating cup, I'm reminded of that ancient day at Teplitz when I did the same for the Earthly Goethe. . . . Strange that I should feel the way I do. Kapell is only a Subsidiary being; yet in his quiet artistic presence, I sense the greatness of Goethe. While I complete my witchlike procedures, Kapell stretches out comfortably in the easy chair next to the piano. He lights up a huge greenish-brown cigar that soon fills every cubic inch of my study with a lung-scratching, throat-grasping smog. As I watch that cigar being chewed and smoked with equal vigor, it seems symbolic of the young man himself. Through the strength of his artistry, he has pervaded every aspect of my coveted musical privacy. When I hand him his cup, he asks the question I knew he would ask:

SK. Tell me, Herr Voskamp. Why have you changed your mind? Why do you suddenly take me in? Your dear wife has told me a hundred times that the day would eventually come when you would do this. At first I shared her optimism, then I began to doubt that you would ever recognize my presence. . . . And now you have! Why?

B. You're too great a musician *not* to be recognized, Kapell, even by a jealous old fool like myself. Many years ago, when I was a little boy, music was literally beaten into me by my loving father. "I do this for your own good," was his answer to my tears. Besides music, he beat into me an abnormal amount of self-confidence . . . so much so that by the time I reached young manhood, my motto had become "Man, help thyself" instead of "God help me!" My success as a musician seemed totally dependent upon a fierce desire for professional superiority and aloofness. I had to be at least a few inches "taller" than every other musician who came my way. If such were *not* the case, then the very basis for my emotional stability began to quiver and quake until I had either improved my relative status or had violently abandoned my gifted contemporary to the total deprivation of my personal acquaintance! But over the years, Kapell, there've been changes, changes for the better! They are attributable almost entirely to the enlightening advent of Voskamp's musical marriage. My love for Anna and my desire to be her husband became greater than even my childish need for personal security. Finding myself married to a pianist and violinist every bit my equal enables me to embrace all genuine performers, whether they be smaller or greater than old Voskamp. Through Anna's inspiration, I've been able to take up the very baton which Sabatini's greatness had caused me to throw down in a fearful fit of admiring despair. This left but one fertile field of my professional life wherein I could still sow and harvest a Voskamp crop superior to that of my contemporaries—the field of composition! Here at least was one activity that I needn't compromise nor share with anyone. It was mine, and mine alone . . . sole . . . unique! . . . Then along came that wife again. She assured me that composing was my most creative activity and, for this reason, should be shared with her. At first, I brushed aside her suggestion as ridiculous. But her phenomenal response to a few lessons in composition made me change my tune and bide my time. Sure enough, just as in piano and violin, there seemed to be no limit to her potential growth as a composer! Within two years, she was snooping into my sketchbooks and helping me make my themes go precisely the way I wanted them to go. My finished pieces took on a smoothness, a flow, a polish, a lack of redundance, which they had seldom achieved before. Though I hated to admit it, there she was, my own little Anna (in less than four years), totally indispensable to the successful operation of my entire composing process!

SK. Then tell me, Maestro, with the successful admission of Frau Voskamp to your composing procedures, why are you reluctant to open your door to *others* who might be of help to you?

B. Anna is my wife! To share my creativeness with her is one thing, to share it with an outsider is something else again.

SK. Then what am I doing sitting here in your den of creativeness? I'm neither your wife nor your son . . . just a humble contemporary.

B. You're my brother!

SK. How so?

B. Long before your first visit, Anna and I had set for ourselves a composing goal that seemed challenging but nonetheless attainable. We decided to evolve a new mode of expression based upon my *E Minor Symphony*, my *B-flat Concerto*, and my *B Minor Quintet*. We tried and tried again. She tried, I tried, we both tried. Nothing happened! We produced music, but nothing at all compatible with our new standard. Then suddenly, along comes a symphony and a concerto beyond my dearest hopes . . . better than the *E Minor* . . . better than the *B-flat*. And it's no coincidence that they arrive twenty months after you have become my wife's student and teacher rolled into one! I have *you* to thank for their success, and for this reason, I call you "Brother" and welcome you to my Court.

SK. Actually, Herr Voskamp, I've done little beyond learning profoundly from you and your wife. . . . Perhaps I've contributed to a theme here and there, to the softening of a phrase, to the deepening of orchestral colors. . . . But these pieces, Maestro, are yours . . . yours alone!

B. Your modesty, Kapell, is what I expected it would be. But you're wrong! The pieces are the children of all three of us, and without your help, they would never have been born. This brings me to the *real* reason for welcoming you to my Court as "brother." Many years ago, and for reasons that I can't explain to you now, I toyed with the idea of collaborating with other composers. Try as I did, I found this impossible for me to do. Each work that I created had to be exclusively the toil of my own hands. For some strange reason, to compose with the help of another seemed like the forfeiture of my very right to exist. In order to be called "Voskamp," each piece had to be written exclusively by me! Yet the deep desire for collaboration remained hidden within my heart, the dream of my lifetime, a distant inaccessible goal. . . . Distant and inaccessible until you and Anna entered my professional life. Thanks to you patient musicians, I have now achieved my life's dream. I have written my two best pieces solely through the extensive help of a pair of gifted fellow composers! And the creation of these works has brought me greater pleasure than composing by myself has ever done.

SK. But, Herr Voskamp. How can you commend us for these pieces? We were not with you when you composed them. Anna and I were working in her study.

B. Ah. . . . But there was something here that you were not aware of. Even though I worked alone, I unintentionally contacted you two in spirit. But that was not all. There was a fourth participant joining me . . . an invisible one that enabled this music to blossom. Sure, I wrote the notes down, but this unseen entity actually guided me in the process. Do you think this was possible?

SK. I'm willing to accept this idea, Herr Voskamp. But it seems hard for me to believe.

B. How else could these pieces have evolved into such greatness? For this to come about, we must expand our minds and open our hearts to higher levels of thought and feeling, such as what makes a melody honest and pure, how is the warmth of love shown, what does it feel like when we've performed a kind deed, how can we visualize peace and serenity, what makes goodwill exist, how does fun and laughter express itself, what is a noble attitude, how can the joy of dancing be portrayed, what makes a glorious sunset awe inspiring . . . If we bathe ourselves in thoughts like these and listen deeply within our souls, we will be open to higher realms with powers beyond our ken and an extra surge of energy running through our veins. Subtle suggestions and possibilities will present themselves in our heads with no effort on our part. All we have to do is write them down and apply them before they leave our minds. I believe these bits of inspiration come from angelic forces who gladly stand ready to help us.

SK. This must be true, Sir. . . . I assume you and Anna work this way.

B. Perhaps in a sense we do . . . but not consciously. We need to bring these ideas to the surface. . . . Begin a piece by preparing our minds first . . . and inspiring results should follow.

SK. You're very perceptive, Herr Voskamp. Aren't we fortunate that such a spiritual force can assist us if only we ask?

B. Yes indeed. It was you and Anna, working on your own, and my sincere effort working alone, all three of us striving for ethereal perfection . . . that alerted the attention of unsuspected celestial beings. This, I'm sure, has caused a symphony and concerto to emerge that has transcended my highest dreams! I know now that "conscious" collaboration can be a real asset to our progress in evolving a high standard of music!

SK. I'm certainly looking forward to this privilege. . . . Now I must tell you about a pursuit that has improved the quality of *my* writing. I have spent much time outdoors in the woods and fields around here, absorbing the sounds and sights of the quiet countryside. Here I'm enveloped by the green sunlit foliage, singing birds, and refreshing breezes. Melodies seem to come up from the ground that I dare not tread upon. There's enough "nourishment" here for me to write a dozen symphonies.

B. Exactly what happens to me! Stroling through the meadows and along streams improves my creative thinking to the point where my crude scratches of phrases and themes seem to transform themselves into real musical meaning. Some of my best sketches have been written in these surroundings.

SK. Isn't it amazing the wondrous ways our Creator displays his love?

B. And we can return this love by sending out glorious music that will enrich the souls of all who listen. . . . Now that you and I have shared our highest aspirations with one another, we should work quite well together as cocreators. This means, Kapell, that I now wish to "knight" you into my Court.

SK. Frau Voskamp has told me of your famous "knightings." And who am *I* to be called?

B. I dub thee, "Sir Hannes."

SK. "Hannes"? . . . "Johannes"? . . . Where under heaven do you get such a name for "Sigmund Kapell?"

B. Never mind where I get it. It fits you perfectly. You must "put it on and wear it" . . . at least in my presence!

SK. Gladly! You can call me the devil himself . . . "Sir Lucifer," just so long as I may kneel at your table and enjoy the hallowed crumbs that fall from it.

B. Not crumbs, nor will you kneel! You'll sit at our table and enjoy whatever food we have—food, which in many cases, will emanate from *your* creative spark.

SK. Thank you, Herr Voskamp!

B. Let there be no more "Herr Voskamps" between us. Our collaboration must vanquish all formalities. Let "Anna," "Hannes," and "Vos" be the names we shall use.

SK. Very well, Vos. I thank you for whatever feasts we are to enjoy together. What are your immediate plans for our collaboration?

B. During the past few months, I've come to view the art of composition in a new and better light. I now realize that there are many things that a composer can do with the help of others, which he could never achieve by himself. For any given composition, it's the *music* that counts—not some self-esteemed, god-almighty egomaniac who might glory in its authorship. The important thing for a composer to leave behind is not so much an impressive list of opuses as an artistic heir, a creative offspring, an evolving force that will continue to create long after the parent artist is dead and gone. . . . Realizing this, it is now my chief purpose to establish such an offspring for myself, and *you*, dear "Hannes," will hopefully be that child.

SK. To be such a child is the real beginning of my adulthood.

B. Good! Then our partnership is secure! Our collaboration will be directed mainly toward making *you* the official successor to Mason Voskamp.

SK. Do you plan to evolve from our present style?

B. No! Anna and I have talked this over many times . . . dozens of times! We've listened long and carefully to the subtle rhythms and lush harmonies of the impressionists. We've exposed our God-given ears to the man-made clangings of our modernists. . . . We've decided that what remains for us to say can best be said within our present idiom. A final block of compositions, and then the rest is up to you.

SK. This I can't believe. . . . Two great composers like you and your wife don't just suddenly put down their pens . . . no more than they would suddenly decide to stop breathing!

B. From my personal standpoint, the composing Muse demands too much of me. She keeps me too long and too far from my wife's other interests, from our friends, from our family. My children now reach an age when I can understand them better, and yet I'm practically a stranger to them. . . . All this must change!

SK. What do you plan for these final pieces?
B. More symphonies and concertos.
SK. A certain number of each?
B. I plan for a dozen symphonies. Voskamp will take credit for the first nine, and Kapell for the final three. We'll write half this many piano concertos, crediting me with the first four, and our "great pupil" with the final two.
SK. I see. . . . In this way, my career as a composer will evolve from yours and Anna's.
B. Exactly! Not too different from the manner in which mine evolved from Von Collins.
SK. Then what happens?
B. You must develop your *own* style—something truly musical, and yet in the modern idiom.
SK. Now there's an impossible task!
B. You'll do it. Anna and I will help you.
SK. But surely the two of you will not stop writing altogether.
B. Anna and I deserve a vacation from the writing desk. This will give us some time for each other and for our children.
SK. How can real musicians be happy without their music?
B. There'll still be plenty of music in our lives. With these new symphonies and concertos, I intend to do lots of serious conducting and piano playing. Anna will follow me about as my official traveling companion. But as to composing, this will be *your* responsibility. I shall be more than glad to conduct and perform your newest pieces, but you must do the writing! .And then before too many years, you must select and begin to train *your* composing offspring.
SK. I already have.
B. Really? Who's the lucky man?
SK. He's still a boy, and quite the musician!
B. Wonderful! I can hardly wait to meet him.
SK. You have . . . on occasion.
B. Really? Who is he?
SK. Your son!
B. Wolfgang?
SK. None other!
B. Wolfgang! . . . I don't believe it. . . . He's a fine little pianist and a good violinist . . . but surely not a composer!
SK. He's a born composer worthy of his mother and his father. Someday he'll put us *all* to shame!

B. Dear Hannes . . . I can't believe it! You see what I mean? I've been so busy at my little composer's bench, that I scarcely know my own children!

SK. They're wonderful children . . . all three of them. All are performers in their own right, all have a deep love for music and for what their parents do. But Wolfgang, he's the new composer in our midst!

B. Strange. . . . Through Anna, I thought I was keeping a pretty good eye on these youngsters . . . at least on their instrumental developments. I'm fully aware of their increasing capabilities. But no one has told me a thing about Wolfgang and his composing!

SK. We wanted to surprise you. Anna discovered his tremendous ear and his huge talent for writing soon after I came here. The two of us have been working on him ever since.

B. I'll be damned! And you ask me why I suddenly open my door to you. Now you must surely know! The patient love that you've shown my children and the unmistakable love they have for you . . . these (no less than your musical ability) have melted down my cold old heart and have permitted me to rejoice in the naming of a brother! How shall I ever repay you, Sigmund Kapell?

My new "brother" responds with a warm smile instead of words. As I rise and walk toward the door to call Anna, I notice him finally stamping out the smelly pulp of what remains of his cigar. Another two puffs, and I would have feared for the fiery demise of his handsome red mustache.

Upon opening the door, I discover my Anna standing there with a girlish smile as warm as the sun. She was neither looking nor listening through the keyhole, but she is certainly close enough and smiling enough to have heard most of my conversation with Kapell.

B. So! . . . My dear little wife has turned eavesdropper!

AR. Considering the twenty months we've waited for this conversation, I just had to come and savor it. Thank you, Mason. Thank you for being a real man, for being true to your art and completely honest with yourself. At the peak of one's powers, it's not easy to pass the torch to a chosen successor, and yet you've done it! This makes me very proud of you, my darling.

We embrace, and Anna rewards me with another of her wonderful kisses, that dearest and sweetest of love potions, which over the years has caused me ever to rejoice in my decision for a Subsidiary life:

B. Forgive me, Anna. . . . When I told you that today would be the day of my little speech, I should have invited you in to hear it. But somehow I was afraid . . . afraid that perhaps at the last minute, I would prove to be less true or less honest than you now commend me for being. But at last it's done, and I'm very happy with my rightfully acknowledged brother. We must now celebrate his formal admission to our Court. Please, Anna, would you fetch a bottle of that '89 champagne and bring little Wolfgang with you? I have a few things to talk over with this young man.

In a matter of minutes, Anna returns with a sixteen-year-old bottle and a twelve-year-old son. How cute and little boyish Wolfgang looks with a shock of soft blond hair brushed neatly forward, almost hiding one of his big blue eyes while the other stares at me with a clear sparkle of admiration. His pink cheeks glow with a health and beauty equal to that of any Second-Order lad I have ever seen. His vitality, his respectful manner, and his piping voice all remind me of young Breuning:

WV. Father! . . . What's "Uncle" Sigmund doing here in your study?

SK. (*Before I can reply, "Uncle" Sigmund reaches over from his chair and lifts young Wolfgang to his lap.*) You, little boy, have got yourself a real uncle as of now. I have just become your father's brother, and this makes me your real uncle—only my name has been changed to celebrate the occasion. From now on, you must call me "Uncle Hannes."

WV. "Uncle Hannes"? . . . But why? . . . You're my dear teacher, Uncle Sigmund.

SK. No, your father has given me a better name. When he approves of our musicianship, he grants us this very special favor. Someday when you're a great musician, he'll be giving you a new name as well. Hey there! What's that hand of yours doing in my pocket?

WV. Have you brought us some candy?

SK. You know I have . . . but it's for after your lessons!

WV. But you're my *real* uncle. May I have some now?

SK. Oh, I suppose. . . . Here's the bag, but mind you, save some for your brother and sister!

WV. I will, "Uncle Hannes."

Wolfgang springs to my piano bench, there to curl up and contentedly explore the contents of his artfully won treasure. While my son celebrates the arrival of a new uncle his way, Anna and I celebrate our new "brother" our way. Hannes receives toasts and handshakes from me; he receives toasts, handshakes, and not a few kisses from Anna! Our official welcoming continues until the Voskamp supply of '89 is diminished by one full bottle!

Once again, Wolfgang is the center of our attention. This time he sits on my lap, and I'm the one who asks the questions. Anna and Hannes are close by, trying but failing to conceal their parental looks of admiration:

B. So you're going to be a musician, young man?
WV. Yes, Father.
B. And a composer?
WV. Yes, Father.
B. Why on earth a composer? Isn't playing music more fun than writing it?
WV. No, Father. Music is even more beautiful before it's written down . . . while it still sings in my head!

A cold fear chills my spine; a warm pride flushes my face. How identical are these words to those which I spoke to my father in the Earthly Bonn of 125 years ago.

B. But Wolfgang, composing is such a difficult thing to do. It keeps you sitting at your desk for hours at a time when you'd much rather be out playing in the sunshine and fresh air.
WV. I love the out-of-doors almost as much as you do, Father, but I love composing even more!
B. This "Uncle Hannes" of yours . . . is *he* the one who's influenced you to become a composer?
WV. No more than you and Mother have done.
B. Doesn't he consider it unusual for a boy your age to be writing music of his own?
WV. No. He tells me that it's the natural thing for me to do since my father is such a great composer!
B. I see. This *is* a fine "uncle" you have, my boy. What about Maria and Karl? Will they too become musicians?

WV. I don't think so, Father. They like their piano and violin, and they love their "Uncle" Sigmund . . . "Uncle" Hannes. But I don't believe they care for music in the way that you and I do.

B. Now tell me, Wolfgang. What about these melodies that sing in your head? Are they really yours, or are they bits and snatches that come to you from other places?

WV. Oh they're mine, all right. They come from inside, instead of through my ears. They change and grow and dance and keep on singing until I finally write them down.

Ah, what fatal and decisive words from a little boy. I look at Anna; Ana looks at me. I stare into Kapell's eyes; he stares into mine. Not a word passes among us—three adults and a child, sitting there in absolute silence, as if waiting for me to digest the startling fact that there is indeed a young composer in our midst. At last, through a proud smile, which could easily have been tears, I'm first to speak.

B. Very well, young man. If you're to be my son *and* a composer, then we must spend much more time together than we've spent in the past. Right this minute, I'm not interested in seeing what things you've brought to paper, but I do wish to sample those tunes that "sing in your head." We'll soon discover whether you're a natural composer or a careful follower of rules. . . . Go fetch your mother's violin from her study, and bring Kietzing's viola from the storage room.

Within a few minutes, our assemblage for Wolfgang's ordeal is completed. My son is seated at the piano, with his back toward the rest of us. There is no music there for him to read. On the opposite side of the room near the full-length curtainless windows sit Anna and I with our violins and Kapell with a viola. On our music racks are the upper parts of the Collins Quartet in A-flat, which Wolfgang's teachers assure me he has neither studied nor heard before. I now speak my instructions to a bright-eyed little boy who smiles back at me with all the self-confidence of a twelve-year-old Ludwig van Beethoven:

B. Wolfgang, we are going to play the three upper parts of a beautiful adagio. I want you to listen to them carefully, even though the harmonies are incomplete. Try to imagine how the bass should sound.

After our performance comes the second installment of my instructions.

B. Now Wolfgang, we are going to repeat the adagio. There at the piano, I want you to play what you think would be a suitable cello part.

To my great enjoyment, the young fellow beautifully passes this first "composer's examination" that I've set for him. He plays a "cello part" that (except for a few rhythms and sustained tones) is close enough to Collins to *be* Collins!

B. Very fine, my boy. How did you know what notes to play?
WV. But. Father, what else could they be? In such beautiful music as this, the bass is clear and definite. It can go no other way!
B. Exactly what I hoped you'd say. Now I want you to listen very carefully while the three of us play the allegro from my favorite trio. Hannes will be our cellist. We will then repeat the allegro, at which time I want you to compose a piano part for it on the spot. In other words, I'm anxious to see if your "composer's ears" are capable of transforming a good string trio into a good piano quartet. Listen for the fugal section in the middle. There are many fragments here, tiny bits that are not fully developed within the movement, but which could certainly be used in your piano part.

As Wolfgang weaves his piano improvisation among our swiftly moving strings, I'm almost overcome with paternal pride. Everything he does is in good taste and blends perfectly with our parts. At the fugal section, I feared that he would clutter things, but no, he plays a simple two-voice structure that actually enhances the tone lines of our strings. How can a tiny First-Order child be such a great musician? But then, why not? After all, this isn't just a little boy who plays for us; this is the son of Beethoven! From the lengthy fugue, Wolfgang scrapes up so many treasured fragments and uses them so masterfully against the restated themes of the allegro that I can't further contain my emotions. I jump from my chair, drop my fiddle, stumble to the piano bench, and lift our still-busy pianist way up and over my head.

WV. Father! . . . What's wrong? . . . Why do you stop?

B. I can wait no longer to tell you what a great musician you are, and how proud I am of you.
WV. Really? . . . Then someday I *will* be a composer!
B. You *are* a composer now . . . in the true sense of the word. . . . You're far greater than *I* was at twelve years of age; in fact, in your own way, you're as great as Mozart himself!

As I speak this authoritative slip of the tongue, I happen to be facing Anna and Hannes. Both look pleasantly surprised; both reply simultaneously with the same embarrassing question:

AR & UH. Mozart! . . . Who is Mozart?
B. (*My rebound is a classic.*) So you haven't met Mozart? Come with me.

I lead us to the "composing side" of my study. There above my writing desk is Judy's magnificent portrait of the Earthly Mozart—that companion painting to the one of Beethoven that hangs on Bonaparte's wall in the May Building. After a careful examination of the beautiful face, Anna is first to speak:

AR. So this is Mozart! . . . At last I learn who he is. You know Hannes, this picture has been with Vos longer than *I* have. It has smiled down upon our entire marriage. Dozens of times I've sought to learn the identity of this face. And now today, I have. Pleased to meet you, Herr Mozart!
UH. (*Hannes raises another question.*) If this Mozart is so great a composer, how come we've never heard of him?
AR. He was more interested in teaching than in a composer's career. In a very real sense, he was my master's prime tutor. When you listen to early Collins, you *are* listening to Mozart.
WV. (*The topic of our conversation is suddenly changed by a tug on my sleeve and a smiling question from Wolfgang.*) Then Father, would you say that I'm now a musician?
B. You certainly are.
WV. A good musician?
B. An excellent musician!
WV. Will you soon be changing my name?
B. Yes indeed. In fact, right now! Downstairs, on the second floor, you will always be my dear little Wolfgang. But up here among

us musicians, I dub thee my dear sweet "Hosenknopf." Perhaps someday I might even call you "Mozart."

For five full years and a few months into 1910, there is once again little to relate in my personal narrative. There is little to relate because during these years, I am once more a happily productive composer, totally involved in my daily work, or more correctly, I am one of *three* busy composers, totally involved in a daily collaboration. By April 1910, the three of us produce our dozen symphonies and six piano concertos exactly as planned. All are in the superb style of a late and wondrous Brahms. Three of the symphonies and two of the concertos are credited to our Hannes, who receives a flattering contract from my still faithful publishers, Schoenbern and Kietzing. The premières of all this music are scheduled for a Voskamp-Kapell Festival to be held in Vienna during May 1910. News of the festival spreads far and wide. Starting in January of this year, it brings young Schoenbern himself to our door on a weekly basis. He can hardly wait to get his printing press on these first scores to issue from the Hildebrandtstrasse in over five years. The pending event brings Sabatini to Vienna on April 2. He stays at our home for the entire month, where he spends twelve hours a day studying the new scores. His great Berlin Philharmonic will be featured in our six-evening festival, and he will be its sole director. Since he wishes to conduct all eighteen works from memory, his visit displays one very busy maestro!

Besides the symphonies and the concertos, we manage to compose my final block of piano pieces—thirty-four in number. They are written with dear Judy in mind and in answer to her long and patient plea for another batch of "mood pieces" to satisfy the eternal appetite of her immortal brush! These pieces are interesting in that they reflect a considerable enlargement of our harmonic idiom through my recent and current studies of Claude Debussy. Judy is delighted with the results and considers them ideally suited for canvas—the closest I've yet come to genuine tone painting. They are filled with whole steps, with towering dominants, and with occasional ear-awakening clusters—yet they are still of Brahmsian spirit! I wouldn't go so far as to call them "German Impressionism." They are Brahms, but they are an evolving Brahms, with an eye and at least one ear to the future!

Countering these initial efforts of Anna and me to "evolve," Ernst Koch (the "Wagner" figure on our SCP) brings out a final cycle of music dramas in the style of the "Ring." His three new operas make extensive use of leitmotifs and have librettos which again derive from German mythology. Koch is granted permission (logically) to become the "Richard Strauss" of SCP 7,900,111. Before the turn of the century, he introduces four of the great Strauss tone poems: *Don Juan, Death and Transfiguration, Till Eulenspiegel's Merry Pranks,* and *Thus Spake Zarathustra.* I'm so impressed by the orchestral extensions of these imaginative works that I spend much of my spare time in studying their scores. For over a decade, there is nothing new from Koch's pen. Then suddenly . . . *POW!* He bursts upon the musical world with a handful of opuses so perfectly timed that it seems as though he had a spy in our midst. In June of 1910, one month after our musical event, he stages a Koch festival at Berlin and invites the Vienna Philharmonic there to do the honors. Since he had put in a conspicuous appearance at *our* festival, Anna, Hannes, and I journey to Berlin in order to reciprocate. There we are treated to *Don Quixote, Ein Heldenleben,* and *Symphonia Domestica,* their first performances on our planet. Although Koch's conducting is a far cry from Sabatini's, I find these new scores interesting enough to want to study them as well. Of even greater interest are four symphonic tone poems that Koch himself has written and which he includes in his festival. These "originals" are definitely in the Strauss tradition, but they contain a greater wealth of good melodies—more like Wagner than Strauss!

My present counselor, Ernst Hergenroeder, seems to be gifted with the ghostly attribute of materializing out of crowds. He did so at the Opera House Ball in 1903; he does so again (seven years later) at Koch's Festival. During intermission on the third evening, Anna and Hannes go backstage with an enthusiastic group of music lovers to congratulate Maestro Koch on his latest compositions. This gives me a chance to step out for a breath of fresh air. As I enter the foyer, I feel a friendly slap on my left shoulder. Upon turning around, there's Hergenroeder with his comforting smile and ruby ring.

HH. Herr Beethoven! . . . How are you doing these days?
B. Well if it isn't my handsome young counselor, Herr Hergenroeder! You certainly show up on schedule. I expected you this year, and here you are!
HH. How about a little smoke?
B. Fine! I was just heading for the terrace.

My friendly "ghost" offers me some genuine Second-Order tobacco that tastes delicious even in my smelly old First-Order pipe!

By the time I get things puffing smoothly, he has already asked his next question.

HH. Tell me, Herr Voskamp, now that 1910 has arrived, what are the chances of your returning to Major-Order life?
B. Nil . . . at present. There is too much to be done here. For our latest pieces, Anna and I have planned extensive concertizing. We wish to continue our efforts on behalf of Sigmund Kapell . . . a truly gifted protégé. And my son Wolfgang has turned into a budding composer; he needs careful looking after. No, I couldn't possibly leave all these responsibilities behind!
HH. Very well, Herr Beethoven; but you must pay the price of staying here.
B. What price?
HH. The sweat and toil of another evolution in your composing style. You must develop a new musical vocabulary . . . more contemporary than your present idiom.
B. In my current style, I've written the best music of my entire career!
HH. Having attended your recent festival, I agree with you. I have little doubt that your corporate BEETHOVEN will adopt this glorious fusion as its permanent speech. Such would be to the credit of our entire Major culture. But here upon this tiny Earth-centered planet, your chosen SCP, there's no more room for music to be written in this particular spirit. For better or worse, SCP 7,900,111 must follow the contemporary trends of Earth.
B. And for this reason, I plan to do no further composing here. With our performances, with Kapell's career, with my talented son, there are still plenty of musical activities to keep old Beethoven happy.
HH. And when you've resolved these challenges, then what?
B. Then I'll probably return to Major-Order life.
HH. Good! This is what I was hoping you'd say . . .

A gentle bell chimes the conclusion of intermission. Hergenroeder and I return to the foyer where we shake hands, and like the final puffs from my pipe, he gracefully vanishes into the crowd.

At the time of this latest visitation, Karl, Wolfgang, and Maria are respectively nineteen, seventeen, and fifteen years of age. Karl is a student of mathematics at the University of Göttingen. (Imagine! A son of Beethoven, majoring in mathematics!) Wolfgang is every inch a composer, as richly talented as his mother or I could ever hope to be, this side of the Third Order. I'm so proud of his dedication and steady progress that I do indeed change his official "third-floor" name from "Hosenknopf" to "Mozart!" Nevertheless, to assure the thoroughness of his training, Anna and I secure his enrollment as a student of composition at the Vienna Conservatory. Maria is as beautiful and sweet as she is lovely. Being the offspring of Paul Rezler's Second-Order physique, my daughter's grace and charm is so unusual that I fear it might arouse the suspicions of her Subsidiary peers.

Beginning in the fall of 1910 and continuing in uninterrupted sequence are four annual concert tours, each lasting until the spring of the following year. Since both our sons are at school, and since Hannes is now an official tenant at the Hildebrandtstrasse and can there look after Maria, Anna and I feel free to map our tours as extensively as conditions permit; and extensive they are, each taking us through Europe and to the United States. For these concerts, I divide my time almost equally between the podium and the piano bench. Occasionally, Anna performs under my baton, but for the most part, she functions as my wife, fellow traveler, and chief critic. The compositions used on these tours are, of course, our newest symphonies, concertos, and piano pieces. They enable us to enjoy Voskamp's final victory as a composer and at the same time to bring Kapell's name before the musical public on each of four succeeding seasons. There is one additional work added to our repertoire for these concerts. It is the *Second Piano Concerto in C Minor* by Sergei Vassilievitch Rachmaninoff. On our particular SCP, the "Rachmaninoff" figure is one Andrej Jakubowicz—a first-rate pianist and Russo-Romantic composer in the Rachmaninoff tradition. Though I admire many of the Rachmaninoff-Jakubowicz opuses, there is something absolutely unique about the "C Minor Concerto." Its composition is more like the birth of an inspired poem than the disciplined writing of notes. From that evening in 1902 when we first hear Jakubowicz interpret the concerto, it is "love at first sound." Anna and I can hardly wait to perform it, and throughout our seasons of concerts, we never tire of doing so.

In the fall of 1914, there is no world tour for Anna and Mason Voskamp; there is no world in which to *have* a tour. Following its Earthly counterpart, the "Europe" of my SCP plunges itself into four years of complete madness—World War I. As on Earth, the spark that triggers the explosion is the assassination of Austria-Hungary's crown prince by a Serbian terrorist. Russian influence in the Balkans had increased, particularly in Serbia. On the eve of the assassination, the Pan-Serb movement had grown to such an extent that it threatened Austria's entire multinational system. In the wake of the assassin's bullet, the Austrian government decides that Serbia must now (or never) be punished and reduced in power, regardless of what the risk might be. She declares war on Serbia on August 3, 1914. By the middle of September, most of Europe is involved in the beginnings of world war. Austria, Germany, Turkey, and Bulgaria are pitted against Serbia, Russia, France, and England. All Germany seems to explode with enthusiasm and patriotic exaltation over the declaration of war. She anticipates her future battles as constituting "a grand and wonderful war," a fresh and happy war that will put pride in her soul, steel in her backbone, and confidence in her national future.

I wish I could share such optimism with my German brothers, but somehow I can't. I feel that Germany and Austria are doomed to destruction. I'm unable to put my feelings into words, but a certain Earthling, Dr. Arthur Bernstein (exhibiting a marvelous gift of prophecy) *is* able to do so. Immediately following Germany's declaration of war upon France, he sends a note of warning to the Berlin Morgenpost. Military censorship, of course, prevents its publication, and only recently have I been able to read excerpts from his uncanny prognosis:

> In a few days, no one will any longer be able to speak the truth, much less write it. Therefore, in this last moment, the warmongers are miscalculating. In the first place, there is no Triple Alliance! Italy will not go along, at least not with us; and if it does, it will join the side of the Entente. Secondly, England will not remain neutral, but will stand with France. England will also not tolerate a German march through Belgium, which (since 1907) is generally known as our plan of strategy. But if England fights against us, then the entire English world, particularly America, will come out against us. Most probably the entire world! For England is respected all over, even though not loved, and this much can unfortunately not be said of us! Thirdly, Japan will not attack Russia; more likely she will attack us. . . . Finally, Austria-Hungary is militarily hardly a match for the Serbs and Rumanians. Economically, it can hunger through three to five years. It can give us nothing! . . . Whether we can be the victors at the end of this most terrible war the

> world will have seen, is questionable. But even if we *win* the war, we will win nothing! . . . Germany is waging this war for nothing, in the same way in which it has entered the war for nothing. One million corpses, two million cripples, and fifty billions in debts will be the balance of this "fresh and happy" war. . . . Nothing more!

During these years of the Great War, there's not much for an eighty-year-old Voskamp to do but sit and wait and worry about his two young sons who are now in uniform. No doubt because of Karl's excellent mathematical background, he is accepted as a petty officer in the German navy, where, except for the battle of Jutland, he participates in very little fighting on the high seas. His main battles are against boredom, inaction, and low morale, resulting from the British naval blockade that (since the outbreak of war) keeps the major portion of the German fleet in harbor at Kiel. Then things change for the better, or worse—depending upon whether your viewpoint is that of the son or the father. In March 1917, Germany embarks upon unrestricted U-boat warfare, and Karl is transferred from the Nurnberg to the U-105. Wolfgang, like most sensitive and creative artists, finds himself an infantryman specializing in front-line duties. He sees action in three different countries: Serbia, Rumania, and Bulgaria. While our Greater Germany piles victory upon victory, the stupid war goes on and on! Our costly victories will be the death of us. *Wir siegen uns zum Tod!*

The final German offensive is launched on March 25, 1918, and lasts until the twentieth of July. It brings a temporary improvement in field positions, but no ultimate victory. At this time, Anna decides that we have been musically inactive for too long. She proposes a Herr and Frau Voskamp morale-building concert tour that happens to coincide with the final month of the offensive. We perform at Stuttgart, Heidelberg, Würzburg, and Frankfurt; but for the most part, our tour follows the Rhine from Karlsruhe to Cologne. Our final concerts are at Bonn, where I derive endless pleasure walking among the old gray buildings with their sloping roofs and their cool shady gardens. How soul comforting it is once again to be greeted by Father Rhine . . . to make countless comparisons between *this* Bonn and the Bonn of my Earthly childhood. Many things have changed . . . grown bigger or smaller. But the essential spirit is still here—the seven green hills and the eternal song of the river!

Our third and concluding Bonn concert is performed Friday evening, July 19. We plan to leave for Vienna, Monday morning. On the Sunday afternoon preceding our departure, Anna suggests a little drive north for a final savoring of the Rhine. Our rough and dusty road soon leads us to a beautiful green spot about halfway between Bonn and Cologne. We walk down a wind-rippled grassy slope and spread our picnic lunch only a few feet from the sun-filled wavelets of the old river. What a perfect place to commune with Father Rhine: no factories, no railroad tracks, no timeworn castles, no battlemented watchtowers, no staring houses, no heaven-piercing cathedrals—just one huge panorama of blue sky, white clouds, green slopes, and sun-warmed vineyards, all perfectly reflecting the calm of the river.

After lunch, we walk along the cool slope for nearly an hour. Then at a particularly warm and sunny spot, we stretch out on the river's bank, my head in Anna's lap. Even upside down, as she gently strokes my brow, her face looks sad and serious:

B. Now come, Anna. Don't let the madness of this wretched war get you down. Let me see that beautiful smile of yours.

Anna tries to smile, but she can't. Her eyes moisten, becoming as deep and reflective as the river itself. Continuing my admonition, I reach up and spank the tip of her nose with my finger.

B. The war will soon be over . . . the fighting will end . . . our sons will come home to us!

AR. No, Mason. For us, the war will *never* end. Our sons will *not* come home.

B. You're being unduly pessimistic. Things will soon get back to normal. Wait and see.

AR. You don't understand what I'm trying to say.

A spastic dryness clutches at my throat—a freezing piercing of my heart almost prevents me from asking that question which my soul fears most to ask:

B. What are you trying to say, my love? (*As she answers me, I rise on one arm and stare directly into her unfaltering eyes.*)

AR. Our dear sons, Karl and Wolfgang, they are *not* coming home to us. . . . They are dead . . . both of them . . . killed in action!

B. God in heaven! . . . How can you speak such bloody and hopeless words?
AR. They *are* bloody, but they are true!
B. Goddamn! . . .

I release my arm, roll from Anna's lap, bury my face in the cool grass. How can there be enough grass to absorb my burning tears? With both fists, I pound the earth to emphasize the shouting of my words.

B. What a dirty, rotten, stinking, damnable place this is! . . . How can we have life and love and creativity in such a world? We give them our sons, and they send us back corpses. . . . There is no reason to go on . . . no reason on this earth!
AR. But there *is* a reason!
B. What? Name one. Where? Show me!
AR. There . . . in the voice of the river. There's your reason!
B. His voice is silent. It chokes red with human blood!
AR. His voice is *deep*, but not silent. . . . He still speaks to his dear ones who have the heart to listen.
B. Tell me, Anna. When did it happen? How did our sons die?
AR. Karl was killed on October 18 of last year. His U-boat was sunk in the North Sea; there were no survivors. Three months later (to the very day) Wolfgang was reported missing in action . . . the Rumanian campaign. On January 28, we received notice of the positive identification of his body. There can be no doubt of it; our sons are taken from us! . . .
B. God in heaven! . . . Dear Anna . . . why did you keep this terrible calamity to yourself these many months?
AR. I haven't had the heart to tell anyone . . . neither you nor Hannes. I feared the sad news would crush you both. But long ago, sweet husband . . . when we spent our first vacation on the Rhine, I observed the wonderful restorative effect this old river seemed to have upon you. It was as though you drew a kind of spiritual sustenance from the mere sight of him. I made up my mind then and there—if ever the day should come when I must break some sad or shocking news to you, this is the peaceful place where I would do so.
B. How lovely. . . . Now I see the reason for our sudden Rhenish tour, not so much a wartime gift to the Fatherland, as your thoughtful and sensitive reaction to my spiritual needs and

emotional quirks. How shall I be able to thank you enough? What a burden you have born alone on my behalf. I should have been the one to comfort *you,* but no, you've done my suffering for me. Well, it hasn't been in vain. Because of you, I've survived the saddest news this world can tell, yet I still hear the voice of the river!

AR. Wonderful! My prayers are answered. Tell me, Darling. What does Father Rhine say to you?

B. He tells us to rejoice in the memory of our fine sons, to be confident in the certainty of our eventual reunion, to be proud of their sacrifice, to be patient and faithful!

AR. Good! These are the same words he speaks to me. I don't understand him, but I do believe in him. Someday . . . somehow . . . we *will* be together again. These tears of our present sorrow will be exchanged for the heavenly rejoicing of a permanent reunion!

The Allied counteroffensive begins August 12, 1918. It's successful from the very first and rages continuously in one sector or another until armistice terms are finally accepted on November 22. Even in defeat, there is some joy. At least the senseless fighting and destruction and bloodshed are ended!

As Anna had predicted, life is anything but normal in the Hildebrandtstrasse. We try pretending that our boys are just away at school, but death's cruel face shows clearly through our little game. No amount of pretense will ever bring Karl and Wolfgang home to us. In spite of Kapell's "family status" in Voskamps' second-floor living quarters, the rooms there seem twice as big, twice as many, and twice as empty as ever before. I run daily to our third-floor studio, hoping that the musical activities of my Court will somehow put an end to the excruciating sadness of the floor below. But no, things are just as bad there . . . even worse. By prewar standards, there *is* no Court, just a few glum students who come and go only to return a week later, a gloom-laden Hannes who sits and stares into space, a fluttering Anna whose attempt at cheerfulness makes me suspect the many tears and broken heart that hide behind her constant smile, and of course, the ghost of a young "Mozart"—our dear Wolfgang whose happy memory fills every corner of our music rooms with constant reminders of the many wonderful things he would now be doing, if only he had returned.

During the years immediately following the war, our concert activities are restricted to Vienna, Berlin, and several other German cities. There are enough expressed and implied cries of "Voskamp the

Hun . . . go home!" to discourage any present tours through France, England, or the United States. As far as Anna and I are concerned, there are no new compositions issuing from the Hildebrandtstrasse. Our sole efforts in the "composing department" are directed toward helping Sigmund Kapell arrive at a successful evolution from our now locally accepted post-Brahms idiom. To do this, we make a thorough study of much of the new music arriving on our SCP, especially the latest scores of Igor Stravinsky, Ralph Vaughan Williams, and Paul Hindemith. Little by little, our Hannes comes alive again. For several years, it appeared as though (musically, at least) he would not survive Wolfgang's death. Even his interest in composing had waned. But now, thank God, the new sounds of contemporary Earthling scores inspire him once more to vigorous activity! He tears into our detailed analyses of complex orchestral tapestries with a thorough determination to master the new material and to develop an adequate style of his own. But as to the training of an apprentice successor, since the death of our Wolfgang, I never hear him mention the idea again!

February 11, 1927, is a bitter cold Friday whose dawning has left our fair old city buried deeply (almost helplessly) under a fresh white snow. It's that "cozy indoors" kind of a day that makes me rejoice in not having to go out anywhere after supper. Naturally, because of this internal coziness, the phone rings and I'm invited out after supper! On the other end of the line is Herr Granville Bloch, our current Second-Order proprietor of the Waldmüller Kaffehaus. Since Anna and Hannes are both downstairs, I'm able to talk freely:

B. Herr Bloch! . . . How unusual for you to call me here.

GB. How unusual is my reason for calling. It is safe to talk?

B. Yes, I'm alone.

GB. Good! You must come to the Waldmüller this evening. I've taken the liberty of arranging an important appointment for you at 8:00 PM.

B. I'll be damned! This isn't how things are done, Granville. You're assuming the authority of my counselor. I don't understand.

GB. You will when you get here.

B. Whatever it is, can't it keep until next week? I was planning to stop by either Wednesday or Thursday for my regular checkup on Second-Order affairs. Why not arrange the appointment for then?

GB. Impossible! This is too important to wait a week.

B. You win. I'll be there at eight.

GB. Come at seven thirty, Rezler. There are some goodies you'll want to read in the *Aaronian News* . . . important background for your conference.

B. Very well. I'll see you at seven thirty.

Anna looks at me as though she thinks I'm crazy, venturing out on such a night, but venture out I do. I take a cab into the Graben, then walk the last six blocks as an after-dinner stimulant. With cold moon and howling stars, the sky is clear and bright, as though attempting to apologize for its ugly misbehavior of the preceding night!

Upon entering the Waldmüller, I'm led immediately to booth No. 6. There Bloch provides me with three glasses and two chilled bottles of fine French wine:

B. Champagne! . . . What's the idea, Herr Bloch? Who *are* these important visitors, anyway?

GB. Never mind. They'll be coming through that panel in about twenty minutes. (*He reaches inside his jacket and hands me a carefully folded first section of the* Aaronian News.) In the meantime, feast your eyes upon this. Then try to tell me that I've overstepped my bounds in making an appointment for you.

Before I can open the section to its first page, Herr Bloch vanishes behind the Kaffehaus side of the booth's red velvet curtain. I'm left there alone to suffer the greatest shock any newspaper has brought me since that bygone day at Dogwood when I first read of the rebirth of Ludwig van Beethoven! The news that surprises me now is also that of a rebirth. For the second time in less than two hundred years, our beloved Prophet Aaron has come to dwell among us in the Second Order of his Major life system. His prior visit was from 1701 to 1733 and was achieved through the spiritual absorption of a seventeen-year-old economics student named Pablo de Cubas. His present arrival on January 25, 1927, involved the absorption of a sixteen-year-old dramatics student by the name of Roger Reavis. Two weeks were spent on Aaron AP making tests and confirmations and holding secret meetings with the entire College of Counselors. Then on February 9 (the date of my newspaper) the blessed event was made public. Because of the frequency of his recent low-order rebirths (Second, Third, and Fourth), Aaron suspects that he will soon be making his ninety-ninth visit to Earth (the First Order of his entire life system). He plans to spend most of his present life in preparing for such a return visit. Aaron's proposed itinerary is already decided upon and is published on the second page of my paper. He has allocated about one month to each of our Cultural Planets and will arrive at BEETHOVEN's CP on March 3, 1933. This means that my firm must prepare some very special music for the occasion. I think I know who my visitors will be. Sure enough, in ten minutes the panel slides open and there stand the Bonapartes—Richard and Marcie Grant! I plant a little kiss on Marcie's brow, then shake hands with her husband:

B. Welcome to the Waldmüller. What a long time it's been since I've seen the two of you. . . . How are things at BEETHOVEN?

Gr. As well as might be expected, considering that you're not there. Now that Aaron has returned to our order, what's the chance of your coming home with us?

B. None, just now. I still have some important business to finish here, then perhaps I will return to the May Building. Any chance of claiming my old partnership?

Gr. Indeed yes! Your Schwarspanierhaus office is still waiting there just for you. In the meantime, will you help us with a major composition honoring Aaron's arrival on CP 75? We have six years to complete it . . . until March 1933.

B. I'd love to, Grant, but it's impossible for me to evolve an authentic new style in so short a time.

Gr. You needn't. Write something in our present post-Brahms idiom.

B. I'm not permitted to write in this style and still remain in Subsidiary life.

Gr. But you *are*. We've got permission from the College of Counselors itself.

B. What do you mean?

Gr. Marcie and I had little hope of your returning with us now. Yet our entire planet has a genuine need for a new Beethoven composition. How else are we musically to honor the return of our Prophet? We explained this situation to SCP Control. They understood perfectly and gave you permission to write one more piece in our present style.

B. Wonderful! Then one more piece you'll have—a huge composition, a musical mountain, the last and the best from Mason Voskamp. It might take me five years to complete, but you'll have it in plenty of time for '33.

Gr. Will it be a choral work?
B. Yes. If Charles Jennens can inspire the Earthly Handel's greatest oratorio, I'm sure he can now do the same for me.
MG. You mean, another *Messiah*?
B. Yes! How better could I honor the rebirth of Christ?
Gr. I agree with you. Your choice is perfect!

The Grants and I spend nearly three hours discussing old times, drinking champagne, and planning BEETHOVEN's future. I comment frequently upon how young and handsome they both still are, and upon how old and decrepit I myself am beginning to feel. They attribute my imagined infirmities entirely to the many years I have masqueraded as a Subsidiary musician.

MG. (*How temptingly Marcie smiles as she reassures me.*) Remember, Darling, when you *act* like gray hairs and wrinkles, you *feel* like gray hairs and wrinkles. But don't despair. . . . Beneath that crinkled "Voskamp" of yours is a vibrant young Beethoven of 118 years, who (physically at least) is nothing less than a sexy, teenaged Paul Rezler

Only after securing my promise to come personally and conduct the CP 75 première performance of the new *Messiah* do my visitors at last bid me farewell and disappear through the sliding panel of booth No. 6.

At this time in my Subsidiary life, there begins a series of inducements that will eventually cause me to transfer my long-established living quarters from Viennese to North American soil. First and foremost is, of course, the downward spiraling degeneration of the Weimar Republic of 1918 into the National-Socialist Germany of 1933. As on Earth, my Subsidiary Fatherland has its continuous bouts with inflation and with the impossible terms of the Versailles Treaty. Almost coincident with the signing of the Armistice, she begins a strenuous program of secret rearmament. She cooks up an efficient National-Sozialistische-Deutsche-Arbeiter-Partei of her own, including among its members a future führer named Ago Humboldt instead of Adolf Schicklgrüber. When Humboldt becomes the indispensable leader of the NSDAP, he is naturally "absorbed" by a Major-Order Aaronian, whose unenviable task is to duplicate the bastard career of Adolf Hitler down to the last "Heil!" As such, he developed into the personification of Pan-Germanism, anti-Semitism, and ruthless ambition, attempting to lead a mighty Third Reich in the dubious direction of Weltmacht oder Niedergang.

Other developments that will combine to separate me from my Fatherland are more personal than the stomping boots of Der Führer. Between 1908 and 1915, my dear friend and great Maestro Arturo Sabatini had spent much of his time in the United States as conductor of the Metropolitan Opera House. Because of his brilliant results there, in 1926 he is offered the post of director of the New York Philharmonic Symphony Orchestra. This position he joyfully accepts and occupies through 1936. During these years, I receive from him countless letters assuring me that America's anti-German feelings have subsided and urging me to come to the States, if not to live, at least to resume my concerts.

An even stronger inducement is provided by my one remaining child, Maria. In 1930, she falls in love with Max Wilding, an American film director who first calls at the Hildebrandtstrasse for the specific purpose of obtaining an original Voskamp score for his current production of *Iron Cross*, a story of World War I, which he is now filming in Germany.

B. Bah! . . . You don't understand me, Wilding, not at all! If you did, you wouldn't ask such a thing. My music is for great orchestras, not for paltry strips of celluloid.

Needless to say, young Wilding does not return to the United States with a Voskamp score; he takes our daughter with him instead. Though they've known one another less than a month, Maria Voskamp and Max Wilding are married on Friday morning, June 20, in St. Stephen's Cathedral at the very altar where Anna and I were married so many happy years ago. After honeymooning about the Mediterranean, they leave for the United States on July 3, 1930. Commencing the first of August, we receive regular letters from Maria and our new son, inviting us to come and visit them at their fabulous home in Beverly Hills.

None of these incentives effects our immediate move to the United States. At first I'm so busy with my *Messiah* project that there's not time even for a brief visit there. How surprised Anna and Hannes are (on that Saturday morning following my visit with the Bonapartes at the Waldmüller) when I call them together and inform them that there is to be one more composition in the late Voskamp style. They both explode with enthusiasm; then Hannes questions my change of heart:

UH. How come? What finally makes you see the light?
B. It's hard to explain, Hannes. I suddenly feel that my life's work here needs a more fitting climax than it presently has—a genuine opus ultimum!
UH. What's this masterpiece to be?
B. I've decided on a choral work. . . . I'm going to do my own version of *Messiah*!
AR. (*These words startle Anna into the conversation.*) You mean the same text used by Krassner?
B. Yes. More inspiring words could not be found!
AR. Nor could one find more inspiring music for these words.
B. I agree. It's not my purpose to give the words a better setting; I wish to give them a *different* setting, the warmth of my present style in lieu of Handel's *Baroque.*
AR. But why an oratorio? Isn't our music better suited to opera?
B. Perhaps it is . . . but my heart is set upon *Messiah.*
AR. Why?
B. This too is hard to explain. It's as though I had a dream, a premonition of the end. . . . And what do I take with me from a lifetime of composing? I must take *something* with me. Should I come face-to-face with the Christ, I must have some little token to cast at his feet. For this purpose, nothing will do but a *Messiah.*
AR. How unusual, Vos. . . . I doubt if any other piece has been composed with such a thought in mind.
B. It is unusual, but what better motivation could there be for a final composition?
AR. None better. When do we start to work?
B. You mean, when do *I* start to work. In spite of all our years of profitable sharing, I somehow wish this final effort to be the product of my own hands.
AR. But this isn't fair, Vos. Hannes and I have toiled long and faithfully at your side; we deserve to share in the birth of your *Messiah.*
UH. (*Hannes replies with a perpendicular waving of his left hand.*) Count me out. I'm too busy searching for something to be of use to you now. Why don't you each write your *own Messiah*?
B. A brilliant idea, Hannes. This is exactly what we'll do. I'll write my *Messiah,* and Anna will write hers. Then we'll select the better

of the two (or the best parts of each) for sending to Schoenbern and Kietzing.

This decision pretty much sets the pace of things at the Hildebrandtstrasse for the rest of 1927. Hannes remains totally absorbed in his comparative studies of our SCP versions of Hindemith, Stravinsky, and Vaughan Williams. Because of the sanctity of a *Messiah,* Anna and I condition ourselves especially to project thoughts of an inspirational nature, ideas that would arouse the presence of spiritual beings, serving as collaborators in this sacred mission. I try to have a clear enough mind that will enable me to "hear" the revelations these unseen benefactors have to offer. And even though we are physically separated in this monumental task, we're humbly united in one true purpose: the earnest desire to please our Creator!

Anna is as one possessed by the Divine Muse. It's as though the spirit of motherhood has descended upon her once more, compensating her for the loss of our sons. On the morning of March 12, 1928, Hannes is with his students at the university. Anna and I are alone, she working in *her* studio, and I in mine. I'm standing there with pages of my *Glory to God* taped on the wall, trying to direct its choral lines through a thick texture of brass and strings, when in comes my little wife.

B. Anna! . . . It's not like you to interrupt my composing. What's happened? Is Germany at war again?
AR. Put down your pencil. There'll be no more composing today.
B. Why?
AR. We must celebrate!
B. Celebrate what?
AR. For me, this is like Christmas morning. . . . My *Messiah* is born!
B. What do you mean, Anna?
AR. My score . . . it's finished!
B. Not the entire score!
AR. Yes! Fifty-three numbers. . . . Nearly four hours of music!
B. I'll be damned! . . . And here I am, still working on number seventeen.
AR. Yours are probably better than mine, but at least I've written the best music I knew how. I've never been so totally inspired by any creative assignment as this. Will you come and read through the score?
B. Note by note! Lead the way, my dear . . .

It takes me over four hours to hear the entirety of Anna's masterpiece. By the time I reach her last Amen, my shirt front is wet from tears of admiration! In its own way, her music is greater than Handel's. She has accomplished everything that I dreamed of doing, and much more—all in one-fifth the time it would have taken me to finish. I rise from my wife's desk, and the two of us meet in one huge embrace.

B. Dearest Anna, my sweet. . . . I'm so very proud of you and of what you've accomplished. A few years ago, you were my little angel, hovering over my shoulder and peering into my sketchbooks. Today, you're a greater composer than I am.

AR. Nonsense!

B. It's true, Darling. I try to create the perfect oratorio; and before I can even get the job under way, you've finished it! There's no reason for me to go on with my struggling choruses. You, my dear (not I), have just completed Voskamp's opus ultimum. If I ever do come face-to-face with Jesus, it will be *your Messiah* (not mine) that I shall be proud to place at his feet.

And so it is that my final composition on SCP 7,900,111 turns out to be written by my wife instead of me! She had indeed been overshadowed by divine adepts and thus was able to capture the magnificence of a heavenly creation! Its world première occurs under my baton on Christmas Eve 1928 at St. Stephen's Cathedral. On January 15 of the new year (due to Anna's insistence), the score is finally sent to Schoenbern and Kietzing, under the title:

Messiah
A Sacred Grand Oratorio
being the
Opus Ultimum
of
Anna and Mason Voskamp

On May 1, our publishers present us with three copies of the full score, one of which I send off to the Bonapartes via the Waldmüller. Within days, I'm rewarded with a dozen letters of overwhelming praise. It seems as though everyone at BEETHOVEN heartily approves of my commemorative opus, proclaiming it the best composition I have ever written, well worthy of honoring Aaron's arrival on CP 75.

If only they knew that the sublimities of this creation were not mine at all, but had fallen like an abundant spring rain from the hands and heart of my gifted Subsidiary wife (and the ethereal impact of the higher realms), I wonder what they'd say!

On December 27 and 29, 1929, Sabatini directs the first performances of our *Messiah* in the United States. The results are explosive, creating a huge demand for our public appearance there. Consequently, for the fall and winter of the next year, I begin planning our first concert tour of the States since World War I. Maria's surprise marriage to Max Wilding in the summer of 1930 naturally results in even more extensive plans for our tour. We schedule six additional concerts on the West Coast and an extra week for visiting our "children" at their Beverly Hills "castle."

On October 7 (a week and three days prior to the first concert of our American tour), I stop by the Waldmüller for a final check on Aaronian affairs before leaving Vienna. What shocking news fills the first page of the *Interplanetary*! Johann Sebastian Bach has died; he died in the early hours of Monday morning! I find this news sad and yet (in a way) joyful: sad, because I had so wished to renew our acquaintance upon my return to Major-Order life; joyful, because our great Maestro had died in the blessed arms of Aaron himself! Interrupting his visit to CP 15, our dear Prophet had spent three days at the musician's bedside! Think what this must have meant to J. S. Bach! The arms of Jesus, those very arms that had nurtured him through a lifetime of joyful suffering on Earth were now the arms that peacefully assured him of the challenge of a Third-Order rebirth.

Our first American tour is so successful that a similar event is planned and executed during each of the next two seasons. The third tour ends in New York City, where I perform a Voskamp and a Kapell piano concerto with the Philharmonic under Sabatini at a pair of concerts given on March 3 and 5. We plan to sail for Germany on Monday the twentieth. Before doing so, we naturally schedule a visit with the Wildings: Max, Maria, and our little grandson, Freddie. Anna leaves for the West Coast on March 6. I promise to join her there the following Monday, under the pretense of having a week of important musical business with Sabatini and with Henry Braunstein, our U.S. concert agent. This gives me the necessary time to translate to our Major Order for my avowed performance of *Messiah* in honor of Aaron's arrival on CP 75.

Aaron first visits BEETHOVEN's Cultural Planet on March 3, 1933, the precise date projected in his schedule. Naturally, his initial days there are spent in being officially welcomed at CP 75's seat of government and in making planetwide TV appearances. My corporation's preliminary musical tribute to our beloved Prophet is an Altburg concert scheduled for Friday evening, March 10. At this concert, I'm to conduct our new *Messiah* and (at the request of Aaron himself) a performance of my Earthly *Symphony No. 9 in D Minor.*

Arriving at Aaron AP on Monday afternoon, March 6, the first thing I do is remove my old Voskamp disguise from Rezler's handsome young body. Although the latter has reached the ripe old age of 124 years, it still has twice the beauty and sexual virility of a twenty-four-year-old Earthling physique. Since this is my first appearance as "Paul Rezler" in eighty-one years, and since the Altburg rehearsals are scheduled for Thursday afternoon and Friday morning, I decide to spend Monday, Tuesday, and Wednesday at Dogwood. What a joyful family reunion these days turn out to be—although a strange experience for me now to embrace a pair of Second-Order parents who are suddenly "middle-aged"! Somehow I must have thought that this couple (at least) would escape the aging process, would still be the handsome "teenagers" who had nurtured my Second-Order childhood and had directed me toward architecture until Beethoven himself came along and changed everything. Freeman and Gina are both there, each with a spouse and a flock of children and grandchildren. Even dear old Culby shows up and dances to my playing. When I'm not greeting friends and family, I'm either studying Friday's scores or reading the latest Beethoven biographies, having concluded that after a hundred years in "heaven," it would be interesting to see what contemporary Earthlings are writing about me. Of the half-dozen "Beethovens" I read, the one by Robert Haven Schauffler is my favorite.

The rehearsals and concert are to be held in the new Beethoven Hall at Altburg. Since this elaborate block-size structure is within walking distance of the May Building, I sign out a room at DeWitt's. After so many years, how strange it is (once again) to be living in this particular complex and to be staring across the busy street at old BEETHOVEN, Incorporated. What a lot of living and growing I've done since my last visit here!

Friday's rehearsal ends at 3:00 PM, only four hours before concert time. I'm especially pleased with the way things have gone; the old symphony, the new *Messiah*—both have responded ideally to my composer's baton. How I wish that dear Anna might hear her great music thus performed to Second-Order perfection!

Next comes a very pleasant surprise in the form of a preconcert supper. The surprise evolves not so much from my being invited to a supper as from the delightful company that assembles for the occasion. There sit the Donovans, the Bonapartes, my parents, Gina, Freeman, Brother Johann, Nephew Karl, and (all the way from our SCP) one Maria Luigi Carlo Zenobio Salvatore Cherubini. What a pleasure to shake Cherubini's hand for the first time as Roy Debbs, to see him clad in the Negroid beauty of his Second-Order body, instead of masquerading about as an ancient Sabatini!

At 7:00 PM, when I first step to the podium, the houselights are not dimmed. This gives me an opportunity to acknowledge Aaron's presence and (incidentally) to observe the huge crowd that has packed Beethoven's Hall to SRO capacity! I have no trouble in spotting our beloved Prophet, who is seated in a flower-draped box of honor. I bow first to Aaron, then to the applauding audience. He responds to my bow by standing and applauding all the harder. Everyone in the hall (including the orchestra and chorus) follows his example, and what was meant as a humble tribute to Aaron turns into a standing ovation for Beethoven!

Facing the orchestra, I raise my baton and within a few seconds am totally absorbed by the opening measures of *Symphony 9.* How wonderful of Aaron to request this Earthly child of mine! How better could he show his approval of my First-Order musicianship?!

Immediately following the *Ninth,* I launch Part 1 of Anna's *Messiah.* This part of her version (like Handel's) contains twenty-three numbers, beginning with an Overture and ending with the Chorus: His yoke is easy, his burden is light. . . . At the conclusion of Part 1, there is a huge burst of applause. Instead of claiming what I'm sure would have amounted to a dozen curtain calls, I direct the tremendous ovation toward that Prophet whom we have come to honor, whose spirit has inspired the greatness of Anna's music, and who finally stands and acknowledges the plaudits of our hearts!

Upon reaching backstage, I receive a hug and a kiss from Judy Donovan, plus a handshake and a tiny envelope from her husband. In the envelope is a crisp white card upon which is scrawled:

> Dear Beethoven,
>
> Would you do me the honor of spending a portion of the intermission in my box?
>
> Aaron

Immediately I cross behind the backdrop, mount a steel spiral stairway, and traverse a narrow marble hall that leads to Aaron's private box. As I do so, I try to imagine what it will be like to come face-to-face with our Prophet himself. The experience is something like climbing those stairs to Mozart's musical abode. There too, I was on my way to meet a giant among men. He turned out to be more the spirit of love and encouragement than an almighty god sitting in judgment upon me. Surely Aaron will now do the same. Before I can realize what's happening, the crowning experience of my living becomes a reality. I turn a sharp right, the empty hall widens and brightens. There, coming toward me with extended hand and smiling face, is (literally) the Father of us all! A mere handshake seems inadequate for the occasion; such relative impersonality soon gives way to a warm and hearty embrace!

In the handsome body of a twenty-two-year-old Roger Reavis, our great Prophet appears almost too young and too handsome to be what he really is. He looks like a typical product of the stage: a crown of curly black hair, a warm healthy glow shining from his clear-cut features, a firm young body flexing impressively beneath its formal garb. His "professional" smile is that of a well-trained Reavis, but oh those eyes . . . those huge brown eyes . . . they're anything *but* the scholarly acquisition of a dramatics student. In them it's possible to see the eternal story of life, death, and rebirth . . . infinite love . . . living faith . . . inexhaustible hope! . . . Fortunately (for the lump in my throat), Aaron is first to speak:

Ar. P. So this is Herr Beethoven, master musician of Earth, maladjusted composer of the Second Order! . . . What a pleasure to meet you face-to-face, my son.

B. And now that we *do* meet, I can't believe you are who you are, except for what I see in your eyes.

Ar. P. Do they speak to you?

B. They confirm everything I've dreamed you to be, and more. . . . When I look deeply into them, I feel that I must fall to my knees and worship the spirit within you.

Ar. P. The purpose of my spirit is more to give direction to my children than to serve as an object of their worship. Whatever you see in *my* eyes, you will one day read in your *own*. After a certain amount of living and growing, you too will be a prophet among humans and will beget an entire race of children to bear *your* name.

B. Now that I stand before you, my Lord, I'm not even sure what I should call you.

Ar. P. Aaron will do. . . . I much prefer a simple "first-name" basis.

B. Throughout our Major system, I've used the name of Aaron to describe so many different people and places and things, it's almost lost its aura of holiness.

Ar. P. Good! . . . So much the better!

B. But if I refer to the mere King of Prussia as "Your Majesty" and to our little Goethe as "Your Excellency," surely there must be some title of honor that I'm to use upon the very spirit of our Creator.

Ar. P. "Father" will do, or why not "Jesus?" On Earth, you were a Christian, likewise as Mason Voskamp.

B. I was *called* a Christian, more a matter of word than deed. As Beethoven, I developed a genuine dislike for the commercialized distortions of the historical Jesus that were then being pumped out by every little priest in Germany. For *me* at least, by the time they finished readying you for "market," they had shrunk you to the size of a tiny Jew who was crucified as a rebel, and who was later deified by a pack of hero-worshiping peasants.

Ar. P. Your reaction to my Earthly Jesus is not unique. Many have found in him little meaning beyond the origin of a convenient curse word. . . . I'm told that you once met Mozart. What title of respect did you confer upon him?

B. "Maestro." . . . Of course! . . . "Maestro"! . . . This is what I must now call you!

Ar. P. Why not? Considering that nonillions of my preprophetic lives were happily devoted to music and musicians, this seems highly appropriate.

B. Wonderful! For me, there is no greater expression of endearment or respect than "Maestro." And you, sweet Lord, are the greatest Maestro of all!

Ar. P. Thank you, my son. Coming from Herr Beethoven, this is a genuine compliment!

B. Dear Maestro, why am I now privileged to meet you face-to-face?

Ar. P. In order that I may personally thank you for the evening of beautiful music . . . a performance of the *Ninth* at my own request, plus the première of a Second-Order *Messiah*, which (so far) is actually a worthy successor to Handel's. And also I wish you to meet some dear friends of yours who are sitting with me.

Aaron pushes aside a blue velvet curtain and beckons me to enter his box. There, two elderly women and an old man are introduced to me as "Frau X," "Frau Y," and "Herr Z." All three wish to remain anonymous as an inducement for me to translate permanently to our Major Order. And quite an inducement this is. As I examine their faces, there's something in the eyes of each that confirms a deep and genuine love emanating from our Earthly relationship. "Frau X" appears to be about 955 or 960 years old. Her face . . . her entire manner has the keenness, the sensitivity, the lean intensity of a middle-aged Madame Curie. "Frau Y" is perhaps the older of the two, though her aging has produced the keenness, the sensitivity, the plump intensity of a middle-aged Victoria Regina. At about 975, "Herr Z" has all the bigness of physique, the graceful aging, the exceptional countenance, the faithful white hair, and the unruly mustache of a seventy-five-year-old Albert Schweitzer.

After introductions, we talk for several minutes about the music of the evening. All three former acquaintances are unanimous in their praise, especially of the new *Messiah*. This leads directly to my personal confession.

B. I hate to admit it, dear music lovers, but the *Messiah* to which you now listen . . . the piece we use to welcome our great Prophet . . . is not the composition of yours truly.

HZ. No?! (*with a look of enormous surprise on his huge face*) Then whose is it?

B. Magnificent though it be, it's the work of Anna Voskamp . . . my dear little Subsidiary wife.

FX. (*This comment brings a sudden reaction from "Frau X."*) But how can such great music be written by a First-Order Subsidiary being?

B. I don't know, "Frau X" . . . I've often wondered this myself. Perhaps Beethoven *is* due some credit in the matter. I'm quite sure that the example of his total dedication influenced Anna to take up such a work in the first place. At any rate, when I *do* return to Major-Order life, my sole purpose will be to lead our corporation in the direction of this *Messiah*.

The sound of a quiet bell signifies the approaching end of intermission. Simultaneously, Aaron shakes my hand and slaps my right shoulder.

Ar. P. Well Ludwig, it's about time for you to return to the podium. We certainly look forward to the rest of the concert.

B. To a Nonillionth-Order musician, our tiny *Messiah* must sound like the babbling of a child.

Ar. P. To Nonillionth-Order ears, it *does*. But this evening, I've been using my Second-Order, Fifth-Order, Tenth-Order ears; and to all of these, your music brings the greatest sounds they've ever heard!

B. Wonderful! Then perhaps we're not boring you. . . . Good-bye, great Maestro. I shall never forget the unbounded joy of these precious moments. Surely our paths will soon cross again.

Ar. P. I'm sure they *will*, my son. . . . Good-bye to you.

B. (*Addresses X, Y, and Z.*) And good-bye to *you*, dear loved ones. . . . When I return permanently to Major-Order life, my first order of business will be a joyous reunion with the three of you. I can hardly wait to learn the secret of the beautiful love that I read in your eyes. . . . Good-bye! . . .

FX. (*As I turn to leave, "Frau X" reaches out and touches my sleeve.*) Wait, dear Ludwig. . . . Tell us one thing more! When *do* you think you might return here to Major life?

B. I can't really say. . . . I guess it depends upon Anna Voskamp. So long as she lives, my place is certainly at her side. You know, "Frau X" . . . there's something strange about those eyes of yours . . . something deep and beautiful . . . something very dear to me. Tell me. Were you by any chance my Earthly mother?

FX. I enjoyed both your love and your respect, but no . . . I was not Frau Van Beethoven!

B. Very strange, indeed. Your eyes tell me that you were as close and dear to me as my mother and yet, you were not my mother! . . . I can think of no other person as close or as dear! Oh well, we'll solve this mystery at our reunion . . . *Auf Wiedersehen*!

When I return to the left wing, there's time only for picking up my baton and for taking a few deep breaths. I then bounce to the podium and resume the Major-Order première of Anna's *Messiah*. When we reach the *Hallelujah Chorus*, which concludes Part 2, Aaron does exactly what I knew he would do—emulating King George of England, he rises to his feet and stands for the duration of the *Chorus*. The entire audience (naturally) does the same. I have no doubt that wherever Anna's *Messiah* is performed, audiences will stand up for *her* "Hallelujah" precisely as they do for Handel's.

Upon returning to my SCP, the next five seasons (from the fall of '33 through the spring of '38) have as their sole musical concern, a series of concert tours of the United States. Though Anna is now in her seventies and has officially retired from the concert stage, she accompanies me on each of these tours and remains at once my chief inspiration and my severest critic!

In January of '38, Paul Knipp, chairman of America's Eastern Broadcasting Corporation, forms the EBC Symphony Orchestra in honor of Arturo Sabatini and offers him a fabulous contract as its permanent director! Our Maestro gratefully accepts the position, then immediately starts a persistent campaign aimed at convincing Anna and me to follow his example and remain in the States, this in lieu of returning to a Germany gone mad with power and ambition. Though it comes as quite a surprise to Sabatini, Anna and I suddenly decide in favor of his recommendation! After all these years, we finally say good-bye to our home in the Hildebrandtstrasse and to our dwindling crop of private students. For the first time in Subsidiary life, poor old Beethoven has no Court to call his own.

At the insistence of our daughter and son-in-law, we move into a private apartment (which amounts to an entire wing) of their huge Beverly Hills home. The three years we spend here together (1938–1941), are among the happiest of our entire marriage. They enable us to escape the senseless tragedy which a berserk Germany now brings down upon all Europe! They permit us to enjoy the companionship of the Wildings and as well, the inspiration of our grandchildren (little Freddie now has a brother, Franz and a sister, Paula). Moving to the States also facilitates our collaboration with Sabatini (and his entire group of superb artists at EBC) in making a complete recording of Voskamp's music. This ambitious undertaking replaces concert giving as our musical project for these years.

All is happy and bright except for the sad note sounded by Hannes Kapell. He absolutely refuses to heed our warnings; none of us can entice him to America, or even to leave Germany! He has completed his studies of Bloch, Hindemith, Vaughan Williams, Harris, and Stravinsky, fusing the entire results into a mature orchestral speech, which is essentially that of an enriched Hindemith. In fact, without knowing it, he has become the official "Hindemith" figure of our SCP—the greatest contemporary composer of Germany. As such, he apparently considers himself immune to the Nazi purging of Jewish music and musicians. Suddenly, the storm breaks. In an explosion of wrath, the Kulturkammer declares the works of Kapell to be non-Aryan, the offspring of a distorted Jewish mind, a pernicious influence, degenerate, unbearable to the Third Reich! Poor Hannes, though he and his music are more German than our Führer himself, they are officially banned from all concert programs throughout Germany. We begin to fear for Kapell's life!

In the late spring of '41, on Monday morning June 9, I enter our breakfast room and am surprised to find Anna missing from her usual chair. This prompts me to peek into the kitchen, where I fully expect to find her planning the day's culinary stratagems with Agnes Moore, our cook and housemaid extraordinary. Upon doing so, I discover that my wife is not there either.

B. Good morning, Agnes. Where's the "boss"?

AM. I don't know, Sir. It's strange that she's not down by this time. I thought perhaps she didn't feel well and decided to sleep in a bit.

B. Why no. . . . When I woke up this morning (as usual) our big old bed was empty of Anna. . . . I wonder if she left me a note or something.

This possibility sends me back upstairs to our bedroom. Sure enough, there on her dresser is a dainty pink envelope marked, "To my dearest Maestro." Inside is a short note that gives me quite a shock, but which doesn't at all sound like the final words I'm ever to hear from Anna Rosecranz:

June 8, 1941

Dear Mason,

Please forgive my sneaking off this way; I'm planning a wonderful musical surprise for you. I should return no later than the middle of next week. . . . You probably don't approve of your seventy-eight-year-old wife gallivanting around by herself. But fear not! . . . On *this* trip, I'm being accompanied by no less an authority on musical surprises than Maestro Sabatini. . . . Let my husband prepare himself for a truly great musical happening!

Love and dearest kisses,
Anna

On the following Monday at 11:00 PM, there is indeed a great surprise—though far from being a musical one. Arturo Sabatini comes knocking at our front door. He gives me a huge emotional embrace and at the same time breaks into tears. When at last he stops shaking and sniveling, he tells me of the death of my Anna! The two of them had flown to Austria in a final effort to convince Kapell that he must leave that country immediately, that his musical accomplishments would no longer protect him from the fate of thousands of other Jews in Germany. "Hannes in America" was to have been my musical surprise. As things worked out, Kapell had agreed to come to America. Early on Saturday morning, he and Anna were speeding along the München-Salzburg Autobahn, when their car was forced from the highway by the sudden stopping of an enormous truck. The car overturned in a ditch and burst into flames; both occupants were killed instantly. What remained of their bodies was stored in a temporary vault at Vienna's Central Friedhof, to be buried there in the Voskamp plot upon receipt of my signature on the certificates that Arturo now hands me. News of the tragedy is kept from the public until Tuesday morning, this in order that Sabatini could arrive in time to inform me of it personally.

For over three months, I live in an absolute daze, a kind of protection from the reality of the loss that has impoverished my life. Maria and the grandchildren attempt to fill the vacuum; I'm hardly aware of their presence. I try to decide whether to return now to Major life; no decision is reached. I listen to music, go for long and lonely walks, attend the theater; nothing gets through to me. It takes another shock to finally restore me to the world of the living, this time, something of a pleasant nature.

On October 11, I receive a phone call from Jack Watts, Second-Order proprietor of the Hollywood Hotel whose subbasement houses the only D-R Chamber in Los Angeles. He requests me to show up Sunday morning at eleven o'clock for an appointment with an Aaronian admirer and seems pleasantly surprised when I tell him I'll be there! Hardly realizing what I'm doing, half hoping that my visitor will be Judy Donovan, I arrive at the Hollywood an hour early. Watts informs me that my ruby-ringed worshiper has been there since 9:00 AM and directs me to booth No. 14. As I enter the cubicle, a handsome wiry chap (with the enthusiasm and vitality of *ten* handsome wiry chaps) jumps to his feet, then falls to his knees before me:

Wg. Dear Beethoven! . . . Great Maestro! . . . I worship the very ground on which you stand.

B. (*I reach for his arms, pulling him to his feet.*) You mustn't do this, young man. There's nothing left in old Beethoven worth worshiping, I assure you.

Wg. Ha! Then there's no beauty in a sunrise, no hope in the singing of birds, no freshness in a spring shower, no promise in anything which Aaron has given us to enjoy!

B. This is kind of you to say. Since the death of my precious Anna, I feel so little of my former self, so weak, helpless, useless! . . . I *do* have need of your praise!

Wg. I've not come to praise you, dear Maestro. The likes of your spirit would never have need for the words of *my* tongue. I'm here to ask you for help.

B. Help! . . . How could I be of help to *you* when I can't even help myself? I fear you've come too late.

Wg. Not too late. On Earth, you were directly responsible for everything of musical value that I accomplished. Beethoven was my Earthly father, and it's never too late for me to come to him for help.

B. Who *are* you, young man?

Wg. I am *Richard Wagner.*

Chapter 49

B. Richard Wagner! . . . What a pleasure to meet you after all these years!

Wg. The pleasure and honor are mine, I assure you. If only you could realize, dear Maestro, how totally indebted I am to you for all that I was and all that I am.

B. If you *are* indebted to me, your indebtedness is no greater than mine to Bach and Haydn and Mozart and Brahms. So you see, each cancels out the other. As Mozart once told me, it's like the passing of a torch.

Wg. How simple and how beautiful!

B. Exactly! Now what makes you think that an old Brahmsian Beethoven could *ever* be of help to the mighty composer of "The Ring"?

Wg. My problem is a musical problem, and you are the spirit of music. Within your sacred realm, there's no problem which you cannot solve.

B. What sort of problem?

Wg. In our attempt to synthesize music and drama, Wagner and his corporation have failed completely.

B. Forty Second-Order operas in less than sixty years doesn't sound like failure to *me.* What makes you think you've failed?

Wg. With all our strength, we have pursued a path that leads nowhere.

B. What path?

Wg. Music drama. There's nothing left for it to say, no important direction for it to take. . . . We've been successful in evolving opera into music drama, but now that it's time for another evolution, a five-year search has led us nowhere.

B. Then perhaps there *is* no further summit to which opera may aspire. . . . You've done the ultimate in musical stage.

Wg. The greatest art form of all, incapable of further growth? . . . We can't believe this . . . at least not until *you've* studied the problem and have personally told us so. From Beethoven, we could accept such a decision, from no one else.

B. Is this the help you ask me for?

Wg. Yes, dear Maestro. Study the course of Wagnerian drama, see if there's any path left for us to take.

B. I'll *do* it, Herr Wagner. Since the death of my Anna, I've been wandering round and round, turning aimlessly in endless circles, being of no use to anyone. Then suddenly, here you are, my musical offspring, standing before me with a brand new artistic challenge, something bigger than myself, outside myself. It's just what I need to send me back to work . . . back to life!

Wg. Excellent! Then I know we're all saved. I know you'll find us something meaningful.

B. Send me a dozen of your newer scores, the best things your WAGNER has done. I'll study them carefully, and I'll let you know what happens.

Wg. Thank you, dear Beethoven. In your hands, I know that our future is secure.

For one solid year, I study the scores sent me by Wagner. The harmonies are good, the contrapuntal textures are good, the melodies are good, but none are really better than those of the Earthly "Ring." Wagner is absolutely correct. There is no justification for more of the same. If music drama is to remain a vital art form within our Major culture, it must evolve into something bigger and better than itself. But what?

During this year of Wagnerian studies, my old and abandoned Fatherland declares war upon my new and adopted country. This it does without proper regard for America's industrial strength, and it does so on the day following Japan's attack at Pearl Harbor, which, in our SCP, occurs Sunday morning, December 14, 1941. A strange paradox arises when the United States embraces a "V for victory" symbol and decides to put it to music. This she does by employing the "dot-dot-dot-dash" from my old *C Minor Symphony*. Thus the rhythm of Beethoven is sent to war against Germany!

After a full year of searching, there is nothing definite or optimistic that I can report to Wagner. Perhaps the motion-picture industry holds the answer to our problem. In this belief, I start snooping about various departments of the Werner-Amick Studio, where my son-in-law is now a vice president in charge of production. Wilding is overjoyed by my sudden interest in his studio. He interprets this to mean that at long last my stubborn resistance to motion pictures is breaking down, that I'll soon be preparing a genuine Voskamp score for one of his films. I try to convince him that this is not the case and that there is *no* sound basis for his optimism. He goes right on smiling and gesticulating: "The fact that you've finally come here to Werner-Amick is good enough for me. I know that you'll soon be writing us a score!"

Christmas 1942 is as "merry" as can be expected with my Anna dead and gone and with most of the "civilized" countries on my SCP dedicated to all-out war! At least there's the memory of Anna living on in our dear Maria and in my loving grandchildren. A deferred Christmas present comes knocking at my door on Sunday afternoon, December 27. You can imagine my complete astonishment when a tall, gaunt figure of a man displays an Aaronian ring on his scrawny finger and introduces himself as Anton Schindler, my old "Papageno" of an Earthling factotum:

B. God in heaven! . . . Schindler! . . . Dear "Papageno"! . . . How can you know to show up just when I need you the most?

AS. In Second-Order life, I am Howard Manning, concertmaster of the Altburg Philharmonic. The child-raising period of my marriage has long since passed, and I've translated here to spend the twenty years of my Subsidiary assignment in service to my old master.

B. What about Mrs. Manning? Has she translated with you?

AS. No. I'm here alone, nothing to prevent me from being once again your full-time factotum. My wife had satisfied her subordinate responsibilities a full ten years before our marriage.

B. But tell me, dear "samothracian ragamuffin," how can you know when my very soul cries out for the likes of you?

AS. Across all the time and space that have separated us, I've been carefully following Herr Voskamp's career.

B. Through Robinson?

AS. First, through Robinson, then through Hergenroeder. When we learned of Frau Voskamp's death, your counselor suggested that now would be the proper time for me to come and try to be of help to you. Perhaps I might be instrumental even in effecting your return to Major-Order life.

B. This is wonderful! You have come just at the right moment. But tell me, as a Subsidiary being, who *are* you? . . . Where did you ever find a body so much like my Earthly Schindler? Except for having no glasses and less hair, I would think you were old Papageno himself!

AS. You're right, there *is* a resemblance to my Earthly body. But I assure you, this is not my reason for translating as Henry Obeldee. I do so because this man is single, is principal violinist with the Werner-Amick Orchestra, and is totally dedicated to music. This puts me in a convenient position for striking up an acquaintance with Herr Voskamp and for becoming once again your loyal and learned factotum.

B. How thoughtful of you, dear Schindler, but I welcome you as a brother, not as a servant. This calls for some serious celebrating. Wait here a minute.

I soon return with a bottle of Rüdesheimer Berg, two wine glasses, and a tablespoon. My new "brother" is smiling with his entire face.

AS. What's the spoon for, Maestro?

B. At the risk of being childishly sentimental, I wish now that your first kind deed to me in Second-Order life might duplicate the last sweet thing you did for me on Earth.

I pour out a spoonful of Father Rhine and hand it to Schindler. He knows exactly what to do. His boyish smile quickly changes to an expression of deep somberness as he tenderly raises the precious nectar to my lips:

AS. Ah yes, dear Maestro, I *do* remember it well. Only there in the Schwarpanierhaus when our Rudesheimer finally arrived at your bedside, your lips were too dry and you were too far gone to sip even a spoonful of it.

B. But not *now*, dear Schindler. Here, let me fill these glasses. . . . Let us drink to our new brotherhood. . . . May it be a long and happy one. And may you be instrumental in helping me solve the latest and most baffling musical problem of my entire professional life.

AS. This sounds interesting. What musical problem?

B. No less an artist than Richard Wagner has asked me for help in determining a new path for music drama to take. I've been searching continuously for over a year and have as yet found nothing! With your help, perhaps I can find the answer. But I'm curious about one thing. What if I retranslate to Major life before the twenty years of your Subsidiary assignment are fulfilled? *Then* what will you do?

AS. I'm here to serve Beethoven for twenty years. If you remain here that long, good! Should this not be the case, then I'll stay behind since you have on this planet no official musical successor to piece together whatever bits and shreds of Voskamp's post career that might need piecing together.

B. You are a fine fellow, dear Papageno. I welcome you to my home as the dearest of friends and as the last official Courtier to Beethoven on SCP 7,900,111.

With Schindler's arrival at the Wildings, everything changes for the better. Agnes Moore continues as our superb cook and housemaid. Maria no longer feels sorry for me since I now have a loving companion. She stops coaxing me to move into their wing of the huge Beverly Hills mansion. This guarantees me the necessary privacy for whatever musical works remain for me to do in Subsidiary life.

My daily visits to Werner-Amick take a new turn during the first three months of 1943. I spend most of my time there viewing some three hundred of the better films produced at this studio during the period from 1935 to date. Twenty-six of these are the artistic offspring of my own son-in-law, Max Wilding. My favorite from his contribution is a magnificent three-hour colored spectacle that turns out to be our particular planet's film version of *Gone with the Wind.* For some strange reason, I view this glorious motion picture dozens of times, only to be promptly attracted to yet another viewing. My total fascination for this film is engendered not by just the story, or just the acting, or just the color, or just the music. It's as though the sum total of its components has a message of profound importance just for me . . . perhaps the very answer to my long and arduous quest!

On Friday afternoon, April 2, my patient search comes to an end. As I suspected, it does so halfway through another viewing of *Gone with the Wind.* It's as though the ceiling splits open and a brilliant stroke of insight falls from heaven directly into my lap. I'm tempted to shout my happiness! Now I know the precise direction that music drama must take. Now I know the answer to Wagner's problem—a problem whose solution tingles with such invigorating musical challenges that I wish to be part of it myself!

In response to my immediate phone call, a hyperzealous Richard Wagner shows up at the Hollywood on Sunday morning at nine o'clock. We drive straightaway to Werner-Amick for a private viewing of *Gone with the Wind.* In spite of Wagner's eagerness, I refuse to tell him a thing until we have both witnessed my pride and joy among films. At 12:30 PM, we return to the Hollywood for lunch, then to a private booth in its subbasement for our long-awaited discussion.

B. The answer to the problem of finding a future course for music drama is so simple and so obvious that we've both lived squarely in its midst without recognizing it!

Wg. What *is* the answer, dear Beethoven?

B. The motion picture.

Wg. Alas! For several years, I thought so myself. I was attracted to this medium like pretzels to beer. Three of our latest and best WAGNER operas were painstakingly arranged for and presented on the screen. After a careful study of the results, our partners and I concluded that motion pictures offer certain advantages over the stage, that the stage has certain advantages over the screen, that neither medium can save music drama from the helpless lethargy into which it has fallen. The impotency of our beloved art form lies within its own structure and can't be remedied by a new and different method of presentation.

B. Exactly! It's the *structure* which now must be changed!

Wg. And how can a motion picture do this?

B. A motion picture can't effect any change, but what we put on film can!

Wg. How do you mean?

B. *Gone with the Wind*—there's your basis for a new evolution in music drama.

Wg. *Gone with the Wind*? . . . Why, that's a movie, not even an opera!

B. Call it what you will. This is the path that music drama must follow. The story of opera began with the Italians: tiny plots, tiny acting, a superabundance of duets, trios, quartets, quintets, and sextets. . . . Then realizing that human conversation is *not* the simultaneous sounding of two to six voices, along came Wagnerian music drama with its truer-to-life "duets." And now, realizing that normal discourse involves the *speaking* of words, along comes *Gone with the Wind* that has no singing at all!

Wg. Grand opera without singing? Surely you're being facetious, Herr Beethoven!

B. Not at all! There'll always be a need and a place for singing in operettas, but not in grand opera . . . not in genuine music drama!

Wg. Take away the singing voice and what's left?

B. Exactly what the Italians must have wondered when they heard that you had dropped from Wagnerian Opera such requisite features as recitatives, arias, and choruses.

Wg. But there was still enough vocalism to make good opera. Without singing, what will you have?

B. Music, acting, scenery, dancing . . . plenty of everything for the evolution we seek!

Wg. *Gone with the Wind* is filled with good acting, good photography, good dance scenes, but it's still only a movie, anything but a replacement for grand opera. Its music, at best, is no more than good orchestral accompaniment. Are you suggesting that our WAGNER give up opera for the mere writing of background scores?

B. What I'm suggesting is as far removed from "background music" as *Tristan und Isolde* is removed from Opéra Comique!

Wg. How do you mean, Herr Beethoven?

B. Visualize that movie we saw this morning, raised to the "tenth power." Instead of three hours with an intermission, think in terms of ten or fifteen acts of three hours each . . . successive acts to be viewed on a weekly basis. Instead of ordinary dialogue chopped down from a great story to fit the paltry time budget of a Hollywood production, imagine a perfect script, taut (yet unrushed) from first to last . . . a polished improvement over the book itself! Instead of a frail score written to the tune of a rat-race schedule and dubbed here and there into the finished product almost as an afterthought, try to hear the impact of a *true* Wagnerian orchestra performing the glories of an artistic score that is written over a period of years instead of days—a score composed as an integral part of the script, a score to which future actors must learn to perform, a score which often fades into the background of a dialogue or a soliloquy, but which just as frequently weaves its magical spell into the foreground, replacing altogether the need for spoken words. . . . If you can imagine these things, dear Wagner, then you must understand the future course of music drama.

Wg. "Nonsense" would be my reply to anyone making such unheard-of suggestions . . . to anyone except Ludwig van Beethoven! Since you are the one who makes them, and at my own request, I shall devote the next ten years (longer, if need be) to the creation of such a work. But tell me, dear Maestro, may I bring this child to you from time to time to see if he grows as you would have him grow?

B. Better still, I was hoping that the two of us might collaborate in his birth.

Wg. God in heaven! . . . I can't believe my ears! . . . Are you actually offering me the chance to create with you?

B. Yes! Why the surprise?

Wg. But such a dream is something I could scarcely hope for in the Fiftieth or the Hundredth Order, not here in the Second! . . . Are you sure, Herr Beethoven? Do you *really* mean what you say?

B. Of course I do. It's no less an honor for me to be working with Richard Wagner! As my Anna used to say, "Each of us will learn from the other." I have *no* doubt that we shall be able to give Wagnerian art precisely the new direction it needs.

Wg. Wonderful! To facilitate our joint project, will you be retranslating to Major life?

B. I'm sorry, Herr Wagner. For personal reasons, it's not yet possible for me to return there.

Wg. Then think no more of it. Within six weeks, *I* shall translate *here.* By the way . . . I hope we can agree upon a story. Have you given any thought to the matter?

B. A great deal of thought. I would like our story to be that of Jeanne d' Arc, the Maid of Orleans, Saint Joan.

Wg. An interesting choice! How did you decide upon Joan of Arc?

B. The ultimate icing for our huge cake is to be a series of semiabstractions—oil paintings done by a great artist whose favorite story, ever since her own rebirth, has been that of the Maid!

Wg. Ah! . . . La belle jeune fille! This sounds like more than artistic admiration!

B. It is! Judy Adams is the only Second-Order girl I have loved (and still love) comparably to my dearest Anna. Since she's now Mrs.

Judy Donovan, I can no longer love her as a man, but only as an artist.

Wg. Judy Adams . . . of course! She's the REMBRANDT artist who does abstractions for so many of your compositions!

B. That's the girl! And I'd be both happy and proud to involve her in our creative enterprise.

Wg. Wonderful! Will she find the time?

B. I'm sure she will . . . especially since the story is of Joan!

Wg. Very well, Herr Beethoven. I'll be translating within a month or so, then we'll immediately start to work. From the bottom of my heart, I thank you for opening your door to me. You've saved not only my soul, but as well the art form nearest and dearest to it! . . . *Auf Wiedersehen*!

On May 17, Richard Wagner shows up on our SCP as Samar Lerman. His choice of Lerman is perfect! In one mighty stroke, he absorbs our Hollywood's prime background composer, thus tempering Wagner's unbelievable passion for the legitimate operatic stage; becomes a Jew, thus administering an effective deathblow to the Earthly Wagner's ridiculous anti Semitism; and translates into a fifty-seven-year-old widower (whose children are now married and living in New York), thus enabling him to spend most of his time at the Wildings with Schindler and me.

For the remainder of 1943 through June 1947, Wagner and I devote ourselves completely to Joan of Arc's story. As *she* grows, *we* grow! I find myself capable of total collaboration, exceeding even that which Beethoven had achieved with his wife and with Sigmund Kapell. The demands of our joint project are so great that each of us needs all the help he can get from the other! Not a *trace* of professional jealousy develops between us, only a deepening admiration and a growing dependence. Poor Wilding! He's terribly disappointed, now that Lerman and I no longer show up at his studio. He knows that we're working on something together, but whatever it is, it's not a score for one of his productions. To prevent my son-in-law from becoming overly curious, I tell him that the two of us are planning a possible revision of the more important of Voskamp's orchestral compositions. This dampens family inquisitiveness, and there are no further intrusions upon my musical privacy. Maria and Max are both happy and grateful for the congenial social setting in which I now find myself: perfect for an aging Voskamp, practically a miniature Court in which Agness Moore and "Papageno" administer daily to my domestic tranquility while Richard Wagner provides old Beethoven with all the musical challenge and inspiration he could wish for.

The genuine masterpiece that results from our four-year collaboration is almost too much to believe. Never has the story of Joan (or any story, for that matter) been told in such totally unrushed detail, yet with such continuous forward thrust: twelve acts of three to four hours each, a superbly developed mood-setting prelude for each act, extended duets for orchestra and motion-picture camera, taut dialogue so polished that it reads with an almost poetic heat, wordless expanses of music and acting alone that enhance the buoyancy of the dialogue when speaking parts do reappear.

Naturally, in any art work of such magnitude, there are bound to be certain sections that become one's favorites. As to the script, my favorite spots are Joan's recognition scene with her Dauphin, her magnificent prayer before the final battles and her captivity, and of course, the great trial scene from beginning to end. As to the music, I feel that our greatest peaks are reached in the Faëry Tree scene at Domremy, during the siege of Orleans, during the coronation scene, and during that soul-shattering hour spent with Joan in the final darkness of her prison cell. And as to the concluding half hour of the entire production, I would never have believed that music drama could rise to such ethereal heights. Indeed it could *not* have, without the master hand and heart and mind of Richard Wagner! What a perfect evolution of his entire Earthly accomplishment! Here, especially in these ultimate scenes, all the beauty of Wagnerian art combines with the simple words of the Maid and transforms her final prayer and martyrdom into a spiritual victory of unbelievable dimension! The impact of these searching words and their divine accompaniment is more than enough to stretch the bounds of a Second-Order human spirit! I'm so grateful that God's spiritual helpers were fully engaged in this divine experience. The entire effect is thoroughly appreciated by Richard Wagner. My consummate partner is pleased no end with the conclusive results of our joint effort magnified by heavenly powers. He is now thoroughly convinced that *Joan of Arc* delineates the one true path for music drama to follow.

Hoping for the earliest possible production and performance of our huge opus, Wagner and I can hardly wait to deliver it into the hands of Max Wilding, who would no doubt descend upon it with all the financial and artistic resources of Werner-Amick. Before doing so, we contact Subsidiary Control through my counselor Ernst Hergenroeder. He suggests that we transfer the score to him for immediate consideration by the College of Counselors. This we do, expecting a favorable response. Within two weeks comes their reply—a great big definite NO! Under no circumstances are we permitted to produce the work on SCP 7,900,111. They are certain that its unleashing within our Subsidiary culture would produce revolutionary changes in motion pictures that would not be in keeping with our SCP's predetermined commitment to parallel the contemporary conditions of Earth. In fact, our Aaronian counselors are so impressed by the novelty of *St. Joan* that they unanimously declare it a new Second-Order art form and strongly recommend the retainment of its score within our Major culture! Wagner and I are nonplussed to say the least. We talk things over for the better part of a week and always come to the same conclusion. If our new music drama will not return to *us*, then we must return to *it*! Disregarding Schindler's chagrin, we both now decide to retranslate *permanently* to Major-Order life!

Chapter 50

On June 25, 1947, I call Hergenroeder and inform him of my intense desire for immediate and permanent return to Major life! True, I'm still reluctant to leave my dear Maria and the sweet memories of her mother in exchange for facing a happily married Judy Adams Donovan, but the beck and call of *Jeanne d'Arc* are now more than adequate to overcome such reluctance.

My counselor is pleased to no end with this decision. He calls back the following Friday and informs me that Wagner's request and mine have both been approved by Subsidiary Control! Things are relatively uncomplicated in both our cases since neither of us is currently important enough (in the broad cultural sense) to require a creative successor. Though Lerman is the best of our Hollywood composers, he is still but a minor figure in the contemporary musical world of SCP 7,900,111. And in refusing to evolve beyond a late-Brahms style, poor old Voskamp is now little more than a respected relic. He has long since been succeeded by more modern "transferees" from our Major culture.

Wagner and I show up Sunday morning at the Hollywood to receive the detailed plans for our retranslations. Wagner's "departure date" is set for Saturday night, July 5. On the Wednesday preceding this date, he is to begin taking a series of special tablets, which (in about forty-eight hours) will produce within his body a composite of pseudo-symptoms indistinguishable from lobar pneumonia! These are to land him in the Sun West Hospital on Saturday morning, where that evening, Lerman's "death" will be staged by a Major-Order physician and his corps of Aaronian helpers from Subsidiary Transfer. Voskamp is scheduled to "die" in his sleep on Sunday night, July 6. Schindler should be of great help to us in effecting this little deception!

Strange and swift is the sequence of events that returns old Beethoven to Major life. My final Monday morning as Voskamp is spent at the Hollywood National Bank and Trust Company, where I transfer one-third of my accumulated (heretofore untouched) Major-Order salary into a trust fund for Maria. I have little doubt that during his lifetime, Max Wilding will adequately provide for my daughter and the grandchildren, but he has never been one to save money! Should something unexpected happen to this son-in-law, then my comfortable trust would be there to carry on in his stead.

Next comes my visit to the Armstrong Warehouse. There I remove Judy's portrait of the Earthly Mozart and temporarily store it in the basement of the Hollywood Hotel. I had long realized that this dear companion of the Hildebrandtstrasse days would be the one material object I would wish to take with me upon my return to Major life! Accordingly, while still living in Vienna, I had a fine copy of it made by Ebbner. Upon moving to the States, I stored the original at Armstrong's; the copy I hung in my study at Wilding's. Thus, following Voskamp's "death," there'll be no clumsy explaining to do about the sudden disappearance of a mysterious canvas which had been with him most of his lifetime.

There is a final phone call to Sabatini in New York. He's elated to hear of my decision and promises to retranslate just as soon as his career can be terminated. I offer him a conducting partnership at BEETHOVEN, which he gleefully accepts.

On Tuesday, there's my final call to Lerman. I tell him of the surprise I'm planning for my return to the May Building, and he promises to say nothing of my retranslation until I have announced the event myself! We agree to meet soon thereafter and commence work on the myriad details leading to the eventual Major-Order premiere of our "Joan."

There are frequent visits with the Wildings, so unusually frequent that I fear these loved ones might suspect that old Voskamp had actually anticipated his own death. How sad it is to hold Maria in my arms for what I know will be a final time, to experience those parting kisses between a proud father and his loving daughter. If only I could tell her who I am and where I'm going, the burden of our separation would seem so much lighter!

Poor Schindler! How grievously the aftermath of Voskamp's "death" will rest squarely upon his shoulders. His chin quivers and eyes moisten as we discuss the final details of my departure. Endless redundant questions remind me of his Earthly concern on that final March when I began talking about "going up there"!

Traditionally, Saturday evenings have become the Wildings' "night on the town." All four servants are given an afternoon off following lunch on Saturdays, and the grandchildren are shipped across town to Aunt Lucy's. This means that from 6:00 PM until the wee hours of Sunday morning, Schindler and I are the sole inhabitants of "Castle Wilding." Accordingly, at nine thirty on Saturday evening, July 5, a huge crate arrives "special delivery" from Aaron AP. The carefully sealed box is long enough, wide enough, high enough, and gruesome enough to contain a coffin. In fact, it *does* contain a coffin! And inside the coffin is all that remains of the eighteen-year-old Voskamp whose spirit I absorbed ninety-five years ago. The remains are no longer those of a young man, nor are they a pile of dusty bones. They are a perfectly preserved body to which has been applied the precise subelectronic disguise that (this very evening) permits a "fortyish-looking" Paul Rezler to spend his final day in Subsidiary life as a "ninetyish- looking" Mason Voskamp. In other words, here is the body which in twenty-four hours will represent the termination of my life on SCP 7,900,111! Four Aaronian technicians who deliver the heavy box help Schindler and me carry it upstairs to my bedroom. There it is safely locked in a walk-in closet, resting quietly until it is needed.

On Sunday evening, I have supper with the Wildings. After our meal, we talk for several hours about the sadness and the suddenness of Lerman's death. Max tries to speculate as to what changes will now occur in the music department at Werner-Amick. It's considerably past nine when I finally excuse myself and Maria sees me to the front door of their wing of the huge house. Paused in this doorway, we exchange those parting kisses that I mentioned earlier.

Standing by the window in Schindler's darkened quarters, he and I carefully spy on the rest of the house. By twelve thirty, the last of the bedroom lights are flicked off. Sleep has finally come to the Wilding home. Not a creature is stirring except two "mice," who may now engage in their little drama of "death and resurrection." Schindler phones the Hollywood to inform our technicians that the "coast is clear." Within a half hour, the four of them enter our wing through a side door whose walk is so thickly shrubbed as to be totally hidden from the rest of the house. The tallest, most official looking of the four bids me to follow him through this side entrance. Before doing so, I turn and once more embrace my dear Schindler, thanking him for all he has done and will do for Mason Voskamp! Just as we're leaving the dimmed hall, my Aaronian leader spots the tiny package in my right hand.

AL. What's that?
B. Nothing. . . . Only a Voskamp diary.
AL. Does anyone here know that you've kept one?
B. Just Schindler.
AL. Very well then. You may bring it with you.

Silently, the Aaronian and I enter the dark street and go walking beneath a skyful of stars. Their sparkling glitter seems actually to welcome me among them. To think that I'll soon be countless light-years beyond the farthest of the lot! We walk for three blocks before coming to a hearselike black sedan. This we enter, and there we wait for nearly an hour while the other technicians place Voskamp's corpse in my bed, there to be "discovered" early the next morning by Schindler. The crate in which the coffin arrived is disassembled and stored in the basement. The coffin itself is taken apart and folded into three convenient suitcase-sized packages, each replete with a handle of its own. At 2:00 AM, our technicians begin joining us at ten-minute intervals, each carrying one-third of a coffin. What would we have done if some dedicated police officer had suddenly stopped by to inquire into the nature of our early morning business?

At three fifteen, I enter a D-R Chamber in the subbasement of the Hollywood. In my right hand is Voskamp's current diary; those of prior years had been sealed and sent to Dogwood for storage. Under my left arm is Judy's painting of Mozart. As the door closes, I can't help thinking what an uneventful farewell to SCP 7,900,111. No orchestra, no music, not even a friendly handshake! And yet what profitable years these have been—ninety-five years of growth and happiness for Beethoven, a growth and happiness which he could never have found had he remained within the Major culture of Aaron's Second-Order system. This then is my farewell to Subsidiary life, the memory of ninety-five happy and well-spent years!

Once on Aaron AP, I sign for a tiny dormlike room in the Subsidiary Transfer Center, and there spend the rest of Sunday night.

First thing Monday morning, I devote a half hour to shedding my old and faithful Voskamp disguise. What a pleasure once again to cast my true image in a mirror! I'm not an old man, but quite the young Rezler with trim round muscles, plenty of dark curly hair, and enough sex appeal to pass for a handsome and virile thirty-five. Since it would be physically impossible to squeeze the vigorous youth of Rezler's firm body into the long-limbed lankiness of my old Voskamp suit, I exchange the outfit for a new one before leaving our Transfer Center.

On Monday afternoon, I arrive at Altburg on CP 75. There I sign out a large and comfortable apartment at DeWitt's, though this time I'm unable to get one directly opposite the May Building. I send out for supper and spend the remainder of a quiet day planning my big surprise for BEETHOVEN.

That night's sleep is rudely interrupted by the coarse "clanging" of my bedside phone. I had asked the operator to awaken me at 4:00 AM. Following an elaborate breakfast at DeWitt's Coffee Shop, I arrive at the May Building one hour later. A stern-looking watchman sits directly inside the only door of the building that can be entered at this time of day. I must present a strange picture indeed, timidly standing there in the early morning darkness, smiling beseechingly into the light of the building, and gently tapping on the heavy glass door with the edge of my comb. The mighty guard shades his eyes and stares me down from head to toe before finally opening the transparent door. At long last, he finishes his silent scrutiny and is first to speak:

Wa. And what could you be wanting here so early in the morning?
B. I've come to visit BEETHOVEN, and I'd like you to help me.
Wa. I see. And who are you?
B. I am Beethoven!
Wa. Oh?
B. I can tell you don't believe me. (*Before continuing, I remove a time-worn scrap of newspaper from my wallet.*) See this picture? It is Beethoven! Surely you can tell we're the same.
Wa. You *are* Beethoven, though you look a little older now.
B. I ought to; this was taken a hundred years ago! You'll help me then?
Wa. Of course! But there's little I can do for you this early in the day. Their studio doesn't officially open before nine. Not even the receptionist shows up until eight thirty.
B. Receptionist . . . she used to be a Ms. Mary Banks.

Wa. Not any longer. Now she's Emma Simpson.
B. Emma Simpson . . . do you know her?
Wa. Quite well. Since I don't go off duty until nine, I'm here to greet her every morning.
B. Have you ever been through the BEETHOVEN studio?
Wa. Several times. Emma herself has taken me through.
B. Good! Then you must have seen the Schwarspanierhaus Room.
Wa. Is that that room they're saving for you?
B. I hope they are. Is it still there?
Wa. Yes indeed! I was in that study just this spring. Emma often speaks of it. It's her job to unlock it every morning at ten, then lock it up again at five.
B. What's it used for?
Wa. A kind of Beethoven chapel den. Off and on through the day, all sorts of staff members stop in for a few minutes of professional renewal and inspiration.
B. Good! It's *this* room I wish you to help me with.
Wa. In what way?
B. Have you a key to it?
Wa. I have a key to every room in the building.
B. Wonderful! I've prepared a little Beethovenian prank involving this den of inspiration. After being away from the firm for nearly a century, I've finally decided to return and claim my position as managing partner.
Wa. And you want to surprise them!
B. Exactly! I'd like you to lock me inside my study. Then when everyone's there, but before Ms. Simpson has unlocked that door, I'll begin playing my concert grand.
Wa. Wow! You *will* give them a shock!
B. You'll do it then?
Wa. Of course!
B. And you'll say nothing to anyone?
Wa. I won't breathe a word of it.
B. That's my boy! But you haven't told me your name.
Wa. Freeberg! Tim Freeberg.
B. Fine, Tim! When do we go?
TF. Just as soon as I can get old Clark to stand here at the door for me. He won't mind. I'm due for a coffee break at half past. I'll get him to come fifteen minutes early.

Freeberg opens a shiny brass panel set in the marble wall a few feet from where he was sitting. Behind it is a miniature telephone. The exchange of a few words soon brings an old red-faced Clark on the scene. With a total lack of formality, there's a "changing of the guards." Freeberg and I head for the elevator. Before its door opens, he notices the package under my arm.

TF. What's *that* you have there?
B. A picture for Beethoven's room.
TF. Do you wish to hang it this morning?
B. Very much so.
TF. Then you'll need some picture hooks and a hammer.
B. I brought both with me. Thank you, Tim.
TF. Very well, then. Thirty-two it is.

The elevator starts its silent scrotum-sinking ascent.

B. I hear that old BEETHOVEN has expanded beyond his thirty-second floor.
TF. That's right! Thirty-two, all of thirty-one, some practice rooms on thirty, and a huge recording studio on ten.
B. Well, it's nice to be home again, Freeberg. And I'm very grateful to you for helping me with my surprise.
TF. Think nothing of it, Maestro. . . . And welcome home!

In a matter of minutes, Freeberg has deposited me within my Schwarspanierhaus study, has bid me farewell, and has locked the door behind him. For a half hour I seat myself at the magnificent Broadwood, improvising softly while the first gray streaks of dawn confirm the reality of Altburg's skyline. By now it's light enough to see my way about the room. I unpack Judy's "Mozart" and hang it directly opposite her vibrating portrait of my Earthly self. Now the room is complete; now it's ready for Beethoven! I have only to roll up my sleeves and start to work on a new symphony. But first . . . that lounging couch. What a delicious looking couch! Why not a short snooze? Then my surprise. . . . *Then* I'll start to work.

My short snooze turns into a sound sleep, a total slumber, a complete loss of consciousness! Instead of me surprising BEETHOVEN, *I'm* the one who's shocked out of a year's creativeness! What a rude awakening. The clanking, rasping, slotting of a key in my door tells me that ten o'clock has come and gone. Before I can fasten my collar, adjust my tie, or don my jacket, there stands Ms. Emma Simpson in all her questioning glory. She looks as though she's about to faint.

ES. Ye gods! What are *you* doing in here? . . . Have you been here all night?
B. Easy, Ms. Simpson. . . . Here, have a chair.
ES. But what are you doing here?
B. I've planned a little surprise for BEETHOVEN, and you mustn't spoil it. Please, sit down.
ES. I think Mr. Grant should know about this.
B. He will, in just a minute. . . . Damn this coat!

In attempting to hurry into my new jacket, I tear a huge gash between its sleeve and shoulder. During that peaceful slumber, the left cuff of my trousers had come unrolled; of course, I now trip and fall over it on my way to the door. The button pulls from my collar; my stupid necktie won't budge one way or another. The more gracefully inconspicuous I try to appear, the more clumsily monstrous I become. Poor Ms. Simpson! By now, she's gingerly sitting on the tiniest edge of my desk chair. One more sudden or clumsy move on my part, and I'm sure she'd faint. Her eyes follow me like those of a frightened deer. You'd think I were about to take a big bite out of her. Somehow I manage to prop the door open a few inches, to raise the lid of the Broadwood, and to seat myself before its keyboard without causing further apprehension on the part of my singularly frightened guest.

Once again, the glorious optimism of the *Hammerklavier*'s *Scherzo* comes pouring from my fingers. This time through, the direct path of the original notes soon gives way to genuine extempore playing, to a grand Beethoven improvisation in the Earthly sense of the word! It sweeps all before it, filling the room, the hall, the entire thirty-second floor! Though completely caught up by the inspiration of my music, I'm aware that the room has filled with people. Then mysteriously, it empties out again. Even so, not once during my entire performance do I take my eyes from the keyboard. After forty minutes of total absorption, the final chords are "hammered" out; I wheel around on the bench, expecting to find a more congenial Emma Simpson and at least a handful of admirers. The young lady has vanished! Not a soul remains! Not a soul except Richard Grant, who now jumps from my desk chair and rushes toward me, as I address him:

B. Monsieur Bonaparte! . . . How good of you to attend my concert. I'm glad there's still someone at BEETHOVEN who appreciates great music when he hears it!

Gr. (*Grant sits beside me on the bench, shaking my hand and slapping my back at the same time.*) Dear Maestro, we *all* appreciate your playing. In fact, I've just taped most of it for the enjoyment of BEETHOVEN-ites yet unborn.

B. Then where *is* everyone?

Gr. This room is too small and too sacred to be stuffed full of people. While I've been sitting here devouring your inspiration, the entire staff has assembled itself in our Junior-Senior workroom . . . the largest room we have.

B. Is that on thirty-one?

Gr. Yes. Even Ms. Simpson is waiting there for you.

B. We mustn't keep *her* waiting, Grant. I damn near scared the poor girl to death. You should have seen the look on her face when she unlocked that door and found *me* in here.

Gr. How *did* you get in?

B. Through the window.

Gr. I see. Well, before we go down, I must ask you something.

B. What's that, Richard?

Gr. Since I'm the one who will introduce you to our staff, I must have your answer to the question of the day. Are you just passing through Altburg on a visit, or have you returned to us for good?

B. I'm here to stay, Grant. And I'm here to do whatever job there is for me to do.

Gr. Praise God! . . . Then come, dear Beethoven, we mustn't keep BEETHOVEN waiting!

As Bonaparte and I enter our new staff room and I first come face-to-face with the BEETHOVEN of 1947, I'm amazed at how much he has grown, almost twice the size of a normal corporate composer! Instead of forty to fifty juniors and seniors, there stand before me ninety-one; instead of twenty principals, we now have thirty-seven; instead of a dozen partners and a managing partner, our count has reached nineteen, including Bonaparte and myself. Such increase in size is permitted only when one corporate musician absorbs the charter of another, and this has been the case with our BEETHOVEN and BRAHMS!

When we enter the room, our entire staff rises in one accord and presents me with a mighty ovation! On and on goes their heartwarming applause. As I stand there before them, I glance from one person to another, attempting to recall familiar faces. Not too many remain. Jon Floyd is present, but there's no trace of the other founding partners. Kreps must still be our business manager; there he is, smiling at me like an expectant father. On either side of him are nephew Karl and brother Johann, likewise smiling radiantly. I'm sorry to find Marcie Sbalzato (Mrs. Grant) missing from our staff. Grant later tells me about his wife's retirement from BEETHOVEN seven years earlier. Most of the admiring eyes are filled with tears. . . . So are mine!

At long last, Bonaparte motions for the staff to be seated. He pushes a high wooden stool in my direction. As I try to make myself comfortable, he takes his place at the lectern:

Gr. Dear colleagues. . . . Almost exactly a hundred years ago, I stood before the staff of BEETHOVEN and proclaimed that our corporation was then and there living through the most important hour of his entire history . . . the hour in which we first discovered Ludwig van Beethoven in our midst. But I was wrong. That was *not* our greatest hour. It was our saddest hour, the hour in which our dear Maestro decided to leave us and go his own way! We've been patiently and impatiently awaiting his return ever since. During his long absence, we've tried the best we could to sense the direction in which he would have his corporation move, were he himself here to lead us. In Subsidiary life, our Master evolved into his magnificent late-Brahms idiom. Here we tried our best to do the same. We must have succeeded in measure because during the interim period, BEETHOVEN has attracted to his staff not only the entire BRAHMS corporation, but Hannes Brahms himself! I must interrupt my little speech long enough to bring our two great men together. Johannes Brahms, would you please come forward and shake the hand of your cospirit, Ludwig van Beethoven?

Almost before I can jump down from my stool, a mighty square stump of a handsome blond youth springs from the crowd and encompasses my hand in his. We exchange worshipful stares, each enjoying the broad smile on the face of the other. For the moment there are no words between us, but with such a spiritual communion, who needs words? Brahms returns to his chair, I resume my wooden perch, Bonaparte continues his welcoming speech.

Gr. But now, dear staff . . . today . . . this hour . . . we *do* experience the greatest moment in our corporate history! Beethoven has returned to us. At long last, he's come to claim his own! My future here is entirely in his hands. If he bid me leave, I shall do so; if he bid me stay, I shall *gladly* do so, and in whatever capacity he might direct. Fellow musicians, may I present to you the living spirit of Earth's greatest music . . . the soul of our corporation . . . the reason for our being here . . . our long and dearly awaited managing partner, Herr Ludwig van Beethoven!

There is another long and flattering ovation during which I replace Grant at the lectern and spend several minutes nodding and smiling especially at Karl and Johann. Suddenly the room is "concert hall" silent—the moment has come for me to speak. I can't tell who best expresses himself within me—Beethoven, Rezler, or Voskamp; but somehow the right words seem to come:

B. Dear Monsieur Bonaparte and staff of BEETHOVEN. Considering what I said when I last stood here before you, considering the century that I've stayed away, considering my apparent total lack of concern over the course of your affairs, you should be unceremoniously dropping me out that window instead of welcoming me with your applause. But since you *do* welcome me, I thank you from the bottom of my heart and promise to remain in your midst until the end of my Second-Order days. And as to our Bonaparte, our managing partner of one hundred years' good standing, you can imagine me now bidding him to leave. Without this great and dedicated musician, without this "emperor" among men, there'd be no BEETHOVEN for me to return to. And so, dear Grant, if I am to be at the helm of this firm, the least I can offer you is a full partnership in charge of whatever operation or operations you wish to be in charge of.

My offer is supported by a spontaneous ovation for Grant. He stands and bows to the entire staff. Now it's *his* cheeks that are wet with tears. We shake hands, and he tries to speak. No words come. But (as before) when true emotion is present, who has need for words? I resume my little speech.

B. When I last stood here before the staff of BEETHOVEN, many of you were not yet born. This is good, for you can't remember the villainous look on my face as I personally declared "war" upon the very firm that bears my name. I pridefully stomped from your presence, vowing to free the professional musician from servility, from corporate impersonality, and vowing never again to return here. Now, the prodigal returns! Why? Why is my return to BEETHOVEN now the overwhelming desire of my present life? The answer is simple. There've been some changes in old Beethoven since he pouted his way from your midst—changes for the better, I hope. With all respect for Rezler and Voskamp, these improvements were not due to something within *me.* They were the direct result of the unbelievably favorable conditions of my hundred years of Subsidiary life. First and foremost was an ideal spouse who, on angel wings, descended upon my career there. Her name was Anna Rosecranz. Though she was only a tiny Subsidiary being, as God lives, her professional attributes were those of a Fourth-Order musician. She became Voskamp's pupil, and then his wife. Soon her piano and her violin were both superior to mine, and yet I had only love for her. Shortly after our marriage, she announced her intention of becoming a fellow composer. Within two years, she had penetrated the secrets of my sketchbooks and was functioning as my own right hand in composition!

Soon after this, a big red-haired bastard named Sigmund Kapell entered our lives. I hated him from the very first, and my hatred was directly proportional to his great talent for composing. Anna, not I, sensed his indispensability to our cause. Between Kapell and myself, she fluttered her angel wings in such a way that her love and musicianship proved too much for even Beethoven's hatred and jealousy. Miracle of it all, through these musicians, I had become a thoroughly collaborative composer!

After serving my apprenticeship with this firm, I left in a fit of rage, convinced that for me (at least), composition could never become a joint effort. I entered a Subsidiary world for the specific purpose of dominating its musical scene through the weight of Beethoven's creative spirit. And what happened? Before long, my monstrous ego was reduced in size. I found myself enjoying every moment of composition with Anna and Kapell. In fact, I could no longer compose without them! . . . And here's another discovery that made me change my mind in favor of collaboration. Once when I was in the throes of composing, I became aware of an invisible power working through me. I could feel a stimulating force flowing through my veins, capturing the best of my thoughts as fast as I could write them down. What an awakening experience! To think that spiritual powers can reveal musical wisdom beyond a person's capacity to imagine was quite a profound idea. Anna and Sigmund both agreed that accepting this divine guidance is the way to go. We decided that if all three of us worked together and acknowledged this spiritual presence, our creations would be of highest quality. So we tried this procedure and were amazed at the glorious results that ensued. To know that a "superior musician" can be at our sides as a sublime collaborator was such a comforting feeling. . . . We were made by our Creator to *be* creators! This divine faculty resides within *all* of us. If we just tap into the ethereal realms of "heaven" where an abundance of musical ideas flourish, our work will be both joyful and rewarding. I'm excited to try this approach when we start working together.

Should you embrace the transition which Beethoven has made into a post-Brahms idiom, then *another composer* will also have earned your respect. When death separated me from Anna and from Sigmund, I felt that my Subsidiary-composing days were at an end. Indeed, they *would* have been, were it not for the sudden appearance of Richard Wagner. Our great music dramatist came all the way to my SCP for what he worshiped as the help and guidance of Beethoven. He expected only that I would point him in a new direction. But lo and behold, within a matter of months, I was working at his side as one *born* to collaborate with other composers. Between the two of us, we found a suitable new course for music drama to follow. And so you see, dear friends, the Beethoven who returns to you now is older and wiser and quite incapable of being other than a corporate composer! I thank you for your welcome; but I would ask that you, the staff of BEETHOVEN, my fellow musicians whom I come to serve, you must confirm the appointment so kindly offered me by Monsieur Bonaparte. Those of you who would have me as your managing partner, please signify your assent by standing.

In one mighty accord, the entire room booms to a stand:

B. Very well, then. As your new fearless leader, here is my first decree. I ask that a representative number of our partners meet with me for the remainder of this week. (Hopefully, these will include our Grant and our Brahms.) I ask that these men fill me in on all the recent and current projects of our firm. We shall then discuss possible plans for BEETHOVEN's immediate future. Others of you . . . all you lucky juniors, seniors, and principals, I request that you take the rest of the week off . . . a sort of presummer vacation . . . a little homecoming gift from your Beethoven!

A gleeful howl shakes the room.

B. But mind you, all of you, we start early Monday morning with an eight o'clock staff meeting. Our recommended plans will be presented for staffwide discussion, modification, and approval. Only *then* will we know for sure which path we must follow. In the meantime, happy holiday! And God bless the lot of you!

Big hands, strong hands, warm hands, fat hands . . . small hands, weak hands, cold hands, thin hands—all kinds of hands I shake. For a half hour I shake hands with BEETHOVEN! Only then does our staff room thin out. Only then do our apprentice musicians accept the reality of their five-day weekend. Only then am I left standing there with eleven partners, including Grant, Brahms, Karl, and Johann. We have lunch together and begin our discussions immediately. That evening, Mrs. Grant entertains the twelve of us at a delightful dinner party in her home. Marcie is the perfect hostess! Somehow I expected her to look much older, but she doesn't at all. Still the same beautiful girl. She jokingly threatens to come back to work now that I've returned and have assumed the managing partnership.

I'm very pleased to learn that nephew Karl and brother Johann are *both* now happy and productive partners at BEETHOVEN. Of course, my recommendations were chiefly responsible for their initial appointments to the firm. But their swift rise to partnership status was due to *their* musicianship and nothing else. Johann is a successful violinist within BEETHOVEN's concert division, but not so, Karl. My nephew rose to the rank of senior assistant in our violin department and then decided that (at least in Second-Order life) the concert stage was not for him. He took an eight-year course in sound engineering, returned to the firm, and is now a full partner in charge of our recording division.

How wonderful and revealing are my initial conversations with Johannes Brahms. I can't resist calling him "Hannes," which seems to please him very much. The only outburst of the famous Brahmsian temper occurs when I offer him a comanaging partnership and suggest changing the name of our firm from BEETHOVEN to BEETHOVEN-BRAHMS. If I insist on this change, he threatens to leave immediately and to reactivate his BRAHMS charter. Of course, I never bring up the subject again, and we remain on the best of terms.

Speaking of charters, I'm surprised to learn at this time that MOZART has been dissolved at Mozart's own request. Haydn, who was acting as the firm's managing partner pro tem, now heads up a HINDEMITH, which he founded in 1943. There seems to be no end to Brahms's praise for my *Messiah.* Again and again I remind him that it was the creation of my dear deceased unbelievable Subsidiary wife; on and on goes his praise. He calls it the most musical music he has ever heard and, in spite of my repeated explanations, in some strange way, insists on attributing it to *me.* Since Handel died out of Second-Order life in 1945, I remark to Brahms how sorry I am that the Master had not lived long enough for me to get his opinion of the "Beethoven" *Messiah.* Brahms smiles enormously as he tells me that in December 1943, Bonaparte and he, in the company of Handel himself, *did* hear my *Messiah* on Aaron AP and that the Master (with tears in his eyes) had proclaimed it greater than his own!

The Grants' dinner party lasts beyond two o'clock, Wednesday morning. It's almost three when I finally return to DeWitt's. In spite of this late hour, our serious meetings concerning BEETHOVEN's immediate future commence that morning at nine sharp and last until Saturday at noon. We all agree that the Beethoven-Brahms style, as currently practiced by our firm, should be continued indefinitely into the future, perhaps for a century or two. As a rich mode of expression, it is well-accepted and extremely popular throughout our Major culture. Our big problem arises from my intense interest in the new musico-dramatic form, which Wagner and I have recently evolved. Naturally, I recommend that our firm plunge wholeheartedly into this new medium. But my colleagues, excepting Johann and Karl, are opposed to such a plan. They feel that music drama is more clearly within the province of the WAGNER firm than that of BEETHOVEN. We argue the matter back and forth until Saturday morning, when a compromise is finally reached. Our major output is to continue to be symphonies, concertos, choral works, chamber music, and piano pieces. As for music drama, I'm to be given afternoons off in order to work with Richard Wagner in subjecting our *Joan of Arc* to its final polishing. When this is finished, the two of us will supervise and direct its production at Altburg Studio, the largest of three motion-picture studios on CP 75. The Major-Order première of our "Joan" will then be given. If the results are artistically favorable, BEETHOVEN will turn immediately to producing a first such work of his own; otherwise he will continue creating pure music and leave experiments in music drama to Beethoven, Wagner, and WAGNER. At our staffwide meeting on Monday morning, July 14, these plans are presented and accepted unanimously. I'm surprised at the unusual interest that "Joan" creates, especially among our junior and senior assistants. With a little pep talk from me, I'm sure I could immediately get BEETHOVEN started on his first music drama. But somehow I feel there is considerable wisdom in the decision of the majority of our partners. I hold my tongue and make no effort to sway the group.

Chapter 51

On Wednesday, July 9, news of my permanent return to Major life is released (at my request) through Translation Control. For the weekend of the twelfth, I stock my pantry at DeWitt's with three dozen bottles of favorite Beethoven wines. I do this in anticipation of the mob of dear Earthly friends, admirers, and loved ones that I'm sure will now be visiting me: the Breunings, my mother and grandfather, Wegeler, Schuppanzigh, Zmeskall, Lobkowitz, Lichnowsky, Archduke Rudolph, the Rieses, Wagner, Liszt, Czerny, Goethe, Neefe, Albrechtsberger, perhaps even a few musical greats, such as Haydn, Mozart, Chopin, Schumann, Puccini, Schubert, Tschaikowsky, Paderewski, Rachmaninoff—but surely not Debussy! You can imagine my surprise when the weekend comes and goes and my only visitors are the Rezlers! As happy as I am with the arrival of the Rezlers, I can't imagine where everyone else has gone. Perhaps they'd rather visit me on evenings during the week. . . . Monday, Tuesday, Wednesday, Thursday, Friday . . . no one! Not even a phone call from Culby!

On Saturday morning, July 19, I prepare thirty-three "Type A" (urgent) cards and send them off to Reunion Control. Surely these will bring favorable results. Another week passes . . . no one! On Friday evening, the twenty-fifth, I phone Counselor Hergenroeder and ask him to please come for a visit. He shows up the next morning at ten.

B. Goddamn! . . . I don't understand, Hergenroeder. Thirty-three A cards I send out, and not a single reply! Does everyone hate me? . . . Don't they know Beethoven's reason for not answering their cards back in the early days of his rebirth? . . . He was sick. He needed time to grow, to build self-confidence, before he could face these people. And now that I *have* grown, I open my arms to embrace them to my heart, and no one comes!

HH. This isn't the case, I assure you. Here! . . . See? . . . These are your cards!

B. What are *you* doing with them?

HH. Through Reunion Control, we've requested that no personal contacts be established at this time between you and your Earthling friends.

B. But why? I've waited long enough!

HH. I'm sure you have. But a special reunion is to be arranged for you in the near future, and its responsibility is mine. . . . Something I've inherited from your former counselor.

B. Robinson?

HH. Hal Robinson! He planned the entire affair especially for Beethoven, and now I must carry out his plans. I wanted to visit you last week to explain things and save you this anguish, but here I am, late as usual. Delay, delay, delay . . . the life story of a counselor these days. I'm told that this is characteristic of the years of an Aaronian visitation. Our first responsibility is to *him*, then come our counseling duties. But at least now you know the reason for your unpopularity.

B. And this should put my mind to rest. When will Beethoven's grand reunion occur?

HH. Six months . . . a year . . . perhaps a little longer. We must first be sure that you're well adjusted to Major life. B. I wrote Reunion Control about a certain "Frau X," "Frau—"

HH. I know exactly who they are: "Frau X," "Frau Y," and "Herr Z." All three will be very much present at your reunion. So don't worry about a thing. Concentrate on your music, and leave the rest to me.

B. "Concentrate on your music"—this seems to be the story of my lives! Very well, Hergenroeder. I've done it a hundred times before, I can do it again. I'll concentrate on my music and forget about the rest of life. But when I *do* finally meet these friends and loved ones, I hope I'll recognize who they are.

HH. You will, Herr Beethoven . . . I'm *sure* you will.

And concentrate on music I do. Each weekday I'm hard at work in my Schwarspanierhaus study by 7:00 AM and never leave earlier than 1:00 PM. During these mornings, I divide my time almost equally between BEETHOVEN's three new compositions, and the enormous task of gathering up my long-neglected piano technique and raising it to the demanding standards of Major-Order Aaronian concert-hall performance!

By the middle of October, our new symphony and piano concerto are finished; the sonata comes two weeks later. Allowing for adequate rehearsals, we decide to première this new music in January 1948. For the present season, the main goal of our firm is to have Beethoven himself representing BEETHOVEN before the Aaronian public. This achievement takes the form of a series of eighteen concerts, beginning in January and ending in April. During these concerts, I appear eighteen times as conductor and fifteen times as pianist. I give the first performance of our new sonata on the evening of January 9; our new symphony is premièred under my baton on January 23, but I purposely withhold performance of the new concerto until the evening of April 9, a deferral that permits me to play it under the baton of our beloved Arturo Sabatini! Early in January '48, we're informed of his pending retranslation from SCP 7,900,111. On March 17, he arrives at BEETHOVEN and plunges immediately into rehearsals of the concerto. All is in perfect readiness for my final appearance on April 9. After so long an absence, I find great pleasure in returning to the concert stage. In no other place does one feel more totally alive through music!

Like other partners and principals, when I represent our firm before the public, I too must don a subelectronic disguise of the Earthly Beethoven. How humorously strange it is, suddenly to reappear in the square-faced, hyperhaired, short-legged garb of my Earthly flesh, to replicate the same ugly pockmarked, broad-nosed face that followed me from one cracked mirror to another, across the entirety of a bygone Vienna! The swollen face is ugly and stupid looking, but the spirit behind the face is not. Because of this spirit, there is a BEETHOVEN within the Aaronian system; and ten centuries from now, there'll still be an ugly little musician with the spirit of Beethoven, composing and performing at Altburg!

During this entire season, most of the afternoons are spent in my music room at DeWitt's with Richard Wagner. We polish our "Joan" until she shines with a total readiness for production. This "happy stage" is reached on the eve of my final concert, the one with Sabatini.

My association with Wagner is not all work and no play, especially Friday evenings, which we usually spend together wining, dining, and socializing until the early hours of morning. Often for these musico-social Fridays, Wagner arranges for Franz Liszt to be present. Liszt is a co-managing partner (in fact, a founding partner) of WAGNER. He's twice the pianist he was on Earth and ten times the composer he was there. Wagner is very proud of the musical improvements in his former father-in-law and can hardly wait to see the effect our "Joan" might have upon him. Starting about the first of the year, Frau Wagner becomes an important part of these Friday socials. She is none other than the same beloved Cosima who made for Wagner such an ideal wife on Earth. It couldn't have been otherwise. Such a perfect union of souls *had* to be continued on this side of the grave. Wagner often tells me that if Cosima had *not* been reborn a woman, a woman who still loved him passionately, then he would not have married until the Third Order. I suppose that most Earthlings who think about it at all, imagine heaven to be the place where successful Earthly marriages are continued "happily ever after." This is not the case. Only between 6 and 10 percent of First-Order marriages are extended directly into the next Order. We're told that the percentage remains about the same, even in much higher Orders of our life system—the prime reason for this being the infinite compounding of human personalities through rebirth after rebirth after rebirth.

My first meeting with Cosima is at a Christmas dinner held at the Donovans' on the evening of December 26, 1947. The Wagners and myself are invited so that Judy might give us some idea of how she and her REMBRANDT are coming along with the series of semiabstractions for our *Joan of Arc*. It is there that I discover Cosima Wagner to be such an altogether delightful person that I insist that from now on we invite her to be a regular part of our Friday evenings!

What a pleasure it is for me to meet my Judy again after so many years. She's still as young and blond and beautiful as ever, and her children, chips off the old Adams's block (two girls and a boy), range from ten to sixteen. Of course, I had been in phone contact with Judy regarding her paintings, but all the personal details concerning "Joan" were handled for me by Wagner. Judy wanted the hour of our latest reunion to be the hour of her big surprise. And what a surprise it is! One hundred forty-one of REMBRANDT's semiabstractions are finished; nine are still in process. From those that are finished, Judy's firm developed a two-hour sequence of beautifully imaginative and creative slides, which Wagner and I now view. Exploding from their blaze of color is the very spirit of Joan's story. We know at once that we must include every precious moment of their message somewhere within our film. But where? Each of the twelve acts has its own prelude; each prelude has a mood-setting film sequence planned for it. Where *can* we insert Judy's pictures? Suddenly, Wagner reaches over and grabs my wrist, his eyes blazing like fire:

Wg. I've got it, Maestro! An *entr'acte*! Between the halves of each act, we'll compose an *entr'acte* to interpret Judy's paintings.

B. But Richard, the message of these paintings is far too important to be relegated to intermission space.

Wg. Not to intermission space, to *post* intermission space—a kind of prelude to the second half of each act.

B. I see! This could mean quite an improvement over our present state of affairs. It *does* seem stupid after each intermission to go racing back into "Joan," like flicking on a bright light in a dark room. With *entr'actes*, our resumptions could be gradual and artistically rewarding. This is *exactly* what we'll do!

And so passes the '47–'48 season. Mornings at BEETHOVEN, afternoons and Friday evenings with Wagner, weekends at Dogwood—now comes an abrupt change. As far as Wagner and I are concerned, "Joan" is completed on April 8, 1948; we've gone as far as we can go with her this side of production itself. After a week of careful planning and discussion at the Altburg Studio, we are informed by their production engineers that a work of "Joan's" proportions would take from three to four years to film, using their entire facility and working at top speed. What discouraging news! The two of us can't possibly wait this long for the birth of our child. We contact the College of Counselors and ask them for help. They recommend Aaron's X-5 Studio, the largest film plant within our present life system. X-5 is so huge that it occupies most of the land area of CP 87. No wonder it's called the motion-picture center of our culture. Wagner and I spend a week at X-5 with much more favorable results. *Their* engineers estimate that our "Joan" can be produced within twelve to fourteen months.

X-5's facilities turn out to be as superb as their production estimate is accurate. Wagner and I each obtain a special leave of absence from our corporate responsibilities. He, Cosima, and I journey to CP 87 and obtain adjoining musical apartments at the administrative center of the studio. Filming begins on May 5, 1948, and is completed on

July 14, 1949. These months are a period of total application. We eat, sleep, drink, and think Joan of Arc. There are no regular weekends at Dogwood, hardly any contacts with the May Building, and only a few hours of my socializing with Cosima and Richard. Within this concentrated routine, an important break occurs, and what a welcome experience it is—my "happy reunion day" as arranged by Hergenroeder and Robinson.

The day of my grand reunion arrives quite unexpectedly; in fact, I had completely forgotten about the "six months to a year" waiting period imposed by Hergenroeder. On Wednesday evening, December 22, 1948, following dinner with the Wagners, I return to my apartment (as usual) for some musical meditation and an early retirement. I remove my dinner clothes and don my faithful lounging robe. The comfortable living room has a modest log-burning fireplace, where I stoke up a friendly blaze. Out comes my old "Bach" pipe that soon blends its fragrance with the woodsy-fall smell of the crackling fire. As I stretch out on the divan, the first thing to pass through my mind is a blending of beautiful themes—melodies from the third scene of Act 4, upon which we've been working for over a week. Then my thoughts turn to the joyful weekend ahead; how wonderful to spend another Christmas at Dogwood! Next comes a mental picture of my shopping list, which I start checking off for last-minute items. Halfway down the list comes a sudden explosion of anguish that quickly replaces my thoughts of Christmas and starts me pacing the floor, talking out loud to myself.

B. When in God's name am I to meet these Earthlings of mine? . . . After a hundred years, we're still apart. Damn Hergenroeder!

The bell rings. I answer the door. There's Hergenroeder!

HH. Herr Beethoven! May I come in for a few minutes?
B. Hergenroeder! I was just thinking about you, and here you are. You always seem to show up when I need you the most.
HH. We try to please.
B. Have you come about my reunion?
HH. Exactly! A Christmas present for you!
B. Wonderful! . . . Here, sit down by the fire. Can I get you something?
HH. No thanks, but I'll join you in a smoke.

As soon as my counselor gets his meerschaum burning properly, he reaches in his pocket, then hands me a crisp brown envelope. Its contents are some final Second-Order words from Hal Robinson, which I read aloud:

January 15, 1894

Dear Beethoven,

Now that I'm finally retired from counseling responsibilities, I find that I must write a few words to several of my choice counselees . . . choice in the sense that their Second-Order transitions have caused me the most sleepless nights and have given me my fringe of premature white hair!

A counselor's chief obligation is to see that his wards have effected a productive adjustment to their present order of life. In most cases this requires translation to a Subsidiary planet; in rare cases (such as yours, dear Beethoven) something more is required. When an Earthly spirit is as strong and as creative as yours, its Second-Order Subsidiary environment must often be carefully selected and controlled. The College of Counselors achieves such control through the waving of traditional requirements of Major-Order identification. . . . In other words, dear Maestro, the Court which you've so long enjoyed in the Hildebrandtstrasse is not just a random falling together of Subsidiary beings. Most of these persons were carefully selected and conditioned by me, then were translated into *your* life under the guise of missing Aaronian rings!

I'm well aware of Herr Beethoven's strong resentment toward being tricked; under no condition should you interpret my actions as a deception. They are a highly specialized form of counseling which meets with the approval of Aaron himself. By *no* means is this counseling a one-way street. The life of each person sent to you has benefitted immeasurably from the association; and, I dare say, your life will never again be the same!

I can't tell for sure whether you'll be retranslating to the Second-Order of Major life. If not, then my secret counseling and this letter will not be revealed to you. But I rather think you *will* be returning to us here. Consider how far you've come already. Without a trace of jealousy, you appreciate the playing of Chopin. You compose the "best of Beethoven" with a composing wife at your side. I predict that you will retranslate.

Upon your return to Major life and your adjustment to things at BEETHOVEN, Ernst Hergenroeder is instructed to present you with this letter and with a list of those Earthling loved ones whom I sent to your Subsidiary Court. Prior to an imminent reunion, I think it best that you know at least the *names* of these persons. This should somewhat lessen the shock. . . . We can't have you fainting on us again. Do you remember how you reacted to your first meeting with Bach and Handel?

Of all the treasures of my counseling years, nothing compares with the marrying off of my Beethoven. Yes, dear Maestro; it is *I* who sent Anna Rosecranz into your arms. She was achieving none of her Second-Order potential as a musician until her life became one with yours. *Now*, look at her!

And so, Herr Beethoven, from the other side of the grave, I greet you once more and bid you *auf Wiedersehen*! . When we meet again, here in the Third Order, perhaps you'll have a little surprise for *me* . . . a musical surprise, that is.

With loving admiration,
Hal Robinson

B. (*Licking my lips, I slam down my pipe.*) Ye Gods, Hergenroeder! . . . Does this mean that my Anna is alive today . . . living here in our own Second Order?

HH. It does, Maestro . . . Anna and Wolfgang both. You'll be with them on Christmas Day.

B. What about Karl?

HH. Your son Karl was killed in Subsidiary life. He's now awaiting you in the Third Order.

B. Oh well, to have Anna and Wolfgang alive again, I could hardly ask for more than this. So Christmas Day is the moment of my grand reunion!

HH. Exactly so.

B. But I've already made plans for Dogwood!

HH. I've just been talking with the Rezlers. They're very happy for you, and they understand perfectly. They've moved their season's festivities back a day, so you'll be celebrating at Dogwood on Sunday.

B. Wonderful! Then Christmas Day is entirely for Beethoven and his friends. . . . Where is the big surprise to take place?

HH. At Altburg . . . in the May Building. Can you be there at 9:00 AM sharp?

B. I'm sure I can, and don't worry, Hergenroeder. This time I won't faint.

HH. Good. Here's the list Robinson wanted me to prepare for you, but I've changed something. I've given you only their Subsidiary names!

B. How come?

HH. Most of them plan to appear in their subelectronic disguises, just as they were on your SCP . . . and they want *you* to try and guess their Earthly identities.

B. Are they in any special order?

HH. Yes. They're listed in the precise order they will appear, roughly in half-hour intervals, beginning at nine. So study your list, and there won't be any fainting!

B. This I'll do, and a Merry Christmas to you, "Santa Claus."

Hergenroeder is scarcely gone when I'm pounding on the Wagners' door. In a few seconds, there stands Richard. As usual, he's draped in a red velvet gown, which is set with pink silk roses from top to bottom. He stares suspiciously at me along the green cylinder of his huge cigar.

Wg. Herr Beethoven! You're as white as a ghost. . . . Is something wrong?

B. No, dear Richard. Something's right for a change . . . very right!

Wg. What is it?

B. At last my reunion with Earthlings is upon me . . . hands I've waited a hundred years to clasp . . . lips I thought I would never live to kiss again.

Wg. When? On Christmas Day?

B. Yes. And Richard, the greatest miracle of all! When you come to visit me next door, I too shall have a little wife.

Wg. What do you mean?

B. Anna Rosecranz! She's *alive,* Richard. She's alive, and she awaits my arms this very night!

Wg. Wonderful! It *had* to be this way. Come in, dear Maestro. This calls for champagne!

I spend the rest of the night drinking champagne with Richard Wagner. We go up and down my list a dozen times, toasting each name on it. . . .

Arriving at DeWitt's on Thursday afternoon, for a day and a half I do little more than pace the floor, study the names on my list, stare through my windows at winter's snowy face, and count the crippled hours that painfully limp their way toward Christmas morning.

When the twenty-fifth finally descends upon me, I enter our May Building office at eight forty-five. No sooner are my ears inside than I recognize the sensitive adagio playing of Johannes Brahms. Unusual, but it's coming from my Schwarspanierhaus room. I tiptoe inside and quietly seat myself beside the piano. Brahms smiles and winks at me, but (fortunately) doesn't stop playing. It's past nine o'clock when the beautiful adagio ends.

B. Hannes, what a lovely Christmas present! Thank you very much!

Bra. You're welcome, Maestro. How are you and "Joan" coming along?

B. We're on schedule; she's better than half filmed. But tell me, what are *you* doing here this morning? I was informed that the entire office would be closed all day except to Beethoven and a group of his Earthly Subsidiary loved ones. The hour of their long-awaited reunion has finally come.

Bra. (*Brahms winks and smiles again.*) Listen to this little scherzo.

I'm somewhat angered by his evasion of my question. But all is soon forgotten in the delightful sparkle of another "Christmas present." His rippling technique reminds me of Mozart's. A surprise cadence for the scherzo brings the hands of my watch to nine twenty. Peering into the hall, I see *no* one, and therefore return to my chair beside the piano.

B. I don't understand, Hannes. My visitors are to come to this room one at a time, starting at nine o' clock.

Bra. So?

B. So it's almost half past, and there's no one here!

Bra. Oh, I wouldn't say that! Who's first on your list?

As I remove the sheet from my pocket, Brahms seats himself in the other easy chair and starts lighting up a cigar.

B. My first guest is to be Sigmund Kapell, my dear co-composer from the Hildebrandtstrasse.
Bra. Is he that "big red-haired bastard" you told us about?
B. Yes. I suppose he'll still have the same old—

A freezing shock cuts off the words in my throat. Of course! How stupid of me! Hundreds of times . . . thousands of times I've seen him light his cigar just that way.

B. We'll wait no longer for Sigmund Kapell!
Bra. How's that, Herr Beethoven?
B. Because he's already here!
Bra. What do you mean?
B. You know what I mean, Kapell. Your red hairs are gone, but you're still a big old bastard!
Bra. Congratulations, "Sherlock"! You've finally discovered my secret.
B. I would have done so years ago, except for your deception.
Bra. What deception?
B. No ring, no Brahms; how could you be Brahms without an Aaronian ring?
Bra. You're right, Herr Beethoven; we did take advantage of you. But without our hiding, nothing would have worked out as beautifully as it has.
B. I agree, Hannes; and I hold nothing against you or anyone else. But tell me, greatest of musicians . . . for so many years, how could you subjugate the spirit of Brahms to the tyranny of Voskamp?
Bra. Discipline, technique, and patient evolution are not subjugation. They are the means for launching one's own creativeness. I played this role in our First Order; how natural for me to do so again. Because of Beethoven, there *was* a Brahms on Earth; and now, because of you, there is a definite place for me in Major life. And that place is here at your firm.
B. But why did you translate?
Bra. In spite of Bonaparte's laudations, I could never really be part of BEETHOVEN until you became his managing partner.
B. Then you translated, hoping to influence my retranslation.
Bra. Exactly so! I had a talk with Hergenroeder; he felt that since you were reacting so favorably to a composing wife, the next logical

step would be to introduce a "nonfamily" composer into your Court.

B. And how you suffered under my childish jealousy!

Bra. Dear Maestro, working and growing in the shadow of Beethoven is *not suffering*! What *must* I do to convince you of this? My Hildebrandtstrasse days with you and Anna are the most productive I have yet lived!

B. No wonder you were able to help us with our Brahms evolution.

Bra. Yes. . . . Being Brahms *did* place me at somewhat an advantage.

B. Just think, Hannes. All the plans we made there in the Hildebrandtstrasse will now come true. You *will* be my musical heir. Upon my retirement from the firm, you will be BEETHOVEN's new managing partner . . . you and Wolfgang!

Bra. And then what?

B. Beyond this, our Second-Order BEETHOVEN is in the hands of fate. His distant future is not for us to worry about. Tell me, Hannes. After all your SCP studies in the contemporary music of Earth, are you really satisfied to go on writing in our Beethoven-Brahms idiom?

Bra. Very much so! For me, it has everything in it that's really music. Several of Earth's newer pieces—those which are honest—have aroused my deepest admiration. But they are *not* superior to what we are doing. The bulk of what I reviewed is sheer nonsense, childish attempts to be new and different . . . meaningless (sometimes mathematical) assemblages of tones, which have no spiritual or philosophical basis for existence. In desiring above all else to write *new* music, they are writing *nonmusic.* Well, dear Maestro, I've overstayed my time. Your next visitor must be getting impatient. I'll see you at our luncheon.

B. Is that to be in the main staff room?

Bra. Yes. Two concert grands have been moved in for this occasion, which is going to be musical, edible, and filled with surprises! But let me tell you my present responsibility. At 3:00 PM, I'm to tear you away from your admiring throng.

B. What for?

Bra. For the biggest surprise of all.

B. Anna?

Bra. Yes!

B. I noticed she's not on my roll.

Bra. No. The reunion of Herr and Frau Beethoven is to be a special affair, and I'm to drive you there.

B. Where?

Bra. To your new home.

B. What new home?

Bra. The home which Anna and Wolfgang have prepared for you here in the suburbs of Altburg.

B. God in heaven, Hannes! It's too much to believe. . . . What a Christmas! I shall never again doubt the sagacity nor the validity of Santa Claus!

The next visitor brings me stumbling to my feet and clumsily crashing into her arms. My vision is so blurred with a burst of tears that I can hardly enjoy the smile on her dear face. For long minutes, as we rock side to side in each other's arms, my trembling lips repeat over and over again the single word: Mother! . . . Here in my embrace, alive, breathing, smiling, crying, and seeing again is dear Mother Voskamp, causing herself to look fifteen years younger than when she "died" out of our Subsidiary lives. When we finally realize that we are united again, we seat ourselves on the comfortable sofa, still holding hands.

B. Now, dear Mother, as our little game goes, I'm supposed to guess the Earthly spirit within you.

BM. And can you, Vos?

B. I think I can . . . but I'm almost afraid to say it for fear of being wrong.

BM. I'm sure you know my secret now. Speak my name, dear Son.

B. Very well! All those years in Subsidiary life, I wondered how the mother of Voskamp could so easily "mother" the Beethoven within me. . . . Now I know! Because you *are* the mother of Beethoven!

BM. Correct, dear Ludwig. I'm the mother of Voskamp, and I'm also the loving mother whose eyes you closed there in Bonn's Wenzelgasse.

B. God in heaven! What sweetness! . . . And now I have you both in one dear being to love and to cherish. Who are you here in our Second Order?

BM. Mrs. Vera Cunningham; my husband is Rothwell Cunningham, the historian.

B. I believe I read his books at Lakemont.

BM. Those were probably his father's. Roth is the third Cunningham to be the author of histories.

B. Are you also a historian, my dear?
BM. In a modest sort of way; that's how I met my present husband.
B. All those years on my SCP . . . didn't these separate you from the Cunninghams?
BM. Yes. But we were married with the understanding that our Subsidiary assignments would come between us for twenty years or more. All has worked out beautifully. Roth is very proud of my having mothered Earth's great musician! He's anxious to meet you.
B. At least your translation explains away *one* miracle.
BM. Frau Voskamp's sight?
B. Yes. When your body absorbed her soul, it restored her sight.
BM. Naturally! Beneath that subelectronic disguise were my perfectly good eyes.
B. How clever . . . and how wonderful. But tell me, Mother, when shall I meet your Second-Order self?
BM. You already have.
B. Really? . . . Where?
BM. At the glorious première of your *Messiah.*
B. I can't remember.
BM. Yes, you can . . . there in the box with Aaron.
B. "Frau X"?
BM. No. "Frau Y," sitting there between Aaron and "Herr Z."
B. "Herr Z" . . . he couldn't have been your new husband.
BM. No . . . my *old* husband . . . the father of Mason Voskamp.
B. I'll be damned! Surrounded by loved ones, yet totally unaware of them. But I'm no longer unaware of you, my dear. Here . . . let me kiss you again.

In one joyous sweep, I pick up the mother of Voskamp and the mother of Beethoven and hold her aloft:

B. Now that you *are* here in my arms, I can't seem to find appropriate words of welcome.
BM. Use tones, dear Ludwig . . . not words.
B. (*Carefully, I seat her on the piano bench, then quickly snuggle beside her.*) What would you have me play, Mother?
BM. Surely you haven't forgotten!
B. Of course, your favorite piano piece . . . that simple *Lullaby* from Voskamp's *Sonata in A-flat.*

My dear mother gently sways in recognition and thorough approval of the tender theme. Now *I'm* the one who's smiling, and she's the one with tear-filled eyes.

At regular intervals I continue to receive visitors and surprises through the rest of the morning. After Mother Voskamp comes (naturally) Father Voskamp. He turns out to have been none other than my Earthly grandfather. How I scold him and joke with him about peering into my cradle and referring to me as an "ugly bastard." He repents in full. To commemorate my first exposure to music, he takes my hand in his and guides it once more through the C major scale. Then I accompany his (still) glorious baritone in six of our favorite Brahms lieder. Next appears Karl Seibert, whom I dubbed "Schuppanzigh" in my Subsidiary Court. Quite an insight on my part, for he *was* the Earthly Schuppanzigh! Seibert is followed by Axel Oberhausen, that dear fellow whose personal and musical solicitousness led me to dub him "Ries." But here I was mistaken. On Earth, this constant companion was none other than Prince Karl Lichnowsky! The final participants in my reunion guessing game are that pianistic pair, Ralph Gay and Victor Pepusch. Perhaps you recall that when these young men first officially entered my Court, Gay was given the name "Czerny" and Pepusch was called "Ries." Remember also that within a few months, I began wishing that I had named them in reverse order. And well might I have done so, for on this revealing Christmas morning, I learn that Ferdinand Ries *did* translate as Ralph Gay and that Carl Czerny *did* become my pupil, Victor Pepusch. How great it is to hear each of these superb pianists playing once again within the revelation of his true identity. After Czerny's departure, I grab Ries and viciously accuse him of using his "Ralph Gay" disguise as a sneaking device for getting me once more to play the piano for him:

R. Surely, dear Maestro . . . after 140 years, you don't still hold my little joke against me.

B. The hell I don't! It was wicked and stupid. And now that I know who you are, I shall never again play for you.

R. Herr Beethoven . . . you *must* be joking.

B. (*Uncontrollably, my scowl gives way to my true feelings.*) I am indeed, Ries. . . . Here, sit down beside me at the piano.

Without a moment's delay (and to Ries's beaming satisfaction), I play through the very *Andante Favori* that caused our ridiculous breach in the first place.

Chapter 52

At about twelve fifteen, Ries and I enter BEETHOVEN's general staff room, where a crowd of over two dozen stands and greets us in the main event of my May Building reunion. Things are so arranged that at three different times during the luncheon, I'm requested to change my seat—a kind of "musical chairs" without the music. This permits me to socialize with three different groups of Earthly acquaintances during the time of a single meal. "Appetizer and soup" are spent with Wegeler and the Breunings. All my dear Münsterplatz friends have been reborn and are now here to welcome me: Madame von Breuning, Eleonore, Stephan, and even Gerhard, my dear "Hosenknopf." The "main course" is devoted to other reborn Earthlings dear to the heart of Beethoven: Zmeskall, Lobkowitz, Archduke Rudolph, Chopin, Haydn, brother Johann, and our great Goethe, whose flowing words color the occasion with a charm and importance equivalent to Christmas itself. "Dessert and coffee" transport me to a third group: Neefe, Albrechtsberger, nephew Karl, Liszt, the Wagners, and Franz Schubert. The latter inquires whether my favorite Earthly Schubert is still the *G-flat Impromptu*:

B. I believe it is, Franz. That dear melody struck its way to my heart the first time I heard it, and it's been there ever since.

FS. Good! For this happy day, I've prepared a slightly modernized two-piano version of the old *G-flat* which Franz Liszt and I would now like to play for you.

B. Wonderful! My reunion would never be complete without some music!

The rest of my "party" is strictly musical. When Schubert and Liszt are finished with their *Impromptu*, I'm introduced to the Schumanns, who perform a set of four-hand variations on Robert's delightful *Träumerei*. Next come Puccini and Tschaikowsky, who (hard to believe) are now collaborating on their tenth grand opera—a delightful tribute to young love entitled, *The Garden*. Tschaikowsky accompanies his partner in three shimmering excerpts from its first act. There's something almost magical about the blending of the diverse styles of these two composers—a magic which, in my opinion, is producing the most irresistible operas of our present culture. Their unusual success explains why Richard Wagner came seeking a new path for his musico-dramatic aspirations. I wonder how these famous partners will react to our "Joan." Now I shake the hands of a pianist long-admired by Beethoven, a pianist whom I sincerely believe to have given my *Moonlight Sonata* its most sensitive interpretation. He graciously consents to perform it for us. His name? Ignace Jan Paderewski! At the conclusion of the *Moonlight*, another young stranger comes up and shakes my hand.

CD. Congratulations, Maestro. The first movement of that sonata is one Beethoven piece I really enjoy!

B. It's nice to have done *something* that meets with your approval. And who might *you* be?

CD. Claude Debussy.

B. What? . . . I don't believe it!

CD. Really!

B. What are you doing at a party given for an old German by a bunch of old Germans?

CD. I'm here to keep Chopin company.

B. Are you now reconciled to the greatness of German music?

CD. Heavens no! The only thing great about *German* music is that it creates the need for *French* music.

My eyes bulge. My chin drops. Everyone laughs.

B. Well, German that I am, I'm beginning to appreciate your music. Will you play some Debussy for us?
CD. Gladly! What have you learned to appreciate?
B. *Clair de Lune.*

There's more laughter than even before. Apparently it stems from the thought of a Beethoven whose ears could master things far more demanding than the *Great Fugue* from his own *B-flat Quartet,* and who professes now to have gotten just as far as the childlike *Clair de Lune* in his appreciation of modern French music. The laughter soon changes to applause and then to admiring silence as the great impressionist plays those familiar (but still fresh) chords that have made his name dear to all students of piano. While I listen, I can't help studying the expression on Chopin's face. What a tribute to the achievement of Claude Debussy. In my reunion's garland of pleasant surprises, the final participant turns out to be Sergei Rachmaninoff. He goes immediately to the piano and performs his magnificent transcription of the *Prelude* to Bach's *Third Partita.* As the tones descend upon us like chiseled raindrops, I try to find thoughts to match my feelings. Franz Liszt helps me in this effort by whispering in my ear: "Now *there's* a Third-Order pianist who puts us *all* to shame."

At the conclusion of his Bach, the great pianist looks directly at me and asks if I have a request.

B. I certainly do, Sergei Vassilievitch. I request my favorite Rachmaninoff.
SR. (*A tremendously sour expression crosses his face.*) Maestro! . . . Not it! . . . Not the *Prelude*!
B. No. The *C Minor*—the dearest of all romantic concertos!
SR. Ah! But who will be my "orchestra"?
B. (*I nod at Liszt; he nods back.*) Franz Liszt will accompany you.

The room fills with applause. How natural, considering this combination of pianists.

Between its second and final movements, the Rachmaninoff Concerto is interrupted by Johannes Brahms. He apologizes for "using spoken words midst such music," but explains that it's his responsibility to see that I'm delivered at my wife's doorstep by three thirty for the biggest Christmas present of all! Now my guests' plaudits are directed toward *me.* I feel that a few parting words are in order:

B. Dear friends . . . great musicians. . . . Of all the reasons for the extension of life as we knew it on Earth, I'm sure the two most important are the continuation of our work and our reunions with friends and loved ones. For the past century, I've thoroughly enjoyed the continuation of my music, but (for the most part) my reunions with Earthlings have remained a bright sun on a distant horizon. For a hundred years, I've anticipated the joy of this day. Quite often, when one looks forward to something for this length of time, its ultimate arrival is unavoidably tinged with an element of disappointment or delusion. Not so in the case of Beethoven's grand reunion. You . . . dear friends who have cared enough to share your Christmas Day with me, you've made my reunion every bit the joyous occasion I've always dreamed it would be. Perhaps some of you have noticed improvements in the old Beethoven you used to know. There *have* been improvements, attributable not only to those of you who translated to my Subsidiary Court, but also to Anna Rosecranz. I would like you all to meet her. Only *then* will you appreciate the "new" Beethoven. Less than one week ago, I thought my treasured spouse was a Subsidiary being and thoroughly dead. Today I understand that she is a Major-Order being, very much alive in our midst. I now take leave of you, dear friends, that I may be reunited with my Anna. Tomorrow, she and I will be visiting the Rezler home on CP 25. I invite all of you to stop by and meet her . . . my pride and chief joy . . . my Christmas present supreme . . . my true musical self. Until then, I welcome you to the hospitality of BEETHOVEN. Enjoy the rest of the Rachmaninoff. Help yourselves to that champagne. And have a Merry Christmas, each one of you. *Auf Wiedersehen*!

Our trip to my new home is filled with silence. Hannes realizes that to any conversation between the two of us, I would prefer my silent contemplation of Anna. The smooth car he drives is quieter than the whispering snow. Its wiper blades play tag with hundreds of puffy flakes at a time. The uniform motion of their game has an almost hypnotic effect upon me. I decide to use a side window for my staring through. Half past three arrives, and we're still not there. Another five minutes does the trick. I would describe Anna's "nest" as a country home. Its grounds are too rambling and its terrain too wooded for it to be called a home in suburbia. The multilevel two-story frame is painted gray with white trim. Its profusion of windows and porches and gables, the fairy-tale slope of its roof, the snow-white blanket covering all, reminds me of that famous home for which Hansel and Gretel had an irresistible attraction. Brahms enters the half-circle drive and stops at the main entrance. We shake hands.

B. Hannes . . . you must forgive my silence. I assure you, it's no reflection on my company. I was ordering a million questions in my mind . . . questions for which I now hope to find answers.
Bra. No offense; I understand perfectly.
B. Will you come in?
Bra. Not now. The rest of this Christmas belongs to the Beethovens. Good luck, Maestro! I certainly envy you the surprise you're about to enjoy. May I visit you tomorrow?
B. By all means, Hannes. Tomorrow at Dogwood. Well, thanks for bringing me; thanks for everything. And mind you, if you come upon that Sigmund Kapell, wish him a Merry Christmas for me.
Bra. I'll *do* that, Maestro.

In spite of my rude silence and careful thoughts, I cannot decide which question should be put to Anna first. I therefore decide to ask no questions. When the door opens, I'll simply grab her in my arms and cover her with kisses. The door opens, and I do just this . . . until I suddenly realize that it's not Anna that I'm kissing.

B. Maria! . . . What in God's name are *you* doing here?
Ma. I'm here to greet you, Father . . . and to wish you a happy homecoming.
B. But you don't *belong* on this planet.
Ma. Oh yes I do. (*She takes my coat and hat, then continues.*) Don't forget that you and Mother are *both* Major-Order beings, which pretty well takes care of your "Subsidiary" children.
B. Of course it does, my dear. After all these years, it's hard for me to think of you as you really are. Somehow you'll always be my little "Subsidiary" daughter. How about that husband of yours? Don't tell me that Max is *also* a Major-Order being.
Ma. No. He's just a darling Subsidiary creature whom I dearly love. I'll be returning to my "Hollywood" on Monday, so enjoy me while you can.
B. I certainly will. How come you're able to slip away for Christmas?
Ma. Max is filming in Mexico for at least two weeks. He took the children with him, and I'm to join him there next Wednesday.

(*She motions into the living room.*) And now, Father, "behold thy son."

Wolfgang jumps from his chair and almost flies into my arms . . . a crushing embrace . . . a real bear hug like the one Ries and I enjoyed so many years ago, only *this* time there's no shaving cream.

B. Wolfgang! . . . Dear Son! Can you possibly know what it means to me to have you alive and in my arms again?
WV. And can you know what it means to *me* to embrace my father as the great Second-Order musician he really is?
B. In time, *each* of us will realize what he has in the other! I'm sure of this, my son! And you, Maria, surely you'll soon be translating to Major life.
Ma. Yes, Father. Just as soon as my dear Max is gone.
B. Now come, children. I can't wait another second. Where *is* this mother of yours . . . this Anna Voskamp, my biggest surprise of all?
Ma. She's upstairs, Father . . . in the master bedroom.
WV. She told us to send you up. It's the first door to the right of the stairs. You're supposed to knock.
B. Sounds mighty mysterious, but here I go! . . .

The stairs are filled with well-built silence; it's my *knees* that do the creaking. The first door to the right is closed. I knock. It opens. And there she is!

AR. And what young devil have we here?
B. (*Her unusual words strike a familiar ring. I decide to play her little game.*) Not a devil, Madame! I am Beethoven. I have come from Bonn to see you.
AR. Oh yes! Just last week I received a post from your elector. He introduced you and included some fine commendations from Herr Neefe and my friend, Waldstein. Come in, I must hear you.

We enter a large bedroom that is fitted throughout in blue and mahogany. The portion of its hardwood floor that shows beyond a feathery blue carpet is an intricate parquet. Majestically posed in front of curtainless French windows is a Steinway Music-Room Grand. As we walk toward it, Anna motions for me to seat myself at its keyboard. I ask her for a theme upon which I can improvise. She stands beside me at the piano and plays a familiar text. It contains an interesting melody, a pregnant rhythm, and a trick—the same melody, the same rhythm, and the same trick given me a hundred-sixty years ago by Mozart. I begin my improvising at once. As I do so, my mind runs over and over the words we have just exchanged. Obviously, Anna has been doing some research in the Beethoven biographies. How else would she know the precise words that Mozart spoke to me? But the theme . . . this is what amazes me. Where could she have found this theme known only to Mozart and me? No amount of reading could have given her this. God in heaven! . . . Could it be that she and Mozart are one and the same? . . . I quickly terminate my improvisation. Sure enough, there she is, standing behind me with her hands on my shoulders. I look up into her face and, with the same dry throat of 1787, manage one quivering question.

B. Tell me, Anna, before you take another breath, could it be possible that you're really Wolfgang Amadeus Mozart?

AR. (*Her reply is neither yes nor no, but another Mozart quote.*) Watch this young chap! He'll make a noise in the world. And we'll all sit up and listen!

I rise from the piano and take her in my arms. Again and again we kiss. Then suddenly, the full realization of her greatness slaps me in the back of my neck like a ten-ton block of ice. A strange, light-headed feeling . . . but there's no mistaking it! In spite of Hergenroeder's precautions, I'm about to faint. It took the combined talents of the mighty Bach and Handel to first steal my consciousness from me. Now for the *second* time in 178 years . . . I faint again! And the entire process is perfectly managed by one dear, sweet, lovable Mozart!

Soon I'm awakened to the pungent scent of ammonia. Hovering over me are Anna and our two children.

B. A monstrous bunch of conspirators, the lot of you! For nearly seventy years, I'm married to the world's greatest musician, and only today find out about it! . . . I've got so many things to talk over with you, I don't know where to start.

AR. (*Anna smiles approvingly.*) Good! Let's start with music. *Tones* are best suited to answering the questions of a musician, not words! Wolfgang and I have written a trio to commemorate your homecoming. He's practiced up the cello, I'll do the violin, the piano is for you, and Maria is assigned the responsibility of our Christmas goose, which should be ready for us in about an hour.

B. And my questions?

AR. After a trio and Christmas dinner, your questions will be no trouble at all.

As usual, Anna is absolutely correct. At about 8:00 PM, when the two of us finally retire to our "blue room," I'm a far more rational and better composed inquisitor. We pull two easy chairs knee to knee, and my barrage of questions begins.

B. Now young lady, first of all, when do I get to see you as you really are? How soon will you be casting off your Anna Rosecranz subelectrons?

AR. You already *have* seen me as I am, my dear.

B. So? . . . When?

AR. Remember your *Messiah* concert? There in the box with Aaron.

B. Of course! The missing "Frau X." How long I've wondered who and where she is. . . . Now the final piece fits into place . . . the picture is complete!

AR. But "Frau X" is far too old for the likes of you.

B. What do you mean, Anna?

AR. On Earth this would be like a handsome young chap of forty marrying a little old lady of seventy . . . certainly unfair to Paul Rezler. So I've decided to retain the disguise of a thirty-year-old Anna Rosecranz, that very girl you married in Subsidiary life and impregnated with three fine children.

B. Wonderful! It's not often that a fellow gets a chance to turn the clock back and start his marriage all over again!

AR. And as Rezler's body ages naturally, I'll see to it that Anna gets enough gray hairs and wrinkles to keep pace. Considering my age, I don't want to suddenly look too young for my husband.

B. But tell me, Anna . . . what about our present sex life? You've donned the flesh of the very girl with whom I've enjoyed my happiest hours in bed. I'm liable to forget myself and come at you as I did in Subsidiary life. Wouldn't this be repulsive to "Frau X"?

AR. Heavens no, Rezler. I thought you knew musicians better than this. Of course, now there'll be no children; but for us at least, sexual love is a never diminishing thing!

B. Good. Then happy days, I welcome you again. Now, here's my next block of questions. Who is "Frau X"? What's the story of

Mozart from the hour of his rebirth until his translation into my Subsidiary life? Why did you decide to become the savior of Beethoven instead of the managing partner of MOZART?

AR. Very well. “Frau X” is really Estelle Forbes, born into our Major Order back in 1778, when Beethoven was only a little boy. Estelle had an enormous talent for music, especially for composition. Her talent showed up when she was first tested at six years of age. By ten, she was majoring in composition and modern forms at EP 41. That same year, her talent was declared “Fourth Order” by our College of Counselors, and she was given permission to head up her own musical corporation. All she had to wait for was her rebirth and the resulting Second-Order status. During the next three years, her studies involved her in an extremely mathematical approach to composition—a sort of advanced tone-row technique, the antithesis of all that is traditional or diatonic. On her thirteenth birthday, her counselor predicted that within one year of its founding, the FORBES corporation would be producing the most modern and aesthetically demanding “Western” music within our Major Order. And then suddenly, one morning at breakfast in 1791, into this explosion of mathematics, into this welter of modernity, into the spiritual subelectron of Estelle Forbes came the simple, traditional, diatonic soul of Wolfgang Amadeus Mozart!

B. Ye gods, Anna! It’s a wonder you didn’t pass right on into the Third Order.

AR. I almost did. . . . Believe me, Vos. . . . The overwhelming demands of Herr Mozart and the unquenchable aspirations of Ms. Forbes precisely cancelled out one another. I could do *nothing* with my music. In other words, I could do nothing at all except cater to one big fat neurosis for the better part of ten years! Seven counselors were assigned to my problem. They *finally* got me to admit that the sole key to my salvation lay in some nonmusical service to others. Through the painful hypocrisy of denying my true selves, a decision was made in favor of nursing. For several years, Estelle and Wolfgang prepared themselves for this profession at EP 10 . . . each biting off the other’s nose, without once suspecting that they had but a single nose in common. In 1811, I began my practice as a nurse at the Debilitation Center on CP 201. For sixty-four years, this remained my sole occupation, my excuse for not marrying, my escape from music. But my counselors were not satisfied. They felt that I had spent adequate time as a nurse, more than enough to overcome my neurosis. Somehow they hoped to redirect my talents toward music and marriage. The problem of a nonmusical Mozart-Forbes became a favorite toy of the entire College of Counselors. They tossed it back and forth like a newly acquired beach ball. And with each successful catch, there'd come some new advice. The path I finally did choose was presented to me by your counselor in January 1876.

B. So Robinson *was* behind it all.

AR. Yes. He made his plan sound so totally inviting that I couldn't resist. Even apart from music, I had learned to find happiness in rendering service to others. My career as a nurse had enabled me to overcome the anticomposing frustration within me. And now all that Robinson seemed to be proposing was an exchange of my *nursing* services for *musical* services—personal services to Ludwig van Beethoven. He explained the details of your Earthly career, your accomplishments as Voskamp, and his grave doubts that you would *ever* be able to return to Major life in the Second Order without some careful and personal help from a fellow Aaronian.

B. And so you became my pupil, then my wife, then my co-composer.

AR. Yes. . . . But the entire sequence was far from a sacrifice on *my* part. After some artful "spying" on Voskamp and Anna, I could hardly wait to become Frau Anna Voskamp. Dear "Stanzi" had been reborn a woman, making it quite impossible for me to extend my Earthly marriage into the Second Order.

B. That mother of mine, she certainly encouraged me to marry Anna Rosecranz. Did she know that you were Mozart?

AR. Yes. Both your parents did.

B. No wonder then. But surely you didn't marry me entirely out of pity.

AR. No indeed. The Mozart within Anna had a profound and musical respect for the Beethoven within Voskamp. I came to you out of true love, and in the desire to help!

B. You've done so much for me! I have you to thank for everything. Without your help and example, old Beethoven could never have adjusted to Major-Order music!

AR. And think what "old Beethoven" has done for me. I thought my composing days were over for God knows how many lifetimes. But you and your Brahms evolution solved my problem. Through *you*, dear Rezler, I experienced the combined joy of music and motherhood. What more could I ask?

B. Well, it's nice to know that you received *something* in return for your sacrifice and love. But you know, my dear, I don't think I'll ever be able to look you square in the eye and call you "Estelle Forbes." Nor can I happily spend the rest of my Second-Order nights in bed with "Herr Mozart." I must go right on thinking of you as my "resurrected" lover, my dear Anna Voskamp!

AR. Fine! This is what I hoped you'd do. And to *me*, you'll always be my "Mason" or my "Vos," not "Herr Beethoven" or "Paul Rezler."

B. Speaking of names, I see now why you called that second son of ours "Wolfgang." . . . A tribute to Herr Mozart.

AR. And I see why you called that *first* son of ours, "Karl." . . . A tribute to Herr Beethoven's nephew.

B. Poor Karl! How come you were unable to save *him*?

AR. As our children approached ten years of age, I took them aside and explained to them who they and their parents really were. Then when you would go on tour, we'd sneak away for little visits to Aaron AP, confirming my unbelievable stories of other worlds! In this way, each child was anticipating his rebirth when it actually occurred. Our overall plan was to wait until *you* showed some signs of wanting to return to Major life. We would then reveal our true identities to you and translate to Aaron as one big happy family! But before you showed such inclinations, along came World War I. I begged our boys to translate, though neither would hear of it. Then came the death of Karl on that U-boat. That settled the matter. I insisted that Wolfgang translate immediately. Heeding my demand, he left Subsidiary life by feigning death on the battlefield. He went straightway to your old alma mater, M93, and spent eight years there preparing for entrance to BEETHOVEN. Once at your firm, he soon worked his way to a principal in the composing division, where (ever since) he's awaited the appearance of his famous father.

B. Then he and Kapell have been working along together up here in heaven; all the while I thought both of them were dead and gone.

AR. They have, and the two of them have grown immensely. I strongly recommend them as joint managing partners when the day comes you decide to step down.

B. Kapell, indeed! What a naughty deception, Anna. No wonder the two of you got along so well: Mozart and Brahms, dancing in each other's arms. Did you request his entry into our Court, or did he come of his own accord?

AR. Hergenroeder sent him. He felt that the time had come for you to learn to collaborate with a composer other than your wife. This he felt sure would be the last big step toward your ultimate retranslation!

B. Well, he certainly sent the right man for the job. My Subsidiary goal was to evolve into a rich Brahms idiom, and along comes Brahms to help me in my task . . . Brahms *and* Mozart! No wonder Voskamp succeeded!

AR. But don't forget, Herr Beethoven—each of *us* benefited immeasurably from our workaday associations with *you*.

B. That's kind of you to say, my dear, but I feel the scales were tipped in my favor. And now, Frau Wolfgang Amadeus Beethoven, I see the reason for your miraculous *Messiah*. Written by *Mozart* . . . no wonder!

AR. Not by Mozart . . . not by Forbes; neither of them could have written a note because of the other. *Messiah* was written by Anna Rosecranz, a brand-new composer born entirely out of love and respect and admiration for the spirit of Beethoven. Without a Beethoven, there would have been no composer Rosecranz . . . no *Messiah*. The work is no less yours than mine, and this is exactly what I told Aaron as I sat there beside him.

B. And think of *me*, moved to tears at the thought that my little Subsidiary wife was not hearing her masterpiece performed to Major-Order perfection!

AR. But I *was*. And how I enjoyed it under *your* baton. And that sweet confession telling Aaron that *Messiah* was the work of your Subsidiary wife when actually it was the product of *her* hands and *Beethoven's* spirit! But most of all, it was the divine offerings of spiritual guides that transfigured its creation.

B. I fully support your humble acknowledgment of these heavenly beings as "partners" in this miraculous accomplishment.

AR. Well, we can thank God for this privilege of helping him fulfill his omniscient plan for the universe.

B. And for permitting us to continue working together in our higher order status.

AR. It took longer than we thought. Brahms and I hoped that you'd retranslate soon after our Subsidiary "deaths," but on and on you stayed, embracing the Wildings!

B. The Wildings *and* my broken spirit. I thought I'd never again find happiness in Second-Order life. . . . Then along came Richard Wagner.
AR. That's right. He and Joan of Arc finally brought you back to us!
B. Dear "Joan." I can't wait for you to meet her. You probably consider movies an unworthy art form, but wait until you see our "Joan"!
AR. That's what I've been doing . . . waiting!
B. What have you done since your retranslation?
AR. Lived here with Wolfgang in this cozy house, made occasional visits to BEETHOVEN, and counted the days until "Christmas."
B. What *music* have you done?
AR. Brahms has been our constant visitor. Between "auditing" his works and those of Wolfgang, I've kept busy enough.
B. Well, my dear, you've answered my million questions, now you must *play* for me.
AR. And what does my dear husband request?
B. Mozart's *Fantasia y Sonata in C Minor* played by Mozart!

As Anna performs this dear and familiar work, I sit next to her on the bench, planting regular kisses on her beautiful cheek. When the music ends, we go to bed—Beethoven and his Mozart in one big happy bed! What a perfect ending for a perfect Christmas Day! How sublime to have this girl in my arms once again! There's something very special about Anna Rosecranz, and now I fully realize what it is!

I'm so proud of my new wife that I want to show her off to everybody. Sunday the twenty-sixth at Dogwood gives me the opportunity of doing just this. Without exception, those present at my Christmas reunion all show up the next day. Also there to meet Anna and our children are the Donovans.

We leave on Monday for Aaron's X-5 Studio on SP 87, where Wagner and I resume our direction of *Joan*. Since the composing part of the project is already completed, there's little for Anna to do except join with Cosima in the role of spectator. And "spectate" she does! Before the end of the week, her enthusiasm for *Joan* is equivalent to Wagner's and mine put together! She considers the perfection of our new-type music drama as a worthy goal for both the WAGNER and the BEETHOVEN corporations—preferably independent of each other. So there's no selling job on *my* part to persuade her that our firm should try such a work of its own.

The filming of *Joan of Arc* is completed on schedule, and July 16 finds Anna and me happily moved into her Altburg home, which is to be our regular weekend residence. To save on commuting time, weeknights are to be spent in my commodious apartment at DeWitt's. I practice a careful speech that I intend to deliver at a general staff meeting of BEETHOVEN on Monday morning. In it I propose to reintroduce Mozart, this time as the wife of Beethoven! And I intend to recommend her as a full managing partner of our corporation. Neither the introduction nor the recommendation is necessary. No sooner do Anna and I enter BEETHOVEN's reception room than Ms. Simpson motions us down the left hall toward "partners' row." Some interesting changes have been made. Bonaparte's office is still at the end of the hall, but Brahms's is no longer next to mine. He has been moved directly opposite the Schwarspanierhaus room, and the plaque on his door now reads,

JOHANNES BRAHMS, PARTNER
WOLFGANG VAN BEETHOVEN, PRINCIPAL

The space vacated by Brahms has been dutifully assigned to my loving wife. An inscription on *her* door reads,

FRAU LUDWIG VAN BEETHOVEN
MANAGING PARTNER

Anna and I no sooner enter the Schwarspanierhaus than doors begin opening and a wave of BEETHOVEN musicians descends upon us. At the crest of this wave are Wolfgang, Hannes, and Bonaparte. They follow us everywhere as Anna and I first inspect my old room and then her new one. On *her* walls are two beautiful oils by Judy Donovan—portraits of the Earthly Brahms and the Earthly Wagner. They are obviously companion paintings to the Beethoven and the Mozart that grace the walls of *my* study.

Returning to my room, I take down Judy's "Beethoven" and place it carefully on my desk. At least twenty people stop breathing as they watch me alter the inscription which I scribbled there a hundred years ago. It *now* reads,

> Man, with the help of *Mozart*, help thyself!
> Ludwig van Beethoven
> October 4, 1848
> July 18, 1949

The Aaronian première of *Joan of Arc* begins at Altburg on Friday evening, September 2, 1949. Each three-to-four-hour act runs a full week before the next succeeding act is premiered. In this way, the entire music drama requires through November for its total presentation. On December 15, the College of Counselors makes its former declaration official: "The music drama entitled *Joan of Arc*, composed by Ludwig van Beethoven and Richard Wagner, is hereby declared a new and original art form within the Second-Order Major culture of the Aaronian system." The document is signed by Aaron himself, among others of the College. Our dear Prophet declares that prior to "Joan," an art form of comparable purpose and dimension was not to be found this side of his Fifth Order. He is very pleased and now looks forward to such musico-dramatic sproutings within his Third and Fourth Orders.

With the successful première of *Joan*, the declaration of Aaron, and the arrival of 1950, our firm goes wild with suggestions for a music drama of its own! In spite of my protestations, the story finally decided upon is the story of my life, it being argued that "Who could better tell the story of Beethoven than the very artistic firm that bears his name?" My first responsibility is to supply the script. Because of total recall, the fifty-seven years on Earth are easy enough. The digging and sweating starts when Paul Rezler enters the picture. Fortunately, sister Gina gave me a first diary on my twelfth birthday. The practice of daily entries became a habit, which (all the more reason) was continued through the "reborn Beethoven" years. I now send to Dogwood for these "treasures" and make a thorough study of them. The result is an autobiographical script that is completed on April 14 and accepted by BEETHOVEN five days later. The polished epic is called *Beethoven 1770-1950*, and our composing staff goes immediately to work on its music.

A totally unrelated, yet miraculously related event occurs the following month. At 9:30 AM on May 15, my Schwarspanierhaus door inches open, and there with neither ceremony nor announcement stands our beloved Prophet himself—Aaron!

B. Maestro! What a surprise you give me! What a *pleasant* surprise! . . . Here, come in, sit down. To what kind providence am I indebted for this happiest of moments?

Ar. P. Nothing so portentous, dear Beethoven. I've come to ask a favor of you.

B. Certainly! . . . Something about *Joan*?

Ar. P. No, not directly. . . . I've come to ask you for the story of Beethoven . . . the story of your life to date.

B. What a coincidence. This is exactly what I've been working on since January.

Ar. P. What do you mean?

B. Our firm has decided to do the story of *my* life as its first music drama. I've just spent three months polishing and compressing it into a script. (*I reach to my desk for a large blue folio and hand it to Aaron.*) Here, Maestro. . . . You're welcome to it.

For several minutes, he carefully studies a random selection of pages. Then he smiles and fixes his huge brown eyes on mine.

Ar. P. This is a fine script . . . well polished. But it's not what I had in mind, Herr Beethoven.

B. No?

Ar. P. What I want is Beethoven's story to date told in the first-person simplicity of your own recollections.

B. That should be easy. I've already done the research for it.

Ar. P. Fine! I've reserved the early part of June entirely for hearing your story. On Saturday the third, we'll meet in an appropriate pastoral spot, then for three or four or five days, you do the talking and I'll do the listening.

B. Just in my own words?

Ar. P. Exactly! It wouldn't hurt to spend a little time reviewing dates and names and sequences, but it's to be *your* story in *your* words.

B. Very well, Maestro. I'll study my data and be ready for you on the third. May I ask how you plan to use the story?

Ar. P. Certainly. I'm sure you're aware that your Prophet's visit to any given planet within his system is usually between twenty-five and thirty-five years. Furthermore, he has nothing to say concerning the sequence of these visits. Each time, he shows up precisely where God's intelligence wills him to be. But there *is* a pattern. . . . Each reappearance on Earth tends to be preceded by a string of low-order visits within the life system.

B. And this is what's happening?

Ar. P. Yes. . . . Five out of my past eight visits have been within the Second or Third Orders.

B. Then you expect an imminent reappearance on Earth?

Ar. P. Yes. My ninety-ninth visit there within the current cycle. And for this visit, I need your story.

B. How so?

Ar. P. This time I don't plan to appear as a prophet, or a teacher, or a worker of miracles. I'm going to function as a psychiatrist. My new crop of "disciples" will be a handful of special patients—patients who can be helped by the simple telling of a story.

B. In what way?

Ar. P. Most psychological breakdowns are preceded by philosophical breakdowns. No man with a strong and meaningful outlook is in need of psychiatric help. But certain patients need to be cured by repairing or replacing their broken-down philosophies. Such curables will then become the disciples of my new gospel.

B. And what *is* this new gospel?

Ar. P. The story of life, death, and rebirth. A believable portrayal of the immortality of man's soul. I've collected over a thousand personal stories of Earthlings who are now living in the Second or Third Orders of our system. These stories, and yours, will be the new Gospel of our First-Order Space Age.

B. Are only a few "sick people" to be helped by this "Good News"?

Ar. P. At first, yes. . . . Then we'll release it to *all* Earthlings.

B. How will you know whose story to use?

Ar. P. The story used will depend entirely upon the patient to be helped. Suppose some Earthling musician, sick at heart and of mind, gropes his neurotic way to my office. He confesses to bearing within his soul a long list of frustrated goals. He knows no way to turn. He no longer has faith in himself. He sees his life as a meaningless hypocrisy, a fevered grasping of material things, a greedy sampling of sex, a total disintegration of youthful goals, a gross disappointment with threadbare talents, a nameless grave, and a muddy mound of smelly clay to crown his less than "three score years and ten." No *wonder* he comes for help. . . . I reach into my spiritual subelectron and draw out the story of Beethoven—word for word, exactly as you'll be telling it to me. I give him your story on tape and recommend that he study it. He does. . . . And as he does, his vision of life and self is expanded and clarified. Material things lose their soul-crippling power. Sex becomes a creative force, not an addiction. Impossible goals and modest talents are no longer victors over those few brief hours called "life on Earth." My patient now has something old to laugh at, something new to believe in. . . . He is cured! We've saved ourselves a musician and we've gained a First-Order Aaronian disciple—someone to preach the new Gospel according to Beethoven.

B. This is wonderful! It's about time old "death" be tickled under his chin and made to smile. He's been the aloof monster long enough!

Ar. P. I agree. As Earthlings enter their Age of Space, their souls will need something more revealing—the revelation of a new Gospel!

B. I don't suppose you'll be using the name "Jesus" on your next visit.

Ar. P. No. Six hours on that cross are enough for a while!

B. What name *will* you use? Have you decided yet?

Ar. P. Curious that you'd ask. Only a month ago, I decided. I was reading an Earthling book called *Caesar and Christ* by Will Durant. Its impact was such that I gleaned from it my new pseudonym. I shall retain whatever first name I'm given, but my *last* name will be changed to . . . CAESAR!

Synopsis

I have often heard people express their wish that someone who has died would return to us and relate what the life-death-rebirth experience is really like. Well, someone *has*! This is exactly what Beethoven does in my third novel, *Beethoven, Then and Now.*

Like Beethoven, each one of *us* is the proud possessor of a "human soul." This clearly defined object is none other than our very own *spiritual subelectron.* Our physical hulk is only a pile of ashes; but our "soul" (spiritual subelectron) is unique, eternal, indestructible.

Because of its high vibrations, Beethoven's "soul" is immediately attracted to the third subelectronic ring of our First-Second-Order universe. Here it awaits rebirth via fusion with the spiritual subelectron of a Major-Order being within our Second-Order-Major universe. Paul Rezler (age seventeen) is the fortunate recipient of this unbelievable prize. He had awakened to the day at hand with his usual *zero interest in music.* Now (1827 Earth-time) he is the *greatest Earth- musician yet to live.*

Try as Beethoven does, he cannot adjust to the Second-Order reality of corporate composers, not even to being the absolute leader of the *Beethoven Corporation.* He must be entirely on his own-- a single man vs. the world!

Counselor Robinson does his best in selecting a *Subsidiary culture* which contains a "Vienna" as close as possible to the one which Beethoven had left behind upon his Earthly death. Within a month, our hero makes his translation and enjoys living where there's not the trace of anything resembling a "musical corporation." Sketches for new "third-period" works begin to flow: a piano sonata, a string quartet, a piano trio, a violin concerto, even some encouraging vibrations of Symphony 10. A handful of piano and violin students emerges, including an exceptional young lady named Anna Rosecranz, who is already a master of these instruments. Her musicianship is so strong that they soon fall in love and are married. How they enjoy performing concerts together! In time, as Beethoven works at his composer's desk, she starts peering over his shoulder. She begs him for lessons in composition. He replies, "I compose, and AM NOT a teacher of composition!" This declaration does not frighten her away.

As Beethoven fumbles and bumbles his way from sketchbook to finished score, Anna carefully watches each step of the process. Her comments are invaluable:

> Use a pedal-point here.
> Not so dissonant a chord.
> Pure melody would fit here.
> Please, not so sustained.
> Too many notes in the melody.
> Avoid more of this rhythm.
> Two-voice counterpoint would do.
> Too much for the brass here.
> This use of strings is perfect.

Thanks to Anna, Beethoven accomplishes the impossible. He realizes that he works far better *with* her help than *without* it. He now loves to share the very process which only yesterday had demanded his total aloofness. As if by magic, he is now prepared to return to Major-Order life as managing partner in charge of the Beethoven Corporation. But considering all that Anna has done for him, he cannot now simply go his own way. As a Subsidiary being, her lifespan is a mere 100 years, compared to his Second-Order-Major span of 1000 years. Being happily married, he plans to share life for the balance of *her* days. But Fate has his own plan for their lives—. After all their years of loving and sharing, Anna is "killed" in an automobile accident.

When Beethoven returns to the Major Order, a super surprise awaits him. There stands Anna Rosecranz, a full Major-Second-Order being, with whom he can share the rest of their 1000 years in joyful creative activity. His first question: "On Earth, who *were* you, my dear?" Her reply causes our hero to faint for the second time in his entire Second-Order life!

CPSIA information can be obtained at www.ICGtesting.com
Printed in the USA
BVOW07s0656201214

380190BV00001B/5/P

9 781499 068184

Life in Picture

Oasis

Christine Kidney

Oasis from The Rain

1991 was the year the First Gulf War started; Tim Berners-Lee established the first website at CERN; unemployment in the UK reached nearly two and a half million; a mortar attack was launched by the IRA on Downing Street; and rock legend Freddie Mercury died. In Manchester a band called The Rain, 'making a racket with four tunes', became Oasis, the band who above all others came to embody Cool Britannia. Initially comprising of Paul 'Bonehead' Arthurs (guitar), Paul 'Guigsy' McGuigan (bass guitar), Tony McCarroll (drums) and Liam Gallagher (vocals and tambourine), it was the arrival of Liam's older brother Noel that changed the band's direction and success.

L-R: Tony McCarroll, Paul 'Bonehead' Arthurs, Noel Gallagher, Liam Gallagher, Paul 'Guigsy' McGuigan.

Before Noel joined, Oasis was a band 'making a racket with four tunes'

First gig in Manchester

Liam and Noel were two of three children born to Thomas and Peggy Gallagher in Burnage in Manchester. Noel was born in 1967, Liam in 1972. Noel was always writing and playing songs but it was Liam who first joined a band, having got heavily into music in his teens. Noel meantime was working in the construction industry before becoming a roadie for another Manchester indie band, Inspiral Carpets. Liam auditioned for The Rain as a vocalist and suggested they change their name to Oasis. They played their first gig at the Boardwalk club in Manchester on 18 August 1991.

RIGHT: Noel Gallagher performs in the UK. He plays one of two Gibson Les Pauls given to him by Johnny Marr of The Smiths.

OPPOSITE: Liam Gallagher

Songwriter Noel joins the band

While working with Inspiral Carpets as a guitar technician, Liam's brother Noel had spent years writing his own songs. When Liam and the other band members of Oasis invited Noel to join, he agreed, on the condition that he would be the only songwriter and the leader. 'All of a sudden, there were loads of ideas,' said guitarist Paul Arthurs. Under Noel's direction, the playing became simplified while the amplifiers were ramped-up, giving them an instantly recognizable distorted sound.

'All of a sudden, there were loads of ideas'

Performing at The Water Rats in January 1994. L-R: Paul 'Bonehead' Arthurs, Tony McCarroll, Liam Gallagher, Noel Gallgher.

Oasis played for over a year without even the promise of a record deal

Noel, above, and Liam, opposite, performing live at The Water Rats

Small local following

Oasis rehearsed and played live gigs for over a year without even the sniff of a record deal, though they had a small local following. In spring 1993 Noel managed to persuade Tony Griffiths of the Liverpool band The Real People to let them use their studio to produce a demo that they could send out to record companies. There were six songs on the final recording, all on cassette, including early versions of 'D'Yer Wanna Be a Spaceman?' and 'Married with Children'. In early summer 1993, the band, having managed to scramble the money together to hire a van, made the six-hour journey to a gig at the famous nightclub, King Tut's Wah Wah Hut in Glasgow.

Six album deal

Although they were invited to Glasgow by Sister Lovers, a band who shared their rehearsal rooms, when they got to their gig at King Tut's in Glasgow, Oasis were surprised that they didn't appear on the set list for the night. The band members used their formidable powers of persuasion to get in and were put in the opening slot. In the audience was Alan McGee, co-owner of Creation Records, who was there to see a band he had already signed, 18 Wheeler. He signed Oasis up almost immediately to a six-album deal with Creation Records.

ABOVE: Noel fronts Oasis at the Astoria in London, 19 August 1994.

OPPOSITE: Liam at the Paradiso in the Netherlands

‘Less is more didn’t really work then.’

Fastest selling debut album ever

Their first song was a limited release of 'Columbia', which had appeared on *Live Demonstration*, the name of their demo collection. Oasis's first official single was 'Supersonic', which came out in April 1994. This reached no. 31 in the UK charts. It was followed by 'Shakermaker' and 'Live Forever', their first song to enter the top ten. Oasis's first album had serious teething problems. They recorded it first at Monnow Valley Studio near Monmouth but something wasn't working: the attack they showed in performance didn't translate into the recording. Later they re-recorded it at Sawmills Studio in Cornwall though that too proved unsatisfactory, with Noel overdubbing several guitars. Paul Arthurs said, 'Less is more didn't really work then.' But producer Owen Morris became involved and turned it into what would become at that time the fastest selling debut album ever.

***Definitely Maybe* sold over 2 million copies in the UK and the album launched Oasis in America.**

Definitely straight to No.1

Oasis's first album *Definitely Maybe* went straight to no. 1 in the UK album charts on its release in August 1994. It sold over 2 million copies in the UK and the album launched Oasis in America, where they sold over one million. It has since sold over eight million copies worldwide and has often been cited as the best album of all time in various polls. Following Blur's release of *Parklife* in April of the same year, *Definitely Maybe* marked a turning point in British pop music, an embracing of old influences and a new energetic delivery that tuned into the boom-seeking mood of the nineties, which would see Labour sweep into power a few years later. They defined Britpop. Left to right: Paul 'Bonhead' Arthurs, Liam Gallagher and Noel Gallagher.

Oasis headlined at Glastonbury in 1995 before 'The Battle of Britpop' occurred. Oasis in the long run sold more records than Blur and achieved more success in America.

Some Might Say...

In April 1995 Oasis had their first number one hit with 'Some Might Say', which was the last to feature Tony McCarroll on drums. He was replaced by Alan White, who was recommended to Noel by Paul Weller. In September 1995 bassist Paul McGuigan also left the band but only for a short period. During that time he was replaced by Scott McLeod who toured with Oasis but left during their US tour. Regretting his decision, he asked to return but Noel famously retorted: 'Good look signing on.' Paul McGuigan eventually returned to the band and remained until 2004.

Paul 'Bonehead' Arthurs and Liam Gallagher at the1995 Glastonbury Festival.

The British press seized upon a supposed rivalry between Oasis and Blur. Previously, Oasis did not associate themselves with the Britpop movement but came to define it.

LEFT TO RIGHT: Noel Gallagher, Paul 'Guigsy' McGuigan, Paul 'Bonehead' Arthurs, Tony McCarroll and Liam Gallagher.

Noel Gallagher playing his Epiphone Union Jack guitar at Maine Road.

OPPOSITE: Left to right: Tony McCarroll, Noel Gallagher, Paul 'Guigsy' McGuigan, Liam Gallagher and Paul 'Bonehead' Arthurs. Bassist Paul McGuigan briefly left the band in September 1995, citing nervous exhaustion. He was replaced by Scott McLeod, who was featured on some of the tour dates as well as in the 'Wonderwall' video before leaving abruptly while on tour in the US.

Cool Britannia

Britpop was a cultural phenomenon that defined music in the 1990s, broadening out into what became known as Cool Britannia (made memorable by figures from popular culture, including Noel Gallagher, visiting Prime Minister Tony Blair at 10 Downing Street). Blur and Oasis were Britpop and started up a rivalry that at first was generated by the media but which became more entrenched, with Oasis and Blur appearing to represent opposing sides of the British North-South divide. Oasis headlined at Glastonbury in 1995 before 'The Battle of Britpop' occurred. On 14 August Oasis released 'Roll with It' and Blur released 'Country House' on the same day. Blur narrowly claimed victory, selling 274,000 copies to Oasis's 216,000, going in at, respectively, numbers one and two in the charts. However, in the long run Oasis sold more records than Blur and achieved more success in America.

Although a softer sound led to mixed reviews, Oasis' second album, *(What's the Story) Morning Glory?* was a commercial success, becoming the fourth best-selling album in UK chart history with over four million copies sold.

ABOVE: Liam and Noel talking on the set of a UK TV show in January 1996.

OPPOSITE: Liam shouting at Patsy Kensit, the actress, singer, model and former child star, at the Brit Awards in 1996. The couple married in 1997 and had a son, Lennon, named after John Lennon; they divorced in 2000.

What's The Story

In October 1995 Oasis released their second studio album, *(What's the Story) Morning Glory?* On it are 'Champagne Supernova' (with Paul Weller on backing vocals), 'Don't Look Back in Anger' and 'Wonderwall', three of Oasis's most enduring songs. It has been the most successful of their albums, selling at least 16 million copies worldwide and breaking record sales in its first week. It won Best British Album at the 1996 Brit Awards and at the 2010 ceremony won an award for the best album of the last 30 years. It made the Gallagher brothers international superstars, with the album staying at No. 1 in the British charts for 10 weeks and reaching No. 4 in the US charts.

The demand for tickets when Oasis announced their upcoming concert at Knebworth in August 1996 broke all previous records.

Half a million ticket applications

In April 1996 Oasis held two concerts on consecutive days at Maine Road, formerly the home of Manchester City Football Club. The video *There and Then*, released on VHS in the same year and then on DVD a year later, features highlights from the second night. The demand for tickets when they announced their upcoming concert at Knebworth in August 1996 broke all previous records. They sold out both shows within minutes. 375,000 were sold though two and a half million people applied for tickets.

LEFT: Liam and Noel performing live in September 1997. Oasis spent the end of 1996 and the first quarter of 1997 at Abbey Road Studios in London and Ridge Farm Studios in Surrey recording their third album. *Be Here Now* was released in August 1997.

BELOW: Noel Gallagher performing at the Reebok Stadium, gesticulates while playing his paisley patterned Fender Telecaster guitar.

OPPOSITE: Liam Gallagher performing at Universal Amphitheater.

More public spats

The next month proved turbulent for the band. Though they were riding a wave of unprecedented success, they were showing signs of exhaustion. Liam pulled out of a concert at the Royal Festival hall and an episode of MTV *Unplugged* with a sore throat. Noel took over the vocals and, demonstrating the sibling rivalry that has always entertained the media and their fans, Liam heckled his older brother from the balcony at the Royal Festival Hall. The band began another US tour that year at first without Liam. After another public spat, Noel returned to the UK during the tour but the brothers soon made it up and finished the tour.

Noel returned to the UK during the 1996 US tour but the brothers soon made it up and finished the tour.

Fastest-ever selling album in Britain

OPPOSITE: Oasis playing KROQ's Almost Acoustic Christmas, the annual concert run by the Los Angeles radio station KROQ-FM at the Gibson Amphitheatre in Universal City.

ABOVE: Noel gets close to his fans on the streets of New York.

Although the quarrels and spats emanating from the brothers seemed more the stuff of pantomime than heartfelt, the rivalry between Noel and Liam began to affect their work. They took longer to record their third album, *Be Here Now*, which was the most anticipated album of their career as a band. On the day it was released in the UK, *Be Here Now* sold 350,000 copies, and reached sales of nearly 700,000. It was the fastest-ever selling album in Britain. However, its sales in the US proved disappointing, peaking at 152,000 copies in the first week, less than half of what had been expected.

The Oasis Masterplan

Be Here Now received more mixed praise than Oasis's previous two albums and after their follow up tour in 1998, the band took some time to keep away from the media glare. Later that year they released a compilation album called *The Masterplan*, consisting of B-sides that were not included on previous albums. They had intended to release the album in the US and Japan, where previously the songs had been available only as expensive imports. It eventually went platinum in the UK. Noel has said of it: 'The really interesting stuff from that period is the B-sides'.

The quarrels and spats emanating from the brothers seemed more the stuff of pantomime than heartfelt.

BELOW: Liam, Noel and Andy Bell at the Coachella Music Festival, in Indio, California. The 2002 event saw a reunited Siouxsie and the Banshees, and Björk.

A darker sound

While they were working on their fourth album, *Standing on the Shoulder of Giants* (a title inspired by a motto on a £2 coin) in 1999, two of the original band members left: guitarist Paul Arthurs and bass guitarist Paul McGuigan two weeks later. The remaining members, Liam, Noel and drummer Alan White continued recording the album with Noel having to re-record some of the guitar parts. They hired a new producer in Mark Stent, who replaced Owen Morris. Noel also chose to try out new equipment and techniques, giving the album a darker sound.

OPPOSITE: Liam Gallagher on stage at Shepherds Bush, London, on 31 August 2001 in London.

ABOVE: Noel Gallagher playing his Gibson Les Paul guitar in October 2001.

Oasis set up their own record label

Gem Archer was quickly announced as new lead/rhythm guitarist and finally brought in guitarist Andy Bell, though he had to learn to play bass guitar. When Creation Records folded in 2000 Oasis set up their own record label, Big Brother: the name is perhaps self explanatory. (Also, each catalogue number begins with RKID – 'our kid'.) It was a difficult time of transition and although it was their lowest-selling and least popular album in their history, Noel has since said of it: 'Even though it wasn't our finest hour, it's a good album born through tough times. I worked harder on that album than anything before and anything since.' This may, of course, be because he had to play the parts of his two recently departed band members.

'I worked harder on that album than anything before or since'

OPPOSITE: Liam Gallagher centre stage as Oasis play in a concert in aid of teenage cancer at the Albert Hall in London.

ABOVE: Oasis play BBC's *Top of the Pops*, 11 April 2002.

Turbulent world tour

Oasis went on a turbulent world tour in 2000, during which drummer Alan White had to pull out because his arm had seized up, and Noel and Liam fell out, resulting in Noel quitting the tour and returning only for the British and Irish dates. Two of these gigs were at Wembley Stadium, the first of which they recorded live – *Familiar to Millions*. The following year they joined bands The Black Crowes and Spacehog in a tour entitled Tour of Brotherly Love (the other bands also had brothers known for their public spats), another tongue-in-cheek acknowledgement of the tensions between them.

OPPOSITE: Noel and Liam at the 2005 *Q* Awards. In May 2005, the band's new line-up embarked on a large scale world tour. Beginning on 10 May 2005 at the London Astoria, and finishing on 31 March 2006 in front of a sold out gig in Mexico City, Oasis played more live shows than at any time since the Definitely Maybe tour, visiting 26 countries and headlining 113 shows in front of over 3.2 million people.

LEFT: Liam Gallagher performs on stage wearing a white parka.

Playing to 3 million world wide

Heathen Chemistry, Oasis's fifth album, was the first to include a song not written by Noel: 'Songbird' by Liam. It was also the last album to feature drummer Alan White, who was replaced by Zak Starkey, Ringo Starr's son. Their sixth album, *Don't Believe the Truth*, which was three years in the making, was released in 2005. It was hailed as their best album since *Morning Glory*. Like its predecessors, it went in at No. 1 in the UK album charts. It was followed by one of Oasis's most successful world tours, performing to over 3 million people in total. It was also noted for its lack of incidents.

LEFT: Liam and Noel performing in the Netherlands, June 2005.

OPPOSITE: Oasis hold a photocall in Hong Kong, 25 February 2006.

The sixth album, *Don't Believe the Truth* was hailed as their best album since *Morning Glory*.

Oasis released a compilation double album entitled *Stop the Clocks* in 2006, featuring what the band considers to be their 'definitive' songs.

OPPOSITE: Noel and Liam at Earls Court in London, February 2007.

ABOVE: Liam Gallagher

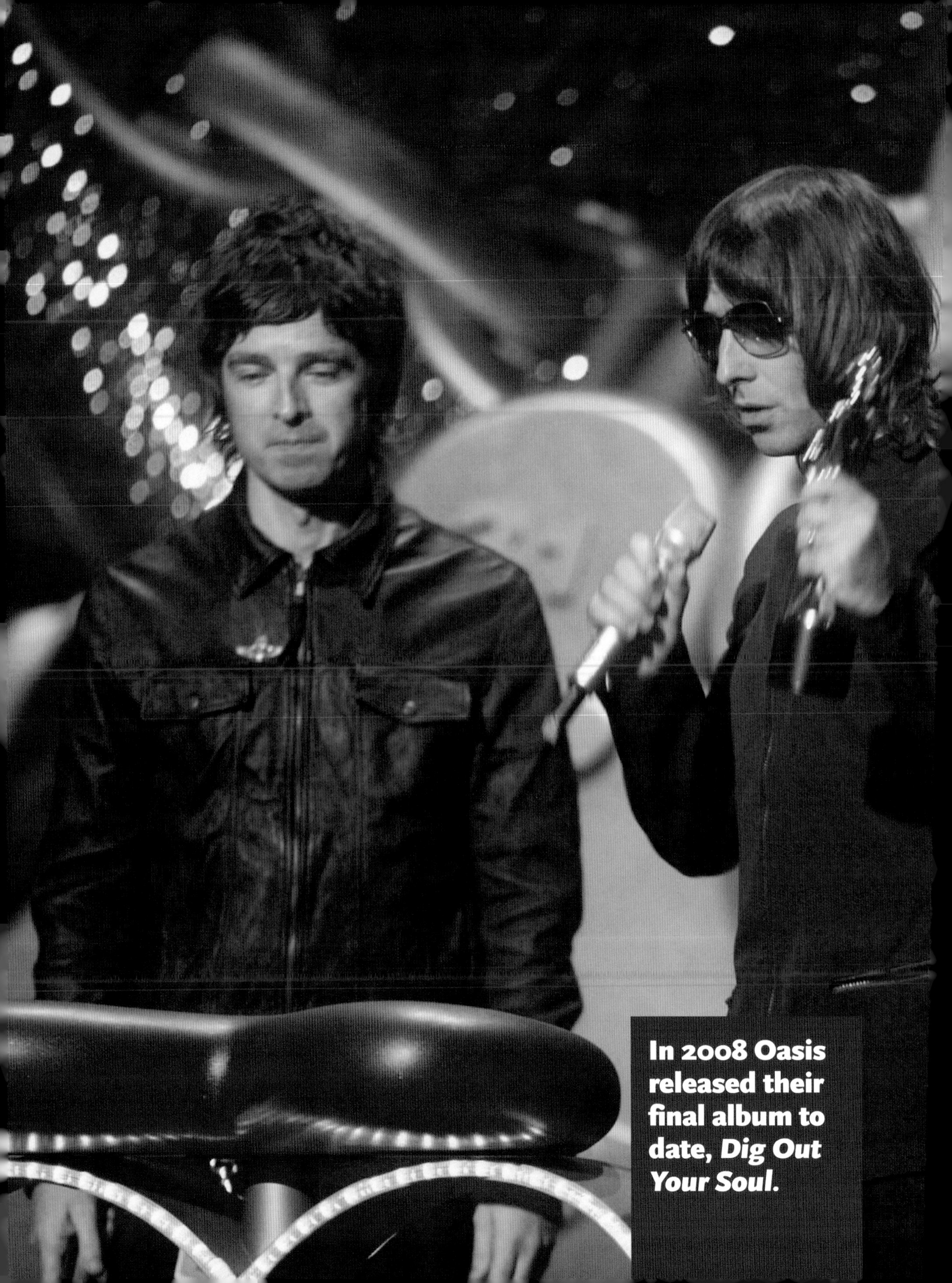

In 2008 Oasis released their final album to date, ***Dig Out Your Soul.***

Dig Out Your Soul: Noel departs

In 2008 Oasis released their final album to date, Dig Out Your Soul. During a major tour Noel finally announced his departure from Oasis in August 2009. Liam formed a new band with the remaining members of Oasis called Beady Eye. Their first album Different Gear, Still Speeding entered the charts in February 2011 at no. 3. Noel confirmed his solo career and Noel Gallagher's High Flying Birds have released an eponymous album which debuted at no. 1 in the UK album charts in 2011.

LEFT: Noel Gallagher, Liam Gallagher and Gem Archer collecting their award for Oustanding Contribution to Music at the 2007 Brit Awards at Earls Court, London.

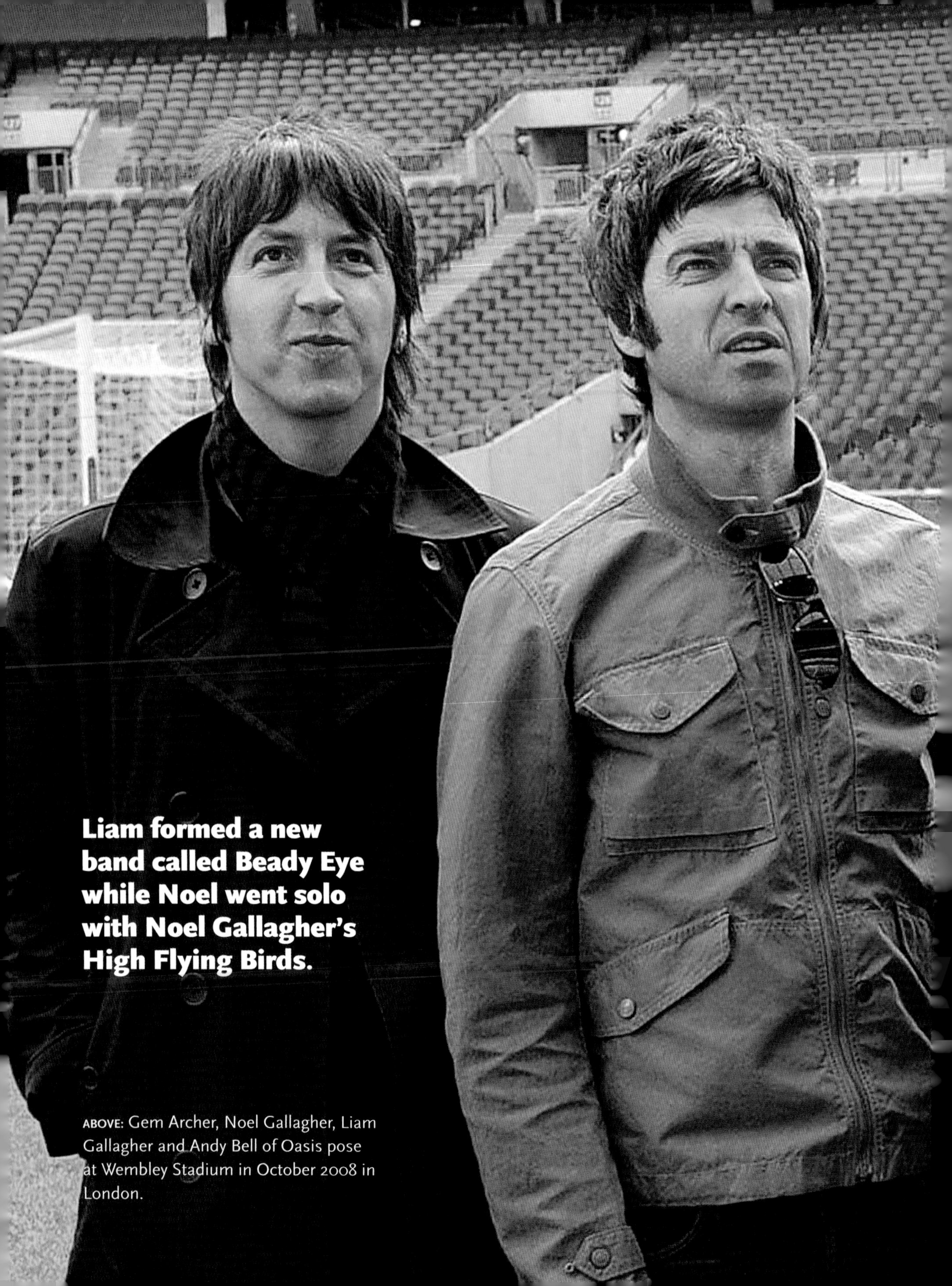

Liam formed a new band called Beady Eye while Noel went solo with Noel Gallagher's High Flying Birds.

ABOVE: Gem Archer, Noel Gallagher, Liam Gallagher and Andy Bell of Oasis pose at Wembley Stadium in October 2008 in London.

The Oasis musical heritage

Noel and Liam Gallagher and Oasis have been at the forefront of British popular culture for the last 20 years. Their musical heritage can be traced back to the great British bands of the past – The Beatles, The Kinks, Led Zeppelin, T Rex, The Jam, Pink Floyd, The Smiths, to name only a handful. But their domination of music in the last two decades has also influenced such bands as Coldplay, The Killers and the Arctic Monkeys. They created a unique sound that harked back to their past and moved music on. The often fraught chemistry of the two brothers created a dynamic energy and creativity that perhaps is an echo of their heroes, Lennon and McCartney.

On 16 February 2010 Oasis won the award for Best Brit Album of the Last 30 Years at the BRIT Awards

The fraught chemistry of the two brothers created a dynamic energy and talent that is an echo of their heroes, Lennon and McCartney.

OPPOSITE: Liam Gallagher of Beady Eye performs at Somerset House, London, on 12 July 2011.

RIGHT: Noel Gallagher of Noel Gallagher's High Flying Birds performs at the Academy of Music in November 2011 in Philadelphia, Pennsylvania.

This is a Transatlantic Press book
First published in 2012

Transatlantic Press
38 Copthorne Road
Croxley Green, Hertfordshire
WD3 4AQ, UK

A catalogue record for this book is available from the British Library.
ISBN 978-1-908849-03-8

Printed in China